THE CHROME BORNE

Mercedes Lackey
&
Larry Dixon

THE CHROME BORNE

This is a work of fiction. All the characters and events portrayed in this book are fictional, and any resemblance to real people or incidents is purely coincidental.

Born to Run copyright © 1993, *Chrome Circle* copyright © 1994 by Mercedes Lackey and Larry Dixon

A Baen Book

Baen Publishing Enterprises
P.O. Box 1403
Riverdale, NY 10471

ISBN: 0-671-57834-0

Cover art by Clyde Caldwell

First printing, October 1999

Distributed by Simon & Schuster
1230 Avenue of the Americas
New York, NY 10020

Typeset by Brilliant Press
Printed in the United States of America

Born to Run

DEDICATION

Dedicated to J.R. and Shirley Dixon, Ed and Joyce Ritche, and to all parents with the vision to listen to what kids *really* wish for—and help them find it.

Thanks to the music of Icehouse (and to Iva Davies for being the visual inspiration for Tannim), a-ha, Midnight Oil, Rush, Kate Bush, Alan Parsons, Thomas Dolby (hope you get the keys to her Ferrari), Edvard Grieg, Shriekback, David Bowie (past and present!), Billy Idol (for visceral fight-scene music), Mannheim Steamroller, the Floyd, Michael Hedges, and the entire Narada Artists catalogue, especially David Arkenstone and David Lanz—we could never have done this one without you!

Special thanks also to Kevin Barry's Pub and Acadia Restaurant (run by none other than the sparkling Trish Rodgers!), Trish Rodgers herself, the Buccaneer Region SCCA, Roebling Road raceway, Professor Russ Barclay (for drilling grammar into Larry's thick artsy skull lo these many years ago), and the faculty, staff, and students of Savannah College of Art and Design (for backing a long-haired hippy-freak dark horse).

MUSTANG SALLY

"Excuse me?" said a low, sexy, female voice.

Tannim jumped in startlement, and turned to face the barn door—and froze as he saw who was standing there. His mind lodged on a single thought, unable to get past it: *It's her—it's her—it's her*—

And it was: the woman who had haunted and hunted him through his dreams for years. The woman he'd dreamed of this morning. *Her.* And she stood there, calmly taking in his look of utter shock.

There was absolutely no doubt of it; she matched his dreams in every detail. Gently curved raven-wing hair framed a face that he knew as well as he knew his own. Amused emerald-green eyes gazed at him from beneath strong brows that arched as delicately as a bit of Japanese brushwork.

"Excuse me," she said again in that throaty contralto. ". . . but I understood that I could find someone here who works on Mustangs."

He looked past her and spotted her black Mustang standing in the midst of the tall grass outside the barn door. "Not—for a long time," he said dazedly.

"Ah," she replied. Then her eyes widened as she looked past his shoulder, and she stepped back in alarm.

Fear lanced him. He whirled to look. There was nothing there.

He turned back, and she was already gone. And so was her car.

Only *then* did his mind click back into gear, as he sprinted to stood where the car had been. There was the imprint of four tires in the grass—but no trackmarks leading up to them. There was no sign that the car had actually been driven through the grass to reach that spot, and there had been no sound of a motor.

She was haunting him still, it would seem. . . .

OTHER BOOKS IN THIS SERIES

The SERRAted Edge
Born to Run
Mercedes Lackey & Larry Dixon
Wheels of Fire
Mercedes Lackey & Mark Shepherd
When the Bough Breaks
Mercedes Lackey & Holly Lisle
Chrome Circle
Mercedes Lackey & Larry Dixon

Urban Fantasies
Knight of Ghosts and Shadows
Mercedes Lackey & Ellen Guon
Summoned to Tourney
Mercedes Lackey & Ellen Guon
Bedlam Boyz
Ellen Guon

ALSO BY MERCEDES LACKEY FROM BAEN BOOKS

Bardic Voices: The Lark & the Wren
Bardic Voices: The Robin & the Kestrel
Bardic Choices: A Cast of Corbies
(with Josepha Sherman)
Fortress of Frost & Fire: A Bard's Tale Novel
(with Ru Emerson)
Prison of Souls: A Bard's Tale Novel
(with Mark Shepherd)
The Ship Who Searched
(with Anne McCaffrey)
Wing Commander: Freedom Flight
(with Ellen Guon)
If I Pay Thee Not in Gold
(with Piers Anthony)

CHAPTER ONE

A dark red Mustang perched beside the ribbon of highway, alone but for the young man resting against its door. It was an unusual sight for such a place, here where the shallow water of the wetlands reflected moonlight, and endless silvered marsh grasses whispered in the breeze. The cicadas didn't care if the man was there, nor did the night-birds, nor the foxes and raccoons—they were used to the comings-and-goings of men in their loud machines, and would avoid him. There would seem to be no reason for him to be stopped here—no smoke or steam poured from beneath the nostrilled hood, no line of shredded rubber marked a newly departed tire. A highway patrol officer would have been very interested—if there had been one anywhere within twenty miles. And that, too, was unusual; this close to Savannah, there should be police cruising this stretch of road.

"One of these nights," griped Tannim to no one in particular, "I'll have a normal drive, with nothing chasing me, pestering me, shooting at me . . . no breakdowns, no detours, no country-western music, no problems. Peace, quiet, and the road. No place to go, no one to save, no butts to cover except my own."

Tannim pulled himself up onto his old Mach 1, faded black jeans *shushing* over the hood. Its cooling engine tick-tick-ticked, radiator gurgling softly as it relaxed from its work, the warm old American sheet metal satin-smooth and familiar. He ran a hand through his long brown hair, catching fingers in his uncountable ratty knots of curls, and snorted in cynical amusement. Casting his eyes skyward, scratching at his scalp, he said wistfully, "Man. They keep telling me, 'Y'knew the job was dangerous when ya took it.' Thanks for giving me the job description *after* I've signed the contract, guys."

The cicadas answered him by droning on, unimpressed.

The road was deserted, the air clear, the bright country sky shining off of the curved fenders. Tiny pinpoints of light twisted into sweeping contours only to be swallowed up in the flat black intakes of the hood.

The beauty and peace of the evening softened his mood. *No finer job in this world, though. When it works out— wish Kestrel were here to help. He's better at this than me.* Tannim thought about his old friend from high school back in Jenks, Oklahoma, with more than a twinge of regret—regret for Derek's curious blend of talents, compassion, and guts. Derek Ray Kestrel was gifted not only with a sexy name but with a knack for magic that just wouldn't quit. Deke spent his time with his cars and guitars, now, and didn't do road work anymore. *Guess he didn't have the stomach for it. It can get gross enough to freak a coroner. Damned if he didn't have more than just talent, though.*

He gave up on his hair and adjusted his jacket, a third-hand Battlestar Galactica fatigue he traded a Plymouth carburetor kit for. Both he and the other kid thought they'd gotten the better deal. They were both right. Tannim didn't know from carbs then, and had let go of a rare five-hundred-dollar sixpack. Deke had sure given him a hard time about that! The other kid had no idea how hard the battle-jackets were to get. *Live and learn.* He dug around in one of the many pockets he'd sewn inside the jacket, and pulled out a cherry pop, whistling along with the Midnight Oil tape on the Mach 1's stereo, occasionally falling into key.

Decent night for a job, though. Not raining like last

time, and no lightning to dodge, either. Tannim was a young man, but he was not inclined to die that way, despite the reckless pace he kept up. *Better to run toward something than away,* he'd always thought, but the scars and aches all over his wiry body testified that even a fiery young mage can be harmed by too much running. Or perhaps, not running hard enough . . . He had been self-trained up to age twenty, and then someone from *elsewhen* had taken him in and really shown him the ropes of high magic. Their friendship had built before their student/teacher relationship really began, Chinthliss admiring the boy's brazen style, wicked humor, and dedication to the elusive and deadly energy of his world's magic. That was, in fact, the reason Chinthliss had taken Tannim on in the first place; it had not escaped the young mage that he and his mentor were a great deal alike in many ways. There were a lot of words to describe the two of them, the best of which were creative, crafty, adventurous, virtuous—well, maybe not virtuous—but their many critics had other choice adjectives, none flattering. Tannim had a way of taking the simplest lesson and turning it around to befuddle his "master," who in turn would trounce the boy with the next one, and giggle about it for a week. It was Chinthliss who had given Tannim his name—it meant "Son of Dragons." It fit, especially since he thought of Tannim as he would his own offspring.

Eventually, the lessons simply became jam sessions of experimenting, and Tannim began teaching Chinthliss a thing or two. What was about to occur on this lonely stretch of road was something he'd come up with himself years ago—something that had scared the scat out of Chinthliss. It was the kind of "job" he had done a couple of times with Deke Kestrel in tow. He unwrapped the cherry pop and began chewing on it absent-mindedly, humming along with the tunes. He crumpled the wrapper and slipped it into a pocket, and his humming became a chant through clenched teeth.

He pulled his shoulders back and stretched, neck and back popping from road fatigue, and let in the rush of energy that heralded a major spell. Around him, the cicadas rose in pitch, to harmonize with Peter Garrett and the young man's chanting. Harmonizing with Garrett was no small feat, and he noted it as a good omen. He kept his arms raised toward the crescent moon overhead, and his eyes perceived a subtle change in the starlight as he entered his familiar trance.

His body went rigid, as if rigor mortis had suddenly frozen him in place.

To say that Tannim died then would be misleading— although he was not precisely alive anymore either. The trance he entered was protected well, and he was being monitored by otherworldly allies, but the young mage's soul was now connected to his body by the thinnest of threads—*much* more tenuous than anything most mages ever depended on during out-of-body work. Most of them would have been terrified at the notion of trusting their lives to so fragile a bond. But most mages weren't Tannim. *He* had been trusting his life and more to far more fragile bonds than this for a long time now.

As he stabilized his spirit-form, there was the sensation of everything being well-lit and dark at once, and of infinite visibility—the dizzying effect of mage-sight in the now-and-then hereafter.

He "felt" completely normal, right down to the candy tucked in his cheek and the feel of the Mach 1 beneath him. He tapped his worn black high-tops against the chrome, focusing his thoughts and getting comfortable, teeth gnawing on the pop's soggy stem as he drew energy up from the earth through the frame of the Mach 1, tempering it through the sheet metal, grounding the wild-magic resonances into the engine block, radiating the excess through the window glass.

Good so far; now to find him.

With that, he pulled his spirit away from his body, his shadow-image standing upright, stretching, and adjusting its jacket while his body remained seated on the hood, connected to it by a shimmering field of gossamer threads, the only traces of the spell visible to the trained eye. He stepped away from his anchor, and crossed the gravel shoulder.

A figure wavered and coalesced before him, a fortyish

man in a plaid workshirt and chinos, standing with his hands in his pockets, looking away from the road. There was a half-smoked cigarette hanging slackly from his lips. He was an ordinary man, the kind you'd see at any truckstop, any feed store in the southern belt, lines etched into his face by hard work, bright sun, and pain endured. The only thing that set him apart now was that he was edged by a soft yellowish glow, which seemed to fill in every shadow and crease in that face, and followed him as he stepped towards Tannim.

His brows furrowed, as if trying to remember something. He took a drag off the cigarette. It glowed, but did not burn down. Smoke curled up around his face, a bright blue and violet. "Haven't seen you here before," the man said. "Hiya. Canfield, Ross Canfield. . . ." The man stepped forward, reflexively offered a hand. Tannim bit his lip, stepped forward again, and grasped his hand. *Well, I've got him. Oh God, I thought this was going to be easier. He doesn't know.*

"Hello, Ross," he said. "I'm Tannim."

Ross nodded; he seemed distracted, as if he wasn't entirely focusing on the moment at hand. "Tannim? Good ta meetcha. That a first name or a last name?"

"Only name," Tannim replied cautiously. "Just Tannim. How are you? I mean, you look a little stressed, Ross; are you all right? How do you feel . . . ?"

If Canfield was surprised about this atypical show of concern from a stranger, he didn't show it. "Been better. Strange night." Ross took a pull off of his cigarette. Its tip glowed again, but still didn't shorten. Its smoke wisped up violet and vanished above his head, and he blew smoke from his nostrils in a wash of reddish-purple.

"Mmm. As strange as usual." Tannim smiled inwardly at the oxymoron. "Where you from, Ross?"

Canfield focused a little more on him as the question caught his attention. "Louisiana. Metairie. You?"

Tannim moved a little farther away, unobtrusively testing the energies coming from Canfield. "Tulsa."

Now Canfield's attention was entirely focused on the young mage. "Why you ask?"

"Just curious; I wondered if you were local." It was time to change the subject. "You know, Ross, you seem like a friendly fella, laid back, able to handle 'bout anything. Got something kinda serious to talk to you about."

"Uh huh." Ross Canfield set his jaw, and the glow around him turned a rich orange. Not a good sign. Red would be worse, much worse, but orange was not a good sign.

"Ah, look, Ross, I have some bad news for you, so don't get mad at me. . . ." *They always blame the messenger don't they?*

"Bad news?" Another drag on the cigarette, which now glowed a fierce red—echoing the glow of energy swirling around him. "My wife just left me, kid, and you say *you've* got bad news?"

Abruptly, Tannim was no longer the focus of Canfield's anger. "That sonuvabitch Marty Lear tore the hell outta my lawn with her in that goddamn Jap pickup of his and—and—took her away—"

So; there was the reason for it all. *Uh oh. Fast work, boy, you hit it right the first time.*

Tannim's eyes narrowed, and he took the mangled pop stick out of his mouth. Power fluctuated around them, silent and subtle, but there. Tannim noted their patterns, setting up buffer fields with a mental call. He saw a fan of lines spread around them both, channels waiting to be filled if needed.

"What did you do?"

Canfield did not take offense at what should have been considered a very personal question. "Went after 'em. We was fightin' and she'd already called the bastard; he showed up and she jumped in. Caught up to 'em. Have this old 'Cuda, hot as hell . . ."

"*Had.*"

Tannim was the focus of Canfield's attention again; he felt the hot glare of Ross's stare. "What?" Canfield asked.

He isn't going to like this. "You *had* a Barracuda. I'm sorry, Ross, but . . . that's the bad news I have for you."

"What you talkin' 'bout, son?" Ross Canfield looked pale for a moment, then his glow pulsed cherry red and his face began to twist into anger. He exhaled bright red smoke from his nostrils, jaw set, threads of energy coalescing around his feet and fists.

Now a quick deflection. "Ross, walk with me a minute, will you?" Tannim started along the roadbed toward the overpass a hundred feet away. "How long would you say you've been standing out here, Ross? An hour, maybe? A couple?"

Ross hesitated, then followed Tannim. The tiny traces of reddish energy crackled and followed his steps.

"Ross, you remember stopping here? Getting out of that car? Lighting that cig?"

Ross absently pulled the cigarette from his mouth and looked at it, brow knotted in concentration.

Tannim stood next to the overpass abutment. It was gray concrete, scarred and cracked, with patches of cement covering half its surface. Bits of glass and plastic glittered in the starlight. Tannim picked up a razor-edged sliver of safety-glass an inch long. *Barrier's in place; might as well tell him straight up. He hasn't taken the hints.*

"Ross . . . this is all that's left of your 'Cuda. You hit this bridge doin' one-forty, and you never walked away from it."

The cigarette slipped from Ross' fingers and rested in the dry grass. It smoldered, but didn't set fire to the grass it landed in. The energy field around Ross Canfield crackled like a miniature thunderstorm, apparently invisible to him.

"Ross, look over there." Tannim pointed at the Mustang, and at the man still sitting on the hood. "That's me."

Ross took a deep breath, stooped to pick up his cigarette, and returned it in his mouth.

Here's where it hits. I can handle it; he's not too powerful . . . I hope. Tannim built up his defenses, preparing for a mental scream of rage. . . . Or worse. *Sometimes they don't just blame the messenger, they kill the messenger. I hate this part.*

Ross bit his lip, shock plain on his face as he realized the meaning of Tannim's words.

"Never . . . walked . . . away. . . ."

Tannim nodded, ready to strike back if Ross broke and gave in to the rage building in him. "So I'm dead, huh?"

Tannim could feel the energies arcing between them, screaming for focus. . . .

Hoo boy. Now so am I.

"That's right, Ross. You died three years ago, right here. I'm sorry, really. . . ."

Ross Canfield pulled himself up to his full height, towering over Tannim by almost a foot, eyes glowing red with fury as he seethed. His fists clenched tighter, then relaxed slowly and finally opened. His broad shoulders slouched as his aura dimmed to orange, red tinges slithering away into the ground. He inhaled one massive breath, pulled a hand back through his hair and said—

"Well, *shit*."

Tannim heard mental giggles from his guardians, felt them skitter away to other business, pulling his borrowed energy reserves with them. He heaved a sigh of relief and lowered his guard against a strike.

Ross swayed as if drunk, then stared at Tannim's spirit-form like he was trying out newly bought eyes.

"So, this is what it's like to be a goddamn ghost," Ross said to Tannim as they stood beside the Mustang. "Just my damn luck. I should've expected something like this to happen to me. What the hell do I do now?"

Tannim stood at the hood, beside himself. "I'll tell you in a second." He drew up the Walking spell's reserve energy and stepped back into his body, trusting his instincts that Ross was not going to disturb his transfer. Back at home, he opened his eyes, stretched and stood, rubbing the ever-present kink in his left leg.

"Just for the record, you could have hurt me pretty bad back there, Ross. Just now, I mean. Stepping into and out of a body is a vulnerable time. I trusted you that you wouldn't—thanks."

"Uh huh. What was I gonna do, rattle my chains at ya?" Ross snorted. "And, uh, if it's not too much trouble, what the hell good is this gonna do me? What am I s'posed to do? If I'm dead, where are the angels?"

Tannim paused, and walked to the door of the car. "Get in; I'll tell you."

Ross reached for the door-handle, and his hand passed through it, a tracing of fire around the point of entry. "That's lesson one, Ross. You're only partially in *this* land of the physical. You can choose whether or not to interact with it. Lotta advantages to being a ghost; I don't get the option of deciding if I want to be hit by a bullet or not." Tannim grinned. "You do. Or rather, you will. You're not up to that yet."

"That's spooky as shit," Ross observed, watching his forearm disappear completely into the door.

"Normally you wouldn't be able to do that to this particular car. As a ghost, that is. It has some powerful defenses. I'm lowering the ones against spirits for you, keyed to you and you only. Otherwise, you couldn't get within a foot of that door. Also, another thing: if you get near my tape collection, I'll kill you." Tannim smiled. "You can fry magnetics with a touch—tapes, computer disks, that sorta thing. The tapes are in that red box there. Please don't touch it."

Ross looked through the window at the red fabric case, and read "NO GHOSTS OR POSSESSIONS WITHIN 10 FEET" embroidered into a panel on its lid. The caution was surrounded by arcane symbols. "Yeah, I see. What are those, spells or something?"

Tannim chuckled and leaned against the roof. "The runes? They're from the back of Led Zeppelin Four. Scares most of the ghosts bigtime, except the metal-heads, they just give me a high-sign and say 'Duuuude!' "

Ross laughed, and pulled his arm free of the door. He shoved his other hand in his pockets, and dragged on his ever-present cigarette. The smoke wisped away, disappearing as blue this time.

"That's another advantage, you can see things living people can't, like that warning. It's for spirits only. Your vision should be changing soon, now that you've realized . . . ah, what you are now. Things'll start getting pretty weird . . . people will have funny glows around them, colors that show how they feel emotionally, the brighter they are the more intense they are. I see that way all the time, it's called 'mage-sight'—that's how I can see you now. Watch out for blind spots, they mean trouble every time. They stand for something you can't see, something someone won't let you see, or something you don't *want* to see."

Ross appeared grim for a second, then turned his head to face the overpass.

He looks like he's seen a . . .

Well, he turned very pale.

"I can't see . . . I never noticed that before. That's where I died, and I can't see it at all." Ross looked visibly shaken, and began walking towards the overpass.

Would he be able to see it? Should Tannim even encourage him to try? But he seemed ready. "The trick is to look past it, and bring your field of focus into it. Concentrate on seeing the road past it, then pull back until it appears; the more you want it, the sooner it will come."

Tannim watched him walk up to the place where he'd died, and stop.

"Ross . . ." he said softly, "you don't have to do this, if it's making you uncomfortable, at least not right away. There are ghosts in this world who haven't been able to come to grips with their own deaths for centuries. It's not easy."

"How th' hell would you know?" Ross snapped, and then immediately looked embarrassed.

"I've helped almost a hundred move on to their next destination," Tannim said. "Not always willingly, but . . . it's for the better."

Ross faced him, skepticism warring with a touch of awe. "You're not—an angel, are you?"

"Me?" Tannim laughed. More often, he was mistaken for something else entirely. "Not hardly. Not even close. I'm just a man who can tell you a thing or two about magic, about dying, and what comes after it. Angels live far cleaner lives, and have cleaner consciences."

"There are angels, then? And Heaven?" Ross pulled a long drag on his cigarette.

"I guess." Tannim shrugged. "Hell, I don't know what your definition of Heaven is, so I can't say. But I will tell you that not everyone who dies waltzes through the 'Pearly Gates' of their choice; they still have things to do. A lot of 'em love this world, and don't want to leave. They don't have to, at least, not right away."

"They don't?" Canfield looked surprised—and bemused.

"Nope. Not if they still have things to do, things on their minds." Tannim leaned up against the Mustang. "Most move on to whatever suits them, pretty much right off. But some, it takes a while to find out what it is they want. You're probably that way. It's a whole different ball game when you're dead; conflicts that were big guns when you were alive don't count for much. You meet all kinds of people from all times. Plenty to talk about. Hell, the drone of sports talk at Candlestick Park from a hundred thousand dead fans is enough to put you over the edge!"

"Uh huh." Ross pulled the butt from his mouth. "So I'm gonna be this way for a while?"

"Yeah, probably." He looked up at the clear night sky for a moment. "Since you didn't—go on, when you really understood what had happened to you. I guess you must have some things to do. The way you are—it's kind of a way to live again, with your senses enhanced and a new way of looking at things. Kind of gives you a second chance."

"I guess it isn't all bad," Ross observed after a moment of thought. "Guy could do a lot, see a lot, like this. Things he never got a chance to."

Tannim nodded. "There's a big tradeoff to it; if there's something you need to take care of, that tie will hold you to a place. Even without that, there's ties to your family. Most ghosts build up a sort of 'monitoring' of their families and loved ones, so they know what they are doing, and can be there to lend support from beyond if they can, while they're still ghosts. Native Americans in particular have a strong tie with their ancestors, and their spirits fill everything around them. If I were you, I'd travel a bit and reconcile your feelings about everyone you've ever loved or hated. Then visit your gravesite. After that, it's up to you whether to stay or to move on."

"Well, ain't this a helluva turn. Life after death is just

as big a pain in the ass as living." Ross planted his hands on his hips, and stared towards the bridge. "I can kinda see it now, Tannim. And I can see . . . my 'Cuda. Holy shit . . . I really did buy it good." Ross shuddered, and swore again. "Damn. I loved that car."

Tannim nodded. "Yeah, I can relate. I've lost a couple of good ones myself . . . Thank it for its services and offer it its own afterlife. Even cars can develop spirits, believe me. Honor everything you knew, Ross, then you'll be happy again."

Ross looked down at his feet. "I . . . I loved her too, more than the car, more . . ." he said, and Tannim didn't have to ask to know who he was talking about. "I cried like a goddamn baby every time I couldn't tell her how I felt. It was easier to drink the booze than to find the words. And I chased after her drunk . . . hell, I didn't even know what road she was on. I couldn't even get dying right. . . ."

Better intervene before he starts getting caught in a downward spiral. "Uhhh, Ross, I've met a lot of spirits in my day, and there've been a lot of them who died 'good deaths,' real 'blaze of glory' stuff. Every one of 'em mentioned how stupid it was after all, you know, big picture stuff. I don't know if there *is* a right way to die. But, they all have had regrets about their lives . . . the real heroes and the regular joes."

"Hmm. Yeah, well, I guess I have a lot to think about, and a lot of time to do it." Ross turned, and pulled the cigarette from his lips. "So now I get the chance to change things, huh? Fix what I shouldn't have been in at all. Fine." He threw the cigarette down and ground it out. "I've wanted to quit smoking for twenty years now, and never could. I'll be damned if I'll do it when I'm dead. Don't start drinking or smoking, boy."

Tannim smiled and said, "Yeah, the stuff'll kill you."

Ross bent down before the concrete pillar, and reached a translucent hand towards a sparkling shard of glass. He crouched there a moment longer and smoothed the dirt over it, then strode towards the Mustang, leaving his death behind him.

❖   ❖   ❖

The Alan Parsons Project's "Don't Answer Me" played on the tape deck as the wind rushed past the Mach 1, its engine thrumming in mechanical symphony. The breeze from the open windows made the young driver's hair stream back against the seat-covers, and that same breeze blew right through his passenger.

Ross Canfield put his hand to his chin, shifted to lean his arm against the sill, and put his arm through it. He withdrew and tried again, this time successfully resting his arm against the vinyl. "Shit, this is gonna be hard to get used to."

Tannim chuckled and leaned forward to tap a sticking gauge. "You're doing fine, Ross. Just remember, things in my world may or may not affect you. It's mostly a matter of what you want to be influenced by; for instance, you could, if you wanted to, fall right out of this car doing seventy now by simply deciding that seat won't affect you. Then, you may choose for the road not to affect you, and you wouldn't be hurt by the fall. But you missed the armrest just now because you forgot to 'want' it to affect you. Tricky, huh?"

"Kinda like—what'd they used to say? Mind over matter?"

"Exactly." He nodded with approval. "Now, until you learn spirit-traveling, you're limited by your old human abilities. One day, you may be able to fly cross-country by will alone, but for now, if you fell out of the car, I'd have to stop and pick you up, 'cause you couldn't run fast enough to keep up with me."

Ross chuckled. "Yeah, but I can run faster now that I'm dead. No wheezy lungs from smoking, no beer gut."

"Yeah, and you can play tennis with dead pros to keep in shape."

Ross and Tannim both laughed. "You know, I never thought being dead would be so damned entertaining. And it seems like I should be more upset about it."

Tannim kept his eyes on the road, but he smiled to himself. Ross Canfield was coming along very well—a lot faster than Tannim would have thought. "Well, seriously, Ross, there are a lot of ways to deal with it, but you're running on instinct. Your subconscious was aware you were dead, but your superconscious wasn't ready to accept it, so you stood there sucking a butt for a couple of years. Now, it's kind of a relief that it's out in the open, and you're able to get to the decisions you've been building towards all this time. And as for it being entertaining, kissing a bridge at lightspeed drunk off your ass is a grim thing, but there are a lot of things about being a ghost that are damn funny, no matter what the circumstances are."

"Like fallin' through doors," Ross supplied.

"Uh huh. So, deal with it now with a laugh, because there are plenty of things in the future that'll make you cry, make you scream—" now he turned to look at Canfield out of the corner of his eye "—make you wish you were more dead than you are."

"Huh. As you can tell by the two-year wait, I don't *spook* easily." His face cracked with a smirk.

"Ross! I'd never picked you for a punster!"

"Yeah, well, that's why I'm not in Heaven right now."

Tannim grinned and thought about the turn of a friendly card. Maybe they were both lucky they'd met.

"Seriously . . . what do I do now? How'm I supposed to learn all these ghost things, and how do I get outta bein' one? This shit's gonna get old eventually." Now Ross looked uncertain. "I don't suppose you'd teach me—"

Tannim shook his head. "I can't, Ross. The best I can do is what I just did—break you out of the stalemate you were in and get you started. Like most things, Ross, you have to get out and practice. Learn by doing. Talk to other ghosts, pick up the tricks. I can't show you what you need to know; I've got too many other irons in the fire, and I've got problems enough with people trying to make *me* into a ghost."

At first Ross snorted; then he looked around, and squinted. His eyes widened, and Tannim figured he had started to see some of the protections on the Mustang. It was enough to impress him—even if he wasn't seeing more than a fraction of the magics Tannim had infused the Mach 1 with. "There are a couple of other things I can tell you: just like you can let the rest of the world affect you, with practice, you can influence what happens in the physical world—or; more accurately, the world I'm in right now. Like back there, when you touched that piece of glass, buried it . . . there's a lotta different kinds of 'physical.' Making a change in this one means discovering how to make yours interact with it. That thing with the magnetics is an example of one you can't control; there are others you'll pick up soon enough."

"Got some simple tips?"

"Sure. Stay away from things that make you tired, don't fiddle with walls that won't let you pass, and if anything tries to eat you, *hurt* it."

"Tries to—eat me?" Ross's eyes widened again.

"There's a lot of unfriendly things out there, including some that used to be human. Remember, don't attack first. Until you have the experience to tell friend from foe, be cautious. It's always easier to hold a defensive position anyway. And there are a lot of things out there that aren't human at all; treat them fairly, they can become very close friends. My best friend isn't human. Pretty simple. Otherwise, things are similar to living. You can have sex as a ghost, ride in an F-15. Fly on the Space Shuttle if you want, if you can find room. It's very popular. Enjoy it, and learn. That's the key to moving on—knowledge and maturity are important."

"But, what about moving on? How—"

Tannim shook his head. "I can't tell you; it's different for everyone. You'll know when. If you didn't know how, you'd have never seen the bridge back there; that was an important move. It shows you're finally ready to accept what you are."

Ross was silent for a while, and the miles ticked away as the skyline of Savannah came into view. Finally he spoke. "Tannim . . . thanks."

"No thanks needed, friend," Tannim said, slowing as he approached the city limit. "You ready to take off on your own?"

Ross nodded. "If you need anything, call. I'll find a way to get there. I guess this is dangerous work you're doing, and I owe you for this," he said through teary spectral eyes.

"I'd better get out there. I lost enough time getting shit-faced before, and I want to see what I missed."

Tannim looked sideways at Ross Canfield, nodded, and turned his eyes back towards the highway, pulled to the shoulder and stopped. The city lights illuminated the car, the driver, and the empty seat beside him.

"Be sure to visit River Street while you're here, Ross. Always a party. Good luck. Here's your exit."

The ghost stepped through the door onto the shoulder, and Tannim watched him in the rearview mirror, an ordinary enough guy, watching the Mach 1's taillights recede into the night. Ordinary—except that only Tannim could see him.

And only Tannim could hear him, as clearly as if Ross still sat beside him.

"You need me, you call."

CHAPTER TWO

"That was Georgia's own B-52s, with 'Rock Lobster,' "
said the radio announcer, his cheerful voice murmuring
from the sixteen speakers of Doctor Sam Kelly's home-built
quadraphonic system. "Next up, Shriekback, the Residents,
the new British release from George Louvis, and an oldie
from Thomas Dolby, but first . . ."

Sam hit the "mute" button, and the commercial laded
to a whisper. The timer would bring the volume back up
in another sixty seconds, and by then the station should
be back to music. Doctor Samuel Sean Kelly might have
majored in metallurgy, but he had minored in electrical
engineering; sensing, even back in the '40s, that the time
would come when everyone had to have some understanding of electronics. After all, hadn't he grown up on H. G.
Wells, and the science-fiction tradition that the engineer
was the man who could and would save the universe? "Not
bad, for an old retired fart," he chuckled to his Springer
Spaniel, Thoreau, who raised his head and ears as if he
understood what his master was saying. "I liked Elvis in
the '50s, I liked the Stones and the Fuggs in the '60s, and
now, sure, I'm on the cutting edge—right, boyo?"

Thoreau wagged his stub of a tall and put his head back
down on his paws. He didn't care how eclectic his master's
taste in music was, so long as he didn't crank up those

17

imposing speakers to more than a quarter of their capacity. When Sam retired from Gulfstream, he'd held a party for his younger colleagues that was still the talk of the neighborhood. There had been complaints to the police about the music from as far away as five blocks, and poor Thoreau had gone into hiding in the back closet of the bedroom, not to emerge for three days.

The desk-top before him was preternaturally clean, with only a single envelope cluttering the surface. Sam fingered the letter from "Fairgrove Industries," as the radio volume returned to normal, and Thomas Dolby complained of hyperactivity. He sat back in his aging overstuffed recliner, surrounded by his books, frowning at the empty room and wishing wistfully that he hadn't given up smoking. Or that he hadn't agreed to talk to this "Tannim" person.

It had seemed very harmless when he first got the letter; this "Tannim"—what sex the person was he hadn't known until the phone call came confirming the evening appointment—wanted to talk to him about a job as a consultant. He had offered Sam an amazing amount of money just to *talk* to him: fifteen hundred dollars for an evening of his otherwise idle time. Sam had said yes before he thought the consequences through—after all, how many retired metallurgists could boost their income by that much just by talking to someone? But later, after he'd had lunch with some of the youngsters at Gulfstream and heard some of the latest news, he began to wonder. There was a lot going on over there right now; the joint project with the Russians, a lot of composite development and things being done with explosive welding and foamed aluminum. None of it was exactly secret, but there was a lot of proprietary information Sam was still privy to—and more he could get clandestine access to, if he chose. What if this "Fairgrove Industries"—which was not listed with the Better Business Bureau, and not in any industrial database that Sam had access to—was just a front for something else? What if this Tannim was trying to set him up as a corporate informant, or looking for some "insider trading" type information? Sam had loved his job at Gulfstream; they were, as he joked, a "growing, excited company." He liked the people he worked with enough to socialize with them, even now, when he had been retired for the past several months. He wasn't interested in doing anything that would hurt the company.

Sam tapped the edge of the envelope on his desk and made up his mind about what he *was* going to do, now that he had realized the implications. "Well, Thoreau, if this young fella thinks I'm some kind of senile old curmudgeon he can fool with a silver tongue and a touch of blarney, he's going to be surprised," Sam said aloud. "If it's looking to make a fool of me he is, I just may be making a fool of him."

If this Tannim *was* trying to set him up as a corporate informant, Sam decided, this old man would turn the tables on him. There was a break-in camera under the eaves; it took snaps when the burglar alarm went off, but it could be operated manually. Very well, then, he'd snap pictures of the man's car and license tag when he arrived. First thing in the morning, he'd call his old bosses, give them the number and the young man's description, and let them know exactly what had gone on. Looking for a corporate informant wasn't illegal, exactly—but the fellows at Gulfstream could certainly put a stop to anything shady.

And Sam would still have the fifteen hundred dollars.

Not bad, when you stopped to think out all the implications first, rather than backtracking in a panic. Assuming of course, the check didn't bounce.

But planning ahead in case things did go wrong was what had made Sam one of the best in his field.

"Or so I like to tell myself," he said aloud, smiling at his own conceit.

The doorbell rang, and Sam reached automatically for the modified TV remote-control that, through the intervention of an old Commodore microcomputer, handled gadgets throughout the house. The poor old thing was useless even as a game machine these days, but it was perfectly adequate to mute the radio—or take pictures of the young man and his car before Sam even reached the door. He made his way to the door with a shade of the limberness of his youth, and opened it, catching the stranger in a "listening" pose that told Sam the man had been trying to catch the sound of his own approaching footsteps.

"Doctor Kelly?" The man at the door was illuminated by the powerful floodlight Sam had used to replace the ridiculous little phony carriage-lamp that had been installed there. And he was a *very* young man, much younger than his deep voice had suggested. He nodded in a noncommittal fashion and the man continued. "I'm Tannim—we had an appointment—"

He was carrying a dark leather folder. Sam first took in that, then the wild mop of curly hair, cut short in front and long in the back, the way a lot of kids on MTV cut theirs—a dark nylon jacket, with a good shirt underneath, and a soft scarf instead of a tie—dark slacks, not jeans—boots—the first impression was reasonable. But not exactly fitting the image of a corporate recruiter. The face was good; high cheekbones, determined chin, firm mouth, fine bone-structure and curiously vulnerable-looking eyes. The kid looked like a lot of the hotshot young engineers Sam worked with. But not like what Sam had been expecting.

"I remember," Sam replied cautiously. There was something about the young man that suggested trustworthiness, perhaps his eyes, or the curious sense of *stillness* about him; but Sam knew better than to trust his first impression. Some of the biggest crooks he had ever known had inspired that same feeling of trust. And some of them had been just as young as this man.

"Can I come in?" A quirky grin spread across the man's bony face, transforming the stillness without entirely removing it. "Or would you rather earn your retainer standing here in the doorway? Or would you like to go somewhere else entirely?"

Well, it wouldn't hurt to let the youngster in. Sam moved aside, and Tannim stepped across the threshold. Sam noticed that he walked with a limp, one he was at pains to minimize; that he moved otherwise with a cat-like grace at odds with the limp. Sam was no stranger to industrial accidents and their aftermath. This was someone who had suffered a serious injury and learned to cope with it. That moved him a little more into the "favorable" column, in Sam's mind. Con artists tended to emphasize injuries to gain sympathy—con artists tended *not* to get injured in the first place. "Follow me, if you would," Sam said, leading the way to his office. This was going to be more interesting than he had thought.

Tannim cocked his head to one side as he entered the office, and caught what was playing softly over the speakers. The playlist had migrated to the outré. His eyes and his smile increased a trifle. "Doctor Kelly—I'm pleasantly surprised by your taste in music."

Sam shrugged, as the Residents gave forth their own terrifyingly skewed version of "Teddybear." He took his seat in the recliner behind his desk and waved at the two identical recliners in front of the desk.

But Tannim didn't take a seat; instead, he put the folder he had been carrying on the desk, and beside it, a set of I.D. cards he fanned like a set of playing cards.

"Before we talk, Doctor Kelly, I'd like to assure you of something. Fairgrove Industries is a brand new entity insofar as the rest of the world is concerned—but we've been around a long, long time in the private sector." Sam looked up to see that Tannim's smile had turned into a wide grin. "We've been around a lot longer than anyone knows. I know what you've probably been thinking; that I'm a corporate raider, that I'm a front-man for industrial espionage, or that I'm looking for information on your former employer. Actually, I don't usually do this for Fairgrove, but the folks back at the plant thought I'd be the best person to approach you."

"Oh?" Sam Kelly replied. "So—just what is it that this Fairgrove does that they want from me?"

Tannim tapped the folder with one long finger. "We build racecars, Doctor Kelly. We have nothing to do with aerospace, and I doubt very much we'll ever be involved in that business. But you have skills we very much need."

Sam looked back down at the top photo I.D., which was, unmistakably, Tannim. And listed only the single name, oddly enough—no initials, no first or last name. It was an SCCA card, autoclub racing, sure enough; beneath it was a SERRA card (whatever that was), an IMSA card, an I.D.

card for Roebling Road racetrack, and beneath that was
his Fairgrove card. That particular piece of I.D. listed him
as "test-driver/ mechanic," which Sam hadn't known was
still possible. Not these days, when either profession
required skill and training enough to overwhelm most ordinary people.

But Tannim didn't give him any chance to ask about
that—he opened the folder, and began describing just what
it was that Fairgrove wanted from him, *if* he would take
the job.

"We need you as a consultant, Doctor Kelly," he said,
earnestly. "We're working on some pretty esoteric technolo-
gies here, and we need someone with a solid background
who is still flexible and open to new ideas. You were one
of the best metallurgists in the country before you retired—
and no one has ever accused you of being stuck in a rut,
or being too old-fashioned to change."

That surprised him further, and embarrassed him a little.
He was at a loss for a response, but Tannim was clearly
waiting for one. "Oh, I would'na know about that," he said,
lapsing briefly into the Irish brogue of his childhood.

"We would," Tannim said firmly, nodding so that his
unruly mop of dark, curly hair flopped over into one eye,
making him look, thin as he was, like a Japanese *anime*
character. "We've looked very carefully at everyone who
might suit us, and who could legitimately work with us
without compromising themselves or their current or past
employers. You are the best."

Sam felt himself blushing, something he hadn't done
in years. "Well, if you think so . . . what's the job, anyway?"

"Metallurgy," Tannim told him. "Specifically, fabricat-
ing engine blocks and other high-stress parts of non-ferrous
materials." He flashed that grin again, from under the
errant lock of hair, calling up an answering smile from Sam.
"Like your music, we're on the cutting edge."

"I don't know," Sam replied, slowly, as Tannim finally
took his seat, leaving his host free to leaf through the
Fairgrove materials. Most of them had the look of something that had been produced on a personal computer, the
great-great grandchild of the one that helped Sam run his

house, and the cousin of the one on the workstation behind him. The specs Fairgrove had on their "wish list" were impressive—and as unlikely as any of H. G. Wells' dreams of Time Machines. "I don't know. Engine blocks—you're talking about a high-stress application there. You want a foamed aluminum matrix for internal combustion, with water-cooling channels, air-cooling vanes, and alloy piston sleeves? In five castings for the main block? I don't know that it's possible."

"Ah, but you don't know it's *not* possible, do you?" Tannim retorted. "We aren't going to pay you on the basis of whether or not common wisdom says it's possible—we're doing research. Applied research, yes, but when you do research, you accept the fact that some of your highways may turn out to be dead ends. That's life. And speaking of payment—" He reached into his jacket, and pulled out an oak-tree-embossed envelope, which he laid on top of the Fairgrove folder.

Sam thumbed it open. There was a cashier's check inside, made out on his own bank, for fifteen hundred dollars. Until this moment, Sam had not entirely believed in the reality of this retainer. Now, holding it in his hands, he could find no flaw in it—and no real flaw with what Fairgrove, in the person of this young man, proposed.

Except, of course, whether or not what they wanted was a pipe-dream, a Grail; desirable, yes, but impossible to achieve. . . .

Or was it? These people certainly had a lot of money to wave around. And there *were* some problems you could solve by throwing money at them.

"I suppose I could take a look at this place," he ventured. "I could at least see what you people have to work with."

If anything, Tannim's grin got wider. He spread his hands wide. "Sure! How about—right now? We're all night owls over there, and it isn't that far away."

Now? In the middle of the night? That wasn't an offer Sam expected. Did they expect him to come? Or did they expect him to say no?

If he showed up now, surely they wouldn't have time

to put on a big display for him . . . and that might be all
for the best, really. He'd see things as they were, not a
dog-and-pony show. As for the lateness of the hour, well,
one of the advantages of being retired was that he no
longer had to clock in—and he didn't have to follow the
company's time schedule. He'd always been a night owl
by nature, and although this was the "middle of the night"
to some people, for him the day was barely halfway
through—one reason why he'd set this appointment long
after a "normal" working day had ended.

And besides all that, if he was going to take a look at
this place, he wanted to see all of it. That meant the metal
shops, too. This early in the fall, daytime temperatures were
still in the nineties, and no matter how good their air-
conditioning was, the shops would be as hot as Vulcan's
forge during the daylight hours. Metal shops always were,
especially if these people were doing casting work.

"All right," he said, shoving himself resolutely out of
his chair. "Let's go. No better time to see this miracle place
of yours than right now."

"Great!" the young man answered, sliding out of his
chair and getting to his feet with no more than a slight
hesitation for the bad leg. "Want to take my car? We've
used it to test out some SERRA-racer modifications;
y'know, suspension mods, rigidity, a little composite fid-
dling. It's street-legal—barely."

There was something challenging about his grin, and
Sam decided to take the dare. "Sure," he replied, taking
just enough time with his remote to tell the house to run
the "guardian" program. He slipped the remote into his
pocket as an added precaution; without that, no one would
be able to disarm the system. Not even cutting the power
would make a difference; the house had its own
uninterruptable power supply, and a generator that kicked
on if the power stayed off for more than half an hour. He'd
installed all that during the Gulf War terrorist scare, when
high-level people at a lot of industries, including
Gulfstream, had been warned they might be targets for
kidnapping or terrorism. He'd gotten into the habit of
arming it whenever he left or went to sleep, and it didn't

seem an unreasonable precaution still. Maybe he was paranoid, but being paranoid had saved lives before this.

Thoreau sighed as he saw Sam reach for his jacket. Sam reached down and ruffled the dog's ears, promising that even though "daddy" wasn't going to be around to beg a late-night snack from, there would be a treat when he got back. Thoreau accepted this philosophically enough, and padded alongside, providing an escort service to the front door.

There, Sam was briefly involved in locking the door, and wasn't paying a great deal of attention to the car behind him. Then he turned around.

Sam had been around hot-rodders all his life; seemed to him that for every four techies at Gulfstream who were indifferent to automobiles, there would be one who cherished the things. Now he was looking at a machine that would impress any of them. It was parked with the front wheels turned rakishly, and he made note of its distinguishing features. Dark metallic red; three antennas. Scuffed sidewalls. Dark windows. It was hardly the "company car" he was expecting.

Tannim was wearing that sideways smile of his, and thumbed his keyring. The Mustang rumbled to life, and its doors unlocked and opened a crack. Despite himself, Sam's face showed his interest in the electronic gimcrackery. Tannim gestured to the open passenger's side door with a flourish, and went around to the driver's side as Sam pulled the door open and got in.

Sam pulled the seatbelt snug as Tannim slid into the driver's side, noting as he did so, that these were *not* standard American windowshade seatbelts, which tended—in his opinion—to allow far too much freedom of movement for safety. And as Tannim closed the driver's side door, he noted something else. . . .

Something besides the door had closed, sealing them inside the protective shell of the Mustang. It had sprung into being the moment Tannim's door closed, and covered car and occupants. It wasn't tangible, like the seatbelts or the roll-cage—it wasn't even visible to ordinary sight. But it was there, nevertheless. Tannim pushed a worn tape into the dash deck, and turned down or switched off most of the suite of other instruments there—the CB, high-end channel-scanner, an in-dash radar detector, and—what was this, a police-repeater sensor? Sam looked over the interior a little more, noting the various boxes in the back seat. Some more electronics gear. Hmm. There was also a trash-box stuffed with candy wrappers, a tissue box, allergy tablets, fire extinguishers mounted next to crowbars, two first-aid kits . . . and an embroidered tape-case. As he peered at it, Sam thought he could almost see words in the threads, and familiar symbols. This vehicle was not just a very unusual car; there was more to it than that. There was a great deal of power under the hood—and there was far more Power of a different sort infused into it.

The differences might not be visible to normal eyes, but Sam had a little more to use than what his granny had called "outer eyes." Sam had not been gifted with the ability the Irish referred to as "the Sight" to neglect using it, after all. Nor had becoming a man of science interfered with that. If anything, he was too much of a scientist to discount a gift that had granted him knowledge he might not otherwise have, with fair reliability, over so many years.

Interesting. Very interesting.

"So," he said, as Tannim pulled out smoothly onto the darkened highway, the headlights cutting the darkness ahead of them into areas of seen and half-seen. "Tell me about Fairgrove. Why did they decide to get into manufacturing? And why nonferrous materials?"

Tannim fiddled with the tape deck for a moment before replying. He had put in a Clannad tape, and made a show of ensuring that the volume exactly matched that of the radio in Sam's office, stalling a little. Sam knew a stall when he saw one.

"Before I tell you about Fairgrove, I have to explain SERRA," he temporized, paying closer attention to the road ahead than it really warranted. "In some ways, they're almost the same entity. Virtually everyone working for Fairgrove came out of SERRA, and the president and board of Fairgrove actually helped found SERRA. Uh, their families did."

Sam was pretending to watch the road, but he was really watching Tannim out of the corner of his eye. And that last, about the board founding SERRA, had been a real slip. Tannim hadn't meant to say that. But what made it a slip?

"So? What's this SERRA?" he asked.

"South Eastern Road Racing Association," Tannim replied promptly, and with enthusiasm he didn't try to conceal. "It's an offshoot of the SCCA—Sports Car Club of America. Part of the problem for us was that SCCA doesn't allow the sort of modifications we wanted, and the folks in SERRA wanted to push the envelope of sportscar racing a bit more, more 'experimental' stuff. Fairgrove also supports an IMSA team, running GTP, but that's for pro drivers, guys who don't do anything but drive, and we've only just started that circuit. Some of us—like me—still race SCCA, in fact, I drive for the Fairgrove team. There's things to like about both clubs, which is why Fairgrove still maintains a team in both."

"You don't drive in the Fairgrove SERRA team?" Sam said. Tannim shrugged.

"We've got some drivers as good as I am on the SERRA team, drivers who can't race SCCA cars. Since I could do both, I opted for the SCCA team, and left rides for the other guys." He grinned. "Don't worry, I get plenty of track time in! If I had the time, I could spend every weekend and most weekdays racing."

Sam had no doubt that Tannim was a professional driver in every sense of the word, despite the disclaimer; the way he handled this car put Sam in mind of an expert fighter pilot, of the way the plane becomes an extension of the pilot himself, and the pilot can do things he shouldn't be able to. There was an air of cocky competence about the kid, now that he was behind the wheel, that was very like a good pilot's too.

"That's not cheap, fielding several teams—" Sam ventured.

"Three teams, each with several cars, and no, it isn't cheap," Tannim admitted cheerfully. "The founding families started out independently wealthy—inherited money that survived the '20s crash—but they've been making racing pay for itself for a while now. Not just purses and adverts—they've been farming out their experts—" he grinned again "—like yours truly, and opening up their shops for modifications to whoever was willing to pay the price. But that could only go so far. *Now* we'd like to hit the bigtime. Indy-style, Formula One, that kind of thing. Getting right up there with the big boys—maybe even have the big boys come to us. But to do that, we have to have something better than just mods. We have to have original advances. That's where you come in."

He braked, briefly, and Sam caught the flash of a bird's wings in the headlights. An owl; a big one. Most drivers wouldn't have known it was going to cut across the car's vector. Most drivers wouldn't have bothered to avoid it.

"Maybe," Sam replied, feeling his way. "I don't know; this sounds like it could be very risky business. . . ."

"Your part won't be," Tannim promised. "Fairgrove will pay half your consultation fee up front, before you even pin on a badge, and put the other half in escrow in your bank." Then he named a figure that would have given Sam cardiac trouble, if not for watching his diet and cholesterol. It was considerably more than his salary at Gulfstream had been. Of course, one of the disadvantages of staying with a firm for years was that your salary didn't keep pace with the going rate for new-hires with similar experience, but—this was ridiculous; they couldn't want him that badly! Could they?

"What about disclosure?" he asked, when he could speak again.

"We've got a tentative non-disclosure clause in your contract, but we can modify it if you feel really strongly about it," Tannim said. "We based it on the non-disclosure clause at Gulfstream, but we made one modification, and that's in the area of Research and Development in safety. Anything that's a significant advance in safety is immediately released, and patents won't be enforced. Think you can live with that? Even if it means a loss of income?"

Since that was the one area where Sam had himself had several heated arguments with his own bosses over the years, he nodded. "Some things should be common knowledge," he said grimy. "That's in a Mercedes ad, but it's true for all of that."

He asked many more questions over the course of the next fifteen minutes, and although Tannim never refused to answer any of them, he kept getting the feeling that the young man was doing a kind of verbal dance the whole time—carefully steering him away from something. It wasn't where the money was coming from; at least, this wasn't the kind of youngster or the kind of operation Sam would have associated with money laundering and organized crime. And car-racing wasn't the kind of operation that would lend itself to that sort of thing anyway. It wasn't what he would be expected to accomplish. It was nothing that he was able to put a finger on. But there was some skillful verbal maneuvering going on here, and Sam wished strongly that he could see at least the shape of this blind spot, so he could guess at what it was hiding.

Tannim pulled off the highway onto a beautifully paved side road, and stopped at a formidable gate, punching in a code on the keypad-box just in front of it. The gate-doors retracted—

And just on the other side of the gate, a miniature traffic signal lit up—the yellow light first, then the green, and the radar detector under the dash lit up. Tannim turned toward his passenger with a sparkle in his eye, and a grin that bordered on maniacal. "Did you know that there's no speed limit on private driveways?" he said, conversationally. Then he floored the accelerator.

Once again, it was a good thing that Sam had been watching his diet for years—and that he was well acquainted with "test pilot humor." As it was, by the end of that brief but hair-raising half-mile ride, he wasn't certain if Tannim had *added* years to his age, or subtracted them by peeling them off; with sheer speed as the knife-blade. One thing was sure; if Sam's hair hadn't already been white, the ride would have bleached it to silver.

Tannim pulled up to a tire-screeching halt beside another miniature traffic light. As they passed it, Sam noted—faintly surprised that he still had the ability to notice anything—that going in the opposite direction, the light was red as they passed it. It turned yellow well after they passed, then green a moment later. A wise precaution, if people used the driveway as a dragstrip on a regular basis. A board lit up with numbers, and Tannim laughed out loud. "Elapsed time and speed, Sam." He cocked his head sideways like an exotic bird. "Not my best run, but not bad for nighttime, and with a passenger weighing me down."

They rolled up to a driveway loop at a sedate pace. In the center of the circular cut-out was a discrete redwood sign reading "Fairgrove Industries." The building itself looked like Cape Canaveral before a shuttle launch, with hundreds of lights burning. Evidently these people *were* night owls.

Tannim pulled the Mustang into a parking slot, between a Lamborghini Diablo and a Ferrarri Dino. "Expensive neighbors," Sam commented. Tannim just chuckled, and popped his seatbelt.

He led the way through a series of darkened offices; the clerical staff was evidently not expected to keep the same hours as the techies. The offices themselves gave an overall impression of brisk efficiency with a touch of comedy; although the desks were clean and orderly, there were toys on all the computer terminals and desks, artwork and posters on the walls, and so many plants Sam wondered if someone had raided a greenhouse. Most of the artwork and toys had something to do with cars. These people evidently enjoyed their work. And these were working offices; had been for some time; there was no way you could counterfeit that "lived in, worked in" look. Whatever else Fairgrove was, it *had* been in existence for some time. This was no façade thrown up to delude him.

Tannim brought him to a soundproof wall—Sam recognized it as the twin to one at Gulfstream, that stood between the offices and the shops—and opened a door into bright light and seeming chaos.

There were cars in various states of disassembly everywhere, each one surrounded, like a patient in intensive care, by its own little flotilla of instrumentation and machinery.

There was a *lot* of expensive equipment here: computer-controlled diagnostic devices, computer-controlled manufacturing machinery behind the cars on their little islands of activity—

There must have been several million dollars in cars alone, and about that in equipment. Oddly enough, though, no one seemed to be using any of the latter; they all seemed to be working directly on the cars. The machinery itself was standing idle. In fact, given the sheen of "newness" on all that expensive gimmickry, most of it hadn't ever been fired up.

Why buy all that stuff if you weren't going to use it?

Tannim was looking for something, or someone, craning his head in every direction. Sam was unable to get his attention, and really, didn't try very hard. There was definitely something odd about this place. There was a facade—and it was in here, not out in the offices.

Finally, as a little group of people emerged from behind one of the cars and its attendant machines, Tannim spotted whoever it was he was looking for among them. He waved his hand in the air, and called out to them.

"Yo!" he shouted, his voice somehow carrying over the din. "Kevin! Over here!"

A tall, *very* blond man turned around in response to that shout, green eyes searching over the mass of machines and people.

And Sam felt such a shock he feared for a moment that he'd had a stroke. Those eyes—that face—they were familiar.

Hauntingly, frighteningly familiar, though he hadn't seen them in nearly fifty years.

He *knew* this man—

—who *wasn't* a man.

CHAPTER THREE

It was the same face—not a similar face, the *same* face, the same man. Identical. There was no confusing it, nor those green, cat-slitted eyes.

Inhuman eyes; eyes that had *never* been human.

Sam fell back across the decades, to his childhood, and his home, and one moonlit, Irish night.

Sam stumbled along beside his father, miserable right down to his socks, and wanting to be home with all his five-year-old heart.

"Da—me tum hurts," Sam whined.

The full moon above them gave a clear, clean light, shining down on the dirt path that led between the pub and John Kelly's little cottage. A month ago, they wouldn't have been on this path. A month ago, Sam's mummy, Moira, would have made them a good supper, one that wouldn't have hurt Sam's tummy the way the greasy sausage-and-potato mix the pub served up did. In fact, a month ago, John wouldn't have been anywhere near the pub, and the pint of whiskey he had in his back pocket would have lasted him the month, not the night. He would've had tea with his good dinner, not washed bad roast down with more whiskey.

But that was a month and more ago, before Moira took

a cough that became worse, and then turned into something awful, something called "new-moan-yuh." Something the doctor couldn't cure, nor all the prayers Sam and his Da had offered up to the Virgin.

She'd taken sick on a Monday. By the following Monday, they were putting her under the sod, and the priest told him she was with Jesus. Sam didn't understand any of it; he kept thinking it was all a bad dream, and when he woke up, his Mummy would comfort him and everything would be all right again.

But he went to sleep at night, and woke up in the morning, and it wasn't all right. His Da was drinking his breakfast, and leaving Sam to make whatever breakfast he could on cold bread-and-butter and go off to stay with Mrs. Gilhoolie, since he was too young for school. John Kelly was going to work smelling like a bottle, coming home smelling like a bottle, and taking Sam to the pub every night for a bad supper and more bottles.

It was cold out, and Sam had forgotten his coat "Da," he whined again, knowing that he sounded nasty but not knowing what else to do to get his Da's attention. "Da, me tum hurts, an' I'm *cold.*" The wind whistled past them, coming around the Mound, and cutting right through Sam's thin shirt and short pants. The Mound was an uncanny place, and Sam didn't like to go there. The Fair Folk were supposed to live there, and they weren't the pretty little fairies in the children's books and the cartoons at the cinema; Sam's granny had told him about the Fair Folk, and she had never, ever lied to him. They were terrible, wonderful creatures, taller than humans, handsome beyond belief, and many were utterly unpredictable. The best a human could do was steer clear of them, for no human could tell whether a man or woman of the Folk was kindly inclined towards humans or dangerous to them. Even when they seemed to be doing you favors, sometimes they were doing you harm, the bad ones. And the good ones sometimes did harm with the idea of doing good.

But right now Sam had more immediate troubles than running into one of the Fair Folk. His tummy hurt, he

was so cold his teeth chattered, his head hurt, his Da was
acting in peculiar ways—

And oh, but he missed his Mummy—

"Daaaaa," he whined, holding back tears of grief. When
his Da said anything about Mummy, it was to tell him to
be a man, and not cry. But it was hard not to cry. The
only way he could keep from crying, sometimes, was to
whine. Like now. "Daaaaaa."

There was no warning, none at all. One moment he was
stumbling along beside his Da, the next, he was sprawled
on the cold ground beside the path, looking up at his Da
in shock, his face and teeth aching from the blow his Da
had just landed on him. The moonlight showed the mur-
derous look on his Da's face clearly. Too clearly. Whimpering, with sudden terror, he tried to scramble away.

He wasn't fast enough.

His Da grabbed the front of his shirt and hauled him
to his feet, then off his feet, and backhanded him. Sam
was in too much shock to even react to the first two slaps,
but at the third, he cried out.

There was no fourth.

John had his hand pulled back, ready to deliver another
blow. Sam struggled fruitlessly in his father's iron grip,
crying—

Then there was a tremendous flash of light; Sam was
blinded, and felt himself falling. He flailed his arms wildly,
and landed on his back, hard enough to drive the breath
out of him.

He wheezed and rubbed his eyes, trying to force them
to clear. The sound of someone choking made him look
up, squinting through watering eyes, still trying to catch
his breath.

What he saw made him forget to breathe.

A tall, terrible blond stranger, dressed in odd clothing,
like something out of the pantomimes of King Arthur, was
holding his father by the throat. John Kelly was white-faced
and shaking, but was not trying to move or fight the stranger.
This was no one Sam had seen in or near the village, and
anyway, most of the people around here were small and
dark, or small and red-haired. Not tall and silver-blond. The

man looked down at Sam for a moment, and even though the only light came from the moon overhead, he saw—clearly—that the man had bright, emerald green eyes; eyes that looked just like a cat's. And long, pointed ears.

This was no man. This could only be one of the Fair Folk, the Sidhe; and the fairy-man's eyes caught Sam like a rabbit caught in the headlights of a motorcar.

Sam couldn't move.

John Kelly made another choking noise, and the stranger turned those mesmerizing eyes back towards his captive.

"John Kelly," the terrifying man said—with a gentleness made all the more terrible by his obvious strength. "John Kelly, you're a good man, but you're on the way to a bad end. 'Tis the luck of your God that brought you here tonight, within my reach and my ken, for if you hadn't struck your lad just now, I wouldn't have known of your troubles and your falling into the grip of pain and whiskey. Now get hold of yourself and get your life straight again—for if you don't, I swear to you that we'll steal this lovely boy of yours, and you'll never see him again, this side of paradise. Remember what your mother told you, John Kelly. Remember it well, and believe it. We did it once within your family, and we can and will do it again, if the need comes to it."

There was another flash of light. When Sam could see, the man was gone, and his father was sinking slowly to his knees. Sam still couldn't move, numb with shock and awe, and feelings he couldn't put a name to.

For a long, long time, John Kelly lay in the dirt, his shoulders shaking. Then, after a while, John looked up, and Sam saw tears running down his Da's face, glistening in the moonlight.

"Da?" he whispered, tentatively. "Da?"

"Son—" John choked—and gathered Sam into his arms, holding him closely, just the way he used to. Sobbing. Somehow that made Sam feel both good and bad. Good, that his Da was the man he loved again. Bad, that his Da was crying.

Sam said again. "Da, what's the matter? Da?"

"Sam—son—" John Kelly wept unashamed. "Son, I've

been wicked, I've been blind with pain, and I've been wicked. Forgive me, son. Oh, please, forgive me—"

Sam hadn't been sure what to say or do, but he'd given his father what he asked for: Forgiveness, and all the love and comfort he had.

Eventually, John Kelly had gathered his son up in his arms, and taken him home. And from that day until the day he died, he never touched another drop of alcohol.

It can't be— he thought dazedly, from the perspective of half a century away. *It can't be*—

Despite the Sight, he'd assumed for decades that the whole incident had been a dream, something his childish imagination had conjured up to explain his father's brief, alcoholic binge and his recovery.

He'd only been five, after all. But this, this tall, blond man striding toward them was the same, the very same person as that long-ago stranger. No matter that the long hair was pulled back into a thick pony-tail, not flowing free beneath a circling band of silver about the brow. No matter that the clothing was a form-fitting black coverall, incongruously embroidered with "Kevin" over the breast pocket, and not the tunic and trews of a man of the ancient Celts. There was no mistake.

Sam knew then that he must be going mad. It was an easier explanation than the one that fit the situation.

The man strode towards them with all the power and grace of a lean, black panther in its prime. As he neared them, he smiled; a warm smile that reached even into those emerald eyes and made them shine. "You've grown into a fine man, Sam Kelly," he said, stopping just short of them, and resting his fists on his hips. "A fine man, like your father John, and smarter than your father, to wash your hands of a dying land and seek your life on this side of the water. Now you know why we chose you, and no other."

"I see you've met," Tannim said, with an ironic lift of an eyebrow.

This man, this "Kevin"—he hadn't aged a day since Sam saw him fifty years ago. He'd looked thirty or forty then, which would make him what? Ninety? A hundred?

Either he had discovered the fountain of youth, or—

"You—" Sam said, finally getting his mouth to work. "You're—"

"One of the Fair Folk?" Keighvin said, with a lop-sided smile, and a lifted brow that echoed Tannim's. "The Lords of Underhill? The Kindly Ones? The Old People? The Elves, the Fairies, the Sidhe?" He chuckled. "I'm glad to see you still remember the old ways, the old tales, Sam. And, despite all your university learning, you believe them too, or at least, you're willing to believe them, if I read your heart aright."

In the face of a living breathing tale out of his own childhood, how could he not believe? Even when it was impossible? He had to believe in the Sidhe, or believe that someone had read his mind, picked that incident out of his childhood, and constructed someone who looked *exactly* like the Sidhe-warrior, and fed him all the pertinent details.

It was easier and simpler to believe in the Sidhe—the Wise Ones who had stolen away his granny's brother, because great-grandfather had beaten him once too often, for things he could not help. He remembered his granny's tales of that, too, for Patrick had been granny's favorite brother, and she'd told the story over and over. Poor Patrick; from the vantage point of near seventy-five years Sam knew what Patrick's problem had been, and it hadn't been willfulness or clumsiness. They'd have called him "dyslexic," these days, and given him special teaching to compensate. . . .

"We helped him," Keighvin said, as if reading his mind again. "We helped him, and sent him over the sea to this new land, and our kin here in Elfhame Fairgrove. He prospered, married a mortal girl, raised a family. Remind me to introduce you to your cousins, one day."

"Cousins?" Sam said, faintly. "I think I need to sit down."

". . . so, that was when the Fairgrove elvenkin got interested in racing," Tannim said, as Sam held tight to his cup of coffee, and Keighvin nodded from time to time. Sam sat on an overturned bucket, Tannim perched like a gargoyle on top of an aluminum cabinet, and Keighvin leaned against one of the sleek, sensuous racecars. Now that there was no need to counterfeit the noise of a real metal shop, things were much quieter, though there was no less activity. "Now roughly a fourth of the SERRA members are either elves or human mages. At first it was mostly for enjoyment. The Fairgrove elves in particular got interested in the idea of using racing to get some of their members out into the human world, the way things used to be in the old days."

"Aye," Keighvin seconded, leaning back against a shining, black fender, and patting it absent-mindedly, as if it was a horse. "In the old days, it could be you'd have met one of the Sidhe at any crossroads, looking for a challenge. You'd have found a kelpie at every ford—and on moon-lit nights, the woods and meadows would be thick with dancing parties. Plenty of the Sidhe like humans, Sam; you give us a stimulus we sorely need. It was Cold Iron that drove us Underhill, Sam, and Cold Iron that drove us away, across the sea. It's deadly to us, as your granny doubtless told you."

"But—" Sam protested, gesturing with his coffee cup. "What about—that? You're leaning against Cold Iron."

Keighvin grinned, white teeth gleaming in a way that reminded Sam sharply that the man was no human. "That I'm not." He moved away from the car, and the car—twisted.

It writhed like something out of a drug-dream. Sam had to close his eyes for a moment; when he opened them, there was no car there at all, but a sleek, black horse, with wicked silver eyes. It winked at him, and stamped a delicate hoof on the concrete. Sparks struck and died.

"An elvensteed," Tannim said, with a chuckle. "That's how the pointy-eared smartasses got into racing in the first place. They transformed the elvensteeds into things that looked like cars, at least on the outside. But once club racing started having *inspections*—"

"I'd have found it damned difficult to explain a racecar with no motor," Keighvin supplied, as the elvensteed nuzzled his shoulder. "Rosaleen Dhu can counterfeit most things, including all the right noises for an engine to make, but not the engine itself. Only something that looks superficially like an engine."

Black Rose. She's beautiful. . . .

Tannim gestured at the lovely creature with his chin. "And *that's* how Fairgrove is setting the pace in aerodynamics, too. Put an elvensteed in a wind-tunnel, and alter the design by telling it what you want. No weeks of making body-bucks and laying fiberglass." Tannim gloated, and Sam didn't blame him. This was better even than computer modeling.

"But—you're still racing now, with a real team—" Sam protested. "With real cars—real engines—"

"With every part we can manage being replaced with nonferrous materials," Tannim told him. "That's what we started doing even before the inspections. It was no challenge to race an elvensteed that can reach half the speed of sound against Tin Lizzies. It *was* a challenge to try and improve on human technology."

Keighvin held up his hands, and only then did Sam notice he was wearing thin leather gloves, black to match his coverall. Sam also noted a black web belt and a delicate silver-and-silk-sheathed knife, more decorative than a tool. "And for those things that can't be replaced by something other than iron and steel, well, some of us have built up a kind of tolerance to Death Metal. Enough that we can handle it if we're protected—and we try not to work much magic about it." He patted the horse's neck. "I'll explain the Laws of it all to you later—and how we're breaking them."

Tannim jumped down off the cabinet, catching Sam's eye, and began pacing. Sam suspected he needed to ease an ache in that bad leg. "Racing and building cars was what lured the elvenkin out from Underhill," he said. "But racing wasn't the real reason that some of the elves wanted more of their company out in the human world, and to be more active in it."

"Some didn't approve—" Keighvin said.

"But most of Fairgrove did," Tannim interjected. "And now we have to get into some old history. That's Keighvin's subject."

The horse had turned back into a car again while Sam had been watching Tannim; Keighvin leaned back against its fender (flank?) and folded his arms.

"Do you have any idea why I confronted your father that night, Sam Kelly?" Keighvin asked. "Or what I was talking about, with your great-uncle and all?"

Sam blurted the first thing that came into his head. "The Fair Folk steal children—everybody knows that—"

A moment later he wanted to go hit his head against a wall. *Now you're for it, Sam Kelly. Why not go into a gay gym and tell the boys there that you've heard they seduce six-year-olds?*

But strangely, Keighvin didn't look the least bit angry "Aye, Sam, we steal children. The Seleighe Court does, at any rate. To save them. Children bein' beaten within an inch of their lives, children bein' left cold and hungry and tied t' the bedpost all day, children bein' sold and slaved. . . . Oh aye, we steal children. Whenever we can, whenever we know of one in danger of losing life or soul, or heart, and we can get *at* them, aye, we steal them." Keighvin's expression was dark, brooding. "We used to do other things, too. There are some problems, Sam, that can be fixed by throwing money at them, as you yourself were thinking earlier. Not all of those problems are technical, either. Do you mind some of the other stories your granny used to tell? About the leprechauns, or the mysterious strangers who gave gold where it was most needed?"

"Aye," Sam replied, again falling into the brogue of his childhood, to match the lilt of Keighvin's speech. "But those strangers were the holy saints, or angels in disguise, sent from the Virgin, she said—"

Keighvin snorted. "Holy saints? Is that what you mortal folk decided? Nay, Sam, 'twas us. At least, it was us when there were hungry children to feed, and naught to feed them with; when there was no fuel in the house, and children freezing. When some mortal fool sires children, but won't be a father to them, leaving the mother to struggle alone. Our kind—we don't bear as easily or often as you. Children are rare and precious things to us. We're impelled to protect and care for them, even when they aren't our own."

Suddenly a great many of the old stories took on a whole new set of meanings. . . . But Keighvin was continuing.

"This isn't the old days, though, when a stranger could give a poor lass a handful of silver and gold in return for a kindness. For one thing, the girl would be thought a thief, like as not, when she tried to trade it for paper money. For another, someone would want to track down whoever gave it to her. We have to truly, legitimately, *earn* money before we can give it away."

Tannim shook his head in mock sadness. "Oh, now that's a real pity, isn't it—you elves having to *work* for a living. What's the world coming to?"

Keighvin cast the young man a sharp glance. "One of these days, my lad, that tongue of yours is going to cast you into grief."

Tannin chuckled, uncowed by the fire in Keighvin's eye. "You're too late, it already has." He turned to Sam. "These boys can literally create anything, if they've studied it long enough beforehand. We've been making foamed aluminum engine blocks ever since Keighvin here got his hands on a sample from a Space Shuttle experiment." He hopped back up onto his cabinet, crossing his legs like a Red Indian. "I'm not even going into how we got that. But, we've been using the stuff in our cars—now, can you imagine what we could charge some of the big boys to duplicate *their* designs in foamed cast aluminum?"

Indeed, Sam could. And the major racing teams had a great deal of money to play with. "So that's why you set up this shop, Fairgrove Industries—but what do you need me for?"

"We need a front-man," Tannim said, leaning forward in his eagerness to explain himself. "We need someone who can give a convincing explanation of how we're doing all this, and show us how to create a setup that will at least look like we're making the things by some esoteric process and not by magic."

"But there isn't any process—" Sam began. "There isn't a firm in the world that could duplicate—"

Tannim waved a negatory hand in the air.

"It doesn't matter if no one else can duplicate what we do," he said blithely. "They'll expect us to have trade secrets. We just need someone who knows all the right techno-babble, and can make it sound convincing. As long as you can come up with something that's possible in theory, that's all we need. We'll keep on buying machines that go *bing*, and you leak tech reports to the curious."

Sam couldn't help himself; he started to laugh. Tannim and Keighvin both looked confused and surprised. "What's so funny?" Tannim asked.

"Do you know much science fiction?" he asked, through his chuckles. Keighvin shook his head. Tannim shrugged. "A little. Why?"

"Because a very famous author, Arthur C. Clarke—who also happens to be one of the world's finest scientists and engineers—said once that technology that's complicated enough can't be told from magic."

"So?" Tannim replied.

Sam started laughing again. "So—sufficiently complex magic is indistinguishable from technology!"

Keighvin looked at Tannim for an explanation; the latter shrugged. "Beats me," the young man said with a lopsided smile, as Sam wheezed with laughter. "Sometimes I don't understand us either."

It was nearly midnight when they'd gotten the basic shape of a plan hammered out. By then, they'd moved into Keighvin's office—a wonderful place with a huge, plate-glass window that looked out into what seemed to be an absolutely virgin glade. The office itself was designed to be an extension of the landscape outside, with plants standing and hanging everywhere, and even a tiny fountain with goldfish swimming in it.

"Well, I'm going to have to go home and sleep on this," Sam said, finally. "Then get into some of the journals and see what kind of a convincing fake I can concoct before I can definitely say I'll take the job."

He started to get up, but Keighvin waved him down again. "Not quite yet, Sam," he said, his expression grave.

"There's just one thing more we need to tell you about. And you may decide not to throw in your lot with us after you've heard it."

"Why?" he asked, a little surprised.

"Because Fairgrove has enemies," Tannim supplied, from his own nook, surrounded by ferns. "Not 'Fairgrove Industries.' I mean Elfhame Fairgrove, the Underhill Seleighe community here." He leaned back a little. "Keighvin, I think the ball's in your—ah—'court.' So to speak."

Keighvin didn't smile. "Sam, how much did your granny ever tell you about the Seleighe and Unseleighe Court elves?"

Sam had to think hard about that. Granny had died when he was barely ten; fifty-five years was a long time. And yet, her stories had been extraordinarily vivid, and had left him with lasting impressions.

"Mostly, she told stories with—I guess you'd say—good elves and bad elves. Elves who wanted to help humans, at least, and elves who wanted only to hurt them. She said you really couldn't tell them apart, if you were a human child—that even human adults could be easily misled, and that sometimes even the good elves didn't know who was good and who was bad. She said the Unseleighe Court even had agents in the Seleighe Court. She just warned me to steer clear of both if I ever met either kind, until I was old enough to defend myself, and could tell a glib lie from the truth."

Keighvin nodded, his hair beginning to escape from the pony-tail. "Good enough. And that fairly sums it up. There's the Seleighe Court—that's us, and things like elvensteeds and dryads, selkies, pukas, owls, things that can pass as humans and things that never could. Oh, and there's creatures native to this side of the water that have allied themselves with the Seleighe Court as well. And for the most part, the very worst one of us wishes is that the humans would go away." The Sidhe looked out into the forest beyond the glass, but Sam had the feeling he was seeing something else entirely. "For the most part, we're interested in coexisting with your kind, even if it forces us to have to change. Many of us are interested in helping your kind. We have the power of magic, but you have the twin powers of technology and numbers. One on one—you humans are no match for us. But population against population—we've lost before we even start."

"All right," Sam agreed. "I can see that. What about the Unseleighe Court?"

"They hate you, one and all," Keighvin replied, somberly. "There are elves among them; and many, many things straight out of your worst childhood nightmares: bane-sidhe, boggles, trolls, things you've never heard of. The Morrigan is their Queen, and a terrible creature she is; she hates all things living, even her own people." His eyes darkened with what looked to Sam like a distant echo of pain. "They hate us, too, for wanting to coexist with you; they're constantly at war with us. They want you gone, and they're active in fostering anything that kills you off. If you run across a human conflict that seems senseless, often as not, they have a hand in it. Not that you humans aren't adept at creating misery for yourselves, but the Unseleighe Court has a vested interest in fostering that misery, and in propagating it. And they don't like the idea that Fairgrove is a little further along the path of easing some of it."

"All right so far," Sam said, a little puzzled, "but what's that got to do with me?"

"We have agents in their ranks, just as they have agents in ours," Keighvin told him. "We've gotten word that some of their lot that can pass as human have found out what we're planning, and are going to try to expose us as frauds."

"It'll be Preston Tucker all over again," Tannim put in, his own expression grim. "Without someone with a spotless reputation fronting for us, they can do it, too. They can claim we've stolen our samples, that the engine blocks aren't what we say they are, and that we have no real intention of manufacturing the products. It's happened enough times in this industry that people are likely to believe it—especially with a bit of glamorie behind their words and a strong publicity campaign. Your actions will be the saving of us—as Keighvin's was of you and your father."

"No one's ever heard of us, except as a racing team,"

Keighvin said, leaning forward in his chair; giving Sam all of his attention. "But they know you. Your reputation can give us the time we need to actually build a few customers. Once we have that, it won't matter what they say. They'll have to come after us some other way. But there's the danger. They will. And not only us, but you."

Oddly enough, the threat to himself didn't bother Sam. In fact, if anything, it added a little spice to the prospect. Terrorists and fanatics who threatened folk just because they were American frightened him; there was no predicting people like that, and there was something cold and impersonal about their enmity. Give him a real, honest enemy every time. You knew where you stood with a real enemy; you knew whose side you were on. After all, hating a country takes away its faces, but hating someone because of what he did was something he could get a grip on.

"To tell you the truth," Tannim put in, "I'd have been a lot more worried before I saw how you've got your home defenses rigged. Even a creature with magic is going to have trouble passing them. And once I add my two cents' worth, I think you'll be in fairly good shape to hold them off if you have to."

"Your two cents' worth?" Sam asked quizzically. Tannim grinned and shrugged—and Sam remembered the odd protections around the car. This Tannim might not be one of the Fair Folk, but there was no doubt he held his own in their company.

More of Sam's granny's lore was coming back to him. There was, surprisingly, a lot of it. And the things he remembered about the Unseleighe Court were unpleasant indeed, especially when it occurred to him that she had undoubtedly toned things down for his young ears. Now he wondered how much she hadn't told him, and how important that information was.

And where she had gotten it from. The "missing" brother, perhaps? He made a mental note to ask Keighvin about that some time.

Still—here was a chance to see things very few other humans had seen. A chance to be useful again. He'd

retired only because he'd had no choice. He had enjoyed
the first few weeks of his vacation, but truth to tell, he
was getting bored. There were only so many things he
could do to improve the house. He hated fishing. He could
only watch so much television before feeling the urge to
throw something at the tube.

"All right," he said. "I'll do it Full speed ahead, and
damn the torpedoes. You've got your man."

The little that remained of the evening passed in a
blur. Tannim took him home again—and this time did not
treat him to a mini-race on the driveway. Neither of them
said much, except to set a dinner meeting for that
evening—since it was already "tomorrow," being well past
midnight.

Tannim waited until he was safely sealed inside his little
fortress before driving off; he wasn't certain if that was a
wise precaution, or real paranoia. Surely the Unseleighe
Court denizens wouldn't already know he'd agreed to help
Fairgrove?

Then again, this was magic he was dealing with; as
unknown in its potentials as a new technology. Maybe they
could know.

Thoreau was lying beside the door, patiently but obviously waiting for his promised treat. Sam headed for the
kitchen and dished out a tiny portion of canned food.
Thoreau didn't need extra pounds any more than a human
did, and these late-night snacks were the only time he got
canned food. The rest of the time, he had to make do with
dry.

Thoreau was one of the more interesting dogs Sam had
ever owned. Instead of greedily gobbling down his treat,
he ate it slowly, licking it like a child trying to make an
ice-cream cone last. Sam left him to it and went to his
library in the office, but didn't immediately pull down some
of the reference materials he'd mentally selected.

Instead, he sat with hands idly clasped on the desk for
a long moment, wondering if, when he did go to bed, he'd
wake up in the morning to find that all this had been a
dream.

Something crackled in his jacket pocket as he took it

off, and he found the envelope with the check in it still in his breast pocket.

"All right," he said to Thoreau, as the dog padded into the study, licking his chops with satisfaction. "Maybe it is a dream. Maybe there are fairy checks as well as fairy gold. But it's here now." He planted the envelope under his favorite paperweight, a bronze replica of the Space Shuttle Challenger. "If it's gone in the morning, I'll know it was a dream. But for now, all we can do is try. Eh, Thoreau?"

Thoreau wagged his stub of a tail in agreement, and put his head down on his paws as Sam got up and began pulling books and bound magazines down off the shelf. He'd seen this before. He knew it was going to be a long night.

CHAPTER FOUR

The Mustang purred happily as Tannim drove into Sam's driveway. There were times, especially lately, when Tannim wondered if maybe he hadn't instilled a little *too* much magic into the car. Or maybe he'd planted something else besides pure Power. Lately it had seemed as if the Mach 1 was almost—sentient. It certainly seemed to approve of Sam Kelly; there was a warmth to the engine's purr that hadn't been there before he turned into the drive, and the car had embraced Sam as if he belonged inside it.

Well, for that matter, Tannim approved of Sam Kelly. He was a smart, tough old bird, and too good to waste on retirement. Now, as long as he and Keighvin hadn't gotten the old man into more danger than any of them could handle.... His conscience bothered him a bit over that. Sam had brains and savvy, but what if he needed that and a younger man's reflexes as well?

He was taking Sam to dinner, after a couple of drinks at Kevin Barry's Pub in Savannah, on River Street. There were several Irish pubs in the area, but Kevin Barry's was the one Tannim preferred. He had the feeling that Sam would feel more at home, easier, in an atmosphere that reminded him of Ireland and all it meant.

He'd chosen a dinner meeting rather than a return to Fairgrove for a very good reason; he wanted Sam's first dose of Keighvin Silverhair to wear off before they talked again. Keighvin's formidable personality had been known to overwhelm far stronger personalities than Sam's, even without a glamorie at work.

Not that Keighvin would have used a glamorie on Sam Kelly. They wanted a willing ally, with all his faculties in working order, not a bemused dreamer.

Tannim wasn't entirely certain how old Keighvin was; certainly at least a thousand. That much living produced personalities that could easily bowl the unsuspecting over. If Sam was having second thoughts, Tannim wanted to know about it without Keighvin around to influence him.

The pub itself, however, was a good place to talk to Sam. The atmosphere, so strongly Celtic, should put Sam in the state of mind to remember and Believe, even though he was going to be completely in the "real world."

And there was no more "real world" a clientele than the bunch that frequented Kevin Barry's. Students from SCAD, business people, locals, artists, holdover hippies, folkies—you name it, and you would probably see it in Kevin Barry's. Except maybe yuppies; the place wasn't trendy enough for them.

Not enough ferns, or drinks with clever names and inflated prices. And no selection of forty-five mineral waters.

Sam must have been watching for him, for he was locking up even as Tannim arrived. He opened the passenger's side door and slid in beside Tannim as soon as the Mach 1 came to a full stop. He was amazingly fit for a sixty-five-year-old man; he looked as if he'd been getting lots of regular exercise and watching his diet—his build was a lot like Jacques Cousteau's, in fact, who at sixty-five had still been leading his own underwater expeditions. Maybe Tannim didn't need to worry quite so much about him after all.

"Am I in for any more impromptu racing today?" Sam asked, with a twinkle, as Tannim pulled out again. And there was no doubt of it; the Mustang was truly purring with satisfaction, a note in its engine he'd never heard before. The Mach 1 liked Sam.

Too bad I can't ever find a lover it likes that much, he thought ironically. *Of course, if I do, she'll probably like the car better than me. I can see it now—my girl and my car, taking off into the sunset without me.*

"No, no racing today," he said, with a chuckle. "I'm taking you into Savannah. I had the feeling you probably haven't been downtown in a while."

Sam nodded. "Not for years," he admitted. "Never had a reason to. And to tell you the truth, I spent most of my time at Gulfstream. There wasn't much of anything I wanted to go downtown for."

"I may be able to change your mind," Tannim replied. "So, how are you feeling about our offer in the cold light of day?"

"Well—the check didn't disappear, or turn into a handful of leaves when morning arrived," Sam replied after a moment. "And my bank was perfectly happy to have it. I wasn't entirely sure it would still be there when I woke up this morning, and that's a fact. I was half convinced I must have dreamed the whole thing. Especially that car-horse-car."

"I don't blame you." Tannim chuckled, watching Sam out of the corner of his eye. "I know how I felt the first time I saw anyone working real magic."

There. The word was out in the open. Sam hadn't flinched from it, either.

"Magic," the old man mused. "The Sidhe, and magic. Maybe I've come into my second childhood, but—I think I could come to appreciate all this." He tilted his head to the side. "So, what happened the first time *you* saw magic at work?"

Tannim laughed. "I freaked. For the first few minutes, I thought someone had slipped me recreational pharmaceuticals without my noticing. Then, once I figured out that everything I saw was real, I just hoped that whoever was duking it out didn't notice *me*. I was—oh, sixteen or so— and I kind of got caught on the sidelines of a magic duel." He waited to see the effect of that revelation on Sam.

"Fair Folk?" Sam asked after a moment. "A duel between elves?"

Tannim shook his head. "No. A witch and a sorceress. The witch was the good guy—or rather, gal. I didn't know who the bad guy was, or that it *was* a female at the time. I was just glad the witch had a good sense of ethics and was trying to keep the mayhem to a minimum where the audience was concerned."

"A witch and a sorceress? Aren't they the same thing?" Sam asked, in a genuinely puzzled tone.

Again, Tannim shook his head. "Trust me, there's a difference between the two. The reason it was dangerous was because although the witch was being careful about innocent bystanders, the sorceress wasn't. And, like I said, in this case, the witch was the good guy. There's a lot of parallels between the Seleighe and Unseleighe Courts there."

Sam nodded thoughtfully, but made no further comments for a moment. By that time, they had reached Savannah proper, and the infamous brick-work streets. Quaint and picturesque, but hell to drive on.

They got a bit of relief at a stoplight. Tannim's leg ached distantly, from hip to ankle. "I keep forgetting about these damn streets," he remarked to Sam, who nodded.

"I remember now," Sam responded. "This was one of the reasons I avoided coming downtown. There wasn't anything down here that was worth having to drive this, and the cobblestones are worse."

Tannim sighed. "I guess it's because I like River Street so much I sort of forget what it takes to get there. I'm sure the tourists like this—but I swear, I know I'm going to have to put the car up and do an alignment when I get home."

"It's the tight suspension, I'd wager," Sam said through clenched teeth. "Makes you wish you had a Lincoln or a Caddy."

Tannim laughed. "Maybe I'll remember this next time I come here, and rent one!"

The Mustang coughed as though its carburetor had stuck, then settled once Tannim patted the dash.

Some things never change, Sam thought, as he watched a trio of black-clad art students walk by in the shade of the old, Spanish-moss-bedecked oaks. There seemed to be an unwritten rule that young artists had to wear black and act morose at least twelve hours out of every day. He'd seen that sort of thing, in a different way, with the Gulfstream engineers, who thought that if they wore blue cotton shirts, club ties, and Cross pens, they would be taken for Brain Trust. Sam had never been able to take that kind of thing seriously after watching a PBS documentary about mimicry in moths.

The art students were a constant source of amusement and amazement for the locals, but the kids always meant well. It tickled Sam that their school was slowly buying out the entire downtown, building by building. "Are those ninjas, or performance artists?" Tannim chuckled, nodding at a duo in black *gis* and black, absurdly baggy pants, like rappers wore on MTV. They lounged beneath a wrought-iron balcony that was old when their great-grandparents were their age. They reminded Tannim of similar sights in New Orleans, and the mix of cultures and ambience there.

"Poster kids for mousse abuse," Sam replied solemnly. "Ninjas would have better taste."

"Geez, you could hide aircraft in those pants," Tannim commented, after a second look. "Better keep them away from Gulfstream, Sam. Some of your planes might mistake them for hangars."

A blue-haired old lady under the trees of one of the dozens of tiny park squares nagged at her husband as the balding man focused his camera on a building across the street. "Wait until the kids are in the *picture*, George," she shrilled. "I want a picture with *art kids* in it. This is where the *art school* is, I want *art kids* in the picture."

The old man just grunted and made minute adjustments of the focus. The art students just ignored it all and continued drifting along in front of the boutique windows, expressions of studied *angst* decorating their young faces.

"Maybe he can't hear her," Tannim suggested. "His shorts are drowning her out." Indeed, the man was wearing possibly the most obscene pair of Bermudas Sam had ever experienced; an appalling print in cerise and chartreuse. He and his wife were completely unaware of the team of video students behind them—taping every move *they* made. Sam nearly died, choking down laughter.

They found themselves creeping along at five miles an hour, stuck behind one of the horse-drawn sightseers carriages. Tannim put up with it for a little, but finally muttered something under his breath and turned off their street at the next light, leaving the coveys of tourists and micro-herds of art students behind. After about a mile, Sam noticed they had left the glass-front boutiques and hole-in-the-wall shops behind as well. The buildings were neglected, now; paint cracked and peeling, windows broken and patched with tape and cardboard, yards full of weeds. The cars here were in the same shape as the houses. There weren't many businesses; what few there were had grates over the windows and rusted bars on the doors.

Sam would not have wanted to break down here, and now he recalled another reason for not visiting downtown. River Street was flanked by two bad neighborhoods. Even in daylight, Sam would not have wanted to be alone out here. The sullen expressions of the toughs lounging on the corners were not feigned or practiced, and their cold, dead eyes gave Sam the chills. He kept his eyes on the dashboard, and Tannim was uncharacteristically silent.

Finally the young man broke the silence. "This neighborhood's economy isn't depressed," he said grimly, "it's suicidal."

They turned another corner and drove for about half a mile, with the buildings slowly improving again. Finally they turned onto River Street itself, and as they hit the cobblestones and the punishment really began, Sam felt able to take his eyes off the dashboard. That was when he found that the dubious sorts weren't limited to the bad neighborhoods, either; there was a cluster of kids in front of a shop with a "for rent" sign in the window, and from the look of them, they were exchanging money for drugs. Sam watched the loitering toughs out of the corner of his eye, and remembered that this was yet another reason why he had avoided the downtown area in general. He certainly wouldn't want to come here alone at night, and maybe not even with someone. He knew he was tougher than he looked—yes, and a lot sprier than he let on—but he was no match for a street-gang.

And he was smart enough to know it.

A cop car rumbled down one of the cobblestone ramps from the street above River, and the gang evaporated, vanishing into the covered alleyways behind the River Street stores.

Well, maybe it wouldn't be so dangerous. The cops were certainly a presence. And then, again, there were a number of Irish pubs around here, and a lot of Irish on the street as well—the ones without the bags and cameras and look of tourists. If he *did* happen to find himself in trouble, it could be there'd be more help here than he first reckoned.

Tannim pulled into a parking place so abruptly that Sam was taken by surprise; cutting in right under the fender of a departing vehicle, and neatly getting the Mustang worked into the slot so quickly it seemed as magical as the car-horse. As the young man shut the engine off, he turned to grin at Sam. "You've got to be quick around here," he said. "Parking places go fast, and the god of parking has a short attention span."

To his surprise, since Tannim hadn't mentioned specifically where they were going, the young man led the way into one of those Irish pubs Sam had been eyeing. And to Sam's great delight, once inside, the place proved to be real Irish, not "tourist" Irish. It looked—and felt—homey and lived-in. There was a small stage in the restaurant section, against one wall, with a folk-group setting up on it, whose instrumental mix Sam also noted with approval. He liked mixing the old with the new, although one could do some quite amazing things with traditional instruments. One of his most cherished memories was of being in a club in Tennessee and hearing the Battlefield Band performing "Stairway to Heaven" on the bagpipes. . . .

Still, although *he* was prepared to spend several delightful hours here, this did not look like the kind of place that would suit his companion. Young Tannim looked as if he'd never encountered an acoustic guitar in his life; a rock'n'roller to the core. The Clannad tape notwithstanding, he couldn't imagine Tannim caring for any music that didn't come with amps and megawattage. It was to Sam's considerable astonishment that the lady bartender greeted his escort by name, and asked if he wanted "his usual table." At Tannim's nod, the lady waved them on, telling them that "Julie" would be with them in a minute.

As Sam took his place across from Tannim, he realized that, once again, he was going to have to realign all his previous ideas about the lad. And that was a discovery just as pleasant as the existence of this pub.

"Well," Tannim said, when the waitress had brought them both drinks, "ready for a little more business?"

Another surprise for Sam—not the question, but the drink. Tannim had stuck to pure cola. He was young enough to take delight in drinking because he could. Interesting.

"I think so," Sam replied cautiously. "You gave me a lot of information last night, but it was all in pieces. I'd like more of a whole picture."

"Fine," Tannim said agreeably. "Where would you like me to start?"

"With magic." Sam took a deep breath. "Just what is it? How does it work? What can you do with it—and what's it got to do with racing—"

Tannim held up a hand. "The discipline people call 'magic' is a way of describing an inborn talent that's been trained. It has rules, and it obeys the laws of physics. It uses the energy produced by all living things; it also uses the energy of magnetic fields, of sunlight, and a lot of other sources. It's a tool, a way of manipulating energies; that's the first thing you have to remember. It's not good *or* bad, it just *is*. Like, I can use a crowbar to bash your head in, or to pry a victim out of a wreck." He shrugged. "It's a tool; just a tool and nothing more. Some people have the skill to use the tool, some don't."

Sam nodded, since Tannim looked as if he was waiting

for a response. "But—how does it work? And who has it? Can anyone work it if they've got the knowledge?"

Tannim chuckled. "Hard to describe, Sam. First of all, you have to be able to see the energies in the first place, or at least know that they're there. That's the key; if you can see them, you can learn to manipulate them with magic—which is basically a way of making your own will into that tool to manipulate energy." He licked his lips. "Here's where it gets complicated. If you've trained your will well enough, you can still use the energies without seeing them. Everyone could use some kind of magic, if they had the training—but most folks never come in touch with what they can use. Know anything more now than you did before I said that?"

Sam shook his head, ruefully. "Well . . . no. Not really. But I can believe in plasma physics without knowing exactly how *it* works. I suppose I can believe in magic too. So long as it follows rules."

"That's the spirit!" Tannim applauded. "Now, what Keighvin won't tell you, because like most elves, he's an arrogant sonuvabanshee, is that humans were applying magic to cars before the elves thought of it. A lot of times they didn't realize that was what they were doing, but a lot of times they knew *exactly* what they were doing, especially on the racing circuit. So when the elves came on the scene, they got a bit of a shock, because there were humans out there already, using magicked cars. That's when they decided it might be a good idea to try and join up with some of those humans." He spread his hands. "Voila—SERRA was born."

"But why racing?" Sam asked, still bewildered. "For the Sidhe, I mean. It seems so—foreign to what they are."

"Boredom," Tannim replied succinctly, tracing little patterns on the wooden tabletop with his finger "They live—if not forever, damn near. But here's something else they won't tell you. The one thing they lack is *creativity* as near as I can figure. Every bit of their culture, with the sole exception of who and what they worship, comes from humans." He looked up through his lashes, as if he were sharing a secret "They can replicate what we do, and even improve on it, but I've never once seen one of them come up with something new and original. So they depend on us to bring new things to their culture; as far as I can tell, that's always been the case. They were bored, and racing gave them a chance to bring back some excitement to their lives, like the old combat-challenges used to give them. Brought them that element of risk back—" his face sobered "—'cause, Sam, if you mess up on the track, sometimes it's permanent, and sometimes it's terminal."

Sam wondered if Tannim's game leg was evidence of the boy's own brush with just that.

"But they won't admit it, even if you confront 'em," Tannim said, with a crooked smile, making a figure eight. "That's the real reason they got into racing though, I promise you. Now as to why Keighvin took it farther, to where Fairgrove is trying to make mundane money—he's not lying, he wants to have that kind of mundane cash to kind of fix things for kids. I've got a hunch he wants to set up some safe-houses for abused kids that we can't take Underhill, starting here in Savannah. All elves have this thing about kids; Keighvin has it harder than most. If he could save every kid in the world from pain, hunger, fear— he'd do it. But he can't do it magically, not anymore." Tannim made a complex symbol that looked suspiciously like a baseball diamond. "For one thing, there's too much Cold Iron around for his magics to work down here in the cities."

"Huh." Sam nodded, but he had reservations. Not that he hadn't heard about all the supposed abused kids, on everything from Oprah to prime-time TV dramas, but he wasn't sure he believed the stories. Kids made things up, when they thought they were in for deserved punishment. Hell, one of the young guys at work had shown up with a story about his kid getting into something he was told to leave alone in a store, breaking it, then launching into screams of "don't beat me, Mommy!" when the mother descended like a fury. Embarrassed the blazes out of her, especially since the worst she'd ever delivered in the kid's life was a couple of smacks on the bottom. Turned out the brat had seen a dramatized crime-recreation show the night before, with an abused-kid episode. Sam was beginning to think that a lot of those "beaten kids" had seen similar shows, then had been coached by attorneys, "child advocates," or the "non-abusing spouse." Wasn't that how the Salem witch-trials had happened, anyway? A bunch of kids getting back at the adults they didn't like?

As for the runaways—they'd had a solution for that back when he was a kid. Truant officers with the power to confine a kid, and reform school for the kids that couldn't toe the line at home. Maybe that's what they needed these days, not "safe-houses."

But just as he was about to say that, he took a second, harder look at Tannim, and thought back about what Keighvin had said. Tannim might be almost a kid himself, but he didn't look as if he was easily tricked. And Keighvin had known what was happening to Sam—and presumably Sam's great-uncle—by supernatural means. It wasn't likely that *they* were being tricked. . . .

They, the elves, had been right about Sam's great-uncle. And who could say what might have happened if Keighvin hadn't intervened that night, so long ago. Would John Kelly have come to his senses before he'd done more than frighten Sam? Or would the beatings have continued, getting worse with every incident, until Sam turned into a sullen, trouble-making creature like Jack McGee, with his hand against every man alive, and every man's hand against him? Jack's father was the mainstay of the town pub . . . Jack's mother a timid thing that never spoke above a whisper, and always with one eye out for her husband, wore high collars and long sleeves, and generally bore a healing bruise somewhere on her face or neck. Now Sam was forced to confront that memory, he wondered, as he had not, then. What did those sleeves and collars conceal?

Maybe the stories were true; maybe the elves were right. . . .

Glory be. Am I thinking as if they're real?

He was. Somewhere along the line, he'd accepted all this—magic, elves, all of it. He might just as well accept the abused kids as well. . . .

"Have you people cast some kind of spell on me?" he demanded. "Made me believe in you? Brainwashed me?"

Tannim laughed. "If we used magic to make you believe in magic, to brainwash you, doesn't that mean magic works?"

Well, the boy had him there.

"I suppose you could have brainwashed me some other way," Sam said, feebly.

Tannim shrugged. "Why?" he replied reasonably, as the waitress brought another round. "What's the point? By definition, someone who's been brainwashed is operating at less than his optimum reasoning capacity. Why would we want you brainwashed, when what we want is for you to be at your sharpest?" Tannim took a sip of his cola, and looked up at Sam from under a raised eyebrow. "Are you having second thoughts about all this, about agreeing to help Keighvin?" he asked. "If you are, Sam, it's nothing to be ashamed of. We need you, but not at the expense of forcing you to make a bargain you regret."

Sam sighed. "No. No. It's just that I find myself believing in the impossible, and it doesn't seem right, all my brave words about plasma physics to the contrary."

The young man took a moment to finish his drink before answering. "Sam," he said, slowly, gazing off into nothing for a moment, "when you were a kid, people said it was impossible for a plane to fly past the speed of sound, for polio and smallpox to be eradicated, for the atom to be split, for a man to walk on the moon. I don't know what's impossible. All I can say is that 'impossible' just seems to mean that nobody's done it yet. There's some people that still don't believe a man walked on the moon. And there's people who still believe the earth is flat. Nobody puts *their* names in the history books. I know it all seems fantastic, but we *are* based in reality. It's just a bigger reality than most people are used to dealing with."

"What *do* you know?" Sam found himself asking, his own meal forgotten for the moment. "You, who's magicked his car, who walks and talks with the Folk and treats them like mortals—what do you know?"

Tannim grinned. "Well—I know your beer's getting flat."

Sam laughed, and gave in.

Tannim finished his third cola with one eye on Sam, and another on the crowd. On the whole, the evening had gone well. Sam had weathered both his initial exposure and the period of doubt that always followed it in good form. Better than Tannim had expected, in fact. Of course, he'd had a dose of the Folk as a child; that tended to leave a lasting impression.

Sam had finally worked himself round to asking specific questions about the elves, and how they were functioning in the human world. And why.

The crowd-noise around them was not too loud for them to be able to talk in normal voices—or at least, it wasn't after Tannim did a little local sound-filtering around their table, a tiny exercise in human magic that was worth the energy he expended on it. "Well, this is something else Keighvin won't admit unless he's pressed. Essentially, the Seleighe Court is split," he said. "One group thinks they should all withdraw Underhill, and leave the world we know to the humans. The other group thinks that would be a major mistake."

"Why?" Sam wanted to know, his head turned to one side.

"Remember what I told you about them, that they can't seem to create anything?" Tannim reminded him. "Keighvin thinks that if they withdraw, they'll stagnate. That's something a little more serious to them than it is to humans. They call it Dreaming; they can be forced into it by caffeine addiction, or they can drop into it from lack of stimulation, and being cut off from their old energy sources by Cold Iron. That's happened to one group in California already. They managed to get out of it, but—it wasn't pretty."

He didn't like to think about that. They had all been *damned* lucky to pull out of their trap. And they wouldn't have been able to without the aid of humans.

He pulled his thoughts away; Elfhame Sundescending was all right now, and thriving. "Like the old story of the Lotus-Eaters; they lose all ambition and do next to nothing, sit around and listen to music and let their magic servants tend to everything, dance, and never think a single thought. Scary. I've seen it once, and I wouldn't wish it even on the Folk who'd be pleased to see me six feet under. Keighvin's got some plans to keep it from happening on this coast, and they involve all of us in Fairgrove."

Just then, his attention was caught by someone that didn't fit with the usual Kevin Barry's crowd. She was clearly underage; he guessed round about thirteen or fourteen. Fifteen, max, but he doubted it. She was tarted up like a bargain-basement Madonna in black-lace spandex tights, a black-lace skirt, and a cheap black corset; wearing entirely too much makeup, so that her eyes looked like black holes in her pale face, with a bad bleach-job that made her hair look like so much spiky dead straw. What in hell was she doing here? This didn't look like her kind of crowd. *God, she looks like Pris from* Bladerunner, he thought.

But then, Sam had been surprised that *he* was a regular here. Maybe she just liked the music.

"I can see that, and I can see why racing, now," Sam said, in answer to whatever he'd just told the man. "But what are they doing about Cold Iron? That's what drove them out of the Old Country, isn't it? Doesn't it bother them now?"

"How much real iron and steel do you see nowadays?" Tannim countered, raising his eyebrows. "Plastic, fiberglass, aluminum, yes—but iron?"

"Hmm. You have a point."

The girl had worked herself in towards the stage, with a look of utter fascination on her face. Tannim felt a twinge of sympathy; he remembered the first time *he* encountered really good Celtic folk-rock. It had been right here—and this band, Terra Nova. Kind of like having your first experience of pizza being Chicago deep-dish. And it wasn't often that the old members of Terra Nova got back together again for an old-time's-sake gig, what with Trish being so busy at the restaurant and all. No wonder this chick had shown up. Yeah, it looked like she was just a punker with Celtic-rock leanings. Too bad she was so young. This was supposed to be an adult club, what with the bar and all.

She could get bounced in no time, if she got herself noticed.

Well, if she behaved herself, they'd probably leave her alone.

He watched her, still a little bothered by something, something not quite right. Then, as he saw her stop and talk to a businessman who shook his head abruptly—and ignore a SCAD student who half-made an approach, it dawned on him.

She was a hooker.

He'd thought he was beyond shock, but this stunned him. So damned young—

He watched her make her way around the floor, most of her attention on the band, but obviously a part of her keeping an eye out for a potential john. *Don't try and turn a trick in here, honey, please,* he pled silently with her. He might be wrong—but the more he watched her, the surer he became. At that age—out here on a school night, dressed like she was—it was long odds against her being on River Street for the fun of it. *If you get too obvious, or bother the customers, they'll throw you out. Stay cool. It's cold and mean out there, and if one of the soft-hearts sees you, they'll get you something to eat and you'll be safe a little longer. . . .*

Sam asked him a question, and he answered it absently. "Well, what's happening is that some of the elves—with Keighvin leading the pack by a length—are trying to build up a kind of immunity to Cold Iron—or a tolerance, at least. I can think of half a dozen, actually, who can handle it with a minimum of protection, and two that can actually tolerate it well enough to work on and drive a stock car."

Donal, he thought fondly. *Wish you were here, man. You could pick up this poor little chick and glamorie her into coming back to Fairgrove with you, tuck her away Underhill until you'd talked some sense into her. And if you couldn't your brother could.*

The more he watched the girl, the less comfortable he felt. She was wandering around the area of the stage, and although she wasn't making any full-fledged tries at picking up the customers, it was pretty obvious that if anyone that she thought had money responded to her tentative overtures, she wouldn't turn him down.

"Keighvin says the Folk have to adapt or die, it's that simple," he concluded, as the band finished a wild polka and went into a still wilder reel. "They haven't got a choice anymore. *He* thinks if they withdraw, they'll do worse than stagnate, they'll fade away. Just—disappear."

"Is that possible?" Sam asked, sounding surprised. Tannim pulled his attention away from the girl long enough to catch his eyes. He nodded, slowly.

"It's already happened," he said seriously. "Mostly in Europe, but even over here, there've been enclaves of the Folk that went Underhill and just vanished after a while. Nobody's heard from them, nobody can find them."

"Couldn't they just have closed themselves off?" Sam wanted to know. "If they became that anti-social, maybe they even got tired of other elves. I mean, what is this Underhill, anyway? We used to say the Fair Folk lived in the mounds, but what you're saying, it sounds more like Underhill is everywhere. Couldn't the missing Folk have just shut the door and turned off the phone, so to speak?"

Tannim shook his head. "Underhill doesn't work that way. It's hard to describe. It's kind of—another world, one magicians can touch, and sometimes get into. A kind of parallel world, I guess. Lots of magic; I mean, of power, and it's readily available, like electricity, only it's like—" He thought for a moment, as the crowd began clapping in time to the music. "It's like having all the power-stations and the power-grid in place and running, only there's nobody manning it, and no electric company to make you pay for what you take. It's yours for the tapping into. The only 'cost' involved is in tapping into it and in using it."

Sam shook his head, but not in disbelief, exactly. "Sounds like free lunch, to me."

Tannim looked around for the girl, but she'd gotten lost behind a screen of taller people. Not that *that* was hard, as tiny as she was. He thought he knew where she'd moved to, though, by the path of mild disturbance along the bar. "Not really; the cost to the individual of tapping in and using it is high, and you have to have the ability in the first place. Kind of like solar energy. Keighvin thinks that's where the power created *here* that doesn't get used leaks off to—if you think of it as bio-energy, the kind that makes Kirlian auras, you're close enough to the truth."

Sam closed his eyes for a moment in thought. "All right," he replied, opening them again. "That much I can believe in. What's it like in there?"

"Parts are like a bad sf novel," Tannim laughed, without humor. "Like some of the old pulp writers described an alien planet. Parts of it are like an architect's wet-dream." He spread his fingers wide for emphasis. "Mostly it's a kind of chaos, a place where things are always changing, always dangerous, and that's where the Unseleighe Court creatures go. Then there's stretches of order, walled gardens or even small countries, and that's where the Seleighe Court enclaves are."

"And those?" Sam prompted.

Tannim sighed, but this time at the memories Sam's question invoked. "I've only been there a couple of times, and each time it was different. Figure every description you've ever heard of Elvenlands, Morgan Le Fay's castle, the Isles of the Blest—that's what those Underhill enclaves are like." He felt his eyes sting with remembrance and the inevitable regret that he hadn't stayed, and pushed the memory away. "Incredible—and they require elven-mages of very high power and a great deal of will to force the chaos out, and the area into that shape. That means they leave a mark on the world of Underhill, very visible, like the Red Spot on Jupiter. When someone like Keighvin goes Underhill, he *knows* where all the other pockets are, at least the ones created by other Folk. Always. He might not be able to get into them without invitation, but he knows where they are."

Sam took a sip of his beer before replying. "So it doesn't matter if the Folk in that place don't want to be bothered, they can't hide themselves. At least not on purpose."

Tannim nodded. "Right. So with the ones that faded out, the places that have gone missing—well, they're not there anymore. Maybe they died, maybe they went to still another world, and maybe they just dissolved back into the chaos. Even if there are still Folk alive in there, nobody can reach them, and they can't find their way back to the rest of us, nor to the real world. Likeliest—according to Keighvin—is that they faded until they were easy prey for the Unseleighe Court critters."

Sam toyed with a napkin, looking troubled. "You mean—they—"

Right on cue, Terra Nova launched into "Sidhe Beg and Sidhe Mor;" a tune that sounded lighthearted—but was about a war between elves of the Seleighe and Unseleighe Courts. The body count, as Tannim recalled, had been pretty high.

He raised an eyebrow at the band. Sam chewed his lip, as the meaning of the tune came home to him. "The Unseleighe Court plays for keeps, and every time they kill a Seleighe Court creature, or a human, they add his life-energy to their own power. Elves can die; they can be killed. Ever think about where the word 'banshee' came from?"

Sam's eyes widened. "Bane-Sidhe?"

"Right. 'Bane' or 'death' of elves. And it's not just a name." Tannim was just glad he'd not had any personal experiences with one. The descriptions were bad enough.

"The stories my grandmother told me—she said some banshees actually came for people." Sam looked a little embarrassed, as if he'd been caught believing in the bogeyman.

Who also exists.

"They do that too; they'll do their damnedest to scare you to death," Tannim said grimly. "That's how they get their energy; from your fear and from your dying."

"Oh." Sam blinked, as if he wasn't sure how to take that. He'd accepted danger last night—but that was with Keighvin, in Fairgrove territory. He was here now, the "real world," in the middle of a pub full of noisy people and a Celtic-rock band.

And a thirteen-year-old hooker.

She appeared again, this time giving up all pretense of working the crowd, just standing close to the stage and hugging herself, as Trish sang "Buachaill on Eire" with a voice an elven Bard would have paid any price to display.

A glitter of Trish's half-closed blue eyes, and the set of her chin, betrayed the fact that she was watching the girl too, and Tannim relaxed minutely. Trish didn't pick up on street-sparrows often, especially not now that she was managing "Acadia," but when she did, she was very kind to them. Like the way she'd adopted that monster wolf-hound of hers, letting it take over her life to the point of buying a house just so the dog would be able to stay with her. She wouldn't let the girl get away without at least trying to see she got something to eat. With luck, she'd keep the child busy until Tannim could take over.

Maybe I can get her to Keighvin. I can't get him out of Fairgrove territory, not yet, but if can get her to him, he'll take care of her. Not for the first time, he wished that he could just lie to the kid, get her into his car and make off with her, but to take her away from whatever life she had chosen, he had to have her consent, and she had to know what she was choosing. Conal and Donal wouldn't have worked that way, but they were Sidhe, and trickery was a part of their nature. Not his. It couldn't be by deception. Even Keighvin could work that way, but he couldn't; he was bound by a different set of rules. Self-inflicted, but nevertheless real. He hadn't liked being lied to, or manipulated, even with good intentions, when he was younger. He wouldn't do that to another kid. *Besides, small incidents have a way of turning around and biting my ass. If the wrong person saw me getting into my car with an underage hooker, it could mean big-time trouble later. Trouble we can't afford.*

As the band finished the set, he saw with relief that Trish definitely had her eye on the girl. As soon as they'd finished their bows—and before the child had a chance to escape—she was down off the stage and beside the kid. She made it look completely casual, and Tannim gave her high marks for her subtlety.

"What's wrong?" Sam asked, startling him. He tore his eyes off the girl for a moment to stare at his companion.

"What do you—"

"Oh, come now," Sam interrupted. "You haven't had more than half your attention on me for the past fifteen minutes. And you've got a frown on your face, so it can't be that you're watching a pretty girl, or that you're enthralled by the band. So what's the problem?" As Tannim paused, debating how much to say, he lost his half-smile and began to frown, himself. "Is it something I should know about?"

Tannim sighed. "Over there, with Trish, from the band. See that other girl?"

"The one that's made up like a cheap tart?" Sam asked, disapproval thick in his voice. "Girls these days—ah well. What about her?"

"She's not only made up like a cheap tart, she probably *is* a cheap tart," Tannim replied wearily. And before Sam could reply to that, added, "Take a good look under all the paint. She's not only underage, she's hardly gotten away from playing with Barbie dolls. What's a kid like that doing out here hooking? And more than that, why? She has to be a runaway—what's she running from that's bad enough for her to be turning tricks at fourteen?"

Sam started to make some snap reply, but it looked as if some of what Tannim had been talking about—the abused kids and all—had penetrated. Tannim could almost read his mind from the fleeting expressions that passed over his face. First, contempt—then disgust—but then a moment of second thoughts, followed by worry. "I don't like it," he said.

"Neither do I," Tannim told him, "but we're going to have to be careful about this. She could be bait in a trap; she could be a trap herself. Some of the Unseleighe Court things can look like anything they want. *I* don't See any magic around her, but that doesn't mean she's not one of them, or even a human kid they picked up to use against me. This is one of my regular hangouts, and everybody knows it."

And they know my soft spots.

"So what do we do?" Sam asked. A frown line was forming between his brows. Obviously he wasn't used to the kind of the multitudinous layers of deceit the Unseleighe Court creatures used by habit.

"We let Trish handle her. If she's after me, she'll find a way to get Trish to bring her over here. If she's a real kid in real trouble, she'll act like one." He watched the two of them, without seeming to. It looked as if the singer was warning the girl against soliciting; Trish was nodding her head so emphatically that her black hair bounced, while the child blushed under all the makeup, and hung her head. But the singer didn't leave things there; she took the girl to a table in the corner, and got her a sandwich and a cola, standing over her and talking until the food arrived. By then, it was time for the next set, and Trish abandoned the girl for the stage.

The kid finished the food in about three seconds flat. Tannim had never seen a kid put away food so fast, and the way she cleaned up every crumb argued that it might well have been the first meal she'd had today. She lingered over the dregs of her cola until Trish was obviously wrapped up in her song. Then a look of bleak determination passed over her face, and she slid out of her seat; and without a single glance at Tannim or even in his direction, she went back to the bar.

Tannim sighed, half in relief, half in exasperation. *All right*, he said to himself. *She's genuine. Now what am I going to do about her?*

CHAPTER FIVE

Just as Tannim asked himself that question, the girl found a mark.

It wasn't one of the regulars, and Julie hadn't even bothered to try to find the jerk a table. He was holding up the bar, more than two sheets to the wind, and up until the kid cruised by, he'd been insisting that Marianne, the barkeep, turn on a nonexistent television. He jumped all over her tentative overture, so much so that it was obvious to half the bar that he'd picked her up. The guys on either side of him gave him identical looks of disgust when they saw how young the girl was, and turned their backs on the situation.

Unfortunately, Tannim wasn't going to be able to do that. Not and be able to look himself in the mirror tomorrow. *Hard to shave if you can't do that. . . .*

Well, he knew one sure-fire way to pry her away from Mr. Wonderful. And it only required a *little* magic. With a mental flick, he set the two tiny spells in motion. With the first, a Command spell, he cleared people to one side or the other of a line between his table and her. With the other, a simple look-at-me glamorie, he caught her eye.

At precisely the moment when she looked his way, down the open corridor of bodies, he flicked open his wallet, displaying his Gold Card, and nodded to her. Her

eyes were drawn to it, as if it was a magnet to catch and
hold her gaze. Only after she looked at it did she look
at him. She licked her lips, smiled, and started toward
him.

Tried to, rather. The drunk grabbed her arm.

"Hey!" he shouted, rather too loudly. "Wa-waitaminit,
bitch! You promised me some fun!"

All eyes went to the drunk, and none of the looks were
friendly. Kevin Barry's was not the kind of pub where the
word "bitch" would go unnoticed.

So much for taking care of this the easy way.

Tannim was up and out of his seat before the girl had
a chance to react to the hand gripping her arm. He grasped
the drunk's wrist and applied pressure. The drunk yelped,
and let go. "I think she's changed her mind," he said, with
deceptive gentleness.

The drunk yanked his hand away, and snarled aggres-
sively, "Yeah? And what's a faggot artsy punk like you gonna
do about it? Huh?"

His hands were balling into fists, and he swung as he
spoke, telegraphing like a Western Union branch office.
Tannim blocked the first blow with a little effort; the
second never landed. Three patrons landed on the drunk,
and "escorted" him outside. And that was all there was to
the incident; Kevin Barry's was like that. Tannim was family
here, and nobody messed with family.

And nobody even looked askance at Tannim, for guid-
ing a kid barely past training bras back to his table. It
would be assumed that, like Trish, his intentions were to
keep the kid out of trouble, and maybe talk some sense
into her. He caught Sam's eye as he made a show of pulling
a seat out for her; the old man was anything but stupid.
"I'll be at the bar," he said as Tannim sat down. "I can
hear the band better over there."

That was a palpable lie, since the bar was far from the
stage, but the girl didn't seem to notice. Sam vanished into
the crowd, leaving Tannim alone with the girl. She looked
around, nervously; tried to avoid his eyes.

But then, young hookers are always nervous.

"So, what's your name, kiddo?" he asked quietly,

projecting calm as best he could, and regretting the fact that he wasn't an Empath.

"Tania," she said, so softly he could hardly hear her.

"Tania. Okay, my name's Tannim. We've both got the same first syllable in our names, that's a start." She looked up at him, startled, and he grinned. "Well, heck, it's not much of a line, but it beats 'Come here often? What's your sign?'"

She smiled back a little. "Wh-what do you want me to do?" she asked bluntly. "W-we could go to your car and—"

My car. So she hasn't even got a place of her own. The thought sickened him. How long had she been turning tricks in strange men's cars?

"What's your rate?" he asked, just as bluntly.

She didn't bat an eye. "Sixty an hour."

Right. You wish. And you'd take sixty a night. He raised an eyebrow, cynically. "Give me a break. That's for somebody with a little more experience than you've got."

She wilted faster than he expected. "Forty?" she said, tentatively.

He watched her over the top of his drink, as Trish belted out one of her own compositions, the notes sailing pure and clear above the crowd. "Sixty and forty. Okay, that makes a hundred. Let me tell you what you're going to do for a hundred."

She looked frightened at that, and she might have tried to get up and run except that he was between her and the door. He wondered if she'd gotten an "offer" like this before. And if she'd gotten away relatively undamaged.

Yes to the first question, from the look of fear in her eyes—and no to the second. It was all he could do to keep up the pretense; to keep from grabbing her hand and dragging her to his car, and taking her straight to Keighvin.

"No, I'm not a cop," he told her; "and I'm not going to bust you. I'm not into S and M and I'm not going to hurt you." A little of the fear left her eyes, but not all of it, not by any means. "I *am* a pushover."

He looked up long enough to signal Julie with his eyes. She hustled over to his table as soon as she'd set down

the other customer's beer. Tannim's tips were legendary
in the River Street bars and restaurants, and that legend
ensured him downright eager service.

"Julie, I need four club sandwiches with everything—
to go." He nodded significantly and she winked at him,
turning and heading towards the kitchen with the order.
He turned back to Tania.

"Okay, that's a hundred dollars for tonight; the first time.
You take it, you go home if you've got one. You get *off*
the damn street, at least for tonight. You get a room if
you don't have a home." He slid the five twenties he fished
out of his wallet across to her. She looked at them, but
didn't touch them. "Use what I gave you for seed money;
start putting a real life together for yourself. I come here
a lot. You find me here and ask me for help, you get
another hundred to keep you going—but only if you aren't
doing drugs. Believe me, I can tell if you are, better than
any blood-test. Got that?"

She was just inexperienced enough to believe him, and
experienced enough to be skeptical. "So what do you get
out of this?"

He smiled crookedly. "I stop having to rescue you from
drunks. I *told* you I was a pushover." He sobered. "Tania,
it's harder to keep believing in dreams these days—but
when you stop believing in them, you kind of stop believing
in yourself. I still believe in them. And I'm just crazy
enough to think that giving an underage hooker a hundred
bucks just might make a difference to her. Maybe give her
a chance to go out and build some dreams of her own."

"I'm not under—" she started to protest frantically.

He covered her hand, the one that was holding the cash,
with his, just for a moment. "And you can start by not lying
to me. Kiddo, you're underage even in Tennessee, and we
both know it. Now there; one crazy, helping hand. This
time, I pushed help off on you. Next time, you ask for
help. All right?"

She nodded, speechless, as Julie arrived with the sandwiches. "Julie," he said, as he shoved the brown paper bag
towards Tania, "I want you to start a tab for Tania here.
Two hundred bucks' credit, food only. Put it on the card."

"Sure thing, Tannim," the waitress replied, plucking his credit card from his outstretched fingers, and flashing a sparkling smile. She winked at Tania, who clutched the paper bag with a dumbfounded look on her face, looking for all the world like a kid in a Halloween costume.

Yeah. "Trick" or treat. Poor kid.

"Now, you get hungry, you come here," he ordered. "Even if I'm not here, you can get fed. Okay?"

"O—okay," she said, letting go of the bag long enough to shove her money into her cheap vinyl purse.

He grinned again. "Go on, get out of here. It's getting nasty out there, and I don't just mean the weather." She whisked herself out of the chair, threading the crowd like a lithe little ferret, and vanished into the darkness beyond the door. Sam returned almost immediately.

"What the hell was all that about?" he asked, sitting himself down in the chair Tania had vacated.

Tannim sighed. "The first step in building trust," he replied. "I just put up a bird-feeder. If I'm really lucky, one of these days the bird will eat from my hand. That's when I can get her back to where she belongs—or over to Keighvin, whichever seems better for her."

Sam shook his head dubiously. "I don't know. You gave her money, didn't you? What's to stop her from blowing it all on drugs?"

"Nothing," Tannim admitted. "Nothing, except that she doesn't do drugs, yet. Kid like that probably doesn't turn more than a couple of tricks a week. I just gave her enough to stay off the street for a while, maybe even more than a week, and promised her more if she asks for it." Julie brought back his card and the credit slip; he signed it, and added a sizable tip for her. "And this gives her a two-hundred-dollar food tab here."

Sam frowned. "You're a fool, boy. She's going to be on you like a leech."

He let out some of his tension in a long breath. "I don't think so," he replied. "I know . . . I don't have a real reason to think that way, but I don't think she's hardened enough to see a potential sugar-daddy and snag him. And even if she did—well, I could insist she come stay with me, and hand her over to Keighvin that way. Frankly, Sam, I'm more worried she'll vanish on me; decide I'm some kind of nut, the Savannah Zodiac killer or something, and never come near me again." He looked up again at the stage, where Trish had just begun "The Parting Glass," a sure sign that the gig was over, at least for her. The rest of the band might stay, but Trish was calling it a night. "Enough of this. That's our signal to move along, Sam, and go find ourselves some dinner. How's tandoori chicken with mango chutney and raita sound? Or lobster with macadamia nuts?"

Sam gave him a look of pure bewilderment. "What in hell are you talking about?" he asked.

"Dinner, Sam," he replied, grinning with anticipation. "Pure gourmet craziness."

"Sounds crazy, all right," Sam said, as they wormed their way through the crowd, and out into the damp, fish-redolent air.

"Trust me, Sam," he laughed, as the mist began to seep across the street, the precursor of one of Savannah's odd, chin-high fogs. "Trish knows wine and food the way she knows music. It might be odd, but you won't be disappointed."

Tania Jane Delaney slipped up the warped steps to the apartment she shared with five other kids, her heart in her mouth. The entrance to the upstairs apartments gaped like a toothless mouth when she'd arrived, dark and unfriendly. The light at the top of the stairs had gone out again—or somebody had broken or stolen the bulb—and she shivered with fear with each step she took. Jamie'd been beaten up and robbed twice by junkies; Laura'd had her purse snatched. If anybody knew she had money—if there was someone waiting for her at the top of the stairs—

But there wasn't, this time, nor was there anyone standing between her and the door as she'd feared when she felt for the knob. She fumbled open the lock with hands that shook so hard her key-ring jingled. There were only three keys on it, and the little brass unicorn Meg had given her for good luck. One key for this place, and the two to the locks of the townhouse in North Carolina—

But she wouldn't think of that.

There wasn't anyone else in the apartment, which was all right. She really didn't want to share Tannim's largess with the other three kids that had the room with the kitchenette, anyway. They'd given her a hard time the last time she'd wanted to cook something, and she thought they were filching things from her shelf in the fridge. Not that there was much to filch, mostly, but there had been things she'd thought she had that came up missing. She and Laura and Jamie never gave *them* any trouble over using the bathroom, and never had any problem with making sure there was paper and soap in there.

Please, don't let them blow all their money on dope again, she pled with an uncaring God. *The rent's due in three days, and old man March sent his kids to collect it last time. I think they could wad us up like Kleenex without even trying hard. They could throw us out on our asses and we couldn't do a thing about it.*

She'd already eaten one sandwich, feeling guilty, but too hungry to leave it alone. She hadn't eaten anything yesterday but a cup of yogurt she'd shoplifted. But that still meant Jamie and Laura had a sandwich and a half each, plus all the chips. There'd been a styrofoam cup of bean soup in there too, and cookies; she'd saved the cookies for Jamie and his sweet-tooth, but she drank the soup, sitting on a stone bench in Jackson Square, watching the fog roll in, listening to the far-away music coming from a bar somewhere. It had been awfully good soup.

Mother had never made soup like that. Mother never made soup at all; she bought it from a gourmet place. And when she bought it, she bought weird things, like cold gazpacho or miso, things that didn't taste like soup at all. When she wasn't on some kind of crazy diet with Father; that is. When Tania ran away, they'd been on one of those diets; some kind of stuff that looked like rice with things mixed into it, and tasted like hay. They'd made Tania eat it too, and she was hungry all the time. She'd have killed for a candy bar or a steak, or even a hamburger.

"You only think about what tastes good," Mother had said, scornfully. "Just like every child."

The only time Tania had eaten real soup was when she was little, and she got it at school or the learning center. It wasn't called a "day-care" center, it was a "learning center," and she'd had lessons stuffed into her every day for as long as she could remember. French, math, music . . . she hadn't gotten bedtime stories, she'd gotten flashcards. She hadn't gotten hugs, she'd gotten "quality time," with quizzes about how well she was doing in school.

Like the Spanish Inquisition, with long talks about how if I really wanted to get into a first-class college like Yale I had to have better grades.

She left the food on her roommates' sleeping beds. Jamie and Laura had an old mattress, with the seams popped and the stuffing coming out. It had been so stained that Tania would have been afraid to use it, because of germs, but they didn't seem to mind. They had a pile of cargo pads stolen from a moving van for bedding, all spread neatly on top of it, plus the blankets and sheets Laura had taken out of the Goodwill drop-box, all different sizes, none matching. Tania had two thin foam mattresses she'd gotten from the open dumpster at the old folks' home, piled on top of each other, and some of Laura's leftover sheets and blankets. Laura had thought the idea of using the egg-crate mattresses was too creepy; they wouldn't have been out in the dumpster if their owner hadn't died, probably *on* them. But the idea of ghosts didn't scare Tania; she'd taken them, hosed them down real good in case the old person had peed on them or something, and she hadn't been haunted yet. In fact, a ghost might be preferable to some of the people who hung out around here.

She went to the bathroom to wash the makeup off. The makeup, bleach-job, the whole outfit was Laura's idea, but she wasn't sure it was working. On the other hand, any tricks she got looking like the way she used to would be real pervs. The makeup at least made her look older, and the outfit like she knew what she was doing. But it itched, and if she didn't wash it off every night, she'd wake up looking like Tammy Faye Baker after a good scam-cry. She saw as soon as she pulled the chain on the bare bulb dangling from the ceiling that somebody had been by the

Hilton again; the toilet-tank lid was covered with little bars of soap, and matching rolls of paper sat on the cracked and grimy brown linoleum. It was probably Laura; she was really good at sneaking in, finding an unattended maid's cart, and sneaking out again. That was how they'd gotten their towels, too.

She ran some water into the sink, ignoring the rust that had stained the gray, grainy porcelain under both spigots. The hot water was actually hot tonight, and Tania decided impulsively on a bath. She had to clean the tub first, though, and by the time she was done, she was ready for a good long soak.

She went to the footlocker where she kept her things, got her tiny bottle of hotel shampoo, and discovered that there were lots more beside it. That clinched it; only Laura would have gotten shampoo for everybody. She silently blessed Laura as she stripped, hurrying because the apartment was cold. She ran some hot water into the tub to warm it, trying not to think about her beautiful, antiseptic, sparkling-clean private bathroom at home.

It wasn't my home. It never was home. It was just a place to live. They probably didn't even miss me when I was gone; I bet they're glad I'm gone, in fact. Now they can buy another BMW or a Porsche and take a trip to Bermuda.

She washed her hair under the tap, kneeling in the bottom of the chipped, scratched tub, then filled it to the top with water as hot as she could stand. Mother and Father had a Jacuzzi in their bathroom, but they'd never let Tania use it.

She sighed, and sank back into the hot water. She was so cold; when the fog came, it brought chilly air with it, and Spandex wasn't very warm. She'd been out longer than she'd intended after that strange guy gave her all the money. She'd stopped to watch *Legend* through the window of somebody's apartment after she'd eaten the soup; the unicorns had attracted her attention, and she stayed when there didn't seem to be anyone in the room who could see her peering in from outside.

What a great movie. Altogether, it had been a good

night, and she felt a little happy for the first time in weeks. First there'd been the music at that bar, then the food the singer had gotten her, then the money for doing *nothing*. That would have been enough, but there was a two-hundred-dollar tab waiting for her, and she'd be able to get one good meal a day for all three of them until that ran out. She wasn't certain the guy was for real, but the tab was. It would be easy enough to avoid him, and still eat on his money.

The movie had put a cap on the night. She hadn't seen it when it was first out, Mother and Father hadn't permitted it. They didn't let her watch any TV at all except PBS, didn't let her see any movies, *ever*, but this had been one film they would have really tossed a hissyfit over.

Fantasy. They said it like it was a cuss-word. If Meg's parents hadn't been one of Mother's clients, they'd have made her throw out the unicorn keychain. She wasn't allowed to read anything but schoolbooks, listen to anything but classical music, but *fantasy* was the ultimate slime, so far as they were concerned. She'd managed to read some at school, by keeping the books from the school library in her locker, along with the unicorn poster Meg gave her, and the dragon calendar. She'd also had a little cache of books she'd hidden under the springs of her bed, books Meg gave her when she was through with them, books full of unicorns, elves, magic . . . and that turned out to be a major mistake. Mother had found them.

You'd have thought it was kiddie-porn, she thought, angry and unhappy all at the same time. *Or drugs. You'd have thought they were Fundies and the books were about demon-worship.*

The way they'd carried on had been horrible; not yelling, no, yelling would have been a relief. No, instead they lectured her, in relays. About how the stuff was going to ruin her mind for logical thinking; about how it was wasting time she could have been using on extra-credit stuff to boost her grades and give her an edge. How they felt betrayed. How if the colleges found out she read this stuff, they'd never let her in. On and on and on—

And then they took it and her into the living room and

burned the books in the trendy gas-log fireplace, right in front of her.

"No living in a dream-world for you, Tania," Father had said, as he fed the brightly colored books to the flames. "It's time to wake up to the real world."

Well, I'm in the real world now, Father, she thought at him, her eyes stinging. *It's more real than yours.*

They hadn't been able to do much to her, other than spend every minute they had to spare lecturing her. What could they do, after all? She wasn't allowed to "waste" her time on clubs, boyfriends, hobbies, music for pleasure— the only time she was ever outside the townhouse was when she was at school or at her after-school lessons: ballet on Monday, piano on Wednesday, tennis on Saturday. She didn't *like* any of those outside lessons; they couldn't punish her by taking any of them away. She didn't have any friends but Meg, she wasn't *allowed* to have any friends but Meg, and she only saw Meg on Saturday, at the club for tennis lessons.

Then she found one Saturday that there was still one thing they could do. They moved her lesson, from Saturday morning, to Saturday afternoon. She'd lost even Meg's tenuous friendship.

They told her Friday night. That was when she decided to run away.

Father always accused her of being unable to plan ahead, of forgetting about the future. *Well, he was wrong.*

She knew the combination of the safe, and how much money her parents kept in it. She went to it by the light of a tiny flashlight, opened it, and counted . . . she didn't dare take too much, or they might miss it if they happened to need money for something on Saturday, but she made sure she had enough for the fare. Then she packed her tennis bag, taking everything she could fit into it, stuffing it and her purse to bursting. Father was on the way to New York, Mother was seeing a friend of Meg's father, helping him find a house for a relocating veep. She did things like that for her clients; that was why she got so many accounts.

Too bad she didn't do things like that for her kid. Or maybe I was like a "declining account" to her.

When Mother dropped her off at the club, she'd gone around to the kitchen instead of to her lesson. She asked one of the busboys how to get to the city bus, figuring they'd know, if anyone would.

It was easier than she'd thought; many of the employees at the club used the bus as their primary transportation. She'd taken the city bus downtown, and from there it was a simple matter to get to the Greyhound depot. Before the four-hour tennis lesson was over, she was on her way to Savannah. There was no special reason to go there, it was just a place somewhere, anywhere, else. She'd picked it more-or-less at random, figuring if she hadn't known in advance where she was going neither would her parents. Research Triangle Park, North Carolina, vanished behind her.

If Father'd been more like Tannim. . . . She let a little more hot water into the tub, and sank back with a wistful sigh.

Money didn't last as long as she'd thought it would. Really, she didn't have any idea how much things cost. She made the mistake of buying a couple of nylon bags and a lot of t-shirts and things to wear so she didn't look so conspicuous. By the time she reached Savannah, she was down to her last twenty dollars, and desperate. The bus arrived after midnight, and had dumped her out on the street, cold and scared. Afraid to hang around the bus terminal, she'd wandered the streets, jumping at every shadow, expecting to get mugged at any moment.

That was when Jamie found her; she found out later he'd just turned a really good trick, and was a little high, and feeling very generous and expansive. All *she* knew was that this really cute guy came up to her, as she was sitting on a bench in some kind of little park, and looked at her kind of funny. Then he'd said, "You're in trouble, aren't you?" and offered her a place to stay.

If she hadn't been so exhausted, she'd have been horrified by the awful apartment. The place was musty, full of mildew, with stained ceilings where leaks had sprung. Two rooms, on the top floor of an old, unpainted building so rickety that it leaned. No furniture, cracks in all the walls, carpeting with about a hundred years of dirt ground into it, bugs crawling everywhere—she'd never seen a place like it before.

Laura had been waiting, and when she saw that Jamie'd brought Tania with him, she started to yell at him. But then she'd taken a second look, and just gave Tania a couple of blankets and a pillow, and said they'd talk in the morning.

They talked, all right. Or rather, Tania talked. When she was through, Jamie'd looked at Laura, and Laura had nodded slowly. "All right," Laura had said. "Y'all can stay. But y'all gotta pay your own share. We ain't got anythin' t' spare a-tall."

She'd thought it would be easy. She didn't know that no one was going to hire a fourteen-year-old with no experience, no phone, and no transportation. Not when there were so many SCAD students looking for jobs. After a week of filling out applications and getting turned down, she was getting desperate. If Laura and Jamie threw her out—

She asked Laura to get her a job where *she* worked. That was when Laura laughed, and told her what she, Jamie, and the other kids sharing the apartment did all night. And offered to show her how.

"It's easy," Laura'd said cynically, in her thick, Georgia-cracker accent. "They pay y'forty bucks, and y'just lie there. Half hour, and it's over, an' ya go find another john."

She'd had sex education; she knew about all of it, from contraceptives to AIDs. As desperate as she'd been, she hadn't thought it would be that bad.

So she'd been deflowered by some guy in the back seat of his car and gotten forty bucks out of the experience; he hadn't even known she'd been a virgin. It had hurt a lot, but she soaked away the pain in the bathtub, and went out the next night. After a while it stopped hurting—physically.

It could have been worse, she told herself. In fact, she'd been incredibly lucky, and she knew it. There were guys who hung around the bus station waiting for kids like her; they'd offer a place to stay, and the next thing the kid knew, she was hooked and he was her pimp. Jamie saved her from that, anyway. At least she wasn't doing drugs, her money was her own, and she could make her johns wear rubbers.

She sat up a little in the tub, thinking she heard the key in the lock. But no, it wasn't Laura or Jamie. It was getting awfully late, and she was beginning to worry.

Especially about Jamie. *He'd* started using drugs; he'd always smoked a little grass, hell, he was high when she'd met him. But she was pretty sure he'd been doing something harder than grass, lately, and she was afraid it was crack.

She couldn't blame him, in a way. She'd naively assumed that he was getting picked up by women the way she and Laura were hooking with men. Then she'd seen him in a car with one of his johns . . . and later, down on Bull Street, with the other cute young boys, cruising for another customer. Male customers.

"I'm not a fag," he'd said fiercely, when she mentioned she'd seen him. "I'm *not*. I'm straight, I'm just making the rent, okay? It doesn't mean anything."

"Okay," she'd said hurriedly, "I believe you." And didn't bother to tell him that it didn't matter to her if he was gay or straight. Her father had referred to one of her Fine Art Appreciation teachers as "queer as a football bat," and she'd always liked *him*. What mattered was that Jamie was careful; that he made sure all his johns wore rubbers, the way she did, and that he stayed *safe*. That he didn't start on heavy drugs, like the kids in the other room.

Because she'd seen what happened when you got hooked. Especially the guys; they wound up going to a pimp, one who'd keep them stoned all the time and take all their money, and when they got stoned, they weren't so careful anymore.

Laura wasn't much better about taking chances. When Tania did anything besides in the guy's car, she never went anywhere with a guy except a motel room, and then she'd meet him there, and if he wasn't alone, she'd leave. She wouldn't do kinky stuff, either. Laura did things Tania never would; Laura took chances all the time.

But Laura was a lot tougher than Tania.

You'd have to be tough to take what she did. Getting raped by your stepdad, then thrown out of the house for telling . . . her mom saying she was a slut, and that she lied about it all. . . . I guess she figures she hasn't got a lot to lose. Except Jamie, I guess.

Laura spilled the same story every time she came home drunk, which was about once a week, even though she wasn't more than sixteen. Jamie didn't talk about *his* past. Tania figured it must have been worse than Laura's; sometimes she'd wake up and hear Jamie crying, hear Laura comforting him. She'd seen him nude a lot, and there were scars all over his body.

Tania was getting all wrinkly, like a raisin; she got out of the water reluctantly, and pulled the plug. As she watched the water run down the drain, making a little whirlpool, she remembered the PBS show bit about how you could tell what hemisphere you were in whether the whirlpool ran clockwise or counterclockwise.

Gravity, Coriolis forces . . . her life was running out like the water. It was so hard to think of anything but the next trick, hard to plan past making the rent.

She used to have dreams, plans. When she first ran away, she was going to get a job, maybe learn to be a model . . . or get into a tech school and learn computers . . . or maybe see if her art teachers were right about her being good at drafting. These days, she watched the SCAD students with a kind of dull hatred. They had it all, and they didn't even know it. How *dared* they pretend they were so tortured, so tormented by art? They didn't know what torture was.

Torture was coming home with cigarette burns on your arms, like Laura; having scars all over your body, like Jamie.

Torture was running fifteen blocks with a guy chasing you, hoping you knew a way to get away from him before he beat you up and took your money. Torture was not having enough to eat, ever; worrying about getting kicked out onto the street because the junkies in the next room couldn't afford their share of the rent.

Tannim had talked about having dreams. What had happened to hers?

She pulled on an oversized t-shirt and curled up in her blankets, waiting for the others to get home. Next week was the end of the month and the bookstores would strip books of their covers, turn in the covers for credit, and pitch the stripped pages into the dumpster. There might be some fantasy or science fiction in there, if she got there early enough. There had been, last month.

If she couldn't live on her own dreams, she'd take other people's. That would do. She thought again about that black-and-white TV she'd seen for ten bucks at the Goodwill store; maybe she could get it with a little of the hundred dollars. . . .

Meanwhile she'd wait for Laura and Jamie to get home, make sure they ate the food she'd brought, make sure they were all right.

They were all the family she had.

She must have dozed off, because she woke up with a start to the sounds of the kids in the other room coming in, all three together, higher than anything. Joe and Tonio were all over each other, and Honi kept telling them to hush in a voice louder than their giggles. Tania didn't know if Honi was a boy or a girl; Honi had awfully big hands and feet for a girl, and a prominent Adam's apple, but she never wore anything but tight black skirts and pumps and fishnet hose out on the street—and this grubby old bathrobe with tatty marabou trim at home.

Joe and Tonio were, according to Jamie, "queer as football bats." Odd that Jamie and her father used the same expression. They said they were lovers, but whenever they got drunk—as opposed to high—they beat each other up something awful. Laura and Jamie ignored them, but Tania always stayed hidden in bed when they started on each other that way.

She glanced over at the other bed, almost by reflex, and saw one lump in it, with long, fire-red hair. Laura.

"Jeezus, ah wish the hail them queers'd take it outside," came a loud groan from the lump. Laura had deliberately made it loud enough for the others to hear, and Tonio just giggled harder.

"But baaaby it's cooold outside," Joe shrieked, and by the thump, fell onto the sleeping-bags he shared with Tonio. The overhead bulb went out in the other room, leaving the harsh light from the cracked ceramic lamp in the corner of their room as the only source of illumination.

Laura sat up, shaking her hair out of her eyes, and peered through the doorway into the other room. "Weahll, theah goes the rent," she said glumly. Tania pulled her blankets back and sat up too, her heart sinking.

But then Laura took a second look. The trio in the other room were already snoring. "Or mebbe not," she said thoughtfully, and slipped out of her bed to creep quietly into the other room.

She came back with a handful of something. "Damnfools didn't spend it all, this tayhme," she said grimly. "Got thutty from Tonio's pants, foahty from Honi, an' twenny from Joe. I got foahty put by. How 'bout you?"

Tania dug into her purse and came up with Tannim's five twenties, handing them over without a qualm. After all, she didn't have to worry about eating for a while.

Laura looked at her with a dumbstruck expression on her face. "Whut in hail did y'all do, gal?" she asked. "Ah found the sammiches. You go to a pahty, or didja get a delivery kid?"

Tania giggled, and shook her head. "No," she said, and the story of the strange guy in the bar spilled out under Laura's prodding. But to her surprise, Laura wasn't pleased.

"Jee-zus!" the girl finally exploded, tossing her tangled hair over her shoulders. "Whut in hail didja thank you was doin'? This ain't no fairy tale, girl! Man don' give away money foah nothin'! You ain't gonna go back theah, are you?"

"Not while *he's* there," she replied, resentfully. "But the tab's real, Laura; I saw the charge slip. I think we oughta eat it up before he changes his mind—"

Laura wasn't convinced, and she scowled, then interrupted her. "That's 'nother thang, now ah'm glad I didn' eat them sammiches—he prolly put dope in there. First taste is free, but—"

"Laura, they came straight out of the *kitchen*. He didn't

touch them! Kevin Barry's is straight-edge, you dummy, they wouldn't do anything like that!" At Laura's continued scowl, she added, "Besides, I already ate one, and it was okay."

"*Jeezus,*" the older girl said explosively. Then, "I reckon it's all right. But don' go near him agin, you heah me? He's prolly a pimp, all that crap 'bout dreams and do-good bull. Only dreams man like that has come in white powdah, or lil' brown rocks. He jest wantsta get you off, get you stoned, an then he's got you."

Tania sighed, and bowed her head in acquiescence. It would have been nice to have somewhere to go for help. She had vague memories of a dream, where Tannim was some kind of warrior, in leather and blue jeans, and he fought monsters to protect her. . . .

But this wasn't a fairy tale or a movie; Laura was right. Nobody gave money away for free, and dreams had a way of vanishing when the rent needed to be paid. Laura was nibbling tentatively at a corner of one of the sandwiches, as if she expected to bite into something dangerous.

That much was real, anyway. Food today, and food for the next week or so, and just twenty more dollars from Jamie and the rent would be paid up.

"Where's Jamie?" she asked, and Laura stopped chewing. Her scowl turned to a frown of worry.

"Ah don' know—" she began, and then they heard the rattle of a key in the lock. From the sound of it, Jamie was having a hard time finding the lock.

When he stumbled through the darkened outer room, it was obvious why. He was even higher than the others had been. But this was a manic kind of high that made Tania sick inside. There was booze on his breath, but that wasn't all.

Crack. He's been smoking crack.

She sat in dumb silence, while Laura scolded him out of his clothes and into bed, holding out one of the remaining sandwiches. But even she went silent at the sight of rope burns on his wrists.

"Whut happened?" she asked, after a long pause. Jamie laughed and snorted.

"I did a party, baby. There was a birthday, and I was the favor. They got a little rough, but they made it up to me." He snatched at the sandwich she held, and devoured it before she could say anything; dove into the bag and got the cookies and ate them, then the second sandwich.

How? With dope and booze? Or did he get that after?

"How many?" Laura asked, finally, flatly. He gave her an owl-like stare, as the food made him sleepy.

"I don' know," he replied, his words slurring. "Four. Five. I wanta sleep."

"Did you make 'em use rubbers?" she snarled, as he lay down. When he didn't respond, she shook him. "Answer me, dammit! *Did you?*"

"Yeah. Sure. I'm gonna sleep now." And he pushed her away. He didn't so much fall asleep as pass out.

Frantic now, Laura scrabbled through his pockets, turning them out on the cargo-blanket and pawing through them. A pocket-knife, a butterfly-knife, assorted change. Keys. Three crumpled twenties. Gum wrappers and half a pack of gum.

Three condoms.

"He went out with six," Laura whispered, her voice tight with fear. "He had six."

Six; three gone—but Jamie had said there were four or five johns. And he had been at a party; no telling how many times each.

Laura started to cry, tears streaking her face with cheap mascara, rent money lying forgotten on the bed.

Tania went to her, hugged her, and held her, rocking, not able to say anything, only able to be there.

"It's all right," she said, meaninglessly. "It's all right. We'll take care of him in the morning, okay? It'll be all right. This isn't the first time this has happened, and he was all right before."

"Yeah," Laura sobbed, "but—"

"If they had the Plague, they wouldn't have partied together, right?" she said, trying come up with something that could soothe Laura's fears—and *not* mentioning her own.

Like, what if they had it and didn't know yet. Or what if they all had it and didn't care?

"But—" Laura couldn't get the rest out through her tears.

"Look. Whatever happens, we'll take care of it," she said, holding Laura and rocking her. "We will. We'll take care of it together."

CHAPTER SIX

George Beecher sighed, pulled his raincoat a little tighter against the damp chill, and lit another cigarette. He moved out of the shadows, walking a little farther along the riverfront, and leaned on one of the cutesy gaslights, staring out at the river as if he was watching for something.

He was, but it wasn't out on the river—which you really couldn't see much of because of the creeping fog. What he wanted was inside that building behind him, in warmth and laughter and candlelight.

Well, the only way he was going to earn some of that for himself was to park out here, in the dark, fog and cold. And wait.

A lot of what a P.I. did was wait, although for the life of him, he couldn't imagine why the gal who'd hired him had wanted her hubby followed. Or what she figured he was doing on his nights out. He hadn't done anything at all this whole evening. He'd thought she was a little odd when the boss first talked to her; now he was sure of it.

The guy had shown up at the Irish bar, like she'd said he would—but it wasn't with a chippie, like he'd expected; it was with an old man, a guy that had that "white-collar worker" look about him. Retired white-collar. Nothing untoward there, either, the old guy was as straight as they

89

came; George had a knack for picking out the bent ones no matter how far in the closet they'd buried themselves. The young guy just had an odd friend, that was all. No big deal. Plenty of guys were buddies with old guys— maybe this was somebody he'd worked with before the old man retired.

They'd listened to the band—along with the rest of the bar. The guy—kid, almost—hadn't even had anything to drink; it had looked to George like he'd stuck to cola the whole time.

Then a chippie *had* shown up, a free-lancer, and way out of place for the bar. For a little bit, it had looked like he was going to get a bite; the guy'd come real close to getting into a fight over the underage hooker.

But the fight never materialized. The rest of the patrons bounced the drunk, and the guy George was following had taken the kid back to his table. The old guy left them alone.

Once again, it started to look like pay-dirt, but he'd just talked to the kid; then got the girl some food, maybe passed her some money, then turned her loose. And when he and the old guy left, it wasn't to go party with the chick—it was to this second-floor restaurant.

They'd been there for hours. The girl had evaporated.

Nobody in his right mind would give a hooker cash and expect her to be waiting for him after dinner. Either the guy was really crazy, or—

Or the guy was a pushover for a sob story. Stupid, but nothing you could prosecute in a court of law. Unless wifey was planning on getting him committed. . . .

You'd need a lot more than giving a panhandling kid some dough to get a guy committed. He hadn't even started the fight in the bar back there—and he'd hardly laid a finger on the drunk. You'd need some serious shit to lock a guy up; some evidence that he was being more than just a pushover for a sob story, something really crazy. So far the guy hadn't obliged at all.

What was more, he didn't look as if he had enough money to make locking him up a profitable deal. He had a nice classic car, yeah, but nothing wildly spectacular, no

Ferrarri, no fancy clothes, and he wasn't parading around with high-class types.

On the other hand, he *had* flashed a Gold Card. And he *was* eating in a gourmet place. A lot of millionaires didn't look or act the part. Maybe—

Well, it wasn't George's business what she did with the information he got her. All he had to do was follow the dude around, and make his report, take his pictures. He'd gotten one of the guy with the old guy, and one going into the restaurant. Funny thing had happened; every time he wanted to get a pic of the guy with the hooker, somebody had gotten in the way. He had only his verbal report, and a picture of the kid as she came out of the bar.

No matter. Wifey would have what he'd gotten. Whatever she did with the full report after he turned it in was her own affair.

He dropped the cigarette on the cobblestones, ground it under his heel, and lit another. It was going to be a two-box night from the looks of it.

Aurilia nic Morrigan leaned over her stark ebony desk and flipped through the pages of the last detective agency's report one more time, frowning. This perusal, like the last, yielded nothing she could use. Bruning Incorporated certainly hadn't come up with much in three weeks of following Tannim around; hopefully the new agency she had hired would be a little more resourceful.

She slapped the folder closed, petulantly, and stared at her perfectly manicured nails. Aurilia wanted Keighvin Silverhair shredded, scattered over at least a continent, preferably by those same perfectly manicured nails. But Keighvin had formidable protections, and at least the grudging backing of Elfhame Fairgrove. She and Vidal Dhu were the only Folk of the local Unseleighe Court who wanted Keighvin's skin; they had *no* backing if it came to an all-out war instead of minor skirmishing. So she and Vidal were reduced to hide-in-corner strategies; one thing she had never been particularly good at. Right now, the only way to get Keighvin, at least so far as she could tell, was through this "Tannim" character. The problem was, she had discovered that beneath a veneer of commonly known information, there wasn't *anything* to give her a clue to the human's nature.

She sighed, tossed the bound folder onto the filing cabinet, and stretched her arms over her head, slowly. The beige suede screens that walled her off from the rest of the room were hardly more than a few feet away, just barely out of reach. There was very little in her tiny office-cubicle besides the desk, the filing-cabinet and the black leather chair she sat in—but unlike humans, she and her associates didn't need much in the way of paper records. The single three-drawer filing-cabinet served all their needs for storage, and all of one and a half drawers was taken up with reports on Fairgrove and the personnel there. The records for Adder's Fork Studios filled barely half of the bottom drawer.

But Adder's Fork didn't need much in the way of paper-trails and record-keeping. Customers came to find *them*, not the other way around. There was no need to go to any effort to keep track of accounting; payment was always in advance, cash only. And if the IRS or any other busy-body agency came looking for them, their agents would find—nothing.

Customers, on the other hand, could always reach them. Vidal saw to that.

Supply and demand, Aurilia mused, a little smile playing about her lips. *A small market, but a loyal one. And one with few options to go elsewhere. . . .*

She stood up, walking around the discreet beige partition to the space taken up by the studio. It was a good thing they didn't need to hire outside secretarial help. A mundane secretary would never be able to handle the environment.

Nearest to the office was the newest sound-stage. Tiny, by Hollywood standards, but quite adequate for the job, it looked very much like an old-fashioned doctor's office. Aurilia looked the new set over again, and decided it wasn't quite menacing enough. There was a definite overall impression of threat, but the customers weren't terribly bright sometimes; they needed things pointed out.

Circles, arrows, and underlings.

She considered the doctor's examining table. The next film would be a period piece, of the 1800s, re-enacting a series of incidents that had taken place during the Chicago World's Fair. With liberal embellishments. The kind their customers really appreciated.

The lead character—one could hardly call him a "hero"—in this movie was a physician who had used the activity and bustle caused by the Fair to cover his own activities. He had lured in young women new to the city by advertising for secretaries, and offering a room above his office as an added incentive. With the Fair in full swing, rooms had been at a premium and were very expensive even in the poorest parts of town. Doctors were respected professionals—and in any case, he (supposedly) did not actually live in the same building as his office. Many young women applied whenever he posted his advertisement.

He only chose select individuals, however. Pretty girls, but ones with no family, or very far from home. Girls with no friends, and especially, no boyfriends. Girls with quiet, submissive natures.

He would scientifically discover their weaknesses, play upon them, and eventually, lure them down into his "special office," with the hidden door. Among other things, he had performed hack-abortions before he had hit on the secretarial scheme. Some of those secret patients had been his victims. It had been no problem to have any number of surprises concealed within the building; it had been constructed from his own plans. Once hidden behind the soundproof walls, he would overpower his girls with chloroform, then strap them to a special examining table—

And once he was finished with them—or even at the climax of his pleasures—he would behead them, with a special device he mounted onto the table.

The bodies he disposed of in various ways, none traceable at the time. Aurilia reflected that he had really been very clever, for a human. His downfall had come when he overestimated his invulnerability and grew careless, choosing a girl he thought fit the profile—who didn't.

But that was not what concerned the studio. They would

use only the barest bones of the original story—and it certainly would not end in the doctor's capture.

Indeed, they were going to take extreme liberties in the matter of the victims' ages. None would be over the age of sixteen. Most would be nine to thirteen, or at least, would look that young. Vidal already had several girls in mind, and there would, of course, be many constructs used to fill out the cast. Aurilia was considering a second version, employing young boys instead of girls, and a female "doctor"—or even a third and fourth with same-sex pairings. After all, why waste a perfectly good set?

But right now that set still needed a few modifications. Aurilia considered the examining table carefully. She couldn't make the restraints any more obvious. Perhaps—

Perhaps a change of color.

She reached out with her magic, and touching the aluminum with the hand of a lover, stroked the surface of the table, darkening, it, dulling the shiny, stainless surface and changing its substance, until the table top had become a slab of dark gray marble.

That did it. That was exactly the touch the set had needed. Now the table called up images of ancient sacrificial altars, without the mind quite realizing it, or wondering why.

Of course, after the first victim, the audience would know what the table was for, and would simply be waiting for the "doctor" to lure another victim to his lair.

But the little touches and attention to detail was what had made Adder's Fork the leading producers of S and M, kiddie-porn, and snuf-films in the business. There was true artistry involved, and centuries of expertise.

Hmm. Perhaps an Aztec theme for the next group. Wasn't there a sect where the sacrifice was first shared by all the participants?

Aurilia busied herself with the rest of the set, checking the apparatus and the camera and sound set-ups, making certain that everything was in place for the shoot tomorrow. It was ironic that both the Unseleighe Court and the Seleighe Court had the same problem in dealing with the modern world. They both had to earn real money.

Different motives, and different ends, but the same needs. For Aurilia, Vidal, and Niall, it was money to pay for the private detectives and to buy property. Money to buy arms to ship to both sides of a fight, be it a simple gang-war or full-fledged terrorism. Money to bribe officials, or those whose power was not official but no less real. True money from human hands, not magic-made duplicates, for the underworld was cannier than the rest of human society and would catch such tricks quickly. The underworld preferred bills in denominations of less than a hundred dollars; preferred old, worn money rather than newly printed. They would not accept money with sequential numbers. The time it would take to gather single, old bills and duplicate them, or to duplicate a single, old bill and make enough changes in it to make every copy look different, was better spent in ways that simply earned that amount of money.

There are times in the humans' world when it is simpler and easier to do without magic.

That had left Aurilia with a few problems of logistics, but nowhere near as many as her opponents were forced to cope with. The Seleighe Court fools limited their ways of earning cash to legitimate means. Fools they were, because "legitimate" and "constricted" were one and the same. And when one reduced one's options, one halved one's income.

Anything illegal was *far* more profitable than anything legal. And, for all of its difficulties, moving and working in the shadow world of the underground was much simpler than coping with all the regulations and laws of the "honest citizen."

Look at everything Keighvin had gone through to establish Fairgrove Industries, for instance. He'd created something that could function totally within human parameters, and yet leave the nonhumans free to work. Resourceful he was, indeed, and though she hated him passionately, Aurilia could admire that much about him.

Whereas Adder's Fork had required only three things once Aurilia and Vidal had arrived at a plan; kenning an airplane and all the equipment they needed, making an underworld contact adept at forging records and getting their electronic copies into the proper systems, and installing a Gate into Underhill inside the plane.

The plane, a C-130 cargo craft, had taken six months to duplicate and another to modify so that it no longer looked like the craft it had been copied from. The lines had been subtlely changed, and the color turned to a light blue that blended in very well with the open sky. Being able to work Underhill had helped; magical energy was much more readily available there. But they had not been able to create the craft exactly; in point of fact, there was no iron or steel anywhere in it, it had no engine, and never needed refueling on mortal aviation gas. That was both an advantage and a disadvantage. There was nothing to break down, and they could land and take off from anywhere, at any time, but they dared not let inspectors or anyone with more than a cursory knowledge of aircraft anywhere near it. That flaw made a dreadful hole in their defenses. Aurilia would have liked a real engine—but the Unseleighe Court shared their rivals' "allergy" to Cold Iron. How Keighvin and his crew could bear to work so near it was a mystery to her. And if they ever broke through the Fairgrove defenses, Cold Iron and humans wielding it would without a doubt be Keighvin's second line of defense. That was fine . . . she had a syringe of human blood with iron filings ready to inject into Keighvin when she had him. It would be very entertaining to watch his reactions to that.

But for that single technical flaw—the authenticity of the aircraft—Adder's Fork was completely in the clear. Gold coins—kenned copies of genuine Krugerrands—had bought the records for plane and pilots, and had bought the human who inserted those records into the humans' computers. More coins, sold one at a time to dealers, had rented equipment long enough for Unseleighe Court mages to ken it. Aurilia had stock-piled many favors over the course of several hundred years; she cashed them all in on this venture.

Then it had only required time. Time to reproduce complicated gear and make sure that it worked; time to build the studio Underhill. Time to make more contacts in the human underworld, offering the kind of product certain humans would literally bankrupt themselves to own.

Adder's Fork did simple porn movies at first—well, relatively simple. All of their pictures had real, if unadorned, plots, and most involved the occult. And every Adder's Fork film involved pain, bondage, S and M; these things raised power, energy the humans never used, energy that would ordinarily have gone to waste, so in addition to bringing in human money, the filming itself was a potent source of power. The favors Aurilia had cashed in were quickly replaced by other favors owed as the denizens of Underhill vied to be in at the filming, acting either on Vidal's direction as camera operators or other technicians, or as extras, if they were attractive enough. Not every creature of the Unseleighe Court was a boggle or troll. Some, like Aurilia and Vidal, were as lovely as any High Court elven lord or lady.

Now that they had both studios up and running, they still did produce that simpler sort of film, for over in Studio One, they'd finished one such film tonight. A gay-bondage party using the Caligula set, to be precise; one with a simple plot that was close to the reality of the situation— a group hires a strip-tease entertainer for the birthday-boy, then they all decide to take things a little farther. The "party-favor" had been a very pretty young male hooker, dark-haired and dreamy-eyed, who Aurilia thought they might use again some time. He was the only one who hadn't known the "party" was being filmed; he'd been plied with liquor at the bar where he had been picked up, and drugged in the cab on the way here. The set was a discreet one, the cameras mounted behind mirrors. The other five men, old customers, had been recruited with a cash bonus and a promise of whatever they wanted from the company catalog.

That was a formidable promise, and one that might have lured them more than the money. One thing that Adder's Fork had that no other pornshop possessed was an unbreakable copy-guard. Adder's Fork tapes could not be duplicated; attempts would only result in both tapes'

signals breaking up—thanks to a special spell in the
Underhill duplicating room. There was a warning to that
effect at the front of each tape—and every time Aurilia
received a request for a copy of something that duplicated
an order to the same address, she smiled. Certain humans
never could believe that there was something they couldn't
get around.

High-tech meets high magic—and loses.

A more economic way to make ends meet. She considered her solution to the cash-flow problem to be just as
clever and creative as Keighvin's. And far less work. His
setup had taken decades to establish; hers mere months.
His was rooted to one spot, and if there were ever troubles,
he would have to vanish with no other recourse. Hers was
as mobile as her "plane," for it did not matter where the
Gate was located in the here-and-now of the humans'
world, so long as it was rooted in something large enough
to serve as an anchor. It was useful to have the studios
Underhill, especially Studio Two. Screams couldn't penetrate the Gate, and even more Unseleighe Court creatures were vying for a chance to serve as extras in the films
Two produced. Adder's Fork Studios had always been
known for high-quality porn, but the Studio Two films,
snuff-pictures with emphasized occult and satanic themes,
really had the customers begging for more.

The customers raved about the "special effects," and it
was not the deaths they were talking about. Vidal's careful camera work, showing every nuance of the snuff and
lingering on the corpse afterwards, so that the customer
could see for himself that it was neither moving nor breathing, made sure the customers knew they had gotten what
they paid for. Most of the dead were magical constructs,
who lived and breathed only long enough to scream and
die, but there were enough true human deaths—and
human reactions of fear and pain—to satisfy both the customers and the thirsts of Aurilia and her partners. No, the
customers were talking about the "monsters" and "demons"
that participated in the sexual rituals, and usually accounted
for half of the deaths. Little did the clients know that these
"monsters" were not humans in makeup and prostheses,

but the Unseleighe Court creatures who thronged Aurilia's auditions every time she cast a picture.

And no one ever went away disappointed. Whoever didn't get on camera, got to help dispose of the corpse when Vidal didn't need it anymore. *Maybe we ought to film that next time. . . .* The Chicago doctor in this version was going to be a satanist as well, and at the moment when the police broke down his door, would summon a demon to carry him to (presumed) safety. On second thought, Aurilia decided to leave the script the way it was, with nothing other than the rituals and the half-seen hints of "the Master," with the supernatural actually entering the picture only at the end. Save all the limb-chewing for the next flick.

It was ironic, Aurilia thought, that human religious fanatics seemed convinced that there were so many truly innocent activities that were inspired by their "Satan" and created by evil, yet they didn't recognize true evil when it walked among them. Adder's Fork was the name of the studio that produced bondage, kiddie-porn, and snuff-films. The holding company that owned the airplane and (supposedly) produced training films was a respected member of the Chamber of Commerce, incorporated as "Magic Mirror, Inc." Vidal went to all the meetings and all the functions, smiled, and passed among the foolish human sheep, even donated money to some of the more fundamentalist churches, and none of them ever guessed that beneath his smooth, flawless exterior lay a creature that would gladly have torn their hearts from their living bodies and eaten them alive. In fact, he was praised by those fundamentalist leaders as a "true Christian businessman."

A shiver of energies touched her spine as the Gate let someone through from the human world. She wasn't worried; right now the Gate was keyed only to herself, Vidal, and Niall mac Lyr. She waited a moment, dimming the lighting with a thought. Vidal stalked through the door from Studio One shortly thereafter, closing it so carefully behind him that Aurilia knew he was angry.

Lovely. What sort of temper tantrum am I going to be treated to this morning?

She turned slowly to face him: He was still wearing his human-seeming, which meant that although he was angry, he had not been enraged so far as to lose control. It was much the same as his true-shape; raven hair replaced the silver, though he wore it longer when he was not passing among humans. The pale skin had been overlaid with a golden tan. Brown eyes with round pupils substituted for the colorless, pale green, cat's eyes . . . But the brow was just as high, the cheek-bones just as prominent, the eyebrows still slanted winglike towards his temples, and the body was still the wiry-slender build of a gymnast or a martial artist. His face wore a cool, indifferent expression, but his body betrayed him.

She, in her turn, did not pretend she did not notice his anger. She simply waited, smoothing the cream-colored silk of her skirt with one hand. She might be the head of this triad, the one with the plans, but he was the strength. He was only a little less intelligent than she, and a better, more powerful mage than she, and she had no intention of ever forgetting that fact. Only his hatred for Keighvin Silverhair kept him at her side, for normally Vidal worked alone. What Keighvin had done to him to warrant that undying enmity, Aurilia did not know and had never asked, but Vidal had tried to destroy the High Court lord for centuries. Until recently, he had rebuffed all efforts at recruiting his aid, even to eliminate Keighvin—but when she approached him with her plan, he had volunteered his help as soon as she had presented it all to him.

So now *she* waited for *him* to speak, and even though she felt a flash of irritation at his superior attitude, she suppressed it. She could not afford to lose him, and she would not antagonize him. Not yet, anyway.

He stalked past her, to the Roman orgy set; they'd finished the Caligula picture last week, but Aurilia hadn't broken the set down yet, because she'd planned to use it for the party picture. Vidal flung himself down on one of the stained cream satin-covered couches, and glared up at her through absurdly long lashes. She seated herself calmly, folded her hands in her lap in a position of calculated passivity, and waited for him to say something. It would have to be verbally; he would not deign to speak to her mind-to-mind. She was not of sufficient rank to warrant that intimacy.

"Keighvin's close to getting the engines into production," he snarled, finally. His command of human vernacular had improved out of all recognition in the past few months. Now it was almost as good as hers. "Very close. He's within weeks."

Aurilia frowned as she recalculated her original plan; she hadn't expected to have to put it into motion quite so soon. She crossed her legs, restlessly. "That's not good— but we've got a counter-plan already in place to discredit him." She blessed the day that she had watched that movie about Preston Tucker. It had given her everything she needed. . . .

"It won't fly," Vidal informed her, his black brows meeting as he scowled. "Somehow he's figured out his own weak spots, and he's ahead of you. He's got a human to front for him. A man with respect and reputation; a retired metallurgist who used to work for Gulfstream. This human knows his field, Aurilia, and he's got contacts we can't touch in the human world. He's going to be able to concoct an explanation that will hold up. And both Keighvin and that human mage of his have placed protections about this new man. I can't touch him magically, not with human and elven magic working against me. I couldn't even take down the first of his shields unless I could catch him Underhill."

That wasn't good; briefly she wondered if Keighvin or the human had seen the same movie she had. She would have to assume that they had, and plan accordingly. She closed her eyes for a moment, and thought. "This human, how old is he?" she asked, finally. "How healthy is he? Could we attack him physically?"

"Well, he's retired, so he's at least sixty-five," Vidal admitted. "He doesn't look terribly sturdy, but he's from the Old Country. You know those scrawny little men—they look fragile, but they're as tough as a briar root and twice as hard to break."

From the Old Country? Eire? Hmm—first generation immigrant? I can work with that. "But their meals are full

of butter and eggs and fatty bacon," Aurilia said with a
sly smile. "And they drink. That doesn't do a great deal
for their hearts, their arteries, or their livers. By now,
Keighvin has convinced him that all of his childhood tales
are really true, and he's thinking of the things besides the
Seleighe Court that might be real. He should have dredged
up a tale or two from his memory about us—hopefully,
a gory one. Why don't you go see if you can't frighten him
into a heart attack?"

Vidal considered the idea for a moment, then smiled,
slowly. His muscles relaxed, and the frown-line between
his brows faded. "Now, that's not a bad notion—and it has
a certain amount of entertainment value as well. A good
thought, *acushla*. Well done."

That last was patronizing, a pat on the head, as one
might pat a dog for a clever trick. Aurilia kept her temper, and smiled winsomely back at him. She was the mind,
and he the strength; as long as she kept that firmly in
mind, she remained in control of the situation, no matter what he might think. Let him break into a froth at
every obstacle. She would keep her head, and guide them
all through to the other side.

As she would keep careful track of every insult. She was
not of high rank in the Unseleighe Court—but rank could
be gained by toppling one higher. There would be an
accounting when this was over.

Oh, yes.

Vidal lounged on his couch, perfectly at ease now, with
a look in his eye as if he might well order Aurilia to wait
on him in a moment. He could get away with that if he
cared to, right now. He could order her to produce refresh-
ment, or even to serve him in other ways, and she was
bound by rank to do as he asked.

She had to sidetrack him, to remind him of her status
in the human world, where he depended on her plans and
knowledge. He'd enjoyed working the Caligula picture; he
didn't much like the Deadly Doctor concept, mostly
because it wasn't decadent and luxurious enough. Aurilia
sought for a distraction in plans for Adder's Fork to keep
him from giving her orders—she wasn't sure she'd be able

to keep her temper if he took the master-slave tone with her.

"What do we do after the Deadly Doctor?" she asked, innocently, looking around at the cream-and-red set, four couches, a couple of marble columns, and a lot of draperies and mirrors. And the series of red ropes lying about. It wasn't an elaborate set; the extras had provided much of the ornament on the Caligula film, and the party picture hadn't needed much more. "It ought to be something demonic. I'd thought Aztec—"

Vidal shook his head emphatically; the one place where she trusted his judgment over hers was in marketing. Somehow he always anticipated what the customers were going to buy. "Not yet. I don't think the customers are going to be ready for anything that exotic yet. It requires too much imagination, and the lead characters are the wrong color. We'll lose a lot of our Southern audience. They want handsome white men as their protagonists. We need something—steamy—decadent—depraved, debauched. Exotic, but not something where the customer can't identify with the master character—"

He shook his head, unable to come up with anything. On reflection, Aurilia agreed with him. She searched for a subject that might do, and suddenly a most unlikely source of inspiration flashed into her mind.

It was the rack of paperbacks at the airport; fully half of them were lurid romances, and she remembered thinking at the time that taken with a little less sugar and allowing the "villain" to win, the plots weren't all that different from Adder's Fork productions. *Passion's Frenzied Fury, Harem Nights, Wild Moon Rising*, they featured stupid, sweet and submissive heroines and some villains who certainly fit the "exotic, depraved, and debauched" description.

"What about a harem thing?" she asked. "We could re-use most of the Caligula set. . . ." But Arabs were not in particularly good odor at the moment, not even with the Adder's Fork customers. And the master character in a harem theme would have to be an Arab. "No, how about pirates; we could do the same there, use this set for the pirate captain's cabin, with one couch and a couple of sea-chests full of bondage gear. The customers won't know they didn't have reclining couches on ships, and frankly, I doubt they'll care. We can open with a boarding party, kill off a few constructs, lots of blood and guts there, take prisoners, and then cut to the cabin."

"Pirates," Vidal mused. "I like that. Snuff, or S and M?"

"Why not both?" she suggested. "A little torture, a little bondage, film from a couple of different angles, mix and match, and leave out the snuff scenes for the S and M flick. But what about the occult angle?"

Vidal grinned, pleased to come up with something she didn't know. "Voodoo, *acushla*. Everybody knows pirates were into voodoo. It's perfect; it's black magic on an exotic island setting, the white stud presiding over a harem of dusky priestesses on a moonlit beach . . . easy to reproduce Underhill with constructs doing all the extra parts. We can even use the arena set for the voodoo rituals, just grow a few palm trees, fill in the seats with foliage, and conjure a moon."

Aurilia felt that cold shiver again, but this time it was not due to someone using the Gate, but to a brush of fear. She did not care to meddle with alien magic—especially alien human magic. She'd had too many bad experiences in the past. . . .

"Be careful with that, will you? We can't afford to bring in something from real voodoo, even by accident. They might not be amused." *They weren't the last time. The Manitou was particularly displeased. If I hadn't been operating against whites, and not against the natives, I might not have survived his displeasure.*

"True." Vidal frowned, this time absently. "I think it's worth it, though. Especially since I suspect we can get extra footage for another couple of flicks out of this. It's going to require some careful research."

By which he means I should take care of it, of course. Well better research assistant than lowly handmaiden.

"Consider it done," she said, with a sweet smile. Vidal looked much happier, and she decided to broach her other idea. "What about making the Deadly Doctor into a foursome, with a female doctor in two of them?" This would be a chance for Aurilia to take her turn in front of the camera. Vidal got plenty of opportunities; even when there weren't any Unseleighe Court volunteers to act as technicians, he could control the camera magically even when he was being filmed by it, and his incredible— attributes—made him a natural for the master character. But they hadn't done anything with a Dominatrix for a long, long time. She'd wanted a chance to be in on the kills personally for weeks.

Vidal pursed his lips, looked sour, but nodded reluctantly. "Not a bad idea, I suppose. How many victims are we talking about? All told, I mean. It takes energy to make the constructs, and it won't be you who's doing it."

As if I didn't know that. "For the first film, I'd say six constructs and two real kills," she replied cautiously. "For the other three, I think the female-male needs a couple of extra real kills, otherwise the customer won't believe in the doctor's ability to overpower young men. But I wouldn't put real kills in the same-sex flick at all; the situation itself is going to be enough of a shocker."

Vidal nodded, after a moment of thought. "We ought to downgrade the same-sex encounters to bondage and torture. The fringe there is a lot smaller market, and I doubt it's worth going after."

She nodded, for once in complete agreement. "That was what I thought—and there's more money available from the leatherboys than there is from the psychotics. The leather crowd never *will* believe that they can't find some way to break our copy-protection."

She rose, so that he followed her lead, subtly answering his superior attitude with body language of her own.

To recover his upper hand, he spoke first, with an order framed as a request. "Why don't you set up your casting-call while I go pay a visit to Doctor Kelly," he suggested. "And get me some parameters for the constructs. I'd prefer file personas, if you have some that will do; they're a lot easier to make than brand new types."

"I don't know why file personas shouldn't work," she replied, already heading for the office and speaking over her shoulder as her cream-leather heels clicked against the marble floor. " I'll just modify the Submissive Secretary, the Street-Sparrows, the Victorian Hookers, and the French and Irish Maids. The hardest part will be the costumes, and I'm a good enough mage for that."

"Precisely," he said, not quite sneering. She ignored the implied insult that she was only a good enough mage to make clothing. He strode towards the door, his soft-soled shoes noiseless on the marble, already reaching for the knob.

"Bring me back some *good* news this time, all right?" she responded sweetly, with the implied insult that *she* was sending *him* out to do her bidding.

But the door closed on her words; he was already gone.

CHAPTER SEVEN

Held aloft by good fellowship and excellent wine—for Trish did, indeed, know her wines as well she knew music—Sam deactivated his alarm system, unlocked his door, and with a farewell wave to Tannim, slipped inside. Thoreau had been waiting, and gave him a tail-wagging welcome, then padded beside him with eager devotion.

Sam smiled down at his faithful companion, and his pleasure was not due just to the wine, the company, or the greeting. This was going to work, this strange alliance of magic and technology, of the ancient Sidhe and modern engineering. It was as real, and as heady a mixture, as the odd gourmet dinner he'd just eaten. And like the meal, it all meshed, so well that the various parts might have been made for each other.

For all his skeptical, cynical words to young Tannim, he'd seen a reflection of the elves' purported concern for the welfare of children in the way Tannim had treated the young prostitute. That hadn't been an act of any kind; Tannim had been worried about the girl, and had expressed that worry in tangible ways that could help her immediately and directly. Money was one thing, but giving her a way to eat regularly for a while was a damned good idea.

He could have bought her groceries—but that would have entailed getting her into his car, and that could be trouble if the police took an interest in the proceedings. And even if he'd bought food for her, chances are she'd not have known how to cook anything. Assuming she lives somewhere that she can cook anything.

It must be a hard, lonely way to live, now that he thought about it. Under the makeup, the child had been thin and pale, wearing a brittle mask of indifference that was likely to crack at any time. He'd always assumed hookers were too lazy to do any real work—but what place would hire a thirteen-year-old child? And what runaway would risk the chance of being caught by giving her real name to get a real job? Under the age of sixteen, you had to have a letter of parental consent to work, and if she was, indeed, a runaway, how would she ever get one?

Of course, she could have lied about her age, and forged a parental consent letter, but such fragile deceits wouldn't hold up to any kind of examination. Perhaps she had tried just that, and been found out. Perhaps she had discovered she had no other choice. Sex seemed less important these days than it was in his day; perhaps selling herself to strangers didn't seem that terrible.

Then again, perhaps it did, but there were no options for her, no way to go home.

He had never quite realized how relatively idyllic his own childhood had been. Why, he'd even had a pony— of course, most Irish children living in the country had ponies, but still . . .

Her life now must be hellish—but as Tannim had asked, if she was willing to continue with it, how bad must her home life have been that she chose this over it?

Sam resolved to start carrying books of fast-food gift certificates. That way, if they *did* run into the child again, or one like her, he'd have a material way to help as well.

And 'tisn't likely she'd find a dope dealer willing to trade drugs for coupons.

But there wasn't much he could do now, not without knowing all the circumstances, without even knowing the child's name and address. He had work to do; Tania's plight would have to wait.

He'd learned long ago how to put problems that seemed

critical—but over which he had no control—in the back
of his mind while he carried on with lesser concerns. He'd
gotten several possibilities for the solution to Keighvin's
needs last night, and he needed to track down the latest
research, to see if anything new could eliminate his bogus
"process" right off.

*At least there's one problem I won't be having. The
engine blocks will be there, and be every thing I claim,
pass every test. This won't be a cold-fusion fiasco—I've
got real results, solid product that I can hand out to anyone
who doubts. If the boys in Salt Lake City had waited until
they had working test reactors producing clean power
before they went pubic, they'd have saved themselves a
world of trouble. And if the process had worked the way
they said it did, well, nobody would be arguing with their
theory or their results, they'd just be going crazy trying
to reproduce what they'd done. That's what's going to
happen here.*

He was looking forward to watching the other firms
going crazy, in fact. This was almost like his college-prank
days, on a massive scale.

Sam walked slowly down the hall, turning on lights as
he passed. He intended to re-arm the security system as
soon as he got to the office so that he couldn't be disturbed. His mind was buzzing with all of his plans, and
he was so wrapped up in his own thoughts that he didn't
even notice the stranger standing in his office until Thoreau
stopped dead in the doorway and growled.

Perhaps the man hadn't been there until that very
moment—for as soon as he saw the creature, Sam's own
hackles went up. There was a curious double-vision quality
about the intruder; one moment he was black-haired and
dark-eyed, and as human as Tannim. The next moment—

The next moment he was as unhuman as Keighvin, and
clearly of the same genetic background. But there the
resemblance ended, for where there was a palpable air of
power tempered with reason and compassion about
Keighvin, this man wore the mantle of power without
control and shaped by greed. Now Sam understood what
his granny had meant when she had said that even with

the Sight it was difficult for humans, child or adult, to tell
the dark Sidhe from the kindly. If the creature had not
been so obvious in his menace, he might have convinced
Sam that he was Keighvin's very cousin.

Thoreau growled again, a note of hysterical fear in the
sound; he backed up, putting Sam between himself and
the Sidhe. Not very brave, certainly not the television picture of Lassie—but very intelligent. Sam was just as glad.
He didn't want this creature to strike out and hurt his little
companion. Sam had defenses; Thoreau had none.

"Samuel Kelly, do you see me?" the Sidhe asked flatly.
It had the sound of a ritual challenge.

"I see you," Sam replied. "I see you as you are, so you
might as well drop the seeming." Then he added, in a hasty
afterthought, "You were not invited." Just in case recognition implied acceptance of the man's presence. Granny's
stories had warned about the Sidhe and the propensity for
semantics-games.

"I don't require an invitation," the Sidhe responded
arrogantly, folding his arms over his chest as he dropped
the human disguise.

One for me, Sam thought. The Sidhe played coup-games
of prestige as well. Every time he surprised the creature,
or caused it to do something, he won a "point." That
intangible scoring might count for something in the next
few moments. The higher Sam's prestige, the less inclined
the thing might be to bother him.

"So what do you want?" Sam asked, tempering the fact
that he'd been forced by the stranger's silence into asking with, "I'm busy, and I haven't time for socializing."

Again the Sidhe was taken aback—and showed a hint
of anger. "I have come to deliver a warning."

To the stranger's further surprise, Sam snorted rudely.
"Go tell it to the Marines," he said, hearkening back to
his childhood insults. "I told you, I have work to do. I've
no time for games and nonsense."

Inwardly, he was far from calm. Tannim had put some
kind of arcane protection on him after dinner tonight, when
he signed a preliminary agreement with Fairgrove. The
young man had said that Keighvin would be doing the

same, but how effective those protections would be, he had no idea. He knew *something* was there; he saw it as a glowing haze about him, like one of those "auras" the New Agers talked about, visible only out of the corner of his eye. How much would it hold against? Would it take a real attack if this stranger made one?

The Sidhe raised a graceful eyebrow, and the tips of his pointed ears twitched. "Bravado, is it?" he asked in a voice full of arrogant irony. "I should have expected it from the kind of stubborn fossil who would listen to reckless young fools and believe their prattle. Hear me now, Sam Kelly—you think to aid yet another rattle-brained loon, one who styles himself Keighvin Silverhair. Don't."

Sam waited, but there was nothing more. *"Don't?"* Sam said at last, incredulously. "Is that all you have to say? Just *don't?"*

"That is all I have to *say,"* the Sidhe replied after a long, hard stare. "But I have a demonstration for fools who refuse to listen—"

He didn't gesture, didn't even shrug—

Suddenly Sam was enveloped in flames, head to toe.

His heart contracted with fear, spasming painfully; he lost his breath, and he choked on a cry—

And in the next moment was glad that he hadn't uttered it. The flames, whether they were real, of magical energy, or only illusion, weren't touching him. There was no heat, at least nothing he felt, although Thoreau yelped, turned tail, and ran for the shelter of Sam's bedroom.

He remained frozen for a moment, then the true nature of the attack penetrated. *It can't hurt me, no matter what it looks like.* After a deep breath to steady his heart, Sam simply folded his arms across his chest and sighed.

"Is this supposed to impress me?" he asked mildly. A snide comment like that might have been a stupid thing to say, but it was the only attitude Sam could think to take. Tannim had warned him about lying to the Sidhe, or otherwise trying to deceive them. It couldn't be done, he'd said, at least not by someone with Sam's lack of experience with magic. And good or evil, both sorts took being lied to very badly. So—brazen it out. Act boldly, as if he saw this sort of thing every day and wasn't intimidated by it.

The Sidhe's face twisted with rage. "*Damn* you, mortal!" he cried. And this time he *did* gesture.

A sword appeared in his hand; a blue-black, shiny blade like no metal Sam had ever seen. A small part of him wondered what it was, as the rest of him shrieked, and backpedaled, coming up against the wall.

"Not so impudent now, are you?" the Sidhe crowed, kicking aside fallen books and moving in for the kill, sword glittering with a life of its own.

Sam could only stare, paralyzed with fear, as his hands scrabbled on the varnished wood behind him—

Tannim cursed the traffic as he waited at the end of Sam's driveway for it to clear, peering into the darkness. Something must have just let out for the night, for there was a steady stream of headlights passing in the eastbound lane—when he wanted westbound, of course—with no break in sight. And there was no reason for that many cars out here at this time of night. It looked for all the world like the scene at the end of *Field of Dreams*, where every car in the world seemed lined up on that back country road.

"So if he built the stupid ballfield out here, why didn't somebody tell me?" he griped aloud. "If I'd known the Heavenly All-stars were playing tonight—"

He never finished the sentence, for energies hit the shields he'd placed on Sam—which were also tied to *his* shields.

The protections about Sam locked into place, as the power that had been flung at the old man flared in a mock-conflagration of bael-fire.

Mock? Only in one sense. If Sam hadn't been shielded, he'd have gone up in *real* flames, although nothing around him would have even been scorched. Another Fortean case of so-called "spontaneous human combustion."

But Sam was protected—the quick but effective shielding woven earlier caught and held. Tannim had not expected those protections to be needed so soon.

He knew what the attacker was, if not who. Only the Folk could produce bael-fire. And the *hate-rage-lust* pulse that came with the strike had never originated from one of Keighvin's Folk. That spelled "Unseleighe Court" in Tannim's book.

All this Tannim analyzed as he acted. He jammed the car into "reverse" and smoked the tires. The Mustang lurched as he yanked the wheel, spinning the car into a sideways drift to stop it barely within the confines of Sam's driveway. He bailed out, grabbing his weapon-of-choice from under the seat and didn't stop moving even as he reached the door; he managed to force his stiff legs into a running kick and kept going as the door crashed open, slamming against the wall behind it.

He pelted down the hall, his bespelled, bright red crowbar clenched in his right hand, and burst into Sam's study. Sam had plastered himself against the wall nearest the door; Tannim flung himself between his friend and the creature that menaced him, taking a defensive stand with the crowbar in both hands, without getting a really good look at the enemy first.

He never did get a *really* good look. He saw only a tall, fair-haired man, a glittering sword, a scowl of surprised rage—

Then—nothing.

Only the sharp tingle of energies along his skin that told him a Gate had been opened and closed.

The enemy had fled. Leaving, presumably, the way he had arrived, by way of Underhill.

It's gonna be the last time he can do that, Tannim thought grimly, framing another shield-spell within his mind, setting it with a few chanted syllables. He dropped it in place over the body of the house, allowing the physical form of the house itself—and, more particularly, the electrical wiring—to give it shape and substance.

It was a powerful spell, and one of Tannim's best. Now no one would be able to pop in here from Underhill without Sam's express permission, nor would they be able to work magics against the house itself.

But it was draining, and Tannim sagged back against

the wall when he was done, letting the crowbar slip to the floor from nerveless fingers. It fell on the carpet with a dull *thud*, and Tannim kept himself from following it only by supreme effort.

He looked up, right into Sam's face.

The metallurgist was reaching for his shoulder to help hold him up, such a mixture of expressions on his face that none of them were readable.

"I . . . don't suppose you have any Gatorade . . . ?" Tannim asked, weakly.

". . . and he set fire to me," Sam continued, after another sip of good Irish. After all the wine tonight, he was only going to permit himself one small glass—but by Holy Mary, he needed that one. His nerves were so jangled that he wasn't going to be able to sleep without it, and he didn't trust sleeping-pills. "He did, I swear it. Only the flames didn't burn. Scared the bejeezus out of poor Thoreau, though."

He reached down and fondled the spaniel's ears. Thoreau had emerged from the closet only after much coaxing, and remained half-hidden at Sam's feet, completely unashamed of his cowardice. Sam had praised the little dog to the sky for doing the right thing, though he doubted that Thoreau understood much of what he was saying; probably all Thoreau knew was that Daddy said he was a Good Boy, and Daddy was going to comfort him after the terrible fright he'd taken. Sam was quite glad that Thoreau had deserted him. One small spaniel was not going to make more than an indentation in a Sidhe's ankle— assuming the animal got that far before being blasted. He'd lost enough pets in his lifetime to old age and illness. He didn't want Thoreau turned to ash by a Sidhe with a temper.

"That was bael-fire, Sam," Tannim replied, refilling his cup from the bottle of Gatorade on the kitchen table. He'd already polished off one bottle, and Sam wondered where he was putting it all. "If you hadn't been protected, you'd have burned up like a match, but nothing around you would have been touched. Charles Fort had a lot of those cases in his books of unexplained phenomena. He called it 'spontaneous human combustion,' and thought it might have something to do with astral travel." The young man shook his head, much wearier than Sam had ever seen him. There were dark circles of exhaustion beneath his eyes, and his hair was limp and flattened-looking. "Nobody ever told Fort that going up in heatless flames is what happens when you get the Folk pissed off at you."

"But I was protected," Sam protested, sensing a flaw somewhere. "You said I had shields, and you said other mages would know that."

Tannim nodded, and rubbed his eyes. "Exactly. He *knew* bael-fire wasn't going to touch you. He'd have to be blind not to know those shields were there. I don't think he intended you to be hurt directly, Sam."

"What, then?" Sam asked in fatigue-dulled apprehension. What worse could the Sidhe have had in mind? "Or was that just intended as a warning? A bit extreme for a warning, seems to me."

"Heh. The Sidhe are always extreme." Tannim cocked his head sideways. "I think he was trying to scare you to death. I think he wanted it to look like you died naturally."

Sam took another sip of Irish, thinking about that for a moment before replying. "He did then, did he?" His apprehension turned to a slow, burning anger. "Sure, and that's a coward's way, if ever I saw one."

"Attacking a human with bael-fire is just as cowardly, Sam," the young man pointed out. "Or going after a human with elf-shot. In either case, it's like using grenades against rabbits. The target hasn't got a chance. I think he must have assumed that since you're retired, you're frail, and he was going to use that."

"Can I assume the blackguard was Unseleighe Court?" Sam asked, the anger within him burning with the same slow heat as a banked peat-fire.

Tannim nodded, and finished the last of his Gatorade. "That's their way, Sam. They never take on an opponent of equal strength if they can help it. I assume they came after you because you're hooked in with Fairgrove and Keighvin. I told you before that if you wanted to back out of this, you could." He capped the bottle and slowly tightened the lid down. "You're still welcome to. Nobody is—"

"Back out?" Sam exclaimed. "Bite your tongue! If the blackguards want a fight, they've come to the right place, let me tell you! Sam Kelly never started a fight, but he always finished them." He bared his teeth in a fierce smile. "I don't intend to let that change, no matter how old I might be."

Tannim's tired face lit up in a smile, and he clapped Sam on the shoulder. "That's the spirit! I was hoping we could count on you!"

Sam let the grin soften to something more wry than fierce. "They should have known better than to try and frighten an Irishman. We're stubborn bastards, and we don't take to being driven off. But come to think of it— what the devil did you do to frighten *him* off? You just popped in the room, and he ran like a scalded cat."

"It wasn't what I did," Tannim replied, tapping the glass bottle on the crowbar that sat on the table between them. "It was what I had. This."

"Cold Iron?" Sam hazarded.

"Twenty pounds' worth, enchanted to a fare-thee-well," the young man told him, one hand still on the red-painted iron bar, a finger trailing along the gooseneck at one end, apparently remembering past uses. "One strong shot with this, and I don't care how powerful a mage he is, he'd have felt like he'd been hit by a semi. Eh heh . . . pureed by Peterbilt."

Sam snorted, then gazed at the bar with speculation. "Can anyone use one of those things? I used to be a fair hand with singlestick not long ago."

Tannim's eyes widened for a moment, then narrowed with speculation. "Huh. I never thought about that, but I don't know why not. I'll tell you what; I can't give you this one, but I can make one for you. And until I finish it, just remember that any crowbar is going to cause one of the Folk a lot of distress. If you'd had one in here tonight, it might even have disrupted the bael-fire spell."

Sam made a mental note to visit an auto-parts store

tomorrow. He'd have one under his car seat and in every room in the house. "I'll get the one out of my car before you leave, and I'll pick up a few more tomorrow. You're sure nobody is going to be able to get back in here tonight?"

"Positive." Tannim took a deep breath, and held Sam's eyes with his own. "Absolutely positive. And as soon as I get back to Fairgrove and tie Keighvin's protections into yours, if the sorry sonuvabitch even tries, the Fairgrove Folk will know. If he brings in enough firepower to crack those shields, he'll touch off a war—"

"Not on my account!" Sam exclaimed with dismay. *That* was far more than he'd bargained on . . . and something he did not want to have on his conscience.

Tannim grimaced, and now Sam realized that the young man had been a lot more shaken by the attack than he wanted to admit. "No—no, don't worry, they won't even try. They aren't any readier for open warfare than you and I are. But—you really can quit, Sam, and no one will hold it against you. . . ."

Sam shook his head emphatically. "I told you before, and I meant it. Tannim, the answer isn't 'no,' it's 'hell no.' In fact—" he grinned, and discovered it was actually a real smile "—you couldn't get rid of me now if you paid me!"

Aurilia sighed, sipped her herb tea, and tried not to look at Niall mac Lyr. She concentrated instead on the delicate, fragile porcelain of her teacup, on the white satin tablecloth, and on the gray velvet cushions of her lounge chair. Normally she would have been enjoying a luxurious breakfast along with the tea, but her breakfast companion was not a creature designed to stimulate anyone's appetite.

The Bane-Sidhe squinted across the table at her, and glowered, its cadaverous face made all the more unpleasant by its sour expression. Every time Niall moved, a breath of dank, foul air wafted across the table toward her. Niall smelled like a fetid ditch—or an open grave. There had been times in Ireland when they were one and the same. The Bane-Sidhe did not at all match his surroundings in

Aurilia's sybaritic sitting room of white satin and gray velvet. He looked like a Victorian penny-dreadful cover, for something entitled "Death and the Maiden," or "The Specter at the Feast." Aurilia sighed again, and pulled the gray silk skirts of her lounge-robe a little closer. She could only hope that when Niall left, he'd take the stench with him.

"Where is he?" Niall asked, for the seventh time. The Bane-Sidhe's speaking voice was a hollow, unpleasant whisper; not even Vidal cared to hear its full-voiced cry. The wail of the Bane-Sidhe brought unreasoning terror even into the hearts of its allies.

Aurilia shrugged. It was no use answering him. She'd already told him she didn't know where Vidal was. The Bane-Sidhe was only interested in his own grievances.

"We have work to do," it continued, aggrieved. "Studio Two should be operational around the clock—*we* don't have to put up with union nonsense or mortal time-clocks. You promised me when I joined you that there would be enough nourishment for all of us. You told me—"

"I know what I told you," Aurilia snapped, her temper frayed by the Bane-Sidhe's constant whining. "I told you that *eventually* we'd have all the pain you could ever need or want. I didn't promise it immediately."

"Pah!" the Bane-Sidhe snorted, tossing its head petulantly. "That was a year ago! You could have had Studio Two in full production three months after you brought up Studio One. It's not as if we have to fret about the cost of sets or casts, or even equipment! But no, you had to chase after Keighvin Silverhair—you had to waste your time discovering what he was up to. And instead of being at full power, I must limp about on the dregs of energy a few paltry deaths supply, and Studio Two has produced only that puny little Roman fantasy—"

"You think humans come running to us to bare their throats to the blade?" Aurilia countered with justifiable irritation. Niall simply would not come to grips with the fact that the world had changed, and she had gotten tired of trying to convince him that things were different now than in 1890. "You think there's no *risk* involved in finding those 'paltry few victims'? This isn't the old days; when people die or disappear, even if they have no relatives to ask after them, someone generally notices! Take too many, and we'll be contending with mortal police at every turn! I'd rather *not* have to fly the anchor off if I don't have to, and if too many people come up missing, or we pick the wrong victims, Folk or not, we are going to be—"

"That is not the point," the Bane-Sidhe whispered angrily. "Your—" It turned, abruptly, its enshrouding wrappings flaring, sending a wash of dank stench over Aurilia, as the door to her sitting room opened and Vidal entered.

She assessed his expression, and her already-sour mood spoiled further. If Vidal had been unhappy before he left on his errand, he was livid now. Aurilia started to ask him what was wrong, then thought better of the idea. The rage that burned behind his thoughts was palpable even to her, and she was not particularly sensitive to emotion.

Well, this time she was not going to play scapegoat. Niall would undoubtedly want to know where Vidal had been and what he had been doing all this time. And just as surely, when the Bane-Sidhe learned of his errand, Niall would sneer at him.

Well and good. Aurilia would stay out of it. If anyone was to suffer Vidal's anger, let it be the Bane-Sidhe.

After all, she thought maliciously, *he spoiled my breakfast by arriving when he did. Let him take it in the teeth. I've had more than my share of My Lord Vidal's temper tantrums. Niall outranks him; let Niall exert himself for a change.*

"And where have *you* been?" Niall snarled. "I have things I wish to discuss—"

"And I don't give a damn!" Vidal exploded, his eyes black with rage, fists clenched at his sides. He turned pointedly away from Niall and snarled at Aurilia. "That thrice-damned human mage! Keighvin has had his little protégé put *shields* on the old man. I couldn't touch him! And what's more, when I threw bael-fire at him, the old bastard *laughed* at me!"

The Bane-Sidhe rose to its full seven-foot height, stood over Vidal, and glared down at the elven-mage, its tattered draperies quivering with anger. "Do you mean to say that you have been wasting your time trying to frighten Keighvin's pet mortals when you could have—"

"I'm doing what *you* should have been doing, you shabby fraud!" Vidal sneered. "You should have been the one trying to frighten the old man into a heart attack, not me! Not even a shield would have stopped your wail—right? Or—"

"Why? Why should I waste my time, waste the energy it takes to cross the Gate into the mortal world?" the Bane-Sidhe countered. "I've not enough to spare as it is!"

Vidal was not to be daunted by height or stench, Aurilia had to give him credit for that much. "Because Keighvin has to be stopped, or he'll stop us. Even *you* admit that! If you'd been here—"

The Bane-Sidhe's eyes flashed angrily, and Aurilia held her breath. If Niall grew enraged, he might lose control. "I would not have been wasting my time pursuing a dead-end vendetta when there are other options open!" Niall whined, his voice climbing dangerously in pitch and volume. "Humans are infinitely corruptible. Just look at the sheer numbers of them that are willing to pay to watch their fellows in torment! Look at our files! All we need do is find these foolish mortals' weaknesses and they will be our allies, not Keighvin's! It's simply—"

"A lot *you* know!" Vidal spat. "You haven't been Outside for a century! The mortals you knew are as dead as the creatures of Tam Lin's time! You can't corrupt a human by dangling a pretty piece of flesh in front of his nose anymore! And they aren't naive little village boys with shit on their shoes and not two thoughts in their heads. It's bad enough that we've got Keighvin against us, but now he has these human *mages* with him, and artificers, and they're not stupid, I'm telling you!"

The Bane-Sidhe grew another half a foot. "I have taken the lives of more mortals than you ever dreamed of; I've the deaths of six knights of the Seleighe Court to my credit. That's more than you've ever *hoped* to do, you elven trash! Destroying the likes of you is less than a pastime—"

By the dark moon, this is getting serious—Aurilia

clapped her hands together, distracting both of them for a moment.

"Niall, unless you really want a duel on your hands," she said coldly, "I think you'd better take back those last words to your *partner.*"

She had dealt with the Bane-Sidhe for so long now that she knew exactly what was running through its head, now that she'd sidetracked it. For all Niall's power—and he *was* powerful—he was old and afraid of losing any of it. He used his hoarded energies sparingly, and he lived in fear of finding himself in a duel of magics and coming out the vanquished. Vidal was young, as elves went, but he was powerful as well. Niall did not know *how* powerful, and that uncertainty would be enough. If he were forced to go head-to-head with the younger mage . . .

. . . who had done away with two of the Seleighe Court single-handedly, in the far past. . . .

"I beg pardon for those hasty words," the Bane-Sidhe whispered stiffly. "I am concerned that you seem to be wasting time better spent elsewhere."

Aurilia turned to Vidal, who stood, still rigid with anger, facing the Bane-Sidhe. "You should explain the problem to Niall, Lord Vidal," she said, in as close to a servile tone as she could manage, given how angry *she* was at both of the fools. "You are right in saying he is not familiar with the world outside the Gates today. You should tell him why Keighvin and his pets are dangerous to us."

Vidal's jaw tightened, but her subservient tone evidently mollified him enough to try to be polite. "Keighvin Silverhair is interfering directly in the world of mortals," he said, slowly, "as I have pointed out to you before. He will stop us in *our* quest for power if he can, for we are on directly opposing sides where mortals are concerned. But he has gone beyond simply interfering. Tonight I discovered that he is *using* them, recruiting and training them. And betraying our deepest secrets and weaknesses."

"*What?*" Niall and Aurilia both gasped. This was news to Aurilia; unpleasant news. If mortals knew how to meet the Folk in equal combat—

"The mage tonight had a bar of Cold Iron as a weapon,"

Vidal continued grimly "Not steel—pure, forged Cold Iron, with Far-Anchored spells keyed to the Folk, and shieldings set specifically against our powers. The bastard *glowed* to the Sight, and he knew what he was doing, I tell you. Keighvin must have told him everything. He's going to be impossible to deal with. Another Gwydion, Merlin, Taliesen."

If Niall could have paled, he would have. Instead, he seemed to shrink, and he fluttered back into his seat, collapsing bonelessly with a moan.

"By the dark moon," the Bane-Sidhe groaned. "Why didn't you tell me this before? We must—"

Aurilia knew what the old coward was about to say—that they should leave, pack up in defeat and leave the ground to the enemy. Not a chance.

"Oh, no," she interjected sweetly. "He won't be impossible to deal with. I already have human informants following his movements. Before the week is out, I will know *his* weaknesses."

When the other two turned to stare at her in astonishment, she smiled, careful to cloak her triumph in modesty. "I simply don't have the power you have, my lords. I have learned to make do with the kind of weapons mortals use themselves. There are many ways to wound the human heart, and I have learned most of them. All I need to know is what the young man Tannim cares for—and he will be powerless against me."

She bowed her head a little, to hide the gloating in her eyes, for both the Bane-Sidhe and Vidal were still staring at her in a kind of awe. "You deal with the old man," she finished. "Leave the younger to me. I will deal with him, Cold Iron and all—for Cold Iron will not save him from a pierced heart."

CHAPTER EIGHT

Tania sat in the farthest corner of Kevin Barry's and nursed her mug of hot, milk-laden coffee between hands so numb she couldn't even feel the cup. The weather had turned cold, out of nowhere, and despite Laura's repeated warnings, she had decided to take a chance and come to Kevin Barry's long enough to look for the strange young man again. The hundred he'd given her was long gone for rent; she'd been eating once a day here for the last week, trying to make the tab last a while, but she hadn't found a single trick in a week of walking the streets.

She had to admit, though, that she hadn't really been trying hard. Laura hadn't bothered warning her about Tannim after that first night; she had troubles of her own. Jamie was mixed up with something. He came home with less every night, and usually came home high. Laura was worried sick about the night he'd done the "party"; she'd gotten him to go to County Health and take the HIV test, but they wouldn't know what the results were for another couple of weeks.

And meanwhile, with Jamie getting high so often, it was only a matter of time before he slipped up again.

In a way, Tania didn't blame him for getting high; it might be the only way he could face what he had to do out there. But he was making Laura miserable.

And just maybe he's getting high because he can't face something else. Like his life. He isn't gonna be a cute young kid forever—and then what's he gonna do? He's already getting picked up by some really rough guys. He's come home with bruises or rope-burns the past three nights. The older he gets, the more of that kind he'll have to go with. And he says he'd rather die than get a MacDonald's job.

He'd told Tania and Laura grandiose stories about getting a job at one of the country clubs, like waiting in the bar, and finding a rich old bored lady to support him, but he wasn't fooling anyone. Buses didn't run out there—and he wasn't exotic or talented enough. Tania had seen the kind of kids the "country-club women" picked up; they were generally very dark and latino-handsome, and they could dance, sing, and pay inventive flattering compliments. Jamie couldn't dance (at least not upright) and his most flattering compliment wasn't printable. "Escorts" were intelligent, and could make some kind of conversation. Jamie was stoned most of the time, and his brightest comments usually had to do with sports.

Tania studied the cream swirling slowly in the coffee. Ever since she'd met Tannim, Tania had felt like she'd gotten slapped awake, somehow. What she had now just wasn't enough anymore. She'd started looking ahead, planning for something besides the next trick, or the cheap TV set at the Goodwill. If Tannim was for real, and not just a pimp with a creative approach—well, maybe she'd see what he had to offer. She wasn't sure *why* she had decided to take the risk, and she wasn't sure why she'd decided to act against Laura's advice. In fact, she didn't really understand what was going on in her own head since she met the guy. But whatever it was, it kind of felt good— and it was a helluva lot better than sitting around listening to Laura try to cry without making any noise, or hustling the dirty old men in expensive suits.

Maybe all he wanted was her. That would be okay, too. She wouldn't mind going to bed with him. He was kind of cute, and was certainly nice. He'd promised not to hurt her; she trusted that promise.

She did know one thing: she'd made the decision to

come here today at least in part because it had been too
damned cold to trot around the street in nothing but
Spandex bike shorts and a halter. Now if Mr. Tannim would
just show up. . . .

At least her hands were finally getting warm.

The pub had just opened for lunch a little while ago,
but she really hadn't been that hungry when she first sat
down. And in the last few minutes, as the place filled up,
she noticed something kind of peculiar: although she'd have
been glowered at for nursing a single cup of coffee instead
of buying a meal or a drink anywhere else, no one was
hassling her here. It had been that way every time that
she had come in to get something on the tab; the girls
smiled at her and were nice, and no one gave her any
trouble, acted just like the night she'd been here with
Tannim, in fact. Right now no one had even bothered her
about getting something besides coffee. They acted like
she was someone important; someone who should be given
privacy and space, if that was what she wanted.

Maybe that man had something to do with it. Maybe
because he had taken notice of her, they had extended that
"courtesy to a good customer" umbrella he seemed to travel
under to include her as well.

Every time someone darkened the doorway of the dining
room, she looked up, squinting against the light, to see
if it was him. As lunchtime filled the place up, she began
to think she'd picked the wrong time, or day, or something.
Even with the best wishes in the world, the waitresses were
going to have to ask her to leave pretty soon, and let a
paying customer have her table.

Of course, she could go ahead and order something.
There was still enough cash left on the tab. And the aroma
of the bean soup from the kitchen was enough to make
a corpse hungry. Bean soup and bread—that wouldn't cost
too much, and she could have some more coffee with lots
of cream and sugar. . . .

She started to look for one of the waitresses, when
movement at the door made her turn her head out of habit
to see who it was. And there he stood, looking a lot like
she remembered, only maybe cuter. A beat-up leather

jacket this time, really nice Bugle Boy jeans and a hot brown-and-gray shirt—he could have been making an ad or something, he had that kind of style about him. She glanced down at her second-hand bike shorts and flushed a little. *She* was tacky. But it was the best she could do, and it was clean, anyway.

She looked up again. On second glance, the young man also looked tired, like he'd been working really hard.

Maybe he won't notice my clothes.

He squinted into the relative darkness, then started to turn away to go into the bar. She threw up her hand in an involuntary wave, then snatched it back, not certain now that she really *wanted* to talk to him again, after all. He might not be real happy to see her here, now. He might, in fact, be mad that she'd shown up, at least during the daytime.

Too late—he saw her signal, hesitant though it was; smiled and waved back, and started across the floor through the crowd.

But someone else had seen him too.

A really gorgeous dark-haired woman, dressed all in black leather and cream-colored silk, intercepted him at the entrance to the bar where she had just materialized as he crossed the room. Tania's heart sank. *This* must be who he was meeting. He hadn't come here looking for her He hadn't even really seen her. He'd only seen the waving hand, and he'd thought it belonged to his lunch date. And God, she was incredible. The kind of woman Tania would have expected him to be seeing, not some tacky kid in Spandex.

She sidled up to him and put one hand on his shoulder, smiling brilliantly into his eyes. Her lips moved, although Tania couldn't hear what she was saying. He continued to scan the crowd in Tania's direction, a slight frown on his face. She blushed so hard she felt hot all over, and wanted to sink into the floor in embarrassment; her eyes burned, and her throat tightened. In another second, she was going to cry, she just knew it. And on top of looking tacky, she was going to get mascara smeared all over her face. She knew what he was looking for; now he wanted to know who had pretended to know him. Probably so he could make sure his lunch date with this fabulous babe wasn't interrupted by some scruffy little—

Abruptly, Tannim shook his head, said a few words, and brushed the woman's hand off his shoulder. His brow wrinkled just a little, and he stared directly into the woman's eyes. Then he drew his right hand up into a fist, slowly extended his thumb, and pointed it over his shoulder towards the door. The woman stood there, wearing the most stunned expression Tania had ever seen on anyone's face. He walked away from her as if she wasn't even there.

And as he got close enough to Tania to make out exactly who she was, his face broke out in a wide, welcoming smile, so warm it dazzled her.

Tannim had the feeling he really ought to go to Kevin Barry's for lunch today . . . it was a very strong feeling, and Tannim never, ever ignored those silent hunches of his.

So, although Keighvin had assigned him out to Roebling Road with a brake-mod this afternoon, Tannim decided to take a long lunch break.

Once again, he endured the bone-rattling cobblestones of River Street. He kept his "feelers" out for an incipient gap, then spotted one. He took instant advantage of the opening, shoving the Mustang into a parking space, right on the tail of a departing Caddy. He grinned at the driver of a Beemer, a suit-and-tie executive type, who scowled at him in frustrated annoyance.

Eat your heart out, buddy, he thought in smug satisfaction. *Here you are in your tie and execu-cut, and here I am in my jeans and long hippie-freak hair—and I know I'm happier than you are. Why don't you just spend the rest of the afternoon trying to figure out what I know that you don't?*

He felt just a little smug as he grinned into the yuppie-type's scowl. He'd gotten one of the primo spots, too; hardly more than a wink and a nod from Kevin Barry's. As the Beemer pulled away in search of another place to park, he eased himself out of the car and headed for the

door to the gift shop—for the tiny gift shop let directly
out into the dining room side of the pub.

He waved at the lovely lass behind the counter of the
gift section, and looked over the new shawls, letting his
eyes adjust to the dim light. It was pretty dark in the stage/
dining area, and really crowded for a weekday; it looked
like half of Savannah had decided to hit the pub for lunch.
All of the tables were full, and there was a line of about
four people waiting for one to clear out. But after a
moment, that sixth-sense tingled again, and he peered off
into the far right-hand corner.

Someone waved tentatively at him from the very back
of the room. Tania?

It might be; whoever it was, she was female and blond.

He started towards the corner, easing his way around
tables surrounded by people obliviously chattering and
munching away. But there was a huge group in the very
middle; they'd put three tables together to form one big
arrangement, and to get to the rear he would have to go
past the pub entrance on the right-hand wall. Well, that
was no problem, as long as there wasn't anyone in *there*
who wanted to have a chat with him.

Just as he reached the double-doors into the pub, someone pushed her way past the stand-up crowd at the bar,
and intercepted him at the doorway.

Before he realized she wanted *him*, she laid her hand
on his shoulder, forcing him to stop whether he wanted
to or not. He turned involuntarily to look at her; she smiled
at him as though she was an old friend. "Hello," she
crooned, in a voice just loud enough for him to hear over
the babble of voices in the pub. "I've been hoping you'd
be here today; I'm glad to see my intuition is working."

She was stunningly beautiful: long, raven-black hair with
a slight wave to it, huge brown eyes, sensuous lips and high
cheekbones, and a flawless, rose-and-cream complexion.
She was dressed in an ivory silk blouse and black leather
skirt, both expensive, both understated in their elegance.

She was no one he'd ever seen before in his life.

Just before she'd touched him, all his internal alarms
went off, for she had donned a glamorie that would have

sent a Vulcan into heat. This was trouble, and all of his shields went up in full defensive mode.

While she spoke, he did a closer check, using mage-sight; as he had guessed, her appearance was nothing like her *real* self. There was no mistaking the white-blond hair, nor the cat-slitted, green eyes and the pointed ears.

Elven. One of the Sidhe. And since she was no one he knew, the odds were high that she was Unseleighe Court.

But she hadn't done anything to him but stop him—at least, not yet. So she wasn't declaring open warfare, not unless you counted attempted seduction as an aggressive act.

On the other hand, she could have assumed that Tannim was just as young and inexperienced as he looked.

I don't think so, lady.

But this was neither the time nor the place to answer her with a challenge. If that was Tania back there, he didn't want a kid to see him having even a verbal battle with a Sidhe. He calculated a dozen possible responses to her approach, trying to figure the one that would leave her the most stunned, and selected one by the time the last word had left her soft, wet lips.

He brushed her hand from his shoulder as if it was an inconvenient bit of dandruff.

"Your friends and mine don't get along, lady," he said, without the least bit of inflection. "Run along and we'll leave it at that."

He indicated the door, and watched the woman's energy fields fluctuate wildly as she tried to process this unexpected stonewalling. It was hard not to laugh, even dire as the repercussions might be.

There was a split-second of astonishment before the woman clamped down her mask of impassivity. He could still see her body stiffen in the universal posture of defensiveness.

Score more status from the Bad Guys. She's trying to play it off, but she's counting me as an equal, or a superior.

He then moved past her as though she was not there.

I'll have to ask one of the girls what her face looked like to them. Heh.

❖   ❖   ❖

Aurilia had perused the new agency's report very carefully. *This* one had quite a bit of new information, besides all the dossier nonsense that anyone with a phone and a lot of patience could pull up out of public records. According to the detective, young Tannim favored one particular pub over every other establishment in Savannah: a pub called "Kevin Barry's."

Well, the lad was young, in his twenties, and if there was one thing a young man was susceptible to, it was sex. There hadn't been a young man yet that Aurilia hadn't been able to lead about by the nose, sooner or later. Generally sooner.

But just to make certain, she put a glamorie on herself that could make a corpse rise. Not even the pure Sir Galahad could have withstood her now. And she smiled to herself as she stood at the bar, sipping a glass of *uiskebaghe,* and waiting for the youngster to make one of his appearances. He would, too—she had that feeling, and her premonitions were never wrong.

Those two fools were so busy persuading themselves that the only way they could dispose of the human was by combat that they never even bothered considering other options. Idiots. Why do anything with violence that can be accomplished subtlely?

She toyed with her glass, signaling the lady bartender for another, and considered what she would do when she had the mortal safely beguiled. *He might be useful, especially if he is any good as a mage. I could take him Underhill, to my own stronghold. . . . Yes, that might be the best solution. He'll be tended to in a gilded cage, and I can drain him slowly of power without the others knowing I have him.*

Movement of power at the edge of her shields alerted her that there was a mage within the confines of the pub; turning to check who had just entered, she saw to her immense satisfaction that the quarry had arrived. She left her glass, and quickly conjured a crumpled twenty, identical to the one she had kenned a few days ago, to leave beside the glass.

She intercepted Tannim just as he passed beside the

door to the pub, placing one hand on his shoulder and whispering something innocuous while she exerted her glamorie. He stared at her for a moment, and she felt a flare of triumph. *I have him; I truly do. Now let's see what Vidal says about me—*

"Your friends and mine don't get along, lady," he said, brushing her hand off with an absent gesture.

He blew me off. I can't believe it. . . .

As she stared after him, stunned, he wound his way gracefully through the crowded dining-room without a single backward glance. He went all the way to the rear, where a tatty little teenager with badly bleached hair was sitting at a table for two—

Belatedly, she realized that not only had the young mage recognized her for what she was, he had broken her glamorie. Not only was she terribly conspicuous, he might well be watching her to see what she was going to do.

She melted back into the crowd as only a Sidhe could, and worked the opposite sort of glamorie—one to make her inconspicuous.

Then she retired to the gift shop and strained all her senses, trying to keep watch on him and his lunch guest.

In one sense she was frustrated; he had placed shielding about himself that he had extended to cover the table and the girl, so that she could not listen in on their conversation. But she could *watch* them, with a bit of the Sight.

After a moment she recognized the girl; she might have been the one in the blurred and darkened photo the new detective had included with his first report. Tannim had befriended the girl, who was evidently an underage prostitute, the first night the new man had been on duty. Then, as now, he had engaged her in conversation, and had bought her something to eat.

Well, that was interesting. What on earth could a teenage whore and a powerful young mage have in common? The report had been adamant that Tannim hadn't *done* anything with the girl, had in fact sent her on her way. Could it be possible that *this* was the weak point Aurilia had been looking for so fruitlessly?

The more she watched, the more certain she became.

The girl did hold some kind of interest for him. Not sexual—but perhaps all the stronger for that. By the time the two of them paid the bill and left, she was filled with satisfaction. She had him. She had the vulnerable point. She didn't know exactly what she could do with it—yet— but she knew what it was.

Tania couldn't help herself; she smiled and blushed as the young man pulled up a chair and sat across the postage-stamp table from her. "Hey, kiddo," Tannim said, looking meaningfully at her coffee cup. "That doesn't look like a very nutritious breakfast." Before she could reply, he signaled one of the waitresses. "My usual," he said, "for two." And as the girl disappeared, he turned back to Tania.

"I've been watching for you," he said, "and I was kind of afraid I'd scared you off when you didn't show up."

She looked down at her cup in confusion. "Laura told me you were probably a—" She stopped herself just in time, appalled at the way she had let her mouth run without thinking. If the guy *was* a pimp, he might get angry and take it out on her, and Laura too. If he wasn't, he might get offended. "—Ummm—somebody I shouldn't get involved with."

"What, a pimp?" Tannim asked. "Or a pervert? Kiddo, you have to know that most of the guys who pick you up are perverts. Nobody really straight would want to make it with a kid as young as you are. And, Tania, the hair and the makeup job aren't fooling anybody."

The straightforward reply—too calm and matter-of-fact to be an insult—brought her up short. And before she could think of any retort, he continued.

"Look, I'm not interested in sex. I've got that elsewhere. I just want to talk to you—and not dirty, either." He looked ready to say more, but the waitress arrived with two club sandwiches and two colas, and he waited until she was out of hearing distance.

She eyed the sandwich dubiously, remembering what Laura had said. He caught her at it, and laughed a little. "Go ahead, Tania, it isn't drugged or anything, I promise."

And as if to prove his point, he exchanged plates with her and bit into his sandwich with hungry enthusiasm. Feeling a little stupid, she did the same.

"Look," he said, when she'd finished half of her meal, gesturing with a potato chip, "I told you the other night that I liked seeing people able to dream—and I like it better when I can help them with those dreams. See, there's some weird shit going on out there, and helping you keeps me balanced. Keeps me in touch with the 'real world.' Dig?"

That was just a little too near the bone. "What are you," she asked defensively. "Some kind of Boy Scout or something?"

He sighed and shook his head. "I'm just a guy," he replied. "A plain old human being. Eccentric. Obsessive. Imperfect. I can't do much, Tania—but I'd like to at least talk a while."

She shrugged, uncertain and trying to cover it with bravado. "I suppose. I'm not really busy right now. You're not my usual kinda client, but you ought to get something for your two hundred bucks, I guess—"

"Have you ever been on a picnic?" he interrupted. "A real picnic?"

Caught off-guard once again, she shook her head.

He took her hand and rose, pulling her to her feet. "Come on, then. Let's see if I can show you a good time."

Before she knew what he was doing, he had left money on the table for the bill, and led her outside into the bright sunlight. She squinted as he donned his Ray-Bans, and tugged her over to the River Street parking lot. The next thing she knew, she was sitting in the passenger's side of his car, while he buckled himself in on the driver's side, staring at a dashboard with more gadgets than a fighter-plane cockpit.

"Buckle up, kiddo," he reminded her. "What do you want to hear?"

She was dazed, and replied with the first thing that popped into her head. "That music the other night—here— is there anything more like that?"

"Good choice," he replied, popped in a cassette, then

pulled out of the parking space before she had time to
say anything else, like "where are you taking me—"

She could have hit herself in the head. If Tannim really
was a pimp after all, in spite of all his talk about "dreams,"
she'd just put herself right into his hands. Willingly. How
stupid could you get?

But he didn't pull out towards the worst part of town;
he just drove up the ramp, onto President. They crossed
a couple of bridges, while Tannim rattled on about music,
and pulled up at a place called The Country Store. He
left the motor running (and the tape playing) and dashed
inside.

*This is nuts—I could take the car right now, drive away.
Take my chances—*

But for some reason, she sat and waited, listening to
Celtic harp and soulful voices as he returned with two
white boxes, a large sack, and a couple of drinks in a paper
carrier.

A faint aroma of food came from both boxes as he
dropped them on the seat behind them, and Tania relaxed
a little more. The idea of a pimp or drug-pusher buying
a couple of box lunches was too ridiculous to contemplate.
Maybe he was for real—

She yawned involuntarily while Tannin wedged the
drinks into the center console. Last night had been long—
and fruitless. She'd pounded the pavement until about four,
then come home to find Laura in tears and Jamie too
stoned to do anything but snore. Then she'd gotten up
relatively early to come to Kevin Barry's—now the short
sleep was catching up to her.

She must have dozed off anyway, for she came to herself
with a start as Tannim turned the engine off. "Well, we're
here," he said, with an expectant expression on his face.

She looked around, baffled. "Where's here?" she asked,
not recognizing anything.

"It's a park, outside Fort Pulaski. This is a place I come
with friends. That's one of the approaches to the docks—
it's very deep here." He indicated the waterway before
them. "See? There's one of the big container ships you see
passing River Street." He opened the trunk of the Mustang

and pulled out a familiar item: a cargo blanket like she used for bedding. Some pimp: blanket over one shoulder, white lunchbox in each hand, and a goofy grin.

She shivered in the sea breeze, and Tannim slapped his forehead after laying out the food and blanket. "I should have given this to you before," he explained sheepishly, handing her the sack. "Sorry . . . hope it fits."

Tania opened the sack, and pulled out—a sweat suit. A *nice* one, with a puffy-ink Hilton Head logo and . . . a unicorn.

He knew. How could he know? Oh, God, it's beautiful . . . it's better than anything I have now. I'd look like a tourist or a college student.

She felt her eyes tearing up, and only her involuntary shivering broke her out of it. Tannim stood with a self-satisfied smirk, then sat on the blanket, his back to her.

God, I'm a teenage hooker, and he gives me credit for modesty. Incredible. . . .

She slipped the suit on over her speedos and immediately felt warmer. It was thick fleece. "I look like . . ." She let the sentence trail off.

"You look confident." He grinned, looking her over. "The unicorn design suits you. They're powerful beasts, very, very magical, and as graceful as you are. And just as capable of miracles."

Tania felt herself blushing. "I don't know . . . this is all so weird, I mean, this feels like some movie. It's stupid, this fairy-tale shit just doesn't *happen*."

"Mmm. No. Normally it doesn't. It doesn't make any more sense than sunlight or trees. Or internal combustion." He gestured with a pickle spear "You turn the key, the car runs. Inside it, water runs through iron, lightning sparks fire, thousands of tiny firestorms, and all people ever think of is 'push the pedal and it goes.' But, Tania, people are like that. Complex, but so taken for granted, with all the powers of the elements in them. Sooner or later, even we forget how wonderful our internal machines are. All we need to be great is to remember how amazing we really are."

"Oh, God, you're not one of those Scientologist people, are you?"

Tannim nearly choked laughing. "Oh my God! Give me some credit! I'm not *that* brain-dead!"

She smiled a little, sheepishly. "It's just that what you keep saying all sounds like some feel-good pep talk to fat executives."

The man had nearly stifled his laughing. He wiped his nose with a napkin. "All right. So it does. I just get enthusiastic sometimes. Guess I've gotten used to things working out."

Tania peered out towards the horizon again. The container ship there was four times larger, but still appeared no closer. "I haven't had that kind of luck lately. The street takes away dreams. Makes them hard to even remember. . . ."

Tannim nodded, as if he understood. Maybe he did. "Yeah. Yeah, I can imagine. But, well, like I said, sometimes all we need is a reminder that we can do about anything."

She shook her head stubbornly. "But how come you're doing all this for me? It doesn't make any sense! You've got to have something better to do than—"

"Than spend my day with a teenage hooker?" he interrupted. "If you were any such thing, maybe so. But I don't believe that any more than you *really* do. You know you hate it, but you think it's all you are. We both know better. And, well, yeah, I could be working. I've got testing to do, but, hell . . . the machines can wait. You can't. Not another day. Or else you wouldn't have shown up at Kevin Barry's looking for me."

They were both silent for a moment, watching the huge ship at last move into the channel. It was at least twelve stories high, marked in a language Tania couldn't identify. It bore a prancing horse atop a globe painted on one stack, above hundreds of multicolored boxes the size of tractor-trailers. Tannim stood up slowly and dusted his jeans off, then raised his arms and waved.

From beside a massive lifeboat a single figure waved back.

Tannim stood, grinning and satisfied, hands on hips. "There. A first welcome home."

❖   ❖   ❖

Tania and Tannim talked for what felt like an hour. He was so easy to talk to, that by the time she realized what she'd done, she'd not only told him about herself, she was telling him about Laura and Jamie, too. She managed to keep from blowing everything, but from the bleak expression on his face, she guessed he was able to figure out most of it on his own. So she tried to change the subject—

But he changed it for her, asking her first about what she liked to read. That got her on the subject of fantasy, and *then* she was spilling the whole story about the night her mother found her books, and what had happened, and she was holding back tears with an effort. . . .

He patted her hand, but didn't try to touch her in any other way—which was just as well, really. She would have felt really stupid and afraid, both at the same time. Stupid, because she was crying over *books*, for chrissake; afraid, because if he touched her, he might try something more, and she *liked* him, she didn't want him to be like another trick. But she wanted someone to hold her and comfort her, wanted it so badly it was a dull ache deep down inside.

She stared out at the river as another ship appeared in the distance, and fought her tears down. Finally, after a long silence, he cleared his throat self-consciously.

"Don't you think maybe you ought to go back to your folks?" he said cautiously. "I know it was bad, but—"

She shook her head, angrily. "No!" she replied adamantly. "It was like being in jail all the time, except I hadn't done anything to deserve it! Hell, even in jail, people get to read what they want!"

"But—" he began. She cut him off with a look.

"I didn't deserve being treated like a criminal, and I won't go back to it," she said firmly, relieved that anger had chased away the incipient tears.

"All right, so you won't go back—but what about one of the shelters?" he replied. "That would get you out of that apartment into somewhere safe, and you could go back to school. You could even get a job if you wanted to; the shelter would help you."

She laughed, sourly. "Haven't been out on the street, have you?" she asked. He shook his head. "Well, the *good*

shelters have waiting lists—or else they only let you stay
a couple of weeks," she said, bitter memories of checking the places out still fresh in her mind. "And the rest
of them either have churches running them, or they're
always on your case about contacting your parents—and
if you won't, they will, whether or not you like it."

He blinked. "Oh," he said. "But—don't you think it's
still better than—"

"I don't need Jesus with my orange juice, thanks," she
snapped in irritation. "I don't need getting told this was
all my fault and I'm a sinful slut. I don't need getting
nagged at, and told by some stupid psychologist who never
met my parents how much they really do care about me.
All *they* ever wanted was something else they could boast
to the people at the club about. They never cared about
me, they only cared about how good I could make them
look." She shook her head. "By now they've probably put
a Soloflex in my room. And they've figured out not having me around saves them enough for a weekend cruise
to Bermuda every couple of months. I'll stay where I am,
thanks."

Tannim just looked sad, and watched the ship grow
nearer. "I never thought I'd wind up here," he said, after
a while. "There was a time when I thought I'd stay in
Oklahoma all my life. Now—sometimes I wonder if I'm
ever going to really settle down in one place."

"Why?" she asked.

"Because I like traveling," he replied, and started off
on a series of stories that lasted until the sun started to
set. Some of them were so crazy they couldn't be true—
and she wondered about the rest. It was weird, like he
was talking around something half the time. Surely nobody
as young as Tannim could have done so much in such a
short time, could he?

On the other hand, why would he lie to her?

She let him talk; while he was telling her stories, he
couldn't pry any more out of her. Finally, though, all the
food had been eaten, all the stories seemed to have been
told, and the sun was going down. She had work to do—

She found herself dreading it; going back onto the street

seemed filthier than ever after this afternoon. But she didn't say anything, and when Tannim asked her if she wanted to go back to town, she just nodded and let him lead the way back to his car.

They were both silent on the way back to the city; it was as if they had forgotten how to talk to each other, or that they didn't know what to say. The silence was as awkward as the earlier conversation had been free. When Tannim asked her where she wanted to be dropped off, she replied, vaguely, "Wheaton Street, near Bee," and hardly noticed his wince.

But she did notice the worried look he wore when he pulled over to the curb and she got out.

"I wish you wouldn't," he said, and she didn't have to ask what he meant. She shoved her hands in her pockets, unable to look him in the eye—

And discovered that there was paper in there, paper that hadn't been there before.

She pulled it out. It was money, cash; several twenties. She wasn't sure how many, because she shoved it hastily back into her pocket before someone could see that she had it. "You believe in magic?" he asked. And before she could reply, continued, "Don't. It's unreliable. Make your own luck."

He smiled, reached over, and closed the door, then pulled out into traffic, leaving her standing on the corner.

With a pocket full of cash.

Make your own luck, he'd said. What was that supposed to mean? Or was it supposed to mean anything at all?

She turned to head down the street, pausing once in the shelter of a doorway to remove the cash again, and count it.

Five soft, old twenties. One hundred dollars. Exactly what he'd given her the last time.

Make your own luck.

Well, there was one thing she could do. She could get off the street for another night. Maybe even another week. That was luck enough for right now.

❖   ❖   ❖

"Sam, old lad, could ye hand me that wee driver?" The Sidhe-mechanic put a hand out from underneath the computer-module, and Sam dutifully dropped a small screwdriver into it. An aluminum socket-wrench; Donal might be one of the three Sidhe at Fairgrove capable of handling Cold Iron with relative impunity, but it was only "relative." Right now Donal was doing something more than a bit dangerous: manipulating some of this computer equipment magically, altering it so that while it looked perfectly normal from the outside, and in fact would pass inspection by any licensed tech, what it would register was *not* what would be going on inside.

Which was, in fact, nothing at all.

But even the tiny amount of Cold Iron present in the screws holding various covers in place was enough to foul Donal's magic. Donal was taking them all out, placing them in an insulating container, then making his alterations according to Sam's instructions. The Sidhe's body twisted about for a moment as he squirmed to reach the tiny screws, then was still.

"There now," Donal said, his voice muffled, but the satisfaction coming through plainly. "That should do it. Turn it on, old lad, and let's see if it lies to us proper."

"Are you sure you want me to do that?" Sam asked anxiously. "You're still in there—that's a direct 220 feed—"

Rob, Donal's human shadow, snickered. "Ah, don't worry about frying Donal's brains. He hasn't any to speak of. All you'll do is reinforce his perm."

"And who was it had to have his phone taken away, 'cause he'd order every damn thing K-Swell ever made?" Donal countered. "Who was it came t'me in mortal terror, 'cause he'd broken a chain letter? Who was it that told Keighvin he'd seen Elvis baggin' groceries at Kroger? Hmm?"

"Beats me," Rob said cheerfully, his round face shining with amusement.

"Well, Skippy, I think I'll take that as an invitation—" Donal started to emerge—fist-first—or at least made motions as if he might.

"All right, all right! So I get a little carried away!" Rob sighed dramatically.

"Turn on the juice, Sam," Donal repeated, suppressed laughter in his voice. "Ye needna worry about me. 'Tisn't electricity I need to worry about; that I can handle—'tis enough like magic as makes no nevermind."

Sam plugged the machine in and turned it on, setting it through its cycle, still worried despite Donal's assurances.

"Well?" came a muffled voice. "Is it lyin' to us the way it should?"

Sam nodded, forgetting that Donal couldn't see him. To all intents and purposes, there was a full-blown smelting operation going on—temperature was rising, the aluminum about to slag down, the vacuum building up preparatory to foaming the molten metal—even though there was nothing attached to the computer console.

Or maybe Donal *could* see him. "How much in the way of 'accidents' do ye want now an' again?" Donal asked.

Sam thought, making mental calculations. "With a process this complicated, I'd expect a fail-rate of fifty percent. I'd be really suspicious if it was less than that."

"Fifty percent it is," Donal answered. "Here, I'll gi' ye a taste of it." A moment later, alarms went off, indicating a catastrophic failure of the injection system. The system powered itself down.

Donal climbed out a moment later, and stood up, brushing his black coverall off. " 'Twon't always be the injection system," he said, full of happy pride at his own cleverness. " 'Twill alternate. And we may get five 'failures' in a row before we get a 'good casting.' Danaa's light, that's amusing! Wish I could do this sort of thing more often."

"What exactly *did* you do?" Rob asked. Donal smirked.

"Nothing you can dup, lad, nor your evil twin, neither. I just engraved a few extra circuits into the machine where they won't show; built 'em on the sensor-connections, then programmed 'em hard. So even if someone comes in an' changes the stuff they can see, 'twon't affect the outcome." Donal's grin got even wider. "Have t'say I'm right glad ye showed me how those computer-things work, now."

"Even though I had to drag you into computer literacy kicking and screaming," Rob taunted. "So, all we have to do is have one of the kenning Sidhe standing by to supply the evidence in the mold or in the furnace if we happen to have visitors, hmm?"

"Exactly," Sam said, feeling a wash of contentment come over him, despite the threats of the morning. Donal and Rob had told him, over and over again, that Donal could make these invisible mods to the computer-driven casting equipment, but until he'd seen it, he hadn't dared believe it.

"I hate to admit it, but you did good, *Conal*," Rob told the Sidhe.

"Thank ye kindly, *Skippy*," Donal replied, slapping the little mechanic on the back so hard he staggered. "Gents, I have t' be off; I've got mods to put in on m' brother's car."

"I don't think we'll need your particular expertise any more today, Donal," Sam said absently, as he ran another "casting" through the system, and this time got perfect "results." "Everything else Rob and I can fake without mucking with the computers."

Everyone was behaving perfectly normally; Sam was taking his cue from the rest, in spite of the fact that tonight would be anything but normal.

Assuming Vidal Dhu carried out his threats. He might not, according to Donal. He might simply have issued a challenge without intending to follow through on it seriously.

"He's done that before," Donal had said, sourly. " 'Tis worth it to him just t' muck us up for a night, make us waste energy and magical strength to counter a threat that was never real. Make us jumpy, make us chase our tails from midnight t'dawn, and all for naught."

The tall Sidhe (who reminded Sam strongly of G.E. Smith from the Saturday Night Live band) turned at the door and sketched a mocking salute before heading for the main shop building. As Sam and Rob finished setting up the rest of the equipment, with Rob running the fork-lift and Sam supervising the placement, Sam finally had the chance to ask a question that had been plaguing the life out of him all day.

"What's with this 'Skippy' business?" he asked, as they

brought the second smelter up online and plugged its controls into the computer console.

Rob laughed, and rubbed his short black beard with a finger. "That's from when I first came into Fairgrove," he said. "They already thought I was nuts, 'cause I do imitations of televangelists and bad game-show hosts at the drop of a hat. But then I kept seeing this one Sidhe all over, like, within seconds of the time I'd seen him somewhere else. And half the time, when I'd call him 'Donal,' he'd glare at me like I was simpleminded and say his name was *Conal*. I thought I was going crazy. Then somebody finally told me that there were two of the bastards, they were twins, and they'd been having a good laugh at my expense." Rob chuckled. "I didn't mind, I mean, if they'd been human that's the first thing I would have thought, but who ever heard of twin Sidhe? The birthrate's so low I'd never have believed it."

"So?" Sam replied. "That doesn't explain 'Skippy.'"

"Well, I turned the tables on them. Half the time when one of them saw me and called me 'Rob,' I'd glare and say my name was Skippy. And when I was Skippy is when I'd do the really outrageous stuff, like try to sell Donal his own tool-kit or something." Rob's grin was so infectious that Sam found himself grinning in return. "They actually started to think I had a really crazy twin myself, named Skippy. It was weeks before anyone ever told them the human bad-movie joke about 'the evil twin, Skippy.' I thought when Dottie finally broke down and confessed that they were both gonna hang me right then and there."

Sam joined in Rob's laughter. "I'm surprised they didn't," he commented.

"I'd rather have been well-hung!" Rob grinned, and made sure the smelter was staying cold even though the computer console said it was red-hot. "Those two have a lot better sense of humor than anyone except Keighvin. I think it comes from hanging around Tannim so much."

Sam's response surprised even himself. "A lot of good things seem to come from hanging around Tannim," he said softly, half to himself. Then, a little embarrassed, he glanced over at Rob to see if the young man had overheard him.

Rob was nodding, uncharacteristically sober. "They do," he said, then—

"Sam, I have to tell you, I've got this *great* deal on a set of Ginsu steak knives, and if you order now, you get a free bamboo steamer—"

Sam chased him out of the building, brandishing a broom.

CHAPTER NINE

Although she had every sense at her command locked onto her quarry, Aurilia "lost" the pair to everything but sight the moment they entered Tannim's car—and she lost the vehicle itself to President Street traffic soon after. The protections on the vehicle might have been set by Keighvin Silverhair, but Aurilia doubted it. Whatever other powers the boy had, he certainly drove like a demon. Once again she found herself forced to admit to a kind of grudging admiration for one of the enemy. . . .

But not for long. The aggravation of losing quickly overwhelmed the admiration. *Damn him, anyway. Crafty little monster. Where did he learn all that? Surely not from Silverhair. If I didn't know better, I'd suspect they'd managed to find some devil actually interested in buying his skinny little soul. . . .*

Still, Aurilia hadn't practiced her own particular brand of subterfuge for so many centuries without learning patience. She found herself an out-of-the-way spot in one of the little "pocket parks" and sat in her Mercedes. Tannim could cloak himself, and even his car—but once the girl left his presence, she would register to Aurilia's mage-senses. And the girl was really what Aurilia was after at the moment.

It took longer than Aurilia had thought it would, but

towards sunset, the girl finally "appeared" to Aurilia's inner eye. She quickly triangulated with a mental map of the town, and determined that the girl was at the corner of Bee and Wheaton streets.

She reached out in thought, and seized mentally on the nearest pigeon, taking over what little mind it had with her own. Pigeons were possibly the stupidest creatures on the planet, but that stupidity made them remarkably easy to enslave. When she was done with it, it would drop dead of shock, of course, but that didn't matter. One more dead pigeon on the sidewalk would excite no one except a feral cat or dog.

She sent the bird winging in a direct line to the area where the girl loitered. With sunset coming, a pigeon was perhaps not the best choice of slave-eyes, but it would do. A grackle would have been better, but like all the corbies, it would have fought back too much, wasting time and energy before she could take it. An owl was the best, but Silverhair used those, the bastard. And frequently owls were not what they appeared to be.

She caught only glimpses of what the pigeon saw; just enough to guide it to her target. Fortunately, the girl was fairly conspicuous with her bleached-blond hair, even from above. Though darkness had fallen, the shock of pale straw made a kind of beacon for the bird's dimmed eyesight. So although the pigeon was not much good at flying by street-lamps, once the bird had the girl in sight, Aurilia had it land on a rooftop, and follow her in short flights, from tree to phone-line, to rooftop again.

Even by daylight the pigeon's eyesight wasn't particularly good, as birds went, but Aurilia made out enough detail that she was forced to wonder what on earth Tannim saw in this appalling little creature. It certainly wasn't her looks. She was scrawny, underfed, a modern version of one of Aurilia's own Victorian Street-Sparrow constructs. Clean—well, Aurilia would give her that much. She was clean. And young, if your taste ran to children. But cheap, tacky—tasteless. Perhaps that was why her glamorie at the pub hadn't worked—maybe Tannim was only attracted to cheap tarts. Maybe he only enjoyed sex with hookers,

children, or both. . . . But that didn't fit his profile, didn't
fit anything she'd been able to learn about him.

Peculiar. Once she'd seen him, he hadn't struck her that
way; in fact, his attitude towards the girl, so far as she had
been able to make out, was positively chaste. In any case,
the girl's parents had to know what she was doing, unless
they were even stupider than the pigeon.

The girl wound her way farther and deeper into one
of the bad areas off Wheaton. Well, now it wasn't much
of a surprise that she'd had Tannim drop her back there
on the corner. Aurilia didn't wonder now why the girl
hadn't wanted Tannim to see where she lived; she was
probably ashamed of her home. If she lived here, her
parents couldn't be much better than what was locally
termed "poor white trash." That might be why they didn't
put any restrictions on her dress, her movement, or her
behavior—they probably didn't care.

The girl suddenly dashed across a street and up an
enclosed staircase, catching Aurilia by surprise. She sent
the pigeon to perch in a tree outside the first lighted
window she saw.

She peered short-sightedly at the window, trying to
determine if the bird could get any closer, and discovered
that luck was with her. The girl passed in front of it,
showing it was the right one; and not only that, it was open,
with no screen to keep her from perching on the ledge.

She moved the pigeon in a fluttering hop from branch
to ledge, and poked the bird's head cautiously inside. The
place was appalling: filthy, bug-ridden, falling to pieces,
with the only furniture being pallets on the floor. There
were two rooms to the place; the girl and two other youngsters were in this one, and voices from the door beyond
proved that there were at least two more in the other
room. There were no parents, no adults of any kind,
anywhere in sight. Within moments of listening to the
conversation between the children, it was clear to her that
there were no adults in residence in the tiny apartment
at all. There were perhaps a half dozen children living
there, and now Aurilia knew exactly why the girl had looked
and acted the way she did—for she recognized one of the

other children. There was a girlishly-pretty young boy on a pallet at the side of the room, sleeping the profound sleep of the drugged with his face turned towards the window. Aurilia knew him very well indeed; she had just spent the past week editing film that had his face—and other parts—all over it.

It had been the "bondage-party" film (now called "Birthday Boy" and with three thousand copies already on order) that had featured five of their customers and one "pickup." The boy, called "Jamie," if she recalled correctly, was a free-lance hooker and a runaway.

Suddenly, given Tannim's notorious do-gooder impulses, many things fell into place. That was the attraction, then. *Tannim wants to save the girl if he can—and that fits right in with his profile. Meddling fool. Typical hero-wishing. Save her for what? A life of food-service?* Well, if he wanted to waste his time and resources on dead-end losers, Aurilia wasn't going to stop him. Particularly not when his little hobby fit right in with Aurilia's own plans. Not only her plans, but the current projects for Studio Two.

She withdrew her power in a burst of triumph, abruptly, allowing the pigeon to tumble unnoticed to the ground.

Tannim had expected Keighvin to jump all over him when he got back to the Fairgrove complex. After all, he had been scheduled to run test laps at Roebling, not spend the afternoon watching container ships and lolling around on the grass, however noble his motives.

Maybe if I just tell him the truth . . . edited. Emphasizing the need the child's in, and leaving out the lolling on the grass and the picnic dinner.

But as he wound his way through the offices, a change in the schedule posted beside the machine-shop door caught his eye. It would have been hard not to notice it; under the track schedule was a red-circled "canceled" notice.

When he read it, he had to grin. *The old luck comes through again. Excellent.* Some time between when he'd left for lunch and when he was supposed to return, Keighvin had changed the scheduling. The track had been closed this afternoon for repairs after some damage from a tire-test this morning.

A tire-test? What the hey?

He grabbed the first person he saw when he got into the shops. "What happened at the track this morning?" he asked.

The mechanic, Donal—one of Keighvin's Sidhe, and Tannim's oldest friend Underhill except for Keighvin—grinned wryly. "Hard to believe, eh? Wouldn't have believed it meself if I hadna seen it. We had a series of new tires for the GTP test mule—same mule you were supposed to check brake mods and suspension geometry on. Well, seems our mods or the tires or both were a little *too* good." Tannim watched the elven man rock back on his heels, eyes glittering.

"So what happened?" he asked, since Donal was obviously waiting for him to make some kind of response.

"Well, the lateral gees put a three-inch ripple in the asphalt on one of the turns." Donal's grin got even wider, and Tannim didn't blame him; Donal was part of the crew responsible for the handling. This was something of a coup—for a mule to hug the track that hard on the turns said a lot.

But—a three-inch ripple? That was a lot of lateral. His expression must have said something of his surprise, as Donal held up a hand as if he was swearing to the fact.

"I promise; I measured it meself. We all saw it—a three-inch lump, plain as Danaa's light, ten feet long. We had to hire a steamroller to flatten the track. Took us the rest of the day. Keighvin figured you'd see the posting and take off."

Now Donal raised an eyebrow, because Tannim *should* have known what had happened, since it had undoubtedly been all over the shop; Tannim just shrugged. He wasn't good enough to lie to a Sidhe, so he simply told part of the truth. "You know there's never anyone to answer questions around here in the afternoon. I had a picnic out at the Fort. So, where's Keighvin?"

"With Sam Kelly, at the forge-shop." Donal grinned again, showing gleaming white teeth, teeth that were a little feral-looking. "Now 'tis a 'forge' in more ways than one. Sam seems to have concocted a process that will pass muster, and he's moved that molten-metal equipment we kenned out to the other shop. Says we'll be ready for a cast of thousands."

"Ech, that's awful. 'Forged' engine blocks, hmm?" Tannim indulged the Sidhe; Donal was fond of puns. "And a 'forged' process. Well, I'd better get out there and see what Keighvin wants me to do now."

He wound his way through metal and machinery to the roofed passage that joined this shop to the formerly-empty forge building. He noticed along the way that a lot of the computer-driven equipment was missing; presumably it had been moved to its new home.

Keighvin *should* have been glowing with cheer; the mods that had warped the track had certainly proved successful, and now he had a "process" that would explain where his engine blocks and other cast-aluminum pieces were coming from. But when Tannim found him, supervising the set-up and activation of some arcane-looking machine by that insanely cheerful human tech-genius Skippy-Rob, he didn't look particularly happy.

Tannim wondered if something more had gone wrong than he'd been told, but it wasn't that kind of expression. He'd seen the Sidhe display all kinds of moods, and it was the "unreadable" ones that he feared the most. Keighvin was a gentleman by any creatures' standards, but he had his breaking points, and when he was near one . . . Keighvin looked up and saw him lurking out of the way, then beckoned the young mage over.

"What's cooking?" Tannim asked casually. "Anything wrong with Sam's phony process?"

"With the process—nothing," Keighvin replied, rubbing one temple distractedly. "But—Vidal Dhu showed up at Sam's this morning. Not inside the house, but he blocked Sam's driveway long enough to deliver a message."

"I think I can guess the message," Tannim said slowly.

Keighvin nodded, grimly. "A threat, of course. At least he didn't say, 'And your little dog, too.' The worrisome thing is that he's managed to recruit a corps of lesser

nasties, and they're putting pressure on *our* boundaries.
Nothing like overt warfare, but—don't go into the woods
after dark."

"Any things we haven't taken out before?"

"Nothing any worse, so far as we can tell. I don't like
it. And I don't like Sam being outside our hardened boundaries. I'm setting up our spare rooms here as sleeping-
quarters for anyone who can't protect themselves, including
Sam."

The man in question had come around the corner
during Silverhair's little speech, and waited until he had
finished before leaving the work crew and joining them.

"You're worrying too much, Keighvin," the old man said
comfortably. "I've been going over my old gran's stories.
I think I can hold off the boggles; enough to permit the
cavalry to come over the hill to rescue me, anyway."

Tannim noticed that the old man was wearing what
looked like an Uzi holstered at his hip; Sam patted it as
he finished his statement.

Tannim frowned, rubbing his eyes. "Sam, I don't mean
to rain on your parade, but plain old bullets aren't going
to stop Vidal, and they certainly aren't going to do anything to a creature like a troll that can heal itself—"

Sam pulled the gun from the holster and handed it to
him, wordlessly. Tannim took it—and it sloshed. It was one
of the old Uzi-replica water-pistols, and not a real gun at
all.

"One of your local geniuses prepared this for me," the
old man said. "That's salt and holy water. That should take
care of a fair number of yon blackguard's friends. I've got
rosemary, rue, and salt in my pocket, and a horseshoe nail
with them. There's an iron plate across every door and
windowsill of the house, horse-shoes nailed up over every
door and the fireplace, and sprigs of oak, ash, and thorn
up there with them. A lass here is preparing iron-filled .357
hollowtips for me Colt, and meanwhile, there's this—"

He touched the sheath on his other side, and Tannim
saw the hilt of a crudely-forged knife. He had no doubt
that it was of good Cold Iron. Sam wasn't taking chances
on a *steel* blade.

"That's all very well," Keighvin warned, "but it won't hold them for long. They'll find ways around your protections and mine, eventually."

Sam holstered his water-pistol. "Doesn't have to keep them busy for long," he countered. "It'll hold them baffled for long enough. All I have to do now is supervise your setup, put my John Hancock to everything and write up my part in this deal. That's a matter of a couple of weeks at most. The rude bastard can bluster all he wants. Once I'm finished, you don't need *me* anymore. You just need my name."

"But what if something goes wrong?" Keighvin asked. "There's nobody here that knows the language—"

"But this Vidal character doesn't know that," Sam replied. "He's like some of the really old execs at Gulfstream, the ones who didn't understand tech. He may even be a technophobe, for all we know. That kind thinks that once something technological is set in place, it sits and glowers and runs itself with no further help."

Both Keighvin and Tannim snorted; Sam shrugged. "I know it makes no sense, but that's the way these people think. All he'll see is me sitting back in my chair, and letting you run the show. He'll figure going after me is a waste of effort."

Keighvin shook his head doubtfully, and Tannim had to agree with the Sidhe. He wasn't convinced that Sam was right, either.

But Sam was an adult, and perfectly capable of making his own decisions. Besides, Tannim had other problems.

"Keighvin, I know this is coming at the worst possible time," he said, reluctantly, "but we've got another problem, too." Briefly he outlined Tania's situation, and the plight of the underage hookers she lived with. He hoped to catch Keighvin's interest, but the Sidhe-mage shook his head regretfully.

"Damn ye, Tannim, your timing sucks. I can't do anything for them right now," he said, plainly unhappy with the situation. "I'm sorry, but we're up to our pointy ears in alligators at the moment. I can't do anything for them out there—and you can't bring them here. I can't have a single non-mage mortal inside the boundary right now," he continued, frankly, laying the whole situation on the table so Tannim could see it. "And I'm stretching things to include Sam, because he believes and he's got a bit of the Sight himself. Who knows what these children would do if they saw a skirmish with one of Vidal Dhu's little friends out there? If they panicked, they could breach the shields. If they were taken in by appearances, they could actually bring Vidal inside."

Tannim had to admit, reluctantly, that Keighvin was right. He didn't want to say it out loud, though. *Maybe, just maybe, I can talk him into changing his mind.*

"If I let you bring them here, they'd at best be targets and weak spots," Keighvin continued. "Can't do that, no matter how desperate their situation seems to be, my friend. Keep siphoning them money; that's easy enough. They've kept their necks above water this long, Tannim, they can keep a little longer. When we've finished with Vidal Dhu, you can coax them in to us, but right now they'd just be in more danger with us than they are now."

Tannim grimaced. He didn't like it—but Keighvin was the boss at Fairgrove. This was his territory, and he knew the strengths and weaknesses better than anyone else.

So be it, Keighvin. I've got more to call on than spells. There's always the magic of folding green.

Keighvin eyed Tannim with a very readable expression— one of tired worry. He could read moods as well as minds. Tannim figured that Keighvin knew what his current expression meant. He met Keighvin's eyes squarely, and a little defiantly.

Yes, I am up to something.

But it was too late tonight to do anything about the situation. Tania was safe for the rest of the night, at least, and with any luck at all, that hundred would keep her off the streets for another couple of days. That would be long enough for Tannim to get Plan B into gear.

Assuming nothing happens between then and now. Like one of her friends getting tangled up with a pimp, or on the wrong side of a dealer, or—

He cut the thoughts short. There was no use worrying

about the kids right now; he'd do what he could, when he could.

"Look," he said, running his hand through his hair, catching on more snags than usual, "I'm beat. If there isn't anything you need me for, I'm going home to get some shut-eye. Are we rescheduling those tests for tomorr—I mean, today? Or is it tomorrow?" He rubbed his eyes, wishing in a way that he could run them now. Although he was tired, he was also full of nervous energy, and he wished he had somewhere to go with it.

"No, Goodyear has the track," Keighvin said, his expression one of mingled relief and apprehension. Tannim had a shrewd idea of why the Sidhe wore the latter. Keighvin had to be wondering now just *what* it was Tannim had in mind to do about the kids.

Keep wondering.

"We have it after Goodyear," Keighvin added. "You *are* going to be fit to drive, I hope? And you don't plan on going anywhere tonight, do you? Sam should be safe enough here." The statement indicated that he wasn't necessarily worried about Tannim's involvement with the kids.

He thinks I'm going to go spend the rest of the night guarding Sam, or trying to hunt down Unseleighe creatures or something. Does he really think I'm that foolhardy?

"Don't worry, I don't plan on running out and hunting the kids—or Vidal Dhu—down tonight," Tannim replied with irritation. "I've got a little more sense than that. If the kids can wait, so can Vidal. He's not going anywhere. If he comes after us here, he's a fool, but you don't need me here to face him down."

Now the relief was so palpable on Keighvin's face that Tannim restrained himself from a sharp retort only by reminding himself that Keighvin didn't deserve it.

It's not his fault that you can't hit the broad side of a barn when you're tired. And it's not being paranoid on his part to worry about having you around when you're wonky. Conal may forgive you in a couple of hundred years, but what if you'd gotten more than his hair?

It was something Tannim didn't like to think about. And he hated being reminded of this new weakness of his. If only there was something he could do about it—

But Keighvin was waiting for him to say something; he managed a tight smile, and flexed his shoulders. "I'm heading straight for bed," he said. "You know where to find me if you need me."

Keighvin was too aware of his own dignity to give him a comradely slap on the back, but Sam wasn't. "We'll be seeing you some time in the afternoon, then?" the old man asked, as Tannim staggered a little beneath Sam's heavy hand.

Keighvin lifted an ironic eyebrow. "Aye, do check in some time, won't you? So we can let you know what the schedule is."

Tannim controlled his expression carefully, so that none of his guilt would leak through. *He's got a suspicion I played hooky. It's a good thing this isn't your normal business....* "I'll call when I wake up, but I'd like to come in after dark, if that's all right with you," he said. "It may take that long to get recharged."

This time he wasn't quite so irritated with Keighvin's reaction to his implied exhaustion, since it was working in his favor.

"Take all the time you need," the Sidhe replied quickly. "I'd rather have you take a couple more hours to get into top form than to come in at less than full strength."

Tannim nodded, trying his best to keep it from looking curt. "See you later, then."

He turned and walked out, back through the darkened office complex, back to the safe haven of the Mustang. It would take more than Vidal Dhu to get through the protections on the Mach 1, and he relaxed a little as he slid into the seat and shut the door.

There were times he wished that he'd taken Keighvin's offer of an elvensteed to replace the Mustang, especially when he was tired. It was a great honor for a mortal to be offered an elvensteed, and it would have been really nice to have a car that could find its own way home. On the other hand, there was enough Cold Iron in the

Mach 1 to give any Unseleighe Court critter more than it cared to handle. Keighvin couldn't even ride in it without pain. Tannim was glad of the new "plastic cars" for the sake of his friends, but when it came to keeping his own hide safe, arcanely and mundanely—he'd take good American sheet metal every time.

He thought, as he drove through the gates, that he sensed a lurking nastiness in the woods. But it was too dark to see much, even with mage-sight, and he was too tired to really want to risk a confrontation with anything. That nervous energy that had filled him was draining away a lot faster than he'd thought it would.

He drove carefully—and slowly, for him—back down the dark, near-deserted highway to his little rented house on the outskirts of Savannah. Normally he wouldn't have bothered renting anything as large as a house—but this place had some advantages that outweighed every other consideration. For one thing, it had a three-car garage almost as big as the house itself; whoever had built it must have been a real car-nut, or needed a hell of a workshop. The Mustang and all the gear Tannim needed to keep it in pristine condition no matter *what* he put it through fit comfortably inside.

But there were even more important considerations. The house and yard were hidden from the road by a thick ring of tall evergreens—which themselves were planted far enough from the house that while someone could have used them for cover, to get to the buildings an intruder would have had to cross a good-sized expanse of bare, weedy lawn, mowed short every week by the rental company.

The ring of evergreens was perfectly circular. It was, in fact, a Circle of the protective variety, and had been that way before Tannim moved in. Possibly even long before; the trees were old, fifty, maybe as much as a hundred years old. Had they been ensorceled that long? It was certainly possible. Sorcery invested in living things, unlike that invested in nonliving things, tended to stick around long after the caster was dust—and could even grow and flourish on its own.

The house itself was much younger, but it had been built on an old foundation. Who had built the place this way, Tannim had no idea. The rental agency simply administered it, kept things repaired, collected his rent. There had been protections on the house and garage, too, but since they had been based on dead wood rather than living, and the electricity had been off so that the protections cast into the circuitry had drained away, those shields had been faded by the time *he* rented the place. The agency had been pathetically grateful; evidently they'd had a hard time finding a tenant.

Maybe the trees themselves kept out people they didn't like. It was possible; there was the same feeling of semi-awareness about the trees as there was to the Mustang. Odd how he didn't even react to such things anymore.

Still, with the privacy and all, it was kind of odd that no one had come along that wanted to rent it before he saw it. On the other hand, for a house, the place was kind of small; too small for a family, and yet the rent was a little too steep for most single people. It was worth it—in an effort to find a tenant, the agency had installed new appliances. But the rent was still a little steep, even so.

For whatever reason, the place had stayed vacant for a couple of years until Tannim came along. The little one-bedroom cottage was perfect for him. The only other thing he wished he had was a Jacuzzi—and if he stayed, he could always install that in the garage.

He thumbed the garage-opener as he drove up the drive; his electronics weren't quite as fancy as Sam's, but then again, he wasn't as much of an engineer as Sam was. Twin floodlights came on over the garage door, two more went on inside, and the door rose majestically on a miniature equivalent of the Fairgrove shops.

The Mustang rolled inside, and the door descended again, noisily. It was a little noisier than most, because it was heavier than most: five joined slabs of steel. Bomb-proof, he would have said. The door predated his occupancy, too.

Every so often he wondered what on earth the owner

had been into that he needed a garage door that would withstand a B-52 strike.

He opened the Mustang's door, then paused, as all of the strain of the past week came down on him with a rush. Up until today, the test runs out at Roebling Road had alternated with sessions on the mods, all day and into the night. And when he hadn't been working on the mods, he'd been working, magically, on Sam's defenses. They weren't as good as the ones here, and he wasn't going to stop until they were—

Or until they buried Vidal Dhu and his friends.

He dragged himself up out of the bucket seat, and stumbled towards the door into the house. Fortunately, it led straight into the kitchen, and temporary salvation.

He leaned up against the fridge door for a moment, until the hum of the compressor starting up jarred him out of his tired daze. He pulled the door open and reached inside, blindly taking out a brand-new, unopened bottle of Gatorade with one hand. The other hand groped on top of the fridge and encountered crackling plastic. He brought down what he had found, and looked at it blearily as he shoved the fridge door shut with his hip.

Corn chips. Close enough to food.

He got as far as the tiny kitchen table, dropping down into the chair like a sack of deer antlers. There was an entire row of brown bottles and jars on the back edge of the table against the wall; vitamins, minerals, amino acids. He opened the bottle of Gatorade, ripped open the sack of chips, and began opening each of the bottles in turn, spilling out a couple of each until he had a little heap of pills in front of him. Then he began popping them into his mouth, methodically, washing them down with swigs from the bottle of Gatorade, alternating pills with a handful of chips until pills, chips, and Gatorade were all gone.

Well, that takes care of the IOU to my body.

He thought about a hot bath, stood up, and decided, when he went lightheaded, that the bath could wait. He turned off the kitchen light and stumbled into the bedroom, past the stark living room. The living room always depressed him, anyway—it looked so empty. There were two armchairs that had come with the house, a floor-lamp, and his old stereo. The good rig was in the bedroom; anyone who broke in would probably figure Tannim didn't have anything worth stealing. Which was mostly true; he hadn't accumulated much in his years of traveling. *Moving fast keeps you from hanging on to much.*

He flipped on the bedroom light; and there was The Bed—the single piece of furniture he had acquired and held onto through so many changes of address that he'd forgotten half of them.

It was the size of two king-size beds put together, and completely filled the bedroom. The basis for construction had been two orthopedic hospital beds, complete with controls, with a flat section in between. The bookcase-headboard behind it went up to the ceiling, and held mirrors, speakers, a lot of his audio gear, bed controls, and remotes for the TV and VCRs across the room on the shabby bureau. Plus a tiny bar-fridge and microwave. It had padded rails, and one section of the padding on each side flipped up like the armrests on a first-class airline seat; inside were tray-tables. When he was really hurt or sick, he didn't even have to leave The Bed except to hit the bathroom.

He'd found it (sans electronic gear, but wired with four power-strips and its own pair of breaker-boxes) in a Goodwill store in Dallas. It had been made in Germany, and he'd always figured its previous owner was one of the victims of the slump in oil prices. Occasionally he looked at it, and wondered why he'd hung onto it with such tenacity. It was a stone bitch to move, and holding onto any piece of furniture was so completely unlike him that keeping this monster was insane. But then he'd get hurt, or he'd have one of his days when he'd wake up after a race or a fight hardly able to move, and he'd *know* why he kept it. He'd never find another like it. And it at least gave him one constant in all of his changes of address.

Too bad that he seldom had anyone to share it with.

He edged into the clear slot at the foot, and peeled off his shirt. Beneath it was his body-armor; one of the other reasons he hadn't been overly worried about an ambush by Vidal Dhu. It looked like a unitard, but it was composed of thousands of tiny hexagonal scales, enameled in emerald green. As he slid his pants off, the cool scales slipped smoothly, silkily, under his hands. It had been a project he and Chinthliss had worked on for three months, to the exclusion of everything else.

There were no seams. That was because every scale was joined magically to every other scale, and it could be opened where and when he chose. Though if he was ever unconscious, it would take someone like Keighvin to get it off him. . . .

So he just wouldn't get in any accidents.

Right.

He crooked one finger, which was the only component of the set-spell to open the suit, and ran the fingernail up the front. The armor opened and he shrugged it off, exactly like a dancer squirming out of a costume.

Beneath the armor were the scars.

Starting from the first, a knife-scar on the forearm he got protecting a potential mage, to the latest, teeth-marks that marked his leg from hip to ankle, his body was criss-crossed with a network of lines. They ranged from the thin white lines of old wounds, to the red of the newly healed.

I'm certainly not going to win any bikini contests.

Without the added support of the body-armor, his leg ached distantly, his shoulders felt like knotted wire ropes, and The Bed looked more inviting than ever.

But there was one more thing to do before he collapsed for the night.

He reached to the nearest shelf, and took out the tiny jar of Tiger Balm he kept there. Actually, he kept more than one in there—there was nothing worse than reaching for the only thing that could ease those constant aches only to find the jar empty.

He sat down on the edge of the bed, on the padded rail. With habit that had become ritualized, he applied the salve over every aching muscle. Before he had finished rubbing it into his shoulders, the heat had begun to soothe his aching leg.

He sighed, put the jar back, and crawled into the bed's

embrace, fumbling for the light-switch and dropping the room into total blackness, without even a hint of outside light. The electronic clocks of the VCRs bothered him though, enough that he briefly considered flinging a towel over them before deciding he could just bury his head instead. His last conscious thought was to pull the blankets up over himself and burrow into them, before the exhaustion he had been holding off with both hands won the battle and flung him into sleep.

CHAPTER TEN

Sam glanced over at Keighvin as Tannim retreated. The young man had looked tired and worried, and Sam knew the "why" of both. Tannim had put in several after-hours sessions reinforcing the protections on Sam's house; that took a lot more out of him than mere loss of sleep. And there was no doubt that he was worried about the kids, Tania especially.

He has reason to be. She takes her health, if not her life, into her hands every time she walks the streets.

Sam had more immediate worries on his mind, and so did Keighvin. There was something Keighvin hadn't told Tannim. The Unseleighe Sidhe had shown up this morning outside Sam's house with more than a personal warning. He'd delivered a warning to Fairgrove as well, in the form of a challenge; time and place specified for tonight, at the Fairgrove boundaries. And despite Donal's attempts at reassurance, Sam trusted Keighvin's judgment, and Keighvin was worried.

"It's traditional," Keighvin had said. "You always warn your opponent before you attack—if they're of the Folk, that is." Then he'd smiled, but without humor. "Of course, the warning can consist of sending back the pieces of someone, appropriately gift-wrapped."

Sam had winced a little; it was one thing to hear about

the bloodthirstiness of the Sidhe in a tale, and another to feel it so close to home. "What about mortals?" he'd asked. "Why did I rate a warning?"

Keighvin had pondered for a moment, as if the question hadn't occurred to him. "Probably because you were protected too well to attack easily. Mortals—well, mortals in general just don't rate any courtesy, Sam. I'm afraid the Unseleighe Court deems mortals one short step above cockroaches."

At that Sam had grinned widely. "Could be they forget what good survivors cockroaches are," he had offered. Keighvin had laughed and slapped him on the back.

As soon as Tannim got out of earshot, he asked the question that he couldn't voice while Tannim was around. "Why didn't you tell young Tannim about the rest of the warning?" he asked the Sidhe. Keighvin shrugged.

"He's too tired to be of much use to us right now," Keighvin said with resignation. "He plays hero too much for his own good, and he'd be right here pitching levinbolts, exhausted or no, if we'd told him. I'd rather not have the lad at my back when he's this worn down." Sam looked at him quizzically, and Keighvin coughed, embarrassed.

"Lately Tannim gets a little—erratic—when he's tired," the Sidhe said, carefully.

Erratic, hmm? Just what's that supposed to mean?

"How so?" Sam probed. "Level with me, Keighvin. What are we talking about here?"

Keighvin shook his head. "Truth to tell, Sam, I'd just as soon not have Tannim anywhere nearby when he's exhausted. His intended targets are safer than his allies. Lack of endurance, I fear."

Sam didn't know whether to be amused or alarmed. It was funny now, but it might not be that funny later, if he found himself having to dodge—what?

"Is this bad aim just with his magic?" Sam asked. Keighvin sighed.

"Magic, fisticuffs, guns, 'tis everything, anything that requires aiming." He spread his hands. "The last time it happened, we were picking slugs out of the walls for a fortnight, and poor Conal still hasn't regrown the hair Tannim scorched from his scalp."

Conal, a few feet away, looked up at the sound of his name, and scowled from under the brim of his baseball cap. Sam recalled now that the Sidhe-mechanic had looked rather odd when he'd removed the cap to scratch his head. He'd had a swath about two inches wide shaved from front to back, in a kind of reverse Mohawk. Sam had wondered at the time if it was some sort of new fashion—many of the younger elves had taken to punk and cutting-edge clothing with a glee unmatched by any human over eighteen. Now he knew better, at least in Conal's case.

"A near-miss," Keighvin continued, "and damned lucky it wasn't nearer than it was. Eh. Poor lad never was very sharp with a gun anyway." He shook his head again. "Wish we could get that glittery friend of his with the odd name to magic him up some endurance, but I fear that's asking for a miracle. He hasna been the same since he got that leg of his chewed on."

That explains the limp. Sam thought about asking about just what had been responsible for that injury, saw Keighvin's face, and decided against it. *There are some things man was not meant to know.*

Instead, he glanced at one of the many clock-calendars mounted around the shop. Not because anyone was on a timeclock, but because it was very easy to lose all track of time in here. Work continued every hour and day of the week—there were deadlines to be met, and later, once Sam and Keighvin had convinced the world that Fairgrove was a reliable, legitimate concern, there would be production schedules for outside clients as well.

It was ten-to-twelve. The Unseleighe Sidhe's challenge had specified midnight as the hour of attack.

And even as he looked up at the clock, folk and Folk all over the shop were putting up tasks and taking weapons from the unlikeliest hiding places. Conal opened the top drawer of his rolling tool-chest and produced a matched pair of filigreed swords; a pretty little human girl Sam had thought no more than eighteen went to the first-aid kit on the wall and opened it up. She took out a closely-wrapped bundle and unwrapped the silk from what it contained: a gunpouch. Keighvin had explained the insulating properties of silk when he'd asked Sam to be sure and wrap anything of doubtful content in a square of the stuff from a pile kept beside the door before bringing it into the shop.

She opened the gunpouch itself, and the gleam of more silk showed Sam that the pouches had also been silk-lined, as double protection against the disruptive effects of that much steel inside the shop. The pouch contained a Glock Model 22. Everyone at Fairgrove that was a marksman used these nine-millimeters; that way all the ammo and magazines matched. Sam was the only exception, and there hadn't been time to find or get used to a new gun.

There was an entire row of those silk-wrapped bundles in the kit. The girl handed one to another mechanic, and slapped her acquisition into a shoulder holster.

Sam patted his water-Uzi to be sure it was still with him. His granny's tales had been very specific about the effects of salt water on some creatures, like boggles—and one of the mechanics, seeing what it was he had on his hip, had stopped him long enough to put some kind of pagan blessing on it. She'd said she'd made it into "holy water"—and Sam's granny had been quite adamant about how effective holy water was on the "bad Sidhe." It made him a little uneasy, though; he wasn't certain that was the kind of "holy water" Granny'd had in mind.

But then, again . . . maybe it was.

He also had a silk-wrapped bag of iron filings in his pocket, but unless he could find a way to use them safely, they were going to stay there. Using an area-effect weapon like the iron filings could be as disruptive to his friends as to the enemy.

Like using a nuclear hand grenade.

Keighvin had spoken of the elven trouble with magic near iron earlier that day as they walked around the Fairgrove grounds. It had surprised Sam that he'd treated it like any other conversation topic, only wrinkling that smooth, passive brow when he mentioned the effects of iron's contact with elven flesh. He'd explained that the

Sidhe's bodies thrived on magic itself, as well as food and drink, and the touch of Death Metal was a poison—a corrosive one. Then he'd gone on. The touch of iron was like a lens focusing light—to burn. It seemed that iron in its purer forms attracted the "frequency" of magical energy the elves used, much like a magnet, and warped it in ways that were often dangerous for the mage. Sam had said it was like a planet's gravity affecting every other heavenly body, always slightly tugging it off-target even from a distance, and Keighvin had nodded energetically. Then Keighvin leaned against a very thick fencepost, and said conspiratorially, "Therein's our advantage in the fight tonight. We've discovered that different iron alloys warp the magic in different ways—and we know how to *see* the alloys now. Magically."

Then he'd leaned back, very obviously smug.

Sam was not going to be in the front lines for this little confrontation; Keighvin had been quite firm about that. He was to be in the second rank, with the archers and others whose distance-weapons could not be fired from hiding. The humans on the crew who were good shots would be firing from cover, or protecting mages from physical attack. The others would be wading in hand-to-hand with weapons of steel and Cold Iron.

Keighvin had produced a shining, blue-sheened sword from out of nowhere (literally) and headed towards the outside entrance. Sam followed the Sidhe out, and stood behind him as he conferred with two other Folk and an obviously retired GI employee. They pointed out sections of Fairgrove on a map, and likely avenues of attack. Sam got the impression they knew the grounds very well, and had a few hundred dirty tricks ready. They nodded to each other, traded code-words, and checked radio headsets. Abruptly, the four split up, and Keighvin motioned Sam to follow him, speaking tersely into his mouthpiece.

The two walked briskly into the parking area, where Sam realized he wasn't quite *yet* used to the mixture of machinery and magic at Fairgrove. Before him were a half-dozen figures; a few humans in Cats Laughing and Ian Falconer concert-tour sweatshirts and faded jeans strapped on ballistic-cloth vests, and checked magazines and radio ear-pieces. The rest of the group stood among them, long hair in braids or falling like silvered snow over the intricate armor of the elven Courts, settling the same sort of ear-pieces into gently upswept, pointed ears. One of them carried a US Army-surplus first-aid kit duct-taped to his enameled armor; another swung a handful of aluminum baseball bats as she warmed up for the coming battle. He watched the Lamborghini and Dino ripple and shift into a pair of tall, glittering "horses." They stamped, and their hooves struck sparks.

Keighvin swept the sword suddenly in a great vertical circle, cutting a groove into the asphalt. Blue sparks traced along its arc, and followed the blade up, leaving a semi-circular "mirror" suspended in midair. Images showed within the mirror immediately, lit in tremendous contrast. "Here is where they are now," he said, "and this is what we know of them. Janie on camera has picked out five boggles, and three trolls on their front line. Four rows of goblins, thirteen each, are after them, Danaa only knows why. Here is their leader." The image sharpened so quickly that a stab of pain shot through his head behind his eyes, and Sam took an involuntary step back from the thing he saw. One of the humans whistled in mock appreciation and a little fear; another human female snorted and pulled the slide on her gun.

"You know the routine—we've gone over it before. Plug your other ear, or make enough noise to disrupt its effects. Dottie, you shouldn't have too much trouble doing that for all of us." The woman giggled and let the slide smack back into place. The rest laughed along as she stroked the extra five magazines she carried affectionately. "Donal, take Sam with you, watch him and watch your back. Dottie, Jim, Cuil, follow me and fan on my signal. Take the creek oak, Kieru. Anything goes sour, medical is here, and escape is by Thunder Road."

Sam ran through what he knew of Fairgrove. *Seven of the lot are medics; Thunder Road is what they call the driveway. Oh, Holy Mother.*

Two more elvensteeds appeared so suddenly that Sam

was startled, and blushed in embarrassment over it. Donal jerked a thumb over his shoulder, and led the way inside again. He half-ran through the corridors to a well-lit room where scores of television screens glittered in the eyes of a single woman wearing a full headset, who spoke information so quickly it sounded like a chant.

"Keighvin, camera three shows the first and second ranks of goblins are splitting to let the leader advance. Two trolls are flanking, past camera six, coming into camera twelve. Wire shows crossing at the creek—camera six shows the other two trolls now, following the first two. Camera twenty has all of the boggles moving as one unit towards the forge. Carrie, you show clear to intercept from the other side. . . ."

Even an armchair general could see what was going on. *These bogeymen havena' plan at all that I can see. They've got a sorry lot to face these people.*

Donal leaned close to Sam and said, "Sarge Austin says a deployment like this shows the leader is such an egotist he thinks he can't be defeated."

"We still haven't seen his second rank, or his reserve. Maybe he's right," someone muttered, sounding nowhere near as confidant as Donal. Nods around the room echoed that sentiment.

On one screen, Sam saw Keighvin look directly into the camera, and unexpectedly smile and wave. He mouthed, "Hi, Mom!" and then moved on. It was obscenely absurd with the battle at hand and the odds so greatly against them, but despite himself, Sam smiled.

Donal only shook his head and said, "Danaa, he's been around that boy Tannim too long."

Janie paused for one long heartbeat, then spoke again: "Keighvin . . . their second rank just arrived. You aren't gonna like it."

Donal spat a curse in elven, and began running.

Panting and with a pain in his side, Sam came to a rest at Donal's back after a sprint through the offices and garages of Fairgrove. They had only paused for a moment in the body shop, so Donal could find an earpiece for Sam;

all they could find was an old, taped-up full headset with a battered power pack, stenciled with a SWAT logo. It crackled horribly when activated, but settled down after the initial protest, and then they were running again. Now they were outside, and Sam heard Keighvin's voice in his ears.

"Janie, dim the cameras in five, then hit the spots. Ready on the Pinball."

Donal crouched down and covered his eyes. Sam did the same, still wondering what this "Pinball" could be. An area-effect weapon? Some kind of spell? Keighvin had told him how all the iron around Fairgrove would disrupt any magic the elves used. . . .

The grounds lit up in brilliant light as hundreds of halogens came to life. Sam squinted against the glare and then gasped as he saw what they faced.

Oh Father who art in Heaven, hallowed be Thy name . . .

Caught in the daylike brightness were creatures out of his nightmares and old stories—although under that much candlepower, they looked only like so many special-effects puppets. All except their leader. It was unmistakably real, horrifyingly real, riding a creature that might once have been a horse, but now was tattered hide stretched over bone, fang-filled mouth, and evil, glint-of-fire eyes. The leader's ragged clothing whipped in a wind that seemed to blow from Sam's own soul, and he knew the Bane-Sidhe for what it was. Around it were rank upon rank of gray-and-green skinned goblins, wicked weapons drawn, and great shambling trolls with glistening knobby skin. Virtually all of them were cringing and clutching at their eyes. Behind them, in the second rank, were—Sidhe. Tall, silver-haired, dusky-eyed, identical to the Fairgrove Sidhe, and yet as different as a surgeon's scalpel and an assassin's dagger.

Unseleighe Sidhe. The first besides Vidal Dhu that Sam had seen. They carried some sort of weaponry that looked vaguely gun-shaped—all but four of the tallest. The quartet raised their arms and gestured, gathering sickly green light around their hands, and Sam knew the attack had begun.

"Come on, ye bastards," Donal muttered. "A little closer. Just a little closer—"

They didn't immediately oblige him; instead, some of the skinnier goblins peered, squinting, through the halogen glare, and the Unseleighe Sidhe raised crossbows. They looked odd; when they fired them into the trees where the hidden humans with firearms were waiting, Sam realized why.

Fairgrove wasn't the only group to have pirated technology, and although this was a simpler level of tech, it was no less deadly. The Unseleighe Sidhe had armed themselves with compound crossbows, and the bolts glowed with the same evil green as the mages were gathering about their hands.

"Shit," Donal spat. "Elf-shot. The pricks brought elf-shot."

And from the sudden cries of pain in the trees, those bolts had found marks among the humans. Some shots rang out from the trees in answer, but the Unseleighe mages cast a curtain of deflecting energy across their front ranks, and four boggle-mages emerged from the woods.

That'll be their attackers—

Encouraged by their success, the enemy leader gestured his troops to move forward under the crossbowmen's covering fire.

The boggle-mages gestured, as if about to throw something.

Keighvin's voice came clearly, calmly through the headphones: "Janie, Pinball now."

Then Sam realized why the elven leader had been so smug. The fencepost he'd leaned on earlier that day—and every other fencepost—cracked open along its top and revealed a dark metal bar, trailing shreds of silk cloth as they rose. The grounds-sprinklers popped up from the ground, refracting the artificial daylight in huge rainbows.

The tricky bastards!

The boggles unleashed their spells, and the bolts of searing energy careened madly across the field. One looped in a devastating arc, incinerating a half-dozen goblins before striking the boggle itself, who fell to the ground writhing in agony.

The beautiful, tricky bastards, they built silk-wrapped iron bars into the fenceposts! Sam's mind swam with amazement. *They ran lines to those posts when the sprinklers were installed, and it only takes turning one valve to raise the bars when you activate the sprinklers....*

The bars themselves warped the paths of both the magical energy blasts and the enchanted elf-shot. And that was why it was called "Pinball," he realized, as he watched the spell-bolts the boggles had unleashed tear through their own ranks like silver balls in an arcade game, until they ran out of targets to burn.

He could see the flashes of gunfire around him, and felt the dull thuds muffled by the earphones. There were bodies down on their side, but most of them seemed to be moving, at least—

And now the odds looked to be even; tech on the Fairgrove side, numbers and bloodthirstiness on the Unseleighe side, as the crossbowmen changed from elf-shot to plain bolts with dark, glittering heads, that flew through the Pinball field with courses unaltered. Keighvin and Janie barked information to the team leaders, and the lines of tracer fire mixed with the enemy's spell-bolt trails. Donal stood behind a wild cherry tree and fired a longbow, measuring his shots very carefully, felling one goblin after another. Then the spells from Fairgrove began, and the odds altered again, this time in their favor.

Pinball. Good Lord they're brilliant.

Keighvin had said that different iron alloys pulled elven magic—and Sam realized that those amounts could be *measured.* Like scientists used a planet's gravity to launch a satellite into orbit, the elven mages were *using* the known effect of iron on their spells to deflect their shots into their attackers, and destroy the enemy's accuracy!

Levin-bolts from human and elven mages lanced out from the buildings, the human ones tracking straight and true, the elven bolts arcing gracefully into their targets as they were pulled by the iron-alloy bars. The enemy's magickers launched spells back, and watched in horror as their attacks not only missed, but circled back out of control like unguided fireworks rockets inside the perimeter marked by the fenceposts. Keighvin ordered someone to fire "the magnet," and began counting backwards. When he reached two, the spellfire of the defenders halted, and Sam watched a crossbow bolt strike the ghastly horse their leader rode a moment later. Although he couldn't hear it, he could see Donal shout "Yes!"

Then the spells started up again, and Sam realized why the layout had seemed so familiar as the bolts disappeared around the other side of the buildings—and reappeared moving faster around the other side, racing around the inside of the fenceposts in a league-wide stream of death. They accelerated.

I'll be damned. Fairgrove's built like a simple electric motor—or a cyclotron. The posts are the electromagnets, the bolts the brushes. . . . I don't believe it! The more power you add, the faster the drum spins . . . and the magnet will—

Sam never even needed to finish the thought, as he watched the spell-bolts swirling around the complex track in, one by one, on the single solid iron bolt embedded in the Nightmare's chest. There was a silent explosion, and a great coruscating ball of fire spread for a hundred feet. When it cleared, there was a smoking pile of shredded flesh and rags marking what had once been a Nightmare.

But the rider was still moving, and had pulled back its hood.

Its face was a contorted image of pain, hatred, sadism, every vile emotion a human could possess, magnified a thousandfold. Its eyes glittered with cruelty and hunger, desiccated skin wrinkling around the sockets as it opened its mouth to scream. A low, painful sound built in Sam's ears, like bone scraping concrete. It rose in pitch as the creature wailed, giving him a shooting pain that ricocheted in his head like the spell-bolts racing around the complex. Sam tried to concentrate on what Keighvin and Janie were saying, not wanting to ponder the fact that a few dollars' worth of surplus police equipment was all that was saving him from the deadly wail of the Bane-Sidhe.

Sam and Donal broke from their cover and ran to crouch in the bushes around the forge building, but the creature lashed out at them with a whiplike tendril of crackling green fire. The blaze caught Donal in the chest, and heaved him off his feet, The Bane-Sidhe strode through the water-sprays, inside the lethal wall of spell-bolts, its head still tipped back in a wide-mouthed shriek.

Sam crouched over Donal while the monster approached, and saw that he was still breathing—but barely. The breastplate had been breached in three places he could see, twisted and seeping a bright red fluid that looked as human as any blood Sam had ever seen. Sam felt a dog-like growl of anger rumbling in his chest, and he stood and pulled the Uzi.

I'll be damned if ye'll get away with that, y'black bastard.

Narrowing his eyes, Sam trained the watergun on the horror stalking towards him, trigger pulled as he leveled it. It primed and fired when the Bane-Sidhe was only two arms-lengths from him, and the holy water struck and burned, burned like sulfuric acid. Its scream turned from one of attack to terror as it caught "fire," deep channels burning into its flesh where the water touched, black blood streaming, and the last thing Sam saw in its eyes before it turned to run—was fear.

In a little pocket of Underhill chaos, hastily built into an island of protection, Vidal conjured another torrent of water. Once again, he sluiced the Bane-Sidhe down. The liquid poured over Niall, who lay face-down on the rubbery, soft floor, in a quivering heap of pain and suffering, rags plastered to his unnaturally thin body. Niall's howl had died down to a whimper, which was a blessing. It wasn't the purposeful scream of a Bane-Sidhe's vocal attack, but Niall's cries of agony had called up corresponding pain in his ally, even through Vidal's hastily-conjured earplugs of wax.

The ultra-pure water, carefully warmed to blood-heat, was having an effect. Finally, Niall's whimpers faded and were replaced by hoarse, exhausted breathing.

Vidal conjured a warm breeze to dry the Bane-Sidhe. He hadn't bothered to remove the creature's rags—he hadn't dared. He didn't want to know what lay beneath them.

Slowly, the Bane-Sidhe uncurled, as the rags dried and fluttered in his artificial wind. "Are you all right?" Vidal asked carefully.

"No," the Bane-Sidhe whispered raggedly. "But I shall mend." Then, as if the words had been dragged out of him unwillingly, "I thank you for your quick thinking. And you are right."

"Right?" Vidal replied, surprised. "About what, pray?"

"Keighvin Silverhair." There was no mistaking the venom in the Bane-Sidhe's voice now, the acidic hatred. "He has become contaminated with these mortals to the point that he is a great danger to us. He must be removed."

Vidal nearly lost his jaw. Those were the last words he expected to hear out of Niall; the Bane-Sidhe's stubborn refusal to admit he was ever wrong was legendary.

"I will help—when I have recovered," Niall concluded faintly. "But what do we do in the meantime? We have been routed."

"Not necessarily," Vidal said slowly, thinking of the silk-wrapped bundle he'd left Underhill. Aurilia had given it to him just this morning, after he'd issued the challenge.

"Keighvin and his fools have one strength," she'd told him, handing the tear-gas grenade to him, after showing him how to handle the weapon with silk-lined leather gloves, and how to pull the pin by means of the nylon cargo-tie she'd fastened to it in case he lost the gloves. "Their pet mortals know our weaknesses and exploit them, and they're using the mortals' weapons whenever they can. You'd best get ready to do the same if you want to defeat them."

He'd laughed at her at the time. Now—

Now he was coming to the reluctant conclusion that she was brighter than he had thought.

"I think I have a way to even the score a little," he said, slowly. "If nothing else—I think I can force one of the vermin out of its hole. The one, not incidentally, that got you."

The Bane-Sidhe's head turned sharply, and Vidal thought

he saw the glitter of eyes inside the darkness of its hood, and despite himself, he shuddered.

"Do that," Niall said tersely, "and every power I have is at your call, without reservation."

Vidal held back the thrill of triumph, at least enough to keep it from showing on his face.

Sam unlocked the door and turned to lock it behind him—for although Vidal could not pop in magically, there was nothing stopping the Sidhe from walking in mundanely through the door unless Sam was very careful. The house was much too quiet without Thoreau padding up to greet him, but Sam was glad now that he had sent the spaniel to a kennel for safety until this was all over.

That's one non-combatant out of the way, anyway, he told himself. He'd done everything he could to cover his tracks, too; he'd paid in advance, then registered the dog under a neighbor's name, with her agreement, telling her he was going to be on a consulting job and might not be home for a while. It would take a great deal of investigation for the enemy to learn that Thoreau belonged to Sam. And by then, with luck, this would all be over.

He made sure that his new crowbar—one of six—was still in the umbrella stand by the door, and headed for the library. He still wanted to double-check something before he turned in for the night—what there was left of it.

Certainly the last thing he ever expected when he took this job was to get involved with elven warfare.

But the moment he reached the library door and turned on the light, something crashed through the window.

Glass shards flew everywhere. Something dark skittered and spun across the floor, banging into the furniture, skipping across the rug, spewing a yellowish gas from one end. It spun like a dervish, and Sam made the fundamental error of gasping in surprise.

The stinging of his throat and eyes told him how great an error that had been.

Tear-gas. Just like Belfast. Only this time he hadn't gotten such a big whiff of it.

Coughing and choking, Sam covered his nose and mouth

with his hands, and ran, stumbling, for the door. His eyes burned painfully, streaming tears, making it hard to see; and his lungs felt as if someone had poured hot lead into them.

He fumbled at the lock and wrenched at the door handle until it opened, slamming it into the wall. He dove through it, tumbling out into the cool, fresh air and dropping to his knees on the concrete, his lungs screaming for oxygen.

Falling to his knees was all that saved him from the knife that thudded into the doorframe above him.

He started back, then jerked his head around in the direction of the curse that came out of the darkness, just as the house alarms—which he had not disarmed—started wailing, and all the exterior lights flared on as the second line of computer-driven defenses activated.

Peering through tears, he made out the dark shape of the enemy Sidhe, Vidal—and only that single foe—as the creature threw up its arm to protect its eyes from the wash of powerful light.

Vidal Dhu—you bastard.

He knew then that he had a few seconds before the Sidhe recovered and renewed the attack—

He was praying under his breath, the old litany of "Hail Mary," the words tumbling off his tongue in a high-speed gabble without his being aware of when he had started. And in the meantime, the rest of him was moving again, scrambling to his feet and making a desperate, tear-blurred, panting dash for the garage.

He reached it a breath ahead of the knife that clattered off the door, punched a key-code on the pad to open it, and ducked another blade that landed somewhere in the darkened interior of the garage. If he could just reach the back—

He did, falling to his knees beside his goal, as the Sidhe came charging through the door behind him. Sam glanced over his shoulder, seeing only the upraised arms, and that black and glittering sword.

ThankyouMotherMary— Sam reached for the switch on the powerful box-fan in the middle of the floor with one hand, and the loosely wrapped packet of iron filings in his pocket with the other.

Just then the Sidhe spotted him, crouched on the floor. The enemy shouted with triumph, cries audible even over the sirens from Sam's alarm system, and raised his sword.

Sam switched on the fan, ripped the bag out of his pocket and dumped the double-handful of iron filings into the wind of its blades.

Howls of triumph changed abruptly to cries of pain, as thousands of tiny lances of Cold Iron bit into the Sidhe's face and hands, penetrating and catching even in its garments.

The Sidhe cried out again, threw his hands up to shield his face, and dropped the sword, which shattered into a thousand glassy bits on the concrete floor. Sam snarled, and rose to his feet, reaching blindly to the tool rack on the back wall, his breath wheezing in his lungs, his face still streaming tears.

Sam grabbed the first thing that came to hand; a solid, antique metal T-square, old and heavy enough to be made of steel.

He charged the Sidhe, swinging the implement viciously, like one of his peasant ancestors with a scythe. The Sidhe broke and ran, and Sam pursued, still swinging, to the end of his driveway. There he had to stop, for his lungs and legs both gave out—though he screamed hoarse curses at his enemy right up until the police first arrived in response to the commotion.

Neither Vidal nor the Bane-Sidhe were anywhere in the studio complex, which suited Aurilia just fine. She had work to do, and she couldn't do it if they were hanging around the studio or even the area of Underhill that had been sculpted to hold it. All they ever did was laze about, doing nothing useful, whining about some imagined grievance or other. Making constructs was tedious, exacting work, and she couldn't do it if there was someone distracting her, critiquing her, generally getting in the way.

The grunt work, of making the blanks, had already been done for her by an Unseleighe-mage who had gotten to play Messelina in the Caligula piece, trading work for the privilege of participation in their epic and a share in the results. They waited for her in their boxes in the Underhill workshop, in a work area Aurilia had pretty much to herself most of the time. The other two couldn't be bothered with sculpting constructs; Aurilia considered herself something of an artist in that area. It took skill to create something that would fool the clients into thinking it was a human being; skill and attention to detail. The latter required a patience neither Vidal nor Niall had, for all that they were powerful mages.

She hadn't planned on building her "extras" for another week, but the discoveries of this evening changed all that. She was working with a limited window of opportunity. Before too long, Tannim would extract his little pavement princess from her surroundings and get her away to safety. If he didn't succeed in that, the girl might be murdered by her own stupidity, or the kids might connect Adder's Fork with the young hookers who had already disappeared. The entire schedule for shooting "Deadly Doctor" would have to be moved up if Aurilia was going to be able to extract the maximum value from the potentials of the situation. That would take a lot of work on her part, but the end result would be worth it.

She opened the first coffinlike box. The creature waiting inside was not "alive" in the strictest sense. It was shaped rather like a store-front mannequin, the modern kind that was utterly featureless, with no eyes, ears, nose, mouth, or other orifices, just a blank face-shaped area. No hair yet, either, and it didn't breathe. If you cut it right now, it wouldn't bleed, for it had no circulatory system. It took all of its nourishment passively, like a plant, from the energy Aurilia channeled into it. If Aurilia didn't use it or feed it, within a month it would die of starvation and never even whimper in pain.

This construct was destined for another fate, however; one it would never understand.

Aurilia had already selected personas for this batch of constructs, and had clipped the pictures she wanted to use to the top of each box. This one would be a "Victorian

Street Sparrow"; Aurilia's term for the underage thieves, pickpockets, and prostitutes that used to throng London's working-class districts.

And humans treat teenage prostitution as if it's something new because now there are mortals with PhDs writing about it.

She took the picture of the full-face shot in her right hand, and placed her left on the construct-blank's chest. The flesh was warm, but a little rubbery under her hand—and much too smooth to be human. That was all right; the clients weren't going to be paying much attention to the skin, after all. If it looked too perfect, they'd assume it was makeup or lighting.

The face would be the first; it was the hardest. She chanted the first words of the spell, calling into being the features in the photograph she held: square chin, slightly undershot jaw, petulant lips. The flesh writhed and obeyed her, clearing away from jawline and neck, mounding up to form the lips, cheeks, and chin. The nose was next; nothing hard there, since the basic shape was already in place. Then the eye area. But there were no eyes there yet; the lids closed over round, featureless balls at the moment.

She selected another photograph and chanted to the body, giving it high, small breasts, a slightly protruding belly as if it was a little bit pregnant, broad hips. Then she sang hair into being, head and pubic; she had intended brown, but it grew up auburn. She decided to leave it the way it was. Sometimes the constructs took on slightly different characteristics than she had intended, though she never knew why.

What she had done up until now was pure sculpture. Now began the hard part; the part that required kenning. She removed her hands from the construct, and flexed them, then cupped them over the body in the box.

She sank herself into deep awareness and her chant changed; the rhythm pattern shifted, until it replicated the beat of the human heart. The words shifted, too, becoming heavier, more potent in sound if nothing else.

But they were potent in other ways.

Now the skin of the construct heaved and rippled, as

beneath it, Aurilia created organs, bones, and a primitive nervous and circulatory system. The latter didn't have to actually do any work; its main job was to carry "blood" to places where the construct was going to be hurt. If Aurilia hadn't been in so much of a hurry, she could have created an exact duplicate of a human, something that would stand up to anything but a tissue analysis—but there was no point in being that thorough.

In the old days, that was why so many changelings sickened and died; no mater what they were fed, the food didn't nourish them and they wasted away. Why create something well made? We wanted the changelings to die. So did the Seleighe fools, though for entirely different reasons. . . .

Lungs were made the same way; mere bellows to simulate breathing and provide air for speaking and screaming. However; the construct *did* need a good pain-nerve net; it was going to have to react appropriately to painful stimuli. That meant a basic spine and some brain functions.

Within an hour, she had her "extra"; one of the creatures destined to die in front of the camera. She'd created dozens of constructs in her time; so long as the raw material was there, it was no strain anymore.

Bending over the box for a close look, she made the creature blink, simulate a variety of expressions, breathe. She fished a long, slender crystal from a pouch at her waist. It looked like a half-melted icicle, but was warm to the touch. This was the key to making her "extras" truly convincing; it was a condensed memory-crystal, containing the reactions of every human who had ever been inside either of the studios. She placed it point-down on the construct's forehead, and pushed it into the "brain." When her palm touched the skin of the forehead, the eyes suddenly snapped open.

The construct screamed itself awake.

She hushed it with a word and a motion.

The creature blinked, looked at her—and cowered away.

Satisfied, she put it to sleep with a thought, closed the lid on the creature's "coffin" and moved on to the next box.

She was half done when Vidal entered the complex, so immersed in her creations that she honestly didn't notice he was there until he knocked something over in the Studio Two bathroom and it broke. That startled her and broke her concentration, and she sensed his presence. She waited impatiently for him to put in an appearance and disrupt her work.

But he didn't; in fact, he stayed right where he was. She heard him moving about the bathroom, but very slowly—unnaturally so.

What on earth is wrong?

She finally left the workroom, too puzzled to continue working. When she entered Studio Two, she realized that the sound she had attributed to the background of disturbing noises that was a constant in the Underhill chaoslands was actually nothing of the sort; it was the sound of Vidal moaning.

She strode over to the bathroom door, her high-heels clicking on the stone of the floor, and jerked the bathroom door open.

She had half expected to find the Sidhe drunk, or otherwise incapacitated with self-indulgence. She certainly did not expect to find him wounded, bleeding, and suffering from Cold Iron poisoning. His face looked like a bloodied sponge.

"By the dark moon!" she exclaimed, shocked, and too startled to keep from showing it. "What happened to you?"

Vidal just groaned. She clamped her mouth shut on further questions, kicked off her shoes, and used the last of her energies to conjure handfuls of silk and bone instruments, tweezers and probes.

When she was finished, Vidal lay on the couch in the old Roman set, swathed in bandages, and she had a blood-stained, silk-wrapped bundle containing a handful of tiny iron fragments. She would have to take it across the Gate into the human side to dispose of it.

She shoved it aside for the moment with her foot. "What happened?" she asked flatly, fearing that Vidal had done something irrevocable. "I thought you and Niall were harassing Keighvin, I thought you'd issued a challenge—"

"We were," Vidal said, after a long moment of silence.
"We were. But the bastard brought the humans into it,
and the humans brought their own weapons. One of them
got Niall with blessed water—the *old* blessing, the touch
of the sun and the full of the moon—"

"*What?*" she exclaimed. "I didn't think anyone knew that
this side of the ocean! Did he—"

"He's all right," Vidal said, sullenly. "He didn't get hit
with a great deal, and I managed to get him back Underhill
before it did too much damage to him. I—"

The shiver of Power behind her warned her of Niall's
approach. "He did the best he could," the Bane-Sidhe said
hoarsely, as she whirled on her knees to face him. Filmy
white rags—much cleaner than they had been—fluttered
as the creature gestured expansively. The charnel odor
wasn't as bad, either.

*Too bad he doesn't get doused with holy water more
often.*

"He did more than most. I pledged my full power if
he could remove the mortal beast that struck me down.
I had come to see if you had triumphed," Niall concluded.

"It was wiser than I had thought," Vidal said bitterly,
raising himself up onto one elbow. "It was craftier."

A hiss of rage emerged from the hood cloaking the
Bane-Sidhe's features. "So I see," it replied.

Aurilia held her breath. Uppermost in her mind was the
fear that now the Bane-Sidhe would revoke its promise.
Without Niall's aid and magic, she would not be able to
restrain Vidal Dhu. He would fling himself at Keighvin's
pet mortals until they destroyed him—and with him, her
plans for vengeance.

The Bane-Sidhe raised itself up to its full height. Aurilia
shrank into herself; Niall towered over her, emanating a
kind of cold hatred. He seemed to pull all the light into
himself—the very air grew dark, thick, and oppressive,
while he himself glowed a faint, leprous blue-white. She
shivered, and her breath caught in her throat. She had
never experienced Niall's full power before this, and now
she understood why mortals died of fright on simply seeing
him.

"This cannot be borne," Niall said hollowly. "Mortals have never confronted us and won. This cannot be permitted. If more of them discover our weaknesses, they may learn also how to travel Underhill and confront us here as well."

That had never occurred to her; and the thought was as chilling as the full effect of the Bane-Sidhe's Presence.

Then she realized what Niall had not said. He was not removing himself and his power from their alliance. He was not insisting that they leave Keighvin and Fairgrove alone. In fact, he seemed to be advocating the very opposite. "But—" she began, feebly.

The cowl bent to regard her, and she shivered again. "We must eliminate Keighvin Silverhair and his mortal allies," the Bane-Sidhe said grimly. "He is the champion of those of the Seleighe Court who wish to integrate their society with that of the mortals. That must not be! I pledge to you, I shall drain every drop of my power to see him defeated and destroyed!"

"But we must be careful," she replied, quickly.

Niall paused for a moment, and then sighed, shrinking back to his normal size as he exhaled, releasing the light. Aurilia sighed with him, but with relief. If she never had to face the Bane-Sidhe in his anger again, it would be perfectly fine with her. "We must be careful," Niall agreed. "Our present state is the direct result of carelessness and overconfidence."

Vidal grunted; Aurilia assumed it was in grudging agreement.

"Thus far," Niall continued, shifting from side to side, restlessly, "the only one of the three of us who has brought plans to fruition scathlessly is you."

"Well," she replied, with a certain amount of hesitation, "I don't know about that."

If Vidal gets his nose out of joint about this—

"The Bane-Sidhe is right," Vidal growled. "It will take the three of us to achieve our goals, working together. We cannot afford to hare off with separate plans."

It's about time you figured that out, she thought sourly. *After all the work I've put in here.*

"Since you have been working here for hours, I assume you *have* a plan," Niall said pointedly.

Now, if ever, was the time to seize leadership, while momentum was behind her. Vidal was temporarily incapacitated and might be influenced; the Bane-Sidhe was already on her side, She gathered her composure, steadied her nerves, and nodded with all the authority she could command.

"Yes," she said. "I do."

CHAPTER ELEVEN

Tannim woke three or four times during the night as random sounds threw him out of dreams, but that was all that they were, pure random sounds, and he drifted back into sleep again. When he finally woke for good, he lay watching the darkness for a while, thinking about getting up for a long time before doing anything about it. Bed felt wonderful, and he wished, selfishly, that he could stay there for the rest of the day. He felt rested, and at the same time, tired—as if he had gone off sleep-fighting, or something. He'd had some strange dreams last night; images of fairy-tale bogeymen mixed up with a Tokomak accelerator, of Nightmares getting hit with Cruise missiles and exploding, and of Sam on a S.W.A.T. team, guarding a rainbow.

Weird.

There was no light at all in the bedroom, other than the clock on the VCR. The lighted numerals said 4:23—which meant it was about eleven. He hated having the damn thing blinking "12:00" at him, so he always reset it to some arbitrary time whenever the power went off or he had to unplug it.

There didn't seem to be any windows in the room. There was one, but he also hated daylight, which was why the floor-to-ceiling headboard blocked the window entirely, so that nothing could leak through.

So, it was about eleven. If he got up now, he could shower, shave, eat—pick out an appropriate outfit—and by one, when the people he wanted to see were in their offices, he'd be ready to see them.

He ran a systems-check on himself, first. About the only thing still not right was his leg, which twinged a little when he flexed it. It had healed about as much as it was likely to, so it always felt like that, except when he was in a hot-tub, so he ignored it and reached for the light in the headboard.

He fumbled around a little before his hand encountered the proper little round knob. It was on a dimmer-switch, which he brought up in microscopic increments. His last live-in lover had hated that, insisting on having bright light instantly in the morning. It was one of the reasons they hadn't stayed lovers for long, although they had parted friends.

His stomach growled impatiently, reminding him that it had been a long time since lunch—most of which he'd pushed off on Tania—and that corn-chips and vitamins were not an adequate substitute for dinner. Chinthliss railed on him constantly about his admittedly horrible diet. He pried himself up out of the bed and headed for the bathroom.

Being a mage means you're never out of hot water. . . .

One very long, very hot shower later, he felt a little more like a human, but not up to choosing clothing. Magery was a very diverse avocation, and some mages could change their form with a thought—but Tannim was not one of them, and so clothing was the closest to shape-changing he was going to get on this world. His choice of garments today would make all the difference in the success of his still-nebulous plan, if he was going to get the maximum clout with a minimum of questioning. He put off the decision and pulled a Salvation Army print caftan over his head. Making a selection that important should be done on a full stomach. Time to invoke the spirit of the microwave.

His last lover *had* been an excellent cook, and had left the freezer full of marvelous microwavable goodies for him, knowing that he would never cook for himself, and knowing that he often forgot to shop as well. Tannim had been making them last for a while, but now, if ever, was the time to dip into the stash. He poked his head into the freezer and contemplated the neatly calligraphed labels.

Calzone, Chicken Kiev, Veal Scaloppini, Chicken Cordon Bleu, Gad. Eggplant Parmesan, ick. That can't have been meant for me. Unless I was out of everything else and couldn't move. Maybe that was the idea. Ah, Huevos Rancheros. Perfect. But it needs something to go with it. Should end in a vowel . . . There, three-cheese zucchini. That'll do.

The microwave *beeped* five minutes later, and he fished clean dishes out of the dishwasher, poured himself a big glass of Gatorade, plucked an old t-shirt off the back of a chair and wrapped it around his hand, then pulled his breakfast out of the nuker. He took a forkful and blew on it to cool it, while he stared at the Ninja Turtles cavorting on his glass for a moment. *Maybe that's what I can tell my mother about what happened to the leg. "There was this glowing ooze, Mom, and—"* Nah. *She's probably seen the movies.*

Besides, right now he shouldn't be thinking about how to explain his scars to his mom. What he really needed was to figure out a persona for his meeting with the shelter directors. Something where he could plausibly fling money at them with a condition attached. They might not care for the condition—that they take in Tania (and her friends, if he could get them to come in with her) with no questions asked, and no pressure on any of them to contact parents. Counseling, yes; pressure, no.

And no sneaking off behind their backs, either. Whatever drove those other kids into hooking, it had to be worse than hooking. If it was, I'm not going to let them go back to it. Tania's folks were trying to make her into a good little Type-A overachiever drone by killing her spirit and imagination. She seems pretty sure it was worse for her than hooking. I don't know if they've learned their lesson yet, since she ran off, and I won't send her back to them until they have.

Getting them into a shelter would get them off the street long enough for Keighvin to clear up the little war with Vidal Dhu. Once that was taken care of, they could all go Underhill while Keighvin's spies found out whether the various parents were worthy of the privilege of having children. If not—Underhill they stayed, like half the humans at Fairgrove.

But meanwhile there was that matter of keeping them safe for a couple of weeks. The way he had it figured, if he threw enough cash at one of the shelters, more than enough to pay for the keep of Tania and all of her friends, they'd take in the strays just as fast as he could deliver them. The shelters were hard up for support; they couldn't afford to turn him down. But he needed that persona to make the offer.

It can't be a Suit. They'd smell Corporation and want to know too much, maybe get greedy, certainly want to see some I.D., which I don't have—except for Fairgrove, and I don't want to leave that kind of trail for Vidal Dhu to find. It can't be my usual look, or they'll want to know where I got all the cash, maybe call the cops on me, figuring me for a pimp or a pusher trying to recruit on their turf, or dumping some poor kid too gone to be useful anymore. He finished his breakfast quickly, hardly tasting it. Then he gulped the last of the Gatorade and went back into the bedroom, flung himself down on the bed, and turned it into a lounge chair while he pondered.

Teacher? No, where would a teacher get that kind of money? That lets out cop or social worker too, plus they'd want to see credentials; ditto psychiatrist or grad student doing research. I could try forging credentials, but if they double-checked, they'd find out I was phony.

He idly flicked on the TV to fill the silence; it was set on MTV already, and the picture and sound came up in the middle of the old "Take On Me" video from A-Ha, where the girl and her comic-book lover are being chased by the comic-book bad-guys. It was one of Tannim's favorites.

Now if life were just like a comic book—

Then it hit him. The perfect answer. He jumped out

of bed and ran to the closet, ignoring the protests of his left leg, and dug through the jeans and soft cotton shirts until he came to an outfit he'd only worn once. He dug it out, and looked at it, then smiled.

Perfect.

Tannim lounged at his ease in the shabby waiting-room, his clothing at violent odds with the tacky plastic sofas. A young woman in her early twenties, with no makeup and her brown hair in a wash-and-wear bob eyed him warily from behind the shelter of her beat-up gray metal desk.

This was the first shelter on his list; the best, the cleanest, and the one least inclined to put pressure on kids. There were rules: you had to go to school, stay clean and off the street, do your homework, pass your courses. There were rules about boy- and girl-friends (group dates only), extra-curricular activities (supervised only), and sex (none). The kids got straightforward lessons in sex-education, and a thorough medical exam when they came in, including the HIV test. They had to spend time with a counselor every day. But if a kid couldn't bring himself to actually talk, he didn't have to—there were counselors who spent whole hours with utterly silent kids every damn day.

And the kids didn't have to give their real names until they wanted to. A big plus in Tannim's book. Understandably, this was the shelter with the longest waiting list. If they wouldn't go for his little bribe—well, then he'd try the next, then the next. . . .

If none of them swallowed the bait, he'd hit Keighvin up for some duplicated gold coins, cash them in with a collector who knew him, and come back to try again, with a new set of clothing, a new face, and a new story. Sooner or later, somebody was going to get bought.

Just as long as they're getting bought for a good cause, taking my conditions to have a chance to help more kids.

He settled the shoulders of his dark-red, full-length rayon jacket over his black silk shirt a little self-consciously. This was a lot more flash than he usually wore. So were the heavy silver-and-turquoise choker and matching *ketoh* bracelet and concho belt. Those he usually didn't wear at all except to pow-wows or when he was with Mike Fighting Eagle and the rest of his blood-brothers out in Arizona.

He watched the young woman at the desk without seeming to look at her; it was easy enough, since she couldn't see his eyes through his Ray-Bans. She was a little nonplussed by his appearance; she obviously wasn't used to having close to a thousand bucks worth of clothing stroll up to the door of Shelter House unless it was a pimp looking for a stray. She scraped the legs of her plastic patio chair noisily against the worn brown linoleum as she tried to find a comfortable way to sit.

Little does she know everything on my back was either conjured by elves or a gift. Never thought this outfit would come in handy a second time.

"Mr. Cleveland will see you now, Mr.—ah—Burgundy," the case-worker currently manning the front-desk said, with only the slightest hesitation. Tannim walked past her into the equally shabby, but pleasant, office. The window blinds were wide open to the sunlight, and there were plants in clumsy, handmade pots on the sill. The wallpaper had faded until the yellow roses were a pale cream, and the leaves a ghost of emerald. The decor was Goodwill-reject; the art on the walls was all posters, posters of rock, sports, and movie stars urging kids to stay in school, to stay off drugs, and to read. The notepad was a giveaway from FedEx, and the letterhead stationery on the man's desk had been printed upon a very spotty dot-matrix printer, probably donated. Obviously this place wasn't wasting money on gold-embossed stationery and collector artwork—or even interior decorating. The dark, harried-looking man behind the desk stood up, surprise flashing briefly across his face before he covered it with a smile. Obviously he wasn't used to seeing clothing like Tannim's, either. He reached a hand across the desk to Tannim. "Alyx Burgundy," Tannim said, taking the hand immediately, and shaking it.

"Harold Cleveland," the director replied, with an equally firm handshake. "What can we do for you, Mr. Burgundy?"

Tannim sat down in one of the three visitors' chairs. Vinyl with an aluminum frame, they were as uncomfortable as they looked. "Mr. Cleveland, my boss sent me over here on his behalf. He's a horribly busy man, but he has the best of intentions. I'm sure you'll understand my being direct. I've got a donation with some strings attached."

Harold Cleveland eyed him with some suspicion. "What kind of strings?" he asked.

Tannim shrugged. "My boss wants to make sure that a little girl and maybe a couple of her friends have a safe place to go. You've got a waiting list—by the time you got around to them, they might be in real trouble. But— you also need money. My boss is very well-known in the music business, and very, very wealthy. He and the girl met after one of his shows, and they started talking. He likes her." Tannim paused for effect. "We'll take care of that money problem you've got right now if you'll move her and her friends to the top of the list." He presented the envelope of cash he'd withdrawn from his bank earlier, and fanned its contents on the desk—a thick stack of fifties and hundreds.

Harold blanched as he ran a quick mental count. Emotions warred on his face, and his hand flinched towards the money.

But the man had integrity. "I don't know," he said, slowly, controlling his immediate impulse. "I'd like to say yes—but we *do* have a waiting list. And I don't know where this money is coming from. . . ." He narrowed his eyes. "If your boss has this much to play around with, why isn't he taking care of this girl himself? Just because we're a charity, that doesn't mean we have no rules and no standards. If I may be so forward, Mr. Burgundy, why is he wanting *us* to take this girl in?"

Tannim sighed, as if exasperated. "My boss—and I'm sure you understand that I cannot reveal his identity—is in no position to do so. It's because she's underage—and as you probably figured out for yourself, right now, she's an underage hooker. My boss is in the public eye—every moment, you might say—and whenever he turns around there's somebody trying to come up with some kind of dirt on him. He feels sorry for the girl, but he can't risk some cop—or a smear sheet—putting two and two together and coming up with 'contributing to the delinquency of a minor' when all he wants to do is get her off the street and back in school."

He allowed his eyes to flicker up to one of the posters behind Cleveland's desk. There were several rock-music idols up there—but only one group was on tour in the area. He watched as Cleveland's eyes followed his "slip," and felt a bit of satisfaction as the man's mouth softened a moment. Good. Tannim hadn't lied. Let the man make his own conclusions—even if they were wrong. Given *that* particular star's reputation as a good-guy, Cleveland should now be very sympathetic. "The guy wants to get a good kid out of a bad situation, but you know what the tabloids would say if they found out."

He grimaced, and Harold Cleveland nodded.

"I see. This is a most . . . unusual proposal, Mr. Burgundy. On one hand, it's hardly fair to the children waiting that we take your three ahead of them. On the other hand, with just the money you have here—" he touched the stack "—we could afford to take in your three and a half-dozen more for a couple of months."

Tannim could see by his aura that he'd accepted the offer. Now it was only a matter of completing the dance.

"Mr. Cleveland, I appreciate your position. It's a tough call." He shrugged, making it look helpless.

Harold Cleveland sighed. "I don't see how we could refuse, Mr. Burgundy. We've got no money to speak of, really. Too few donations, and the problems are getting worse. We'll take the offer."

Tannim nodded, then bowed his head.

"Good. Good. Her name is Tania, and she will be here with her friends within the next couple of days. I hope. She will have a lot to talk about—but nothing relating to my boss." He handed over a small polaroid. "If your outreach workers see her, I'd appreciate it if they talk to her. She might be shy about coming."

"Sworn to secrecy, I assume? To protect his reputation?"

Tannim looked back up, through the Ray-Bans.

"My boss is also my friend. When it comes to kids, he's a pushover. He's spent his life trying to understand them, and be like them, and make things easier for them. He said before I came over that he had a good feeling about this place. I am constantly amazed at his faith in human nature. Times like this—" he said, palming from a pocket "—I understand why. Thank you for being suspicious, Harold, and for being kind. This one's from me."

Tannim left a paper-clipped roll of twenties, stood and smoothed the jacket, and walked out smiling.

Tannim swung himself into his driver's seat, and indulged himself in a moment of self-satisfaction. *So much for Part One of Plan A. Now for Part Two.*

He closed the door and sat quietly in the Mustang for a moment, searching for a particular energy track, drawing on the energies stored in the car and on the faint traces still lingering about the passenger's seat. Negotiating with Harold Cleveland had taken longer than he expected, though it had been worth every second spent. Cleveland's outreach people would be looking for Tania now, as they made their rounds of Savannah. If they spotted her, they'd try to make contact and tell her there was a bunk for her and her friends. Tannim really didn't think they'd spot her before he found her, but there was always a chance, and one he couldn't pass up.

Sunset created a brilliant sky right out of a Maxfield Parrish painting over the marshes to the west. He sought through a maze of energy patterns as brightly and as subtly colored as the patterns in the sky, searching and discarding—

Then he found it; less red-tinged than before, and shading more towards the blue of intellect and acceptance, and away from the vermilion of anger and unreasoning emotion. But full of the warm gold of earthy good sense, too, which hadn't showed before, and the tingle of humor—

Tannim started the car, and pulled out of his parking place, which was filled as soon as the Mustang's tail cleared it He scarcely noticed; he was too intent on tracing that energy trail back to its source, in the real world as well as in the spirit world. It wound through all the other traces, touching briefly at River Street before drifting on, heading off past the edge of Savannah.

After a little while, he got a sense of distance as well as direction, and realized where the trace was leading him. *Oatland Island, huh? Never figured Ross for a wildlife fancier. But then, I never picked him for a punster, either.*

Now that he knew where he was going, he was able to take a more direct route than following the trace through Savannah. By full dark, he was at the gates of the Oatland Island Education Center, parking before the carved wooden sign. A little conspicuous—but that could be remedied.

He turned off the engine and got out of the car; placed his hands palm-down on the warm fender, and frowned with concentration, activating one of the permanent spells that was as much a part of the Mustang now as its paint. He straightened after a moment, satisfied that the eyes of any passerby would simply slide right over the car without ever noticing it was there. That spell—which he had dubbed "Hide In Plain Sight"—was one of the most useful he'd ever come up with.

He stretched, flexing finger and neck muscles, taking deep breaths of the cool, sweet, air. Ross Canfield wasn't likely to be as hard-nosed a negotiator as Harold Cleveland; with luck, he could get this over quickly and get back to Fairgrove before Keighvin started to get annoyed.

He pulled a sucker from the inner pocket of the expensive jacket, unwrapped it, and tucked the cellophane back into the pocket before stowing the candy in his cheek. The flavor startled him for a moment. *Pina-colada? Where'd I—oh, that's right. Donal thought I ought to have fancy suckers to match the jacket. Elves.*

He sat himself cross-legged on the warm hood while the crickets chirred in the grass beside the road, glad that the pants were a practical set of Bugle Boys instead of the unwashable dress-slacks Donal had wanted to put him into. One snag, and they'd have been ruined—

He relaxed all over, and began a low chant, drawing more power up from the stores invested in the Mustang. He had no intention of going for a spirit-walk this time, though. Not tonight, especially now that Vidal Dhu and company knew he was a player in the game. This time, all he intended to do was to call, sending out a very specific identity-sign along a specific trace. And if Ross Canfield was still willing to keep that promise he'd made—

The crickets stopped chirping. "Didja know that bluejays sing like damn canaries?" said a gleeful voice in his ear. Tannim jumped.

"Uh—" he said, cleverly, telling his rattled nerves that this had *not* been an attack and he didn't *need* all that adrenalin, thank you. And no point in yelling at Ross; the spirit didn't know about Vidal Dhu's vendetta, or that Tannim was one of his planned targets. "No, Ross, I didn't. I thought all they did was scream."

Ross sat himself down on the hood beside Tannim, a big grin on his face, oblivious to the shaking he'd just given the young mage. "They do," Ross said gleefully, as if he were imparting the greatest wisdom of the universe. "And starlings are 'bout the only birds that'll eat Junebugs an' Jap'nese beetles, an' bears have their cubs while they're hibernatin', an' there useta be cougars around here, an' gray foxes c'n climb trees—"

"Whoa!" Tannim held up his hand. "Now I know why you were hanging out here! Ross, why the sudden interest in wildlife? Or is it sudden?"

Ross grinned, not at all embarrassed. "Always wanted t' be a Park Ranger when I was a kid, but they gotta have college degrees an' my folks couldn't afford college. So—" He shrugged, then brightened. "Now, shoot, I can walk right up t' birds, sit practically on their tails an' watch 'em—found out about this place an' been hanging around listening t' everything. Better'n goin' t' college, 'cause there's nobody givin' tests! So, what can I do for you? I don't s'ppose this is a social call. Some'a my new buddies know you pretty good, an' they told me that when you said you was kinda busy, you weren't tellin' more'n half the truth."

Tannim blushed, unaccountably embarrassed. "Yeah, well, you can't believe all you hear, either. But no, this isn't a social call, I'm sorry to say. Wish it was, actually. I've got a favor to ask you."

Ross scratched his head, and Tannim noticed that he looked a lot younger—and definitely slimmer—than the last time they'd met. He'd noticed that effect before, with spirits that had adjusted well.

Being a ghost seems to be agreeing with him.

"Ask away," the ghost said. "I told you, I owe you."

"I don't know, Ross," Tannim replied slowly. "You might not want to do it once you've heard what it's all about."

"Try me," Ross suggested, and sat patiently while Tannim explained everything he knew about Tania, the trouble she was in, and how he needed someone to keep a close eye on her until he could get her into the shelter, and from there, to Keighvin and Fairgrove.

Everything was fine until Tannim worked up to telling Ross that the girl was a runaway—and a hooker. Then the ghost frowned, and scratched his head again. "I don't know, Tannim," he said, reluctantly, and Tannim's hope slipped a little. "I mean, that's the kinda kid I'd've said was a punk an' a tramp—before—but—"

That "before" gave Tannim reason to let his hopes rise again. "But?" he prompted.

Ross wrinkled his brow. "Well—I kinda found out somethin'. I can kinda see when people get worked up. I found out there's a lotta things goin' on, stuff I useta think were just media people makin' up stories t' sell papers. Lotsa kids in trouble out there, Tannim. Heard a couple of stories from ones that wound up—out here. They didn't have a reason t' make things up, y'know?"

Tannim nodded; Ross had changed, in more ways than showed in his aura. "She's not mixed up with drugs, Ross— and I don't think she will be—voluntarily. But if she gets picked up by a pimp before I can find her and talk her into the shelter—"

Ross scowled. "Yeah. That's what one of them kids out here said. Damn pimp picked her up at the bus stop, made all friendly, gave her what she thought was just grass—next thing she knows, she's hooked on crack with the bastard sellin' her for a hundred bucks a shot an' makin' her do all kindsa pervo kinky stuff—" He shook his head, and his aura swung into the bright, clear red of suppressed and controlled anger, anger carefully focused. Genuinely righteous wrath. "If I could make a ghost outa *that* bastard, I would."

"So would I," Tannim said sincerely. "I know it's not a lot of comfort—but you ever noticed there aren't a lot of *old* pimps and pushers? His lifestyle is real likely to get him killed—and Ross, when *he* comes over to your side, there are going to be a lot of things waiting for him. Remember what I told you about things that might try to eat you? Well, they think that low-lifes like him are mighty tasty, and they'll actually hang around, waiting, on the off chance that somebody'll put a hole in him."

"So that's what they were doin'—" Ross mused, half to himself. Then he shook his head. "Okay, Tannim, I'll see if I c'n find this girl an' keep an eye on her for you—though I don' know what help I could be if she got into trouble."

Tannim folded his arms over his chest, and grinned. "More help than you think, Ross. You been practicing what I told you about affecting the real world?"

Ross nodded. "Been learnin' some. Ain't fallin' through the hood, am I?" he replied, with a chuckle. "But that's *me* lettin' the real world affect *me*. When it comes t'me actually doin' things, I can't do much more'n flip a bottlecap."

"That could be enough," Tannim told him. "One thing you could do, you could come get me if the kid's in trouble. If you can't get me," he paused as he called up an image of Sam from an open palm, "you go to this man. His name is Sam Kelly, and he's a friend. He should be able to see you. But remember—not everybody can. Moving a bottlecap at the right time could make a big difference; you just have to start thinking on your feet."

"Easy for you to say," Ross grumbled, but he was smiling a little when he said it.

Tannim let out the breath he'd been holding in a sigh of relief. "Thanks, Ross," he said, sincerely. "When this is over and Tania's safe, I'll owe you."

But Ross shook his head emphatically. "No way, partner. I think I got one thing figgered. You kinda gotta earn your way upstairs. I didn' earn it when I was alive, so now I gotta do somethin' about it. What'd *you* think?"

Tannim had to shake his head, laughing. "Damn if I

know. Never had a chance to talk to somebody who'd been there."

Ross laughed. "Well, if I turn up missin' when all this is over, you can figure I was right, huh? So show me what this kid looks like, and I'll get outta here."

Tannim called forth an image of Tania as he had last seen her and projected it into the spirit world. Bad bleach-job, too much makeup, Spandex shorts, and all. Ross studied the image for a moment, then nodded, and Tannim let it evaporate.

"Poor kid," the ghost commented. "Looks like trouble lookin' for a place t' happen."

"Yeah," Tannim said. "That's what I figured. Oh, and another thing. I have friends at the police department I give tip-offs to. You see anything from your side I could use, let me know."

Ross nodded, paused for a moment, then said, "Done. Well, I'm outta here. Got what I need. See you later, Tannim."

And with that, he was gone, instantly. Tannim stared at the place he had been, and snorted. The crickets started back up again.

" 'Been learnin' some,' my ass! That was a teleport, or I'm the Pope!" Then he chuckled. "Ross, you're a good man, and a sneaky bastard. Glad you're on my side."

Tannim stretched again, climbed down off the hood, started the Mustang and drove off into the night, heading for Fairgrove, and another set of duties.

Now if he could just keep them from becoming conflicting duties. . . .

Ross Canfield hadn't teleported, no matter what Tannim thought. He'd *translated*—or at least that was what The Old Man had called it, explaining that the literal meaning of "translate" was "to change one thing into another." What Ross had done was to change from being partially in the real world, to being completely in the spirit world. Or, one of the spirit worlds, anyway; he'd gotten the feeling from The Old Man that there was more than one, but this was the place that folks that were something like him

wound up, until they were ready to go off elsewhere.
Whatever, wherever "elsewhere" was. The Old Man
wouldn't say anything more about that than Tannim would.
Ross had started to think of it as being like tuning a radio
station—sometimes you were right on the frequency, sometimes you drifted between them.

It was a peculiar sort of "place," not really a place at
all. But it was a lot easier to find other ghosts from here.
It was no use looking for The Old Man, though; Ross never
found *him*, he found Ross, when and where he chose.
Sometimes he taught Ross things; sometimes he just said
something that only made sense a lot later. Sort of like
that David Carradine movie his wife had liked so much.
Ross was even starting to understand that now, though
every time she'd played it on the VCR when he'd been
alive, he'd gotten mad, 'cause it didn't make any damned
sense.

He'd figured on doing what Tannim had suggested,
looking her up, trying to come to terms with what had
happened. And he'd run into her all right, but not when
and where he'd expected. Turned out she was married to
Marty now, looked happier and younger, more like the girl
he'd married, and she had a kid, a little baby, about six
months old. He hadn't thought he'd be able to forgive
either of them, but they'd shown up at his grave and left
flowers—

That was where he'd first seen them, as he was standing
by the headstone, wondering what he should do next. It
had been kind of a shock; he'd just stood there, staring
at them, while they left the flowers and talked about him.
And they hadn't said anything mean or spiteful, either. He'd
listened to them for a long time, and had to conclude that
the girl he'd thought he'd married, and the one he really
had married, had been two different people.

He'd felt a lot better when he'd realized that, as if he'd
got rid of a poison that had been in him. That was the
first time The Old Man showed up, right after they left;
taught him a couple of things, like how to *translate*, and
vanished again. He'd left the grave and hadn't looked back.

Right now, Ross was looking for Vanessa, the kid-hooker

he'd told Tannim about. He figured that if anyone knew where the other hookers would be operating, it would be her. Once he knew the streets to look on, he'd be a lot likelier to find this Tania kid.

When he'd first run into Vanessa, she'd been scared as a little baby bunny, with some of the annoying things that liked to pick on the weak and the frightened mobbing her. The damn things were cowards, even if they did look like some kind of deep-sea horror, and he and his new buddy Foxtrot Xray had scared them off. He wasn't sure what Fox was; he was native to the spirit world, and he changed his appearance all the time, sometimes more-or-less human looking, sometimes no more human than a ball of light. Called himself by that name 'cause it was military-talk for FX, and since he was kind of a spirit-soldier and kind of a special effect, it fit.

He wished he could enlist Fox's help on guarding Tania, but it wasn't Fox's kind of thing. Oh, Fox would be willing enough, but he could only operate in the spirit world, though, so he wasn't going to be any use on this job.

Not like when they'd found Vanessa under siege, and he and Fox had chased off the bullies. Ross had stayed around to give Vanessa a hand, and a shoulder to cry on; taught her about being newly-dead, like Tannim had done for him, and how it wasn't so bad.

He sometimes wondered if she thought of *him* as The Old Man. Maybe for her, he was.

Moving around in the spirit world was pretty easy; you just had to think of who you wanted to be with, and unless they had you blocked out (which you did by thinking you wanted to be alone and felt like putting up walls), you were there. He found her wistfully hanging around a radio-station control-room, watching the DJ and listening to the music. He wrinkled his nose a little; not his kind of music at all, but it was making her happy, so what the hell.

"Hey, Vanessa," he said, quietly, so as not to startle her. She startled easily.

She looked up, big brown eyes wide, from under an unkempt mane of raven-black curls, her aura draining to muddy yellow-green. There was fear in her eyes which quickly faded, and she smiled shyly, the colors of her aura coming back. "Hi, Mr. Canfield," she said diffidently. "Mr. Xray, he was here an' showed me how t' find the radio station when I said I missed rock'n'roll."

"Honey, you c'n go backstage of every concert there is now, y'know," he reminded her gently. "No reason t' miss out on stuff now. Ain't nowhere y' can't go if y' want."

She shook her head. "I can't. Not yet. It just—reminds me too much—makes me mad 'cause all those kids are alive an' I'm not—

He nodded, understanding perfectly. "When you're ready, honey. Listen, I got a question for you. Friend of mine needs t'find a girl, 'fore she gets herself inta trouble. You got any idea where the areas are that the hookers hang out?"

Vanessa's eyes widened. "Bull, President, an' the alleys between President an' River Street," she said promptly. "Mr. Canfield, she's not—anyone I know, is she?"

He shook his head. "Don't think so, honey. She's workin' alone, but she's just a little bitty baby, like you was, an' we need t'get her somewhere's safe." He didn't add, *before she winds up like you;* he didn't have to.

Vanessa's hands balled into fists, and tears welled up in her eyes. "I wanta help," she whispered hoarsely, "an' I *can't.* I wanta do somethin' an' whenever I try'n get near Bull, the world just sorta goes away—"

Fox said that Vanessa had died on Bull street, victim of a heart attack brought on by one too many hits of crack. She still hadn't come to terms with her life, much less her death, and Ross sighed with helpless frustration.

"Look, honey, you just now helped, okay? An' someday you'll do better. Right now, you gotta learn to stand up f'r y'self, fight back, don't let nobody push you around. Then maybe you c'n do more."

Vanessa scrubbed at her eyes, and sniffed. And just when Ross began to feel really badly, wanting to comfort her, but needing to go find Tannim's girl in the real world, help showed up in the guise of Foxtrot. Today Fox looked like a cartoon hero, pipestem legs and wild hair. He just appeared out of nowhere, like always, and Vanessa looked up at him and smiled through her tears. Somehow they both always recognized Fox, no matter what he looked like.

"Heya, lady!" Fox crowed, as if there was nothing wrong. "Got something I want to show you." Then he looked over his shoulder at Ross, and grinned. "Sorry old man, no fossils allowed. It's just for people who believe in the magic of rock'n'roll."

"Ah, go on," Ross said, relieved. "You wouldn't know good music if'n it sat up an' bit your ass."

"That wouldn't be where I'd want something to bite me," Fox replied insolently, and reached for Vanessa's hand. She took it hesitantly, and they vanished in a glittering shower of sparks.

Fox was a pistol, all right. Maybe he'd picked Vanessa as his vixen of choice.

Ross smirked, then furrowed his brow in concentration, picturing Bull Street . . . building it up in his mind . . . then, *deciding* to be there.

Then he *was* there. Now *that* was a teleport.

He grinned widely. It was also his first teleport.

But there was no time to gloat about it; he had a girl to find, one who might be getting herself into trouble she couldn't get out of right at this very moment.

He sharpened his real-world focus, bringing himself as far into the world of the living as he could without interacting with it; he wanted to be able to walk through people and things if he had to. He had noticed that he no longer had any trouble seeing even in the darkest places; the street was as bright as daylight to him, with every person on it outlined with his or her own little glow of colored light. The faces were the clearest, but it was as if every living creature carried its own little spot-light with him—and from the way the females tended to be dressed and act, it was pretty obvious that there was no lack of "professional ladies" on this section of Bull. They ranged in age from teenagers in punk gear to women with a fair amount of mileage on the meter. He noticed that their glows were all in muddy colors, sullen and angry; dirty red, murky yellow, dirt brown. Just like Vanessa, when she first came over. Her colors were clearing now, but she had a long

way to go before she looked like Ross—and he was no
match for the clear, blue-white light of Fox or The Old
Man.

He spotted the pimps right away, too—and interestingly
enough, the colors of their glows were sharp and less
muddied, but acutely painful to look at. Reds and yellows
that swirled together in eye-hurting combinations, screaming, clashing pinks and yellow-greens—and the intensity
was somehow *too* much; a fluctuating, pulsing brightness,
as if they were burning themselves out with every heartbeat. There were little ribbons of evil yellow connecting
each pimp to his "ladies," and Ross wasn't sure just what
that meant; was there some kind of emotional or mental
dependency there? And if so, who depended on whom?
And there was something else, too. Just as Tannim had
said, there were *things* lurking about the pimps, vulturine
creatures of shifting shape and shadow, watching and
waiting with infinite patience. One of them looked in Ross's
direction as if it felt his eyes on it, but its glance was indifferent, as if he was of no use to it. It blinked leprous-silver
eyes and turned away, back to the pimp. He shuddered
anyway. If these jerks only knew what was waiting for
them. . . .

But none of the girls he saw, in their tinsel and flash,
short skirts and glorified underwear, was Tania.

He drifted along Bull Street for about a mile, seeing
no sign of her. When he noticed that the street had gotten emptier, that the girls he saw were no longer plying
the trade, he realized he must have come to the end of
the "district," and turned back, taking the opposite side
of the street.

It all was pretty different from what he had expected.
There were no "Irma la Douce" girls here, no "Pretty
Women," or "Happy Hookers." This sure was a far cry from
the way most movies portrayed street-walkers. There was
nothing playful or cheerful here. Most of 'em looked like
whipped dogs, spirits broken, minds numbed. Oh, there
were a few who were different, but none of *them* were
hooked up with pimps. It looked to Ross as if the best
these kids could muster was the same blank business-like

approach as the kids in the fast-food places, selling burgers. No wonder Vanessa had called a night on the job "hanging on the meat-rack."

Suddenly, his musings were broken into by a glimpse of blond hair with the streetlight shining off of it, and the arch of a nose and cheekbone that seemed familiar, an aura that wasn't as muddy as most. The girl moved, and he got a better look—

It was her, all right. Then something else caught his eye, and he realized that he wasn't the only person hunting her.

There was a man stalking her; a man in a suit, with an aura that was completely black, and a swarm of shadow-creatures around him that was three times the number around any of the pimps.

Ross moved in on the man, quickly, fearing the worst. But before he could reach the girl's side, the man had already maneuvered so that he was between her and the rest of the people on the street. And just as he got within touching distance, the man managed to crowd her into an alcove, where she pressed herself back against a locked doorway, a look of fear and shock on her young face.

"What—" she said, her voice tight with panic. "What do you want? Leave me alone! I don't have any money, I don't have any drugs—"

Ross crowded in, trying to think of something he could do. He couldn't hit the guy, he couldn't drag him away, or even shout in his ear to distract him. And suddenly there didn't seem to be anyone else on this side of the street, as if the rest of the denizens of Bull had sensed the trouble and evaporated.

"It's you I want," the man said, in a cold, utterly expressionless voice. "If you come along, there won't be any trouble." He pulled back his coat, and terror spread across Tania's face as she saw the gun he was reaching for. "But if you won't be a good little girl—I'll have to—"

Ross didn't even think; he just grabbed for the gun, desperately, reaching right through the kidnapper's back and somehow getting his hands on the gun-grip and the trigger. And realizing that he couldn't take it away. That in fact, there wasn't much he could do. Except—maybe—

His next move was pure instinct. He cocked the hammer, and, as the kidnapper started in surprise at the telltale *click,* pulled the trigger.

The gun went off in the shoulder-holster, the bullet tearing its way through the leather and down his side, with a roar and a muzzle-flash that would have blinded and deafened Ross if he had been alive. The jacket blew away like a rag in a hurricane, and the man's body whip-cracked against the opposite wall of the alcove. Tania jerked back, screaming, then spun and bolted for the street.

The kidnapper clutched at his side, nearly doubling over as his legs and torso went slick with hot, red blood.

Tania made it across the street, just as the firefight began. Gunmen appeared from nowhere, the pimps and pushers he'd seen before, firing wildly; and Ross realized as he ducked out of sheer reflex that none of them knew why they were shooting. But they certainly knew what they were shooting at; the kidnapper, as the originator of the first shot.

The kidnapper went down, blood spraying, in the crossfire; Tania ducked into an alley, and sirens began to wail in the distance.

The firefight continued as Ross dashed across the street after her, while the red and blue flashes of approaching cop cars lit up the sky in both directions.

CHAPTER TWELVE

Tania's side was afire, pierced with pain, but she ran anyway, gasping for breath as her lungs ached and her throat rasped. Behind her, sirens split the night air with unearthly wails, though the *crack* of gunfire no longer echoed down the alley. She didn't care; or rather, she had no room in her mind for anything but the desperate need to run, run until she was somewhere safe.

She couldn't see at all; her eyes were still dazzled by the flash when the gun had gone off. She lost her balance when she stumbled over a trash-can and fell face-first in the slimy alley, ripping the knees out of her tights and scraping the skin of both palms. She was up again in the next heartbeat—dashing out of the alley and into the lit street, across it, and into another alley again. She ran into a dumpster she hadn't even seen, pushed away from it, and stumbled off into the dark. At the end of this alley she slowed, then stopped, doubling over with one hand on the brick of the wall beside her, sucking in huge gulps of breath, her belly heaving as if a dull knife carved at it deeper every time she breathed.

Panic ebbed, slowly. Her palms burned, and so did her knees. She stood up, slowly, as the blinding white light of pure fear flickered and went out, freeing her mind, letting her think again.

This wasn't the first time she'd been approached by a pimp, but they'd never *come after her* before. No one had ever pulled a gun on her. If it hadn't gone off like that—

She started to shake, and not just from reaction to her narrow escape. The gun—the gun had gone off, in the guy's holster—before he even touched it. He'd just pulled his jacket open to show it to her. He *had* been reaching for it, but he hadn't actually gotten his hand on it, when the hammer had gone *click,* he'd gotten a startled look on his face, and the gun had flashed and roared.

It had misfired. She had to think that. Anything else was too weird.

Besides, she didn't want to think about it at all. All she wanted, she realized desperately, was to get home. Back to the apartment, where she could soak her knees and hands before they got infected, soak her tired body in a hot bath, hide in her bed with a book, and never, ever come out again.

She stood up, still shaking but determined to get home, knees and palms sending little stabs of pain up her arms and legs every time the raw skin flexed.

She ignored that, and the distant ache in her side, and stepped out into the dim light from the streetlamp, trying to muster a show of courage. She couldn't help but glance over her shoulder, up and down the street; trying not to be obvious about it, but looking furtively to see if there was anyone else likely to make a grab for her. It wasn't just that she was afraid of another muscle-boy coming after her. In her current disheveled condition, she knew she looked like prey, easy prey. Even someone who might ordinarily leave her alone could be tempted to go for her the way she looked right now. And there were muggers, rapists, kids just looking to make some trouble, and she was all too obviously a good target. She started to shake again.

She saw only a couple of people on her side of the street, and neither of them looked terribly dangerous. One was an old bag-lady who tottered down the street peering into corners, clucking and muttering to herself; the other, of indeterminate gender, wandered all over the sidewalk, clutching a bottle in a paper sack.

That didn't mean there wasn't someone lurking around the corner, or in the mouth of an alley; someone she couldn't see. But at least she'd see them and have a head start if they came after her. . . .

She started up the street, in the direction of the apartment, forcing herself to walk normally, with her head high. The wino stared at her as she passed him, but he didn't seem to really see her; the bag-lady ignored her entirely in favor of an old sneaker she'd just found.

Nothing happened; no one jumped out of shadowy doorways to grab her, and no one pulled any more guns. One or two kids, alone, dressed in variations on jeans and gang-jackets, looked her over carefully, but evidently decided she wasn't worth hassling.

By the time she made it back to the apartment, she was ready to pass out from fear and from exhaustion. But at least tonight there was a lightbulb illuminating the staircase, however faintly. There was no way that there could be anyone lurking on the landing, waiting to ambush her. She took the stairs slowly, carefully, pausing every few stairs to catch her breath. It took her a long time to fumble the key out of her tiny purse, and even longer to unlock the door.

The apartment was completely empty.

In a way, she was glad; that meant she wasn't going to have to explain what had happened to anyone until she'd managed to sort it all out herself. But the emptiness of the apartment meant she was going to be alone for a while. What if that pimp had friends? What if they knew where she lived? What if they'd been following her?

They couldn't know where she lived, she told herself, as she shut and locked the door behind her. All she had to do was stay away from the windows, and not turn on any extra lights that might be visible from the street. That wouldn't be too hard.

The sound of her own heart was so loud she was certain that if anyone did break in, they'd find her by that alone.

She edged her way around the first room. Tonio, Joe, and Honi were nowhere to be seen, and the bedding hadn't been slept in. She kept between the wall and the light, so that no betraying shadow could fall to tell anyone watching that there was now someone inside the apartment. The bathroom was dark, and once in its comforting shadows she heaved a sigh of relief. She stripped off the ruined tights, whimpering as she pulled the fabric away from abraded flesh. They were useless now; huge runs had already started unraveling the black knit, and by the time she got the tights off, there wasn't much left of them but a weblike snarl of threads.

My best tights, too, she thought, angrily, tears in her eyes. They'd cost her a full two dollars at Goodwill, and had been brand-new, out of a batch donated by some store or other. SCAD students had snapped up the rest; she'd practically had to fight to get this pair. And now some goon with a gun had ruined them. Her knees started bleeding again, and she caught the blood with a hastily grabbed wad of toilet tissue. She probably ought to let the scrapes bleed for a while, to clean them out.

She waited until the bleeding slowed, then wrung out a wash rag in hot water, and sat on the toilet in her panties and cotton minidress, carefully dabbing at her knees and the palms of her hands, trying not to get any blood on anything else. Each touch of the damp cloth brought an involuntary hiss of pain from her, and she rinsed the cloth and wrung it out, over and over, then dabbed at her knees again, wondering if she ought to use the peroxide Laura did her hair with on the scrapes. But soap and water were free, and peroxide cost money.

Finally the scrapes looked pretty clean, and the bleeding stopped. Her knees looked awful, though. She could hide the palms of her hands, but how was she going to cover up her knees? She still had to hustle tomorrow, if not tonight.

She finally decided to wear the black garter-belt and the black opaque stockings for the next couple of days. Men never asked her to take those off, not even the suits. And if she never told them that the hose were a little old

Italian lady's black support hose, they'd never guess. Those stockings were dark enough she could tape her whole leg and they'd never know it.

A great Goodwill find, courtesy of Laura, who could see potential in anything.

It was easier thinking about what to wear than it was to think about what had just happened. She filled the tub with hot water and slipped out of the rest of her clothing, then climbed in, hissing a little as the water set her knees and hands afire. The pain didn't stop, it only leveled off, and she relaxed back into the tub with a sigh and closed her eyes.

The pimp was dead; she had no doubt at all about that. The minute his gun had gone off, he had been dead. There were enough pimps and pushers nearby to start a small war; they all went armed, and they were all as paranoid as hell, especially the pushers. The minute a shot rang out, every muzzle on the street would have been pointed in her would-be kidnapper's direction, and a microsecond later, every one of the triggers would have been pulled. The law on the street was, "assume they're shooting at you." That was why she'd run for cover, hoping to reach the protection of brick and concrete before the fire-fight began.

She'd kept running once she was out of the line of fire because she also couldn't afford to get caught up with the dead, wounded, and witnesses when the cops came. Somebody might remember the guy was trying to grab her—might even finger her for the one who shot first. The Savannah cops were some of the best. They'd never let a private little war go on for long; she had to be out of there before they arrived and sealed the area off.

But who was that man, and *what* was he? Was he a pimp himself, or somebody's muscle? She didn't recognize him, but that didn't mean anything. New pimps moved in every week; he could have been someone new trying to expand his stable. She knew why he'd try for her; she was working alone, which made her a tempting target. Blondes, especially young ones, were always in demand. That was what Laura had told her when she'd insisted on bleaching Tania's hair.

But he hadn't looked or acted like a pimp; he'd had none of the flash, none of the surface style and smoothness. Hired heat was more like it—but if he'd been hired, who had done it? Why hire muscle to bring her in—was she that valuable, or was it just that there was just a scarcity of young blondes worth recruiting? And would they try again—or hunt her down and take the loss of the muscle-boy out on her?

Her head swam, and not just from the heat of the bath. It was all too complicated ... and none of it made any sense.

She'd have to wait until Laura got home. Laura knew the street, Laura would be able to help her sort it out, and decide what to do.

I ought to at least change my territory, she thought drowsily. *That's a good idea. I could start working President Street.* It would be a little hazardous to move into a new area, since she'd be competing with girls who already had established territories, but maybe she could trade one of them for her old beat on Bull.

Or maybe she could see if she could hit Tannim up again—

But what if *Tannim* had sent the muscle?

The thought made her sit up straight for a moment. It was possible. He knew where her beat was; he knew when she worked. He'd already advanced her three hundred bucks and gotten nothing for it. Maybe he'd decided to collect. . . .

The thought made her sick. She'd trusted him. But wasn't that how the really sick people operated? They got you to trust them, and then they did horrible things to you.

Maybe *he* was the one behind some of the disappearances that had been going on for the past couple of months—the hookers that went off somewhere and never came back. The ones that weren't in the shelters, hadn't been busted, and hadn't moved to Atlanta. Maybe she wasn't the first kid he'd approached; maybe she was just the latest one in a series. She'd read a discarded newspaper's article about serial killers the other night; about how they always chose the same kind of people, that they seemed real nice until they were caught. Regular people; folks you'd never suspect.

She could only sit in silence and cry, her shivers making ripples in the steaming water.

The minute Tannim pulled up to the gate and keyed it open, he knew that there was something wrong. The radar detector on his dash whined as the gun hit it, but the run-lights didn't come on.

Suddenly he recalled his dreams last night; all of them had been about Unseleighe critters attacking and being countered. And he remembered the careful way Keighvin and the others had handled him before he'd left last night. There had been something about to go down—and they'd been keeping it away from him.

He flushed with anger, half tempted to turn the Mustang around and go home, his good mood vanishing. They were treating him as if he was some kind of invalid, a risk, just because he was a little tired and his aim got a little erratic—

Unbidden, the memory of Conal and the near-miss during the last little altercation rose up before his mental eye, and the flush turned to a blush.

He had been more than a "little" tired last night. It had been all he could do to get home and into bed. And his aim was worse than erratic when he was that weary. The last near-miss had been funny, but if someone from Fairgrove got plugged by Tannim's friendly fire, it would be a lot worse than Conal's hair-loss. Last night he'd been too exhausted to have been any use magically—it would have been firearms, then, and no mage-fire shield would deflect a steel-jacketed slug if the mage wasn't expecting one to come winging in.

But he was in good shape now . . . and he'd better get up there and see what Keighvin had for him.

The radio announcer finally ended his commercial spiel, and the first notes of the next half-hour's series of songs started.

There was no mistaking *that* horn riff, even without the lyrics. "Dead-man's Curve," by Jan and Dean.

With a shiver of ill-omen, Tannim snapped the radio off before the singing started.

The radar detector continued to whine as he pulled up the drive, at exactly two miles per hour under the posted limit of thirty. Whoever was on the cameras—probably Janie—would know by that speed that the car she was tracking was a friend and not a stranger or an enemy.

The glare beyond the trees told him that the parking lot was lit up like the yard of a maximum-security prison. In fact, all of the halogens were probably on tonight. Whatever had gone down, it must have been big. . . .

He cursed his own weakness. He should have been there. He should have. He longed to floor the Mustang and race up the drive, to get there all the sooner—but that would give Janie and everyone else heart failure.

Instead, he pulled sedately into a parking lot so brilliantly illuminated that every stray pebble showed clearly. It was a good thing the lot was square, or pilots would be mistaking it for the runway at the airport.

Sam's old Mark IV Lincoln presided over an otherwise empty lot. There were no other cars there, elvensteeds or otherwise. Of course, most of the other Fairgrove humans would be gone by now; the few that were left tended to have gift-steeds, presents from their foster-parents, like the Diablo and the Dino. And any elvensteeds would have gone back to native form for a fight. Still, the empty lot gave Tannim the shivers again.

He parked and locked the Mustang—normally he never locked it here, but there was no point in giving anything to the enemy. If the enemy was still here.

Once he was outside the Mustang's protective shields, there didn't seem to be any sign that the Fairgrove complex was still under siege. There was nothing in the air but the scent of honeysuckle and wet grass; no tremblings in the power-flows betrayed any disturbance of the protections around the place.

But out beyond the parking lot, there were more glares

of halogen lights. The lights at the fence were blazing at
full power, so there was something going on at the borders tonight.

He gave up on speculation and headed for the shop.
Whatever had happened, he'd find it out a lot quicker by
just going in.

The shop was quiet, with no one working on prototypes. No elvensteeds waited in car-form for someone to
suggest modifications to their lines to add to verisimilitude. There was a huddle of bodies, standing and sitting,
at the far corner, beside the prototype Victor he and
Donal had been working on, and Tannim headed that way
at a limping trot.

Sam looked up first, and his wide grin of relief was a
welcome sight. Keighvin finished whatever he was saying
to Sarge Austin, then turned his own emerald eyes up to
greet the young mage.

"We had a visitor last night," the Sidhe said without
preamble.

"And a fair horde of his friends," Conal said with a
grimace of suppressed pain. "He'd sent a challenge with
yon mortal, but we hadn't reckoned on his bringing as
many as he did."

Tannim glanced around the circle, and came up quite
a few names short. And there was a gloom about the Sidhe,
combined with the reddened eyes of the humans, that
spoke volumes.

We lost somebody. Shit.

"Casualties?" he asked carefully.

"Donal," his twin replied, and the lack of expression in
his voice told Tannim just how deep and raw the wound
of loss was. Tannim closed his eyes briefly, and extended
a tentative mental "hand" to his elven friend. It was
clasped, and Conal accepted the comfort that flowed across
the link.

"And one of the fosterlings," added Kieru. "Rob van
Alman. Dinna fret yerse' lad, 'twouldn't have changed
matters if you'd been here. The black bastard sent a
Bane-Sidhe, an old, powerful one, and he'd gi'en his
lesser Sidhe compound crossbows loaded wi' elf shot.

'Twas the shot that got yon Rob, and the Bane-Sidhe that did for puir Donal. Ye'd ha' been no use 'gainst either one."

Tannim kept his eyes closed for a moment more, as he mentally ran through every swear-word he knew twice over. None of them were enough. Rob had been the most cheerful guy he'd ever known, always ready with a joke at his own expense, keeping the place laughing at the worst of times and under the most stressful conditions. And Donal—the Sidhe driver was Tannim's own replacement as mechanic on the SERRA team. He'd taught Donal everything he knew, and he could always count on Donal being there at the track whenever he ran— ready with a cold towel and a squeeze-bottle of Gatorade—

His throat tightened. He opened his eyes, and asked, hoarsely, "And wounded?"

"About a score," Keighvin replied with the carefully impassive expression of a war-leader. "We know that they're learning from us now; we won't underestimate them again."

Tannim took a deep breath to force his throat open, then another. He'd have his own private mourning session later. Maybe, once it was safe, he'd try to visit them on the other side. . . .

"What do you want me to do?" he asked.

"Mine-sweeping," Phil Austin said.

He blinked, puzzled. "But we don't—"

"What Sarge there means is that there's bits of steel all over the grounds," Sam stuck in. "Bullets that missed, that kind of thing."

And none of the Folk would be able to do any precision magic except in the protected rooms until the stray metal was gotten rid of. He nodded. "And when I'm done?"

"Reinforcement on the perimeter," Keighvin replied decisively. "I want a shield ye couldna bring tank nor mouse through."

He nodded, and turned to go.

"Take Sam with you," Keighvin added. "There was

enough ordnance flyin' about last night ye'll need four
hands, an' he can tell ye the full of the story."

And that was definitely toned as a dismissal. Tannim's
liege he was not, but the young man knew that the Sidhe's
terseness was caused by pain, and not the arrogance of a
nobleman. They walked out to the lighted perimeter, with
Tannim stopping long enough to pick up a couple of chisels
to dig bullets out of trees with, from the silk-lined tool
locker where steel implements were kept. A half-dozen
other humans prowled the grounds already, most of them
sporting stained bandages, but none of them were mages.
They were looking for bullet holes by eye alone; digging
the steel-jacketed rounds out, and marking the hole with
a splash of paint. Others were wrapping the Pinball bars
in their special silk sheathes and shoving them down into
the fence-posts. Someone with her face obscured by a
bandage—Dottie, he recognized after a confused moment—
came up and handed him a can of paint and a brush.

"Glad you're here now and not earlier," she said. "I just
sent Fred home and you're the best mage we've got. Fred
found all the easy ones; we know there's more out here,
but they're probably buried in the dirt or twenty feet up
in a tree."

Tannim nodded, a little relieved. He wouldn't have been
any use, earlier. The presence of the other rounds would
have obscured the ones that were harder to find.

"If you find something in a tree, dig it out, and slap
this stuff on it real good," Dottie continued tiredly. "There's
fungicide, wood-sealer, and growth-hormone in it. The least
we can do is make sure the poor trees have a fighting
chance after the way we damaged them."

"Are you all right?" Tannim felt impelled to ask.

"What, this?" she replied, touching the bandage. "Just
a graze. Bled like hell and hurts worse, but I'm good for
duty."

Unspoken—that there were plenty who weren't. Tannim
nodded again, and as she turned back to her own task of
putting the Pinball bars to bed, unfocused his eyes and
reached into himself for the spell that would let him detect
any amount of iron and steel, however small.

Sam asked quietly, "Uhm, lad, can you call up any of your friends to help?"

Tannim absent-mindedly sniffed the paste, and closed his eyes. "No . . . no, Sam. I'm not going to call in any favors for something we can do ourselves."

We may need them later.

While Sam waited in silence, he gathered power from inside himself, chanted in a mechanical drone to set the spell in place, then triggered it with a hissed syllable only Chinthliss would have recognized.

There was a bullet not ten feet from him—straight up. It didn't take a prophet to predict a lot of climbing tonight.

"So," he said, waving to Sam to follow him and handing the older man the paint and brush to hold as he climbed the tree, "tell me what went down."

Sam took a visible breath, and began.

The tiny office was too small to contain Aurilia's rage. "You *fool,*" Aurilia stormed at Vidal. "You empty-headed *witling.* I told you that I had a plan, that it involved the child-whores, especially Tannim's chosen slut; why couldn't you wait until I got the girl here?"

Vidal Dhu glowered and sulked, but Niall stood behind Aurilia, radiating cold anger, and finally Vidal deflated, slumping down into his seat. "I thought it would be better to act directly," he muttered. "I thought that if we left the girl out on the street, anything could happen. She might decide to return home, she might decide to go into one of the shelters, she could even get herself killed being stupid."

"And *you* nearly got her killed!" Aurilia snapped. "Now you've frightened her; she'll be twice as wary as before! You've undone everything I built, in a single moment of genuine idiocy!"

"Maybe not," Niall rumbled thoughtfully. She turned to stare at him.

"How on earth can you say that?" she asked. "This—man—sent out a stupid human to kidnap the girl. He died trying to coerce her, and she was so frightened she ran, the gods only know where! You say he hasn't undone everything I worked towards?"

"Think a moment, child," Niall replied, as she chafed at being called a "child." "The girl has been affrighted, it is true. She may keep herself from the street for some time, it is also true. But you know who one of her friends is. And it seems to me that if she were offered a chance of employment that appears to be safer—at least, safer in the light of the attempted kidnapping—than whoring on the street, she may well take it."

Aurilia licked her lips thoughtfully. It was true, she did know the boy called "Jamie." It would be easy enough to find him in the course of a night. And if she offered him another "movie job," not only for himself, but for a female friend, he might bring in the girl. The ploy might not work the first time, but if Aurilia made it tempting enough, and added offers for other friends, sooner or later, she'd get Tannim's protégé, especially when the "movie work" was mild bondage, some sado-eroticism with only the trappings, not the actuality, or perhaps a staged "satanic ritual" before the cameras; nothing that would frighten them. It would mean a delay in her plans—for she had expected to go directly to where the girl was, and make the "movie offer" in person, but it wouldn't be too great a delay. Right now if anyone or anything approached the girl directly except her trusted friends, she'd bolt—and Aurilia wasn't certain she had the resources to try and catch a fleeing child without complications.

"I'm going to explain what I have in mind clearly this time," she said waspishly to Vidal Dhu, "so that there will be no mistakes, and no ill-advised attempts to anticipate the capture. I will find the boy I used in the party-film. He knows the girl. I will offer him more work, work for himself and a female friend. If he brings the girl in the first time, well and good—if *not*, we will be patient. We will offer him another night of work, this time with two females, and ask him if he has any more friends. Eventually, especially after we gain their trust, the girl will come of her own accord."

"Then we send Keighvin Silverhair a special little tape, or perhaps some pictures," Niall rumbled in satisfaction. "But—do we bring him here? That could be dangerous—this place is full of the kind of machinery and creations of Cold Iron his humans use so well. Even if it is on our own ground—"

Aurilia shook her head. "No, we will let him think that we have the children on our ground, Underhill. He will bring humans and Cold Iron weapons there trying to thwart us. We will ambush him, but more than that, we will portray him and his dogs to the Seleighe Court as a danger to us all. His position is tenuous enough; this violation of custom will have even his supporters against him. If he survives our ambush, he will never be allowed to set foot in the human world again."

"Leaving this place open to our hunting—" Vidal breathed in surprise. She nodded.

"And leaving us the children to dispose of in front of the cameras, accomplishing two tasks in one."

She smiled at Vidal's stunned expression. *You never gave me the credit for that much intelligence, did you?* she thought with viperish satisfaction. *When Keighvin is a memory, and I no longer need you, I think I shall challenge you, Vidal Dhu. With Niall's backing, I will not only humiliate you, I may even be able to destroy you.*

But she allowed no hint of her thoughts to appear in her speech or her body-language. Vidal studied her for a moment, but evidently read nothing, and shrugged.

"Very well then," he said. "I will go and prepare the ambush site. I can still conjure or cajole more than enough underlings to take on Keighvin and all of his allies—"

"Just be certain you do not underestimate him," Niall said coldly. His eyes glittered red within his pitted face. "As you did the last time."

Aurilia watched Vidal seethe with anger, but he held his tongue. "This time the confrontation will be on prepared territory of *our* choosing," he replied, just as coldly. "There will be no mistakes this time."

"I will find the children," Aurilia said quickly, sick to

death of their posturing. "After all, I know what they look like."

Niall sighed gustily, breathing a wash of air straight from the grave over her. "And I shall ready the studio," he said. "I am weary, very weary. That is ample employment for me at the moment." Then he added as Vidal Dhu turned to go, as if in afterthought, "And Vidal, if we are able, I would like very much to have the destruction of Silverhair on videotape."

Vidal reddened again, but said nothing. Aurilia smiled.

George Beecher stared at the report on his desk and ground his teeth in anger and frustration. Bad enough that everything he'd collected on this "Tannim" character showed him to be the kind of guy George could easily have been friends with. But when he'd mentioned his client to an old buddy in Vice, hoping to find something that would make him dislike the guy, if not something he could take to the bitch, Terry had given him a strange look.

"You know I don't mix into your business, bud," he'd said, "but I think maybe you took the wrong client this time."

George had wondered about that remark—and now, today, *this* had arrived in the mail. A copy of a police file, with a note, "Burn this when you get done, okay? T."

Slim, as police files went, it nevertheless held more than enough to make George seethe with rage. His client, that charming, lovely young woman with the face of an old-world madonna, was up to her pretty little ear-lobes in a porn ring. And not just plain old garden-variety smut, either; George wouldn't have cared about that. She was definitely linked to S and M, B and D—and tentatively to kiddie-porn and snuff-films.

Whatever hold she wanted over Tannim, George wasn't about to give it to her. If he hadn't been dead sure that not even Terry could cover for him, he might have been tempted to go put some large-caliber holes in her wide, smooth forehead.

Now he was in an ethical quandary. He'd just gotten paid for his last invoice; he had a couple of days' worth of hours on the new one, but nothing he couldn't live without. If he hadn't already deposited the cashier's check, he'd have been in an even more serious quandary; as it was, the bills had all been paid and there was no way he was going to get the money back to throw in her face.

And I wondered why you always paid with a cashier's check. I thought it was so ex-hubby wouldn't know you'd hired me.

Bitch.

He chewed on his lip and stared at the police file lying in the pool of light cast by his desk lamp, and made some hard decisions.

He couldn't do what he *wanted* to do; go to her office, throw the file down on her desk, and tell her she could keep her damned filthy blood-money. For one thing, that would throw Terry's investigation. For another, these people never operated in a vacuum; she could have mob contacts and bosses, and certainly could hire muscle herself. If she knew *he* knew, it wouldn't take more than five hundred bucks to erase George Beecher, P.I., from the face of the earth.

So, no dramatic gestures.

No gestures at all, in fact.

With his jaw clenched, he swiveled his chair to face the old Smith-Corona on the typing stand beside his desk and laboriously typed out a letter on the agency stationery.

Ms. Morrigan: In light of the fact that I have uncovered nothing substantial in my investigations, I voluntarily dissolve our contract with no further payment expected. G. Beecher.

He dated it, folded it carefully, slipped it into an envelope, and left it for the secretary to mail in the morning.

And there was another thing he could do; he knew Tannim's address. Not that the kid hadn't lost him a million times when he'd tried to follow, but there were other ways of finding someone than tailing them. When the City Directory had come up dry, and the phone company proved uncooperative, he'd turned into a prospective creditor and called American Express. The kid had a Gold Card, after all. And he'd been oh, so puzzled, because Mr.

Tannim didn't seem to have a first name . . . this amused the person on the other end of the line, who'd confided that Mr. Tannim was very eccentric in that regard.

Bingo; name, address, phone, current employer, and the fact that the kid paid all bills in full on time.

So he had Tannim's address. Now for a little anonymous letter to ease his conscience.

Sir: I wish to advise you that you are being investigated by a Ms. Aurilia Morrigan, of no known address, who operates a business from Hangar 2A at the Savannah Regional Airport. I do not know why Ms. Morrigan has chosen to have you investigated, but her motives are suspect, since confidential information given me reports she herself is under investigation for possible involvement in illegal activities, including child pornography. Please be advised that she may be dangerous, and take what seem to you to be sensible precautions.

There. That was all he could say without blowing his cover. This letter would not be entrusted to the secretary; it would be hand-delivered.

He folded it and inserted it into a plain, white envelope, turned off his desk lamp, and took his coat off the back of the chair: He knew where Tannim would be tonight: Kevin Barry's pub. He was probably looking for that poor little teenage hooker again. So, while Tannim was at the pub, George Beecher would be slipping this warning under his door.

It wasn't much, but it was something. And a damn sight better than doing nothing.

He flipped off the office lights and picked up the police file, leaving it and the copy of his letter to Aurilia Morrigan on the boss's desk. In the morning when he came in, there'd be a new case on his blotter, the files would have quietly disappeared, and no mention of the case would ever be made again. There was a little calligraphed piece in the boss's office, where he could see it when he sat at his desk.

Responsibility. Accountability. Integrity.

It wasn't the agency motto, but it might as well have been. Nice to work for someone with a bottom-line like that one. Yeah, the boss was a good man to work for. Even if sometimes it meant that you sweated a little at the end of the month. Better sweating a little money than not being able to sleep at night. Being a hardworking, average joe with a relatively clean conscience wasn't a bad way to live.

George flipped the latch and closed the door of the office quietly, patting his coat pocket to be certain that the letter was still there, and looking forward to a good night's sleep.

CHAPTER THIRTEEN

Tannim drummed his fingers idly on the phone-tap detector, and waited for his police contact to pick up. There had been a few too many coincidences lately for comfort—and his nerves told him that anything could be a setup. This anonymous tip in his mailbox reeked of an inept trap.

On the other hand, why would any of his enemies be that inept? Unless it was to throw him off, and make him think it was too inept to be a trap—

Circular reasoning like that is gonna make me too dizzy to see in a minute.

At last a voice answered. The detector showed nil.

"Yeah?"

"Hiya, Terry? This is Greeneyes. Hey, look, you need a good bottle of scotch? I need a fingerprint check." He crossed his fingers and hoped Terry wasn't busy . . . or rather, *too* busy. Vice was always busy with something. Terry sounded annoyed, but not angry. "Aww, jeez man, you *know* I hate to do those! They take freakin' *forever*."

Tannim sighed. The balance sheet was a little too tilted in Terry's direction lately. He'd have to do something about that, later. Maybe when he got Tania safe he could talk her into fingering some pimps or pushers. "I know, I know, it's just that there's something weird going down,

and there are a couple real young civilians in the middle
of it. Dig?"

The growl Terry produced sounded only halfhearted.
"Damn Boy Scout. All right, three bottles of Amaretto and
a Bob Uecher card."

Well, that was an easy bribe, and just a little too quick
for something off the cuff. Tannim had always suspected
Terry of keeping a list of items he wanted for doing favors.
"Done. Thanks. Here's the story: got an anonymous letter in my mailbox, no address or postage, tipping me off
to the whereabouts of Bad Guys. Letter says these Bad
Guys are into everything that pushes my piss-off buttons.
All I've got to go on is this letter, and I don't know if it's
genuine. If it is, well . . ."

Terry snorted. "If it is, we'll find out about it after you've
played vigilante, same as usual. Dammit, Greeneyes, this
covert hero-crap of yours is going to sink us all. You and
your friends're gonna get shot by a cop one of these days
while you're out being white hats. You dig that?"

Tannim bit his lip. It was *not* the most encouraging
thing he could have heard at the moment, but Terry had
a good point. The police were damned good at their job
in Savannah, and a lot of Tannim's activities could look
mighty suspicious if someone that wasn't a friend happened
upon them. He could picture it, too. His armor could stop
a bullet, but he'd still lose a couple ribs from the impact,
and then there were the explanations. . . .

And there was nothing armoring him from a head-shot.

"Greeneyes? You there?"

"Yeah . . . yeah, I'm here. I'll be careful, Terry. And look,
you're right. If things get too rough, I'll call you for help."

Terry produced something that was closer to a bark than
a laugh. "If it's that bad, I'll bring an ambulance."

Tania rubbed sleep from her eyes, her mouth tasting
like her sweat-soaked, musty blankets. She'd tossed all night
in half-sleep, haunted by images of gun-toting maniacs forcing her against grimy walls, and awakening was at best a
hollow improvement. The creaking from the apartment's
warped steps had snapped her into attentiveness—but she'd

calmed as she heard a familiar voice. It was Jamie, high as a kite, staggering up the stairwell.

Oh, God. Not again. This is too much. . . .

Tania pulled the strands of hair from her mouth—that always seemed to happen when she slept, no matter how short her hair was. Jamie giggled uncontrollably, amused beyond belief by how difficult it was to get his key into the lock. Tania heard the unmistakable sound of his forehead thumping against the door, but the giggling didn't stop even then. He was wasted but good this time.

Laura was not waking as readily as Tania had; the two had spent the wee hours hugging and comforting each other before finally crashing. Laura had seemed unusually tense over the threat to Tania, and it had amazed her no small amount that the normally suspicious, cynical girl could be so open about her fears when Tania'd confided in her. Both of them had talked about suicide as some solution to put the street out of their minds forever, but neither could do it. There was something, somewhere, to live for, and they could cry in hope over it—and if nothing else, they had each other.

And they both agreed that Jamie was in trouble. The drugs, the recklessness, his frailty . . .

By the time Jamie had gotten the door open, Tania had pulled her sweat suit top on, and was pulling the bottoms on over her still-stinging, scab-caked knees. Laura had roused, too, and had pulled on a tattered black shift. She'd obviously had better nights herself, and gave Tania a significant look as the door came open.

Jamie stumbled in, a red scarf around his neck despite the sultry night, tight jeans torn at the knees and a wad of something in his pocket. Dozens of rubber junk-jewelry bracelets covered his wrists, falling down his forearm as he hung his keys on an exposed nail. He turned heavily dilated eyes to his roommates.

"Heya! Miss me?" Another fit of giggling overtook him, and he made a great show of trying to control it. "Okay. Okay. Before you ask—no, I did not mug Ed McMahon." He turned his pocket inside-out, and a shower of crumpled twenties fell to the rotting floor.

With them fell a pair of tiny plastic bags full of white powder. Laura's breath hissed when she saw them. Tania's heart froze.

Jamie fished a last bill out of his pocket, smoothed it carefully, and dropped it onto the floor with the rest. He then tottered off into the kitchen and turned on the tap, and splashed his face obsessively. By the time he returned, Laura had picked up the money and counted. She'd avoided touching the bags as if they were pit vipers.

Three hundred forty dollars.

"Jamie, how'd you get this money?"

"You oughta be in pictures . . . you oughta be a star. . . ." Jamie sang off key. "I'm in show business, baby. Big time mooo-vie star Want my autograph?"

Laura's brow was knotted up in rage. "What ah wanta know is what's goin' on, Jamie. What d'you do for all this cash?"

. . . And how much was there before you got stoned . . . ?

He gestured wildly. "I have starred . . . in a major motion picture, clothing optional. I agented myself and found my contract agreeable."

Laura's fist clenched, white-knuckled, on the cash.

"I was so very surprised to find that acting was so easy. Heels in the air and speak into the camera—it was so much like my day job I may go full-time." He snickered again, and bowed.

Tania tucked her knees up into her chest and rocked slowly on the mattress. This was the worst Jamie had ever come home wasted. It was like seeing your little brother slice at himself with a dirty knife, and laugh at the spectacle.

"Did they give you the drugs, Jamie?" Tania asked softly.

"Oh no. No. They don't like drugs on the set, baby. They say it affects the quality of the performance. I got my buzz later. I like to celebrate. Party, 'arty, 'arty . . ." His voice trailed off.

Laura stashed the bills in Jamie's pocket and took his face in her hands. "You are effed-up, boy."

"Yeah, but I'm rich. Money, money, money for hooking easy." Jamie smiled, the kind of look he'd give with a birthday present. It was like sunlight through thunder-cloud. "And they want girls, too. Money for you, and it's in cash. Straight sex, some kink, a little bondage, but not worse than street johns, and they even call you a cab when you're done. You wanna come?"

Laura was still far from happy, but Tania knew that chilling look in her eyes. It was the same look she used sizing up johns, or buying clothes at Goodwill.

Tannim leaned back in the vinyl chair in Terry's office, and gazed in wonder at the hundreds of baseball and football cards in frames covering every wall. This was the first time he'd been allowed inside the Sanctum Sanctorum, but Terry had insisted he show up in person. Behind a coffee-stained desk cluttered with file folders, Terry jawed on the phone with one of his team. After a few minutes of mind-numbing technical talk, he insulted the caller's sexual prowess, then hung up grinning.

Tannim looked around conspiratorially, winked, and withdrew three bottles of Amaretto, a small paper bag, and the plastic-wrapped letter from his backpack. With a flour-ish, he opened the bag to reveal a colorful card between two thick slabs of Lexan.

"But it's not a bribe, of course," he said, grinning.

Terry nodded. "Of course not."

"That would be illegal." Tannim held it out. "I'd never do anything illegal, and even if I thought about doing anything illegal, I'd never, ever ask you to do anything illegal."

"Heaven forbid." Terry leaned over the desk, took the card-holder, and held it up to the light. "Thirty-proof Uecher." He put it down on top of the file-folders. "A token of your undying esteem, I'm sure."

"Naturally." Tannim somberly handed over the letter. "Here it is, pretty much as I found it. My prints are on it, of course."

Terry took it out of the plastic and unfolded it with a pair of tweezers, and glanced at the contents. Then he snorted and passed the note back to him without taking the same elaborate precautions. "Greeneyes, I don't have to run prints to know who sent you that. It's legit, from one of the most principled P.I.'s I know. He's a buddy, and he managed to acquire a little confidential information from the usual impeccable sources. And he was really pissed off about working for this woman once he had the dope on her."

Tannim raised an eyebrow. "The impeccable source was someone for whom I have undying esteem? You're investigating her?"

Terry went stone-faced. "Can't answer that. You just watch yourself if you go anywhere near her. She's not only pretty poison, she's gonna find herself hip-deep in alligators real soon now. And I'd hate to see a friend caught in the alligator pit."

Tannim nodded. He knew Terry had grown up on cop shows where the good guys worked outside the letter of the law. That was the only thing that had kept the cop in him from pushing Tannim away for interfering in police business, any number of times. Terry knew there was something strange about his friend "Greeneyes," and that favors could one day be called in. After all, he'd tipped off Terry to some goings-on around town before, ones that by-the-book police work would never have revealed. The baseball card bribes were only part of the dance.

But that meant there was another debt that needed to be put to rest. "All right, credit where it's due. He take a personal check?"

Terry opened a worn Day-Timer, then scribbled on stationery marked "From The Desk Of Hank Aaron." "Here's his address. His rate is fifty-eight an hour plus expenses, and he has a car to pay off. You were never here, I never saw you, pay no attention to the cop behind the curtain. Later."

Tannim took the note. "Just let me know when you're in need of another token of my admiration."

"Out," Terry ordered. "Let an honest cop get some work done. Go."

Tannim went, whistling "Take Me Out To The Ball Game."

❖   ❖   ❖

Tania tried, but couldn't erase the image of twenties falling to the floor. They fell in slow motion, or in sharp detail, and crept back into her thoughts no matter how hard she tried to forget them by reading.

Laura and Jamie were her family now, like it or not. All three of them knew they were too young to be trying to survive out here on their own, that the world was a cold, uncaring place that made no allowances for their weaknesses. It was never more plain than the past few days, and going through all of the old magazines she'd collected only reinforced how hopeless the future looked for her almost-family. Page after page showed perfect teeth, made-up faces, clothes that cost more than Tania had made in a year. Here on one page was a cigarette-smoking model, showing how glamorous a stick of burning weeds could be. On this page was a bare-chested Adonis in designer jeans. On this page . . . Tania closed the magazine on the camper ad. Was this the way the real world was, or was this what the advertisers expected people to be? The Suits at the ad agency hyped what their demographics told them to: that upper middle-class whites were their target audience, blue-eyed, clean-cut, blond. . . .

Like my family . . . was. . . . And there they were, laughing and happy, in their pressed slacks and forty-dollar haircuts, mocking the decay around Tania from glossy pages.

Tania chewed on her lower lip. That, among other things, was something her mother had nagged her about constantly, calling it a "bad habit," or "unladylike."

I wonder if she chews on her lip now when she thinks of me. She probably told the social clubs that I was kidnapped, and milked her grief for the attention. The neighborhood probably used my disappearance as an excuse to double their security patrols, while setting up a politically-correct fund to find me. Papa probably bought that third BMW he wanted with it, and the money he's saved on my French tutor and racquetball coach. . . .

It all would have been so much better with one less imported luxury car, and a camper instead, out in the woods once in a while, where there were no neighbors to impress.

It seemed like a ragged lifetime ago, those days when her posture and manners were always on her mind for fear of verbal punishment later. There could always be somebody watching, her parents had drilled her, and looking like you were everything they wanted to be would make them do exactly what you wanted. Now, Tania was in a world where invisibility was what one desired most; trying to be unnoticable to the ravagers.

Money was one thing her parents had that she envied— but all that ready cash hadn't kept her from running. If money hadn't kept the all-American yuppie dream family together, how could it help a trio of tramp runaways?

It hadn't escaped Tania that their shared poverty was the glue that kept them together. If each of the three had enough money to live independently, wouldn't her new family dissolve?

God, I wish they were back.

The other three roommates hadn't returned yet, either. In fact, they hadn't been seen in a couple of days, not here, nor on the street. Tania's imagination painted grisly images of what had happened to them, none of which were likely, but still—they had probably only hopped a train, or stolen a car, and were in another state by now.

Or gotten shot by a—

Enough. Worry about how to pay the rent if they'd gone for good, not about what might have happened to them. You couldn't worry about everybody. *Save the worrying for the people you care about.*

Tania opened one of the books in her small stack of paperbacks. She was bright enough to know that escapism was a myth; she read now to find solutions. The science fiction and mystery writers she loved the most were the ones who taught as well as they entertained, and whose characters understood human nature. There were heroines and heroes, aliens with kind eyes, fire-breathing dragons and silver unicorns. . . .

Like the one on the sweat suit Tannim gave me. . . .

And there *he* was in her thoughts again. Maybe she had

believed a few too many fantasy stories. Maybe she'd been tricked by her own wounded heart into believing there could be someone who did good things for no other reason than that they needed to be done. Why would anyone do that? It didn't make any sense at all. . . .

No more sense than treating a kid as property.

There was the burden of proof: if her world were cruel enough to make her an alien to her own blood, then it had to have another extreme to the good. One crusty, drunken old john had babbled about odds last week, saying that if something hadn't happened yet, it was statistically likely to happen soon. He called himself a gambler, but he'd never gambled with disease and death the way a streetwalker did. Maybe Tannim was the long-awaited proof that a human being could be kind for kindness' own sake in a risky world full of self-serving pricks.

If her world was one of insane gambles, then Tannim's brand of insanity was the better.

And, no matter how restricted she had been in Research Triangle Park, her life had never been in danger. Her folks had always seen to it she'd had the best health care their money could buy. She'd never had to worry about guys with guns coming after her on the street . . . or someone with a knife waiting for her on the landing with the lights out.

Maybe they'd changed once they'd lost her. Maybe. People changed—God, people changed. Maybe they'd welcome her back and have things her way, now that they knew what assholes they'd been. They'd forced her to run by not giving her enough credit, but Tania was damned if she'd be that insulting even to them. Anyone could change if they were kicked hard enough.

And that, Tania knew, was the single good thing that being on the street had done for her. She wasn't the mewling brat she saw herself as a couple of months ago, she was a hardened survivor. If they were going to get her back it would be on her terms. She'd have her privacy, her room inviolate, her own choice of clothes, her own choice of books. . . .

And their love. . . .

Tania sat a few minutes, and realized a smile had come to her face. The dream the ads showed could be real, if everyone loved everyone else, and gave them the choice to be themselves.

Her brow furrowed as she realized that was why Jamie had gotten the way he had, though—she and Laura had wanted so much to stay out of his business that they'd let him get progressively more out of control. He was just as much a kid as she was, and he needed someone to say "no, stop that, you're screwing up" once in a while. The three all loved each other, even though they'd never said it. The way Laura and Jamie had insisted she stay home until whoever was looking for her got tired of looking was proof of that. And, as his family, the two girls were obligated to help him out of the drugs and danger, just as they were obligated to help each other improve their lives. Maybe the money could keep them together after all.

A car engine outside roused her from her thought. She rose, knees protesting, and edged next to the window. She peeked around the frame, and saw a glossy yellow taxi at the broken curb. Jamie and Laura were getting out, wearing new outfits, and laughing. The taxi left as they climbed the stairs, and Tania met them at the door, an expectant look on her face.

Laura arrived, sailing through the door like Marilyn Monroe at the premiere of *The Seven Year Itch*, her face aglow. "Hey, sugah! We're baaack! Jamie here picked a good one, honey. Ah been keepin' his sweet tush outta trouble."

Jamie blushed, and giggled a little self-consciously. Laura got in his face and pinched his cheeks, saying, "Jamie-wamie, you'se the best lil' studmuffin ah ever been gigged by."

Tania stammered, taken aback by their happiness. And Laura being sexed by Jamie? That was a first—none of the three had ever had sex with each other. It must have been some gig indeed.

"S-so, what was it like? You both okay?"

Laura twirled in place, making her bright red mini-skirt flare. "Honey, we're better than okay. It's easy tricking, soft kink, and they'se payin' enough I ain't gonna rag on 'em about rubbers, 'specially since it's with mah Jamie, an' we know he's clean. Lookie lookie."

Laura opened her clutch purse and thumbed open a roll of twenties. "Three hundred *each*, sugah. And they need another girl." She licked her lips and winked. "Baby-doll, I think you're exactly who they're looking for."

"She turned about her milk-white steed, and took True Thomas up be'hind, and aye whene'er her bridle rang, the steed flew swifter than the wind. For forty days and forty nights he wade thro red blood to the knee, and he saw neither sun nor moon, but heard the roaring of the sea."

Tannim lay back in the worn driver's seat of the Mustang, hands caked with dirt, clutching the three dozen or so slugs he and Sam had dug out of the trees and grounds. "The Ballad of True Thomas" came unbidden to him, one of many songs and fables he'd learned to fascinate and entertain the Folk Underhill. He closed his eyes, seeing neither sun nor moon, and the breeze washing over the car sounded like the sea.

"For forty days and forty nights, he wade thro red blood to the knee. . . ."

It hadn't just been fatigue that had kept him down the night before, he'd surmised. Conal or Keighvin had no doubt influenced his sleep, playing on his own desires to deepen it. He remembered, now, the other elements of his dreams: the lover that had come with him into a room of green and gold, and laid him down . . . they had no doubt arranged that, too, to occupy him, keep him in the dream for as long as it took for his body to heal itself of the strain he'd been putting on it. And in the room with them had been a sleeping golden eagle, and a tapestry of a kind dragon holding a child, gently, as a parent would.

Oh, the dreams of mages. They were sharp and powerful, second only to the waking world, but just as real in their influence on the mage. The lover had been that *woman* that had plagued his dreams for so long; the one he'd seen while with Chinthliss, so far away. He had seen her a half-dozen times, but never spoken to her; black hair, green eyes, grace beyond words, cheekbones. . . .

Little wonder he had been enthralled by her, and by the dream. Even with all that had just happened, she still could dominate his thoughts.

The Queen of Air and Darkness. . . .

But she wasn't Sidhe, he was certain of that, not even Sidhe in disguise; there was too much of mortality about her, a mortality that made her beauty all the sweeter. . . .

More to be done.

With the slugs in the car's protective envelope, the Sidhe could resume their great magics on the grounds, and safely call up the Lesser Folk to assist. The grounds would be changed, from above and below. Although it might look the same to a casual observer, below the surface would be thousands of tricks and traps that not even the souls at Fairgrove would know completely. That was for the better, too—anyone could be broken, and made to betray their friends, when magic and guile were involved. Tannim didn't *want* to know the place's secrets; he had too many weak spots that could be manipulated. Chinthliss had laid him bare one time, to show him how easily it could be done, then helped him build up defenses against the most likely attacks. Tannim had countered by dissecting him with words. The great creature had twitched uncomfortably as he repaid the test, using no magic at all. It had been the most trusting moment of Chinthliss' life, and his best friend had never forgotten the lesson his human friend had taught him.

There were many ways to destroy someone—with magic, knives, or scalpels of language. Nothing could save a victim from a determined and resourceful enough foe. Nothing could save a human trapped by the Unseleighe Court. Or one of the Seleighe Sidhe, for that matter.

It couldn't save . . .

Enough.

There were two boxes still in the back seat, aside from the tape case; both of them had been gifts from Donal. One was a CD player that Tannim hadn't had time to install since it had been given to him eight months ago.

"So that you may stop fearing for your precious songs, my friend. These little disks cannot be harmed by the passing of spirits."

Oh, Donal.

The other was . . .

He reached back with one hand, cupping the spent slugs in his lap, and brought the small box up into the front with him. He thumbed it open, and pulled from it an emerald green silk scarf with edges of silver and gold. A birthday gift from one of the Fair Folk, one that showed great trust and friendship. Silk, spun and woven Underhill, with all of the magic of Underhill twined in its warp and weft. A single shred of this could open doors into Underhill for Tannim that few mortals had even guessed at.

God, Donal, this is never what you intended it for. Danaa watch over you, dear friend. Tannim solemnly placed the bullets on the scarf and tied it into a bundle, then nestled it on the dashboard.

A reminder to me of what you have to pay for, Vidal Dhu.

Tannim drew the crowbar from its resting place, and slipped it into its leather and silk sheath. The gooseneck crowbar was one of the most elegant designs ever, he'd always thought. A single piece of simple formed iron, direct and unadorned, flat blade at one end, strong hook at the other. No one he knew of besides himself had ever used that hook quite the way he did. He'd found that it would fit comfortably over a shoulder, and never be noticed under a loose jacket even when you were shaking someone's hand.

Chinthliss and his other friends had warned him about his temper. Told him how mages affected everything in the area when they became emotionally upset. How he had to be in control all the time. How he couldn't let revenge be a motivator.

Good thing they can't see how much I want to crease Vidal Dhu's skull with this crowbar right now.

But they were right, and he knew it. If he let the rage inside him take over, let the grief overwhelm him, he would be operating at less than peak performance. Vidal Dhu was a past master at seeing weaknesses that were waiting to be exploited, and his own anger was just such a weakness.

"*When you're angry, you aren't thinking, you're feeling,*" Chinthliss had said. "*That's all well and good when you're putting power behind something, but it spells disaster in a fight.*"

Yeah, well, the old lizard was right. He ran his hand through his sweaty hair. He had to calm down; he had to. He wasn't ready for any kind of a fight in this state.

Drive. He could just drive, and let the thrum of motor and highway be his absolution. Actually, that was not such a bad idea—there was tension by the bucket at Fairgrove right now, and some of it might be the result of ordinary hunger. A quick burger run might do everyone a lot of good.

Tannim started the car with the key and the foot-switch under the brake pedal, and pulled onto Thunder Road, not even thinking of making a speed run. His head was filled with replays of what had happened lately—the fights and intimidations, the pain of little Tania. Vidal Dhu's incessant vendettas. The dreams. Donal. There they were again—Donal and Rob. Damn. So much of this could be dealt with by calling Chinthliss and teaming up with him, but his friend and mentor had problems of his own, and was just as likely to call for Tannim's help. So, no dice there. That familiar feeling was back—of having all the pieces but not *quite* fitting them together yet.

Keighvin's building like a volcano. Conal's suppressing his grief for his brother, but it won't hold for long. Skippy-Rob's death is hurting us all, and Dottie's out of it along with a half-dozen more, easy. Sam's turned out to be stronger than we'd thought, but Vidal knows it too— plus, whatever's left of the Bane-Sidhe will want a piece of him. The production schedule's at a complete standstill. Janie's probably been on the phone all day letting the rest of SERRA know what's happened, so there'll be help soon, but if anything happens before then, we're sucking fumes.

The overcast skies didn't help his mood any, and the drive-through burger order was in a monotone, not his usual cheerful banter. The girls at the window, who usually flirted with him, could tell there was something wrong, and mercifully said nothing while Tannim sat and stared through the Mustang's front glass, eyes unfocused, chewing on his knuckles in concentration.

That's not even considering what this is doing to me. My concentration is going straight to hell. Fighting Eagle could probably snap me back into shape with a sweatlodge, but that's a couple thousand miles away. I'll have to call in allies before this is done, and I'm running out of bribes for them. No Guardians around either. I'd call that P.I., but he's a civilian. First sign of magic and he'd freak. Can't call in the cops, or Terry would catch it but good, plus they're civvies too, at least where magic is concerned. My power reserves are okay, plus what's in the car, but against pissed-off Sidhe? Hard to say.

A polite cough startled him out of his thoughts. The cheeseburgers and chicken were ready, and the drive-through girl waited patiently with all six bags. Tannim sheepishly took the bags, and used the old trick of seatbelting them in place before driving back towards Fairgrove.

Get a grip, man. You could be broadsided by a Peterbilt and never see it coming in this state. He shook his head and began paying more attention to the road, before he ran into someone. *Never drive angry or distracted. Rule one, boy. Innocent people out there . . .*

Innocent people. Damn, with all of this going on, he hadn't had time to get word to Kevin Barry's about Tania and her friends having a place at the shelter! Tannim again regretted not having installed a cellular phone—it would have made that a moment's work. Instead, he had to pull over to a pay phone and root through the phone book for the number.

Before his hand could touch the receiver, a psychic blow slammed against his shields. He whirled and flared out his shields into a barrier, scintillating and probing in the light ranges humans couldn't see.

Before him stood Ross Canfield, hands curled into fists, ready to strike at Tannim's shields again. Tannim leveled a blade of magical force at the ghost's throat, and held it there until Ross relaxed.

"Jeez, boy, come on! Just trying to get your attention. Ya couldn't seem t'hear anythin' else I tried!"

"You got it, Ross. Bigtime. What's the damned problem?"

Ross backed off—evidently, the young mage was projecting irritation like a bad country station. Tannim reduced his shields after checking Ross over, and nervously ran a hand through his hair for the umpteenth time that night.

"It's your little girl, Tannim. She's in bad trouble. She . . ."

Tannim looked around a moment, then gestured at the car with a thumb. "Get in."

The shields around the car turned transparent for a moment, and Ross slipped into the passenger's seat and waited, food-sacks visible through his body. Tannim sat down next to him and fastened his harness, then started the engine and pulled away from the pay-phone.

"Sorry, Ross. Lost a couple friends last night. Still on edge over it."

Ross nodded; could be the news of the fight had made it over to his side.

"Tania?"

"I've been following her. Last night, a real nasty fella tried to kidnap her. I stopped him. Today, she's gone off with her friends to be in a porn movie. A limo picked them up, and as soon as they stepped in, I couldn't see them anymore. There was just something about it that wasn't right—a wall, like you've got on this car."

"Oh, shit." Pieces were falling into place. The car accelerated.

"Fox is watching her now. Last time he talked, he was furious. I haven't heard from him in a couple'a minutes, though an' I'm startin' t' worry. She's—"

"Fox? Who's this Fox?"

"A friend of mine from the other side. Foxtrot Xray, he calls himself. Smartass shapechanger. Powerful. Anyway, the limo lost me, but Fox could follow it. I came to you, soon as I could."

The gates of Thunder Road were coming into view. As

the Mustang rolled up, Tannim could see that there were three of the Fairgrove crew, including Conal, standing around a foot-wide smoking hole. They turned at the sound of Tannim's approach, and Conal walked a few steps to stand next to the open driver's window.

"What's the burn-spot?"

"A messenger," he spat. Conal peered into the Mustang, noting the burgers and the ghost at once, and appeared unimpressed by either.

"The ghost is with me. That"—nodding at the hand—"must be bad news."

"Aye, you can bet your last silver on that." He handed the envelope to Tannim. It bore the black seal of Vidal Dhu.

The main bay was eerily quiet. There were no screams of grinders, no buzz of technical talk or rapping of wrenches. There was no whine of test engines on dynos coming through the walls. Instead, there was a dull-bladed tension amid all the machinery, generated by the humans and the Sidhe gathered there.

Tannim laid the envelope on the rear deck of the only fully-operational GTP car that Fairgrove had built to date, the one that Donal had spent his waking hours building, and Conal had spent track-testing. He'd designed it for beauty and power in equal measure, and had given its key to Conal, its elected driver, in the same brother's-gift ceremony used to present an elvensteed. Conal now sat on its sculpted door, and absently traced a slender finger along an air intake, glowering at the envelope.

Tannim finished his magical tests, and asked for a knife. An even dozen were offered, but Dottie's Leatherman was accepted. Keighvin stood a little apart from the group, hand on his short knife. His eyes glittered with suppressed anger, and he appeared less human than usual, Tannim noticed. Something was bound to break soon.

Tannim folded out the knifeblade, slit the envelope open, and then unfolded the Leatherman's pliers. With them he withdrew six Polaroids of Tania and two others, unconscious, each bound at the wrists and neck. Their

silver chains were held by some*things* from the Realm of
the Unseleighe—inside a limo. And, out of focus through
the limo's windows, was a stretch of flat tarmac, and large
buildings—

Tannim dropped the Leatherman, his fingers gone numb.
It clattered twice before wedging into the cockpit's fresh-
air vent. Keighvin took one startled step forward, then halted
as the magical alarms at Fairgrove's perimeter flared around
them all. Tannim's hand went into a jacket pocket, and he
threw down the letter from the P.I. He saw Conal pick up
the photographs, blanch, then snatch the letter up.

Tannim had already turned by then, and was sprinting
for the office door, and the parking lot beyond.

Behind him, he could hear startled questions directed
at him, but all he could answer before disappearing into
the offices was "Airport!" His bad leg was slowing him
down, and screamed at him like a sharp rock grinding into
his bones. There was some kind of attack beginning, but
he had no time for that.

*Have to get to the airport, have to save Tania from Vidal
Dhu, the bastard, the son of a bitch, the—*

Tannim rounded a corner and banged his left knee into
a file cabinet. He went down hard, hands instinctively
clutching at his over-damaged leg. His eyes swam with a
private galaxy of red stars, and he struggled while his eyes
refocused.

Son of a bitch son of a bitch son of a bitch. . . .

Behind him he heard the sounds of a war-party, and
above it all, the banshee wail of a high-performance engine.
He pulled himself up, holding the bleeding knee, and limp-
ran towards the parking lot, to the Mustang, and Thunder Road.

Vidal Dhu stood in full armor before the gates of
Fairgrove, laughing, lashing out with levin-bolts to set off
its alarms. It was easy for Vidal to imagine what must be
going on inside—easy to picture that smug, orphaned
witling Keighvin Silverhair barking orders to weak mortals, marshaling them to fight. Let him rally them, Vidal
thought—it will do him no good. None at all. He may have

won before, but ultimately, the mortals will have damned him.

It has been so many centuries, Silverhair. I swore I'd kill your entire lineage, and I shall. I shall!

Vidal prepared to open the gate to Underhill. Through that gate all the Court would watch as Keighvin was destroyed—Aurilia's plan be hanged! Vidal's blood sang with triumph—he had driven Silverhair into a winless position at last! And when he accepted the Challenge, before the whole Court, none of his human-world tricks would benefit him—theirs would be a purely magical combat, one Sidhe to another.

To the death.

Keighvin Silverhair recognized the scent of the magic at Fairgrove's gates—he had smelled it for centuries. It reeked of obsession and fear, hatred and lust. It was born of pain inflicted without consideration of repercussions. It was the magic of one who had stalked innocents and stolen their last breaths.

He recognized, too, the rhythm that was being beaten against the walls of Fairgrove.

So be it, murderer. I will suffer your stench no more.

"They will expect us to dither and delay; the sooner we act, the more likely it is that we will catch them unprepared. They do not know how well we work together."

Around him, the humans and Sidhe of his home sprang into action, taking up arms with such speed he'd have thought them possessed. Conal had thrown down the letter after reading it, and barked, "Hangar 2A at Savannah Regional; they've got children as hostages!" The doors of the bay began rolling open, and outside, elvensteeds stamped and reared, eyes glowing, anxious for battle. Conal looked to him, then, for orders.

Keighvin met his eyes for one long moment, and said, "Go, Conal. I shall deal with our attacker for the last time. If naught else, the barrier at the gates can act as a trap to hold him until we can deal with him as he deserves." He did not add what he was thinking—that he only hoped it would hold Vidal. The Unseleighe was a strong mage;

he might escape even a trap laid with death metal, if he were clever enough. Then, with the swiftness of a falcon, he was astride his elvensteed Rosaleen Dhu, headed for the perimeter of Fairgrove.

He was out there, all right, and had begun laying a spell outside the fences, like a snare. Perhaps in his sickening arrogance he'd forgotten that Keighvin could see such things. Perhaps in his insanity, he no longer cared.

Rosaleen tore across the grounds as fast as a stroke of lightning, and cleared the fence in a soaring leap. She landed a few yards from the laughing, mad Vidal Dhu, on the roadside, with him between Keighvin and the gates. He stopped lashing his mocking bolts at the gates of Fairgrove and turned to face Keighvin.

"So, you've come to face me alone, at last? No walls or mortals to hide behind, as usual, coward? So sad that you've chosen *now* to change, within minutes of your death, traitor."

"Vidal Dhu," Keighvin said, trying to sound unimpressed despite the heat of his blood, "if you wish to duel me, I shall accept. But before I accept, you must release the children you hold."

The Unseleighe laughed bitterly. "It's your concern for these mortals that raised you that have *made* you a traitor, boy. Those children do not matter." Vidal lifted his lip in a sneer as Keighvin struggled to maintain his composure. "Oh, I will do more than duel you, Silverhair. I wish to Challenge you before the Court, and kill you as they watch."

That was what Keighvin had noted—it was the initial layout of a Gate to the High Court Underhill. Vidal was serious about this Challenge—already the Court would be assembling to judge the battle. Keighvin sat atop Rosaleen, who snorted and stamped, enraged by the other's tauntings. Vidal's pitted face twisted in a maniacal smirk.

"How long must I wait for you to show courage, witling?"

Keighvin's mind swam for a moment, before he remembered the full protocols of a formal Challenge. It had been so long since he'd even seen one. . . .

Once accepted, the Gate activates, and all the Court watches as the two battle with blade and magic. Only one leaves the field; the Court is bound to slay anyone who runs. So it had always been. Vidal would not Challenge unless he were confident of winning, and Keighvin was still tired from the last battle—which Vidal had not even been at. . . .

But Vidal must die. That much Keighvin knew.

CHAPTER FOURTEEN

There could be no mercy this time. Those mortal folk who had raised Keighvin in the tradition of the mortals' forgiving God had been wrong—there came a time when there could be no more forgiveness.

But neither could Keighvin afford to accept Vidal's Challenge. In a straight mage-duel right now, he was no match for Vidal; and in his current state of physical exhaustion he could not even best his enemy blade-to-blade.

That left only one thing he could do: stall for time, trigger the trap when Vidal was not looking, and hope that someone or something would intervene and tilt the balance back his way.

Pray for luck, in massive quantities—to Danaa and the humans' God, who also cherished children—that all the pieces could somehow come together at once and Keighvin could save himself, Fairgrove, and the hostage children.

"Why here, Vidal?" he asked, keeping face and voice impassive. "Why now?"

"To prove to Seleighe and Unseleighe Courts alike that you're a fool, a brain-sick, soft-headed fool, Keighvin Silverhair," Vidal snarled, scarlet traces of energy crackling down his hands as he clenched them, his pitted face twisted with sick rage. "You and your obsession with these mortals, with their works and their world, when you should be exploiting them!"

So far he hadn't noticed that Keighvin hadn't formally accepted the Challenge. Until the Challenge was accepted, with the proper words, any means of defeating Vidal was legal. Until Vidal noticed, Keighvin intended to keep stalling, while he tried to think of some way of alerting his people back at the complex to his need.

From a half mile away, his sharp hearing picked up the burbling growl of a high-performance engine; a particularly odd growl, closer to the sound of a racing plane than a car. Long familiarity let him identify it instantly as Tannim's Mustang. And a plan occurred to him with a blinding flash of insight.

All he had to do was keep stalling, for a little longer. The trap would not be needed after all.

Blessed Danaa, thank you. Sacred Mother of Acceleration be with us. . . .

He swept his arms wide, flinging his cloak to either side as if he had unfurled wings; at the same time he magically keyed the gate-control behind Vidal, so that the twin panels receded and locked in the "open" position.

"Oh, impressive," Vidal mocked. He had not noticed that the physical gates behind him were open; all his attention had been centered on Keighvin's extravagant gesture— precisely as Keighvin had hoped.

Behind Vidal, the engine-sounds screamed and dopplered as Tannim gunned the Mustang and turned her. Vidal Dhu had not noticed the telltale noises at all; or if he had, had thought it was another car on the highway somewhere in the distance.

Or perhaps, in his arrogance, he accounted the things that mortals did of no importance.

He sneered, and the vermilion glow about him increased. "What is your next trick, Keighvin Witling? Do you make an egg appear from your mouth? Or a coin from your ear?"

The engine's growl pitched up; and behind Vidal's back, the speed-run lights flashed from green, to yellow, to red.

❖   ❖   ❖

Pain from Tannim's abused knee sent streaks of red lightning across his vision. It felt as if someone had driven a glass knife into his kneecap, and his leg got heavier with every step he took. Very much more, and his leg wasn't going to hold him.

Just a few more steps. . . .

Light. Light from the parking lot ahead of him, through the office windows. The Mustang was close enough to "hear" the remote now.

The keys were in his right hand, although he didn't remember groping for them. With his left hand clutching his thigh just above the knee, he thumbed the remote while staggering for the door, and was rewarded with the growl of the engine.

A few more steps. . . .

The door, the last barrier between himself and the Mach 1. He hit it, hoping it would open, hoping it hadn't quite caught the last time someone had come through. It flew wide, spilling him onto the concrete outside. He tried to roll, but didn't quite make it, and his left knee struck concrete, leaving a red splotch of blood where he'd hit.

JEEEEsus!

Gasping for air, he got to his feet again, and made the last few steps to the Mustang. He fell inside, sobbing, unashamed of the tears of pain.

He hauled himself into place with the steering wheel, and stole a precious few seconds to jerk the harness into place, yanking it tighter than he ever had before. As he reached over for the door-handle and slammed it closed, he averted his eyes from the hole in his jeans and the mess underneath. If he didn't look at it, it might not hurt so much.

Oh God, don't let me have taken my kneecap off, please. . . .

And he was profoundly grateful he'd followed an old cop friend's advice—that he "couldn't shoot and drive" without an automatic tranny. Right now, there wasn't enough left of his leg to manage a stick-shift.

He reached blindly for the T-shifter and threw it into

reverse, gunning the engine at the same time. The rear of the car slewed wildly, spinning in a cloud of exhaust and tire-smoke and a screech of rubber, until the nose of the Mustang faced the driveway.

He smoked the tires.

Gees threw him back into his seat, and his leg howled in protest; tears blurred his sight, but he knew Thunder Road like he knew the colors of his magic, and he kept it straight down the middle.

Fifty. Seventy. Ninety.

The Mustang thundered defiance, getting louder as it built up to speed, the war-cry of the engine thrumming through the roll-cage, vibrating in his chest, filling his ears to the exclusion of any other sound. The trees to either side were a blur, made so as much by acceleration as by his watering eyes.

Hundred ten.

The road narrowed, and he felt every tiny irregularity in the asphalt in his tailbone—and his knee. The passing-lines down the middle started to strobe—then seemed to stop—then appeared to pull away from him. It was one of the most unnerving optical illusions of high-speed driving, daring the driver to try and catch them. He clamped his hands on the steering wheel so hard they hurt, and still the tiny corrections he was making sent him all over the road like a drunk.

And the road got awfully narrow when you were going this fast. . . .

The Mach 1 shuddered and vibrated, as its spoiler and ground-effects fought against lift. Now would not be the time to research a Mustang's airspeed velocity.

One thirty.

The trees on either side seemed closer—much closer. The speed made them bend right over the road, cutting off the stars above the road. There was light from the streetlamps at the end of the tunnel of trees. The gates were open. He keyed in his mage-sight.

His mouth was dry. His knee still screamed pain at him, but *he* was no longer capable of feeling it. Somewhere, deep inside, he knew he was going to pay for this later—

but that was later and this was now, and he was in the grip of his own adrenalin.

The speedometer had already pegged, and he was going to run out of road in a few seconds.

Keighvin counted under his breath, keeping himself and Rosaleen squarely in front of the gates, occupying Vidal's complete attention. The Unseleighe Sidhe was still blissfully unaware of the engine-howl behind him, but Keighvin saw the tiny dot of Tannim's Mustang growing larger, and knew that his timing would have to be exquisite.

He's going to have to start braking soon. . . .

One heartbeat too soon, and Vidal would escape the trap, for Keighvin's jump would warn *him*. One too late, and he and Rosaleen would go down with the enemy.

Better too late than too soon, he thought, and felt Rosaleen, the darling of his heart, agreeing silently with him.

:I could jump for him: she added, mind to mind.

Blessed Danaa. . . . It was a brilliant notion. Vidal would probably not interpret *that* as either an attack or an attempt to escape something coming up behind him. It would certainly get his attention. And it might look as though Rosaleen had bolted out of nervousness or battle-anger her rider couldn't control.

But Rosaleen, as strong and clever as she was, would not be able to make the jump in one bound. She would have to take a second leap at the very last instant to clear the Mustang, and that would leave her wide open to an attack by Vidal.

:So be it,: she said, and then it was too late for second thoughts—the Mustang was braking, the engine-howl was near enough that even Vidal was likely to sense something wrong, and there were only seconds left—

Rosaleen leapt.

Vidal started; shouted in contempt. "Idiot! It'll take more than one horse to—"

Rosaleen gathered herself a second time, muscles bunching beneath Keighvin's legs, and Keighvin heard Tannim inexplicably hit the gas—again.

Rosaleen threw herself into the air, as high as she could, flinging herself *over* Vidal, and over the Mustang. But the Mach 1's sudden acceleration threw her timing off—

She strained—tucking her hooves as high as she could—

One trailing hoof caught on the Mustang's roof, sending a shower of sparks up, just as Vidal whirled, and saw a silver horse below two flaring nostrils—framed by a hood the deep red of heart's blood—and his mouth formed a scream he never had time to voice.

Tannim pumped the brakes furiously, pleading with all powers that they wouldn't lock up. He looked *past* the gates for the first time.

There was something blocking his way.

The glow of magic—flavored unmistakably with the screaming scarlet of Vidal Dhu.

Screw it.

The foot went down again—on the accelerator. Vidal turned, sensing something wrong—his eyes grew wide in horror—

And Tannim saw, over the tied bundle on his dashboard, the final moment of Vidal Dhu's life.

The Mach 1 impacted his body squarely, as Tannim used the hood's air-intakes to sight on his hips—and Vidal folded, his face mating with the Mach 1's hood in a soggy, splintering crash like a melon below a hurtling cinder-block.

Suck sheet metal!

Tannim threw a burst of reinforcing energy into the windscreen just as they hit, praying the glass wouldn't shatter. The pyrotechnic-glare blazed out from the car's every seam, as long-stored energy was tapped, obscuring Vidal's impact on the windshield. Then Vidal was flung up in the air like a rag doll. The glass held, then cleared enough to reveal the next problem.

Tannim had just run out of road.

Oh shit. . . .

Rosaleen stumbled, throwing Keighvin against the saddle-bow; recovered, stumbled again, and went to her knees. Keighvin thanked Danaa that Rosaleen was not a horse; the first stumble would have broken her legs off like twigs; the second would have broken her neck *and* his.

The elvensteed lurched to her feet and whirled. Keighvin heard the whine of another car approaching, registered it absently as Conal's Victor, and leapt from Rosaleen's back, his hands clenched into fists as he watched Tannim's Mustang slewing sideways.

Dear Danaa, let him pull this off—

Tannim didn't have the room to brake; instead, he slung the car around, gunning the throttle to break loose the drive-wheels, putting the tail squarely in the direction of momentum, with the still-spinning wheels now working to arrest the car's movement.

The tires smoked like an erupting volcano, with a scream like the death-wails of four Bane-Sidhe. The cloud of smoke and dust hid the Mach 1 from view, and Keighvin held his breath—

The screaming stopped; it did not end in a crash of sheetmetal and glass. The smoke and dust lifted, to reveal the Mustang sitting beneath the streetlight, with steam and smoke coming from the wheel wells, its tail tucked neatly into the embankment on the opposite side of the road.

Blessed Danaa—he did it. In all of his long lifetime, Keighvin had not seen a piece of driving to match it. He sucked in a deep breath, only now aware that he had forgotten to breathe entirely.

Before Keighvin could take a single step towards the Mustang, the engine coughed and roared, and with another screech of tires, Tannim pulled the Mach 1 back onto the road and screamed off towards the airport . . .

. . . Just as Conal braked the Victor beside Keighvin. Conal took in the entire scene in a single glance, swore a paint-blistering oath, and burned rubber in hot pursuit of the human mage.

Keighvin took another deep breath and walked, slowly, to what was left of Vidal Dhu.

The Unseleighe Sidhe was still alive. His body was a broken wreck, his face a shapeless ruin, but he still breathed, and Keighvin could Feel the hatred rising from him like the stench of decaying flesh.

He looked down at his lifelong enemy, and knew that Vidal was still conscious, could still hear every word he spoke.

He stared down at the body for a long time, then chose his words with precise care. "Once before I left you for dead, Vidal, and once before you returned to make war upon me. Once I gave you mercy and let you live—and you repaid my mercy with blood." He drew the tiny, hand-forged *skean dhu*, the little "black knife," from its silk and leather sheath at his belt. Fitting that it should be a gift from Tannim, who never believed the gift of a knife severed a friendship. This stroke would be from both of them. "No more mercy, Vidal Dhu."

With a curious lack of passion, he drove the knife of Death Metal home to the hilt and stood, leaving it buried in what was left of Vidal's twisted heart.

Tannim's leg felt as if he'd been soaking it in lava, but it was bearable. The hood of the Mach 1 bore a huge dent where Vidal Dhu's face had made its first impression. Tannim wanted to hammer the dent out with what was left of that face.

But that could wait until later. Right now, there were three kids in trouble, and personal vendettas could wait—assuming Keighvin left anything of the Unseleighe Sidhe for anyone to play with. He didn't think Keighvin Silverhair had even an atom of mercy left for Vidal Dhu.

And, of course, before Tannim could get any more licks in, there were others with more right than he had to dance on Vidal's little corpse. Conal, most notably.

Tannim still wasn't certain how he'd pulled that slingshot maneuver off, and he wasn't sure he'd ever be able to duplicate it.

Then again, I devoutly hope I'll never have to.

He looked reflexively in the rear-view mirror, not expecting to see anything, but as an automatic reaction—and saw the front end of the Victor filling the rear windscreen, with Conal, helmeted as if he was on the track, grimly clutching the wheel. For one startled moment, it felt as if his earlier thought had summoned the Sidhe.

Conal?

The Victor was so close he could hear the high-pitched whine of its engine over the brawling thunder of the Mach 1's.

Jeez—the radio!

If Conal had his helmet on, he *might* have plugged in his radio-mike. Tannim reached over and flipped on the FM scanner between two four-wheel drifts; it hit two broadcasts too faint to hold, then stuck on—

". . . . *Tannim will ye turn yer bloody damned receiver on, I've been . . .*"

". . . tryin' t' raise ye fer the past five friggin' minutes, ye demon-blasted muddle-headed excuse fer—" Conal broke off his tirade as Tannim waved frantically.

"It's about damned time!" the Sidhe exploded. "Keighvin's bringin' up th' rear-guard; the rest is mostly behind me. I don't s'ppose ye've got a plan?"

While waiting for a reply, Conal cursed under his breath, as between the tight suspension and the low ground clearance, the Victor bottomed out for the thousandth time since this desperate run began. He was certain they were leaving a trail of sparks and grooved pavement. Not to mention what this run was doing to the undercarriage of Donal's precious car—

Donal. Sweet Danaa. . . .

Tannim stuck his hand out the window, miming shooting a gun. Repeatedly. "Ah, blessed Danaa, th' boy thinks he's Mel Gibson now," Conal muttered. " 'Tisn't a plan he's got, 'tis a deathwish."

He raised his voice a little. "Yon Sam's wi' Dottie an' her 'steed. You an' I have th' only real metal beasties, an' we're leadin' the pack. They should be on my tail in a trice. An' *you're* leadin' *me* b'cause I don't have any bleedin' headlights!"

Plan, we need a plan . . . there's going t' be damn-all interference at the airport. Conal thought fast, speaking his thoughts aloud, and watching the mage-sight-enhanced silhouette of the young man ahead of him for any signs of agreement or disagreement.

Staying right on Tannim's tail was no easy feat—it was a good thing the Victor had better brakes than the Mustang. "We're goin' t' have t' breach th' mage-shields on their stronghold—an' we're goin' t' have t' break down a fence there too, if I recollect. Now, the shields, they're likely t' be just like any *reg'lar* Sidhe defenses—an' that's pure Sidhe magery, w'out any human backup. So if you an' me should happen t'hit it wi' all that sheet metal, seems t'me it should go down. . . ."

Tannim nodded vigorously, and raised a clenched fist in the air.

Conal continued to think aloud. "That still leaves th' fence. But if we put our magics t'gether, you an' meself, an' armored up th' point on yon Mustang—ye think it'll fly, lad?"

There was no doubt that Tannim thought it would fly. Conal grinned in savage satisfaction, even though it included a twinge of guilt.

The Mustang was Tannim's pride, joy, and precious baby. He was going to have to spend weeks on it as it was, repairing the damage that had already been done to it. Conal hated to ask him to put the Mach 1 on point—but there wasn't much choice. "I know how ye feel 'bout that car, old son. But ye've got 'bout twenty-five thousand worth there, an' *I'm* pilotin' near half a mil. I promise, ye'll have every tiny atom of magery I got on that nose. So—do we brace for rammin' speed?"

In answer, magic energy flared up all over the Mustang, a vivid coruscating aurora of every color Conal could name and some that had no names, as Tannim released more of the energies he had invested in the Mach 1's body, adding his own to them. After the initial flare, they settled into a thin skin of light, with a vivid blue-white glow somewhere near the front end. Conal unleashed his own powers, letting them meld with the human's work. He Felt Tannim direct the shape and force of it, as Donal and the young mage had so often when working on the Victor. . . .

He choked back a sob, and shook his head to free his

eyes of the stinging tears that threatened to obscure his sight.

This one's for you, Donal.

He let his grief and anger build, containing them within himself until they were too painful, too powerful to hold back any more. And *then* he added both to the mixture, strengthening it as only emotion could, giving it a wild power no dispassionate, cold, controlled magery could ever hope to rival. *Oh aye, my brother, my friend. This one is for you. . . .*

Tannim triggered the remainder of the Mach 1's defenses, letting the energy run wild for a moment before shaping it into a pointed ram over the Mustang's nose. To his mage-sight it outshone the headlights—and when he added in his own, personal power, it flared again with arc-light brilliance.

One eye on the tach to keep her from red-lining, one eye on the road—he needed a third eye for the magic—

Well, he could manage that by inner eye and feel; he waited for Conal's input, and it came to him, smooth and controlled, from the hand of an expert. And so like Donal that his eyes stung with unexpected grief.

Christ.

He and Donal had worked so closely together on that vehicle behind him, working complex collaborative magics. The Victor wasn't pretty, not yet; the bodywork was immaculate, but the paint job was hardly more than a promise, and it still had tech-bugs to work out. No, it wasn't pretty. But it was beautiful, a work of pure art and genius, magic on four wheels.

A complete whole, in its own way. Even if it didn't have headlights yet.

A lump of sorrow threatened to choke him; just before he could swallow it down, he felt another surge of energy coming down the link. This one was pure emotion, and the feelings matched his own. Grief. Rage. A burning need for vengeance.

He gave in to his mourning, to his anger, and let his emotions join with Conal's to reinforce the magery they

had just created. He rode it like a wave, then wrenched
the wave into a coruscating barrier/weapon sheathing the
front chrome.

Never fight when you're angry. Chinthliss had told him
that, over and over. But there was a counter to that. Yes,
anger destroyed control, disturbed the ability to think. But
it *granted* a force that no controlled magic could match;
and this, if ever, was a situation that called for that extra
edge.

Deliberately Tannim forgot everything except the road
ahead and his memories of Donal and Rob; and of little
Tania, somewhere ahead, in mage-forged chains.

In the hands of people who tortured and killed children, and filmed it for profit.

He linked himself into the mage-ram, and filled it, laying
its channels so the ram would dispel moments after impact
with the fence, exposing the steel of the Mustang's nose.

Finally, when he had to dim his own mage-sight because
the front of the Mach 1 had gotten too bright for *him* to
bear, he became aware that Conal was trying to get his
attention.

*Tannim! Wake up lad! Th' rest of th' cavalry's behind,
an' Keighvin says ye're lightn' up th' sky like a bloody
fireworks display!*

He shook himself loose, and took the eye he'd had on
the tach and spared a glance for the rear-view mirror. Yeah,
they were behind him, all right. All the elvensteeds were
in car-shape, and they streamed behind him as if he were
a demented pace-car driver, in a LeMans race to hell.

It wouldn't be long now; the beacon from the airport
was on the horizon.

*"Tannim! Sarge says Hangar 2A is second off the com-
mercial access road!"*

He hadn't noticed any civilians on the road—either
they'd been lucky, or—

*"By the way, ye've run a brace a' station wagons an'
a Miata off onto th' shoulder. We better get there pretty
quick-like, or th' next lad ye run off is likely t' be a
black'n'white."*

And he hadn't noticed. *Great. Just great.*

Then he knew where his other-worldly allies were—they were ahead of him, forcing people off the road so they wouldn't be hit. Bless them, bless them, and thank God for mage-sight—there was the sign for commercial air. It couldn't be far now. . . .

Hang on, Tania. Help's on the way—

The movie people sent a limo; that alone impressed Tania. She and Laura got in the forward-facing seat, while Jamie (wired and irritable, and in need of a fix) bounced into the rear-facing bench. The driver closed the doors, and Tania ran her hand over the armrest, only to discover that it was really a cellular phone. Intrigued, she and Laura began exploring all the amenities this rolling room offered.

The dark blue upholstery hid a myriad of surprises: a TV and radio, wet bar and a little refrigerator, and—

She looked up at Jamie's sudden exclamation of pleasure, and lurched across the intervening space between them. Too late; he'd not only gotten one of the little bags of white powder open, he'd stuck his nose inside it and snorted directly from the packet.

As she and Laura stared at him, appalled, he lay back in the embrace of the seat-cushions and grinned at them. "Oh, chill out," he said, mockingly. "It's no big deal. I just need it for the shoot—"

Then he stuck his nose in it and sniffed *again*.

Oh God—how much of that has he done—

That was when the driver turned to look at them, and something odd about his eyes made Tania glance at him.

She froze, as his glowing, red eyes glared at them through the glass of the screen and the growing darkness of the interior. Eyes like two little candle-flames in the middle of a completely featureless face.

Tania screamed; Laura jumped and gurgled—Jamie started to turn—

And then, with no warning, everything went black.

She woke to moaning, in the dark, with her hands cuffed behind her back. She held absolutely still for a moment, wondering if she was stuck in the trunk of a car, or in a completely darkened room.

Her left arm was numb where she was lying on it, her legs knotted with cramps, and she was horribly cold. She stretched out her legs, tentatively, and encountered no resistance, rolled, and learned she was on some kind of hard, cool, stone-like surface; probably a cement floor.

Somewhere off in the darkness, someone was cursing. Someone else was moaning, crying. After a moment, she recognized the voice. Laura.

Oh God—

At just that moment, lights came on again in the darkness off beyond her. The huge bulk of something was between her and the light, and it took her a moment to recognize it as an airplane.

The moment the lights came on, Laura stopped moaning and started to scream, cry, beg her unseen captors to leave her alone, to let her loose. The sharp *crack* of a hard slap echoed across the building, but Laura didn't stop.

"Get her inside and across the Gate," said another female voice. A cold hand of fear clutched Tania's throat; *these* must be the people who'd sent that thug out after her! Whatever they'd done to Laura so far, what they were about to do must be much, much worse for her to be shrieking like that. They must be monsters—

Then she remembered the faceless thing in the limo. Maybe they really were monsters, and Laura was screaming in mindless fear because the limo-thing—or something worse—was what had hold of her.

Oh, God— The ice of fear threatened to paralyze her, but right now nobody seemed to be watching her. She might have a chance to get away, get help. She rolled over, whimpering with the effort and pain it cost her, closing her eyes to concentrate on moving quietly—

And when she opened them, she was staring straight into Jamie's dried, wide-open eyes.

She couldn't help it; she screamed, and kicked away reflexively, pushing herself across the concrete away from the corpse, which gazed at her with a frozen expression of horrified pain. There was no doubt that Jamie was dead;

he never blinked, never moved, never took a breath; his body was twisted up in a careless heap—a discarded puppet, with the ghastly evidence of violations no sane mind could inflict.

"What's that?" the female asked. Footsteps out of the dark heralded the arrival of someone. A moment later, a hand caught a fistful of Tania's hair and pulled her face up. She just caught a glimpse of a blond man, handsome in a movie-star way, before he slapped her hard enough to lose his own hold on her hair and she dropped back down to the concrete, too much in shock and pain even to cry out.

"Just the little bitch, my lady," the man called out, staring down at her and smiling. "She seems to have been startled by her bedmate. I think she'll be quiet now." He leaned down and crooned, softly, "Won't you?"

She nodded, tears cutting their way down her cheeks. *He has pointed ears. And green eyes—*

"Fine," the woman snapped. "Come give me a hand with this one."

The man smiled and locked eyes with her, and Tania shuddered at the promises in that smile. With a toss of his head, he flung his long mane of blond hair over his shoulder, and walked off again, turning only once to say, "He's sure to be hard for you now."

He had pointed ears. First the monster, then this—elf? He matched all the descriptions of elves—at least, the evil ones. . . .

They killed Jamie. The tears fell harder; she put her bruised cheek down on the concrete, and sobbed. *They killed Jamie, they're going to kill Laura, and then they're going to kill me—*

At that precise moment, the lights went out with an explosive flash; Laura screamed again, high and shrill, and the woman cursed.

"Hold still, little lady," came a harsh, Louisiana-accented whisper in her ear.

She jumped, and stifled a yelp.

"Come on, now, I cain't help ya if ya won't hold still," the voice scolded. *"It's hard 'nough doin' this shit without ya'll movin' around."*

"Who are you?" she whispered back, unable to hear or feel anything behind her, in spite of the fact that the whisperer must be on top of her. "What—"

"*Ross Canfield, honey,*" he whispered back. "*I'm tryin' t' get these damn cuffs unlocked. I'm a friend 'a Tannim.*"

Her heart leapt and pounded, and she started to try to struggle, then remembered to hold still. "Tannim? Oh God, does he know what's happening? Mr. Ross, they killed Jamie, they've got Laura—"

"*I know, honey,*" came the grim reply. "*Tannim's comin' as fast as he can, but there's a couple miles between him an' us, an' a lotta things c'n happen in a couple'a min- utes. I keep puttin' out th' lights t' kinda delay 'em, an' now that you're awake, I'm gonna try and get you loose.*"

"Don't bother about *me*, get to Laura before they do something horrible to her!" she said, hysterically.

"*Honey, I cain't help Laura,*" Ross replied. "*There ain't a lot I can do, but I'm doin' all of it right now.*"

"Why not?" she whispered through her tears, as Laura screamed again. "Who are you? Why won't you let me see you?"

There was a *click* behind her, a grunt of satisfaction, and the handcuffs suddenly loosened. She jerked her hands, freeing them, and pushed herself into a sitting position, feeling frantically for her rescuer.

"*Ya cain't see me 'cause I couldn't get visible an' work on th' damn cuffs at th' same time,*" said Ross, from right in front of her, where her hands were groping. She blinked; a glowing shape was forming in front of her. "*I'm sorry, honey,*" he continued, apologetically. "*There's only so much a ghost c'n do.*"

As he finished his sentence, the glow took shape and sharpened—and she sat there with her hands buried to the wrist in the chest of a transparent redneck.

She jerked her hands back, and stuffed them in her mouth, choking on another scream.

CHAPTER FIFTEEN

Five thousand, six thousand, seven thousand, hold on, hold on . . .

Tannim's eyes flicked from the road to the tach to his mirrors, each split-second's attention divided. The RPM needle swept up as the engine's exhaust note built to a lusty whine, but Tannim refused to lift. He wanted every ounce of power he could get from the 351, and he was timing its peak torque to coincide with the impact on the fence. There were only a few hundred feet for the Mustang and the Victor to build up speed once the last turn was made. Then, the fence faced them: chain link and pipe.

This isn't a movie; they don't just break away, Tannim thought grimly, at last slapping the T-bar up into drive and stroking the throttle. Four hundred horses' strength thrust the car forward and pressed Tannim back into the seat as the distance to the fence closed—

—and the chainlink disintegrated, shattering like crystal shards as the magical field disrupted it and cast flaming shrapnel high into the air. The Mustang exploded through it onto the tarmac, and barely a breath behind it came the Victor. Crackling sheets of flame swept over the Mustang and then curled off into nothingness, exposing unscorched paint and chrome and four headlights stabbing the darkness.

Mage-sight showed flickering patterns of energy all over the hangar door, and more beyond—there was no doubt this was the right place. Any hope of surprise would be lost, though, if the field could not be breached all at once—and doing that meant punching a hole.

I'm going to miss you, old car, really—it's been good. . . .

Tannim braced himself as the RPMs climbed again, and the hangar door swept inexorably closer.

Alarms and klaxons burst into life, while rotating scarlet lights sent flashing signals of danger.

Oh shit. The cops will be here any minute. We'd better get this over with fast.

The bulk of Hangar 2A loomed ahead, the alarm-lights strobing against its flat metal sides. It looked locked up tight from where Tannim sat. He went through a very short list of bones he could afford to have broken, but still, there seemed to be no other way to sunder the magical defenses against elven magery. Lacking a helmet to protect his eyes, Tannim used the only defense he had against the inevitable flying, shattered glass from the windshield. He drew the Ray-Bans from his jacket and flipped them open, raised them to his eyes. . . .

A sliver of light grew from the ground as the main door of Hangar 2A rose, clanking and protesting.

What in—

"Hurry up, hotshot," came a voice so close to his ear it might have been from the passenger's seat. *"I hit th' damn door button, but I ain't gonna promise it'll stay that way fer long!"*

"Ross!" Tannim could have kissed the ghost. "You ever-lovin' *genius!*"

"Save it,"' Ross said shortly. *"You got a reception committee. An' I ain't up t'arrow-catchin'."*

Tannim backed off the throttle. For once, he had all the concrete he needed, and guided the Mustang into a wide arc which would very soon place him at the tail of the aircraft he saw inside the hangar. The Victor didn't need to follow, not with its superior handling. Conal gunned the beast and pulled up alongside, then ahead of him, the elvensteeds overtaking both of them, having no need to conform to the apparent laws of physics. The steeds streamed into the open hangar, a fantasy of black, white, and screaming scarlet Ferrarris, Lotuses, Jags, show cars, all bearing inhuman warriors in enameled armor and humans with high-powered firearms.

Every light in the place came up full, much to the obvious surprise of those inside, giving the Fairgrove team a clear view of their enemies. The enemies ran for what little cover the hangar and the C-130 inside provided—

And one small peroxide-blonde in a torn taffeta minidress spotted the Mach 1, lurched to her feet, and stumbled to a run. And a silver-haired Sidhe darted out of cover, in hot pursuit of *her*, hands stretched to seize and hold her.

Aw shit— Tannim hit the door-release keypad on the console and yanked the wheel sideways, so that the momentum of his spin swung the passenger door wide open just as the Mustang came to rest a few feet from Tania. She flung herself in the general direction of the passenger's seat, crying hysterically, her face streaked with mascara and tears. Tannim leaned as far over as his race harness would allow, offered his right hand, grabbed her outstretched hands and dragged her the rest of the way inside. Then he gunned the engine again, slewing the car to the right on the slick concrete, and as the pursuing Sidhe came charging, glittering blade drawn, Tannim opened the driver's door right in his path.

The side window shattered as the Unseleighe Sidhe went down and the rear tire rolled over him. Tannim jammed on the brakes and bailed out, forgetting his bad knee—

Which promptly collapsed under his weight, with a stab of agony that made all the previous pain seem like a day at the dentist's. He fell, mouth gaping; saved himself from complete collapse by grabbing the door, and hauled himself back up. Tania stared in shock, tears still pouring from her eyes.

"*Shut the damn door!*" he yelled. Galvanized by his angry command, she reached over and shut her side, head snapping back to face him instantly. "*Lock* them," he continued. "Please! Stay down, and *don't move!*"

She stared at him dumbly, as if she had seen too much for her brain to take in. *Aw hell, she's probably seen Ross, boggles, trolls, God knows what—*

"Look," he said pleadingly, taking his crowbar out as the firefight erupted all around him. "When this is over, I promise I'll show you a unicorn. Just *lock* the doors, *stay* down, and *don't move*."

She nodded, and he slammed the door, waiting just long enough to see her push the lock down and duck under the safety of the dash next to the battered CD-player box before turning to stumble into the fray.

Dottie let the elvensteed do the driving; she simply checked over her ammo and the rest of her gear as best she could with only one unbandaged eye. The headset looked very odd, wired in place over the bandages. She had assured Sam that the damage was slight, just a cut eyelid rather than a gouged eye, but it meant she couldn't use that eye until the lid healed. Sam noticed, however, that she had *not* mentioned the rest of the cut, a slash that continued up over the top of her head and had taken forty-seven stitches to close.

She finally took her main weapon onto her lap, and patted it the way Sam patted Thoreau. He stared at it, and her, still fascinated and taken a bit aback by the mere existence of a shotgun with a bore the size of the Holland Tunnel, never mind that it was tiny Dottie who was toting the thing. And then there were the shells, in double bandoleers that made her look like a Mexican bandit. She smiled gleefully when she noticed the direction of his stare.

"Triple-aught steel shot and salt," she said fondly. "Packed 'em myself. Forget the Force. Trust in the spread of the gauge, Sam."

He took a mental inventory of his own weapons. He'd left the water-Uzi behind, figuring that the enemy already knew of that, and were expecting it. *Two penny nails, Colt revolver and steel-jacketed bullets, six-inch circular saw blades . . . good thing Thoreau and I play frisbee a lot.*

He'd been saving the damn sawblades for months, collecting them from all his friends, since his neighbor

Mary had started painting daft little landscapes on them and peddling them at craft fairs. He'd not trusted her around even a dulled edge, and he'd ground every bit of sharpness off, lest she slice open a finger while dabbing paint.

Still, dull or not, they'd play merry cob with an Unseleighe Sidhe's day when thrown hard enough.

I d'know about that baggy of iron filings, though, he worried. *Is the plastic likely to break on impact or not?* He wanted to have at least one weapon that couldn't possibly harm anyone but a Sidhe. There were three children in there, who might still be alive. If one of the nasties grabbed one to use as a shield . . .

Ahead of them, the Mustang impacted the gate with a fiery crash that sent sparks in a thousand directions, and lit up the place with every alarm known to the mind of man. Dottie only sighed. "So much for subtlety," she muttered, then frowned as she listened to something on her headset.

"Sam, Keighvin wants us to check the offices and make sure nobody gets out that way," she said absently, after a moment. Sam nodded, though Dottie looked a little disappointed as her elvensteed made an abrupt direction change, throwing him against the door, then screeched to a halt outside the darkened glass of the office entrance.

The doors dissolved and he and the mechanic bailed out like a pair of commandos. The elvensteed waited until it was obvious that they weren't going to need it in its current form—then it rippled, transforming into horse-shape, before rearing, pivoting on its hind hooves, and shooting off through the night towards the open hangar door.

Dottie moved in fast, blasting the thick glass door open with a single shell and darting through to throw herself against the wall. Sam followed, Colt in his hand and heart in his mouth, plastering himself to the wall on the side opposite her.

Nothing: desk, chairs, a painting on the wall behind the desk, now all full of holes. Typical receptionist area. But two hallways branched from it—one to the right, and one to the left. Glass crunched under their feet. Dottie jerked

her head leftwards; Sam nodded, and eased into the hall
to the right, ripsaw blade from the ammo-box at his side
in his odd hand. Funny thing, that. Even though he was
right-handed, he'd always been ambidextrous at frisbee.
Thoreau had no idea at all what a good doggie he'd been.

He inched along the hallway with his back against the
wall. When he reached a door, he opened it from the side;
waited, then felt along the wall for the lightswitch and
flicked it on before poking his nose and the barrel of the
Colt inside. The first two doors he encountered led to
storage rooms full of cardboard boxes. He checked one
box that was open; it was full of videotapes in blank plastic
holders. The third, however, was a little different.

He blinked in astonishment; this was a reception area
that would have done justice to any of Gulfstream's high-
powered execs. In one corner was a wide-screen TV with
a discreet VCR on top; surrounding it were couches covered in what Sam was willing to bet was black leather.
Matching black leather chairs were arranged in little conversation circles, each centered on a stylish walnut table.
A wet bar took up one entire side of the room. Sam licked
his lips, and tried not to think how much money was
invested in the plush gray carpet, the black marble of the
bar, the lush seating and furniture.

He eased along the wall to make sure no one was hiding
behind the bar, sliding on the soft cushion of the bag of
iron dust in his pocket. If only he'd had time to think of
a better delivery system for it. . . .

The bar itself was magnificent: rare scotch and decanters
of cut crystal, goblets, stem glasses, silver-chased antique
seltzer bottles, shot glasses. . . .

Holy God, I could use a whisky and soda right—

He froze. Soda. Seltzer bottles—the old fashioned,
rechargeable kind—their nozzles were big enough that
nothing would clog them—not even iron dust. At least not
right away—and the seltzer would make a good vehicle for
the dust.

Now if the bastards had just gone all the way with this
yuppie image of theirs, and had really invested in expensive crystal seltzer siphons and not the fake kind, the kind

that could be opened and recharged at the bar, instead of the sort that took refills of cheap canned soda-water. . . .

He stuffed his gun back in the holster and dropped the sawblade into the ammo box, and began rummaging through the stock under the bar itself.

Armed with overcharged seltzer bottle in one hand, sawblade tucked under that thumb, and Colt in the other hand, Sam resumed his explorations.

There wasn't much else to find. The rest of the suite was one enormous room, with tables piled high with video-tapes, mailing boxes, and more supplies beneath the tables. Two postal machines graced the far end of the room.

He started to cross it—and Dottie's personal Howitzer thundered from across the hall.

He sprinted back the way he had come; it was longer, but this way he'd be coming up from behind her, not arriving in the line of fire.

This side of the office complex was a set of small, empty rooms, barren even of furniture. The shotgun spoke twice more as he passed them. He began to pant as he reached what would have been the executive lounge; he was an old man, and not used to running so much—

The shotgun roared again as he reached the door and flattened himself to one side of it. It looked as if this place was set up as a kind of rudimentary video studio. He couldn't see Dottie at all—

But he *could* see the back and shoulders of a tall, slight young man hiding behind a screen with a crossbow in his hands: blond-haired—

—pointy-eared—

He didn't even think; he just acted. He dropped to the floor, putting the seltzer bottle aside, drew up the sawblade and pitched it—then dodged aside without waiting to see if it hit. The worst it would do would be to distract him.

The Sidhe must have seen the movement out of the corner of his eye, for he turned just as Sam dropped, reflexively firing the crossbow.

The bolt *thudded* into the wall above his head—just as the sawblade hit the Sidhe in the neck.

He shrieked and gurgled, and fell back into the screen, knocking it over, and Dottie's shotgun thundered again.

There wasn't much left of either Sidhe or screen when Sam got to his feet again. With the screen gone, the rest of the room was in plain view, and it was pretty evident that Dottie didn't miss with that thing.

And the bodies of the Sidhe—were smoking and evaporating.

Sam stared at them, repulsed, but unable to look away. The bodies were literally dissolving, leaving only the sprinkles of iron buckshot behind. Dottie stood up from her hiding place behind an overturned sofa across the room, and made her way across the smashed lights and broken video equipment to his side, absently reloading from her bandoleer.

"Why are they *doing* that?" Sam asked, fighting down nausea. "Our people didn't—"

"Our people weren't killed by Cold Iron, holy herbs, and blessed rock-salt," Dottie said. "It's mostly the iron that does it—" She caught sight of what Sam had in his right arm and frowned. "Sam, this is a bad time for cocktails."

He took his eyes off the remains soaking into the industrial-brown carpet. "Here," he said, thrusting it at her. "Put that pagan blessing of yours on it, like did with me watergun."

She raised an eyebrow, but freed her right hand to cup over the bottle. She whispered a few words, then sketched a sign in the air over it—

And this time Sam saw for certain what he hadn't quite caught the first time. A flash of light traveled from her hand to the bottle, and the water lit up for a moment. Her brows furrowed.

"There's Cold Iron in the water in that thing!" she exclaimed, half in accusation, half in admiration. "How in hell did you manage that?"

Sam just grinned. "Never piss off an engineer."

Ross was livid, and ready to murder—if he could. They'd already tortured and killed the boy. One of the bastards had taken the other girl, the dark one, across the Gate into Underhill before he could do anything about it. That was Foxtrot's territory; he'd have to handle it now. But Ross had managed to get the hangar door open, and to keep it open, long enough for everybody to get inside.

The little blonde was safe inside Tannim's car—or at least, as safe as any physical body was going to be with all that steel-jacketed lead and those magic lightning bolts in the air. The firefight was spectacular; and the Bad Guys were losing it. . . .

Ross decided he'd better go keep an eye on Miss Bad News, the one duded up like a fashion model who seemed to be in charge. If she had any rabbits to pull out of her pert little hat, now would be the time.

He scanned the area for her aura, a peculiar purple-black like a fresh bruise. It was easy enough to spot; she was heading straight for the C-130—or whatever it was. It wasn't exactly a plane, although it used the electronics of one. The engines didn't run on any fuel *he* was familiar with. There weren't any fuel cells in the wings, just peculiar spongy things filled with sullenly glowing energy.

He blinked himself into the body of the plane, avoiding the dead-black area of the Gate in the tail. He didn't know where that led, and Foxtrot had whispered into his head that he didn't *want* to know where it went. For a moment he was afraid that Queen Bee there was going through—

But no; instead of turning towards the tail, as soon as she climbed the stairs to the side entrance, she turned towards the cockpit, taking strides as long as that tight executive skirt of hers would permit, her high-heels clicking determinedly on the flooring. He followed her, growing more and more alarmed.

Jeez. She got a gun up there or somethin'? She can't be plannin' t'take this thing off—

But that, it seemed, was precisely what she intended to do.

She dropped herself down into the pilot's chair, and reached for the controls. Ross looked around, frantically, for a way to stop her—he was just a plain old country boy—he didn't know anything about gear like this, not like Tannim did.

But that reminded him of what Tannim had told him about how he could glitch gear—and none of this stuff was armored against spirits. In their arrogance, the Bad Guys must never have counted on finding a ghost ranged up against them.

As the motors caught, and the rotors started to turn, Ross grinned savagely, and began taking a walk through the control panels.

Aurilia strapped herself into the pilot's seat and reached for the controls, glad she'd taken the time to rob that young pilot of his memories. It was time to cut her losses and run for it. Vidal was gone, and since the Fairgrove hosts were *here* instead of at the ambush site, presumably they had either killed or captured him. She'd already lost personnel, including some lesser Sidhe. Since the hangar door had malfunctioned and let the enemy *in*, she might as well take advantage of the situation and fly the plane, Gate and all, *out*. There were other cities to exploit; Atlanta wasn't that far away. She could return one day in force, and take Keighvin at her leisure.

She heard the first engine catch; the second. All the instruments were green—

She'd take the aircraft out on the runway, and too bad for anything that happened to be in the way. Maybe she'd waggle the wings at the Fairgrove idiots shaking their fists down on the ground. Then head for new, fresher meat—

The engines coughed once, twice—the rotors slowed— and the engines died. Lights began flashing all over the cockpit, and warning buzzers whined like hornets in a blender.

She stared at the instrument panel, which now displayed readings that made no sense at all. The oil-pressure was off-scale; an engine was overheating. One had never started. Five airplanes were about to hit her according to radar. The airspeed read one hundred twenty knots. The altimeter showed her to be in a steep climb.

She pounded her fists on the panel, but succeeded only

in hurting her hand. Somehow, *something* had glitched the electronics. And as she stared at the display panels, movement ahead of her caught her eye.

The hangar door was closing. Even if she could fix what had just been done, she'd never get the plane started and moving before the door was closed.

She snapped the belts off and flung herself out of the seat. *Niall,* she thought, a red rage beginning to take hold of her, making her shake. *Niall will have to go call in his debts, the stinking corpse. If Keighvin wants a war, a war he'll get!*

The girl lay where one of the Sidhe had flung her, on the couch in one of the movie-sets, too hysterical and fear-crazed to touch. Foxtrot left her alone. He couldn't do anything for her mental state, and at the moment she wasn't in any physical danger.

There wasn't a *lot* he could do in this Sidhe-built pocket of Underhill, anyway. His realm was a different sort of space. Right now he was little more than a glowing spark, hovering at about eye-level for a human, beside one of the video cameras. Still, whatever he could do to help the cause—though he couldn't do much here, at least he could do *something*. He couldn't even enter the human plane at all, not like Ross and the true ghosts could.

Changes in the energy level rippled across him, alerting him to the fact that something had just crossed the Gate. He bounced in place, torn between the urge to see what had crossed it, and the fear that if he left the girl alone, something would happen to her. Finally he gave in to the former, and raced across the studios to the staging area in front of the Gate. It didn't look like much; just an expanse of flat, brown stone, walled on one side by the studios, on two sides by the gray, swirling chaos of Unseleighe Underhill, and on the fourth side by the utterly featureless, black void of the Gate. The two pillars that held it in place on this side glowed an eye-jarring blackish-green. If Fox forced himself he could see through to the other side, very dimly, as if he was peering through dark smoked glass.

The Bane-Sidhe paced impatiently on the other side, rags fluttering as he moved. *It* must have been what caused the disturbance in the Gate energies, Fox reasoned. But—why?

Movement in the gray chaos caught his attention. There was someone out there—coming in response to a call?

No—

There were *hundreds*. Lesser Sidhe atop Nightmares, trolls and goblins and boggles and red-caps and worse—every variety of Underhill nasty Fox had ever seen—headed this way—

Making for the Gate.

If they came through, Ross's friends would be outnumbered and outclassed. He had to stop them, somehow. All he had here in the way of special effects was the power of pure illusion. . . .

And there was only one entity powerful enough in and of himself to stop an army of the Unseleighe Court. It would be a gamble; they might not believe the illusion. They might decide to take him on anyway. By his reckoning, the trick had only a fifty percent chance of working.

Well, that was what being a shapechanger and a trickster was all about, and he'd played worse odds happily.

He took his most recent memory of the High King and held it up before his mind's eye. The memory was about five hundred years old, but it would do. That wasn't so long in the lives of the Sidhe.

He Manifested in a flash of light, calculated to blind and surprise them, and when they recovered from the blaze, they saw the majesty of King Oberon striding towards them.

As he raised his remembered image of Oberon's sword in a threatening sweep, the foremost riders pulled their beasts up on their haunches, pure fear on their faces. As he took one step forward, they turned tail and ran, panicking the ones behind them, until the entire army was in flight.

Fox howled with maniacal glee, conjured the illusion of an elvensteed below him, and gave chase.

❖   ❖   ❖

Aurilia snarled with impatience, kicked off her high heels, and summoned her armor and arms. She ran down the stairs of the plane and headed aft, wondering what could be holding up Niall. Surely it didn't take *that* long to summon his followers! And while the Bane-Sidhe dawdled, the last of Vidal Dhu's flunkies were falling, and her own troops were coming under fire. *Fatal* fire too; most of Keighvin's people were armed with a variety of Cold Iron weapons, and those that weren't were using the presence of the two steel-bearing cars to bend the trajectories of their magics in unexpected ways.

Damn them!

She could hardly see, she was so angry. The feel of the hilt in her hand was not enough; she wanted to slash something with it—

Just as she reached the tail of the plane and the ramp down onto the concrete, the Bane-Sidhe let out a wail of despair and stumbled down the ramp to cling to her with both skeletal hands, babbling, desiccated eyes wide in horror.

"What?" she shouted at him, daring to shake him, hard. "*What?* What's the matter?"

"Oberon!" Niall wailed. "It's Oberon! He's here, he's on Keighvin's side, he—chased off the army—he might return—"

Oberon! For one moment, she panicked as thoroughly as Niall. But then—

"It can't be Oberon, you fool!" she said fiercely. "He's vowed to stay clear of things involving mortals!" Niall continued to babble, and she pushed him away from her in disgust. "Come on, you worm," she snapped, turning, and hoping the insult would wake some sense in the Bane-Sidhe's skull. "There's still time to—"

She froze. There was a mortal between her and the battle; an old man brandishing a gun—and a seltzer bottle.

While Dottie marched straight into the fray, pumping her shotgun and picking off targets as calmly as if she was shooting skeet, Sam worked his way around the edge of the hangar towards the C-130. The sawblade-frisbees proved lethal indeed; by the time he was twenty feet from the tail-ramp, he'd used them all, and to good effect. Dull or not, they *acted* as if they were sharp when they hit any of the enemy—and even if all his hits did was to wound the creatures, that gave one of the other Fairgrove Folk a chance to get in a killing blow.

He made a dash from cover to the tail-ramp of the plane without getting worse than his hair scorched—and a steel-jacketed round into his attacker's face took care of hazard from that quarter. That was when he heard voices—and recognized one of them for the Bane-Sidhe by the evil whine under its words.

Blessed Mother Mary—if that thing starts to howling, in here, with all the echoes—

He froze with fear and indecision. He remembered all too well his last encounter with the thing. And that was with the protection of his ear-pieces. Here, at short range, the thing could fry his brain.

You're for it, lad. This is it. It's you between that thing and all your friends. He squared his shoulders. He was the only one within striking distance of it. And if it took him down—well—there were worse ways to go.

He stood up and walked calmly around the ramp; the Bane-Sidhe was there, all right—and curiously shrunken. It clung to the shoulders of a stunning woman in dark, shining armor, and babbled fearfully at her. She pushed it away, and turned. And froze as she saw him. He brought up both his weapons to bear.

The Bane-Sidhe took one look at the bottle in his hand, and stood paralyzed with fear, unable to speak, much less howl.

The woman stared at him—then began to laugh. "What *is* this?" she said scornfully. "Which are you, Moe, Larry, or Curly?"

The Bane-Sidhe pawed her shoulder and babbled something about "It's him, it's him, Holy Water." She shoved the thing rudely away and began walking toward Sam. "You're a fool, mortal," she said, her eyes narrowing as she slowly unsheathed her sword. "I know all about guns and gunpowder." Her free hand sketched a symbol in the air, where it glowed between them for a moment.

"There," she continued, "your gun is useless. Go ahead, try it—"

He did, he couldn't help himself; he pulled the trigger convulsively, and the hammer simply *clicked*. She laughed.

"I don't necessarily have to play by elven rules any more than Keighvin does. What my magic can't touch, the magic of an elemental can. And as for that silly little water bottle you have, it might give Niall problems, but it won't hurt me. Holy Water is only good against the Bane-Sidhe, not a full-Sidhe. I might even find it—refreshing—"

He shook the bottle frantically to get the maximum amount of spray, as she neared him, forcing him to back up against the corrugated metal wall of the hangar. She raised her sword. "Good night, court jester," she said—

And he hit her full in the face with the metal-charged water.

She screamed; he raised the stream above her as she dropped to her knees, pawing at her face, and sprayed the Bane-Sidhe. It opened its mouth to shriek, and he directed the stream into its mouth—saw it splash out for a moment—and then come out the back of the Bane-Sidhe's head, boiling the decayed skin off of its bones.

The nozzle clogged, then, but it didn't matter. Both the woman and the Bane-Sidhe were out of the battle and no hazard to anyone. The woman knelt, keening in pain; the Bane-Sidhe writhed on the ground unable even to do that.

I did it. By God, I did it. . . .

He took one step to the woman, raised the seltzer bottle, and brought it crashing down onto her skull. His old legs gave out, then, and he sat down on the concrete, and waited for the rest to find him.

CHAPTER SIXTEEN

Tannim limped away from Tania and the Mustang, crowbar unsheathed and at the ready. Three black elvensteeds thundered past him, ridden by spell-casting Sidhe in cobalt blue armor. They cut across his path, in pursuit of two red elvensteeds ridden by gray-clad Unseleighe, whose armor already showed burn marks and holes from bullets and elven arrows. As he watched, the three chasing split into an inverted vee, one to each side and one pulling back between them. Seeing they had been flanked, but not immediately noticing the third fighter, the Unseleighe slowed and whirled, to be caught in the throats by that third Fairgrove warrior sweeping a silver longsword in a massive arc. Both riders fell, and the Fairgrove fighters dispatched the red 'steeds with swordstrokes. Then the three turned as one, seeking new targets. *Padraig, Sean, and Siobhan,* Tannim noted absently. *I guess polo is good for something after all.*

And so the battle went; the Lesser Sidhe their Unseleighe opponents had rallied were being steadily routed by Keighvin's tactical skill—and the unpredictability of the magical and technological weapons brought to bear against them.

Tannim had not yet engaged any Unseleighe in hand-to-hand combat since leaving the car—but he held no illusions that his freedom would last. For now, he was taking the lay of the situation magically, while he had the time to do so. He Felt the hangar's defensive net being drained away around the battle; someone had given up on this place, and was going to use its energy elsewhere. The airplane's engines had started a moment earlier, but had then gone silent, propellers seizing. Maybe Ross had glitched the airplane, and now whoever had been trying to escape was gathering power for a last stand. Maybe it was one of the Fairgrove mages stealing the power away.

Maybe it was part of a trap.

In any case, the flow was heading in the general direction of the airplane; he narrowed his eyes to home in on the focal point—

And was struck sharply from behind, strongly enough to go to the concrete.

Dammit! I missed one . . . ?

A heavy arrow clattered to the ground beside him, from where it had struck him in the back. Its tip smoldered—elf-shot, made to kill humans instantly by disrupting their tissues and lifeforce at once. It had not penetrated, thanks to Chinthliss' armor, but left a ragged, seething hole in his beloved jacket. He whirled, hands blazing with energy, to face a seven-foot-tall Unseleighe who had fired point-blank at him from behind several huge wooden crates.

The bow was raised again, arrow leveling at Tannim's face this time—and Tannim took three stumbling steps towards him and lashed out with the crowbar's hook. He caught the bow, which splintered as if touched by an arc-welder.

Enchanted. Damn I've got a good one here. . . .

The Sidhe's face contorted with a snarl; apparently he had felt about the bow much the way Tannim felt about his jacket. Tannim looped the crowbar's path up over his head and brought it down on the Sidhe's upraised arm, where sparks flew again.

Enchanted armor, too? Oh, hell, I don't need this right now.

Tannim's shoulder blades ached from where the arrow had hit; the armor had done *nothing* to arrest the shaft's momentum. The knee, and now the entire leg, were threatening to freeze up, and only dogged determination was keeping him on his feet. That, and a strong sense of self-preservation.

The Sidhe staggered back, and dug his fingers into the crate beside him, coming away with a two-by-four the size of Detroit. He dearly intended to beat Tannim into a liquid with it. The fellow hadn't drawn his sword, doubtless assuming that Tannim was armored the same as he, but like as not, he'd noted that the arrow's impact alone had hurt the human. The young mage could only limp backwards, mind working furiously to find an easy save—or *any* save!—while the towering Unseleighe stalked him.

The two-by-four swung; Tannim deflected it downwards with the crowbar. Its owner brought it back around much faster than Tannim would have thought possible and swung again, too fast to deflect, this time just catching Tannim in the left side above the kidneys. He flew sideways, landing on his back, and the crowbar slipped from his fingers and clanged against the concrete.

The visor on the Sidhe's helm was down now, a silvery metal skull shadowing slit-pupiled eyes. He stepped swiftly to the downed human, drawing the board up over his head for the final blow, one to Tannim's skull. Tannim's fingers grasped the pointed end of the crowbar as he propped himself up with his left arm, and he did the only thing he could—

The crowbar struck again, this time hooking the Sidhe's right ankle, and Tannim put all his weight into pulling on it. The warrior went off-balance and toppled back, as Tannim recovered and leapt to the warrior's chest, pressing the crowbar's point under the visor and prying up. The metal skullface bent until the bone underneath gave. The body twitched once, then fell still.

Tannim withdrew the dripping bar and staggered back, falling against the crate he'd nearly bodyslammed a moment before. The three riders shot past him then, one raising a high-sign to him before decapitating another

Lesser Sidhe, and then all three disappeared behind another stack of crates. Above them, a flash of white—a barn owl, no doubt giving aerial information to Keighvin. To his right, shotgun blasts and other gunfire marked Dottie's arrival with a pair of mechanics. And at the tail of the airplane was—

Tannim broke into as good a run as he could manage, sending out a desperate mental call to all of his allies, and even Chinthliss. He'd spotted the focus of the tapped energy—and she was just about to unleash it on Sam Kelly.

Sam backed away from what he'd done, inching on his buttocks like a kid in a sandbox. This was all so absurd, and so deadly—maiming fairy tales with a slapstick gag. At his age, anyone else would be sipping prune juice and weeding petunias in Florida, not acting like Batman in mail-order slacks. It was ridiculous, all of it, but there it was—a gibbering, discorporating Bane-Sidhe scratching its last moments on the tail-ramp of a C-130 with no throat or mouth left to scream with, and at the foot of the ramp, a former Joan Crawford look-alike knelt, doing the ultimate death scene.

He could hear her sucking breaths, sobbing, and despite what she'd no doubt done, it was a heart-rending sound— that of a near-immortal dying. Funny, he'd never thought of it that way before—it made him shudder. Or *was* that the reason his skin was pricking . . . ?

The woman raised her head, and gazed hatefully up at him with a marred, bloodied, but by no means dissolved face. She clenched her fists. Sam's heart froze.

Bloody hell, her makeup. It wasn't water-based, God help me—the iron-water didn't touch her skin enough to kill her—

Tannim kept a weather-eye on all sides while running, not wanting to be blindsided again. And much as he liked Sam, if there was a greater danger to be met, he'd have to answer that first. But as far as he could tell, the Unseleighe were at fourth and ten, with no kicker and no linebackers left. The hangar door was closed now, and they weren't going to be able to escape—what was left of them, anyway, unless they had a Gate up their sleeves. Tania was still in the Mustang; the Victor was still in one piece. Keighvin was on the farthest side of the hangar; astride Rosaleen. With no other threats apparent, he allowed himself to narrow in on the one immediately before him.

The woman Sam had been backing away from was standing now—the primal energy building up in her like floodwater against a dam. It did not Feel exactly like Sidhe magic, either—this was something Tannim knew well, something he was familiar with himself—it was elemental magery. It swirled about her in a sullen eddy as she raised her hands to spell-cast.

And where in hell did she get that? *The Sidhe don't do elemental stuff—*

Well, evidently this Sidhe did. But there was something wrong with the flavor of it.

Never mind that; right now Sam was a sitting duck—literally, so far as the sitting part went—and the Unseleighe was about to let loose. He couldn't deflect it, and he couldn't shield Sam from it—he had his hands full keeping his own shields up. There was only one thing handy.

He threw the crowbar.

It wasn't exactly made for throwing, and Tannim was badly off balance. *He* went down on his ass, as his leg gave out altogether—and the bar just barely hit the woman's upraised hands, knocking them aside, aborting the spell she had been about to cast. She whirled and saw him—and he recognized her as the woman from Kevin Barry's—probably the same "Aurilia Morrigan" that had sicced the P.I. on him. And she recognized him, too; though her face was red and swollen, blistered in places from what could only have been Cold-Iron contagion, she snarled with an unmistakable rage and turned her attention towards *him*.

He clasped his hands, arms braced towards her in a desperate warding-spell, and cowered inside his shields as she unleashed a deadly combination of Sidhe and elemental magic on him. She overloaded his mage-sight; his eyes burned with the raw power flung at him. He Felt his shields eroding, being peeled away a layer at a time. He kept throwing more of them up, but he was quickly running out of energy. He'd pumped too much into the ram, and he'd already drained all the reserves in the Mustang.

A lick of fire got through, and he cried out as it scorched his cheek before he managed to cut it off. She was just throwing too much at him—it kept changing with every second—forcing him to change his protections just as quickly. He couldn't see anything; he was trapped in the heart of a swirling maelstrom of multicolored magics, all of them subtlely wrong, but enough so to make his stomach churn with distress and his eyes ache and water.

Another lick of flame came through, touching his legs. It burned away patches in his jeans, but could not eat through further. His armor was proof against that, but not against everything, as the Sidhe with the two-by-four had figured out. The argument his knee had lost with the file cabinet had bruised or broken his kneecap—and had torn newly-healed gashes open again. There was blood seeping through the armor there—if Aurilia saw that and figured out the implications, she could call up a stone elemental to pulverize him, and his friends would bury him in the armor because it would be the only way to keep him from oozing all over the bottom of the coffin. . . .

There were two determined firelords and an air elemental striking at him, relentlessly. They were beginning to hurt him seriously—all of his magical deflections were being undermined second by second. He'd never been oriented towards force-versus-force war—all his life he'd been the clever one using a tiny bit of leverage in the right place. Like the crowbar—but it was likely slag by now, and soon there would be nothing left of him but smoldering ashes in green-scaled armor. He was nearly blind, crippled, and thoughts of submission or suicide lanced his mind. . . .

No! There's gotta be a way I can turn this stuff against her—there's always a way. She's got the elements Bound—if I can break the coercive spells, the elementals will—

The Hammer of God crashed down about ten feet from him. He clapped his hands to his ears; a reflex, it was too late to effectively protect them.

The magics around him swirled and evaporated—

Aurilia stood with hands outstretched, a look of complete surprise on her face, and a hole in her chestplate. As she crumpled, her eyes left Tannim and tracked to his right—

Where Sam was getting slowly to his feet, smoking Colt revolver in his hand, an expression of grim satisfaction on his face. He walked wearily to where Aurilia lay, and stared down at her for a moment.

Then, slowly and deliberately, he sighted down the barrel of the Colt. This time Tannim had enough warning to cover his ears and look away to protect his eyes from muzzle-flash. Sam Kelly planted a second steel-jacketed round right between Aurilia's eyebrows.

Tannim's ears were ringing; ringing hard enough to make him dizzy. Or maybe that was the pain in his knee. When he looked back, Sam had holstered the gun and was walking towards him.

"Why—why in hell didn't you use that before?" he said in frustration.

"What?" Sam's voice sounded very faint and far away through the cacophony in his ears.

Right. Neither of us can hear after two shots from the Colt.

"I said," he shouted, "why didn't you use that before?"

"She got me damn bullets!" Sam shouted back. "They wouldn't fire!"

"So?" Tannim yelled.

"I guess she saw too many movies!" Sam screamed, with smug, self-satisfied anger.

"What?"

"Guess she never heard of speed-loaders!" Sam laughed.

So. She'd neutralized the bullets in the gun with her elementals, but not the ones in Sam's speed-loaders. That was the drawback of coercing elementals; wherever they had the option of taking you literally—if it was to your disadvantage—they would. They had done *exactly* what she told them to, and had not touched one bullet more than that.

Tannim felt his lips stretching in a grin; a feral grin that Sam answered with a nod. She'd underestimated Sam, too.

She'd surely thought that once the old man was down, he was helpless.

"I saw you were in trouble, so I took a chance!" Sam continued; his voice seemed a little louder over the ringing. Maybe their ears were starting to recover. "I figured the gun might fire with fresh bullets—an' if that hadna worked, I'd've dubbed th' bitch with it!"

He offered Tannim a hand; the battered mage took it, and hauled himself to his feet. Or rather, foot—his left leg flatly refused to bear his weight. With Sam's help, he limped over to get his crowbar to use as a makeshift cane.

"That's what happens when ye piss off an engineer, lad," Sam continued, at a slightly lower volume. "We keep pitchin' things at ye until something works."

"So you do," Tannim observed, with a smile. "So you do."

Their troubles weren't over yet, however; for although the Unseleighe Sidhe and their troops had been destroyed to the last troll, there was a mundane problem still out there. Dottie galloped up on the back of her 'steed, shotgun still smoking, to remind them of just that.

"Tannim!" she shouted. The 'steed's hooves skidded on the concrete when she reined it up abruptly beside them. "Tannim, Conal says the cops are outside! We've got them barricaded out for the moment, but how are we gonna get out of here?"

"Oh, shit." The rest were pulling up beside him or running to meet him, including Keighvin and Conal in the Victor. He looked about frantically for an avenue of escape, but couldn't think of anything. "Keighvin, there isn't any time to build a Gate, is there?"

"Large enough to take the 'steeds—and especially, the cars?" Keighvin shook his head. "And we dare not leave them. They would point straight to us and Fairgrove."

Tannim tugged at his hair, frantically, trying to think. "Can't you transform them or—"

"Hey hotshot!" A familiar misty form, visible only to mage-sight, appeared at his elbow.

"Not now, Ross—" He wondered, briefly, if they could all pile into the plane and fly off—

"Hey!" The ghost slammed into him, jarring what was left of his shields, shaking him. He turned to glare, but Ross ignored it. *"If you want a goddamn Gate, I got one for ya!"*

Those beside Tannim who could hear the spirit stared at Ross. Keighvin seized him by the insubstantial arm. Ross started, and stared back at the elven lord in shock. Keighvin was probably the first real-world creature Ross'd met who could grab and hold a ghost when he chose.

"A Gate? Where, man!" Keighvin demanded.

Ross pointed at the tail-section of the C-130. *"Right in there. That was how they was bringin' in reinforcements, until Fox scared 'em off. You could bring the cars up the ramp, see?"*

Keighvin started to smile, for the first time in this long, harrowing day-and-night. "Fitting," he said, with great satisfaction. "Fitting, that we should use *their* Gate." He looked about him, and began issuing orders. "Dottie, get Tannim back to his car; you and Frank armor it to protect Underhill from it. Conal, you and Kieru do likewise with the Victor. Deirdre, Siobhan, Padraig, Sean—you help me incinerate the corpses that are left. The rest of you, collect the wounded, and up through the Gate! We'll gather on t'other side and make our way home at leisure—after we destroy the Unseleighe holdings Underhill!"

Keighvin set the last of his spells in place, and double-checked them. He glanced around the hangar once to make certain that there were no further signs of Sidhe or Fairgrove or anything out of the "ordinary"—

Though he doubted that the police would think what they found was ordinary. Hundreds of porn-tapes, including several of kiddie-porn and snuff-movies. One young man, obviously tortured to death—

And a hard time we had getting young Tania to turn loose of the body, too. He shook his head in pity; he hadn't blamed her for not wanting to leave Jamie's corpse here for the police to find, but he'd convinced her that it was the only way to cover the Fairgrove trail and give the police enough to think about that they wouldn't look for complications.

The complete sets and equipment from the Underhill Studios, dumped near the crates, including what they had used on Jamie—and what few records the trio had kept.

Danaa only knew what the police would make of it all. There would be no bodies save that of Jamie; nothing but the wreckage of the offices and hangar; evidence of a fight—and a mystery.

Yon Tannim thinks that the police will assume that some organized-crime contract went sour, and this was the result. Well, I care not.

All the preparations had taken less than fifteen minutes; meanwhile, the police were outside, trying to find a way to crack the wall of protections on each doorway, and shouting to them to come out and surrender on their bullhorns. Keighvin heard them through the corrugated metal walls—but while he stood here, this place was made of sterner stuff than corrugated aluminum.

Let the police concoct an explanation for how a fight took place, but bodies and survivors vanished. So long as there is nothing linking this place to Fairgrove or the Sidhe, it matters not to me what they say.

Well, he was ready. Siobhan was the last of the cleanup crew, and she had gone through the Gate a moment ago. It was time.

He mounted Rosaleen, and galloped up the ramp. As soon as he passed across the Gate boundary, the spells he had set activated; the substance of the plane, of Underhill itself, tried to go back to Underhill through the only portal available.

The Gate.

Let them explain this.

The plane imploded, taking the Gate with it, and leaving nothing of itself behind.

The protections on the outside walls collapsed.

Tannim's Mustang was the first up the ramp, with Sam in the seat beside him, and Dottie and Frank in the passenger's bench. Dottie's 'steed—transformed into a proud, ethereal unicorn, a glowing snowy white, with silken mane and tail, silver hooves and horn, and golden eyes—was right behind with Tania on her back. The Mach 1 was doing a good job of glowing itself, from all the magics Dottie and Frank had layered on, insulating Underhill from the devastation so much Cold Iron could cause.

Riding just ahead was Kieru, with his 'steed back to its normal shape—though not even for Tania's sake could Kieru convince it to put on a horn.

Kieru vanished into the dead-black nothingness at the end of the ramp, dissolving into what appeared to be a hard, solid wall. Tannim shuddered, and tried not to look—but his turn was next, and he sent his much-abused American-built steed following in Kieru's wake. He closed his eyes, slowing to a crawl as the Gate sucked up nose, hood, and approached the windscreen—

There was a shiver of energy all over his body as he passed through, and every hair on his body stood on end for a moment. When the feeling had passed he opened his eyes again—

There, Kieru had pulled up, his mouth agape with astonishment and a little fear. Just beyond him stood a tall Sidhe; blond hair streaming to his waist, armored with gold-chased silver, brandishing a sword. His face was—impossible. *Too* beautiful, even for the Sidhe—and he was crowned.

"The High King," Kieru said aloud, as his elvensteed backed. "Danaa! 'Tis High King Oberon—"

Then, before either Tannim or Kieru could do or say anything else, the High King shifted shape—

And in place of the breathtakingly handsome Oberon, there was a red-haired young man in black coveralls, with an aircraft carrier flight-crew cap, mirror-shades, ear-protectors, and a pair of aircraft batons—who began directing the new arrivals, as if he was parking fighter planes.

Tannim looked at Sam; Sam shrugged. "Do what the man tells ye," Sam suggested.

Seeing no reason why he shouldn't, Tannim did, eventually parking at the edge of the "pavement" that marked the end of the Unseleighe-built area and the chaos of the unclaimed places of Underhill. He turned the engine off, pivoted, and watched the stranger.

The red-haired youth walked up to the Mustang, saluted with a baton, and vanished—leaving only the afterimage of an embroidered chest-patch on his flight suit, which read "FX."

CHAPTER SEVENTEEN

It had been a long few months of healing and rebuilding. Conal, thorough as ever, had stroked every last bit of information out of the Victor's diagnostic computer after returning to Fairgrove, and had already forged enough redesigned parts to keep the crew busy testing for a year. The local and national news had enjoyed a field day with the high-visibility "Mystery of Hangar 2A"—no doubt Geraldo was plotting an exposé by now.

Tannim had mentioned to Keighvin that someone would eventually discover the Fairgrove link, possibly even one of the few Fed-employed mages he'd run around with a couple times, but reassured the elven lord that they were generally pretty cool, and cynical in the way only Government employees could be.

They also knew when to leave things mysteries.

It was no mystery, though, how well Tania had recovered from her ordeal. She and he had talked often, and she admitted to having lost faith in Tannim before her kidnapping—but Tannim suspected seeing him coming to her rescue had helped restore her faith in other things, too. And being brought to the wonderland of Underhill, astride what at least *looked* like a unicorn—that is, before meeting a real one—had jolted her from her fears. Her friend, Laura, had been badly broken by what had happened, but was being cared for Underhill by the Court. It was certain that when she was seen again, she would be strong and well, and had promised Tania to be her friend always.

Then Tania had been advised to go to the counselors at the Shelter House back in Savannah, to talk out what the people of Fairgrove could not help with. Her heart of hearts had healed well in her talks with the counselor—and that had led to today.

Tannim bent forward in the seat, pressing the scan button on the new CD/FM/AM tuner, installed at long last. It skipped from WRDU in Raleigh to WYRD in Haven's Reach. Haven's Reach was a tiny community with one of the highest per-capita counts of mages in the United States, right between Raleigh and Fayetteville. Somehow, WYRD stayed on the air year after year regardless of its eclectic playlist.

Now it played Icehouse: "Hey Little Girl." The DJ must be psychic. Actually, in that town, he probably was.

Tannim's left knee hardly ever hurt anymore; Chinthliss had finally showed, embarrassingly apologetic that he hadn't come to Tannim's aid. His dear friend had finally, apparently, had a romantic encounter, and was *very* distracted when Tannim had screeched for help. To make up for it, he'd called in a favor from a Healer-friend—now the knee moved just fine, and the muscles had finally gotten the detailed attention they'd needed for months.

That had made the drive to Research Triangle Park bearable physically—but he was still on edge emotionally over what was happening now.

The counselors had been more than professional—they had sincerely worked for the girl's best interests, and Tania decided, after going over all of her options, that this meeting would be best. So, her parents had been contacted, and Tannim had driven her here, to her old home, to see if the pieces could be fit together anew. She'd told him on the way there that she'd know the moment she saw her parents whether it was right or not, and if she was going to stay, she'd turn and wave.

Tania was walking up the steps, across a yard that had at one time been perfectly manicured. Now it showed signs

of neglect, at odds with the *Architectural Digest* showpieces
to either side of it. In the looping driveway was a gold
BMW with a "For Sale" sign on the dash. And in one
window of the house, a crystal sun-catcher glittered, etched
with a white horse sporting a single spiraling horn.

That was a good sign. The DJ segued from Icehouse
to a-ha: "Out of Blue Comes Green."

The door opened, and two figures rushed out, embrac-
ing her for one glorious minute. They stood at the door,
then motioned for her to come inside with them. Tania
stepped towards the threshold, stopped, and slowly faced
the Mustang. Her arm raised, trembling, and Tannim could
see tears streaming down her face even from this far. She
shakily waved, smiling sweetly but obviously choking back
more tears.

Tannim slipped the Mustang into drive and pulled away
slowly from the curb. Tania was going to be all right, that
much he knew. She had loving parents who had finally
learned what raising a child was about, and she would be
just fine.

After all, once touched by a unicorn, growing up
couldn't be too hard.

AFTERWORD

Tania's story is, unfortunately, not unusual. In fact, Tania got out of her troubles relatively easily. If your situation is like Tania's—alone, out on the street, with nowhere to go and afraid to go home, there *is* help for you. *Real* help; not elves, not magic, and you don't even need a quarter to get it.

Call 1-800-999-9999 for the Runaway Hotline. There are people on the other end of that phone that will help you: they'll find you a safe place to stay, they'll help you with any other problems you might have, from drugs to getting away from a pimp, and they'll get you back with your parents if that's the right thing for you.

You can call an 800 number from most payphones for *free*. Check the instructions on the front of the phone; you shouldn't even need a quarter to use it. Just wait for the tone, and dial the number. You won't be sorry.

Make your own luck—and your own magic. And then go and build yourself a good life.

Chrome Circle

CHAPTER ONE

Gently bending the speed limit, eh? Turnpikes were fine things, out here in the Southwest; long stretches of arrow-straight macadam where you could really burn up some hydrocarbons. With one eye on the radar/laser detector and one ear on the CB radio, Tannim was confident there weren't too many Smokies, plain brown wrapper or otherwise, that he wouldn't know about long before he had to back down.

Heat waves distorted the landscape on either side of the Mustang, and made false-puddles on the asphalt ahead. Tannim had forgotten how hot it was in Oklahoma at the end of May, and how intense the sun-glare got by midmorning. Despite the protection of his ultra-dark Wayfarers, he still squinted against road-shimmers, the glare of sunlight off the metal and glass of other vehicles, and the occasional flash from reflective debris beside the road. In Savannah, Georgia, it was still spring; here it was already summer, and the long grass in the median showed the first signs of sun-scorch. Not as much as there would be by the end of June, but enough to make the ends of the cut stems noticeably brown, even at the speed he was moving.

One good thing about traveling by day. No ghosts. Usually. He wouldn't have been entirely surprised to have seen a weary spirit trudging along the shoulder, equally weary ox beside it, pulling a wagon that would not have been much larger than the Mach I Mustang he drove now, laden with all the worldly goods the long-dead pioneer owned. *Or an Osage or Cherokee, trying to defend the last corner of the homelands he'd been promised.*

He chuckled at his overactive imagination. In all the times he'd driven this stretch of the turnpike, he had yet to see a ghost, and he wasn't likely to this time, either. Not unless there was another Ross Canfield somewhere down the road, existing in an endless loop of time and replaying the mistake that got him killed, over and over again—until Tannim or someone like him happened by to free him.

Shoot, by now, Deke Kestrel's cleaned up every high-way ghost between here and Austin.

The Mach I's air-conditioning worked overtime against the heat outside the car. This morning in the motel out-side Little Rock, the weatherman on CNN had predicted temperatures in the upper 90s for all of Oklahoma. Tannim suspected it was closer to 110 than 90, at least out here on the open road with no shade. He recalled working on his first cars in heat like this, spending every free moment during the school year and most of his summers out in his old barn, with no a/c and scarcely a breeze to dry his sweat. He'd come a long way from that barn, and the kid with all the dreams. Never had the dreams included any-thing *like* what had really happened.

Funny, when I was a kid, I thought the things I "saw" were nothing more than oddball hallucinations, entertaining as hell, but no big deal. Like an imaginary friend, only better, some a lot sexier than any imaginary friend a high school kid would imagine. I just chalked it up to puberty, but they're still on my mind. Hell, back then I even thought Chinthliss was an "imaginary friend," and I figured that still seeing him just meant I had a better imagination than everyone else. Until the spring dance, I never knew it was all real.

How old had he been? Young enough to think he knew everything; old enough to impress that visiting writer playing chaperone with his "maturity." *Then things at the dance got ugly. Somebody there was using the emotions as a power source. I noticed, and so did that lady writer— Tregarde? Was that her name? She not only saw what I saw, but knew it was trouble. An adult, seeing it as sure as I did. It wasn't my own little fantasy anymore. Showed me I'd have to stop playing around with magic, or it'd eat my lunch.* He'd had a long talk with Chinthliss that sleepless night. Given how things looked on the surface, intensive psychotherapy seemed like a fine option until his not-so-imaginary friend had confirmed it all. The magic he'd been playing with was real; the things he'd been seeing were real. In pilot parlance, it was time to get out of the simulators and take a real stick, or give it up. *I grew up on heroes; I opted for taking a shot at becoming one and doing something about the bad guys. Clever me, I thought that just having magic would let me take care of everything. Always happened that way in the comics.*

Since then, he'd seen things no "rational" person believed in anymore; he'd been shot at and beaten up and chewed on—as his often-aching left leg reminded him—by creatures nobody'd ever heard of outside of myths and horror movies. The magic had brought him good times, too, but plenty of moments when he wished he'd never taken the particular path his life was on. Sometimes he wondered if it had been worth it. If the green-eyed kid had known what was going to happen to him, would he still have gone for it? Or would he have sold off every piece of chrome, burned his little notebooks, and gone into accounting?

Well, maybe not accounting. Maybe art, like my folks thought I would.

His eyes itched, and he groped reflexively for the package of antihistamines on the seat beside him, popping one out of the foil and into his cupped hand without taking his eyes off the road. This was the time of day when people suffered highway hypnosis, especially people in cars with no a/c; more than once he'd had someone in front of him start to swerve into his path as they dozed off. And there were always the "Aunt Bee" and "Uncle Josh" types, who thought forty-five was *way* too fast to be driving; you could come over one of the deceptively gentle rises and be right on top of them before you knew it. Especially out here. But the double-nickel was just too slow, and the sixty-five limit wasn't much better.

He washed the bitter pill down with lukewarm Gatorade, and tossed the now-empty foil packet in the back seat with its crumpled brethren. Hopefully the pill would kick in before his nose started again.

Right. Your Majesty, may I present the Incredible Hero Mage with the dribble-nose. He'd learned pretty quickly that magic was like any other ability—you needed to be aware of it to use it, and not only did it not solve everything, it didn't solve *most* things. It was about as miraculous as a lug wrench. Hell, he couldn't even cure his own allergies with it!

He never had any trouble remembering why he'd left Oklahoma; his allergies never failed to remind him, usually long before he crossed the state line. He sighed and downed another mouthful of his drink. *The planet must dump every substance I'm allergic to on the state when I head this way.* The only good thing about his allergies was that by the time he graduated from high school, they were so bad that he needed no excuse to leave the family farm. *Not when I can't get within twenty feet of a cow without my eyes swelling shut.* Never mind that the antipathy between Tannim and farm animals seemed to be mutual. Cattle took a perverse pleasure in chasing him, geese hated him on sight, chickens went out of their way to shed feathers on him, and as for horses—

The only horses that don't try to flatten me come under sheet metal hoods.

That was most of the reason for his sinking feeling of dread as he approached the outskirts of Tulsa, headed ultimately southward toward Bixby. His father's last several letters and phone calls for the past year had all been about the changes he was making. Since he had resigned himself to his son's career-track in car testing and racing and Tannim was not expected to take over the family farm, his father had decided to turn the farm into something more lucrative. Not incidentally, it was also now more likely to sell when he retired. The old homestead was no longer a farm, it was a ranch. A horse ranch. Doing well, too, it seemed.

Quarter horses. Just what I need. They're going to take one look at me, and I know what they'll do. Tannim had never once gotten within a foot of a horse without it stepping on him, kicking him, biting him, or attempting other assorted mayhem on his person. Dad would expect some help, even if it meant that Tannim had to take allergy pills until he was stony. *Well, Al told me that Joe likes horses. Maybe I can talk him into helping Dad out, and getting me off the hook, at least until we can head back to North Carolina and Georgia.*

Young Joe was the other reason for this trip, besides the Obligatory Familial Visit, though the connection between the young man who now called himself "Joe Brown" and Tannim was a convoluted one.

Yeah. Once upon a time.

It all started with Hallet Racetrack.

Hallet International, the small and slightly silly monument to the desire of men and women to hurl their bodies as quickly as possible around a loop was not all that far from Tulsa, or more importantly, Bixby, where the old family farm stood. And last summer, Hallet was where two Fairgrove Industries mechanics had been sent to help out in track-testing the first Fairgrove foamed-aluminum engine block to leave their hands.

Fairgrove also "employed" Tannim as a test-driver, mechanic, public relations, and general "outside" man. Or, as Rob had called him, a "gentleman flunkie." He also drove for their SCCA team, but he'd have done that without the pay.

So far, so good. Ordinary enough; plenty of racing concerns had a guy who was that kind of jack-of-all-trades. And plenty of racing concerns hoped to become big enough one day to field engines or parts of them to other teams. But that was where the ordinary took a sharp right and snapped at the apex.

One of those two Fairgrove mechs that had found themselves out in the heart of Oklahoma just happened to be a Seleighe-Court Sidhe.

In other words, Alinor Peredon, "Al Norris" to the real world, was a genuine, pointy-eared, long-haired, green-eyed, too-pretty elf-guy, just like the kind that clogged sci-fi bookstore shelves and played Tonto in the comic books. So, too, was the head of Fairgrove, one Keighvin Silverhair, Tannim's long-time friend and employer.

The other mech, a laconic fellow by the name of Bob Ferrel, was human enough—but *he* just happened to be a wizard. A minor wizard, whose magics mostly had to do with making engines purr like kittens, but a wizard nonetheless.

Not that he's in my league, but he isn't bad in his own area. Al's better, of course, but you don't dare send an elf out into the Land of the Mundane without a human helper to keep him from blowing his cover. They may be competent enough Underhill, but out here in the wild world, they're rubes.

Perhaps if Tannim had been sent along on that little junket, things would have turned out differently.

Then again, maybe not. Some way or other, though, I'd have wound up with severe bodily injury. I always do. Why is that?

Somehow Alinor had gotten himself mixed up with a desperate mother, her kidnapped and mediumistic child, and a looney-tune preacher. The preacher called himself "Brother Joseph," and manufactured bargain-rate zealots that made skinheads look like cupcakes, and called his little social club the "Sacred Heart of the Chosen Ones". . .

. . . add in a Salamander from the era of the Crusades, the ghost of a murdered child, and a bigger bunch of incendiaries than the Branch Davidians. Naw, I don't think anything would have been any different if I'd been there, aside from my hospital bills. The situation was too unstable. The Feds would still have moved in, and the Salamander would still have blown things sky-high. Nasty creatures.

Alinor and Bob had to handle the whole mess on their own; Keighvin Silverhair and Tannim had their own fish to fry at the time. A spiteful bunch of Unseleighe Court creatures had made themselves nuisances over a crucial period out at Roebling Road Racetrack in Georgia. They'd

almost cracked up the Victor GT prototype, and they'd
managed to cream Tannim's *good* knee while they were
at it. Coincidence? Maybe; maybe not. The Unseleighe had
ears and eyes everywhere; like Murphy's Law, they always
chose the worst possible time to act.

For the most part, Al and Bob had handled it all very
well. Alinor had been rather sloppy towards the end,
though; he'd had to play fast and loose with the memories of several of the humans involved, and he'd had to
do a quick identity switch on himself. But by and large,
there hadn't been too many loose ends to deal with, and
most of those had been taken care of within a month.

All except one: young Joe, the teenage son of the lunatic
preacher Brother Joseph, a boy who had taken his own
life in his hands to expose the crimes going on in his
father's compound. He'd turned informer partly out of a
revolted conscience, but mostly hoping to save the little
boy Al had been looking for—Jamie Chase, the kid who'd
been kidnapped to the cult by his own father.

When everything was over, Al had forgotten there would
be one person around who still knew something about the
supernatural goings-on. He couldn't really be blamed for
that. He was a mechanic, not a military strategist or superhero. Young Joe still had unclouded memories, and he had
no relatives, nowhere to go. For the short-term, the Pawnee County Deputy Sheriff, Frank Casey, had been willing to take the boy in. Joe was eighteen—barely—but did
not have a high school diploma and was not particularly
well socialized. Frank felt the young man deserved that
much help.

Young Joe had seen a little too much for his own peace
of mind, and not enough to keep him from getting curious once most of the furor had died down.

Turned out that he was both curious and methodical.
It wasn't hard for him to find out *some* of what had gone
on, not when his little friend Jamie Chase and Jamie's
mother Cindy were spending a lot of time with Bob at the
track. Between one thing and another, he'd managed to
ingratiate himself with Alinor and Bob before the test runs
ended, and that was when they discovered that the kid was

a potential wizard himself. He was telepathic and also had that peculiar knack with human machines that Bob, Al, and Tannim shared.

Now, there were several options open to them at that point, including shutting his newly awakened powers down. But while he was not quite a child, he was still close enough to that state to qualify for elven assistance, at least so far as Alinor was concerned.

Alinor had an amazingly strong streak of conscience, and was quite a persuasive master of argument when he put his mind to it.

He had stated his case, articulately and passionately, to his liege lord, Keighvin Silverhair. In the short form, Al wanted "Joe Brown" brought into the Fairgrove fold, as many other humans had been in the past. Bob backed him up. They both felt the kid had earned his way in; certainly Jamie would have been dead two or three times over if Joe hadn't protected him.

Joe sure was emotionally and spiritually abused by his old man, which qualifies him for help as far as my vote goes. Poor kid. I wouldn't have wanted to go through what he did for anything. Then you figure out what he must have felt when they told him that the compound went up and that the Feds shot it out with his dad and killed him. Poor Joe; everything and everyone he knew either went up in smoke or is rotting in a federal pen. And rescuing that little Jamie kid by going public and turning his nut dad in—that took some real guts. From all Al said, the cult played for keeps; people like that usually find ways to deal with "traitors." Permanently.

Keighvin listened and Keighvin agreed, allowing Al and Bob time enough in Oklahoma to reveal something of their true natures to the boy. If he accepted them, he could be invited to join the human mages, human Sensitives, and elves of Fairgrove Industries. That organization was loosely affiliated with SERRA—the South Eastern Road Racing Association, which itself had more than a few non-mortals and magic-wielders in its ranks. And if he freaked, they would wipe his memory clean, shut his powers down, and let him go join the normal world.

Joe didn't freak; in fact, he was relieved to find *some* kind of explanation for what had happened at his father's compound. Either the kid was very resilient, or this was a side effect of being taught so many half-baked, conflicting notions that nothing really seemed impossible anymore. Bob was convinced that the kid would make a first-class Sensitive and a fine assistant to Sarge Austin back at the Fairgrove compound. Sarge would make a good role model and father figure for young Joe; a true rock of stability, with honest, simple values. The one place where Joe had actually been happy was military school—working under Sarge should do wonders for him. The only potholes in the road were the facts that the kid was barely eighteen, being watchdogged by the Feds, under the temporary guardianship of the local sheriff, and they couldn't just kidnap him.

So they reached a compromise, worked out with Frank Casey: Joe would finish his last year of high school in Oklahoma, so that he had a genuine diploma. When he graduated, someone would come from Fairgrove to pick him up with a "job offer." And meanwhile, Al and Bob would keep in touch with him through letters, phone calls, and occasional visits, by means both mundane and arcane.

Enter Tannim, who hadn't been back home in more than a year. The elves felt very strongly about the ties of kith and kin, and took a dim view of people who treated such things carelessly. Around about March, Keighvin had begun to hint that it would be a good idea for Tannim to "spend some time with his family." By the end of March, the hints had turned about as subtle as a ten-pound sledgehammer upside his head.

In April, Tannim thought he *might* get off the hook; a major disaster Underhill and in the more mundane lands of North Carolina had left Elfhame Outremer in ruins and all of the Seleighe Court in shock. Virtually everyone on the East Coast was needed to help put the pieces back together again. But by the middle of May, with Joe about to graduate, Keighvin's hints turned into an order. Tannim *would* go visit his family, and while he was there, he would pick up young Joe and bring him back to Fairgrove. But not until he had spent *at least* two weeks in the family bosom.

Go rest, he says. Spend time with your family. They miss you; they need to know you're all right. Relax, he says. Like I'm going to be able to relax around my parents! I can't tell them more than a tenth of what I really do! And good old Chinthliss—if he gets wind of the fact that I'm not busy, he'll want to show up, and the last time he showed up—

"Hiya, boss!"

Tannim yipped in startlement and rose straight up in his seat, narrowly avoiding running off the road. He was no longer alone in the Mach I.

Lounging at his ease in the bucket seat next to him was James Dean, famous boyish good looks, Wayfarer sunglasses, red leather jacket, and all. There was just one small addition: in fancy chrome over the right breast of the jacket was a tiny logo composed of two letters.

FX.

"Mind if I come along for the ride?" Foxtrot X-ray asked with a lopsided smile.

Tannim calmed his heart and his temper with an effort. There was no point in getting mad at Fox; the Japanese *kitsune*-spirit operated by his own rules. There was no point in complaining. Fox wouldn't understand why Tannim was upset. And Fox was good-hearted. He'd done Tannim plenty of favors since they'd met.

"Can anyone see you but me?" Tannim demanded, his attention torn between his sudden passenger and the road. Having a James Dean lookalike along was going to complicate an already complex situation. . . .

Why couldn't I just be gay? It would be a lot easier to come out of the closet than to explain any of this to my parents. . . .

"Of course not!" Fox replied. "Why? Do you want to show me off? That could be fun—"

"*No!*" Tannim shouted. "No, I do *not* want anyone else to see you! *Not* my parents, *not* the neighbors, *not* the people in the next car—"

"Oh, they won't be able to see me," Fox said, shrugging

dismissively. "I don't know whether your parents have the Sight, but even if they do, I can keep them from seeing me if you really want. They won't think I'm real, and that's half the battle. Half the fun, too!" Fox cracked a vulpine grin. "But what about that kid you're supposed to pick up? He could probably see me even if I shield from him, unless I made a point of not coming around while he's with you. That could be fun, too. I could make it a game. You sure you want me to stay hidden?"

Tannim paused a moment before saying anything, thinking hard. It could be useful to have Fox appear to Joe— could it cause problems as well?

"I don't know," he said finally. "Just do me a favor and stay out of sight until I get a feel for the situation, all right?" It was useless to ask Fox to just go away; there wasn't a chance in the world that he would if he thought Tannim was going to be doing anything really interesting. Fox had more curiosity than a zoo of raccoons, and every resource imaginable to indulge that curiosity. There was no place here, Underhill, or in any plane known to Tannim, that the charming and often annoying fox could not go. He was not a powerful spirit, as power was measured among such beings, but what he had, he used cleverly.

Fox sighed and shrugged his leather-clad shoulders. "I 'spose so," he said with some reluctance. "It won't be as much fun, but I 'spose so. Hey, how 'bout some tunes?"

Glad for something to distract his uninvited passenger, Tannim fumbled for the still-unfamiliar controls of the CD player in the dashboard. Not exactly stock equipment for a '69 Mach I, but then, neither were the in-dash radar-detector, the cassette player, the CB, the police-repeater scanner. Tannim had never been one to let authenticity get in the way of gadgetry.

Even if he had been, *this* CD player, gift of a friend, would still have become the crown jewel in his dashboard.

Donal, my friend, I never jack up the volume without honoring your memory. Miss you, pointy-ears.

He'd forgotten what he'd left in the player, but the first bars told him. *Icehouse.* "*Great Southern Land.*" *Appropriate.* Fox certainly appreciated it; he slouched down in his seat with every appearance of pleasure, propped his black fox-feet on the dash, and surveyed the rolling hills beyond the window. An Australian "digger" hat appeared from nowhere to cover Fox's head.

"So, where are we going?" the *kitsune* asked innocently. "For that matter, where are we?"

"Oklahoma," Tannim said in answer to both questions. Fox's brow wrinkled in puzzlement.

"Isn't it supposed to be—like—flat?" he asked. "No trees? Covered in dust?"

Since that was what virtually everyone said, Tannim only sighed. Fox wasn't stupid; he had perfectly good eyes. "If you want flat and treeless, I'll take you to West Texas," he said. "Not everything's the way you see it in the movies. Most things about Oklahoma are filmed out in California anyway." He had no idea if that was really true or not, but it probably was.

"Except *UHF*," Fox reminded him with glee. "Supplies!"

Trust a Japanese kitsune *to remember an obscure Asian joke from a Weird Al Yankovic film*, Tannim thought, grinning in spite of himself. "Okay, you're one up on me. How about sitting back and enjoying the ride while I get us through Tulsa rush hour?"

"Tulsa rush hour? Both cars and a mule?"

Tannim smirked. "Just you wait, silly fox."

They survived rush hour, although Tannim had never been able to get used to the schizophrenic traffic patterns even when he still lived here. The mix of granny drivers too timid to merge, urban cowboys determined to prove their macho behind the wheel of their pickups, guys who'd stopped off for "one for the road" before heading home after work, midwest Yuppies in Range Rovers, and people who just plain shouldn't have been allowed in the driver's seat all made for some white-knuckle maneuvering. By the time they escaped the stream of traffic headed out of the city toward Broken Arrow and outlying bedroom communities, Tannim's tangled hair was sweat-damp and he had to force the muscles in his hands to relax.

No way am I going to go through this on the way back. I'll wait until after dark and start the drive at night. I'm a racecar driver, I don't need commuter craziness. It's too damned dangerous.

Fox wasn't the least bit perturbed, which was aggravating. Then again, if there was an accident, Fox wouldn't have to stick around and suffer the consequences of someone else's stupid driving. *I've been in fights that were more relaxing.*

Never mind. The last of it was behind him now. In a few more minutes, he'd have an entirely new set of problems to worry about.

"Don't try to talk to me when my folks are around, okay?" he said to Fox. "Don't try to crack me up, don't make faces at me, don't play practical jokes. Don't try to distract me. Whatever you think about doing while they're there, *don't.*"

"Would I do that to you?" Fox replied, all injured innocence.

"Yes," Tannim said shortly, and left it at that.

Fox pouted. Tannim ignored it.

Hi, Mom. Hi, Dad. Look what I brought home. Oh God, all I need now is for Chinthliss to show up.

He resolutely put the thought away, because sometimes simply thinking about Chinthliss would conjure him up.

No. I do not need that.

Finally, with a mixture of anticipation and dread, he turned down a county section-line road running between two windbreaks of trees. Beyond the trees were fields that hadn't seen the touch of a plow in decades, dotted with the fat brown backs of grazing cattle. The road itself was bumpy and pitted; they didn't exactly pave roads out in the county, they just laid asphalt over what ruts and holes were already there, and hoped it wouldn't wash out too soon. As long as it stayed flat enough that VW-swallowing valleys didn't form, it would usually do.

He crossed two more section-line roads, ignoring the rough ride. Not a lot of money in the county budget for fixing these roads. Well heck, a few years ago they hadn't even been paved, just graveled, and wasn't *that* hell to drive on? The blackened remains of an old barn loomed up on his right out of a sea of uncut grass, and he averted his eyes. *That,* if anywhere, was the place where his current odyssey had begun, in the ruins of that barn, and his budding "business" of restoring cars. If the barn hadn't burned, would he be the person he was now?

Rhetorical question. One that did not need answering. One thing led to another, and if one path was not taken, who was to say that another would not have brought him to the same end?

One more section-line road, and then a bright red, oversized mailbox with "Drake" in reflective letters on the side, and "RT 4 Box 451" appeared on the left. It was his father's little surprise for mailbox-bashers; it was really two mailboxes, a smaller one inside a larger, with a layer of concrete poured between them. Anyone who hit that with a bat was going to regret it, and anyone who tried to run it over with a truck was going to be a *very* unhappy camper. Depending on whether they were driving a tall truck or a short one, it would end up in their radiator or in their laps.

He signaled, and turned into the gravel drive. There were changes evident immediately.

He replaced the fences! That was an expensive proposition, especially since the post-and-barbed-wire had all been replaced with welded pipe. *He must've dug out my old welding rig—I didn't know he knew how to weld!* Behind the fences, instead of cattle, horses looked at him with interest, while foals sparred with each other.

The house looked a little more prosperous, too. And—

I don't believe it. I do not believe it. He put in a satellite dish!

The mesh dish presided over a front yard patrolled by guinea hens, birds which were noisy as a Lollapalooza tour, but the only sure-fire means of getting rid of ticks without spraying. Tannim pulled up in front of the garage, beside a pair of shiny aluminum four-horse trailers.

Altogether it looked as if the quarter-horse business was doing well.

"Vanish," he growled out of the corner of his mouth,

as the front door opened and two middle-aged, slim people in jeans and work shirts came out to greet him.

Fox vanished, eyes wide, obeying the warning in Tannim's voice. Parents. Now things were going to get scary.

Tannim had always known that his father loved techie-toys as much as Tannim did. He just hadn't realized that Trevor Drake *knew* as much about techie-toys as his son did.

"... so we've got a LAN hooking up the office, the stable, and the kitchen, since your mom has to access the database if we get a call from a customer and I'm out in the fields," Dad said, as Tannim's head spun under the burden of all the computer neepery. "We're using dBase for our data, and I've got a record not only of full pedigrees but everything I've ever done with every field. Got a plat of the property in a CAD program, can keep track of where every buried line and fencepost is to the tenth of an inch." Trevor's voice filled with pride. "We're doing as much without spraying and chemicals as we can, and we let the horses free-range all year except for foaling and really bad storms. The file-server's a 486 with a 2-gig read-write optical drive—it's in the closet in your old room so don't kick it or drop something on it."

There was no doubt that Trevor was Tannim's father; the two had the same slim build, although Trevor's hair was lighter as well as laced with gray and cut as short as a Marine's. Their faces had some superficial similarities in the shape of the jaw and the high cheekbones; Trevor's was tanned to a leathery toughness by years in the fields in all weathers. But there the resemblance ceased; Trevor was as muscular as a body-builder from all those years of hauling hay and wrestling calves, and if he looked like anyone, it was Will Rogers. For all his strength, Tannim really didn't look as if he could defend himself in a fight against a wily garden hose, and he looked more as if he belonged on MTV than behind the wheel of sophisticated racers. Unlike his father's buzz-cut, he'd had his hair styled short in front and on top, but let it grow long in the back,

where it formed a tangle of unruly curls. That changed
due to the couple of months he usually went between haircuts, though. He was expecting to hear something about
the length of his hair, but so far the only comment had
been from his mother, a compliment on the style. Peace
flag up and accepted.

Trevor cocked an eyebrow at his son, a signal that
Tannim knew meant he was waiting for a reply.

"It's very cool, Dad," Tannim replied dazedly. "I didn't
know you'd been doing all this—"

What he was thinking was, *Where did he get the cash?
The beef market hasn't exactly been booming. Even if he
liquidated the whole herd, he wouldn't have had enough
for all those horses, let alone computers, software, satellite dishes, renovations. . . .* There were a number of ways
he could *think* of where his father could have gotten a
bankroll, but none of them were on the Light Side of the
Force, so to speak. It worried him. *If I'd known he really
wanted all of this so badly, I could have found a way to
make it happen, somehow.*

"Well, I wouldn't have been able to, if it hadn't been
for that boss of yours," Trevor Drake said, with a certain
fond satisfaction. "You signed on with a good firm, there.
Remember when you had that pile-up a couple of years
ago that landed you in the hospital, and he sent you off
for some rest?"

*When that mess with the Unseleighe against the
Underhill side of Fairgrove happened, and I creamed my
knee the first time, yeah.* He nodded cautiously. *Dad had
been talking about wanting to convert to quarter horses,
but he didn't have the bread.* A certain suspicion dawned,
hardening into certainty when he dredged up a vague
memory of drugged hallucinations while healing. Yeah, he'd
been babbling something in a dream about his parents'
money troubles, how he was worried about who'd take care
of them if something happened to him, and how it would
take a big load off his mind if only he could do something
about it.

"You wouldn't believe how well he has you insured,"
Dad continued. Tannim nodded cautiously again. "Turns

out he's got a basic load of policies on you, with us as beneficiaries on some of 'em. And when you tore up your knee, once the fuss all died down, they sent us a check. A *really* big check. I thought it was a mistake, so I called Fairgrove, but your Mister Silver said no, it was right, and I was supposed to keep the money, and then he asked if the herd was still for sale. Paid me top dollar for 'em. Between that and the insurance money, we had enough for some top stock and all the rest of this."

That pointy-eared— Tannim bent down to adjust his pant-cuff as an excuse to keep his father from seeing his face flush. He throttled his reactions and simply shook his head, expressing mild appreciation of "Mister Silver's" generosity. Actually, he wasn't quite sure how to feel. Not that he wasn't pleased that his folks had been taken care of, but—

It felt like a cheat.

You've got no right to feel that way, he scolded himself, as his father led the way to his old room and showed him where the file server lurked in the back of the closet, humming to itself. *Dad's worked hard all his life. He earned all this, it wasn't just given to him! Yeah, Keighvin was making sure that Mom and Dad were going to be okay. That's the way he operates. No matter how modern he acts on the surface, underneath it all he's still a medieval feudal lord, and medieval feudal lords take care of their people and the relatives of their people. It comes with the territory.*

Put that way, he felt a little better about it all. But it would have been nice if Keighvin had *asked* first.

Medieval feudal lords don't ask, they dictate. It's just— dammit, he took it all out of my hands, and they're my parents! I thought I was doing all right by them, and then Keighvin comes in and trumps me! I feel like he took me right out of the loop, and he eavesdropped on my dreams to do it. I suppose I ought to be grateful he didn't send them a bag of gold or something.

"It was pretty funny, son—Mister Silver had the check for the cattle sent over in a Wells Fargo bag marked 'gold bullion.' I thought I was gonna bust a gut laughing!"

That does it. Silverhair Stew when I get back to Georgia.

"When you're ready, come on down to the stables," his dad was saying while Tannim brooded over the file server as if it was personally responsible for all this. "I've got some stuff down there that I have to take care of right now, and a lot more I can't wait to show you."

"Great—" Tannim began, but his Dad was already gone.

He turned around slowly, and shut the door. The Ferrari poster he'd hung on the back of the door when he was ten was still there; so were all the models he'd built, although *he* had never arranged them quite so neatly on the shelves. And he didn't remember all those shelves being there, either.

The plain wooden desk was empty, except for a clean blotter, a phone, and a single pen next to a cube of notepaper. It had never been that empty when he'd lived here, not even on the rare occasions that he'd actually cleaned the room. It was always piled with car magazines, comics, rock rags, books about art, and paperback science fiction books. His autographed picture of Richard Petty had been neatly framed and now hung right over the desk, but the holes where he'd thumbtacked it to the wall still showed near the edge of the mat. The drawers of the desk and the matching bureau beside it were empty, but all of his paperbacks were in a new bookcase on the other side of the desk, with a set of magazine-holders taking care of the magazines. There was a metal Route 66 sign hanging on the wall opposite the Petty photo, and his tattered Rush 2112 banner.

Someone had refinished the desk, and done it well enough that all the stains from oil and WD-40 he'd made when he rebuilt carburetors on it were gone. He ran his fingers slowly across the edges and surface. It felt as if someone had erased part of his life with the stains, even though he had tried to remove those stains himself a hundred times.

The room had been repainted and there were new curtains, but the carpet was the same, and the bedspread. But in place of his old clock-radio on the stand beside the bed there was a new digital clock-radio that included a CD player. Replacing the old black-and-white TV he'd rescued from the junkyard and repaired with Deke Kestrel's help, there was a new color portable. No cracked case, no channel knob that had to be turned with vise-grips; this television had an auto-tuner. It could effortlessly lock in a vivid image, just like he had tuned in those strong images in that very bed, so long ago, of the dragons and magic and *her*. All she had done with him—and to him—had seemed so rich and real, erotic and more. But only a few of those images of dragons and adventure had come true, and his ethereal lover had yet to appear in the real world.

This, the real world, where he stood like an artist who has walked into a gallery to see his life's work re-framed while he was away for lunch.

The room felt both familiar and alien at once. *This is surreal. Very, very surreal.* He just wasn't certain of anything at the moment; he felt unbalanced, uncomfortable, as if he had tried on clothing that was too tight.

This is why I don't come back. Because you can't come back. I can't be what I used to be, I can only try to fake what my folks remember. If I just act . . . no . . . if I'm just myself, they'd never be able to handle that. They'll wonder what they did wrong. Parents are as fallible as anyone else, and they made mistakes with me. They want to know what they did right—but like anyone else, they have rigid ideas of exactly what's right. It doesn't take a rocket scientist to figure out that a boy-genius grease monkey isn't what a farmer wants or expects.

As he stared down at the worn red ribcord bedspread, Fox materialized on the bed. He looked a little less like James Dean now, and a little more like the lead singer of the Stray Cats.

"Hey," he said cheerfully. "Nice place! You seen the stables yet?"

"No," Tannim replied cautiously. "Why?"

Fox just snickered. "You're in for a big surprise."

Tannim stared at the horse. The horse stared back and laid its ears down in an unmistakable expression of threat.

"Just hold the reins, son," Trevor repeated patiently. "He won't hurt you."

"Dad—that's a *stallion*. Stallions are aggressive, even I know that much. And he doesn't like me." Fluorescent lighting hanging from the metal rafters of the ceiling showed every nuance of the stallion's expression, and it was not a friendly one. Tannim would have backed off another pace, but there was a cinder-block wall in the way. The horse bared its teeth at him and stamped its foot on the rubber mat covering the cement floor.

Trevor sighed. "That horse is a kitten. Tannim, your *mother* can hold that horse."

"Then why isn't she here instead of me?" he asked, as the stallion stamped his foot a second time—possibly indicating what he wanted to do if Tannim's feet got within his reach.

"He's not interested in you," Trevor replied, patiently. "He has other things on his mind right now."

"I'll bet," Tannim muttered, trying to inch away.

Trevor stood beside something that vaguely resembled the gym apparatus known as a pommel-horse, holding an object like a cross between a large hot water bottle and an elephant's trunk, he referred to as an "AV." He *said* he was going to "collect" the stallion, and he wanted Tannim's help. Tannim did not want to know what an "AV" was, and he certainly did not want to help in what he *thought* his father was going to do.

"Dad, that horse is going to kill me." He said this slowly and carefully, so there could be no mistake. The horse confirmed his words with a neigh, a snort, and another exhibition of teeth. "That horse *wants* to kill me. I did not drive all the way from Savannah to be killed by a horse, *or* to assist you in giving one a good time!"

Trevor shook his head, whether in denial or in disgust, his son wasn't entirely certain. But at that moment, Tannim's allergies realized that he was standing in *straw*, in a stable full of *hay, dust,* and *powdered grain,* and not more than ten feet away from a large, sweaty, dander-laden *animal*.

He exploded into a volley of violent sneezing. The

horse lost all interest in killing him, and backed away
from him in alarm as far as the lead on the halter would
permit. The horse's eyes rolled alarmingly, and it uttered
a pitiful whine as it danced around and jerked on the
rope holding it to the side of the stall. Trevor swore
under his breath, put the "AV" down, and worked his
way hand-over-hand up the rope to the stallion's head
to try and calm it. Tannim took this as permission to
escape.

He retreated immediately, eyes streaming, nose running,
only to meet his mother at the kitchen door. "Dad deeds
you, Bomb," he got out between sneezes. "Dable. Wid da
dallion."

Correctly interpreting this as a message that Trevor
needed help with his champion stallion, Tannim's mother
thrust a box of tissues at him and trotted across the back-
yard in the direction of the stables. He continued his
retreat to the bathroom across from his room, where he
had prudently stashed everything he was afraid he might
need.

He turned on the shower as high as it would go, and
steam poured over the top of the curtain-rod, giving him
a little relief. As he popped pills out of their plastic-and-foil
bubbles and gulped them down, he heard the shower-radio
come on all by itself.

It can't be heat- or water-activated. So— He stripped
off his clothing and ducked into the shower, putting his
head under the hot water to ease his aching sinuses. *It's
him. Maybe if I ignore him—*

"Hey! It's Fox-on-the-Radio, taking the third caller who
can tell me Elvis Costello's favorite flavor of chewing gum,
or answer the Super Mondo Nifty Keen-o Boffo Kewl
Bonus Question: Just what is Tannim, the most eligible
bachelor mage in southern Bixby Oklahoma, listening
to?!" came an all-too-familiar voice from the waterproof
speaker.

Tannim took his head out from under the stream of hot
water long enough to look blearily at the white plastic radio.
"Fox," he said at last, "you are *weird.*"

"Hey! That's the *right* answer, caller number three! And

you win—a *bar of soap!*" A bar of soap popped out of the bottom of the radio, forcing Tannim to grab for it before it got under his feet, only to discover that it was an illusion. "That's right, it's WYRD, *weird radio!*"

"WYRD is in North Carolina," Tannim corrected automatically. "In Haven's Reach. This is Oklahoma."

"So how *'bout* that reception?" Fox replied gaily. "It must be something in the pipes. Yes, it's WYRD, all-talk-talking, all day, all night, all the—"

Tannim reached over and turned off the radio with a firm *click.*

One super-hot shower with lots of steam, half a bottle of eyedrops, two antihistamines and a few squirts of lilac-scented "prescription stuff" up his nose later, he felt as if he might survive until suppertime, at least. Even if he *was* groggy now, it was better than being unable to see or breathe.

Maybe I can just stay in the bathroom for the whole visit?

No, that would be the coward's way out. Besides, Fox would DJ him to death. Or worse. The fox was shameless.

He ventured out into the hallway, hearing voices from the kitchen, and decided he might just as well face the music. The kitchen had been redone, too, but he *knew* that he had paid for that, at least—it had been his Mother's Day gift about three years ago. Right now, that made it the one place in the house he felt the most comfortable in.

His father was sitting at a stool at the wood-and-tile breakfast bar while his mother did something arcane with a piece of raw meat. Both of them looked up as he came in, and to his relief, both of them were smiling.

"I was beginning to think I'd failed my Test of Manhood," he began, and his mother giggled. She still looked a lot like her old high school pictures from the late '50s; a little grayer, a little older, but still remarkably like a Gidget-clone.

"I'm sorry, son," Trevor said, with real apology in his voice. "I keep forgetting about your allergies—that is, I *remember* them, but I keep forgetting how bad they really are. I shouldn't have even asked you to go out there with me."

This, of course, immediately made Tannim feel even more guilty than he already did. *Didn't live up to their expectations, again.* "Look, I should have known better," he interrupted. "I brought a respirator, like we use for painting cars. It's in the trunk. I could wear that and—"

His mother shook her head, still giggling. "Oh no—dear heaven, no, don't do that! The horses would be terrified!"

Well, that'll be a first. Usually they terrify me.

"It's all right," his father said hastily. "Your mother can help me, it'll be fine. She's the best hand with a stallion I've ever seen, anyway."

Tannim bit his tongue to keep from saying anything really crude, and managed to dilute all the things that sprang immediately to mind down to a mild, "Well, she *did* rope you, didn't she?"

That made his father roar with laughter, and his mother blush and giggle, and eased at least a little of the tension among them.

He managed to keep the conversation on safe subjects up to and through dinner—mostly on what those few of his classmates who were still in the Tulsa area were doing. He didn't really *care,* if the truth were to be told, but it gave his parents something to talk about, and when they were talking, they weren't asking him questions he couldn't answer.

In a way, it was rather sad. The stars of the high school athletic teams had all, to a man, washed out in college or in the minor leagues and were now selling cars, or working oil field or construction jobs. Most of the girls that were still in the area were married, and on either their third kids or second divorces. Tannim hadn't kept in touch with any of them, for good reason. He'd had nothing in common with them in high school, and had even less now.

The only kid he *had* kept in constant touch with was Deke Kestrel, and he knew right where Deke was. Down in Austin Texas, working as a studio musician, and doing a damn fine job of it. Deke was sitting in with Eric

Johnson and the other local heroes of the Oasis of Texas. He was also training *his* more "esoteric" skills, but once again, that was something he couldn't talk to his parents about.

"What ever happened to that girl you used to date, honey?" his mother asked, breaking into his thoughts. "The one who was so into science? Trisha, Trixie—"

"Trina," he corrected without thinking. "She finished her doctorate. She's at Johns Hopkins, doing research into viral proteins."

"Oh." From the rather stunned look on both his parents' faces, this was not something they had ever anticipated hearing over the dinner table. *How nice—and you drive cars for a living, dear? Congratulations Tannim, you certainly killed that subject dead in its tracks.* But his mother was persistent, he had to give her that. "Well, what about that friend of yours that went into musicals—"

"I don't know," he lied. "I lost touch with him after he went to New York." *I lost touch with him after he died of AIDS, Mom.* This was turning into the most depressing dinner conversation he had ever had. *I'd better talk about something cheerful, quick.* "I heard from Deke Kestrel just a couple of days ago, though—he's doing backup work for a really incredible guitarist in Austin. It's the guy's fourth CD, and Deke says the guy might do a guest shot on his first solo project."

That revived the conversation again, and he managed to keep it on Deke and how well Deke was doing until the dishes were safely cleared and in the dishwasher.

Then he pleaded fatigue and fled to his room. At least he could call Joe and get that much accomplished. Set up the meeting, feel the kid out, make sure he wanted to go through with this. Try and tell him what the pros and cons of the job were. That was one thing Chinthliss had never been able to get through *his* head, but Joe already had a taste of the "cons." And at least with Joe, he would not have to hold anything back.

It wasn't very comforting to think that he had more in common with Joe, someone he didn't even know, than he did with his own family.

He moved the phone over to the bedside stand, called directory assistance for Frank Casey's number in Pawnee, then took a deep breath to steady himself and dialed.

"I'd like to talk to Joe Brown, please," he said carefully. "This is Tannim, from Fairgrove Industries. . . ."

CHAPTER TWO

Joe nodded as he spoke, forgetting that the man from Fairgrove couldn't see him. The window-unit a/c in the living room came to life with a shudder. The banter of a news-show anchor harmonized oddly with the hum. A drift of cold wafted down the hallway at ankle-height from the direction of the living room. "Yes, sir," he said. "I can do that, sir. I'll be ready."

Joe hung up the old hall phone with a feeling of anticipation mixed with trepidation. So, it was finally going to happen. This whole strange year was finally over. "That was the man from Fairgrove," he called into the living room. "He's in Bixby. He says he'll meet me tomorrow for lunch."

His guardian, the sheriff of Pawnee County, Frank Casey, got up out of his chair with a creak of wood and leather audible over the television and the air conditioner. He turned down the volume on the television and came out into the hallway of the tiny house he shared with Joe, blocking off most of the light from the living room. Frank was a big man, one who truly filled the doorway, and his Native American ancestors would have identified him immediately as a warrior, even without paint, honor-feathers, or any other traditional signs. It was the ambient radiation of *warrior,* a halo of not-quite-there colors that Joe was able to see now, after some coaching and training from Alinor and Bob. There were other colors in that aura, colors that told Joe that his guardian was just as hopeful, and anxious, as he himself was, despite Frank's impassive expression.

"You don't have to go through with this if you don't want to," Frank said solemnly, while the a/c shuddered into silence and the sound of cicadas outside the front door behind Joe grew louder. "I don't care what you promised that fellow from Fairgrove. If you aren't comfortable with this, we can find somewhere else for you. Maybe you should consider college again?"

Joe shook his head as the cicadas wound down for a breather. "No, thanks," he said awkwardly. "Sir, I appreciate your thinking about it and all, but this is going to be for the best. You know I won't ever fit in around here. These Fairgrove people, they know about people like me. I don't think college is the right thing for me now. I'm not ready for it, and I really don't think any college is ready for me. Besides, Fairgrove promised me a full ride if I want to go to college later."

Frank grunted, and the wooden floor creaked beneath him as he shifted his weight. "Sounds too good to be true, like the things recruiters promise you to get you to sign up."

It was Joe's turn to shrug. How could he ever explain to his guardian *why* he trusted these people to keep their promises? Frank would never believe him. Even though he'd been right there to see the worst that the Salamander could do, he no longer believed in the creature's existence. Somehow he'd managed to convince himself that more than half of what had happened during the raid had been optical illusions and the rest was delusion. He'd even forgotten how the Salamander had warned the cult followers about police raids and the like.

That happens to people, Al said. When something happens that just doesn't fit with their idea of reality, they'll chip away at it and twist it until they make it fit. I guess that's what happened to Frank.

"They have a good reputation, sir," he replied. "You checked them out yourself."

His guardian nodded slowly. "I did, and I admit they came out clean on all counts. And you are old enough to make up your own mind. Still—you're also old enough to change it if you want, and if you do, well, you've got a place here."

Joe flushed, but with pleasure as well as embarrassment. He knew there were more things that Frank could not bring himself to say. The lawman was nothing if not stoic. "Thank you, sir," he replied awkwardly. "I—ah—I probably ought to get some sleep. Good night, sir."

"Good night, son," Frank said softly, as Joe retreated to the little guest room that had been his home over the past year and more. "Pleasant dreams."

The ten-by-ten room was tiny, especially in comparison with the luxurious suite his father had bestowed on him just before he had defected from the cult. The walls, with their faded floral wallpaper, sometimes leaked cold air in the winter, but it was nothing compared to the cold fear he'd always endured around his father. The ancient window air conditioner wheezed every time it came on, and it vibrated so hard that it rattled the windows in their frames, but the machinery that kept the underground complex of his youth running had been just as loud. The only furniture was a single bureau, a tiny corner-desk where he did his homework, and an equally tiny nightstand with a gooseneck lamp from K-Mart on it. Joe's own belongings all fit in that bureau with room to spare. But this was a more comfortable room than anything in the mansion in Atlanta or the Chosen Ones' compound could ever have been. He felt welcome here, as he had not there.

For one thing, he didn't need to worry about hidden cameras watching his every move. He didn't have to worry about his father breaking the door down in a psychotic rage, destroying everything in his path in the name of his own holiness.

Joe piled up pillows at the head of the iron-framed bed and leaned back into them, contemplating the poster Bob had given him, now framed on the otherwise empty wall. It was an artist's rendering of the Victor GT prototype, over the Victor logo and the logo of Fairgrove Industries itself.

The latter was a strange piece; at first glance it was simply a pair of trees against the sky, but when you looked closer, you saw that the trees formed the face of a lovely woman, wearing an enigmatic smile. Then you looked again, and it was only two trees.

Which was the reality and which the illusion?

Bob would have shrugged and said it didn't matter. Al would say, "Both. Neither."

But it *did* matter. So much of what he had thought was true turned out to be deception. Just one illusion after another.

Everything my father told me was a lie. He thought about that for a moment, then realized that he actually had more of a start than he'd thought. *If everything he told me was a lie, then the truth would be the opposite of what he told me, wouldn't it?* That made sense—and what was more, a lot of what Al and Bob had told him *was* the very opposite of what his father would have said.

That meant he could trust what the two Fairgrove men had told him. He had no reason to doubt them, and every reason to believe them. But this—it was jumping off a cliff into a sea of fog and no way of knowing if what lay below him was the warm, friendly pool he'd been promised, or rocks he would be shattered upon.

Would it be better to change his mind, and see what Frank could find for him? He could still do that.

Could he, though? He'd spent a whole year here, and every moment of it had been as an outsider. His father had done one thing for him that was decent—he'd had a better education than most of the kids here. Even if half of it had been laced with the manifesto of a lunatic. At least what he'd gotten in the military academy had been sound. He'd tested out of just about everything, and he was able to go straight into his senior year with no trouble.

That was one thing that Frank, Al, Bob, and Mister Keighvin who ran Fairgrove had all been adamant about. Joe *had* to get his high school diploma. "It may not seem like it's worth much," Bob had drawled, "but without it, if for some reason something happens to us, you'll never get anything better than a fast-food job. You won't even be able to get into the Army. That diploma is your safety net."

He'd breezed through his classes with no academic trouble—and despite the doubts of the principal and many of the teachers, no other kind of overt trouble, either. He knew what they thought—or feared. There were those who were certain he would take up where his father had left off, corrupting the other students with the poisonous doctrines his father had taught. Others expected him to bully the other students, start fights. A few simply expected fights to find *him*, whether he wanted them or not.

They were all wrong. The other students were afraid of him, most of them, but even the worst bully in the school was too cautious after the first time he disrobed in gym class to try to pick a fight with him.

Just as well, since I could have wiped the floor with his face. No boast, just fact; the cult of the Sacred Heart of the Chosen Ones had emphasized that there would be battles, and the faithful would be in the thick of them. Every child, Joe included, was trained in self-defense from the moment they entered the compound. Joe had the added advantage of years of training in military school. When he walked into Pawnee High School in the fall, he knew that he had no intention of starting fights—but if they started, he knew that he would be the only one left standing afterward.

There were no fights; no one even *said* anything to his face. But they whispered behind his back and watched him with wary eyes, as if they expected that at any moment he might pull out an assault weapon and start shooting. Despite his powerful build, none of the coaches asked if he wanted to be on a team. Despite his looks, the few girls he'd asked out were not interested.

He really couldn't blame them, not after what had happened at the cult compound. People were still talking about it, and a year later, the FBI and ATF still had the place cordoned off. Joe wouldn't go anywhere near the place; the very idea made him sick. But how were the ordinary people of Pawnee going to know that? For all they knew, he was just like his father. He didn't blame them for being scared of him. In fact, it was probably only the fact that Frank Casey was his guardian that kept them from running him out of town.

From time to time someone in a car with darkened windows would pull up to Frank's house after school and ask to talk to Joe. It was always a different person, but the questions were always the same: Do you remember any more bunkers, or places where there might be weapons or ammunition stored? Whoever the person was, he would always bring a new map of the compound, and there was generally one more tunnel or bunker drawn on it than there had been before. It was hard for Joe to picture where things might be, since he was always working from the memories of having walked through the compound and not from any recall of a map, but with the aid of the ever-growing layout the Feds were building, he could at least say things like, "I think there's another tunnel there—I wasn't allowed down that way."

They may never find it all. Only his father had known where everything was. He'd told one of the men that once. "Why does this not surprise me?" the man had answered—and in the voice used by that parrot in the Walt Disney movie. It had kind of surprised him, that a supposedly grim FBI guy would have seen the movie, and delighted him more that the guy would have enough of a sense of humor to do that. In its own small way, it reaffirmed to Joe that he was dealing with human beings and not faceless chesspieces.

But strange cars pulling up to Frank's house did not add anything to Joe's popularity at school. Would it be any better in college, where he'd turn into the subject of every psych major's term paper and master's thesis?

The cicadas started droning again, right outside his window, loud enough to carry over the sound of the a/c unit. He didn't mind—in fact, he kind of liked it. In the bunkers you never heard anything but the drip of water in the tunnels, and the hum and clank of machinery.

And sometimes, the marching boots on concrete. That

sound haunted his dreams—sometimes in the dreams, the marching men were coming to get him, sometimes he was leading them. Both were horrible.

Frank thought that college would be easier for him, and better than high school, but Joe wasn't so sure. *How long before everyone found out who I was?* Even if they didn't, he *still* wouldn't fit in, not unless he went to some other military school. He was just too—too—

Too straight-edge. It didn't seem to matter that he liked trucks and cars, the way a lot of the guys did, that he liked the same kind of music and listened to Edge of Insanity after midnight when he could. He got rid of that swastika tattoo right off, before he ever set foot in school. That had to go before he grew his hair or tried to. None of it mattered. The differences were bone-deep. They slouched; he stood and sat at rigid attention. They wore grunge, or cowboy-chic; he wore carefully laundered blue jeans and spotless t-shirts or slacks and button-downs. He said "sir" and "ma'am" reflexively. Even the nerds looked more normal than he did.

But with Al and Bob, now—he had felt comfortable for perhaps the first time in his life. However strange he was, they were stranger, they had far more secrets to hide.

And they understood this knack he had for seeing into peoples' minds, for knowing something about what was going to happen, for seeing *things.* Things like ghosts. . . .

Bob said that this Tannim guy could see ghosts. Said he could do a lot of other things, too.

The a/c went off, leaving only the drone of cicadas and the chirp of crickets. This Tannim guy—he sounded interesting on the phone. Easy to talk to. He'd mentioned that Joe's first job would be as assistant to a "Sarge" Phil Austin, running Fairgrove security, a man who had some of the same knacks as Joe. So he was going to get picked up by a guy who talked to ghosts, and he was going to be errandboy to a guy who ran security for a place where they built racecars with magic.

Sounded like the kind of place where one Joseph Brown just might seem ordinary.

Right now, that didn't sound too bad. At least these

people wouldn't be staring at him all the time, waiting for him to go off the deep end, and whispering about him at PTA meetings.

Funny thing; every time he looked at the Fairgrove logo, the lady seemed to be smiling a little more.

Tannim didn't have too much trouble finding Pawnee, even though he'd never actually been to the county seat. The address and the directions Joe had given him were perfectly clear; it was equally clear that there wasn't much of a town to get lost in. Like the rest of the area around Tulsa, this was not a place that had suffered in the Dust Bowl; the trees here were probably as old as the town itself and lined the streets on both sides, giving shade and the illusion of cool. To Tannim's amazement, the streets surrounding the courthouse were cobblestone. Hell to drive on, like River Street in Savannah, but very picturesque. The town itself probably hadn't changed much since the 1920s.

The tiny house belonging to Deputy Sheriff Frank Casey could have been built any time in the last seventy-five years: a white-painted, single-storied frame house with a native rock foundation. It was trimmed with just a little bit of "gingerbread," sporting a huge front porch with a cement floor and a pair of porch swings. Tannim pulled up into the vacant driveway, which was two overgrown and cracked parallel strips of concrete. Before he could get out of the Mustang, two men emerged from the house and stood waiting for him on the porch itself.

The older man of the pair would have dwarfed most people; he made Tannim feel like a midget. He was huge, copper-skinned, hawk-nosed, with intelligent dark eyes, wearing a dark brown uniform shirt and tan pants. He wasn't wearing his badge at the moment, but he didn't have to. This could only be Joe's court-appointed guardian, Sheriff's Deputy Frank Casey.

But Joe was big enough not to be dwarfed even by his guardian. He looked as if he'd been pumping iron since he was a fetus; blond and blue-eyed, he'd have been a perfect model for a Nazi recruiting poster, except that his blond hair had been done in a fairly stylish cut that looked a lot like Tannim's, only shorter. There was a pale patch on his upper arm that made Tannim suspect he'd had a tattoo there, once.

Tannim got out of the car and went around the nose to meet them. There was no breeze under the trees, and he was glad of their shade. It was probably close to 90 out in the sunlight.

Frank Casey stepped forward to intercept Tannim. "I'm Deputy Frank Casey, Joe's guardian," he said, in a carefully neutral voice, holding out an immense paw of a hand.

Tannim met his firm handshake with a clasp that was just as firm. "I'm Tannim, from Fairgrove Industries in Savannah," he said, looking straight into Frank's eyes. "My folks are from around here, though—the Drakes, over in Bixby. They used to have cattle, but they're running quarter horses, now."

He had figured that invoking local ties would relax Casey, and he was right. The man's tension ebbed visibly. "Bixby, hmm? Good horse country," he replied.

Tannim shrugged and grinned.

"Couldn't prove it by me," he answered cheerfully. "The last thing I know is horse-stuff. Well, I'm supposed to bring Joe Brown here over to my folks' place; they want to meet him. Fact is, they insisted on it." He turned to Joe. "I'm not going to inflict them on you until we've had lunch, though. Dad wants to show off his stallions. I wouldn't do that to anyone on an empty stomach."

Frank chuckled, as Tannim had hoped he would. Joe probably thought he was managing a pretty good poker-face, but Tannim read any number of conflicting emotions there.

"Well, *my* lunch hour is about over, so I'd better get back to the office and find out what disasters came up while I was gone." Frank shook Tannim's hand again and clapped Joe on the shoulder. "Enjoy yourselves."

He strode off down the street under the ancient trees, heading in the direction of the aged county courthouse only three blocks away.

Well, looks like I passed inspection. Now let's see what

Joe has to say. Tannim waited until he was out of earshot before speaking again.

"Okay, just so you know, Bob Ferrel is a pretty good friend of mine, and Alinor is some kind of cousin of my boss, Keighvin Silverhair. I've been working for Fairgrove for a good few years now, and I was told pretty much the whole story." He quirked an eyebrow at the youngster, who looked a bit uncomfortable. "I'm sure this is going to sound unlikely, but I promise you, I've seen things weirder than snake shoes and Mets pennants. I've had stuff straight out of Tim Burton films happen to me before breakfast. So don't worry about my thinking you're crazy if you let something slip. You're more likely to think that about me."

A faint hint of skepticism crept over the young man's handsome face, but he didn't say anything.

"So, how about that lunch?" Tannim continued. "I wasn't kidding about Dad and the horses. He's doing something kinky with them. 'Collecting them,' he said. Whatever that is, I don't want to know." He shuddered. "They hate me, I'm allergic to them. Seems to *me* those are pretty good reasons to keep a decent distance between us."

Joe finally smiled. "I like horses," he offered. "There were horses at the military school I went to, and I learned how to ride and take care of them. I'd have been able to get on the horse-drill team, but Father pulled me out—"

His face darkened momentarily, and Tannim nodded sympathetically. "Look, from here on, no one is going to tell you what to do with your life, all right? If you decide to back out of this before we leave, that's okay; if you want to leave Fairgrove after you've been there a while, that's okay, too. Keighvin'll cut you a ticket to anywhere you want to go. Hell, he might even be able to get you into West Point or Annapolis, if that's what you want."

Joe blinked, as if the idea of an elven lord having the ability to influence people in the normal world had never occurred to him. "He can do that?" he asked.

Tannim allowed a hint of cynicism to enter his expression. "Keighvin has money. Politicians need money. Senators are the ones who make recommendations to West Point. Got it?"

Joe nodded. "I'd like to make sure I gave Fairgrove my best shot, though," he replied a little shyly. "I mean, it's only right."

I like this kid. How in the name of all that's holy he turned out this good with that fruitcake for a father— "You about ready for that lunch?" he said by way of a reply, and waved Joe over to the Mustang.

Joe's eyes widened at the sight of the Mach I, and widened even further when he got into the passenger's seat and saw all the electronic gadgetry in the dashboard. He didn't say anything though, until Tannim asked him if he had any preferences in music.

He shrugged. "Rock, I guess. Anything but country." There was something behind that simple statement; something dark. Was there someone in Joe's past who *had* preferred country and western? His father, maybe?

Tannim's fingers closed on the Rush CD, *Roll the Bones.* He took that as an omen, and put it in the player before pulling out into traffic.

God, Donal would have loved this album.

One advantage of the CD player was the extraordinary clarity of lyrics; the title track began, and Joe seemed more than a little startled by the chorus, then began paying attention. Very close attention.

Though Tannim was not one for placing life-guiding meaning into most rock lyrics, Rush was a pretty darned articulate band. And Joe could do worse than get a dose of "hey kid, sometimes things happen just because they happen—for no other reason, not your fault, not anybody's fault." He left it on.

He wasn't in the mood for franchise food, so he picked the first good-looking roadside diner that came along and pulled into the parking lot. GRANNY'S DINER, the sign said, painted on a cracked wall that looked as old as any "granny." The place was crowded, which argued for decent food, and the interior could have come right out of any movie from the fifties. So could the waitress, from her B-52 hairdo to a pink uniform with "Peggy" embroidered over her right pocket. *Fox would love this place. Thank God he isn't here; he'd be freaking out Joe by now and giggling about it.* Kitsune. *I'll never understand 'em. As bad as dragons, I swear. Thank God I don't have to deal with them too often. Well—except for Fox and Chinthliss.*

Joe's tastes were simple: big, juicy hamburgers, a large salad instead of fries, milk . . . just amazing quantities of all of it. Unlike Tannim, he didn't talk while he ate, so Tannim kept up a one-sided ramble about the more mundane side of Fairgrove between bites.

"What do you do?" Joe asked, when the waitress came to take their orders for dessert. "Al and Bob never really told me." His brow wrinkled a little. "I hope you don't mind my saying this, but you don't seem very old."

"I seem too young to be doing anything important, right?" Tannim chuckled. "I guess I started kind of young; a lot of people in racing did. As for what I do—I'm a test-driver and a mechanic, I drive on the Fairgrove SCCA team—"

"SCCA?" Joe interrupted.

"Sports Car Club of America," Tannim explained. "We have three teams: GTP, SERRA and SCCA. The ah—people like Al drive the GTP and SERRA cars; I handle most of the SCCA driving, since SCCA doesn't allow modifications like aluminum engine blocks and frames. It's a racing club, but for regular people with regular budgets."

Joe nodded, then accepted his apple pie à la mode from the waitress with a smile and a polite "thank you." He spooned up a mouthful, and looked at Tannim expectantly. "That can't be all you do," he said.

Tannim chuckled. "You don't miss much, do you? No, the people like Al and Keighvin can't go out much, so I do a lot of outside contact work—Sarge Austin will probably have you doing the same, before too long. We can always use someone who's smart enough to know their way around, and straight-edge enough to make the suits comfortable. I'm afraid a lot of the folks at Fairgrove look kind of like a cross between a rock group and a Renaissance Faire."

Once again, Joe nodded—but then he knew all about needing people for "outside" work. From what Tannim had heard and guessed, Brother Joseph hadn't let too many folks outside the barbed-wire walls of his compound, once they got inside.

The rest would have to remain unsaid, at least until they were safely inside the Mustang again. Joe evidently realized this, for he remained silent until the meal was finished and Tannim had paid for it, with a generous tip for the smiling "Peggy." They walked out into the midday heat, the air so full of dust that there was a golden haze over everything. Tannim thumbed the remote on his keychain; the doors of the Mach I unlocked and popped open, and the engine started. Joe looked startled, then grinned his appreciation as they both got in.

Joe buckled up, fumbling a little, as he had the first time, with the unfamiliar belts. Not too many people put on a four-point harness like it was second nature, after all.

"So," Joe said, with a tension in his shoulders that told Tannim he was bracing himself for the answer to his question, "just what comes along besides the ordinary stuff in this job?"

"How about me?" said a voice from the backseat.

Tannim looked into the rearview mirror. His jaw dropped.

Oh, it was Foxtrot all right. But he was a five-foot tall *fox,* a cartoon-style fox, only one with three tails and a little collar with "FX" on the gold tag dangling down in front.

But just as startling as Fox was Joe's reaction. His eyes were wide with surprise, but also with recognition.

"Long time, no see, Joey," Fox said genially. "If I'd known it was *you* they were talking about, I'd have come for a visit months ago!"

Tannim said the only thing he *could* say under the circumstances. He pointed to the back and locked onto Joe's eyes. "You know this lunatic?" he asked calmly.

Joe's mouth was still wide open, his eyes dazed. "I—uh—he was my imaginary friend," the young man managed, weakly. "When I was a kid."

"Not so imaginary, Joey," Fox replied. "Of course, I'd much rather look like this—"

The whole figure shivered, blurred, and changed back into a leather-jacketed James Dean lookalike. "Hard to pick up chicks when you look like a stuffed toy," Fox offered, leaning back in the seat. "Well, most places. By the way, what *are* you doing here? You were supposed to be in Georgia."

"It's a long story, Fox," Tannim interjected, and sighed. "Well, at least now I don't have to worry about you freaking Joe out by showing up out of nowhere."

"Yeah," Joe said faintly. "He already started years ago."

Tannim decided that he might as well seize the moment and use it for a short lesson. "I told you weird things show up around me. This is one of them," he told the young man as he pulled the Mustang out onto the highway. *Thank God he didn't materialize while I was actually driving.* "Fox isn't human, never was, never will be."

"Hey!" Fox exclaimed, feigning injured pride. "I resemble that remark! I *happen* to come from a very distinguished pedigree!"

"Pedigree is right." Tannim nailed the throttle for a quick pass around a slow-moving haywagon. "He's just what you saw as a kid: a fox-spirit, a shape-changer. Take a good look at him. No, *really* look at him, the way Alinor taught you."

Joe turned around and stared at Fox, who posed for his edification, magicking a white sparkling gleam off his teeth as he grinned. As Tannim had hoped, the order to look at Fox steadied Joe considerably. Having your imaginary friend from childhood suddenly pop up as real was enough to take the starch out of anyone. "Well, he's just a little see-through," Joe said slowly. "That means that he's a spirit, using everything he's got to make people like us *see* him. And there's a kind of an outline around him, and it isn't like a human aura."

"Good," Tannim said with satisfaction. "Right. He's a *kitsune*—to be precise, a Japanese fox-spirit—and *don't* ask me how he ended up in Georgia, 'cause I don't know."

Fox smirked. "I'll never tell. My lips are sealed."

"I wish," Tannim muttered. "Anyway, he's tricky—that's

what he enjoys doing, seeing new things and playing tricks on people. He has absolutely no ability to change anything in the real world, unlike a human ghost, but he's pretty hot stuff Underhill or in the spirit plane. The reason you can see and hear him is because you *can* see into the spirit plane and he is making the effort to be visible. He's kind of half here and half there—and again, that's unlike a human ghost, who can choose to be all here and affect the material world in a limited sense."

Joe nodded, his forehead wrinkled with concentration as he tallied this with whatever Bob and Alinor had already taught him. "So there's things like ghosts that can be *here*, and things like Fox who can't, really?"

"Pre-cisely," Fox replied for Tannim. "I can make you *think* I can affect the real world, though." He snickered. "Like I did to you, hotshot, with the soap."

"Yeah, well I'd like to know how you did that trick with the radio, though," Tannim grumbled.

"Hey! It's Fox-on-the-radio!" The *kitsune's* voice came from the four speakers, even though the radio was off. "Betcha caller number three can't guess how I'm doing this!"

Fox put his hands behind his head, leaning back, looking unbearably smug. His mouth had not moved at all.

"I know!" Joe said suddenly, looking pleased. "It's because since he's really talking with his mind, he's just making us *think* his voice is coming from the speakers instead of his mouth, which it isn't doing either."

A bit tangled, but Tannim got the gist of it, and muttered imprecations under his breath. Fox looked crestfallen.

"Awww," he said. "You *guessed!* That's not fair!"

"Life's like that," Joe and Tannim said in chorus and complete synchronization. They exchanged a startled glance, then both broke up in laughter. Fox pouted for a moment, then joined them.

Either he's handling this really well, or he's so blitzed by Fox and all that he only seems to be. I think my bet's on the kid. "Well now that Fox has joined us, I was wondering if you wanted to tool around Tulsa for a while." Tannim looked at the young man out of the corner of his eye. "Keighvin told me to outfit you while we were here, and I can put it all on the company card. I kind of figured you didn't have a lot of stuff."

"Take him up on it, Joe," Fox advised from the backseat. "Tannim's a Fashion God."

Tannim flashed the *kitsune* a withering look. "I'm supposed to get Nomex for you—that's fireproof underwear, basically, real popular back at Fairgrove. Some jeans and boots, too, and a few other things. And—" He paused. This was a delicate subject. "And personal gear. It can't be a lot, since the Mustang will hold only so much, but Keighvin seemed to think you ought to get yourself the same kind of things you'd be furnishing a dorm room with. You know, CD player, clock-radio, that kind of thing. And clothes."

Joe's face darkened. "I don't take handouts," he said stubbornly.

Tannim sighed. "Look, it isn't a handout, all right? You're going to be meeting people, some of them important. If you're gonna be Sarge's assistant, you'll have to escort Big Guns from places like Goodyear and March and STP all over the plant. You can't do that wearing jeans and a t-shirt. And as for the rest of it, well, if you had anything to move, Fairgrove would be paying moving expenses, right? But you don't, so you're getting it in gear."

Now Joe looked confused. "I don't know," he said uneasily. "I never knew anyone who got a job with a place like Fairgrove. I don't know what's right."

And until you get to Fairgrove, you won't *ever meet anyone who's gotten a job like this.* "Trust me," he said persuasively. "It's perfectly normal."

For Fairgrove.

"If you say so, sir," Joe replied, looking very young and uncertain.

"I say so," Tannim said firmly, taking the Mach I onto the on-ramp for the interstate. And in his head, though he was certain it was only in *his* head, he heard Fox snickering.

"That's right, he says so! Now how much would you

pay?" the radio blared in Fox's voice. "But wait, there's more if you order by midnight tonight! You get two free neuroses, a fixation, and your choice of—"

Click.

There weren't a lot of bags in the back of the Mustang, and not just because Joe had balked at purchasing too much. It had occurred to Tannim that "shopping for Joe" could be the way out of the house that he had been looking for. In fact, "shopping for Joe" might become his salvation. He could use it as an excuse to flee the house even when Joe *wasn't* with him.

So, Joe was now wearing a good pair of Bugle Boy pants and a snappy shirt ("You want to impress my folks, don't you?"); and there was a bag of Nomex jumpsuits in red and black in the trunk of the car, and a box containing a clock-radio. It was *not* the one Joe had selected; Tannim had switched it on him for a pricier model with a CD player in it. But since it was going to remain in the trunk of the Mach I until they reached Savannah, Joe wasn't going to find that out.

Fox was gone; he'd lost interest in the proceedings early on and simply vanished. He'd claimed he had a karaoke tournament to judge. It hadn't been easy persuading Joe that clothing could look good *and* be comfortable, but Tannim had managed.

The kid looked really good, actually. He was probably going to cut a wide swath through the secretaries at Fairgrove. Tannim guided the Mach I through the traffic of south Memorial on the way to Bixby, feeling relaxed and pleased with himself. *Modest, polite, and a hunk. And he has round ears. Uh huh. They aren't gonna know what hit them. He isn't going to know what hit* him. *Oh, things are going to be interesting around there.*

Well, heck, why limit the mayhem to the secretaries? There weren't too many unattached female mechanics and engineers, but there were a few—and the elven ladies would probably be just as intrigued with the polite young human.

Tannim grinned, but only to himself, and freed a hand

just long enough to pull his hair away from the back of his neck to let the sweat dry. Joe's mere presence would get some of the ladies, human and elven, off *his* back. Not that they weren't charming, but they tended to get possessive, and there just wasn't a one of them that Tannim found—right.

Yeah, throw Joe into the pool and see all the lady-fish go into display, ignoring me. *Good plan!* Keighvin would see to it that they didn't eat him alive or get him into any trouble, physical or emotional. And if he didn't, Bob, Al and Sarge would. *Do the lad some good. Loosen him up.*

With those thoughts to elevate his mood, he pulled into the driveway and into his "spot" beside the horse trailers, reflexively checking his watch as he turned off the engine. *Right on time for dinner, just like Mom asked. Perfect. The folks always said, "tardiness is the height of conceit, punctuality the height of respect."*

His parents came out to meet them, both obviously very curious about Joe. They climbed out, and Joe waited diffidently beside the passenger's door while Tannim made introductions. He charmed Tannim's mother immediately with his politeness, and impressed Trevor Drake with his soft-spoken attitude. Supper was waiting for them, and it went *much* more smoothly tonight, since Trevor could not say enough good things about Keighvin Silverhair and Fairgrove, and Joe could not say enough good things about the food. He completely won over Tannim's mother by volunteering to do the dishes afterward, and by insisting that he help clear the table. Tannim vetoed the former, and helped with the latter. "You and Dad can go enjoy the horses," he said. "I'll give Mom a hand. I'm *not* allergic to dishwashing."

So Joe changed back into his jeans and t-shirt for a trip to the stables to inspect the horses, leaving Tannim alone with his mother.

"I was a little worried about this Joe," she told him, as she stacked the dishes he rinsed in the dishwasher. "We saw so much about those awful people on the news, and I was afraid he'd be—oh, I don't know—just someone I wouldn't feel comfortable around. But he's a really *nice* boy, honey." She paused to fix him with a look he knew only too well. "He's so polite, and he looks respectable."

She did not say "why can't *you* be more like him?" but Tannim knew that was what she was thinking.

"Well, Mom, when your father puts a gun in your mouth to discipline you, you learn to be polite pretty quick," he said, off-handedly.

"He *didn't!*" she exclaimed, eyes round. At her son's nod of confirmation, she turned just a little pale. "Well, the poor boy," was all she said, but Tannim sensed the thoughts running around in her head. Joe had just gone from "that nice boy" to "that sweet, mistreated boy" in her mind, and he had an idea what might come next. Actually, he was all in favor of it.

Joe and Trevor came in then, talking horses. Tannim joined them at the breakfast bar, letting them do all the talking, just observing. Joe had relaxed a good bit; Tannim knew his dad probably wasn't like anyone the young man had ever met in his short life, and that was all to the good. *Expose him to something normal, and let that show him how abnormal his own parents were.*

"Listen, Joe, you don't have much to pack up now, do you?" Trevor asked, finally.

"No, sir," Joe replied, looking faintly puzzled. Tannim held his peace; this was what he thought might be on his parents' minds.

"Well, it's a long way out to Pawnee—if your guardian doesn't mind losing you a little early, why don't you come move into our guest room until you and Tannim leave?" Trevor asked, making it very clear that he meant the invitation. "That way you and my son can talk whatever business you need to, and he won't be spending a lot of time driving around in the heat."

"I think that's a great idea, Joe, if you'd like it," Tannim seconded enthusiastically. "A *really* good idea, in fact."

It means I can continue some of those magic lessons without worrying about interruptions. I know every good place around here to go where we won't be disturbed. And maybe if my folks feel like they've got a replacement son, they won't look at me as if I'm not really what they wanted.

Some of the same might be going through Joe's mind. "I can call and ask him," he said tentatively. "If he says it's okay, I can pack up tonight and be ready in the morning."

"Go call," Tannim's mother urged, adding her vote to Tannim and her husband's. "I'd love to have you here. Tannim doesn't eat enough to keep a bird alive, and I love seeing someone who appreciates food."

Joe blushed and excused himself. Tannim grinned at his folks. "Thanks, Dad, Mom," he said sincerely. "Joe is going to need a lot of help getting used to the way things are in this world. I think we can help him out quite a bit in two weeks."

Absolutely true, complete truth, but not the way they think.

"I kind of figured that, son," Trevor said warmly. "Boy's been sheltered in a pretty peculiar sense. He knows everything there is to know about the way lunatics think, and nothing about the way normal folk tick. And we raised you, so we know how to talk to lunatics. We can translate for him."

Tannim mock-threatened his father with a hand and then said, "Well, you have a point, actually." Tannim patted his mother's hand. "And he could use seeing a lady who stands up for herself, too. Where he comes from, women are supposed to go hide themselves in the kitchen and let their men do all the thinking for them."

"Well, he won't get that here," she replied, forthrightly. "I think he's lonely, honey. It would be nice if we could make him feel as if he had a home to come back to, if he wants."

Well, it sounds like they've adopted him! Heh. He could sure do worse.

"Thanks, folks," was all he said, but he put feeling into it.

At that point Joe returned. "Frank said to make sure I wasn't making a nuisance of myself," he reported, looking anxiously at all three of them. "And if this is going to be an inconvenience to you—"

"Well, if you're worried that much about it, you can give me a hand with the horses," Trevor said comfortably. "Tannim can't; boy takes one look at 'em and starts sneezing. Help me run some of the friskier ones on the lunge, maybe saddle up a couple of the mares and give them some exercise in the mornings. Some of those ladies are getting a little pudgy."

"Could I?" Joe's face lit up. "You have beautiful horses, sir. They're so great, are you sure you can trust me with them?"

Hoo boy, wait until the kid gets a look at the elvensteeds. Did Al ever show him Andur and Nineve in their true forms? He thought back over what Alinor had told him in his briefing. *No, I don't think he did. Didn't want to put the kid into overdrive. A Sidhe was bad enough. Heh. He and Rosaleen Dhu are going to get along just fine, and that'll make him one of Keighvin's favorite "sons."*

"If I didn't think I could trust you with them, I wouldn't have asked you to help," Trevor said, invoking logic. "That's a lot of cash tied up in horseflesh, son, and I know you'll be as careful with them as I am. I saw for myself you can handle them fine, and you know your way around a barn. So, can you move in tomorrow morning?"

Tannim sighed. The way his father said "morning," he knew that Trevor meant it. That meant rising at seven A.M., no excuses.

"Sure thing, sir!" Joe was eager now. His blue eyes were alight with anticipation. "If I can tell Mr. Casey that you want me to help out, he'll know I'm not imposing on you."

"Good, it's settled then." Tannim's mother nodded firmly. Her curly hair bounced with the nods. "I'll have the guest room ready for you, and we'll expect you tomorrow morning."

Joe looked at his watch. "In that case, Mr. Drake, Mrs. Drake, I'd better be getting back. I don't want to wake up Mr. Casey coming in."

Tannim rose, stretching. "Right. Mom, Dad, I'll get Joe here back to Pawnee, and I'll probably take the long way home. It's a nice night for a drive."

He watched his mother's face twitch as she repressed the automatic response of "don't stay out too late."

He winked at his father and led the way out for Joe. The sun had set while Joe and his dad had been out in the stables; now it was full dark, with no moon. Their feet crunched on the gravel on the driveway, and off in the distance, the whisper of a distant highway beckoned. It really *was* a good night for a drive, and Tannim intended to take full advantage of the solitude. He'd been promised some rest, and he was, by God, going to *get* some. He found driving restful, particularly when he had no place to go and no time he had to be there.

They climbed into the Mustang, and Tannim joined the stream of traffic on Memorial. Joe was far more talkative on the way back; for a wonder, Fox did not appear. Joe was a lot more relaxed now than he had been when they first drove out here. Tannim took that as a good sign; *he* already liked young Joe, and it seemed that Joe was far more comfortable with Tannim than the boy had expected to be.

"So, how are we shaping up?" Tannim asked, as he took the turnoff to Pawnee, headlights cutting twin cones of light through the darkness. "Me and Fairgrove, I mean. Are we anything like you thought?"

"I—" Joe faltered for the first time during the drive. "Sir, you're not at all what I expected. You're not like Al or Bob, I mean."

Tannim threw back his head and laughed. "Yeah, I can imagine! Sieur Alinor Peredon would probably be *horribly* offended if you thought he was like me! No, I'm not like anybody at Fairgrove, and neither is anyone else. That's the beauty of the place. You're supposed to be yourself, and no one else."

Joe's face was in darkness, but Tannim sensed his sudden uncertainty. "What if—what if you don't know who you are, sir?" the young man asked hesitantly.

"Well, wherever you are is a good place to find out. And Fairgrove is a good place to be," Tannim said firmly. "And quit with the 'sir' stuff. I'm not a knight like Alinor, and I'm not your guardian. I'm just Tannim, nothing more, and heaven knows that's enough for anyone. Okay?"

They entered the outskirts of Pawnee, and a few street lights dimly illuminated the cobblestones. Leaves made dappled, constantly moving shadows between each light.

"Okay," Joe said, although he didn't sound very sure. "Uh, if you don't mind my asking, what kind of a name is 'Tannim'? I never heard anyone by that name before. And why don't you use your last name?"

Tannim chuckled. "I use it, because one of my teachers gave it to me. 'Tannim' isn't the name my folks gave me, but I guess it must suit me since they started calling me by that right after I started using it. And I don't use my last name because I don't really need it." He shrugged. "People remember a guy who only goes by one name, and in this business sometimes you need people to remember you."

I'm not gonna bring Chinthliss up unless I have to, and that is the only way I can tell him where the name came from. Kid's got enough to cope with already. He's got Fox; he sure as heck doesn't need Chinthliss.

He pulled up into the Casey driveway at the stroke of ten; the lights were still on, and the flickering blue in the living room windows showed that the television was also going. Good. That meant they wouldn't be waking the deputy up.

"I'll pick you up in the morning, Joe," Tannim said, unlocking the doors from his console. "Some time between eight and nine, all right?"

"Great!" Joe said with an enthusiasm that made Tannim wince inwardly. *Terrific. The kid's a lark. Ah, well, he and Dad can mess around with the horses while it's still cool, and I can sleep in with a clear conscience.*

The young man slid out of the car, shutting the door carefully, waved a cheerful farewell, and trotted up the porch steps into the house. Tannim backed the Mustang carefully down the drive, and headed out of Pawnee.

He stopped under a streetlight to make a selection from his CD box, since there were no other cars in sight. *Driving to relax, let's see. Kate Bush, Rush, Icehouse, Midnight Oil, a-ha, Billy Idol . . . there. Cocteau Twins. That'll do just fine.*

He slipped the CD into the player, and turned the nose

of the Mustang out into the darkness. No fear of getting
lost; he knew the area around Tulsa like the back of his
hand, every section-line road, every main drag. All he had
to do was look for the glow of Tulsa on the horizon to
orient himself.

He thought about checking out Hallet Racetrack, but
thought better of the idea. It was probably locked up, and
although he could get around just about any lock ever
made, you just didn't trespass on a racetrack. Right now,
when it came down to it, he just wanted the night, the
tunes, and the road.

A brief tingling of energies warned him of a "friendly"
coming in; Fox materialized in the seat next to him, but
uncharacteristically didn't say a thing. Tannim let the
Mach I set her own speed, and rolled the windows down
to let in the night and the air. Music surrounded them
both in a gentle cocoon of sound as the Mustang rolled
on through the darkness, and the wind from the open windows whipped Tannim's hair and cooled his face.

Night, stars, and sound, and the open road. He felt
muscles relaxing that hadn't unknotted for a long time. Fox
leaned back in the passenger's seat, resting one long arm
on the window-frame, graceful fingers tapping in rhythm
to the song.

Stars blazed overhead. The headlights reflected from
the bright eyes of small animals in the grass beside the
road; once a rabbit dashed across in front of the car, and
he braked instinctively to avoid hitting the owl following
her. The owl was hardly more than a flash of wings and
a glimpse of talons. *Barred owl? Looked like it. Be a little
more careful, lady; the next guy might not know you were
going to be on that bunny's tail.*

"I'll warn her," Fox said quietly, picking up Tannim's
thoughts so easily that Tannim realized he must have
relaxed enough to drop his shields. Well, that was safe
enough in the Mach I; there were shields layered on top
of shields, magics integrated with every part of this car,
and the only reason Fox could get in and out so easily was
because Tannim had made those shields selectively
transparent to him.

The music ended, and Tannim reached for the CDs, trusting to his instincts to pick something appropriate. For the first time, he regretted the fact that Fox couldn't interact with the physical world; it would be nice to have someone in the passenger's side to change the CDs for him. This wasn't quite like changing a cassette; still, he managed with a minimum of fumbling.

A great rush of strings flowed from the speakers, and he relaxed still further. *Alan Hovanhess, "Mysterious Mountain." Good old instincts.* Not a lot of mountains in Oklahoma, but right now, with only the stars and the swaths of headlights, the hills seemed mysterious enough.

"This is good," Fox said quietly, his voice full of approval. "Really good."

Tannim made an ironic little bow in his direction, but did not reply; he didn't need to. Fox was so rock-obsessed, he probably didn't realize that any other kind of music existed. The music spoke for itself, sweeping through the Mach I like the night breeze, cutting brilliant streaks across the sky like the occasional meteor. He gave a sigh of regret when it finished; *someday* he was going to find a store that stocked enough obscure records that he'd be able to pick up more from this particular composer. He'd heard another piece on the radio once, "And God Created Great Whales," that he'd snap up in a heartbeat if he ever found it.

But when his hand sought the CD box for the third time, and the first notes screamed from the speakers, he was startled at what his instincts had chosen. *Billy Idol? Not very relaxing—*

Just as he thought that, Fox sat bolt upright in his seat, glancing to the rear in alarm. "Oh-oh," the *kitsune* said.

And vanished.

What the—

He glanced in the rearview mirror, to see a pair of headlights coming up on him from behind. Fast. Too fast for him to do more than react.

He winced away from the mirror in pain, squinting. Whoever this was, he had his brights on, and he was not going to drop them. The headlights filled his mirror, glaring into his eyes, as Billy Idol snarled over the speakers.

Some hot rodder? Got to be, but why alone and why out here? This is a lousy road for dragging.

He edged over to the side, a clear invitation to pass. The unknown didn't take it, moving up to hang right behind his rear bumper, engine growling.

Trying to pick me? Out here? Who is this jerk?

And why had Fox vanished like that?

He edged over further, until his right-hand wheels were actually in the grass, and waved his hand out the window. He wanted to flash the guy the finger, but the idiot was probably drunk and Tannim was not in the mood for a fight.

This time the answer was clear and unmistakable.

The car behind surged forward to hit the rear bumper. Not so hard that it knocked the Mach I off the road—or his hands off the wheel—but hard enough to jar Tannim back in his seat and bang his head and neck against the headrest.

"You *sonuvabitch!*" Pain blossomed in his neck. Savagely he jammed the pedal to the floor, spinning the wheels for a moment before he jarred into acceleration. The Mustang's engine thundered in his ears, drowning out Billy Idol, vibrating through him, a cross between a growl and a howl. For a moment, the headlights receded behind him.

But only for a moment.

The headlights grew again. The car behind caught up as if it had kicked in a jet engine. He had only a moment's warning, and then the vehicle pursuing him swerved to the left, accelerated again—

—and passed him, not quite forcing him off the road.

He got only a glimpse of the driver, just enough to see that it was either a very long-haired guy, or a woman. The car itself was clear enough; a late-model Mustang, '90 or '91. It was either black, or some other very dark color.

Then it was past him, accelerating into the night, impossibly fast unless the driver had a nitrous-rig under that hood. All he saw was the tail, red louvered lights winking mockingly at him, then disappearing.

You arrogant bastard!

His jaw clenched painfully tight, an ache in his neck and the base of his spine. He forced himself not to pursue his tormentor. He slowed, then stopped, right in the middle of the road, turning off the engine.

The license plate had been from no state. And he had not been able to read it. *Could not.* His eyes had blurred around the letters and numbers, although everything else about the car had been crystal-clear.

His hand reached out of itself and turned off the CD player. In the absence of the music, the singing of crickets and rustling of grass in the breeze seemed as distant as the farthest stars.

He reached under the seat for a flashlight, opened the door and got out. Heat rose from the asphalt as he went to the rear to see what the damages were.

He kicked rocks aside savagely as he took the few steps necessary to reach the rear of the car, certain he was going to find a taillight out at least, and a crumpled bumper at worst. He moved slowly, played the beam of the flashlight over the rear of the car, and couldn't see even a scratch.

What the hey—? If I didn't get hit, then what did happen?

Then he turned, and froze, as movement toward the front of the car caught his attention.

There was something on the driver's side door.

He approached it, slowly, cautiously, playing the light over the door, and felt anger burning up inside him, hot bile rising in his throat.

There in the circle of light from his flashlight, pop-riveted to the door-panel, was a fingerless black leather driving glove.

With a growl of pure rage, he grabbed it and tore it off, the thin leather ripping away and leaving the rivet in the middle of his otherwise pristine door-panel.

I'm going to find him. And I'm going to kill him.

Something rustled inside the glove, and a strip of white paper peeked out at him impudently. He had the uncanny feeling it was moving in there on its own.

He pulled it out and unrolled it. His hand trembled as he held it in the light from the flashlight.

It was a thin strip of antique parchment, with a quotation written on it in black ink in a clear, if spidery, hand.

> *I have now found thee; when I lose thee again,*
> *I care not.*
>
> > All's Well That Ends Well
> > Act II, Sc 3

He stared down the black ribbon of asphalt under the stars. There was no way that driver could have done this. No way on Earth.

CHAPTER THREE

The warmth from the asphalt road seeped through his boots and the cool breeze whipped the ends of his hair around his face as his rage ebbed, and the fear began. Not fear for himself—any setup this obvious wouldn't make him fearful for himself—but for his parents, for Joe. *They* were vulnerable, and only because they were related to him, or connected to him. His first impulse was to get in the Mustang and start driving and not stop until he was back in Savannah, at Fairgrove. But that was no more than a momentary impulse, and he preferred not to act on impulse alone. Impulsive decisions were for when he had less than ten seconds to think before he acted.

Besides, that might be exactly what this challenger wants me to do: take off for help and leave them all unprotected. He throttled down every emotion with a fierce determination to leave his reasoning unclouded. *I have to think this one through before I do anything.*

He opened the Mach I's door and slid into the driver's seat, throwing the glove down on the passenger's seat. His mind hummed. *Music. I think better with music.* He started the engine and put the Mach I gently into motion, then punched the radio on. It was after midnight; time for the alternative rock program, Edge of Insanity, that took over the midnight-to-six slot from the classical station. With

348

real luck, the program would work for him the way WYRD did, the play-list acting as a goad to his thoughts.

He tuned in right in the middle of a techno-trance piece; excellent. That was good, logical, thinking music. *Okay, I need to analyze the heck out of this. There's a reason why they talk about "throwing down the glove," and using a glove can't have been an accident. This was a gauntlet, a direct challenge. Not just the glove, though, all of it was meant to impress me so that it couldn't be ignored. Whoever this was, she managed to produce enough of a magical shove to the back of my car that I thought she'd rammed my bumper. And she slammed that glove and rivet into my door, also magically, and in such a way that I didn't even know she'd done it.* He realized he had already come to think of his adversary as a woman; well, it was a reasonable assumption, given the silhouette, the small size of the long-fingered glove, and—the finesse. Not a bit of wasted energy; when males issued a challenge, they generally overdid it. Testosterone poisoning, clouding the brain.

Right. That's what she did. Now, what she didn't do. She didn't shove the left bumper, although she made me think she had; if she'd done that, she would have sent me off the road, and I could have been seriously hurt. She didn't damage the rear of the car. The damage to the pristine door panel was enough to send him into a rage all over again. *Don't be an idiot; you have enough equipment to make that hole disappear. Borrow Alinor or Keighvin, and they might even be able to stand the touch of Death Metal enough to* ken *the hole out of existence. No, the point is she didn't do anything at all that would really have harmed me or the Mach I. All she did was make me mad. And she did it with style. This was very carefully calculated. She could easily have done me some serious hurt if she'd tried.*

This also had the feel of something planned to enrage him, put him off balance, make him stop thinking.

But if she knows anything about me, she has to know that I've got pretty good control of my temper, and I think quickly. So if her ploy didn't make him act on anger or fearful impulse—what did that mean? Maybe this wasn't something planned to make him act impulsively. It was supposed to make him angry, there was no doubt of that. *If she can send a pop-rivet into my door, she could have sent something else through it. An iron spike. A crossbow bolt. Hell, a bullet. All right, rethink everything. Let me assume she's as brilliant and complicated as anyone I've ever seen. In that case, she'd do something that could have multiple outcomes. It might make me angry enough to chase after her, or afraid enough to run, but that wouldn't be her primary objective.*

And her primary objective must have been—

The challenge. An invitation to single combat.

Yeah. Everything she did points to the conclusion that this was a formal challenge, properly issued, artistically issued. Executed to show me clearly that I was dealing with a certain level of finesse and power, without giving anything else away. And done by the rules.

The road passed over a creek; a gust of damp, green-scented air wafted over him, and he thought he heard frogs. If this was a challenge, that meant a great deal; challenges were only meant for the person to whom they were issued. She who flung down the gauntlet would allow him time enough to *realize* that it was a formal challenge, and further time to think about it. Even the worst of the Unseleighe played challenges by the book.

There weren't supposed to be any Unseleighe living out here, though; that was one problem. So the questions of *who* and *why* still remained.

And a new question arose: *what next?*

If he turned and ran, he might very well make things worse. Creatures who played the game of "challenge-response" often took the refusal to accept the challenge as the signal for a no-holds-barred attack, for the once-honorable opponent made himself into "prey" by fleeing. A worthy foe would not act on impulse. An unworthy foe should be disposed of as quickly as possible, for it not only hinted at treachery by breach of format, but also threatened the system of honorable challenge itself.

Easier to be the honorable opponent. When you know the rules, you know the pattern. Thrust and parry.

The parents and the associates of the honorable opponent were not part of the challenge. The parents and associates of prey were—

More prey. No, I'll have to play this one clean until I know the answers to my questions.

He found himself headed toward Bixby and shrugged. *All right. I shield and armor the farm right up to the limit. Joe's going to be a lot safer there than at Frank Casey's. His education is just going to start a whole lot earlier than either of us thought. Damn. Now there's something else. He might be the ultimate "prize" in this little contest if I'm not careful. I have to keep that in mind. He might be what she's really after, and she's challenged me to get me out of the way, or to set things up so that he becomes, literally, the bone of contention. Winner take all.*

He vaguely recognized something by the McGarrigles playing in the background—"Mother, Mother," perhaps—and he turned the radio down until it was a mere whisper of sound. Good omen or bad? Good, if it was meant for Joe, as a warning to protect the young man; but maybe bad, very bad, if it was meant for him.

Another impulse was to call Conal or Keighvin at Fairgrove, but that was likely to be another mistake. First of all, calling in help might be a bad move at this early point. Secondly, this was not the sort of thing you could do much about over the phone. His associates at Fairgrove were not going to be able to help at long distance, and it had not yet come to the point where he could legitimately ask for help, reinforcements. The dance of "liege lord and equal ally" that he and Keighvin trod had its own patterns and measures. If he was to retain Keighvin's respect, he would have to deal with this quickly and appropriately.

But he had another source of help available to him; one with a different set of liabilities attached, but one for which the accounting was definitely on *his* side. Chinthliss owed him at the moment. Time to ask—politely—for a little payback.

One did not skimp on protocols and propriety when talking to dragons.

Tomorrow, he decided. *Tonight, just in case this lady doesn't play fair and I'm misreading everything, I put up the defenses.* That certainly matched the last song: the "house of stone" and the "cage of iron."

The house was dark by the time he pulled into the driveway; only the porch light left on, and a solitary lamp in his room still burning. He used his key and let himself in, and moved to his room, shadow-silent on the carpeted hallway.

He stripped out of everything, including his body-armor; donned a clean bikini-brief, and slipped into bed, turning the light off as he did so. But he was not going to sleep, not yet anyway.

All the old protections and shields he had put in place around this room as a kid were still here; dormant, but ready to be brought up at any time. That, at least, felt like "home." He closed his eyes, stretched in the comfortable and comforting embrace of mattress, clean sheets, and blankets, letting his body relax itself, feeling shoulders and neck pop and release their tension.

He chanted under his breath, old song lyrics invoking all the familiar energies he had learned when he first began his mage-training here. As the chant harmonized with the hum of the machinery within the house, his physical eyes drifted shut, and his body went rigid.

So far, so good.

He opened another set of eyes; everything around him glowed softly, each object clearly delineated in its own faintly-luminescent aura. It could have been dusk in this room, rather than fully dark, so far as the Othersight was concerned. A bit more concentration, and he could have lit up every item that he had cared for or spent time with, according to emotional attachment.

He "sat up," although his physical body remained lying in the bed; his spirit-self rose from the bed, went to the exact center of the room, and took a fighter's stance. As he had when he was a teenager, he readied his magics and sent a spell of deeper sleep into his parents' minds.

Not just because this would be a very bad time for him to be interrupted; if, for some reason, one of them walked in on him at the moment, they'd have the scat scared out of them. They'd be sure that he was dead—and certainly, his heartbeat and breathing were so faint at the moment that they would have every reason to believe just that. He was just short of death, connected to his body by the thinnest of willed tethers. Few people dared to go out-of-body this way, but the advantages were worth the risk.

Oddly enough, he had never used that power to keep his parents sleeping when he was a kid and had wanted to sneak out and raise some hell. Only when he had to meet with Chinthliss, or practice some of what he'd been taught.

Ah, I was just too lazy. I had to be in trance to make them sleep, so there was no point in doing all that work just to keep them from catching me. By the time I went into trance, mucked with their sleep, and came out again, half the night would be gone. Time's already burning away.

The old patterns of shield and armor were still in place; he examined them with a critical eye. He'd based his old constructs on the smooth dome-shapes of the silly, bad-effect "force-fields" of his favorite old science fiction books and movies. The basic *shape* was still good, but he knew a lot more now than he had then; he tore the structure down and began rebuilding it from within, constructing a crystalline structure after the pattern of a geodesic sphere, with his room as the center. Bucky Fuller, mage of logic that he was, would have been proud. He knew better, now, than to assume that because his room stood on solid ground, the earth afforded as much protection as a shield. No, now his shields extended below ground as well as above. The geodesic structure was a lot more stable than a smooth dome, able to bear a great deal more pressure. Once the initial structure was in place, he really went to work. Over that, he layered shields and shunts to drain off excess energies, and not a few traps for the unwary: magical deadfalls and power-sinks.

When he was finished, he sat within a beautiful, radiant construction that could have been a work of computer-generated art. Multicolored energies iridesced over the surface of his basic shield. Satisfied with what he had done at last, he repeated the patterns on a larger scale, weaving a web of energies and barriers around the house and stables, around the entire farm. Layer on layer on layer—it would take someone who *knew* what he had done to untangle it, and he would be warned and ready to deal with the intruder himself long before an enemy actually penetrated those protections.

He worked feverishly, right up until dawn. Then, and only then, he turned his trance into a true sleep and let weariness take him into a light slumber.

As Tannim drifted into the deeper realms of sleep, the dreams started again.

Warm gray mists surrounded his body, evaporating the clothing he wore. The tiny scales of his body armor whisked away, falling in a rain of silent sparkles. As he turned, the shadows from his lower body coalesced into a bedroom of night-black satin. Flames without candles lit the room, atop hundreds of fluted golden rods.

And when he turned around completely, she was there, indescribably beautiful, irresistibly seductive, waiting for him on a bed of silver satin, imploring . . . please . . . now. . . .

The alarm clock went off *far* too early, even though he was more or less ready for it. He opened one eye and blearily looked at the display.

Oh God, six in the morning. No choice, though; the sooner he got Joe under a safe roof, the happier he'd be. He dragged himself out of bed, picked out clothing, grabbed his armor with it, and slipped across the hall to the bathroom.

What was it about mothers and waterfowl? This *had* been a perfectly ordinary, plain bathroom when it had been his, but now that it was the "guest bathroom," his mother had gone berserk with decorating. Ducks. There were ducks *everywhere*. Wooden ducks with dried weeds in them on the vanity, duck plaques on the wall, a duck-bordered, pseudo-early-American wallpaper, ducks carved on the tissue-holder, even a matching potpourri warmer.

"Ducks," he wondered aloud. "Why did it have to be *ducks?*"

"What, dear?" his mother said, and opened the door to the bathroom before he could stop her.

"Oh!" she exclaimed faintly, as he flushed with embarrassment at being caught by his *mother* in his underwear. Even if it did cover more than a pair of Speedos.

But then she paled. "Oh, dear," she whispered, even more faintly, her eyes running with horrified fascination over the scars crisscrossing her son's body.

Thank God none of them are new—

But there was no denying the fact that his entire body was interlaced with a fine network of scars, from the first, a knife-wound in the forearm, to the latest, four talon slashes running from the right nipple to the left hip. Not exactly the way a loving mother likes to see her child. Especially since he couldn't explain most of them.

She was staring at those talon-slashes at the moment, and he knew what she was going to ask.

"It looks worse than it was, Mom. They're just scratches. I was shopping at K-Mart," he improvised hastily, "And I got knocked through a plate-glass window during a blue-light special."

"A blue-light special?" she replied, recovering her poise a little, one eyebrow rising.

"I'm telling you, Mom, those women were *crazy.* There were almost knife-fights over those Barney dolls." *Sure. It could happen. . . .*

But her eyes were already traveling to the teethmarks that crossed his left leg from hip to ankle. "That—ah—was the wreck," he reminded her. "Remember? They had to cut me out of it."

"Aren't those bites?" she asked, in horrified fascination.

"Jaws of Life," he lied frantically. "They slipped. *Mom, please!* I'm in my *skivvies!*"

"And I changed your diapers, young man," she responded automatically, but at least she closed the door.

And at least she hadn't seen the glittering body-armor under the pile of clothing on the floor.

He locked the door to prevent any further incursions and turned on the shower. There were a few things he could do to recharge his body and make up for the lack of sleep, and the shower was the best place to do them. *Writing an IOU to my body. Oh, well. It won't be the first time.* Chinthliss was always on his case about doing things like this, but— *But sometimes there's no choice. If I get a choice, I'll catch a nap after I get Joe over here.*

He stood under the shower and let it literally wash the fatigue from his body as he drew upon his reserves. There was more in those reserve stores than there usually was, thanks in no small part to some payback on Keighvin's part, and a healer-friend of Chinthliss'. By the time he turned the hot water off, he felt better than he expected to. Almost human, in fact.

Certainly alert enough to deal with his mysterious lady in *her* Mustang.

Ersatz Mustang. Boy-racer fiberglass and recycled pop cans. Might as well have a plastic model. Nothing more than the sum of its parts, any of which you can pick up at Pep Boys off the shelf. Heh. If you can't have the real thing, why bother?

Maybe that was why she'd put a hole in his Mach I; pure jealousy.

Sure. It could happen. And Carroll Shelby will join the Hare Krishnas. But if she can have anything she wants, why pick a Mustang at all?

He reached under his clothing for the armor; glad now that he never, ever went anywhere without it, even if it *did* mean he had to wear long-sleeved shirts in the hottest weather. He and Chinthliss had worked on it together for three solid months, and no few of the scars on his body were the result of being in a situation where he *couldn't* wear it. It had saved his life more than once, and was worth all the trouble it posed. If the mysterious lady *had* fired a crossbow bolt, a bullet, or a spike through the door, she would have gotten a rude surprise. He might have gotten broken ribs, but she probably wouldn't have killed him. Not unless she *knew* about it, and how to get past it.

He squirmed into it, like a dancer getting into a unitard, and that was what it most resembled. Made of thousands of tiny hexagonal scales, enameled in emerald green, it was better than Kevlar because it offered as much protection from magic as it did from bullets or knives. The cool scales slipped under his hands as smoothly as silk; the entire suit of body-armor weighed about as much as a garment of knitted silk, and moved with him as easily and naturally as a second skin.

He crooked his finger and ran the nail up the split down the front to close it up again. There were no seams, for every scale was linked magically to every other scale, so it could be opened anyplace that he wished.

It wasn't perfect—he could, quite easily, be *clubbed* to death while wearing it. He could be injured *through* it, by impact. And it didn't protect his head, neck, or hands. But it gave him a lot of edge over someone expecting to do his arguing with a bullet, knife or elfshot.

His clothing slipped on easily over the armor, and he made sure that none of the green scales showed before he opened the door to the bathroom to let the steam out.

When he'd finished with hair and teeth, he sprinted to the kitchen just long enough to grab a banana and down a glass of orange juice, kissing his mother quickly in passing. "Gotta go pick up Joe," he said as he ran for the door. "I'll have a real breakfast when I get back."

Her protests were lost in his wake.

Personal shields were up before he left the static shields of his room and the farm, and he activated every protection he had on the Mustang once he was inside it. With every sense, normal and magical, alert, he drove the entire distance to Pawnee in a familiar state of controlled paranoia.

Nothing happened.

Once or twice he thought he saw a late-model Mustang that *might* have been hers, but it always drifted away in the traffic. There were no attacks, no probes, not even a whisker of power brushed up against his. The attack—or challenge—of last night might never have happened.

Except that there was still a pop-rivet in the driver's-side door, and a black leather glove on the seat beside him.

It taunted him; in no small part because he had been able to learn so little from it. It simply lay there on the black vinyl seat, a palpable presence. Finally he couldn't stand it any longer; at a stoplight he grabbed it and shoved it into the glovebox.

Good God, I just put a glove in the glovebox. That'll be a first.

Well, if she thought she was going to be able to winkle any of her magics into the Mach I via that glove, odds were she was wrong. The glovebox had its own little set of diamond-hard shields, and they worked *both* ways, shielding what was in the box from outside influence, and keeping what was in the box from getting any influences out. This wasn't the first time he'd had to carry something small and potentially dangerous. And for things large and potentially dangerous, there was the trunk.

Heh. Big enough for a body or two, if need be.

Jeez, his thoughts were bloody this morning!

He shook his head. This woman and her little "present" were affecting him in ways he didn't like, turning him savage. A single steel pop-rivet in the door panel and a stiff neck should *not* be doing this to him.

Whoa! Back up! A steel pop-rivet?

He pulled the glove out of the box for a moment and examined it with one eye still on the traffic before shoving it back in. *Why didn't I notice this last night? And steel eyelets on the back of the glove. Whoever, whatever this broad is, she's not Unseleighe. That glove's been worn; there's scuff marks and creases in the leather. No Unseleighe would be able to tolerate steel on a glove, and no Unseleighe would be able to use his magics to manipulate a steel pop-rivet. I don't think even Al or Keighvin could, and they have the most tolerance to Cold Iron of any Sidhe I know.*

That didn't mean, however, that she might not be in the hire of the Unseleighe, or an ally of some kind. They even had human allies and servants. But if she was that good, why would she be working on behalf of someone else?

He sighed, and mentally shrugged, as he took the turn-off to Pawnee. Maybe the pay was extraordinary. Maybe she wasn't with the Unseleighe at all. Maybe she was the local hotshot, somebody who'd moved in after he left, and she was pulling the equivalent of the young gun going after the old gunfighter.

She obviously knew a great deal about him; she had a distinct edge over him in that department. He *had* to learn more about her, and fast!

Joe came bounding out of the house before he even came to a full stop in the driveway, full of energy and enthusiasm, with a pair of duffel bags and a couple of boxes waiting on the porch to be loaded into the trunk. His guardian was right behind him. Tannim helped the young man stow his gear in the trunk, trying to sound and look as normal as possible, all the while reassuring Frank Casey that this was no imposition. Somehow he managed to smile and act as if everything was exactly the same as it had been when he'd dropped Joe off last night. Somehow he remembered to mention that Joe would be helping Trevor with the horses; evidently that was what finally convinced the deputy that Joe would indeed be pulling his own weight.

Being out here made Tannim nervous; he had to consciously force himself not to look over his shoulder. The last place he wanted to bring trouble to was the sleepy little town of Pawnee; they'd already had enough trouble to last them well into the next century, and Casey was obviously able to take care of anything normal that arose.

When Joe was buckled into the passenger's seat, and they pulled out of Pawnee with nothing sinister manifesting, Tannim heaved a sigh of relief.

"Is something wrong?" Joe asked immediately. "Did your parents change their minds or something?"

"Yes," Tannim replied. "No. Yes, there's something wrong, but it doesn't have anything to do with my folks, and they don't know anything about it. They still want you out there. Dad's making his famous omelettes and Mom is doing pancakes so we get 'proper breakfasts' when we get back. No, the problem's with what's in the glove compartment."

He nodded at the glovebox, and Joe opened it, pulling out both glove and quotation.

"A glove?"

"Yeah, weird, huh? After I dropped you off last night, someone in a late-model Mustang rammed the back of the Mach I and left that pop-riveted to the door. Except that she *didn't* ram me, she used magic to shove me forward hard enough to make me *think* she'd rammed me, and she whanged that into my driver-side door with magic, too, so that I didn't notice it until after she'd passed me and was gone."

Joe was quick; he cut right to the chase. "Why?" he asked.

"I think it's a challenge." He chose his next words carefully. "The trouble is, I don't know for sure. I don't know what the stakes are. And I don't know who or what she's going to drag into this."

"Like me, maybe?" Joe hazarded, turning just a little pale. "Tannim, I hope you don't mind me saying so, but I could have gone a long time without hearing that. I was hoping I wasn't gonna have to deal personally with this magic stuff for the next couple of years."

Tannim could only shrug. "Sorry. Sometimes stuff just shows up and bites you in the ass. Look, I've got major protections on the farm, you, my folks. I'm going to try to keep you out of this. *Maybe* this is as harmless as a drag race; she could be the local hotshot trying to pick on me. The main problem I've got is that all I know about her is that she planted *that* on me with magic. The rest is speculation. Except for one thing: she can't be Sidhe. Pop-rivet and the fasteners on that glove are Cold Iron, and that glove's been worn."

"So what are you going to do?" Joe asked, apprehensive, but covering it fairly well. Tannim negotiated a tricky bit of passing before he answered, using the traffic to buy him time to think of what he was going to tell the kid.

Everything. Teenage sidekicks notwithstanding, he's got guts and he's got combat experience.

"Use that glove to try and find something more about her," Tannim replied grimly. "Right now, I'm at a major disadvantage, since she obviously knows something about me, maybe a lot. And for the rest—besides being *very* careful, we're going to act as if this was all business as usual. We'll leave here on schedule for Fairgrove, unless there's a good reason not to. If we let her think she's disrupting our lives, she wins a moral victory, if nothing else."

Joe nodded slowly. "Just tell me what to do, and I will, sir," he said bravely.

Tannim smiled crookedly. "Besides putting that glove back, the best thing you can do is give my mom some-one to fuss over, and someone for my dad to show off his horses to. Occupy their time. That'll keep them from wondering what I'm up to, and maybe keep them out of danger. I'm still thinking this through. Unless you really *want* to stay out of everything, I'm going to at least keep you informed."

"Right." Joe accepted that, and stowed the glove back in the box. "Ah—where's Fox?"

"That—" Tannim replied quietly "—is a darned good question." And one he hadn't considered until now.

He saw her coming. No—he sensed *her coming. He looked back over his shoulder before I knew anything was up, said, "Uh oh," and vanished. And he hasn't been back.*

Fox knew something. He had to. There was no other explanation for the way he'd acted.

Did he recognize her? There had to be something there that he knew, or sensed—something that slipped right by me, because I thought she was just some hot-rodder, or an obnoxious drunk, right up until she rammed the rear of the Mach I. I had no clue she'd done anything with magic until after she was gone. So what does Fox know about all this?

"You're thinking about something," Joe observed, watch-ing his face alertly. "Something to do with that woman and Fox."

"Yeah." He ran his tongue over dry lips. "He was with me right up until the moment she showed up, then he just blinked out, and hasn't been back."

"Can you make him show up?" Joe asked hopefully. "It sounds like he might know something."

But Tannim had to shake his head with regret. "No. Not without violating a lot of trusts, as well as protocols. My friends—the ones like Fox—wouldn't ever really trust me again if I *forced* him to show up. That's part of the reason they like me. He knows I'm thinking about him, I'm sure. He'll only show up if he wants to."

Joe shook his head sadly. "Sometimes it's really *frustrating* to be the good guy, you know? The bad guys never have to think of things like this."

Despite the tension, Tannim had to chuckle at that. " 'Fraid so, Joe," he replied. "I'm afraid so."

They reached the ranch without any kind of incident, but Tannim was not about to be lulled into lowering his defenses. If this was a challenge, that would be precisely the sort of thing she would be looking for. No, if anything, he had to redouble his efforts.

But before he did that, he was going to have to refuel and get some real rest. He'd done everything he *could* do to protect the innocent bystanders without having specific information on his opponent. Now was the time to get himself back up to top shape.

Joe had already gotten breakfast with his guardian, but he showed no reluctance to eat when presented with a second breakfast. Tannim marveled yet again at the way the young man could dispose of food, as he munched his way dutifully through as much of the "farmhouse meal" as he could handle at one time. *One thing for sure, he's solved our leftover problem for awhile.*

After breakfast, when his mother and father *both* mentioned work in the stables, he seized on the excuse to get a little more sleep. "You guys go right ahead," he said, trying to sound relaxed. "I have a ton of books with me I haven't had time to get to. I'll go read in my room, if you guys don't mind, and I'll catch up with you at lunch."

That gives me another three hours to sleep. I can pack six hours worth into those three, with a little hard mage-sleep. That should put me back up to par. Or at least as close to par as I've been in the last couple of months.

After the exhibition of allergic reactions Tannim had

shown the last time he'd entered the barn, neither of his
parents were eager to have him along. They accepted his
statement with a minimum of fuss and ushered Joe out
the kitchen door, all three of them looking eager. The proprietary way his parents flanked the young man made
Tannim smile. They had definitely "adopted" him.

He shoved the dishes into the dishwasher, cleaned up
the kitchen hastily, and practically ran into his room. He
spread a book open on the nightstand, to make it look as
if he really had been reading, but—

*But if they happen to come in and find me asleep, it's
not that big a deal. They know I need rest, they'll just think
I'm actually getting it.*

He thought, given the tension that he was under, that
he just might have to will himself to sleep. He had not
reckoned with the exhaustion, long- and short-term, he'd
been enduring for the past couple of months. He laid
himself down on the bedspread, closed his eyes, and fell
asleep even as he was preparing the first stages of willing himself into that state.

He woke to the sounds of voices in the house; Joe and
his dad. He lay motionless for a moment, with the memories of vivid dreams in his mind.

Dreams of *her*.

He'd dreamt of her, at least once a week, since he'd
first encountered Chinthliss. Nightly, sometimes. And interestingly enough, she had aged at approximately the same
rate that he had; when he'd been an adolescent, so had
she, and now she was a full adult, although it was no longer
possible to tell exactly how old she was. She could have
been twenty or forty; showing nothing that pointed to
chronology, only that she was no longer an adolescent and
not yet showing any signs of middle age.

With raven hair that cascaded down below her shoulders, enigmatic green eyes, and beauty that was both
cultured and wildly untamed, *she* was, in a sense, the
perfect lover he'd never been able to find in anyone else.

Not that he hadn't looked.

For a long time he'd been certain that he would find
her. He'd assumed, as most young romantics full of

hormones do, that the dreams meant the two of them were destined to meet and become lovers. But as the years passed, and he never found anyone remotely like her, he became convinced she was nothing more than an unconscious expression of his wish for that "perfect" lover. Not that she was slavishly devoted to him in those dreams; far from it. *That* would not have interested him, once he was past the macho cockiness of every adolescent that demanded absolute devotion, or worse, ownership. Luckily, that unflattering phase of his development had been brief.

No, she was very clearly herself in those dreams, perfectly capable, perfectly competent, and quite able to take him on in a game of wits, in a game of intellect, of purely physical challenge, and in any other games as well. That was what made her so perfect. And so damned impossible.

He wondered why he'd dreamed of her now, though. And *that* kind of dream: erotic so far past what he thought were his ordinary fantasies. He'd been entangled to the point where he'd awakened in a state of sexual tension that was as demanding as the state of nervous tension he'd been in when he started this little nap. His undershorts felt two sizes too tight. And he was in his *parents'* house, for God's sake. Not in a position to do anything about it.

Oh, she was something special, though. She was just the kind of otherworldly succubus that would make all the sacrifices to get her worth it. He wouldn't *care* if she was going to eat him alive, if there was a chance he could win her heart. But, instead of *her*, he had some crazy woman in a hot-rod Mustang forcibly planting leatherwear on him.

The voices in the hall drew nearer, and Tannim hastily put his dreamy musings out of his mind. He grabbed simultaneously for the paperback on the nightstand and a throw-blanket to cover himself with, then assumed a posture of reading. When his mother tapped on the door and opened it, he was able to greet her with a reasonably calm demeanor.

"Ready for some lunch?" she asked.

"Sure," he told her, putting the book down and stalling a bit for his blood to cool. "I hope you three had a good time out there. I already know it was work."

That kept her busy, chatting about what she and her husband and Joe had accomplished; while she was talking, she wasn't asking him any questions. Joe had clearly enjoyed the morning's workout. A few minutes later, while they all ate, Trevor couldn't say enough about how well Joe had handled the horses.

"Well, if you haven't got anything planned for him this afternoon, I'd like to borrow him," Tannim interjected. "There's quite a bit of outfitting we still need to do."

Joe paused in mid-bite and raised a single eyebrow at Tannim in inquiry. Tannim nodded, ever so slightly.

"There's not much for him to do in the afternoon," Trevor replied, "not in this heat. Remember, we were counting on that. I know you two have a lot of business to take care of, and I figured you were going to take afternoons and evenings to do it. And maybe just spend some time driving around together; if you're going to be working together, you ought to get to know each other."

Tannim smiled; if he hadn't had these current worries, that's precisely what he *would* be doing. Sometimes his folks showed some amazing insight. They always *had* seemed to get smarter the older he got.

"In that case, we'll take off," he said. "As soon as you're ready, Joe."

Joe made the last of his third sandwich and glass of milk vanish with a speed that meant he *had* to be either magical, ravenous or enlisted-Army, then pronounced himself ready to go. Tannim stayed only long enough to clear their own dishes away, leaving his parents lingering over coffee, before leading the way back out to the Mustang.

Which had, unfortunately, been sitting in the hot sun all morning.

He popped the doors open with the electronic gadget on his keyring and started the engine the same way, but waved Joe away from the car. He opened the driver's side long enough to start the a/c, then stood with the door closed beside it for a moment while the interior cooled a trifle. He tried *not* to think about that shiny pop-rivet in the door panel, but it seemed to be winking at him, mockingly.

Heck, I ought to at least hit it with a dab of touch-up paint so it isn't so blatant.

He finally couldn't stand it any longer and waved Joe inside, pulling open his own door and sliding gingerly over the hot black vinyl. The steering wheel was almost too hot to touch, and he made a vow to find some shade, somewhere, that would cover the car in the mornings. Joe winced away from the hot seat, sitting forward a bit to keep his back away from it. *He* didn't have the protection of the armor; all he had were jeans and a white t-shirt.

"Where to?" Joe asked expectantly. "I figured you didn't have shopping on the brain."

"Wish I did." He eased the Mustang around in the graveled half-circle in front of the house, pulled up to the end of the drive, and headed down the way he had first arrived. No more backing down the drive; not when that put him in a vulnerable position so far as a getaway was concerned. "No, I told you I needed to get more information on this woman; I'm going to a place where it's safe to work some magic to see if I can't get hold of—well, he's an old friend, and he's something of an expert on challenges."

When his encounters with Chinthliss had gone beyond *real* dreams and into situations he had originally thought were "waking dreams" or entertaining hallucinations, the old barn he'd rented for his Mustang restoration business had been the place where he'd first encountered his mentor. That would be the safest place to try to contact him again, even though there wasn't much left of the building. No one would bother them there, and the shield-frames Chinthliss had put in place were still there.

He hadn't intended to come back, but now he had no choice.

The track leading up to the place was long overgrown, visible only as two places where the grass was a little shorter and a little paler than the rest. He turned off through the broken gate in the fence that no one had ever bothered to mend, and pulled the Mach I up through the waving tall grass. If he hadn't known exactly where the safe track was, he would never have dared this with a car that was *not* an off-road vehicle. But the earth was packed down here, and there shouldn't be anything lurking to slash tires or foul the undercarriage. Still, he kept the car at a walking pace, just in case, bringing it up to what was left of the east side of the barn, pulling it into his old parking place in the shade of a blackjack oak.

He retrieved the glove from the glovebox and stuck it into his pocket. He climbed out of the car, and waded through the weeds and grass to where half of the barn door hung from one hinge, the other half lying in the grass. Joe followed, diffidently.

He stepped across the threshold. "You know," he said, conversationally, as he stared into the empty, weed-filled space that had once held his workshop and all his beloved Mustangs in their various states of repair, "I had a dream about this place, before I ever set foot in it. I dreamed that I came up to this door, opened it, and looked around. The place was mostly empty, full of shadows. And right there—" he pointed to the west corner "—there was a tarp with something under it. In my dream I would come up to that tarp, and pull it off, and there was an engine under there. Not just any engine, but a 428 CobraJet, in absolutely perfect condition. Mint, like the day it had come off the line. And it had just been waiting for me to find it."

He contemplated the corner for a moment; there was no sign now that there had ever been anything there. Somewhere under the weeds, there probably lurked all the bits of junk the guy he'd sold salvage rights to hadn't carted off, but you wouldn't know that from here. "Anyway, that was what convinced me to rent this barn; to begin my Mustang restoration business, to go ahead with the whole plan. I did just that, rented it sight unseen; walked up to the place with the key in my hand and unlocked the door and swung it open. And sure enough, in that corner, there *was* a tarp, with something under it. I walked up to it; my heart was pounding, let me tell you. I grabbed the end of the tarp, and I pulled it away—"

"And the engine was there!" Joe exclaimed when he paused.

Tannim shook his head, smiling. "Nope. Nothing but

a pile of musty old lumber and some odd bits of farm equipment. And just at first, I was horribly disappointed. I felt like the dream had let me down, somehow."

He let his gaze drift upward to what was left of the walls, to the blue sky above where the roof had been. And he realized that coming here did *not* hurt, as he had feared it would. He'd given up the limited dreams this place meant a long time ago—outgrown them, so to speak. He might just as readily have felt pain at seeing his old tricycle, or his playpen.

"But then," he continued, "I had this revelation. The dream hadn't let me down at all, because it had spurred me to make the commitment to try the business. I might not otherwise have done it. And I knew at that moment that the things I would build here would be so much *better* than that phantom engine, there'd be no comparison. Everyone wants to hit it big and have something great just happen, like winning a lottery. But—the things I would create here would be all *mine*, built out of the work of my own hands and my own sweat, and not just thrown into my lap."

"Yeah . . ." Joe said, and nodded. "Yeah, I see what you mean." And although not everyone *would* have understood, Tannim had the sense that Joe did.

He took another step or two into the barn, and felt all the protective energies of Chinthliss' magics close around him. The blackened walls took on a peculiar golden haze as he reactivated those magics; gaps in the walls closed up, and a glowing golden field arched upward, between him and the open sky.

Joe stared, wide-eyed, open-mouthed. Tannim grinned, gazing right along with him. He still loved this place.

"Well, there it is, Joe. Real magic. Don't know how much Al and Bob showed you, but this is it: two-hundred proof."

"They never showed me anything like *this*," Joe replied, still ogling around with unabashed astonishment.

Tannim permitted himself a chuckle. "Well," he said, "there's more where that came from."

◆   ◆   ◆

Joe hadn't imagined why Tannim had brought them to this burned-out hulk of a barn, except out of nostalgia. He *did* understand what Tannim meant with his story about the dream-engine, though. He'd had more than enough experience with how gifts out of the blue could backfire on you, or have strings attached you didn't even know about until you began your puppet-dance. No, it was better to earn what you got, that was for sure.

Still—the place was not exactly prepossessing. The roof was gone, and although the remains of the four walls lifted ragged and blackened timbers to the sky, he couldn't imagine what Tannim could find here that he couldn't get in—say—a brush-filled ravine, or a tree-packed ridge, both of which would offer the same amount of privacy that this barn would.

Then Tannim had done—something—and as his skin tingled with the feeling of a lightning storm building, the walls came alive and rose unbroken to the sky in solid sheets of power.

More than that, a kind of roof appeared overhead—a roof of glowing golden light.

All of it was rather ghostlike, since he could see right through it, but it *felt* powerful, and he had no doubt that it would protect them in its way as well as armor plating.

That left him with a lump in his throat. Witnessing magic like this was an electrifying and bewildering experience.

Al and Bob had shown him a few things, including something they'd called "personal shields," but it had all been small stuff compared with this. Was this the kind of thing Tannim did all the time? Would he be expected to work with this kind of stuff on a regular basis? And what about the other people at Fairgrove? Were they all as— well—as powerful as this?

"What do you want me to do, sir?" he asked, pleased that his voice shook only a little.

"Just watch," Tannim replied, taking a relaxed pose in the center of the barn, legs spread apart almost like a pistol-shooting stance, arms raised over his head. "Nothing else."

Well, that was easy enough to do. . . .

He watched, and for awhile nothing much seemed to happen. Then he felt that funny tingling along his skin that he had learned meant something magical was going on, and a faintly glowing ball of green-and-gold light formed in front of Tannim, hovering in the air at about chest height. Soon it was quite solid, as if someone had hung a light bulb right in midair. He could not imagine what this thing was, but he watched it with wide eyes. This wasn't the sort of thing he saw every day.

Tannim stared into the ball, and Joe had the sensation that he was somehow talking to it. He dropped his right hand long enough to pull the black driving-glove out of one pocket, and held it up to the globe for a long time.

Then he tucked the glove away again, raised his hand back over his head, and stared at the globe for a moment longer.

This was as creepy as anything Brother Joseph had ever done, and only the sense that this was *not* anything evil or even harmful kept Joe standing where he was. He knew what evil felt like; whatever it was, this wasn't evil.

But he almost lost it when the ball suddenly brightened until it rivaled the sunshine and cast a tall shadow of Tannim against the wall behind him. And he *did* yelp when it vanished in a clap of thunder.

But Tannim only dropped his hands, dusted them off against his jeans, and stared at the walls for a moment. Abruptly, the glow disappeared, leaving only the fire-blackened timbers again.

"I love that effect!" Tannim laughed.

"What was that?" Joe blurted. "What did you do?"

"Call it—a magical version of a fax machine," Tannim replied after a moment, his green eyes luminous in the bright sunshine, as if there was some power making them shine. "I have a friend named Chinthliss who's like a more powerful version of Foxtrot, though he'd choke if you ever said it to him. I want him to help me, and that little glow-ball is how I told him pretty much everything we know." He grinned then, and pulled his Wayfarers out of his pocket, putting them on. "Now, we just wait."

A magical version of a fax? Joe shook his head; this was

way beyond anything Al and Bob had ever showed him. Even though he knew that when they came to visit they hadn't ever come by airplane much less driven across the country, they hadn't once explained how they *did* manage to cross the miles between Pawnee and Savannah whenever they chose. They certainly hadn't *shown* him things like this. Tannim turned away from him for a moment and bent his head down to peer at something in the grass growing up through the barn floor.

Joe might have asked more questions, except that at that precise moment, someone coughed delicately behind him.

"Excuse me?" said a low, sexy, female voice.

Tannim thought he saw something give off a bit of mage-sparkle in the grass at his feet, and he peered down for a moment.

"Excuse me?" said a voice that was *not* Joe's.

Tannim jumped in startlement, and turned to face the barn door.

And froze as he saw who was standing there behind Joe, his mind lodged on a single thought, unable to get past it.

It's her—it's her—it's her—

And it was: the woman who had haunted him and hunted him down through his dreams for the last decade and more. The woman he'd dreamed of this morning. *Her.* And she stood there, nonplussedly taking in his look of complete and utter shock.

There was absolutely no doubt of it; she matched his dreams in every detail. Gently curved, raven-wing hair swept down past her shoulders and framed a face that he knew as well as he knew his own. Amused, emerald-green eyes gazed at him from beneath strong brows that arched as delicately as a bit of Japanese brushwork. The regal nose was just short of being hawklike, and gave strength to the prominent cheekbones. The sensual mouth hinted at a hundred secrets. And the body, the perfect, slim, small-breasted body . . . did more than hint.

She stood as he remembered her standing; poised, and not posed, graceful movement arrested for the briefest of moments. She wore silk and leather; a red silk jumpsuit that flowed in an exotic cut that spoke of expensive designers, tooled and riveted black leather belt and boots. She wore them beautifully, flawlessly, unselfconsciously, as if they were the stuff of her everyday attire.

"Excuse me," she said again, in a throaty contralto that he remembered whispering intimacies into his ear, ". . . but I understood that I could find someone here who works on Mustangs."

He took one step toward her; another. At the third step, he looked past her and spotted her black Mustang standing in the midst of the tall grass outside the barn door. The grasses waved gently around it, like something out of a commercial. Joe simply stood frozen in place, staring at her. She waited, calmly. She looked as if she would be perfectly ready to wait all day.

Tannim started to speak, and had to cough to clear his throat before his voice would work.

"Not—for a long time," he said dazedly.

"Ah," she replied, with a smile tinged with something he could not read.

But then her eyes widened as she looked past his shoulder, and she stepped back in alarm.

Fear lanced him. He whirled to look.

There was nothing there.

Quickly, realizing that she had pulled the oldest trick in the book on him, he turned back.

She was already gone. And so was her car.

Only *then* did his mind click back into gear, as he sprinted past the broken-down door, and stood where the car had been. There was the imprint of four tires in the grass—but no track-marks leading up to them. There was no sign that the car had actually been driven through the grass to reach that spot, and there had been no sound of a motor.

Belatedly, recognition. The car that had stood there had been the same Mustang that had shadowed him last night.

The grasses waved and parted; he looked down when his subconscious recognized that the shadow there was not a shadow. There was a second black, fingerless driving glove in the grass at his feet.

He picked it up, and immediately banished the thought that he might have dropped last night's glove and not have noticed. *That* glove had been torn where it had been riveted to the door and he'd ripped it off. *This* glove, also for the right hand, was intact.

And it, too, contained a small strip of parchment.

He took it out, and there was another quotation handwritten there, in the same spidery hand.

> *The painful warrior famoused for fight,*
> *After a thousand victories, once foiled,*
> *Is from the books of honour razed quite,*
> *And all the rest forgot for which he toil'd.*
>
> Sonnet 25

He stared at it, the meaning burning arc-light bright in his mind. *The challenge has been made. Chicken out of this one—or be defeated—and everything you are and ever were will be erased, and everything you ever did will be forgotten.*

CHAPTER FOUR

Tannim tucked the slip of parchment back into the glove with special care. The sun burned down on his head, as the quotation burned in his mind. Of all the ways he'd ever imagined of meeting *her*, this had never once crossed his mind. He'd pictured himself simply running into her in some exotic place, imagined finding her on his side in a desperate combat, wondered if some day she might simply appear at Fairgrove as a new "employee" even as he had. He had fantasized rescuing her, fighting by her side, having *her* rescue *him*, even. It had never once entered his mind that she could be an enemy.

No—not an enemy. Have to call it like it is; I don't know that yet. An opponent, but I can't put her in the "enemy" column yet. Maybe that was wishful thinking, but he couldn't get all those dreams out of his head. Surely they meant *something*.

Grass swished and crackled behind him, and young Joe moved out of the barn to stand next to him. "There was a lady there a minute ago, wasn't there?" he said, his voice remarkably steady, given the circumstances. "And a car?" In the brilliant sun, his hair looked almost white, and his vividly blue eyes mirrored the Oklahoma sky.

"Uh-huh," Tannim confirmed. "I'm beginning to feel like Prince Charming. She left me another glove."

Joe regarded the glove in Tannim's hand with a dubious expression and made no move to touch it. "I don't think you're gonna have too much luck going around Tulsa getting women to try those on to see if they fit."

Tannim smiled faintly. *Not bad; the kid's keeping his sense of humor.* "Not as reliable as a glass slipper."

No maker's mark in these gloves, though. No tag, and no sign that one had been cut or taken out. No identifying marks at all. Wasn't that a little odd?

Come to think of it, they didn't really look mass-produced. Huh. Custom work? If so, they might be as good as a glass slipper if I can find out where they came from.

He was just about ready to take the gloves apart, stitch by stitch, when a warning tingle along his personal shields alerted him. *Something* was manifesting in the barn!

He tested the energies, and recognized one he had not really expected to encounter quite so soon. But it was more than welcome, especially in light of this second challenge.

He sprinted back to the barn and reinvoked all the protections; the golden walls of power came up around him, enclosing him in a safe zone that only he, Chinthliss, or their sendings would be able to pass. He held his hands out at chest height, preparing the space in front of him to receive whatever Chinthliss' answer would be.

A thunderclap announced its arrival in his hands, and a flash of golden light that lit up the inside of the protective dome as it passed through the shields.

It came in the form of the same green and gold message-globe he himself had sent out, which confirmed his surprised and delighted guess that Chinthliss had answered him *immediately*, interrupting whatever else he was doing to do so. There *were* times when the dragon came through for him.

The globe settled in his hands, weightlessly, and pulsed for a moment, as it confirmed his identity. Then it deepened in color, turning from golden green to a deep bronze, and he felt a familiar touch on his mind. He relaxed and let the message flow into his thoughts.

:I have heard, and am intrigued, Son of Dragons.: The

deep bass, purely mental voice tolled sonorously in his head. *:I will arrive at the usual place at the hour the sun has vanished. And in case you have forgotten, the "usual place" is the building in which you once kept all your machines.:*

The globe spun on its axis then whirled and changed, fading as it discharged its energies into the air, the shields, and anything else that was able to absorb a little extra power.

Including Tannim, who was not too proud to get a little of the charge he'd put into the thing back again.

Once again, he brought the protections down, and took a quick glance at Joe. The young man was not watching him; instead, he had taken up a "guard" position at the doorframe, and his alert stance told Tannim that his erstwhile protégé was perfectly prepared to fight anything that tried to cause trouble. Obviously Joe had not made the assumption that because the challenger was a woman, she could be dismissed.

Good. At least that's one lesson he won't have to learn the hard way.

"Joe?" he said quietly. The young man turned and nodded.

"Nothing out there that I can see," he said. "Nobody watching us as far as I can tell. Did your friend send you a return fax?"

Tannim had to smile at the ease with which Joe had accepted his own offhanded terminology. "As a matter of fact, he did," Tannim replied. "He's going to be here tonight. We'll have to come out here to meet him."

"And until then?" Joe asked, his expression stolid, only his eyes showing his nervous tension as he continually glanced from side to side, making certain nothing could creep up on them.

"First I need to make a phone call, and I want to do that from a private phone, not from home," Tannim told him. "My friend's going to need a hotel room, so why don't we go arrange that for him, and I can use the phone in the room."

Joe nodded, and Tannim reflected that it was really

useful having someone like Joe around, a young man who was used to taking orders without question. Questions like, how was this friend going to get out here, and why couldn't he arrange his own room, or stay with Tannim's folks?

Setting aside the fact that Joe was in the only other guest room besides Tannim's old room—Joe could, after all, return to Frank Casey's house. No, Joe simply accepted that Tannim knew what he was doing, and waited for explanations instead of demanding them. Sometimes repressed curiosity was a lot easier to deal with than open curiosity.

Well, there was no point in standing around here in the hot sun; already his scalp was damp with sweat, and only the armor kept him relatively cool. Joe must be ready to drop; there was sweat trickling down his forehead, and his t-shirt was damp. "Let's get out of here before anything else happens."

"Right." Joe turned and strode to the barn door.

And there he stopped, crouched over, scanning quickly from side to side. Tannim watched in amazement; he had never seen anyone so young with such moves! These kinds of tactics had apparently become second nature to Joe. *Jeez, another good reason to have him around.*

He waited until Joe waved an "all clear" to him before joining him at the door, crouching beside him with one hand on the rough wood. "I can't spot anything out there, sir," Joe said in a soft voice. "The birds aren't disturbed, either, so I don't think there's anybody hiding in the grass."

"You can work point any time, Joe," Tannim told him quite seriously.

Joe flashed him a shy grin before returning his gaze to the field beyond the barn. "I'll go first."

"Go," Tannim said, and pulled out his keychain, pushing the button for the radio-transmitter that controlled the doors and the engine. On the other side of the wall, the Mustang rumbled into life. "There. The doors are unlocked."

Joe nodded and was gone in a flash, scuttling through the weeds in a bent-over run, rather than crawling. There wasn't a real reason to crawl, unless bullets or other projectiles started flying, and a formidable reason in the form of ticks and chiggers *not* to crawl. Tannim followed in the same way as soon as he got around the corner of the barn and out of sight.

He felt a little foolish as he crouched beside his car door, listening intently. But better to feel foolish than not feel at all. "Dead" was a hard condition to cure.

He slipped into the Mustang and punched up the a/c, backed into position so that he could drive straight out, and waited. Nothing rushed at them from the weeds, and there were no vehicles in sight in either direction once they reached the road. It looked exactly as it should: a sleepy section-line road that seldom saw much in the way of traffic.

Tannim did not drop even a fraction of his watchful caution, however, and it was easy to see by Joe's tense posture that he felt the same. Out here it would be easy enough for someone to perch in a tall tree and watch their progress. Not that he could really picture *her*, in that flame-red silk jumpsuit, clambering up a tree.

But if she can make herself and her Mustang vanish, she can certainly change her wardrobe as easily, he reminded himself. *Or, for all I know, she has flunkies out here keeping an eye on us.*

For that matter, she was a mage, and she *could* be using any of the birds around here as "eyes." There was nothing he could do about that—not without endangering himself and his passenger. Anything he did to make the Mach I less visible to birds would make it less visible to other human drivers. The drivers around here were bad enough without complicating the situation by tricking their minds into thinking he wasn't there.

He passed both gloves to Joe, who locked them in the glovebox without a word. There was one thing he could do; birds had distinct territories, and in the summer they didn't tend to venture out of them. Right now, the best thing he could do, if she was using birds as her scouts, was to drive some distance before stopping at a motel. With luck, she'd lose him and not find him again.

Unless, of course, she's using something like a bald eagle.

Well, there was only so much he could do without his precautions hedging his actions so much that he couldn't move.

He drove around in circles for about an hour, stopping once at a convenience store for Gatorade for the two of them, before finally seeking out a motel for Chinthliss.

The south side of Tulsa was a lot more upscale than Bixby; it was where the Yuppies collected in expansive, milling herds, and was thick with condo-complexes with gates and expensive, fenced-in houses set on quarter-acre lots. The blight crept farther south with every year. Tannim figured that he'd be able to find something to suit Chinthliss out here. Nothing less than a palace would make the dragon happy, but at least he wouldn't complain as much as he had the time he shared a room at the Holiday Inn with Tannim and FX.

High and mighty dragon couldn't unwrap the little soaps by himself. Poor baby.

With a little bit of searching, he found exactly what he was looking for: one of those high-end "suite motels." If it became too dangerous to stay with his folks any longer, he and Joe could just move in with Chinthliss. He pulled up to the office, and left Joe in the car with the motor running and the a/c on while he took care of throwing money at the clerk.

He returned with a grin on his face and slid into the seat. "Amazing what a paid-up Gold Card will do, even in this neighborhood. I got a two-bedroom with a parking slot guaranteed to be in the shade all day," he said, and tossed Joe a key. "That's for us, if we need someplace else to go. Hang onto it for me."

"Sure," Joe said obediently, pocketing the key.

"Now, let's go see what kind of digs poor Chinthliss will have to stoop to." He pulled the Mustang around to the side of the complex and found the slot assigned to Chinthliss' suite. As promised, it was in the shade. They locked the car and ventured into the depths of the complex. The suite was supposed to be like a townhouse: two-story, with two bedrooms upstairs and living area and kitchen down. The door wasn't more than a few feet from the parking slot, and when he opened it, cool air rushed to meet them, faintly perfumed with disinfectant.

It was as advertised, and would probably suit His Draconic Majesty just fine. Joe went immediately to the living room and turned on the TV. Tannim let the a/c blow through his hair for a moment, then went to the kitchen. As the clerk had instructed, he filled out the grocery list with things he knew Chinthliss liked. Someone from the staff would be around in the next couple of hours to stock the refrigerator; an extra service invoked by the Gold Card's near-bottomless cornucopia effect. After this, the maids would keep the fridge stocked the same way. This was going to make life much easier for him, even if he was in for over a grand already. *I'll have to put the old lizard up in places like this more often. He can prowl around and poke into things to his heart's content, take showers as long as he wants without using up all the hot water, pop every bag of microwave popcorn in the place. This's going to be a lot easier than taking him to restaurants.*

He did not want to think about the last time he'd taken Chinthliss to a real restaurant. Fortunately, it had been one that catered to the elves at Fairgrove, and the staff was used to some of the customers acting peculiarly.

Like ordering escargot and jalapeño pizza with bleu cheese, and eating it with chopsticks.

While Joe relaxed for the first time since *she* had shown up, sprawling in the living room and watching cable, he left the grocery list on the doorknob and found a phone in one of the bedrooms.

Dottie answered it on the second ring, which was a relief. There was no mistaking her sugar-sweet phone voice. *She* would know that if he *said* he needed to talk to Keighvin, he really *needed* to talk to the boss there and then.

"Fairgrove Industries, Kevin Silver's office," she chirped. "How may I help you?"

"Dottie, it's Tannim," he said. "I need to talk to Keighvin. Something came up out here."

That last was a code signal among Fairgrove employees;

it meant something had gone seriously wrong. "I'll page him, I think he's out in the plant," she said immediately, every trace of sugar gone from her voice. "Hold on a minute."

She didn't put him on hold, just put the phone down on the desk, so he heard her when she used the pager. "Keighvin, Line One. Keighvin, Line One. Charlie Tannim."

That would tell Keighvin that he needed to get to the phone *immediately* without telling any visitors to the plant that there was something wrong somewhere. It would also tell him that he needed to get to a secure phone, one without any outsiders anywhere around.

"Okay, I've paged him," Dottie said, picking up the phone again. A moment later a *click* and the background whine of turbines signaled the fact that Keighvin had just picked up a phone somewhere in the complex.

"I have it, Dottie." Keighvin Silverhair's resonant tenor was as unmistakable as Dottie's phone voice.

"Yes, sir," she said, and hung up.

"It's Tannim, Keighvin," the young mage said. "And I've got a problem here."

Briefly he outlined the appearance of the mysterious lady and everything that had happened associated with her. Except for one small detail; he did *not* reveal that she was the one he had been dreaming about for years. Somehow he just couldn't bring himself to; the dreams were so intimate, so much a part of him. And how could they be germane to the situation, anyway?

Keighvin remained silent all through the narrative, but Tannim knew him well enough to know that his mind was working at a furious pace, analyzing everything Tannim had told him.

"You've been challenged, lad," he said at last. "It's definitely in the style of the Sidhe, too. But I canna explain those bits of Death Metal; in no way could any Sidhe handle those. She canna be Seleighe nor Unseleighe herself, but she knows our style. Is this the lady ye've been dreamin' of all these years, lad?"

Tannim felt himself flush with anger. "Damn, Keighvin, have you left *anything* in my mind alone?"

"Aye, more'n ye know, lad, but that's na important now. It's her then, is it?"

"Yeah. I think."

"Mmm."

"That's it, just *mmm*, Keighvin?"

"Mmm-hmm. As I said, ye've been challenged with the gloves."

"So what's it mean, really, having gloves delivered?" he asked. "Other than the obvious challenge."

Silence on the other end of the line, as Keighvin Silverhair tried to twist Old World feudal customs into words that a twentieth-century hot-rodder would understand.

"It implies one of two things," he said finally. "I believe that we may eliminate the notion that you hae somehow insulted the lady's honor."

Not unless she somehow found out about my dreams. . . .

Keighvin's accent always thickened when he harkened back to his "other self," Lord Sir Keighvin Silverhair, ruler of Elfhame Fairgrove and all who dwelt therein. "So 'tother implication is that you hae been chosen by th' lass t'prove her ain worth. She didna slap ye with yon glove, did she?"

"Not unless you call pop-riveting the first one to my door a slap, no," Tannim replied. "Unless her slamming into the back of the Mach I counts. Does it?"

"Nay." Keighvin was firm on that. "The *glove* wasna physically involved. An' you mind, she was very careful to have no impact when she delivered the glove, aye?"

"Oh, absolutely," Tannim said. "No impact at all, or I'd have noticed it for sure. I had no clue she'd done anything until I was out of the car."

"Then she's not issued th' challenge mortal, or at least, she's not been insulted to th' point where she's wishin' your heart an' head on a platter, an' yer privates for remembrance," Keighvin replied, relief clear in his voice. "The meanin' is simply that she sees you as bein' the best t' measure hersel' against. 'Tis a bit like yon drag race; she wishes t' cast ye down, an' rise hersel' in the process. Like the young knights that would challenge their elders, the Lancelots and Gawaines—or challenge us at the crossroads of a midnight if they were truly bold. Now mind, it can still go t' the challenge mortal, but at th' moment, I'd say she wishes t' gae only to first blood."

"In other words, she's picked me. She can keep it civilized, or she can decide to go for the whole enchilada."

"In essence, aye." Keighvin went silent again as he thought. "I dinna think ye can count on her staying civilized, though."

Tannim heaved a sigh. "Yeah, we have to figure on worst-case scenario. We also can't count on her working alone."

"She could be in th' employ of our darker cousins, aye." Keighvin echoed his sigh. "For that matter, though her intent be innocent now, still, once th' Unseleighe learn of her and her intent, they may yet make it worth her while t' make this more than a contest of wits an' skill."

"Got any ideas?" Tannim asked, hoping against hope that Keighvin, with all of his centuries of experience in situations like this, just might know of a loophole somewhere.

"*Don't* reject th' challenge, an' don't run," Keighvin said firmly. " 'Twill reduce ye t' th' hunted animal. That's the rules of th' game: run, an' ye become a coward, an' th' coward can be squashed like a bothersome insect. Aye, and anyone with him. Run, an' Joe an' your parents coul' be sacrificed, or used as bait t' bring ye in."

Tannim cursed softly, hearing his own thoughts confirmed.

"*But,* for all that she seems t' know a fair bit about ye, she canna assume she knows all," Keighvin continued, raising his hopes. "So—my advice is pretend ye dinna understand."

"You mean play dumb? Like I've never heard of the challenge game?" The idea had its appeal. "How long can I drag things out that way?"

"Depends on how much she knows, an' who she knows. If she's hand-in-glove wi' our cousins, she'll find out soon enough 'tis an act, and challenge ye outright." Keighvin put one hand over the mouthpiece and spoke to someone else for a moment. "Conal reminds me of another aspect t' all of this. As th' challenged party, 'tis *you* who has the choice of weapons. Ah, here—"

Some fumbling on the other end of the line, then Conal's thicker accent and deeper voice sounded over the speaker. "Eh, lad, has she not yon Mustang too, ye said?"

"Yeah, it's a late-model number. Depending on what she's done to it, if she's *not* kicking in nitrous injection or magic, we're probably a match in that department. Hers is lighter, it's reliable, it handles better. It's easy to boost the power on it with after-market stuff. Are you saying," he continued, "that I should accept her challenge and pick the *cars* as weapons?"

"Make it a race, lad," Conal agreed. "Set the conditions. Use yer expertise and yer magery on yon pony-car yersel'. I've not seen a mage here t' match ye i' that department. An' I know for a fact that t'only driver we hae that is as good as ye is young Maclyn."

"What if she wants to make it—what did Keighvin call it? The challenge mortal?" He gritted his teeth, waiting for Conal's reply.

"There is that." Conal took a deep breath. "Well, an' ye find yersel' wi' the challenge mortal—where would ye rather find yersel'? Behind yon blade, i' th' mage-circle, or behind th' wheel?"

He thought long and hard before replying. "Behind the wheel," he said slowly. "I'm better off there than anywhere else."

"I wouldna say *that*—but I would say this. I think ye'd be safer there. I think she canna be th' driver ye are. An' once ye learn whence her magery an' her trainin' come, I think ye can best her. Ah, here's Keighvin back. The luck to ye, lad."

A moment more, and Keighvin came back on the line. "I agree with everything Conal told you, Tannim. Stall her while you learn about her, then when she delivers a challenge you can't refuse, take her to the road. *Don't hesitate to call us.* There's only a limited amount we can do, but what we can, we will. And we'll see to it that yon Joe and your parents stay safe. In fact, we'll begin on that this very moment; 'tis a fair amount we can do even at long distances."

"I'm working on getting someone here who can help

me," Tannim told him. Relief spread through him and made him limp as Keighvin *offered* Fairgrove's help. That took a tremendous amount off his mind. With Sidhe mage-warriors watching over the noncombatants, he could deal with this lady with all his attention. He had the feeling she would *require* his entire attention.

"Keep us informed," Keighvin concluded. "Call once a day from now on, perhaps about this time. I'll be havin' some of the rest dealin' with keeping your parents shielded and safe as soon as I hang up."

"Thanks, Keighvin," Tannim said fervently, running his hand through his tangled hair. "I can't even begin to thank you enough for that."

I can even forgive you for funding the horse ranch without telling me.

" 'Tis nothing you don't have as your due, lad," Keighvin replied, warmth in his voice. "Now, I'll be off."

"Same here. And thanks again." He waited for the *click* that signaled Keighvin had rung off before hanging up himself. Protocol, protocol. Never be the one to hang up on an elven lord.

Joe looked at him inquisitively when he descended the staircase using every other step and entered the living room. "Good?" the young man asked.

"Good," Tannim replied. "Keighvin's taking care of some of it, and he and Conal gave me some good advice on the rest." He leveled the most authoritative gaze he had on the young man. "The moment—the *instant* we know that this might mean more than a simple magical drag race, you are out of here. Keighvin's going to see to it. Got that?"

"But—" Joe protested weakly. "But—"

"You're not a two-stroke engine, stop imitating one," Tannim told him, crossing his arms over his chest. "No arguments. If this gets serious, you haven't got the training, the experience, or the power to handle fighting between two mages *or* between two drivers. If this turns into a Mustang shootout, I don't want innocent bystanders making it into Death Race 2000."

Joe flushed and looked chagrined. "All right," he said reluctantly. *Very* reluctantly, for someone who had just yesterday told Tannim that he had not wanted to get involved with magic anymore.

Sheesh, the kid's decided he's responsible for me. Or else he's feeling guilty about leaving me to take this on alone.

"Look, Joe," he said, lowering his voice persuasively, "if this were a regular fight, there isn't anyone I'd rather have working point or tail. I'd rather trust you at my back than anyone else in the state. But it's not a regular fight—it'd be like you going out into a firefight with an ordinary college freshman backing you. See?"

Joe nodded, his flush fading. "Yes, sir, I do see. You're right. I understand."

Oh, the wonders of a paramilitary education. Authority actually means something! Try telling that to one of the Fairgrove fosterlings, and you'd find him following you as closely as if you'd hooked a tow-bar to his forehead.

"I'll tell you what you can do," he continued. "You can help me keep my folks from finding anything out about all this. And if anything happens to me—well, you and Keighvin take care of them for me, okay?"

Joe straightened at that, and came very close to saluting. "Yes, sir. I can do that, sir. I *will* do that; your parents are—wonderful people."

"Yes," he said simply. "They are. And you have taken an enormous weight off my mind, knowing there will be someone who'll look after them. And speaking of my parents, we'd better get back; it's almost suppertime, and I think Mom is planning pasta. I know it seems kind of stupid to go back home after all this, but there are reasons for it."

Joe rose with alacrity and followed him to the door, making certain that it locked after them. Tannim found himself liking the young man more and more with every hour he spent in Joe's presence.

The odd thing was that having a promise from Joe to "take care of" his parents *did* take an enormous weight off his mind. He was an only child, and while he had every intention of staying alive a long, long time—well, the racing business alone was dangerous, as his own wrecks proved. Then, once you added in the other complications, well—if he'd been an insurance agent, *he* wouldn't have written a policy on himself.

One thing that had always troubled his sleep—besides the *special* side effects of those dreams about *her*—was what his untimely demise would do to his mom and dad, and at times like these it troubled him even more. Now, if everything went badly, they'd have Joe there to help them through the mourning and be a second son to them afterward.

And if everything goes well, they'll still have their first son, plus a second son. One that can stand horses, to make up for me.

This was nothing that Alinor and Keighvin could ever have foreseen when they asked Tannim to pick up the young man. No, this was the kind of magic that had nothing to do with elves, and everything to do with the human heart.

Sometimes, he reflected, things worked out okay. As he popped the locks on the Mustang, he decided that letting the good things happen was the best magic he knew.

SharMarali Halanyn examined herself in the mirror with a critical eye. Her facial fur was perfect; her ears were groomed immaculately, as always. In the reflection of her own green eyes she could see the mirror's glinting circle; she then banished the silvered glass with a thought. All was well. If she looked this cool after being out in the sweltering Oklahoma sunshine, she must have been devastating when Tannim had seen her. She smiled with satisfaction and no little anticipation as she sat back in her overstuffed red-silk chair and gazed at the flower arrangement that had taken the mirror's place.

This looked remarkably like an upscale Manhattan condo, except there were no windows anywhere, and no doors to the exterior, either. There were no windows because there was nothing to look out upon except the emptiness of mist-filled Chaos where she had created her home. And there were no doors, because there was no need for doors. The only possible way in or out of here—other than stumbling on the place by sheerest accident—was by Gate.

Her own Mustang rested in a heavily shielded shelter attached to this apartment, and it had its own Gate large enough to drive through. It had not been easy, bringing so much Cold Iron into this place; the very fabric of Underhill rebelled against the presence of the Death Metal, and the magics of her allies became unreliable and unpredictable around anything ferrous. That was one reason why they did not seek to visit her in her own "den"; and that was the main reason she had insisted on keeping the car here. That, plus the masking properties of silk, kept them just wary enough to suit her needs. Good.

Tannim had looked so wonderfully stunned. That old deer-in-the-headlights look. It was such a marvelous feeling, being able to wipe that self-assured grin off his face and leave him completely off balance. Without a clue! And without even a dime to buy one with!

And it had been so gratifying to know that she could do that to him anytime she wanted. She knew all there was to know about him; he knew nothing of her.

Had he guessed that she was his challenger from last night? There had been some kind of recognition, so perhaps he had. *Or perhaps, just perhaps, he recognizes you from something else entirely,* whispered the little voice from within. *Perhaps he has dreamed of you, even as you have dreamed of him. Remember the candles and satin, and the warmth of his body over you, in you, cupping you and pouring deep. . . .*

She shook the voice into quiescence with a toss of her hair. How could he possibly dream of her? He had no notion that she even existed! Whereas *she* had known of his existence from early adolescence. Hadn't she been trained and groomed to be his opposite number, his ultimate rival, yin to his yang, even as her father was Chinthliss' ultimate rival? She had watched him, studied him for years, and she *knew* he had no inkling that she—or someone like her—was anywhere in any universe.

Even Chinthliss had never told him, although Chinthliss knew very well that she existed, though he did not know where she was. Her father Charcoal had seen to it that Chinthliss was kept abreast of her progress.

The jerkoff. Her father Charcoal, that is, not Chinthliss. Charcoal was no longer a part of her life, and that was the way she wanted it.

No, there was no reason to think that Tannim had recognized her from dreams. Particularly not the kind of dream passages that *she* had about *him*.

Erotic? Oh, a tad. They had certainly been far more satisfactory than anything shared with her Unseleighe lovers.

She frowned a little at that. There would be no more dalliances with the Unseleighe; she had cut them off from that years ago when she realized how much they were using her. They had no consideration for her pleasure in their spurious loving intimacies; their only thoughts were for their own satiation. She preferred a fantasy-dream with Tannim any night over a real-life assignation with an Unseleighe, however comely the elven twit might be.

Not that the Sidhe were extremely attractive to her. It was just that Tannim was anything but uncomely. When it came down to it, he was far better looking in the bright sun of day than he ever had been in her misty dreams, or in much of the covert spying she had done on him. If he were *kitsune*, she'd be even more in lust with him.

She closed her eyes, and he sprang into her mind with extraordinary vividness.

He looked far younger than his true years; he shared that with her, despite his purely mortal origins. He had a fine face; not handsome in the classical sense, but one that was not likely to be forgotten: high cheekbones, broad brow, firm and determined chin, sensual mouth given to smiles and laughter.

Unlike these dour Unseleighe, who smile only when they kill and laugh only when blood spills across their hands. They all think they are such great kings and warriors. What a bunch of complete weenies.

Despite the fact that Tannim was as slim as a young girl, there was strength to him, in the broad shoulders, the wiry muscles. *Good bones,* her mother would say. And, ah, that wild mane of dark and curling hair; women must go mad to run their hands through it!

But it was the eyes that caught you, when he wasn't

staring at you like a rabbit trying to guess the make of the car about to run it over. Huge green eyes that changed hue with the changing of his emotions. Vulnerable eyes; eyes that promised something wonderful to those whom he gave his loyalty and affection. And she had every reason to believe those implied wonders were real, for she had seen how generously he gave of himself once his trust and heart were pledged.

Ah, lucky one, who becomes his true lover. . . .

It was that little internal voice again, and with annoyance she squashed it down. She had *no* business with such thoughts; he was a human and she was most decidedly not, for one thing. And for another—

She was his mirror.

Whether she would be his fate, as the Unseleighe wished, remained to be seen.

She opened her eyes again and interlaced her hands over the red silk covering her knee, thinking in silence. Unlike Tannim, music distracted her. For him it was a focus.

He had, as yet, given her no sign that he recognized the challenges for what they were. Then again, she had given him no chance to respond. She enjoyed this game; she wanted to stretch it out as long as possible, and by teasing him like this, she fulfilled the letter of her agreement with the Unseleighe without actually taking any action against him.

Given how much time he had spent with Keighvin Silverhair, though, he surely must have recognized a Challenge by now. But she could continue to tease him for several days without giving him an opportunity to answer the Challenge. Eventually, of course, the Unseleighe would become impatient with her, and force her to conclude the opening steps of the dance, but for now, she was free to improvise her own patterns on the stage.

A glissando of subtle energies chimed upon her inward ear, and a rustle of stiffer silk than she wore alerted her to the presence of someone who had just crossed the Gate into her private pocket of Underhill. Since that Gate was guarded against everyone but her parents—and since she had long since barred her father from coming anywhere *near* her without her specific permission—there was only one person it could be.

"Mother!" she exclaimed with pleasure, rising to her feet and whirling to meet the Honorable Lady Ako with outstretched arms. The Honorable Lady Ako stepped across the threshold in a flutter of ankle-length, fox-red hair and a rustle of blue-green kimonos, serene as a statue of a saint and graceful as the most exquisitely trained geisha, and she smiled to see her daughter running to greet her.

The Honorable Lady Ako—magician, healer, shapeshifter, bearer of some of the most noble blood in or out of Underhill, and nine-tailed *kitsune*—met her daughter's embrace and accepted it. But something in Ako's eyes told Shar that this visit was not a social call.

Nevertheless, the amenities of civilization must come first.

Shar led her mother to the seat of honor, and with a brush of her hand, changed the silk of the couch to a blue-green that harmonized with her mother's kimonos. *Should there be a tea ceremony?* she wondered, as she settled at her mother's feet. *Perhaps*—

But Ako laid one gentle hand on her daughter's before Shar could summon the implements for a proper tea ceremony. "Tea, but no ceremony, my love," Ako told her firmly. "I must speak with you, and I have little time."

Shar summoned perfectly brewed tea and translucent porcelain cups with a gesture, handing the first cup to her mother before taking up her own. Ako took a sip, then placed the cup back down on her own palm. The amenities had been observed. Now for business.

"I have learned that you have been abroad," Ako said delicately. "That you have been there at the behest of—your father's friends."

Ako would not mention the Unseleighe by name, nor Charcoal. She had long ago fallen out with the blood-father of her daughter—rightly, Shar thought, since Charcoal was insufferable in all ways. She would have no commerce with Charcoal's friends and allies. And when Ako declined to mention someone by name, it meant that she declined to acknowledge their existence, given the option of doing so.

Reluctantly, Shar nodded. She was too well-trained to flush, but the feeling of faint shame was there, as if she had been caught in something dishonorable.

Ako studied her daughter's face, her green eyes grave in the white-porcelain doll-face beneath the crimson waterfall of her hair. It was all that Shar could do to maintain eye contact with her mother. "I know what it is that they wish you to do," Ako said finally. "You know that I do not approve. This young man has done nothing to harm you; he has done nothing, save to be the protégé of Chinthliss. But that is not to the point. Are *you* so certain that you wish to visit destruction upon this young man?"

For a single, bewildered moment, Shar wondered if her mother could somehow have learned of her years of dreams. She shook her head, and bit her lip. "Honorable Mother, I am not to be commanded by such as—my father's friends. I do what I will. At the moment, it amuses me to occupy this young man. It may amuse me to deliver him to them. But it will be of *my* will or not at all."

She raised her chin defiantly, willing her mother to recognize that she would not be tamed by any creature.

Ako looked deep into Shar's eyes, and the young female found herself hot with the blushes she had conquered earlier. "I will say only this to you: look deeply into your thoughts and your heart, your instincts and your memories, before you commit yourself to any action," she said. "Do nothing irrevocable until you have determined that you can live with the result for all of your life. I say this, my dearest child, so that you do not follow in the path of your mother. Do not make mistakes you will regret, and prove unable to correct."

And with that, as Shar sat in stunned silence, Lady Ako rose with the grace of a bending willow, and summoned the Gate to life. She glided toward it, and paused on the threshold.

Then she turned, and caught Shar's eyes, so like her own, one more time. "Remember the past," she said simply.

Then she stepped across the Gate, and was gone.

❖   ❖   ❖

Stuffed full of pasta and garlic bread, Tannim and Joe arrived at the old barn just at sunset. Once again, Joe spotted for Tannim as he drove—carefully—into the long grass and parked the Mach I beside the barn. Joe was the first one out of the car, and Tannim waited for him to give the "all clear" signal before he got out himself.

If the mysterious woman was watching, and she meant no more than a simple challenge, their behavior would seem very consistent for someone who had not understood the meaning of what she had done. And if she meant worse than that, well, she would see that they were alert and would be hard to catch off guard twice.

Once he and Joe were inside the barn, he activated the *entire* set of protections on the place. It was a pity he couldn't get the Mach I in here anymore now that the door was a wreck, but the Mustang had its own defenses.

The protections rose, layer on layer, forming a shifting golden dome inside the barn. It would take something like a magical bomb to penetrate the shields on this place now, plus a physical one to do otherwise.

"Remember, you can't leave till I take this all down," he reminded Joe, who stared in wonder at the glowing dome over them. "Chinthliss did a lot of this; I don't know everything it's set against, I only know that I haven't come across anything that can break in or out."

"Won't somebody see the light and think—I don't know, maybe it's a UFO or something?" Joe worried.

Tannim laughed and hit the young man in the shoulder lightly. "You've been hanging around elves too much," he chided. "Turn your mage-sight *off*."

He watched as Joe frowned in concentration, then grinned with relief. "Nothing," the young man said. "There's nothing there."

"Right, it's only visible to those with the *ability* to see it." He considered the lovely golden dome overhead. "I suppose there might be a few folks around here who would notice it if they looked this way, but they're also the kind who'll stay out of anything they haven't been invited to. Not because they aren't curious—but because they'll have learned 'don't touch' the same way I did. The hard way.

Nothing like getting your hand burned to teach you to watch that fire."

He grinned, and Joe shook his head in mock sadness. "Maybe you shoulda had a dose of military school," Joe told him with a spark of impudence.

Tannim blinked at the unexpected display of wicked humor. "That's what my dad kept saying," he admitted. "I guess I ought to be glad he didn't have the money for it."

Joe sized him up as if he were looking at Tannim for the first time. "You'd either have done real good, or real bad," the young man replied at last. "Depending on whether you got to be the brains of an outfit or not."

"Probably real bad," Tannim told him. "When I was younger, I never could learn to keep my mouth shut. Only thing that kept me out of trouble in high school was that the jocks knew *I* knew how to fix cars, and if they beat me up, next time they were stuck out in the parking lot with a fuel-line block or worse, I'd keep right on trucking."

And the fact that people who beat me up tended to get blocked fuel-lines or worse—and always when they were miles away from a gas station and I had cast-iron alibis. Not my fault they never bothered to get their cars serviced regularly. A little regular maintenance, and their mechanics would have found my little presents.

Ah, well. His former tormentors were like snow on the fired-up gas grill of life, and he had a whole *new* set of tormentors to deal with.

So who's after my hide now that Vidal Dhu and his crew are out of the picture? That was a good question, actually, and one he would really like to have an answer to. The Unseleighe were less cohesive than a rolling barrel of bullfrogs; it was hard to get them to agree to anything long enough to get beyond the "nuisance" stage. Vidal Dhu had nursed a feud with Keighvin's folk for centuries before Tannim ever came on the scene, and he had targeted Tannim for elimination largely because he was Keighvin's most reliable outlet to the human world.

Could it be that they've decided I'm dangerous to the Unseleighe as a whole, even without my connection to

Keighvin? That was possible, and it had happened before. When one human came to know too much about Underhill, that knowledge was often seen as a threat by the Unseleighe. Rightly so; they relied on invisibility in their predation on humankind, and when a human knew what they could do and how they operated, he would be able to tell when something was simply misfortune and when it was *caused.* And he could move to stop what was going on. Humans always had three things going for them against all the magic of the Sidhe: cleverness, sheer numbers and Cold Iron. Those things alone could stop the Sidhe dead in their tracks.

And when a human knew how to make Cold Iron into a *weapon . . .*

That made him much more of a danger.

And I'm training Seleighe Sidhe in Cold Iron Magery 101. Yeah, I can see why they might tag me as a problem.

The sun set with a minimum of fanfare; after a cloudless, hot day there was very little color in the west, nothing but a fattened, blood-red ball gliding down below the horizon. *It won't be long now,* Tannim thought. *Chinthliss has a lot of faults, but tardiness isn't one of them.*

Full dark came quickly; within fifteen minutes the first stars were out, and within a half hour the only light was from the half moon directly overhead.

Moonlight poured down through the open roof, and Tannim frowned a moment as he contemplated the slowly twisting patterns of moonlight crossing the barn floor. Then he realized what was affecting the moonlight. *Jeez! The Gate!*

As he ushered Joe out of the way, he felt a little smug for noticing the patterns. Did Chinthliss know that his magic interfered with moonlight just before mage-senses could feel it? For *now* he sensed that odd internal chiming that meant someone had called up a Gate between this human world and another, and a moment later, the Gate itself appeared.

He'd seen it all before, of course, but Joe never had. The young man's eyes widened as the air where the Gate would be twisted in geometries no mathematician of this world had ever encountered. *Something* darkened, rotated through dimensions human eyes were not built to perceive, and formed into a gossamer arch made up of hundreds of thin threads of pure power, as if an unearthly spider had been coaxed into spinning the structure.

Then it flared, plates formed across the threads, and sheets of light played with each other in oil-on-water colors.

Tannim patted Joe's shoulder. "Don't worry about it," he said easily. "It's just Chinthliss' way of being invisible."

"But—" Joe said, gesturing at the light show. Then he grinned as he realized what Tannim really meant. "Oh. Yeah."

The entire Gate-structure flared again, and the mage-light built until it would soon be impossible to look at. Tannim pulled out his Wayfarers and flicked them open. Joe shielded his face and winced away. Tannim simply put on his shades and smirked.

Then a note deeper than that of a huge bronze temple-gong vibrated across the barn. It thrummed in Tannim's chest, and he had to close his eyes behind the protection of his dark glasses when the final flare ended.

And then came the deafening silence. Magic was like that sometimes.

The crickets resumed their interrupted nuptial chorus, and Tannim reopened his eyes and took off his glasses.

Directly below where the peak of the arch had been, framed by the blackened walls and silvery moonlight, stood a gaunt but obviously powerful man. His thin features were vaguely oriental. He wore an impeccably-tailored Armani suit, and Tannim knew, although the moonlight was too dim to see colors, that it would be bronze silk.

The man straightened his bolo tie, and the eyes of the little dragon curling around the leather winked with bright topaz flashes.

The man raised one long eyebrow at Tannim in a gesture that Tannim knew perfectly well had been copied after long study of Leonard Nimoy.

"Could you manage subtle, do you suppose?" Tannim asked wistfully, thinking of all the Sensitives for miles around who would be suffering with strange dreams and unexplained headaches thanks to Chinthliss' lust for the dramatic.

His mentor simply raised that eyebrow a little higher, though Tannim could not imagine how he'd done it.

"No," he replied.

CHAPTER FIVE

"Well," Tannim said as they walked into the suite. "It's not home, but it's much."

Chinthliss gazed about with delight and immediately began exploring all of the amenities. Joe was perfectly willing to show him around.

Once they reached the bedrooms, with amazingly spacious closets, Chinthliss produced *luggage* from somewhere. Armani, of course. Tannim had no idea where the luggage had appeared from, since the dragon hadn't brought anything across the Gate and hadn't loaded anything into the Mach I. Still, Chinthliss spent the first half hour unpacking.

And people accuse me of being a clotheshorse! Then again, Chinthliss didn't wear this form very often, and Tannim knew he found the concept of clothing-as-persona fascinating. *Just please, God, don't let him have brought any leisure suits.*

Tannim waited, joked, and curbed his own impatience. There was no point in rushing Chinthliss. He would get around to the problem at hand when he felt settled, and not before. Rush him, and you were apt to end up with more trouble than you had in the first place.

At least he was happy with the suite, which was a relief. When Chinthliss was annoyed, he grew uncooperative, and right now, Tannim needed glasnost more than detente.

His old friend finished with his prowling and settled

onto the sofa in the living room as Tannim tuned in the local classical station on the radio/TV console. On the table at his mentor's elbow was a tall cola with a great deal of ice; unlike the elves, Chinthliss had no trouble with caffeine, and unlike most of his relatives, he hated tea with a passion. His jacket had been tossed carelessly over the back of a chair, and he had rolled his silk shirtsleeves up to his elbows. He was ready to work.

"Now, tell me again everything that has happened when this young lady appeared, in as much detail as you can recall," Chinthliss ordered, leaning forward to listen intently. The topaz eyes of the dragon bolo tie at his neck glowed with their own muted power.

Tannim obeyed, closing his eyes to concentrate. When he finished, he fished the gloves out of his jeans pocket and handed them over. "They're custom work, I can tell that much," he said as Chinthliss studied the gloves minutely, then applied the same care to studying the parchment slips. "I didn't realize it until later, but they're both from the right hand, so evidently she doesn't mind wasting whole pairs of custom-made gloves. There's no maker's mark on them, no labels, and the leather isn't stamped. I think they're deerskin, but they're made of very light leather, lighter than any deerskin I've ever seen. They seem to be hand-stitched—"

"They are," Chinthliss interrupted. "With silk thread, which is unusual, to say the least. And the 'string' of the backs is also silk."

Tannim gnawed his lip, and reached into the pocket over his right thigh for a cherry-pop. "Where would anyone get silk yarn like that?" he asked, as he unwrapped the candy and stuck it in his cheek.

Chinthliss shook his head. "It is available in your world, but not in too many places," he replied. "And the supply is very limited. It is silk noil, made from the outer, coarser threads of the cocoon. It is normally used to weave heavier material with a rougher texture than this—" He pointed to his shirt. "Under most circumstances, one would not waste such threads, however coarse, on making string for driving gloves. Unless—"

"Unless?" Tannim prompted.

"Unless the wearer wished to make use of some of the magical properties of silk as an insulator," Chinthliss said, and shook his head. "The leather is unusual also; not deerskin, but *fawnskin*. Very difficult to obtain, and unless I mistake your laws, not legal in this country. The paper, as you probably noticed, has no watermark, and the texture is *too* even; it might not have been manufactured, it might have been produced magically. The quotes were written with a real quill pen, not metal, but a goose-quill; you can see how the nib has worn down on the longer piece by the time she reached the end of the quote. See there, where the lines are just a little thicker. The ink is of an old style that does not dry quickly and must have sand sprinkled over it to take up the excess. Here—"

He held out the second quote, and tilted the small square of paper to catch the light. Sure enough, the light sparkled off a few crystals of sand stuck in the ink.

"All of this points in only one direction, unless your mysterious lady is so *very* eccentric that she drives modern cars yet uses the most archaic of writing implements. And unless she is so very wealthy that she can afford to discard hand-tailored driving gloves made with materials one would have to search the world to find."

"Well, we knew she must be using magic," Joe said thoughtfully. "But you're implying there's more than that."

Chinthliss nodded. "These small things indicate a radically different upbringing than you would find in your America, Tannim. I believe these things indicate that she cannot be from this culture, perhaps not this world. She may well not be human."

Joe looked queasy. Tannim wasn't so sure about his own health at the moment.

"Unless she was using illusion to change her eyes, she isn't Sidhe," Tannim interjected. "The Sidhe all have cat-eyes, with slit pupils, not round."

"But most, if not all Sidhe, Seleighe and Unseleighe, use illusion to cover their differences when dealing with mortals," Chinthliss countered. "There is no reason to think that she would change that pattern with you."

Tannim sucked thoughtfully on the cherry-pop and nodded. "Why two right-hand gloves?" he asked.

"Because at the moment she does not wish to kill you," Chinthliss replied. "As my brother taught me once, there is a reason why the left hand is called the 'sinister' hand."

Tannim swallowed. "Well, that's handy," he said as dryly as he could. Which was not very. He could not help thinking that she had two perfectly good *left*-hand gloves somewhere, doing nothing, taking up drawer-space. . . .

And where in the hell was Fox? He hadn't shown in over twenty-four hours!

Wait a minute. . . . "FX was *with* me just before she showed up the first time. He took one look out the back window of the Mach I, said 'Oh-oh,' and flat disappeared," he said. "He hasn't been back since, and he *had* been bugging me hourly. Old lizard, I think he *recognized* her. I think he *knew* her. Wouldn't a *kitsune* recognize another *kitsune*, even if a human didn't pick up anything at all? Sort of like a scent on the wind—"

"You are more likely being hunted by a succubus or the like, but that is a very good point, and the answer is probably yes," Chinthliss responded. His brow creased and his eyes narrowed. "Bear in mind though, just as a Sidhe would be sensitive to the 'scents' of those creatures from *his* world, a *kitsune* is going to be more sensitive to the 'scents' of those from his. A *gaki,* for instance, or a nature-spirit. But that does give me something to work from."

"Can't you do something magical with those gloves?" Joe asked. "I mean, can't you use magic to find out something about her from them?" He bit his thumbnail as Chinthliss turned to look at him, obviously ill at ease with the whole concept. "Isn't that why you shouldn't let something that belonged to you fall into a wizard's hands, because they can use it to put a hex on you or something?"

"Cogent," Chinthliss agreed. "And if these were ordinary gloves, from an ordinary person, such things would bear fruit. But they are the gloves of a mage, and she has made use of the properties of the materials to remove as much of the essence of *herself* from them as she can."

"Which means it will take some real work to get anything useful out of them," Tannim translated for Joe. "And probably a lot of time."

Chinthliss put the gloves down and stretched. "I shall be comfortable here, and I will need nothing. It grows late. *You* should sleep, Son of Dragons." He lanced Tannim with a penetrating stare. "You were in need of rest when you came here, as I know only too well. I will consult with my allies and send them sniffing along the path these gloves have traced."

Tannim stood up, and Joe followed his example. "Yes, Mother," he said mockingly. "And I'll take my vitamins and brush my teeth before I go to bed."

Tannim chuckled, and he and Joe let themselves out, leaving Chinthliss sitting on the couch, studying the gloves.

Shar smiled and petted the little air elementals that flocked around her, vying for her attention. Cross a kitten with a dragonfly and you might have something like these creatures. Less like a classical sylph than a puffball with wings, they were some of her chief sources of information when she did not care to go and gather it herself. They were not very bright, but they could be very affectionate. They seemed to like her.

One in particular was very affectionate, and extremely reliable; that was the one she called "Azure," and set him the particular task of keeping a constant eye on Tannim. She sent him off on his duties with a shooing motion and continued with her own preparations. She had a scheduled meeting with Madoc Skean, the chief of her "allies," and she was not looking forward to it.

The Unseleighe Sidhe was a sadistic, chauvinistic, selfish braggart, and a traitor to his own kind to boot. Most Unseleighe were born "on the dark side," so to speak: boggles and banshees, trolls and kobolds. But some, like Madoc, chose that path. Until recently, he had served as a knight in the court of High King Oberon. Oberon was a fairly tolerant fellow when it came to his subjects and their "games" with mortals—outright mischief was well within the bounds of what was considered amusing.

Further, if he felt some foolish human deserved punishment or needed to learn a lesson, he saw no reason why a Seleighe shouldn't do whatever was needful so long as he stopped just short of killing the mortal. But some things he would not abide—and he caught Madoc at one of them. What it was, precisely, Shar did not know, though she could guess—but it had been enough to send Oberon into a red rage. He had *physically* cast Madoc out, blasting him through several layers of Underhill realities before he came to rest in a battered, broken heap.

It took Madoc some time to recover; once he did, he used the powerful charisma that had made him a brilliant manipulator in Seleighe Court politics and turned it on the Unseleighe left in disarray after the demise of Vidal Dhu and Aurilia. He not only organized them, but he attracted others to his side, including Unseleighe Sidhe far more powerful than Vidal Dhu had been.

Powerful Unseleighe Sidhe tended to be solitary souls; they did not like to share their power with anyone, and would support a "retinue" composed of vastly inferior creatures that were easy to control. They formed a "court" mostly as a means of amusement; they seldom agreed on anything. Innate distrust made alliances tenuous at best— an "I won't destroy your home if you don't destroy mine" cold war. But somehow, Madoc won them. And won them to his pet project.

Get rid of Keighvin Silverhair's little pet, the mortal called Tannim.

He managed to persuade them that Tannim, knowledgeable as he was in the ways of the Sidhe and Underhill, was far more of a danger to them than their traditional enemies, the Seleighe Court elves. He convinced them that Tannim was unlikely to turn against his friends, but that there was nothing stopping the young man from marching on Underhill and taking over the areas held by Unseleighe with a small army of Cold-Iron-wielding humans.

He even half-convinced Shar. She had been trained as a youngster by the Unseleighe, after all, in the time before she had broken off with her father. Why shouldn't Tannim think that she was just the same as them? She was the

daughter of Charcoal, Chinthliss' great enemy—and she
had been groomed by Charcoal to be Tannim's rival in
magic ever since Chinthliss took Tannim as a protégé.
Allying with Madoc Skean became a matter of self-defense.

Until she came to learn more about both Tannim and
Madoc, that is. Then it became obvious, at least to her,
that this tale Madoc had spun about a human mage mad
for power was full of what they threw on the compost
heap. Tannim was no more a conquering Patton than she
was. He might consider moving into some little unused
section of Underhill one day, just as she had, but conquering vast sections of it would simply never occur to him.
It was only Unseleighe paranoia that made such a thing
seem possible.

But by then she had already committed herself to
Madoc. She'd been having second thoughts for some time
now.

The very fact that her blood-father was friends with the
Unseleighe was enough to make her think they were
worthless. What she had learned about them since she had
cut off all ties to him only confirmed that. Only her own
paranoia had made her listen to Madoc in the first place;
only his incredible charisma had persuaded her to give the
Unseleighe one more chance.

But Madoc had grown more and more arrogant with
her every time she had spoken with him since she first
pledged her help. *He* needed her; she was the only creature allied with him that could handle Cold Iron with
impunity. He knew that, and yet pretended that it was
otherwise.

And the more she saw and learned of Tannim, the less
she liked Madoc or wished to put up with him.

So she donned her armor; armor that the Unseleighe
would understand. Her hair she braided back in a severe
and androgynous style that left the impression of a helmet. She wore tunic and pants of knitted cloth-of-silver
that cleverly counterfeited fine chain-mail and minimized
her femininity. Her belt *was* a sword-belt, with a supporting
baldric, and the empty loops that should support a sheath
spoke eloquently for her capabilities.

She looked herself over in the mirror, analyzing every nuance of her outfit and stance for clues that might hint at weakness. She found none.

She banished the glass again and turned toward the Gate, activating it and setting it for an Unseleighe-held portion of Underhill where she could Gate to Madoc Skean's stronghold. Although this was a poor strategic move, coming to him like a petitioner, she would not permit him here. Allow him here but once, and there was no telling the mischief he could cause.

Or what he might leave behind, besides his smell.

Her Gate had only three settings: Unseleighe Underhill, her mother's realm, and her father's. The last, she would not use. To go to the human world, she must use the Gate in the "garage." A bit awkward, sometimes, but necessary.

She stepped through her Gate, felt the shivering of energies around her as it sprang to life and bridged the gap between where she *was* and where she wanted to be.

As usual, it was dark. She blinked, and waited for her eyes to adjust. Many Unseleighe creatures simply could not exist in bright light, so most Unseleighe realms were as gloomy as a thunderstorm during an eclipse, or dusk on a badly overcast day. She stood at the head of a path that traveled straight through a primeval and wildly overgrown forest. Forests such as this one had not existed on the face of the human world since the Bronze Age, if then. It was the distillation of everything about the ancient Forest that primitive man had feared.

And it contained everything dark and treacherous that primitive man had believed in.

The trees were alive, and they hungered; strange things rustled and moaned in the undergrowth. There were glowing eyes up among the branches, and as Shar stepped out on the path, the noises increased, the trees leaned toward her, and the number of eyes multiplied.

Something screamed in pain in the distance, and something nearer wailed in desolation.

Shar looked about her with absolute scorn, as the sounds and eyes surrounded her, and the trees closed in.

"Will you just *chill out*?" she snapped, putting a small

fraction of her Power behind her words. "I've been here before, and you know it. I am *not* impressed."

A moment of stunned silence, a muttering of disappointment, and within a few more seconds, the trees were only trees, and there were no more scuttlings in the underbrush or eyes in the branches overhead.

"Oh, thank you," she said sarcastically, and made her way to the second Gate. So much of the power of the older Unseleighe depended on fear that the moment anyone faced them down, they simply melted away. That might be why there were so few of these unadapted creatures active in the humans' world these days, and Cold Iron had nothing to do with them fleeing to dwell Underhill. The modern world was frightening enough that most people *couldn't* be scared by these ancient creatures. Where was the power of glowing eyes to terrify when rat eyes looked out at children every day from beneath the furniture of their ghetto apartments? How could a man be terrified by reaching tree branches when beneath the tree was a crack-addict with a gun? Moans and cries in the darkness could be the neighbor pummeling his wife and children to a pulp—and he just might come after anyone else who interfered, too, so moans and cries were best ignored.

The supernatural lost its power to terrify when so much of the natural world could not be controlled. These elder creatures were forced to abide in places like this one, where, if they were lucky, some poor unsuspecting being from another realm might stumble in to die of fright.

But the Unseleighe who had adapted found the modern human world rich in possibility. They fed on human pain and misery, so anywhere there was the potential for such things, you found them in the thick of it. Sometimes they even caused it, either as sustenance for themselves or as a hobby. Some considered inflicting suffering on humans to be an art form.

She had been taught by her father and his friends that humans were no business of hers. They were cattle, beneath her except to use when she chose and discard afterward.

But she had been taught by her mother that humans were not that much different from her. More limited, shorter-lived—but did that mean that a human confined to a wheelchair was the toy of humans with no such limitations?

For a long time she had been confused by the conflicting viewpoints, especially while the handsome Unseleighe Sidhe had been courting her, seeking her favors. They seemed so powerful, so confident. They had everything they wanted, simply by waving a hand. They were in control of their world, and controlled the humans' world far more than the mortals knew. They were beautiful, charismatic, confident, proud. . . .

But after a few bitter and painful episodes, she began to see some patterns. Once an Unseleighe got what he wanted, *he* discarded *her* exactly as they urged her to do with the humans. Her father, whom she tried desperately to please, cynically used her childish devotion to manipulate her.

The lessons were branded deeply; as deeply as the ones she was *supposed* to be learning. Little by little, she changed her own approach. She began learning, fiercely, greedily. She stole knowledge, when it was not given to her.

She spent more time in her mother's company. No one, not even the powerful Unseleighe lords, dared to block the approach of a nine-tailed *kitsune* to her daughter, and Ako made certain they were given no reason to think she was undermining their teaching.

Then, when the time was right, after Shar had established her own tiny Underhill domain, and she had learned everything she could, she began severing her connections to the Unseleighe and to her father.

She had cast Charcoal out of her life first; he had made the mistake of trying to coerce her when she refused to cooperate with some unsavory project of his. She no longer even remembered what it *was;* it had been trivial, but she had not wanted to have any part of it, and for the first time, she had the power to enforce her own will.

After barring him from her domain, she began pursuing her own projects—the first of which was to spend an entire year with her mother and her mother's people.

That year had been the most eye-opening time she had ever passed. She had moved among *kitsune* with poise, not posturing. She had learned manners rooted in respect, not fear of repercussions. She had heard laughter that was not aimed at anyone but instead filled the room with its warmth. At the end of that year, she had withdrawn to her own domain and begun planning what she truly wanted to do with her life, and more importantly, plotting how to rid herself of the Unseleighe influence without a loss of power or status.

She shook herself out of her reverie as she approached the Gate that would take her to Madoc Skean. This one was guarded, by literally faceless warriors, but she had the signs and the passwords, and they ignored her. There were four of them, of the "immortal" type; no weapon would kill them except Cold Iron, and even then it would have to penetrate their mage-crafted armor. The Gate was a real, solid structure, four pillars supporting a dome above a platform, all of black-and-red marble. The faceless ones stood at each corner, staring out into nothingness. They had no wills of their own, never tired, never needed food or drink; they were enchanted flesh and metal, sustained by the mage-energies of their master.

She walked up onto the platform beneath the dome, closed her eyes, and "knocked" with her power. At the third "knock," she opened her eyes on the audience chamber of Madoc Skean, Lord of Underhill, Magus Major and Unseleighe commander.

As if to emphasize how *different* he and his Seleighe rival Keighvin Silverhair were, everything in Madoc's domain was of the most archaic mode. This "audience chamber," for instance. Shar was fairly certain that he had copied it from a movie about a barbarian king and his barbarian rivals—all the Sidhe seemed to love movies. Built of the same black-and-red marble as the Gate, the main body of it was lit only by torches in brackets along the walls, so that the high ceiling was shrouded in gloom.

Pillars ranged along each side of the room, their tops lost in the shadows. The floor, of the same marble, held a scattering of fur rugs. A fire burned in the center of the room, held in a huge copper dish supported on bronze lions' feet. At the end of the room, on a platform that raised him above the floor by about three feet so that anyone who approached him would be forced to look up at him, was Madoc. He sat in a Roman-style chair, made of gold and draped with more furs. Torches burned in golden holders on either side of him, and the rear wall was covered with a huge tapestry depicting Madoc doing something disgusting to a defeated foe. Two more of his faceless guards flanked his throne; their black armor was ornamented with gold chasing and rubies the same color as drying blood.

Madoc wore a heavy, primitive crown of gold, inscribed with Celtic knotwork and set with more rubies, on his handsome, blond head. He made no attempt to disguise his cat-pupiled green eyes or pointed ears. His costume was an elaborate and thickly embroidered antique-style tunic and trews made of gold and scarlet silk; on his feet were sandals that laced up over the legs of the trews. The leather was studded with gold, as was the heavy belt at his waist. A crimson mantle of silk velvet was held to his shoulders by matching Celtic circle-brooches. His jewelry, aside from the crown and the brooches, consisted of a pair of heavy gold armbands and a gold torc with monster-head finials.

Shar could not help thinking that he looked like an art supply catalog on two feet.

Shar stepped carefully down from the platform, which held the physical counterpart of the Gate in the Forest, and made her way across the vast and empty floor. She kept her face impassive right up until the moment that she came to Madoc's feet.

Then she allowed her face to assume an expression of amused irony. "I think you owe Frank Frazetta licensing fees," she said.

Madoc frowned, a flash of real anger, as his impassive mask slipped for a moment. Shar smiled. Madoc hated being reminded that the elves copied everything they did from humans, and he hated it even more when she recognized the source.

"Don't mention Frazetta's name to me again. He has caused the Unseleighe enough trouble. You're making no progress in dealing with Tannim," he said abruptly, as she crossed her arms over her breasts and took a hip-shot, careless stance designed to tell him without words that she was not impressed.

She shrugged. "It's coming along. You know as well as anyone that Oberon has been taking an interest in Keighvin and his crew, and that includes Tannim. Challenge him without all the proper protocols and you could wind up answering to the High King. Again. Just because he threw you out of the Court once doesn't mean he can't choose to come after you."

Madoc flushed. "You haven't stayed long enough to get Tannim's response to your challenge!" he accused. "You're toying with him! Enough of your foolishness! We are not engaged with this plan to amuse you. Deal with the man and have done with it!"

She lowered her eyelids to hide her anger at the tone of command he had taken with her. He should know better than to take that attitude with her—

Suddenly, a soft popping sound signaled Azure's arrival into the throne room, speeding towards her with obvious excitement. *Something* must have happened to make her pet seek her out here! She raised her hand to warn Madoc not to disturb the creature—

Too late.

He was already irritated with her, and this intrusion gave him an excuse to vent that anger on something connected with her.

He blasted the hapless creature into the back wall with a flick of his hand. It whimpered once, and died.

Shar felt stunned, as if she had taken the blow herself. She stared at the remains of her pet, then transferred her gaze to Madoc. The Unseleighe yawned, rubbed his chin, and smiled at her lazily.

"Next time," he purred, "curb your dog."

At that moment Shar made up her mind about which side she was on.

She gave no outward sign of her thoughts. Instead, she said, "What do you want me to do? Don't you realize what weapon he's likely to choose for the Challenge? *Cars*. Racing. His Mustang against mine." She gritted her teeth and went on with the deception. "In anything else, I could best him, but not that. He's better than I am or ever will be, and no amount of magery is going to counteract his skill."

Madoc frowned, as if that had never occurred to him. "Well, *kill* him, then!" he snapped.

But again, she shook her head. "Oberon," she said succinctly. "If you don't want Oberon's attention, play by the rules of the game. We've *issued* the Challenge; we can't kill Tannim out of hand now. Remember, if you violate the rules, no Unseleighe will ever trust you. He has to accept the Challenge, and you're going to have to figure out some way of making him choose magery or some other weapon I am superior with. That's why I've been drawing things out; I've been trying to get him off balance enough that he won't think of racing as the response when I finally let him respond."

There. Bite on that awhile.

She seethed with anger at the wanton, *pointless* destruction of Azure; she would mourn the poor little creature later, when her privacy was assured. But the best way to get revenge on Madoc was to frustrate him, to make *him* angry. If he lost control of himself, he would do something stupid, and he might lose all of his allies. That would put him right back at square one, all of his plans in ruins, all of it to do over again. But this time it would take much longer to undo all the damage. Look how long it had taken Vidal Dhu to regain *his* reputation after losing to Keighvin Silverhair the first time!

Madoc frowned fiercely at being confronted with the truth—but then, unexpectedly, he smiled.

"But he cannot choose *racing* if he has nothing to race *with*, can he?" the Unseleighe lord said with glee. " 'Tis simple enough: we steal his precious Mustang with magic, and bring it Underhill! There are pockets we can armor against the harmful effect of so much Cold Iron—and I myself have enough power to bring the vehicle here!"

She blinked, taken aback—then quickly recovered. "What if he comes after it?" she countered. "What if he brings help with him, armed with Cold Iron weapons?"

"Then he but proves my point to Oberon," Madoc retorted with triumph. "And we can lay a trap for him. Oberon cannot object to our squashing him like an impudent insect if he brings Death Metal into Underhill!"

She was too well-trained to panic, but her mind raced as it never had before. "Let me deal with the car and set the trap," she said quickly. "Why waste your energies on dealing with something I can handle with impunity? Then you can confront him yourself, power intact."

Madoc nodded slowly. "You have a point," he admitted. "It would exhaust me to bring the car Underhill; it would serve us little if I cannot be the one to defeat him here." He straightened regally on his throne. "Very well," he said, his arrogance as heavy a mantle as the red velvet shrouding his shoulders. "Deal with it, Shar. Bring the car to the Underhill pocket nearest the Hall of the Mountain King. The Norse are used to the presence of metals; it should cause a minimum of disturbance to their magics. And if it troubles them—" he smiled, a snake's smile as it prepared to sink its fangs into the neck of the prey "—well, I offered an alliance, and they refused me. They can deal with the consequences."

She nodded shortly and turned on her heel, striding to the Gate at the other end of the hall and presenting him with her back instead of retreating, walking backward, as an underling would do. In that much, at least, she could offer open defiance. Her jaw was clenched so hard it ached, and her hands twitched as she forced them to remain at her side without turning into fists.

He had gone too far. He had neither the right nor the cause to callously slay Azure. Now it was time for her to think, plan everything with absolute care, and then act. She must kidnap the Mustang; she must make sure that Tannim *would* follow it. But the result of that would not be what

Madoc supposed. She would best Madoc at Madoc's own game.

And, fates willing, feed him his own black heart at the end of it all.

Shar crouched in the gravel of the driveway of Tannim's house. Her fur was almost black under the pale moon, and she laid out the last components of her spell with care. Her tail lashed as she spun out the energies, linked them all in together, and *flung* them with handlike paws at the Mach I—

She held her breath, waiting, as the spell settled into place, a gossamer web of her power laid carefully over the layers and structures of Tannim's spells on his Mustang. As delicately as this was made, it *still* might set off his alarms—

It didn't, and she let out her breath in a rush. It had been damned difficult to get past all his mage-alarms and shields and this close to his parents' house, even wearing the true-fox shape. She had never been so close to triggering someone else's protections in her life, and she suspected that only her form had kept her from setting off all those alarms. It would have been disaster if she somehow set off the protections on the Mustang.

She had known from the moment Madoc opened his mouth to order the Mach I's capture that Tannim would, if the car was merely *taken,* simply write it off as a loss. He would *know* it was going to be bait in a trap. When he refused to come after it, Madoc would insist that she make good on the Challenge, assuming that Tannim would have to choose some other weapon.

The trouble was, Tannim could *still* choose racing. He could have the damned Victor GT sent down here to him if he wanted. He could buy two identical cars off a show-room floor.

Madoc would know she could not match him on a race course. He could do something stupid to hex the race, but he would do it in the mortal world, where he could not operate as freely as she could. Yes, she could work this into Madoc's downfall, but there would be a sacrifice she no longer wanted to make.

Madoc would murder Tannim, as he had murdered Azure. SharMarali Halanyn vowed, on the spirits of her ancestors, Madoc Skean would have no more victims.

She had to do something to make it look as if the Mach I's disappearance was an accident. If it happened while *he* was doing something to the car, he would not assume it was a trap.

So, she laid in a spell to open a Gate to the appointed place the moment Tannim tried to set another spell of any kind on his car. With her nipping at his heels, it couldn't be long before he did just that. She would be ready to snatch his car away before he knew what was happening.

And since the Mach I would *not* end up anywhere near Unseleighe domains—as per Madoc's orders—he would assume that something had backfired in the spell *he* had set, and come after his wandering Mustang.

Or so she hoped, for his sake. If he did that, she had a chance of saving him *and* engineering Madoc's downfall.

The only other way of saving him would be for the two of them to join forces and take Madoc on. She knew how strong she was—and in a head-on confrontation, Madoc would win over her. He was the better fighter. The strengths of the *kitsune* lay in subterfuge, trickery. The strengths of the dragon—

She had not learned. Not well enough. Her father had not taught her enough to become a rival to his power. If Ako had remained with Chinthliss, perhaps—

Perhaps changes nothing, she scolded herself, and crept carefully down the driveway, still in fox-shape. She was strong enough to hold her independence only because Charcoal would not challenge Ako and her family, and because the Unseleighe did not realize how she had come to despise them. *They* thought they still ruled her, and permitted her what they thought was the illusion of independence. She could not protect Tannim alone. He could not withstand the full power of the Unseleighe alone. His friends from Fairgrove could not reach him before Madoc murdered him, if Madoc struck without warning.

They would have to join forces, and for that, she would have to show herself as his ally.

She looked back over her shoulder at the house once she was safely outside the perimeter of Tannim's shields. A single light burned in the room she knew was *his*.

What was he doing? Trying to extract information from her carefully Cleansed gloves? Thinking? Dreaming?

Of her?

She shook her head violently, her ears flapping, and sneezed. Then she spun around three times, a little red fox chasing her tail, and reached through the thrice-cast circle for her Gate to home.

Tannim pulled the Mustang into Chinthliss' slot just before sunset. His mentor had told him on the phone when Tannim called him this morning not to bother to appear before then; his own researches would not be completed before dark.

So he and Joe cruised around Tulsa in the afternoon. Fox still hadn't put in an appearance.

But the mysterious, dark-haired woman in her black Mustang certainly did. She was tailing them.

She made no attempt to hide, but she also made no further attempt at contact of any kind. In fact, the two times he had tried to turn the tables on her and force a confrontation, she had managed to vanish into the traffic.

She stayed no less than three cars behind him, and no more than five, no matter what route he chose; even when he was certain he'd managed to shake her, she always turned up again. He thought he'd lost her when they pulled into one of the malls, but when he and Joe came out again with more clothing for Joe, she was there, parked three rows away from the Mach I, watching them.

When he stopped to fill up the tank, she was in the parking lot of a fast-food joint across the street. When he turned onto the Broken Arrow expressway, she followed right behind. He got off and thought he'd lost her for sure when he didn't see her following on the little two-lane blacktop road he'd chosen—but as soon as he came to a major intersection, there she was again, as if she had somehow *known* where he was going.

She finally vanished when he pulled into his folks' driveway, hot and frustrated, and doing his best not to take his frustration out on Joe.

He certainly hoped that Chinthliss would have better news for him than all of this.

She hadn't shown up on the drive to the hotel, so that was a plus. Maybe following them around all day, between the power-shopping and the aimless driving, had been driving her as buggy as being followed had driven him.

She sure as hell hadn't learned anything interesting. Unless it was which stores had his favorite brands of clothing.

They piled out of the car and started up the walkway in the blue dusk. Chinthliss met them at the door, letting them in without any of his usual banter. That was enough to make Tannim take a closer look at his friend. Chinthliss had a very odd, closed expression on his face.

"What's wrong?" Tannim asked bluntly.

Chinthliss shook his head and waved them both to seats on the couch. The two gloves lay on the table, in the exact middle, side by side, both of them palm showing. As Chinthliss took his own seat, Tannim watched him closely. Something was definitely up.

"I believe I have the identity of your challenger," Chinthliss said, abruptly, with no warm-up. "I don't know *why* she has challenged you, for certain, but I can guess. And I hope that I am wrong."

"So who *is* she?" Tannim asked when Chinthliss had remained silent for far too long.

Chinthliss drew himself up and tried to look dignified, but succeeded only in looking haggard. "I would rather not say," he replied. "It involves something very personal."

That was the last straw in a long and frustrating day. Tannim lost his temper. Chinthliss liked to play these little coaxing games, but Tannim was not in the mood for one now.

"*Personal*, my—" Tannim exploded, as Joe jumped in startlement at his vehemence. Then he forced himself to calm down. "Look, lizard," he said, leaning forward and emphasizing his words with a pointed finger. "I've told you a lot of stuff that was *damned* personal over the years, when it had a bearing on something you needed to know. You know that nothing you tell me will leave this room. Time to pay up. I have to *know* this stuff. It's my tail that's on the line, here!"

Chinthliss licked his lips and tried to avoid Tannim's eyes. Tannim wouldn't let him.

Finally Chinthliss sighed and let his head sag down into his hands. "It is very complicated and goes back a long time," he said plaintively, as if he was hoping Tannim would be content with that.

Not a chance. "Ante up, Chinthliss," Tannim said remorselessly. "The more you stall, the worse I'll think it is."

Chinthliss sighed again, and leaned back in his chair, eyes closed. "It all began twenty-eight years ago, in the time of this world," he said, surprising Tannim. *Huh. He wasn't kidding about it being a long time. That's a year longer than I've been alive.*

"This occurred in my realm. There were two young males, constant rivals. One was called Charcoal, and one, Chinthliss," his mentor continued. "They both courted a lovely lady of the *kitsune* clan. She was young and flirtatious, and paid the same attentions to each. Very—ah— personal attentions. Chinthliss was the one who temporarily won her, mostly because Charcoal became insufferable. But it was not Chinthliss who fathered the daughter she bore."

Tannim sat bolt upright. Chinthliss—and a *kitsune*?

"The daughter was charming and talented, and Chinthliss had no qualms with accepting her as a foster-daughter, even though Charcoal had gone beyond being his rival and had become his most vicious enemy. But—he had many things on his mind, and eventually the Lady Ako became disenchanted with the lack of attention he paid her, and left him." There was real pain on Chinthliss' features, the ache of loss never forgotten and always regretted. "When she left him, she took her daughter. He never saw either of them again."

He opened his eyes at last, and Tannim locked his lips on the questions he wanted to ask. "That was when Chinthliss realized that he needed others, and began looking for someone—yes, to take the places of Lady Ako and SharMarali. Stupid, I know, for one person can never *replace* another, but I have never been particularly wise, no matter what my student might say to flatter me...." His voice trailed off for a moment, then he looked Tannim straight in the eyes. "I never found anyone to match Ako, but I did find an eager young mind to teach, a protégé, someone to take the place of little Shar. That was why I gave him the name, 'Son of Dragons'; not only as a joke on the name of his real, blood parents, but because he became a kind of son to me."

Tannim licked lips gone dry, and prompted him gently. "Is this—Shar—the one who's been following me?"

Chinthliss nodded painfully, as if his head was very heavy and hard to move. "I don't think there can be any doubt," he said. "Especially since there is only one *kitsune*-dragon I know of, and in the past, I heard rumors, rumors I had thought I could discount. I *thought* that Lady Ako had Shar safely with her; the rumors were that not long after I began teaching you, Charcoal asserted his parental rights over the girl and took her off to be trained by himself and by his allies. The Unseleighe."

At Tannim's hissing intake of breath, Chinthliss grimaced. "You see, the rumors I heard were that he intended to make her into the opposite of you."

Joe scratched his head thoughtfully. "I can see that," he said. "It all matches, if she's supposed to be the anti-Tannim. Even the car she drives is a Mustang. Late model, old versus new. The same, only different."

"So you see why she would be challenging you," Chinthliss continued unhappily. "And why it's happening here and now, in Oklahoma, where I first found you."

Tannim shook his head and groaned. "Oh, God. I'm in an evil twin episode. If this were a TV show, I'd kick in the screen about now."

Joe snickered; Chinthliss made what sounded like a sympathetic noise deep in his throat.

Tannim looked up at Chinthliss again. "Okay, we can figure it's Shar; we can figure she's sleep—ah—working with the Unseleighe. She's challenging me, and figures she's going to wipe me. Keighvin and Conal said that since I have choice of weapons in a Challenge, I should choose racing."

Chinthliss brightened a little at that. "The laws of challenge are clear on that point; you have the right of any weapon you choose—and I rather suspect that they would never think of racing as a weapon. I cannot imagine how even Shar could best you in a contest of that sort. Unless her allies make it something less than a fair fight."

Tannim leaned back in his chair and ran his fingers through his hair thoughtfully. "Okay. Let's assume they do. What can they do? Booby-trap the course, do something to *her* car to turn it deadly, do something to *mine* to make it fail on me."

"I can prevent them from interfering with the course," Chinthliss replied quickly. "I have more practice working in this world than they."

"No matter what they do to her car, they have to get it close to mine to make any weapons work." Tannim unwrapped a pop, stuck the paper in the ashtray and the cherry-pop in his mouth. "That just takes a little more finesse on my part. *I've* had nasties after me. If she's never done combat-driving before, she's no match for me."

Chinthliss shrugged. "Where would she have learned?" he asked. "Who would have taught her?"

"More to the point, where would she have gotten the practice?" Tannim put in. "SERRA keeps an eye out for reports of driving 'incidents'; things like that sometimes mean there's a mage out there that isn't trained or mentored. I think we'd have a tag on her if she'd been messing around on her own. Hell, she'd have run into one of ours by now, for sure."

"That only leaves—sabotaging the Mach I," Joe said. "But how do you keep someone from messing around with your car when they can do it magically?"

"Easy," Tannim and Chinthliss said in chorus. "More magic."

Joe sighed. "I shoulda known."

Tannim half grinned. "So," he said, looking into Chinthliss' eyes, "feel up to anything tonight? Time might not be on our side. Your wicked stepdaughter was trailing us all over Tulsa today."

"Mmm. I will help, yes," Chinthliss replied. "Most of today's work was not mine. And I have a few ideas that I would like you to try anyway."

"Shall we?" Tannim rose and bowed, gesturing toward the door.

"Let's shall," Chinthliss said with a sigh. "Tannim, this is not how I wanted to find her again."

"I can imagine." Tannim led the way out to the Mustang. It was fully dark now. The stars above dotted the sky even through the light-haze thrown up by Tulsa. Out in the country they would be able to see the Milky Way.

Joe automatically wedged himself into the backseat, leaving the front to Chinthliss. "If this girl's half kit-whats-it," he asked, leaning over the seat as Tannim pulled out of the parking slot, "would that be why Fox just disappeared and hasn't come back?"

"Exactly so," Chinthliss told him. Tannim let his mentor make the explanations; he was too busy watching for that black Mustang. "Shar's mother is a nine-tailed *kitsune*; she can shape-change into a *real* fox if she chooses, or into anything else. She can act and be acted upon as a real human woman. She has powers I could wish I enjoyed. Nine tails is an enormously high rank, and I have never personally heard of or met a *kitsune* with more tails. The number of tails indicates the rank and power in a *kitsune*; I doubt that Shar, in her *kitsune* form, has less than six. FX has only three tails, which is why he can affect nothing in this world; he could not possibly best her, and if he crossed her, she *could* take one of his tails."

"So?" Joe wanted to know.

Chinthliss shrugged. "So, he would definitely lose rank and power—and there are some who say that the number of tails also means the number of *lives* a *kitsune* has. Lose a tail and you lose a life."

"Oh." Joe sat back to digest this.

Tannim knew that the young man must be confused as all hell. *Kitsunes*, dragons, magic-enhanced cars . . . it could have flattened a less stable person. Maybe in some cases old what's-his-name was right: "that which does not kill us, makes us stronger." It sure seemed to work for Joe.

Helluva way to grow up, though.

The barn seemed the right place to go, even though they'd have to do any magic on the Mach I "without a net," outside the protections available inside the barn. But with two mages here, one of them a dragon, what could go wrong that they couldn't fix?

Joe went out ahead with a flashlight, just to make sure that their little playmate hadn't booby-trapped the access with tire-slashers. He walked all the way to the side of the barn, examining the flattened lines in the grass, and waved an "all-clear" when he reached the barn itself.

Tannim pulled up beside the barn and got out. Chinthliss followed.

He stood looking at the Mach I for a long time, fists on his hips, feet apart and braced. Then he took a deep breath, and stepped back.

"All right folks," he said quietly, as the crickets and mockingbirds sang in the distance, and a nighthawk screamed overhead. "It's show time."

Although Tannim had never done anything synchronized this way before, Chinthliss wanted to set up all of their spells in a complex net, so that they all meshed and could all be triggered together.

Tannim had argued against that, but not very forcefully, because he had known Chinthliss was right about one thing. Once Shar got a whiff of magics out here at the barn, she'd *know* that Chinthliss was involved. And once she knew that, she might change her mind about keeping her distance. They'd really better do everything at once, because they might not get a second chance.

The trouble was, he had no idea how well all this stuff was going to "take," given the protections that were already on the Mach I. And he had no idea how it would integrate with what was already there. *Hell*, he thought ruefully, as Chinthliss laid out the last of his webs of power over Tannim's own "crystalline" geometric structures, *I've got no idea how half of what he wants to do is going to work!* It was worse than computer programming.

Chinthliss surveyed his handiwork and stepped back a pace. "Ready?" he asked.

"Ready," his former pupil replied, though not without considerable misgivings.

"Right. On my count." Chinthliss walked to the tail of the car and raised his hands, and Tannim copied his gesture, standing at the nose. "Four. Three. Two. One. *Fire.*"

Tannim triggered his spells.

What *should* have happened was that a structure a great deal like the dome inside the barn would form, then shrink down to become one with the Mach I's skin.

What actually happened was that the dome formed and shrank, all right—

But as soon as it touched the skin of the Mustang, there was a blinding flash of light.

Tannim shouted in pain, and turned away, eyes watering, swearing with every curse he had ever heard in his life. He scrubbed at his eyes frantically—*What did we do to my car?*

There were spots dancing in front of him, but it was perfectly clear what they had done to his car.

Because the Mach I was no longer there; only a flattened place in the grass, and a single chrome trim-ring from one of the wheels, gleaming in the moonlight.

"Ah, *hell!*" he half groaned, half shouted. "*Now* what am I gonna do? How do you explain *this* to State Farm?"

CHAPTER SIX

Tannim stared at the chrome trim-ring for a moment longer, then waded through the tall grass and picked it up. It felt warm, as if it had been sitting in the sun for a long time. "The Mach I can't have gone far," he said finally. "At least, I don't think it could have. We didn't put *that* much power into those spells, not enough to have teleported a car for miles—"

"If it went Underhill, 'far' is relative," Chinthliss warned. "My guess is that's where it went. It would not take a great deal of power to open a Gate into some truly outré realm."

Tannim felt himself blanch, and the bottom dropped out of his stomach. Underhill. It wasn't just Keighvin and his "good" elves who lived Underhill. So did the Unseleighe, the efrits, and a lot of other nasty characters. Underhill wasn't *one* place, it was many places, all lumped in the same generic basket. Some of those places held people who didn't care for Tannim very much. "If it went Underhill," he said slowly, "and the bad guys get ahold of it, I am in deep kimchee. I've got a lot of personal power invested in that car. They could get *at* me through it. I've got to get it back before they know it's there."

"Do you think that is wise?" Chinthliss asked, looking skeptical and a tad worried. "You could end up in more difficulties than if you simply left it there."

"I don't think I have a choice," he retorted. "It's either that, or cut it off from me entirely, which I'm not sure would work, then try to explain to my folks where my car went. They know I'd never sell it. Shoot, I'd rather deal with Unseleighe."

Not to mention the long walk back. *I could say some-one stole it. But then I'd have to go through the whole police show, and meanwhile I* still *have Shar on my tail and I wouldn't have all the protection I built into the Mustang.* It did occur to him that he could borrow an elvensteed from Keighvin—after all, if Rhellan could look like a '57 Chevy, surely another 'steed could look like the Mach I. But that would mean calling in yet another favor from Keighvin, and that would still leave the problem of the Mach I in possibly unfriendly hands. *It won't take them more than a couple of days to figure out that it's down there; all that Cold Iron unshielded is going to make a helluva distortion in the magic fields Underhill. It'll only get worse the longer I wait. If I just get in and get out again, everything should be fine.*

Besides, he loved that car. There were a lot of impor-tant memories tied up in it. It had carried him through a lot of bad situations, and more than a few good ones. He wanted it back.

"It hasn't been down there that long; I can't imagine anyone would have found it this soon. I can use this to scry with," he continued, holding up the trim-ring as he pushed through the waist-high grass to get inside the barn. "It shouldn't take me long to find it. Once I know where it is, I can go get it and bring it back with me. It's easier to open up a Gate from there to here than vice versa. Right?"

"That depends—" Chinthliss began.

But Tannim ignored him. After all, if it hadn't been for Chinthliss insisting that they trigger *all* the spells together, none of this would have happened. Although how that particular batch of spells could have conspired to open up a hole into Underhill, he could not imagine.

Of course, no one knew how programmers got Win-dows 3.1 to run, either, and it had at least as many ways to go wrong as their cobbled mass of spells.

He put the trim-ring down on the ground once he got inside the protected area of the barn, triggered some of the primary protections, and then laid a mirror-finished disk of energy within the trim-ring. That turned the whole trim-ring into a scrying mirror, very like some of the scrying pools Underhill, but set specifically for the Mach I. Chinthliss came in behind him and conjured up a mage-light that provided real-world illumination. In the dim, blue light, Joe wore an expression of worry and puzzlement. Chinthliss was, as usual, inscrutable.

He crouched down on his heels beside the ring as Joe and Chinthliss joined him. Joe stared nervously down over his shoulder, but Chinthliss kept chewing on his lip and casting suspicious glances everywhere except at the ring.

The surface of the mirror glowed with a milky radiance like fog lit up from within. Silently, Tannim commanded it: *Show me the vehicle of which you were once a part. Show me where it is, and the condition it is in.*

He continued to stare down at the ring as the light within it shifted restlessly, showing only vague shapes, and hints of wavering forms within its misty depths.

Finally, faint color tinged the fog, red and gold, purple and deep blue. He willed more power into the mirror, and the image within it strengthened and the colors intensified.

Then the whole image trembled violently, and settled; the huge oblong of deep, deep red in the center cleared and became the Mustang, while the rest of the image focused into the background.

The Mach I sat sedately in the exact middle of what could only be a huge audience chamber, literally fit for a king. She looked terribly odd there: the only modern object in a room that resonated with a feeling of *ancient times*. Her four tires rested on a floor of polished amber; behind her was a wall covered with a geometric tapestry of red, blue, purple, and gold. Benches of gold and amber sat beneath the tapestry, and in between the benches were ever-burning lamps of gold and tortoiseshell, or stands holding antique weaponry.

A thick patina of dust lay over everything except the car.

Tannim chewed his lip, trying to figure out just *where* this was. Underhill, obviously, since of the humans of this world, only a Russian Tzar could ever afford to have a room with a floor of amber, but the question was, *where* Underhill?

Chinthliss finally looked down at the image within the mirror and frowned. "That's the audience chamber of the Katschei, the one he used when he was in a good mood," he said. "It's not that far from the Nordic elven enclaves. Once the Katschei was dead, I'd have thought for certain that something else would have taken over his Underhill holdings, but it looks abandoned. Maybe there's a curse on the place or something."

"Yeah, look at the dust. Well. The Nordic elves are deep Underhill. Keighvin says some of them haven't come out for centuries." That gave him distance and direction; he ought to be able to Gate from here to there with Chinthliss' assistance, using the trim-ring as an anchor, then return the same way. The ring, having been part of the car, should keep the path between them open and clear.

He stood up. "Well, if it's as abandoned as it looks, this should be a piece of cake. I can Gate over and Gate back before three in the morning." He grinned at Joe, crookedly. "Be glad you're with me, otherwise Mom would have you under a curfew."

"I really don't feel comfortable with this," Chinthliss began, then shook his head. "Never mind. I fear it was my work that caused this; I shall have to defer to your judgment."

"I told you why I can't just leave it there," Tannim replied. "If we were home, I'd grab Keighvin and a bunch of the polo players and go riding cross-Underhill to get it. But I'm not, and we don't have time to call them in. If I go now, before anyone realizes the big anomaly that just plopped down there has a physical focus, we should be fine. Underhill's not that stable, and stuff causes magequakes all the time down there."

And people are always watching for mage-quakes, bonehead. Sometimes interesting things surface after one. Yeah, you'd better get your tail moving before somebody finds this particular "interesting thing" and gets the pink slip on it.

Chinthliss shrugged and stepped back a pace. "Have it your way. I can at least establish the Gate for you."

Tannim nodded, and cast a glance back at Joe. The young man looked very worried, but he said nothing, perhaps because he felt so out of his depth with two obviously practiced mages.

Chinthliss stared fixedly at the trim-ring for several minutes, then raised his hands slowly. The trim-ring rose smoothly and rotated sideways until it was facing Tannim and balanced on edge, forming a shining "O" that hovered in midair. Joe's eyes widened. Chinthliss spread his fingers, and the trim-ring shivered and expanded, an inch at a time, thinning as it did so, until it was about a half an inch thick and tall enough for Tannim to pass through. The scene inside the ring remained the same: the Mach I, crouched on the amber floor as if in the heart of a showroom. As the ring widened, the scene expanded so that it was possible to see a bit more: the geometrics on the tapestry proved to be only a very wide border; now the legs and lower torsos of humans and other creatures engaged in combat were visible, all of it woven in the same flat but colorful style, like a lacquer box. Then, as Chinthliss shifted the focus of the spell from *seeing* to *going*, the scene vanished, replaced by a dead-black wall.

"I can't hold it long," Chinthliss warned in a voice that showed strain. "If you're going, go now!"

Tannim did not hesitate. He stepped across the edge of the ring, closing his eyes involuntarily as he felt the internal lurch and tingle that a Gate-crossing always gave him. He experienced a moment of disorientation and blackout, accompanied by a jolt as he dropped about a foot. He flexed his legs automatically and dropped into a crouch, one hand touching the floor.

When his eyes opened again, he found himself not more than a couple of feet from the Mach I, one hand resting in about a half inch of dust. Beneath the dust, the amber floor glowed slightly, adding to the illumination in the room with a warm, buttery light.

The same depth of dust lay everywhere—except around the edge of the room, in a path about three feet wide. *Odd.*

He repressed a sneeze, straightened, and turned around. It was virtually the same behind him. The tapestry on that wall showed twelve lovely maidens dancing around a tree loaded with golden fruit, in the heart of a walled garden. The chamber itself was immense, as big as a high school gymnasium at least. The benches were pushed up against three of the four walls; gold and transparent amber, rather than the opaque butter-amber of the floor and walls. The fourth side held a raised platform with a gold-and-amber throne standing in lonely splendor on it. The hanging on that wall was plain purple with gold fringe as long as his arm on the bottom hem. There was no hanging on the opposite wall; it held a set of huge golden double doors, both gaping open. Beyond them lay darkness; light from the audience chamber was swallowed up by that darkness immediately, as if it was just as big as this room. Above the doors, the wall had been inlaid with mosaics of cabochon gemstones forming a pattern of flowers.

He tensed as sound came from beyond those doors. Instinctively, he sprinted to the side of the Mach I and crouched down beside the headlights, ready to use it for cover.

The noises continued; they sounded like someone shuffling, out there in the darkness. He listened carefully and caught another set of sounds: a steady brushing in a rhythmic pattern, scraping, and something like the sound of squeaking cart wheels.

What the—

Something moved out there in the darkness. He tensed, and crouched a little lower beside the fender, one hand in the dust and one clutching the chrome. He smothered another sneeze. He strained his eyes into the murk; magical ever-burning lamps might have been a neat touch, but they didn't give off a heck of a lot of light, and neither did the glowing floor. The sounds neared.

And finally, the maker of the sounds appeared.

A gnarled and twisted old man, dressed in nondescript rags, shuffled in and stood by the hinge of one of the open doors. He was mostly bald, but with a ring of long, unkempt, yellowish-white hair straggling down the back of his head, and he had an equally unkempt white beard that reached to his knees. He held a push-broom and shoved it in front of him with laborious strokes. There was a cart tethered to him by a rope around his waist, which followed him, wheels squeaking, creeping forward with every shuffling step. He made short, hesitant strokes with the broom, then put the broom down painfully, leaning it against the cart; he then reached into the cart, and picked up a whisk-broom and a dustpan.

He got down onto his knees with little whimpers of pain, felt his way to the edge of the area he had just swept, and brushed the little ridge of dust he had collected into his pan.

He got back up to his feet in the same laborious fashion, turned, and felt around the cart. His hand touched the mouth of an open bag resting in the cart, and he carefully tapped the dust into the bag. Then he picked up the broom and began it all again.

What the heck is this—the janitor of the damned?

The old derelict came fully into the audience chamber— and only then did Tannim see *why* he was doing his work with such slow and stilted motions.

Where his eyes should have been there were two gaping, old, but still unhealed, wounds.

Tannim's hissing intake of breath alerted the old man to his presence. The old fellow turned his sightless eyes in Tannim's direction, holding the broom defensively in front of him.

"Who be ye?" he called in a quavering, rusty voice. "What ye want?" His country-English accent was so thick that Tannim could hardly make out what it was he had actually said. *I haven't heard an accent like that since I watched one of those BBC nature shows. It's almost another language entirely.*

Tannim stood up slowly, but he made no move to approach the man. Appearances could be deceptive

Underhill. It was hard to tell what was a trap and what was harmless.

"My name is Tannim," he said slowly and carefully, so the old man could make out the words through his own American accent. "I am here to retrieve something that was lost."

"Lost? Lost?" The old man shook his head in senile bewilderment. "Naught's been lost here, boy, 'cept me." He grimaced with pain, his face a mass of wrinkles. "This be no place fer an honest Christian. There be boggles here." He turned his head blindly from side to side, as if looking for the boggles he could no longer see. "Ye seem a good, honest lad. There's danger here. Best leave whiles ye can."

"I found what it was I was looking for, sir," Tannim said placatingly. "But I've seen no danger."

"What ye cain't see kin getcha," the old man retorted, and cackled crazily. "I come here lookin' fer treasure, an' see what it got me! No doubt ye look at all th' gold, an' there's lust in yer heart fer it. Pay it no heed, boy! 'Tis fairy gold, an' not fer any man of God! Take yerself and yer lost thing away, afore them boggles git ye, an' ye find yerself like me—" the voice shook, and tears trickled from the eyeless sockets "—all alone, i' th' dark, ferever an' ever. Never t' see m' lovely Nancy, nor m' ol' Mam. Never t' see nothin' an nobody again. . . ."

The old man stood there, weeping horribly from the ruins of his eyes, rattling on about how he had come to be here, as he clutched his broom. Tannim pieced out from the rambling discourse that the man had somehow come upon one of the rare doors into Underhill that opened at specific times—one of the solstices, for instance, or at the full moon. He had seen a rich hall beyond the door and had returned with bags to carry away the loot, full of greed.

But those who had owned the hall beyond the door were not Seleighe elves, who would have tricked him, terrified him for the sport of it, but let him go relatively unharmed. They were Unseleighe, who used that hall as a tasty trap for the unwary. They throve on pain and fear, and nothing pleased them more than to have a human captive to inflict both on.

They had tormented him until they grew bored with his antics, then had decided on one last torment. They blinded him and sent him here. Where "here" was, he had no clue. His task was to "keep the place clean"—and his life depended on it, for once a day he was to return to a specific spot somewhere in the depths of this place, and the dust he had collected would be transformed into an equal amount of bean-bread. Ironically, the rope that held him to his cart, the sack in the cart, and the cart itself were all tools he himself had brought to carry away his loot. It was an irony that obviously had not been lost on the Unseleighe.

Blinded, he could not see where he had cleaned, and apparently he was a fairly stupid man, who had not figured that he could tell where he was in a room by the echoes from the walls, as many blind people Tannim knew had learned to navigate. That was why he cleaned no farther into the room than he could reach with his broom, despite the tantalizing fact that he *knew* there was thick dust just beyond that point. He had ventured into the middle of a room once, and had been hopelessly lost until he had managed to crawl into a wall again. After that, he never dared make a second attempt.

He was in constant pain, he was more than half mad, and the two oozing holes where his eyes had been made Tannim sick to his stomach to look at. If he remembered his name, he never told it to Tannim. But he was—or had been—a human being, once. However stupid or greedy he had been, he did not deserve a fate like this one.

Yet when Tannim offered to take him away, the man cowered against the wall, wept, and babbled in sheer terror. Clearly, he had been tricked by Unseleighe pretending to "rescue" him before this. Every time Tannim tried to touch him, he only winced violently away. The only way Tannim would ever get the oldster into the Mustang would be kicking, screaming, and utterly mindless with terror. Which right now, could attract a whole lot of unwanted attention and get them both caught.

Finally, Tannim did the only thing he could think of to help the man. He cut bits of the gold fringe from the bottom of the tapestry at the end of the hall and knotted the pieces together until they formed a very long, heavy rope, which he gave to the old man.

"Tie this to the rope on the cart," he explained patiently. "Tie the other end to your waist. You can go as far into the center of a room as you like, and as long as you *don't* pull the cart after you, you can always follow the rope back to the wall."

He had to explain it several times before the old man finally grasped it, and if the lesson would last past the next meal, Tannim would never be sure. But he had tried. And the old wreck was weepingly, pathetically grateful. But *not* grateful enough to lose his suspicion of Tannim's motives or identity—his paranoia was too deeply ingrained for him to trust anyone to take him away.

There was something else that occurred to Tannim: time passed oddly Underhill, and the Seleighe and Unseleighe had ways of staving off old age from mortals when they chose. But those methods did not work in the human world, where magic was not as strong. Assuming that he *could* persuade the oldster that he was to be trusted, Tannim could rescue the poor old goat and bring him across a Gate, only to see him crumble into dust on the threshold.

Would that be a kinder fate than the one he currently had? Given a choice—

Yes, but it's his choice, not mine.

There was enough cutlery in this audience chamber alone, in the weapon-stands, for the old man to have ended his life long ago if he chose. Evidently he preferred living, however miserable that life might be. Maybe it wasn't all that miserable by his standards. Presumably he still had a home, something in his memories worth living for. Perhaps the unknown of death presented a more terrifying prospect than the quiet horror of his daily existence here.

He doesn't trust me, and I can't promise him anything, anyway.

The old derelict filled his sack to the top and shuffled

off into the darkness, muttering happily to himself. The cart-wheels creaked, marking his progress, until at last the sounds were swallowed up in the thick darkness.

Shar shuddered and came awake with a smothered gasp.

The internal lurch as Tannim triggered Shar's trap caught her asleep in her own pocket-domain, and took her completely by surprise. She really hadn't expected him to try anything magical for another twenty-four hours at least! She had been so tired after all her work of last night and the ruse of tailing him today that she had thrown herself down on the couch as soon as she returned "home," and must have fallen asleep. The aftershock of so much Cold Iron linked to her hitting the fields of mage-energy Underhill resonated through her as she sat bolt upright, shaking hair and sleep-fog out of her eyes.

She swore to herself as her head rung with a very physical sensation of impact. There was no way that Madoc would ignore *that!* And since he knew that Shar was bringing the Mustang Underhill, he would know what had caused this particular mage-quake. She massaged her temples and swung her feet down to the floor, and wondered what particular imp of ill luck she had annoyed enough to plague her with all these miscalculations.

Oh, most excellent, she told herself sarcastically. *Madoc knows where I was going to dump the car. He'll be there, either as soon as or before I can get there. He won't wait for me to tell him I've caught Tannim—he'll go to gloat over the car! He might even decide not to trust me further and set up an ambush of his own! Why didn't I think of that in the first place? I swear, I get tired of having to second-guess these Unseleighe pricks!*

Tannim would, probably, follow his car as soon as he knew where it had gone. He might already be there. Oh, damnation, if he'd been *in* the car when it made its little journey, he *would* be there already!

Better count on it. If he's not, I can revise things.

Her mind buzzed with a hundred plans, but all of them hinged on one thing—whether Madoc went to the Katschei's Hall alone, or with his troop of mage-warriors.

Alone, she and Tannim could probably best him and be away. But with his troops backing him, there wasn't a chance.

Ah, damnation, I've never seen him leave his hall once without a full escort. He'll have them with him.

Her plans had been based on the notion that she could bring the car Underhill without Madoc knowing when she did. Why hadn't she foreseen that the Mustang would cause such a ruckus?

Because I was basing it on my *car, and I plain forgot how much of Tannim's car is steel and Cold Iron, and all of it filled to the roof with spellwork. I should have done my homework, and now it's too late—*

How soon would Madoc get there? How much lead time would she have? *Better plan on not having a lot. Better plan on none. Better assume that he'll beat me unless my short route is faster than his.*

If Tannim was there, and she had a few minutes, she would probably be able to give him some kind of warning. If she had no time, perhaps she might still be able to do something. *Convince Madoc—no, wait! He must have a dozen Unseleighe lords who all have their own plans for Tannim! If I let them know Madoc has* the man, *I can get them all tangled up in arguing with each other long enough to get him out of there—maybe . . .*

The more she thought about it, the better it sounded. The beauty of it was that she would not even have to identify herself to let the information loose. All it would take would be a few well-placed anonymous messages. If all they had was the car, and Tannim *didn't* follow it immediately, Madoc's allies would be all the more annoyed that Madoc hadn't told them of his plans to trap the human.

So she delayed her departure just long enough to send Madoc's allies their little messages, magicked into pockets and other handy places by the same means she'd used to tack her first note to the panel of Tannim's Mustang, though this time sans pop-rivet. In a few moments, as they discovered their messages, they would all go looking for their titular leader. If Madoc showed up now, it wouldn't be with his own hand-selected guards, but with a following of "allies," all of whom had their own axes to grind on Tannim's skull.

She faced her Gate and set it for that first Gate in Unseleighe lands, from which platform she could descend through another series of magical portals and wind up in the Katschei's Hall, in the room beside the audience chamber. There were very few places Underhill that led directly into each other. For reasons of defense on the part of the Seleighe and neutral realms, and paranoia on the part of the Unseleighe, one could only Gate into halls, Elfhames, or other residences from carefully guarded external Gates, which in turn could only be reached from Gates in friendly or neutral territories. Her one advantage would be that she knew a way to the Katschei's Hall that involved fewer Gates than Madoc did.

She set the Gate and stepped through, but remained on the platform where she had arrived. With a chanted phrase and a sigil drawn in the air, she reset it to another currently vacant domain.

That's where I did do my research, she comforted herself, stepping through and arriving at the edge of a swamp. *If you know who used to be allies, you know where the Gates are set.* Each Gate had a maximum of six destinations; many were not set for more than three or four. No one ever went anywhere in a straight line Underhill, and often a traveler would have to physically walk from one Gate to another in neutral lands in order to reach a Gate that would take him in the direction he wanted to go, and not likely even close to his true destination. It was like trying for connections at Dallas/Ft. Worth airport.

Fortunately, this was not one of those places. Shar would not have enjoyed a stroll across any swamp, but this one, which once had housed Egyptian crocodile-spirits, was particularly unpleasant. *They* had simply vanished over time; the theory was that something had used these swamps as hunting grounds, and picked them off, one by one. Life was dangerous Underhill; the creature that trusted in his own invincibility and immortality often discovered how misplaced that trust was.

But the Egyptians once allied with the efrits, and the efrits with the vampires of the Balkan states. Those in turn had alliances with the Nordic elves—the sort that corresponded to the Unseleighe—and they contracted an alliance with the Katschei. All of those connections were as long distant as the things that once prowled this marsh, but Shar made a point of discovering such alliances and making mental maps of all the Gates that interconnected. Such maps had served her well in the past, and no doubt would again.

Five Gates later, she walked into the audience chamber of the Katschei, a Russian creature, half-monster, half-mage, who had been defeated and killed by a clever human and a benevolent Russian bird-spirit, the Firebird. A great many of the Russian counterparts to the Seleighe and Unseleighe were bird and animal spirits. The Mare of the Night Wind, for instance, and her sons inhabited the same realm as the Firebird.

According to all that Shar had learned, there were not many creatures who cared to share the Katschei's realm with him. Most of the Katschei's underlings had either been his own creations, or creatures which quickly fled as soon as he was no more. No one had ever taken over this domain afterward, partially because of a superstitious feeling that a place where an "immortal" had been destroyed was very unlucky for other "immortals."

Most of the Katschei's palace now lay in complete darkness, except for the gardens outside and the audience chamber. The garden contained a Gate to the human world, but it came out in the heart of Old Rus, not far from what was now Moscow. Probably not the best place for an American with no passport, no luggage, and nothing but his vehicle to appear, even in the current enlightened times. . . .

Assuming Tannim was already here, and that she had *so* great a lead time over Madoc that she could help him get the Mach I out of the palace, into the garden, and through a Gate that hadn't been used in centuries. Assuming Tannim would cooperate.

The glow from the audience chamber lay ahead and to

the right; she moved carefully across the hallway, and paused for a moment on the threshold.

He was there, all right, standing with his hands in his pockets and his legs braced apart, staring at the car. Already it was a disruptive presence Underhill: little crackling tendrils of energy crept across the hood and roof from time to time, and the longer it remained here, the worse the effect would be.

She stepped into the room, making no effort to be quiet. The heels of her boots made muted ticking sounds on the amber floor.

He whirled, hands held out to attack or defend.

She waited for him to say something, but he remained silent. She kept her own hands down at her side, and walked slowly toward him. She did *not* hold her hands out; in a mage, empty hands did not mean "no threat," and such a gesture could be construed as aggressive. He showed no sign of relaxing.

She stopped when she was a few feet away from him. Already she sensed the Gate in the other room gathering energy; it would take longer to transport Madoc and his guards than it had to bring only her, but her time was still short.

But he spoke first. "I know who you are, Shar," he said flatly. "I know who your teachers were, and who you've allied yourself with, and they're not exactly friends of mine."

His use of her name shocked her into unconsidered speech, and she flinched as if she'd been slapped. *How* had he learned her name, much less anything else about her? Unless—

Chinthliss? Could he have contacted Chinthliss?

"They aren't exactly friends of mine, either, monkey-boy," she snapped before she thought. Then she shook her head, and continued, talking so quickly she sounded like a New Yorker so that she could get everything out before Madoc arrived. "Look, you don't have to trust me, you don't have to believe me, but I want to help you. I'm not what I seem, or what you think. But I'm going to have to play along with these jerks to get some room to act, so cut me some slack until the next time you see me, okay? Things are changing faster than you can guess, and I don't much like the idea of being your opposite. I really don't like being forced into it."

He started to answer; she waved him to silence. The Gate had just opened again. She backed up several paces, then said, "Sorry about this," and slapped a spell of paralysis on him just as a clamor of metal signaled that Madoc had come with his guards. Madoc walked through the door into their midst.

"I told you I would bring him, Madoc Skean," she said calmly, without turning around. "I told you, and I have."

Madoc didn't quite run, but he certainly hurried his walk, pushing his escort aside. His eyes gleamed with eager greed as he surveyed Shar briefly, and her prisoner in a more leisurely manner. "You did. Well done," he replied absently. "Now, if you'll just turn him over to me and—"

"Not so fast, Madoc Skean!" said another Unseleighe, who joined Madoc at her side. The sounds of many boots behind her warned that, as she had hoped, the rest of the Unseleighe lords had gotten her message and had taken it seriously. "Not so fast! I have my own claims on this mortal! Did he not slay my own sister's son, Vidal Dhu, with that Death Metal chariot? I swore I would have revenge on him!"

"And what of *my* claim?" cried another. He was joined by the rest, all of them claiming a piece of Tannim. Shar waited; it was *her* spell that held him, and protocol dictated that they could not have him until and unless she let him go.

When the clamor of voices ceased, she spoke into a moment of silence. "My claim supersedes all of yours," she said flatly. "My Challenge to him still holds. And you dare not touch him until it is discharged—you know well the rules of the Challenge. Once issued, it must be answered unless the challenger is willing to be otherwise satisfied. I am not satisfied. And High King Oberon will be less than pleased if you violate so simple a tenet of the laws that bind us all."

There was an uneasy stirring behind her as soon as she

mentioned the name "Oberon." Madoc's face was set in a frozen snarl.

She could not look at Tannim's expression; she confined her gaze to a point just below his chin. She was afraid to look in his eyes and see the bleakness of betrayal there.

"But his vehicle is causing harm in the aether of Underhill," she continued. "I will release him to you, Madoc Skean, only if you pledge to hold him unharmed until I can deal with the vehicle and take it somewhere safe. Only I have the ability to handle so much Death Metal—as well you know."

Madoc's snarl increased a trifle.

"You cannot leave this metal beast here," she reminded him. "Look you, how already it causes rifts in the energy-fields, and warps magics about itself. It will not be long until its influence reaches even to your own realm."

He nodded slowly, reluctantly. "I will hold him unharmed," he said finally. "I pledge it upon my True Name."

"Then give me your True Name," she replied immediately. The True Name did not have the power that some granted it—to give absolute control over another mage—but it *did* make it possible to penetrate most of his defenses. That effect was largely psychological, rather than magical.

With a growl, he leaned over and whispered it into her ear. She kept herself from smiling in triumph, and released the spell into Madoc's hands.

"Remember," she warned, "you pledged to hold him unharmed until my return to your court."

"Aye," he said, tightening his "grip" so that Tannim paled. "But mind, we all have our claims as well."

She gave him a look of warning, and he loosened the cocooning paralysis spell enough to let Tannim breathe easier again. "I will not be gone long, Madoc Skean," she told him. "Be aware of that. This man must be in good health and unharmed, ready to take my Challenge, when I return to your court."

Madoc merely smiled. She dared not stipulate more than she had; she knew very well that Madoc had any number of ways of inflicting suffering that caused no permanent damage to body or health. She only hoped that Tannim's tolerance of such things was as good as she had been led to believe.

She did not watch as Madoc had his guards surround his prize and then released the paralysis spell. She turned her back as Tannim was escorted from the room inside a ring of guards, followed by the dozen or so Unseleighe lords who wanted a piece of him, and then by Madoc himself. She feigned indifference and pretended to study the Mach I. The less real interest she showed in the mortal, the safer he would be. Madoc would not hesitate to use him as a weapon against her, if he thought her interest was anything other than the Challenge itself.

When they were all gone, she studied the Mustang in earnest, for there was no doubt in her mind that she had better do something to make it safe, both for the sake of Underhill and for Tannim. She cast a spell of Creation, reweaving it three times before it fell correctly, and summoned a sheet of silk. That, at least, helped ease some of the disturbance its mere presence was creating, and made it less likely that the neighbors, those surly and unpredictable Nordic types, would come storming across the threshold in the next few moments.

I'll have to actually build another Gate-spell of the kind I put on it in the first place, she decided. *I can't just drive it off. For one thing, I don't have the keys and I bet he's put some nasty surprises in there for anyone who tries to hot-wire it. For another, the only Gate big enough for this thing is the one in the garden. I could certainly fake my way as a Russian, but this is not a Trabant—and how in hell would I get it back to the USA, anyway? Slap a FedEx sticker on it?*

So, the question now was, how much power did she have to spare to move the Mach I somewhere else? She didn't want to send it to her "garage"; that was too obvious a place, for one thing. For another, she wasn't certain she could manage to bridge that much physical distance.

Whoa, wait a moment. I told Madoc I'll be moving it, and that's just about as good as actually moving it. The very last place he'll look for it is here, *and if I put enough shrouding spells on it to negate the effect of all that Cold Iron, no one will ever know that it's here. Except for that poor old blind beggar that sweeps this place, and he won't know it isn't supposed to be here, he won't even know that it's not some peculiar sculpture or piece of furniture.*

The amount of power she would need for those shrouding spells was much less than the amount it would take to open a Gate for even a short distance. Look what bringing the thing here had done to her—she'd slept like a mortal for a dozen hours, then fallen asleep again as soon as she relaxed at the end of the day. There were better uses for that power.

And there was a distinct advantage to not using all that power. Madoc would assume she was drained, as he would be after such an attempt. Or else, he would believe her to be stronger than she actually was. In the latter case, he would not presume to block her, and in the former, he would seriously underestimate her strength.

She nodded to herself as she made her decision and began spinning the gossamer webs of spells that shielded the Mustang from the aether here, and the aether from the Mustang. Each spell settled over the bulk of the car like a delicate veil. Such spells broke the moment whatever they protected moved away from their protection, but that was all right. The only person who would be moving this car was Tannim himself, and if she had him in the driver's seat, it probably wouldn't matter how much disruption they caused.

Finally, the last veil settled into place, and the mists of power flowed through the hall with scarcely a ripple of disturbance.

Shar turned briskly and headed back out the door. She had done all that she could here.

Now she needed to see what she could get away with under the eye of Madoc Skean. Her draconic side knew how deadly a contest of powers this would be—but beneath all the seriousness, her *kitsune* heritage kept reminding her gleefully how much fun this contest would be, especially if she won.

This much was sure; if ever there was to be a test of her full abilities of craft and cleverness, this was surely it.

Things were happening a little too fast for Tannim to react to them. But he had least had one thing straight. *No point in fighting six guys armed with sharp, pointy things. Especially since they'd really like it if I would. It would give them the perfect excuse to use those sharp, pointy things on my soft little body.*

So Tannim stayed uncharacteristically meek and polite—and silent—as the six faceless guards marched him out of the amber room and into the darkness. Their very appearance had given him a bit of a shock, when he'd realized that behind the faceplates of their helms was nothing but empty darkness. He'd never seen this particular kind of Unseleighe before, and he wasn't certain if it was some creation, or something that had intelligence and will of its own. It really didn't matter; in either case, the guy who thought he was in charge, the one Shar had called Madoc Skean, would be only too happy for an excuse to have Tannim roughed up. It was in Tannim's best interest to make sure he had no excuses.

He was still trying to recover from the shock of Shar's little speech. He prided himself on his ability to read people, to pick up on the most subtle of body language, and everything he had "read" indicated that she was telling the truth. She sounded—she acted—as if she wanted to be on his side. Could he believe her? Could he trust his ability to read body language when he was dealing with a *kitsune*-dragon hybrid who only looked human?

After all those years of dreaming about her, he wanted to believe her; he wanted to believe it with an ache of longing that he simply could not deny. Yes, it was stupid to believe her. Yes, he might be pinning his hopes on a creature as evil and devious as Aurilia nic Morrigan. Like her, Shar could be a female who would betray him simply because it amused her to do so. But long ago he had made up his mind that his life was always going to be precarious at best. He could expect the worst of everyone, be paranoid and fearful, and spend his life being

miserable and driving away people who really *did* want
to be friendly. Or he could expect the best out of everyone, treat them that way, and enjoy himself. He might
not increase his potential lifespan, but it was even odds
that he wouldn't shorten it, either. And he just might gain
himself a whole lot of allies against the day—like today—
when the real enemies he had made or inherited caught
up with him.

Some of the Unseleighe had left mage-lights hanging
in the air of the corridor and one room beyond. They
weren't much—as a whole, the Unseleighe preferred a
gloomy twilight—but they helped keep him from stumbling over his own feet. By the time the guards marched
him up onto a stone platform in the middle of a very dimly
lit room, he had made up his mind to believe Shar, or at
least believe that she intended to help him. If half of her
heritage came from Chinthliss' enemy Charcoal, still, half
of it came from a *kitsune*-woman who was clearly someone Chinthliss still cared for and admired deeply.

Besides, he reminded himself, *evil isn't a genetic trait*.

He and the guards stepped through the archway over
the stone platform. The mental and physical jolt that
accompanied a Gate-crossing hit him and disoriented him;
one of the guards shoved him when he didn't move quickly
enough off the new platform, and he sprawled facedown
on the ground beyond it. Fortunately, it was soft turf, but
he scrambled to his feet quickly before one of them could
follow up the shove with a kick in the ribs.

He had expected that he would be marched immediately off into a prison or some other place where he could
be locked up, but to his surprise, he found that they were
standing beside a huge, naturally flat stone in the middle
of a grassy meadow. To either side of them was a row of
long, turf-covered mounds. It was twilight here, the per-
petual twilight he'd noted in many places Underhill; the
"sky" overhead looked like that of an overcast day. His
guards moved forward, and he perforce had to move with
them. They marched down the row and turned between
two of the mounds; there were openings in the middle
of these mounds, dark holes with no doors, the sides

supported by stones. His escort waited while the rest of the party caught up with them.

While they waited, he tried to remember where he had seen this Madoc Skean before, or had heard the name, and could come up with nothing. Not altogether surprising; there were a lot of Unseleighe, in a vast number of sizes and types, and he'd collected enemies from among many of them just by being Keighvin's friend. Hell, look at Vidal Dhu, for instance; he'd never done a *thing* to that particular Unseleighe lord, but Vidal had sworn to exterminate Keighvin's entire clan, and Tannim stood in the way of that. No doubt Keighvin or Conal could identify this particular Unseleighe lord, and likely tell off at least part of his family tree, but it took one of the elven folk to do that. It was enough to know that he wanted Tannim disposed of, and if Shar hadn't intervened, he'd likely have done the disposing then and there, back in the amber room.

That made him wonder about something else. Shar had said that *she* had brought Tannim Underhill; could she have been responsible for what happened to the Mach I? If so, when had she decided to turn her coat? Or had she been on his side all along, but forced into helping capture him?

His head swam with possibilities, and in the long run, none of them really mattered. What did matter was that she had forced Madoc into keeping him alive and unharmed for a time, and if she could be trusted, before that time was up she would find a way to get him out of here.

Once the entire party had assembled, the guards marched him forward into the mound. Or that was what he thought—but as he passed under the capstone of the arch, he felt that same disorientation of a Gate-crossing as he had before.

And once again he found himself on a stone platform; this time a simple slab in the middle of the mist of the Unformed areas. They took him through ten or twelve more Gates before they were through, and from the impatience he thought he felt from his captors, he didn't think all this was for the purpose of confusing him. No, they had no choice but to take this route.

Other than very occasional visits to Elfhame Fairgrove, he'd never been Underhill except to visit a couple of the other Seleighe Elfhames and the one ride through the Unformed lands between the Gate Vidal Dhu had established and Elfhame Fairgrove. He'd had no idea that travel around here was so complicated.

And now a new twist entered the picture. If travel was this difficult, it was going to make escaping a stone bitch. Without someone who knew the way from realm to realm and to the human world, he could wander around in here forever.

Finally, after passing through a Gate into a dark and eerie forest, taking a path right out of a horror movie through that forest, they reached a stone platform guarded by more of the faceless warriors. After this last crossing, he found himself at one end of a huge room of black marble that seemed hauntingly familiar. Finally, after a moment, he realized why. He'd seen it, or one just like it, in the cover paintings of sword-and-sorcery barbarian epics.

He almost earned himself a whack on the head right then by laughing out loud. *Creativity*. The elves just didn't have it, and here was a striking example of exactly how much they lacked it. Given the power and resources of one of these Greater Lords, a human would have come up with something at least a *little* original.

The elves simply couldn't; it wasn't in their natures. Everything they had was a copy of something that humans had already done, from the chrome-and-glass Art Deco splendor of Elfhame Fairgrove to the Tolkienesque groves and tree-dwellings of Elfhame Outremer. Elsewhere, he'd been told, there were realms copied from such diverse sources as Italian science fiction movies and King Ludwig of Bavaria's famous palace. It didn't matter if the source was real or fictional. There had never been a "barbarian kingdom" in the history of humanity that would have produced a throne room looking like this; the mythical, fictional character those books purported to describe never existed, nor did his kingdom and palace. But the elves had copied it as faithfully as if it were real.

In fact, this was a much more slavish copy than anything the Seleighe elves ever produced. They generally elaborated, and often improved, on the originals. Apparently the Unseleighe lacked even that ability.

He wasn't given long to gawk, however; as soon as the rest of the little party had passed through the Gate, it was time to march off again, this time down to a Hollywood nightmare of a dungeon. While part of him tried very hard to seem nonchalant, and another part of him gibbered and groveled in stark panic, a detached third part wondered if they had any idea how to use half of the stuff in here.

Of course they do. It's their specialty, he chided himself. *The one place you can count on an Unseleighe to show some originality is in the ability to hurt someone.*

Beads of sweat trickled down his forehead and neck, making him shiver. *My only hope is that the guy in charge is going to keep his promise to Shar. Oh, please, please, make him keep his promise to Shar.*

Tannim was not a coward, but at that moment he came as close as he had ever come to flinging himself at Madoc Skean's feet and blubbering. He'd had enough injuries to know only too well how it felt to have bones broken, flesh slashed, skin burned. . . .

There was a peculiar contraption hanging in one corner—literally hanging, in fact. It was a cube about four feet on a side, suspended at one corner by a chain; he couldn't decide if it was made of stone or metal. It lacked the sheen of metal, but seemed too heavy to be stone. That same detached part of him wondered what it was; he'd never seen a device quite like it before.

As two of the guards seized him by the arms and dragged him toward it, he realized that he was about to find out just what it was.

One entire side pivoted up on hinges, revealing an interior composed of panels of blunt-pointed, fat spikes, about six inches in diameter at the bottom and three inches tall, set into the walls of the interior so that their sides touched. As he discovered when the two guards grabbed his elbows and heaved him unceremoniously up off his feet and tossed him inside, they were not sharp enough to pierce, but they were certainly sharp enough to bruise. And there was no way to escape them.

They slammed the wall shut on him, leaving him in almost total darkness. Almost—because a little air came in through the top corner, where the chain was strung through a pair of holes. The box was not big enough to stand in or lie down at full length, and the spikes made it impossible to sit comfortably in any position. Despite the ventilation holes, it was stuffy in there. And to add insult to injury, water dripped in steadily from the chain.

Very clever. The "room of little comfort," new improved version. This would certainly not harm him, but it would exhaust him and keep him in a state of constant discomfort, very nicely obeying the exact letter of the promise.

But the situation only made him think faster. *What else would I do if I was one of them? Ah—I'd put a telepath on watch, to see if I was thinking of escape, and glean information.*

He settled himself in a position that was as close to comfort as he was likely to get and waited, listening, both with his ears and his mind. Though no telepath himself, Keighvin had taught him how to recognize the touch of a telepath on his thoughts some time ago.

Interestingly enough, they hadn't taken anything from him, neither his watch nor the contents of his pockets. Granted, some of it, like the pocketknife, could hurt them, but he had no doubt they could find some way around that. Perhaps they meant to show him how contemptuous they were of his abilities. Perhaps they simply assumed, with typical elven arrogance, that there was nothing a mere mortal could do against their magics once they had him in their grasp. The watch alone was a godsend; with it, he knew exactly how much time was passing. After about thirty minutes, he heard the scrape of a chair on stone outside. And a moment later, he felt an insidious little brush against the outside of his mind.

Keighvin had taught him that it took a moment for a telepath to accustom himself to his target's mind, but that once he was inside it, only determined effort would keep him from learning what he wished.

Unless, of course, the target could provide something else to completely distract himself and his eavesdropper. Something as insidious as advertising jingles, for instance.

For the first time since his capture, he grinned. *So. They want to know what I'm thinking about, hmm? Let's see if I can provide them with something . . . completely unexpected. Oh, Yogi, the ranger isn't gonna like this!*

He cleared his throat, took a deep breath—and began to sing.

"I'm your only friend, I'm not your only friend, but I'm a little glowing friend, but really I'm not actually your friend but I am—"

Beat, beat, beat—

The manic grin spread widely over his face as the chair scraped again.

Ladies and gentlemen of the Unseleighe, you are about to be treated to a nonstop concert of They Might Be Giants. Have a nice day.

The thing about the lyrics of a lot of the songs that particular duo came up with was that they were so completely illogical that it required concentration to remember them. You couldn't just infer the next line from the line previous to it. He caroled at the top of his lungs, concentrating *only* on the incredibly infectious melody and the unbelievably bizarre lyrics. *Get that out of your head, not-friend. I sure as hell can't!*

As he began the second verse, and got to the part about ". . . countless screaming Argonauts," he thought he heard a faint whimper.

As he began his second tune, "She'd like to see you again, slowly twisting in the wind," the whimper was no longer faint.

Just wait until I start on the Apollo 18 *album.*

He settled back, protecting the back of his head with his hands, and sang with great gusto at the holes in the metal above him.

CHAPTER SEVEN

Joe stood back in the murky shadows cast by the ruined walls of the barn, where Chinthliss and Fox wouldn't notice him unless they really looked for him, and kept his mouth shut. Fox hadn't been here long—just long enough for Chinthliss to get both their tempers to the boiling point.

When Tannim didn't return, Chinthliss decided to do something—the first thing that apparently came to his mind was the need to interrogate FX. And despite what Tannim had said about not being able to bring FX here, Chinthliss was evidently not bound by any such constraints. A few mumbled words, a clenched fist slapped into a palm—and there was Fox, the photo-image of James Dean, except for his fox-feet and the three tails that lashed furiously behind him, his whole body tense with anger and apprehension.

This was the first argument Joe had ever seen between two mythological creatures; there was no telling in what direction it might explode, or who might get splattered when it did. He decided to stay out of it for the moment, while he let his subconscious work on the problem of getting Tannim back.

Chinthliss had backed the *kitsune* into what was left of the wall beside the door, and he must have done something that made it impossible for FX to disappear, because so far Fox seemed stuck right where Chinthliss wanted him. Surely Fox had made at least one attempt to get away by now, since he certainly looked as if he wanted to be far, far, away from here. Whatever he'd tried, though, it hadn't worked.

"Look," FX said, his eyes widened pleadingly, as Chinthliss loomed over him. Fox spread his hands to either side in entreaty. "What was I supposed to do? I couldn't cross her, I didn't *dare!* I'm a lousy three-tail, she has *nine!* I get in her way, and I end up being called 'Stumpy' for the rest of my short life!"

"You could have told Tannim what she was," Chinthliss growled, looking less human with every passing moment. "You could have called on *me.*"

"How was I to know you knew her?" Fox retorted, tails rigid for a moment.

"You knew she was challenging Tannim; you knew that Tannim is like a son to me. *Of course* I would be interested in anything or anyone challenging him, whether I actually knew the creature or not!" Chinthliss thundered, standing tall and dark against the glow of magic shields. Joe shivered; when Chinthliss talked like that, he sounded powerful. Very powerful. Scary, too.

"You don't understand *kitsune* politics," Fox retorted, dropping his eyes and staring at his furred and clawed feet sullenly. "Hell, that's what got you into trouble with Lady Ako in the first place."

Chinthliss' expression darkened perceptibly, and he seemed to grow a little. Joe decided this might be a good time to intervene.

"None of this is getting Tannim back," he pointed out. "We don't even know where he is. We don't know if he's in trouble or not—"

But FX shook his head and raised his eyes to meet Joe's. "He's in trouble," Fox replied glumly. "When I ducked out, I ran back home to check on the nine-tail who was following Tannim. There was only one unaccounted for; that was Lady Shar, and everyone knows that Lady Shar's been playing footsie with the Unseleighe. And whether or not you can smell it, old man," he added, regaining a little courage to glance insolently at Chinthliss, "this young nose tracked the scent of her all over his Mustang. She's probably the reason it went AWOL in the first place."

Chinthliss' eyes narrowed, and he tensed. For a moment, Joe was afraid that Chinthliss might actually strike the *kitsune*. Or worse. But Chinthliss regained control of himself with an effort after a sidelong glance at Joe.

"Fine," he said acidly. "And if you are so very clever, why don't you find out where he is now?"

"Because I can't," Fox replied, deflating abruptly. Now he looked depressed, and no longer even remotely insolent. "I tried, and I can't. Whoever has him crossed through too many Gates and I lost the scent."

Chinthliss growled and turned away. Fox hung his head and his shoulders drooped. Joe tried to pat him on the back consolingly, but his hand went right through Fox's body.

Funny: Chinthliss could touch him. . . . Never mind. The important thing was to find Tannim.

"Well, we know where the car is," he reasoned out loud. "If Tannim *has* been caught by somebody, that's the first place he'll go, right? And if he's just gotten lost or something, it's still the first place he'll go! Why don't we just wait there for him to show up?"

But Fox only looked panicked at that idea, and Chinthliss shook his head. "This is not like a trip to the mall, young friend," he said, just a little patronizingly. "Tannim will not simply return to where the car is parked. He may decide to abandon it; he may decide that it is wiser to come back after it with a force. He may—be unable to come."

Chinthliss' voice faltered on that last, and Joe's resentment at his patronizing tone faded into worry. "Well, what can we do?" he asked. "Should we go there and see if we can track him or something?"

Fox shook his head fiercely, his eyes wide. "No! Oh, no, no, no! She's been all over that place, and I bet she comes back! That's a very bad idea!"

"But it would be no bad idea to try tracking him from somewhere Underhill," Chinthliss mused. "Magic is more

available there, and more reliable as well. We still have
the chrome circle to keep track of the Mustang, and we
have other things of his to use to find Tannim. Hmm. I
believe we could do this."

"If you're going to start messing around with *her,*
I'm—" Fox began, as he sidled away from Chinthliss. The
latter shot out a hand and caught his jacket collar before
he could sneak out of reach.

"You will remain with us to help," Chinthliss rumbled
dangerously. "A nine-tailed *kitsune* is not the only creature that can change your name to 'Stumpy.' *I* can change
your name to 'Mulch.' It is at least in part your fault that
he is missing; you *will* help us to find him. And if you
try to slip away, the first item I conjure will be *hedge
clippers.* Understand?"

Fox shrank in Chinthliss' grasp, but said nothing and
did not struggle.

"Now, the question is, where are we to go?" Chinthliss
continued, with FX still dangling from one outstretched
arm. "Not a Seleighe Elfhame; the very nature of the place
would make it impossible to find him from within one.
Besides, we need somewhere less—law-abiding."

"Jamaica?" Fox suggested hopefully. Chinthliss shook
him a little, and his teeth rattled.

"Are there neutral places there?" Joe asked. "Like
Switzerland?"

Chinthliss nodded. "The trouble is they are most often densely inhabited. There are more creatures that are
neither good nor evil than there are creatures of either
persuasion."

Joe thought for a moment. "Is that bad?" he asked. "I
mean, would it be bad for people to know that Tannim's
missing and might be in trouble? Maybe some of them
would help us if we came up with the right price. And—
well, if the bad guys have got him, how can it hurt to have
other bad guys know? Either they're going to know already,
or else they just might be pissed off that somebody else
got Tannim first and try and get him for themselves."

Fox brightened considerably as Chinthliss tightened his
lips and drew his brows together in thought. "We might

be able to spring him while they're fighting over him," Fox pointed out. "Maybe some of the neutrals would help us because they owe Tannim a favor. You know how the neutrals are: if the scales ain't balanced, they're not happy. I know of a real good place to go looking for critters that might owe him, too. Furhold. News travels faster there than anywhere else Underhill."

Now Chinthliss smiled, a thin sliver of a smile full of sardonic irony. "Oh, yes. Indeed it does. Not surprising. The Furholders have a privileged life, and a rich economy. They have little else to do but find new ways to entertain themselves, and invent exotic drinks. Chocolate khumiss, indeed."

Joe looked from one to the other and back again, and a strange idea occurred to him. "Is this place—the one you want to go to—anything like a Mexican border bar?"

Chinthliss' lips twitched with reluctant amusement. "It is a comparison that has occurred to me, yes," he admitted.

Joe nodded, feeling a little more on secure ground. Not that he had ever been in a Mexican border bar, but plenty of the men in the Chosen Ones had, before they were "saved," and a lot of loose talk went on in the barracks. The *shapes* might be different, but there would be drunks and bar girls, pushers and pimps, out-of-town tourists, students looking for a thrill, out-of-work self-styled mercenaries—and he should be able to recognize each type for what it was, no matter what shape it wore.

"Let's go," he urged. "I'm not too bad in a fight."

Now Chinthliss let go of FX, turned, and looked at him sternly. "I did not mean for you to go," he protested. "Tannim would be most displeased."

"No, he wouldn't," Joe lied fluently. "Besides, I bet I'm a better shot than either of you."

"He can't take a gun across the Gate, can he?" Fox asked, looking interested and eager. His tails twitched with nervous energy.

Chinthliss shrugged. "If a Mustang can cross over into Underhill, I fail to see why a gun should not. The only question is, where can he get a weapon at such short notice?" He tilted his head in Joe's direction and waited for an answer.

Joe grinned. He was in! They were already talking as if his presence was an accepted thing. "I've got one in my baggage, back at Tannim's house," he told them both gleefully. "A .45 M1911A1, GI-issue. And ammo, too. I didn't tell Tannim, but Frank didn't want me unarmed, in case some of the old Chosen Ones might have gotten away the night of the raid. It's not that far a run; I can be there and back in no time. Besides, I'd better leave a note for Mr. and Mrs. Drake, otherwise if we aren't there in the morning, they'll be really worried."

That was something else he'd considered—what if they couldn't bring Tannim home by dawn? His parents would think something bad had happened to him. Well, something bad *had* happened to him, but Joe didn't want the Drakes to know that, and he was certain Tannim didn't, either.

"You don't want me there alone, if we can't get him back soon," Joe continued with warning. "They'll start asking questions I can't answer. But if I leave a note saying that an emergency came up and Mr. Silver from Fairgrove needed us to run up to Kansas City, they'll probably figure we're fine."

Chinthliss sighed and shrugged. "You are an adult by the laws of your land," he admitted. "You are fully capable of making your own decisions. We will wait here for your return."

"And I'll be back before you know it," Joe promised, and turned and vaulted the doorframe into the tall grass. Excitement chilled his skin and gave his feet extra spring as he ran out into the night.

Shar did not go straight to Madoc's domain; she was fairly certain that he would keep the exact letter of his pledge. Tannim would be alive, sane, and in relatively good health when she returned. Bruises, hunger, thirst—all were easily cured, all were trivial.

She needed advice, and there was only one completely trustworthy source for that advice.

She returned to her own place and composed a carefully worded message, writing it properly in elegant calligraphy on rice paper, folding it into the shape of a flower, before finally encapsulating it and sending it away with a brief exercise of power.

Then she waited, with folded hands, for her little Gate to activate. If Lady Ako did not appear within an hour, she would take her own chances, unadvised, with Madoc Skean.

She forced herself not to look at her watch. The minutes crept past with agonizing slowness. She kept thinking of all the things that could be going wrong. And what if Tannim had contacted Chinthliss before he came Underhill? What if Chinthliss was looking for him? That was another complication that she had not counted on.

The hour ticked slowly to the end, and she rose, preparing to activate the Gate herself to take her to that relatively neutral point in the Unseleighe lands. She had actually touched it with her power, although she had not yet done anything, when the Gate came alive under her hand.

She disengaged her own magics and backed up a pace. Her mother stepped through the dark haze within the doorway as soon as she had cleared the way.

But this time Lady Ako was *not* the image of the proper *kitsune* lady.

She looked scarcely older than Shar; her long hair had been braided into a single tail in the back, and she wore a spotless white t-shirt and form-fitting black jeans. She raised a perfectly manicured eyebrow at her daughter, and set her hands on her hips.

"I have been making some inquiries among the lesser *kitsune*," she said without preamble. "There is a young fox that you have rattled badly, and I fear that your actions will have effects reaching up to the highest tables."

Shar flushed, although she could not imagine what her mother was talking about. Unless—

"Saski Berith, who calls himself Foxtrot X-ray, is now among the missing," Lady Ako continued. "I believe that he is in the humans' world even now. He is known to have been a friend of Tannim, and he told some of the others that a lady of nine tails was interested in 'one of his friends' in a way that was likely to jeopardize that friend's health.

I can only conclude that he sensed you and ran. And, unfortunately, talked. I am probably not the only *kitsune* who has put all the pieces together by this point in time."

Shar flushed more deeply. "I didn't know there was another of our kind about," she confessed. "Actually—to tell the truth, Mother, I didn't think to look."

Lady Ako shook her head. "Draconic carelessness," she chided, none too gently. "It may cost you. There are questions being asked. *Kitsune* of nine tails are not to involve themselves seriously in the lives of mortals unless that mortal is a relative, or unless the *kitsune* is under divine direction, you know that. And when it comes out that the young man was being challenged by you because of your involvement with the Unseleighe—"

Shar hung her head; she couldn't look into her mother's eyes. "I did not think that it would matter."

"Say rather only the first four words of that statement, and you will be closer to the truth, my daughter," Lady Ako said sternly. "And have you brought the mortal to harm by your meddling, or is the situation yet salvageable?"

Shar raised her head slowly. "He is in the hands of Madoc Skean, but will not be harmed until my Challenge is satisfied or revoked," she replied. "That is what I wished to ask your advice upon, Mother." She put pleading into her gaze, but her mother's youthful face did not lose its expression of disapproving judgment.

"You knew what you were doing," Lady Ako replied implacably. "I warned you, and you did not heed the warning. Now there is a mortal in Underhill in the hands of his enemies, it is your fault, and it has come to the attention of the clan. This is not a good thing. You will be asked to balance the scales. It would be better for you if you even them yourself, before you are ordered to do so and find you cannot, because the one you should aid is dead."

Shar clenched her jaw in anger. "How?" she demanded. "If I help him, it is only the two of us against all the Unseleighe that Madoc Skean has under his sway!"

Lady Ako shrugged, as if it mattered little to her. "The way of the *kitsune*," her mother said. "Trickery. Guile. Craft.

Divide them; make them quarrel amongst themselves. Plant rumors; engineer incidents that make the rumors appear to be the truth. Fling the pebble among the bandits, and see them argue over which of them tossed it. I need not tell you these things; you should know them already."

Shar remained silent, waiting for her mother to answer her real question, the one that had been in her letter.

Lady Ako pulled her braid over her shoulder, and toyed with the end of it for a moment. "As for the rest—it is sufficient that you have placed yourself in a position of obligation to this mortal. Discharge that obligation; get him free. Only then can you proceed in any other directions."

"And if I don't?" Shar asked, with a touch of rebellion.

Her mother did not respond to the tone of her voice, only to the words. "If you *choose* not to, you will be liable to answer to the clan; what will happen then, I cannot say. It will depend on how cleverly you argue your case. You could lose a tail; you could get off with little more than a reprimand. If you try, but cannot aid him, what happens to you will depend on whether the Unseleighe detect your meddling." She shrugged. "If you escape the Unseleighe alive at all, I suspect the clan will judge your attempt enough to balance the scales. You will be lectured, and shamed, but no more than that."

Trust Lady Ako to answer her literally! What she wanted was advice of the heart—which, having given it earlier, Lady Ako would not give a second time.

But she had to admit, her mother was right. Before she could decide what to do *about* Tannim, she must even the scales between them—yes, and confess what her part had been in all of this. If he could not deal with that, well, then there was no point in pursuing a mouse down a hole. All that would happen would be sore paws from trying to dig through granite.

And meanwhile—well, she had an answer of another sort. Her status among the *kitsune* was in danger because of her own actions. If the clan had never come to hear of this, or if that lesser *kitsune* had not been frightened, she might have come through this with an unsullied reputation. Now the least of it would be a blot in her record.

How big a blot would depend on how well she managed to set things right. If she managed to not only set things aright, but did so in archetypically *kitsune* manner, spectacularly, she would even gain status from it. *Kitsune* respected style in any form.

She bowed formally to her mother. Lady Ako nodded her head in return. While Shar remained bent over her knees, the lady turned and left, without a farewell.

A bad sign, both for the state of her mother's temper and the temper of the other high-ranking *kitsune.* For a moment, Shar indulged in a fit of resentment.

Didn't she used to be a rebel? Can't she remember what that was like? To have two suitors, to ally with one but bear the child of the other? Isn't that as scandalous as anything I have done?

But her conscience came up with the answer.

It had not involved mortals. It had not changed the lives of humans. Like it or not, human mortals were considered to be beings deserving of pity for their limitations. Ako's had only changed her life—and Ako had no scales to even. That was the difference.

Scandal was one thing. Upsetting the balances was far more serious.

What could she do? She could deal with it. She could follow her mother's advice.

Or she could ignore it all, stay here, and face the consequences.

But her feet were already on a different path than indifference to what she had done to Tannim; they had taken the first steps the moment she asked him to trust her. She was under an even heavier obligation than Lady Ako knew.

So I deal with it. She nodded to herself, faced her Gate, and activated it. *Now—just what kind of pebble can I throw among the feasting bandits, I wonder?*

And despite her mother's real anger and the gravity of the entire situation, she felt herself smiling a true vixen's-grin.

This had the potential to be so much *fun!*

❖   ❖   ❖

The dripping water turned out to be less of a nuisance than Tannim had thought; it gave him something to drink to ease his throat. At least he wasn't too hoarse yet. His singing voice wasn't too bad even after a couple hours of abuse, though he didn't think there were any recording contracts in his future.

"This is where the party ends, I can't sit here listening to you and your racist friends," he sang, wondering what his enemies were making of all this. Most of the Unseleighe he'd seen with Madoc looked as if they hadn't been out of Underhill since the sixteenth century—the very meaning of many of the words he sang had changed since that time, and some words hadn't existed. They were probably analyzing every little syllable, trying to find some meaning in it. He *knew* he'd heard someone cry out in tones of despair, "The White Eagle I know, but what in the name of the Morrigan is the *Blue Canary?*" The White Eagle was an alchemical term; were they trying to find alchemical formulas in the lyrics? No wonder they were going crazy out there!

He had held the thought firmly in mind since he had begun that he was working on some kind of spell to set him free. Halfway through the lyrics of the *Flood* album, it had occurred to him to concentrate also on the accordion as a vessel of incredibly potent magical power just to confuse the issue even further. So now they were trying to make sense of senseless lyrics and wondering what the heck made an accordion so magical. Would there be a rash of mysterious accordion thefts from pawnshops and music stores all across the USA after this? Had he just inflicted the madness of the accordion upon the Unseleighe?

The horror . . . the horror . . .

In fact, if he hadn't been so damned uncomfortable, this would have been a lot of fun. He was pretty certain he was on his third telepath by now; one had collapsed, and the second had begun moaning and been taken away a few minutes ago.

Mom used to claim my music drove her crazy. I didn't think it would ever be the literal truth.

Since about the third song, they'd stopped giving the cube occasional shoves to set it swinging. He was rather glad of that; one major disadvantage of being so thin was that he didn't have a lot of padding between him and those spikes. He was going to be black and blue by the time they let him out of here.

There was a scrape of chair legs. "No more," a voice said firmly, and the light touch on his mind went away. "I will bear no more of this. And I do not think you will find another to take my place, Madoc Skean. There is no treasure and no revenge worth this madness!"

Tannim grinned wider in the darkness of his prison, and sang lustily, at the top of his lungs: "When you're following an angel doesn't mean you have to throw your body off a building. . . ."

More footsteps retreating, and the muttering of voices. Were they actually giving up?

No point in taking any chances. Better start repeating the most infectious song he knew.

"Throw the crib door wide, let the people crawl inside. Someone in this town wants to burn the playhouse down. They want to stop the ones who want a rock to wind a string around. . . ."

Take that, Madoc Skean!

Shar stepped through the Gate to find Madoc Skean's throne quite empty. The Unseleighe prince was in the center of a huddle of his allies and underlings. Two of them were simply monsters: an ogre, and something Shar suspected was a Greek lamia. There were about a half dozen of the Unseleighe elves, dressed in their ornate brocades and silks, enchanted armor, and elaborate jewels, the evidences of the power of their magic. The rest were retainers, each in the livery of his master's colors. "No more," one was saying, firmly, his face creased with strain. "He tortures us with his conundrums more than we torture him."

At that moment, one of the little hobgoblins that served as lower servants trotted by, singing to itself. The melody was incredibly catchy, but the words—

"They want to stop the ones who want prosthetic foreheads on their heads," the little hunched-over creature crooned happily. "But everybody wants prosthetic foreheads for their real he—"

A tremendous *smack* interrupted the song, as Madoc Skean whirled and slapped the small creature into the wall. "Enough!" he roared into the sudden silence. "Is it not bad enough that the fool mortal carols us with his arrant nonsense? Must I hear it from the basest servants as well?"

The hobgoblin whimpered, picked himself up off the ground, and scampered away.

Madoc turned and saw Shar. He was appallingly easy to read; she wondered if he had any idea how easy it was. Even if she had not heard him arguing with his putative allies, she would have known from his thundercloud expression that things were not going well for him. These Unseleighe made no effort to control themselves or their emotions.

Throw a pebble among the bandits? Ah—when better than right now?

"I have investigated the vehicle, Lord Madoc," she said smoothly, offering him the title of honor although she seldom accorded it to him. "I have come to some disturbing conclusions. I am not entirely certain that the creature we have now is truly the human Tannim."

Madoc's blank look of shock came very close to making her smile; she repressed it and continued, with the gravest of expressions, pitching her voice so that all the assembled Unseleighe heard it. "There are a great many traces of magery on the vehicle. They are not magics as a human would practice them; they are not Seleighe. I cannot identify them."

That much was the strictest truth; the very best kind of misdirection.

"If I were to hazard a guess, I would say it was not impossible that these traces were from a neutral creature, or even—" she hesitated a moment, then continued "—even an Unseleighe. I do not think it would be going too far to warn you that this thing we have taken prisoner might

be a shape-shifter, or a changeling. It might even have been
sent as a kind of expendable assassin by one of your
enemies. For that matter, Lord Madoc, *you* might not even
be its target; it might have been intended for one of the
other lords and ladies here."

She nodded at the gathered Unseleighe, who were
eavesdropping without shame, their sharp features betraying
their alarm at this unwelcome news. "It could be that one
of your allies is the real target, and whoever sent this
creature intended the blame for the death to fall upon you,
Lord Madoc."

The ploy was working! Already the other Unseleighe
edged slightly away from each other, casting glances of
suspicion at one another and at Madoc. Lovely! Now if
she could just make Tannim vanish from his place of
captivity. . . .

Wait a moment—

"Perhaps we had best see if your prisoner is still there,
Lord Madoc," she continued earnestly, wondering if he had
noticed by now that she had called him "lord" no less than
three times now. That was more honorifics than she normally accorded him in the course of a week! "If this creature is a shape-shifter, he may already have escaped. If he
is more powerful than we realized, he could have vanished
without you ever knowing."

One of the others laughed scornfully. "Escaped? How?
When we have heard him a-singing like a foolish jongleur
this past hour and more?"

She leveled a glance at the speaker, an ogre, in a way
that made him snap his mouth shut on his laughter. "And
how better to make you think that you had him still than
to leave a voice singing there? It need not even require
magic! Did this creature not *come* from the human world?
Have none of you heard of the mechanical wonders the
humans build? Did any of you think to search it for one
of those human devices by which words and music may
be captured and replayed? Why, such things are made that
are no larger than this!" She measured out the size of the
palm of her hand. "It could easily have concealed such a
thing in its clothing! And there are spells enough to

accomplish the same thing. Am I to understand that you are no longer keeping a mind-reader a-watching of his thoughts?"

At Madoc's reluctant nod, she shook her head, as if she was impatient with all of them. "The moment this creature knew that its thoughts were no longer subject to scrutiny, he could have made his escape. Any shape-changer could become a snake, and slip through holes. A vampire could become a mist or a fog and do the same. A changeling—who knows what it could become at the will of the one who sent it?"

"This is all speculation," snapped one poisonously lovely woman, a pale blond in an Elizabethan gown of deep green brocade with a huge ruff of silver lace about her long neck. "Let us go and see whether he is the mortal we wanted or no! If not, and if it has escaped somehow, we must recapture it and discover what it wants. And if so, well, this *lady* wishes to discharge her Challenge, and the sooner this is done, the sooner we may deal with the mortal."

Whatever Madoc wanted was moot at this point; the rest of his allies clamored for an immediate visit to his dungeons. Shar simply looked grave, and let them carry her along with them.

And while they were arguing about it all, she exercised just the tiniest bit of her powers in a spell of illusion.

The entire group pushed and shoved through the doors, still arguing. Shar brought up the rear, confident of what would happen and wanting to be out of the way when it did.

"Sir!" one of Madoc's guards called out over the noise. "The mortal seems to be repeating his songs now. I thought that it might be a ruse to make us open his prison; I restrained Lord Liam's liegeman from breaking the seal."

"Yes, my Lord Liam, *he* kept me from the performance of my duty!" another guard called out resentfully. Shar raised an eyebrow in surprise at the number of guards crowding the room. It looked as if every one of Madoc's allies had insisted on having his own guard here.

Good. That meant they trusted each other even less than she had thought. She reached into a pocket while they were looking at each other and palmed the first thing she touched that would serve for her next ruse; a cheap pocket-calculator she had broken and shoved into a pocket, then all but forgotten.

"Open it now!" Madoc ordered, waving peremptorily at the guard. This was not one of the faceless creatures Madoc generally favored, although Shar would have preferred one of those to this monster. It wasn't so much the single eye that bothered her as the very pink skin that glistened around it. The creature bowed and propped his pike up against the wall, then turned to the suspended cube and broke the seal on it. Then he swung the side up—to reveal an empty interior.

The singing stopped in mid-phrase.

The heavy side slipped from his fingers as he gawked in startlement and slammed it back into place. Another guard quickly pulled the side back up, though everyone here had already seen that the cube was completely empty, just as Shar had predicted. She reached out herself and "plucked" the calculator from the interior with a neat bit of sleight-of-hand palming.

"Look!" she said, waving it aloft. "What did I tell you? Here is the device the mortal used to trick you into thinking he was singing in there! Now he has fled, and who knows where he might be?"

She flung the calculator down at Madoc's feet. No one here would recognize it for what it was; they'd have to take her word for it. Since it was already broken, they could play with it forever and not get it to "work." And just as she expected, pandemonium erupted as one of Madoc's servants hastily scooped the device up.

Accusations flew for a moment, most of them leveled at Madoc, who had gathered his bodyguard around him and was backing up toward the door. Shar prudently got out of his way; it was never a good idea to be between an Unseleighe and his exit. But after a moment, the accusations and counter-accusations became general. Each of the Unseleighe gathered his underlings to him (or her), and followed Madoc Skean's example, backing toward the exit while screaming imprecations at everyone else. Shar's suggestion that Tannim might be an assassin had fallen on fertile ground; none of them were willing to risk the chance of being the target of that assassin.

There were some tense moments as the several parties collided at the door; those who had more retainers with them intimidated those who had fewer. Madoc, with the most, was the first out and heading toward some place where he might barricade himself into relative safety. The ogre was next, followed by the beautiful Unseleighe elven lady. The rest sorted themselves out, glaring at each other in mingled fear and accusation, until they all got out into the freedom of the hall. Then they headed elsewhere. Where, Shar did not particularly care, so long as they left her in sole guardianship of this room for a few moments.

When she was certain that the last of the Unseleighe were gone, she swung up the unlocked side of the cube and banished the illusion of the empty interior. Tannim sat there for a moment, arms wrapped around his legs, chin resting on his knees, regarding her with a wry expression and the hint of a tired smile.

"I'd love to know how you managed that," he said finally. "I figured I was about to become Spam when I heard all the voices out there. And when they all stared at me instead of grabbing me, I couldn't figure out what was wrong. That *was* your doing, wasn't it?"

"Yes," she replied. "But unless you've grown fond of that thing, I suggest we might find someplace else to have a discussion about what just happened. They could be back any moment."

Tannim took the hint and scrambled out of the cube in a way that suggested to Shar that he had probably acquired a few bruises in there. He brushed himself off as he straightened up, and gave her a look that clearly said, "Now what?" But wisely, he kept silent; she had to give him a lot of points for that.

She simply gestured to him to follow. The less talking they did, the better; there were spells that could reach back in time to see what had happened in a particular area, and if there was no dialogue to *tell* the spellcaster what they

planned to do, following them out of this room would be
a matter of hit-or-miss.

Tannim seemed ready enough to trust her; or at least,
he was going to trust her until he had a chance to strike
out on his own, or *she* explained herself sufficiently to him.

Well, as long as they were in this palace, he would be
very stupid to try and strike out on his own, and she hoped
he had the good sense to realize just that.

There was noise enough in the direction of the audience chamber; she had a fair notion that at least two or
three of Madoc's former allies were fighting their way to
the Gate there. Madoc's men, in absence of any other
orders, had probably assumed that the "allies" had become
"enemies" and were trying to keep them from the Gate.
The Faceless Ones assumed nothing, and there was no
telling what they were doing. Madoc might have told them
to oppose anyone who tried to leave, he might have told
them nothing at all. In the latter case, the Faceless Ones
would let anyone who was already on the approved list to
go through the Gate as they wished.

She hoped that was the case; their own escape
depended on it. The Gate in the audience chamber was
always guarded, but the Gate she intended to use would
very likely be as well.

There was no point in putting a dungeon underground
when you were already Underhill; the reason for having
a prison beneath the earth was to prevent easy escape.
Well, there was no such thing as an "easy" escape for
someone in Unseleighe lands and Unseleighe hands. Even
if you made an escape, you were forced between one of
two choices. You could take your chances on whatever
Gate you might find unguarded, or you could take your
chances in the Unformed. You might run into a solid wall
out there; you might not. One's sense of direction went
all to pieces, and people had wandered in small circles
until they dropped without ever reaching a barrier or the
place they had left. You might discover that the "land"
you had escaped and the Unformed surrounding it com-
prised an area of less than one hundred acres. You might
discover it was the size of a small continent—or, as in

Shar's case, the size of a generous townhouse with attached garage.

Just to make matters even more entertaining, you might or might not find a physical opening into another realm or domain. Shar knew where a few of those were, but no one knew them all. Few cared to trust their safety to the Unformed to explore the possibilities. The mist was strange stuff; very sensitive to magic and to even the thoughts of those within it. Your fears, if you dwelled upon them for too long, could become reality. . . .

Well, just at the moment, Shar had no intentions of dashing off into the dangerous mist outside the walls of Madoc Skean's realm. She had a better plan.

As soon as they penetrated beyond the prison section, she made a sharp right, away from the black-marble corridors lit with torches in gold-chased sconces, and into a hallway built of some dull gray stuff that could not even be identified. Two lefts and a right later, and they were deep into the maze of passageways that only the servants used.

There weren't too many of those about; the noise of fighting, shouts, and the occasional clash of metal-on-metal penetrated even here and warned all but the very dullest that it was not wise to be abroad just now. Only the occasional hobgoblin skipped by, humming to itself, oblivious to everything except the last task it had been given.

The corridors remained the same: gray walls, floor, and ceiling made of something that might even have been taken for plastic elsewhere. Maybe it was, anyway. Out of sight of anyone to impress, Madoc might well have eschewed tradition for sheer practicality. Plastic was one of the easier substances to *ken* and reproduce, after all.

There was no mistaking the light source, however. Dim witchlights bobbed at intervals near the ceiling. Madoc was not one to waste energy on creating comfort or convenience for the sake of mere servants; there was *just* enough light to keep from falling on your nose, and no more.

No matter. Shar already knew where she was going and could have felt her way in the dark, if need be. Madoc might not know it, but she had prowled the halls of his

domain in several shapes until she knew it better than he
did. She had been a hobgoblin, an Unseleighe elven lady,
even one of his very own Faceless Ones. And wouldn't he
have been surprised to know what she had seen in *that*
form!

It was not the brightest of moves, to invite a shape-
changer to be your guest. . . .

Two rights, a left, and a smell that just bordered
between savory and unsavory wafted down the hall, telling her that she was nearing her goal. Tannim followed—
flowed, actually; for a mortal, he was surprisingly graceful.
A little knife in his hand told her that he was not as
guileless as he looked; she wondered where he'd hidden
it. A leg sheath, perhaps?

She motioned him to wait as they neared the door to
the kitchen. She straightened and concentrated for a
moment, shutting her eyes as she shifted her form.

When she opened them, she was quite a bit shorter,
and her neck strained from the odd angle she was forced
to hold her head at. Never mind; she wouldn't have this
form for long. She glanced back at Tannim and grinned
a little at the dumbfounded expression on his face.

Well, it probably wasn't every day he watched a "human"
woman shift into a hunchbacked female troll.

*Now, if luck is on my side this little while more, every
servant in the Hall will have fled to places of safety while
their betters are squabbling.*

She shuffled into the kitchen door as if she had every
right to be there—which in this servant-form, she theo-
retically did. The strange mix of smells nauseated her for
a moment until she dimmed that particular sense down
to something bearable. Some of Madoc's allies and servants
ate perfectly palatable foods. But then there were creatures like that ogre—

Best not think about what might be floating in the soup
kettle on the hearth. Not all the bodies from midnight gang
fights on the streets of big cities ended up in the hands
of the coroner. Not all the old winos who vanished in the
night were ever accounted for.

Enough; her guess was correct: the kitchen was empty.

The work tables were clean, since the evening meal was long since over, but the soapy water and pottery shards on the floor and the heaps of soiled dishes showed that cleanup had not been completed when the servants learned of their masters' quarrels. They might be routed out and sent back to work, but not within the next hour.

She shifted back to her preferred form and waved Tannim in, then headed to the doorway on the opposite side of the room. If it had been gloomy in the hallway, it was positively dark in the kitchen, and hot as Hades. All the light came from the fires in the two fireplaces, and both put out enough heat to melt lead on the hearthstones.

She wrestled with the bar across the door for a moment, then it came free; she lifted it and pulled the latch, slipping out into the eternal dusk outside. Tannim followed, and stood looking cautiously around as she closed the door behind them.

They were in what would have been the kitchen garden in the manor-house that this hall had been copied from. Here Underhill, in Unseleighe lands, where there was no reason to grow things for a purpose, this was simply a rank and weed-filled annex to the main garden. Black vines covered with decaying leaves clung to the walls, their branches infesting the brickwork. Where plots of herbs and vegetables would have been, spiky, gray weeds and limp, dispirited grasses attempted to choke the life out of each other. Trees reached clawlike branches against the deep gray sky beyond the weedy plots, marking the edge of the "pleasure gardens."

But Shar's interest lay here, not out there. Food for Madoc, his guests, and the horde of servants had to come from somewhere, and it was not from anywhere within his realm. Instead, there was a Gate out here, a Gate set to a neutral area where Madoc's servants could obtain the needed foodstuffs. It would probably be a fairly unpleasant place to visit, but Shar didn't intend to be there for long.

She signaled Tannim to follow her, across the garden to the wooden platform and arched roof that marked this Gate position. Somewhat to her surprise, it was *not* guarded; a dropped spear proved that the goblin that usually guarded this Gate had deserted his post. Beside the platform were burlap bags full of garbage, and it occurred to her then that the Gate could be as useful for disposing of kitchen refuse as it was bringing the raw material in. For a moment she toyed with trying that setting—

No, I think not. I don't believe I want to visit an Unseleighe garbage dump.

Not so much because it was a garbage dump as because such a place would be a fine place for scavengers. Unseleighe scavengers were generally not things you wanted to meet under any circumstances.

Unless, of course, you happened to be toting an AK-47.

In her guise as a kitchen servant, she had been once to the "market," and she had noted then how the Unseleighe seneschal had set the Gate. She triggered the spell herself this time, and the crude wooden arch filled with a dark haze. She motioned to Tannim to enter; he bowed mockingly and shook his head.

"After you, lady," he said quietly. So, he didn't trust her? Well, she couldn't exactly blame him.

She walked right through the Gate, ignoring the brief internal jarring as she crossed the boundary between *here* and *there.* A moment later, Tannim joined her, and she banished the Gate quickly, before anyone in Madoc's hall could stumble into the garden and notice that it had been activated.

After the relative silence of the garden, the noise here left her a little numb. The stench of the place could only be compared to a cross between a feedlot and a garbage dump. Fortunately, the merchants here were too busy trying to sell their wares to pay any attention to a couple of human types standing beside the Gate platform looking stunned.

"Come on," Shar said, nodding her head at the Gate. "We aren't going to be here long. I can reset this thing to a place that's a little friendlier." She saw that he was staring at the rows of meat merchants and added, "You really don't want to know what they're selling. Trust me."

He was already about as pale as a human could get; he swallowed hard and nodded. "Ah—by the way, I don't suppose we could get to my car from here, could we?"

She considered the question for a moment; his suggestion had a lot of merit. She already knew the Mach I had some very complex spells worked into its fabric, and there was every reason to think that he might be using it as a kind of magical storage battery as well. It might prove very useful.

"Not directly," she said after a moment. "Why?"

"Because it has a lot of protections on it," he replied with open honesty. "Other things, too. It's Cold Iron; lots of things down here can't cope with it. We're already in trouble; couldn't we really use a safe haven, a rolling base of operations?"

She nodded, and not at all reluctantly. "It's going to take us about a dozen Gates to get there, but yes, I can get us there from here eventually."

Tannim looked over his shoulder at the marketplace and shuddered. "How about if we start now—before someone out there needs to replace his inventory?"

One of the meat merchants, a boggle, had noticed them, and his eyes narrowed with speculation. Granted, a lot of the Unseleighe had human servants, or rather, slaves—but such slaves usually didn't loiter anywhere. They didn't dare.

"Good idea," she said shortly, and turned to reset the Gate to one of its other destinations.

Anyplace with fresh air. . . .

CHAPTER EIGHT

Tannim slid into the driver's seat of his beloved Mustang, shut the door, and simply leaned back in the familiar surroundings. He had never been quite as happy to see any material object as he'd been to see his Mustang still waiting there in the middle of the amber room. The journey to reach it had been a harrowing one in terms of all the strange and menacing slices of Underhill they'd had to traverse. He was still astonished at Shar's ability to pick her way across all of those Gates. She must have an incredible memory. . . .

But they made it, and without any opposition to speak of. For the first time since he'd come Underhill, he felt relatively safe. There was Cold Iron between him and any enemies now, and lots of it. There were spells of protection and defense built into the very sheet metal. He had reserves of magical energy stored here as well; energies that he badly needed.

And his magic-imbued crowbar, his weapon of choice in any confrontation with the Unseleighe, was right under the seat where he could grab it.

The other door opened and closed as Shar slipped into the passenger's side and shut the door as soon as she was seated. He noted that she *locked* it, too, and did the same on his side. She fumbled for a moment with the controls

on her seat before getting the hang of it and sliding it back
as far as it would go.

Shar. Now, there was a mystery wrapped in an enigma:
half-*kitsune*, half-dragon, all perplexing—

*And one I'd better figure out before she turns around
and stabs me in the back.*

Chinthliss himself hadn't known where she stood but
had assumed she was not on the side of truth, justice, and
apple pie. Tannim had been so happy to see her, though,
back in that Rubik's Prison, that he hadn't given a thought
to what Chinthliss had said about her. Or, frankly, a fat
damn about her motives in cracking him out of there. Her
motives didn't matter, as long as she was getting him free.
If she was leading him into another and different trap,
well, maybe it would be easier to escape or talk his way
out of than the last. The important thing was that he was
buying a little more time, and in an uncertain universe,
every moment counted. It gave him a little more opportunity to think things through. Something unexpected
might happen.

So far, so good.

"All right, we made it. Now what? Aren't Madoc and
his Merry Men going to come straight here as soon as they
get over fighting with each other?" he asked, opening his
eyes and blinking them wearily. How long had he gone
without rest? Long enough; his eyes felt puffy and swollen, very heavy.

He looked over at Shar's lovely profile; she smiled a little
and shook her head. "No," she said with a ghost of a
chuckle. "No, I put a lot of masking spells on your car
to deaden the effect of so much Cold Iron here—then I
told them that I'd moved it to a safer place. Madoc won't
go anywhere in person if he has the choice. The spells work
like that silk sheet we put in the trunk; your Mach I is
insulated from the energies Underhill now—which means
that they are not going to be able to detect it by its effect
on the world around it. They have absolutely no reason
to think I left it here. I don't believe any of the Unseleighe
Madoc's got know these masking spells are even possible,
so they're going to take me at my word if they don't see

Death-Metal effects here. And scrying is so costly in terms of time and energy that I don't think they'll make the attempt. They'd have to have something of yours, mine, or the vehicle's for scrying to find it anyway. We can actually afford to get a little rest, then be on our way."

"How?" he asked skeptically. "Drive out of here?"

To his surprise, she nodded. "This place was meant for creatures larger than this vehicle; the doors and hallways will all accommodate it, and this room is on the ground floor. We can drive it out into the garden; there is a Gate there as well as the one in here. We will have to take our chances on *where* it goes, though; the only setting that I know of would land us in a fairly unpleasant and unfriendly place. I can see how many other settings there are, and you can pick one, and we'll hope it takes us somewhere familiar."

He nodded. She turned to him then, pulling her hair away from her face and looking at him rather wistfully. "I don't suppose you have anything in the way of food in here, do you? I'm awfully hungry. I *could* get something from the garden, but I'd rather not leave the car, frankly. This is about the first time I've felt safe outside of my—my own place."

He lifted an eyebrow at her, quite well aware of gnawing hunger in his own innards. "You mean our gracious host didn't offer you dinner?"

She made a little face. "You saw the kitchen; you saw what was in it. Would you eat anything prepared there?"

He had to grin, just a little, and reached behind the seat. "Here—" he said, handing her one of the high-energy sports-bars he kept back there. "I fool my body into thinking this is food all the time. It's not exactly cordon bleu, but it'll keep you going." He looked back around the side of the seat. "I've got crackers and Spraycheeze back there too, if you'd rather."

"This will be fine," she responded, unwrapping the bar and nibbling on it.

There were dented drink-boxes of Gatorade back behind the seat as well; he fished out a pair and handed her one. She nibbled at the bar daintily, but not as if she disliked the taste. He wondered what a *kitsune* normally ate; not sushi, surely. Somehow she didn't seem to be the sushi type.

He made short work of his own share and reclined the seat to its fullest. After sitting in that cube for hours, the car seat felt as luxurious as a featherbed. He was going to have to get some sleep; this seemed to be the safest place for it.

But worries swarmed through his mind, preventing any relaxation. How long, real-time, had he been Underhill? Time often moved very differently here; by the chronology of his own world, he could have been down here a few minutes, or a few months. His folks would be frantic—

I hope somebody thought of a story to tell them.

Chinthliss had obviously lost the link to the Mustang; *he* might be able to reach back to the human world with a Gate, but only at the price of expending everything he had and leaving himself open to any attacker.

That might be just what Shar was waiting for, in fact. Just because she'd been chummy with him so far today, that didn't mean she was on his side. She could be waiting to catch him in a moment of vulnerability.

Yeah, like asleep in this car.

But he didn't want to think about that. He didn't even want to consider it. He wanted to hear that she had somehow seen what her former allies really were like and had rejected them.

I want to find out that she's turned into a good guy, darn it. I want—hell, might as well admit it. I want her to be the girl in my dreams.

Well, there was another objection to opening up a Gate on his own. He was no Chinthliss; he would need quite a bit of time to establish that Gate, and such a huge expenditure of power would signal his presence as effectively as a Las Vegas-style neon sign.

Yeah. "Good Eats Here." Bad. Very bad.

So how was he going to get home again? Drive cross-Underhill? What was *that* going to do to the Mustang? He could create small planes of force, like magical ramps, all day long. They weren't too tough to make. He could even create those from inside the car, while it was in motion, so that should take care of stairs, lumps, and small ravines.

And where in heck are the gas stations down here, anyway?

Where did Shar figure into all this? What *was* she all about? Was she friend, foe, or neither?

"So," he said carefully, staring through the windshield at the throne at the other end of the room. "Why don't you start with some explanations? Like, how come you're suddenly my friend?"

She stiffened a little, then wrapped both hands around her drink-box, propping it on her knee. "You know who I am," she stated. "Who my father is." Her voice was completely neutral, and he nodded just as neutrally.

"Your name is Shar, your father is a dragon named Charcoal. He is an enemy of my mentor, Chinthliss, and an ally of the Unseleighe." He waited for her response; it was a curt nod. "I'm assuming you are, or were, an ally of the Unseleighe yourself. Your mother is a *kitsune*; Charcoal and Chinthliss both courted her, and Chinthliss won her, temporarily at least. That's basically all I know."

"My blood-father is a manipulative control freak," Shar replied bitterly. "I was raised supposedly as *your* opposite number. I was supposed to be everything you are not. Fortunately, Mother made certain that Charcoal wasn't the only creature with a hand in my upbringing. I parted company with him some time ago; our parting was less than friendly and he has forgiven neither Mother nor myself."

She glanced at him to see how he was taking this; he kept his expression neutral, but nodded.

"Unfortunately I was taught by Unseleighe and spent a lot of time in several of their domains. I began severing as many ties with his old allies as I deemed feasible, but—much as it galls me to admit this—there were some I didn't dare cut off completely. If I had, they would have been mortally offended." She bit her lip, and looked at her hands.

"And offending an Unseleighe prince can have very

permanent results," Tannim commented. He could understand that; heck, he lived it. "They hate everybody, and it's only when they want something out of you that you can trust them within limited bounds. It's just a good thing that there are rules even they don't dare break."

"Exactly." She blinked rapidly, and rubbed her eyes. "I was still *supposed* to be your opposite; I went on studying you, partly because it didn't do any harm, and partly because if Father wanted me to be your opposite, I wanted to see what I was supposed to be the opposite of. You posed something of a challenge, actually, trying to come up with things I could do to match your skills. I've been watching you, on and off, for years. Since you were in high school, in fact."

She'd been studying him? For *years*? He couldn't conceal his shock and surprise—and it was that shock that made him blurt out what he would not otherwise have revealed. "Did you dream about me the way I—"

She brought her head up like a startled deer and stared directly into his eyes, her pupils wide with shock and surprise. "You dreamed about *me*? When?"

Good one, Tannim. You really stepped on your dick that time. Well, it was too late now; might as well fess up. "At least once a month, sometimes as often as every other night, for years. Since Chinthliss first came across to my side of the Hill, anyway." He couldn't help himself; he felt his ears turning hot as he flushed. Would she guess just what some of those dreams had been about?

But she averted her eyes, and pink crept over her cheeks. "I—dreamed too, about you. I thought it was just because I was studying you."

Quick, get the subject back on track before you really stick your foot in your mouth. Don't ask what she dreamed about! "Right," he said more harshly than he intended. "So—now what? How do you figure into this mess? Besides challenging me, I mean; I suppose that was on this Madoc Skean's orders. Why'd you get me out of that prison?"

"I caused it," she said in a very small voice. Her blush deepened to a painful crimson, and she stared fixedly at her clenched hands crushing her empty drink-box. "It's my fault you're Underhill in the first place. I was the one who brought your car here."

So that's why—! Damn it—

"I didn't expect you to follow it so fast!" she continued, an edge of desperation in her voice, as she finally turned to meet his accusing gaze. "I was—oh, I was under pressure from Madoc Skean. I didn't know what to do, I mean, I really got a rush out of challenging you, but he kept pushing for me to—"

"To get rid of me," he supplied, flatly. "So?"

"So I was trying to buy time for both of us! I couldn't risk a direct confrontation with Madoc Skean, I didn't want to actually consummate the challenge, and I was trying to buy us both time!" Her hands tightened on the drink-box. "I thought—I thought you'd follow the car in a few days at best, and by then, I'd have some idea of how to put Madoc off further, or I'd have managed to create a rift among his other allies, or you'd have gotten in touch with your Seleighe friends. And I had no idea this car was going to make such a huge disturbance when it came across!" The muscles of her throat looked tight, and there was a line of strain between her brows. "Madoc had a lot of ideas; he thought that without the Mach I you might choose something other than 'racing' as your weapon. And in case you decided to go chasing after it, he expected to use the car as bait in a trap, and I was the only one that could bring it Underhill for him. My plan was to keep the fact that I actually had it hidden from Madoc until I could talk to you. . . ."

Her voice faltered and died, and she licked her lips unhappily. But she did not avert her gaze, and she seemed sincere. He looked into her eyes and saw no falsehood there.

Could he believe her?

Ah, hell, why not?

"Okay," he said into the thick, leaden silence. "Okay, I'll accept that. Now, why are you helping me?"

She dropped her eyes for a moment, then looked up again, with a spark of defiance in her expression. "Because I got you into this," she said. "The scales have to be balanced before we decide on anything else; that's *kitsune* law and custom. I got you into this, but now I've gotten you out of this. You have to release me from that debt."

But he shook his head slightly. She was not going to get off the hook that easily. *He* was still Underhill, and so was the Mach I; springing him from Madoc Skean's little reception didn't even things out. "Sorry," he told her. "I can't do that. I'm not *out of this* yet, I'm only out of Madoc's clutches, and that may just be temporarily. I can't release you from your debt until I'm back in my world, and my car, too."

She flinched, but she nodded; she obviously saw the justice of his demand. Her cheeks were so pale that he longed to touch her and reassure her.

He wanted to do more than just touch her, if it came down to that. Unbidden dream-memories told him of any number of ways this could go—

But this wasn't a dream. He couldn't make that kind of assumption.

He tore his gaze away from hers and stared out the windshield again, trying to calm the chaos of his mind and heart.

He just wasn't certain how to act—did he behave as if she was a stranger, or as if she really *was* the person he had dreamed about? This was as confusing as all hell; it felt as if he *knew* her, as if he had known her intimately for years! It was all those damned dreams, where she'd figured as his lover. They'd had a solid feeling, a reality to them, that made the current situation positively schizoid. He didn't *know* her in any sense; they'd never met before she'd nailed that glove to his Mustang. Yet at the same time, all the little things she did, the tiny quirks of behavior, the ways she reacted, the bits of body language, were all exactly the way he "remembered."

"I hate to ask you what your dreams were about, if they were anything like mine," she whispered across his confusion.

"If you knew," he replied, trying desperately to make a joke about it, "you'd slap me into next week."

"Oh, I don't know about that," she said, which was exactly

what he would have expected her to say if this was a dream, and not at all what he had rationally expected to hear. He looked over at her in startlement to find her smiling wanly at him. "After all, I am half-*kitsune*. We have a certain reputation; one that's been known to attract even dragons."

His body reacted in a predictable manner before his mind took over and gathered up all the reins firmly. *This isn't the time or the place,* he told his galloping libido firmly. *We're surrounded by potential enemies, we're exhausted—and on top of that, the front seat of a '69 Mustang is absolutely impossible. These are bucket seats. The backseat is practically nonexistent. You'd have to be a contortionist.*

"Trust me," he said firmly. "You'd smack me so hard I'd lose teeth."

He closed his eyes for a moment—just for a few seconds—

It was long enough; she struck as swiftly as a cobra. Before he could open them again, she'd writhed around in her seat, leaning over the center console, and planted her mouth firmly on his. One hand snuck around behind the back of his head, holding him so he couldn't jerk away.

Not that he wanted to!

Without the use of anything as confusing as words, she was letting him know that her dreams had probably been along the same lines as his own. And in no uncertain terms, she was telling him that she had enjoyed those dreams.

When she'd succeeded in setting every nerve afire and causing a complete meltdown of his brain, she let him go, returning to her seat with a teasing smile on her lips. "I don't think I would smack you, if those dreams were like mine—unless you asked nicely," was all she said.

"I—guess not." He blinked and tried to make his frontal lobes function again, after having the blood supply to his brain rush off elsewhere. Should he follow up on this?

If I do, I could get into more trouble than I can handle right now. If I don't, it could still be trouble, but not as complicated.

"This isn't a—a good time to get into anything—ah— distracting," he ventured. "We aren't really *safe* here, just safer for the moment than a lot of other places." He hoped she understood; the lover who had shared more than just his bed would have.

"You don't like it dangerous?" she purred.

"No, and you wouldn't, either."

She nodded; reluctantly, he thought, but in agreement. "Damn. You're right. I'm not happy about it, though." She smiled weakly. "I shouldn't have done that, but I couldn't resist. Let's just call that a—a promissory note, a raincheck, until a better time."

Jeez, some raincheck! Makes me want to call Fighting Eagle for a thunder-dance! He yawned, exaggerating it a little. "Look, Shar, I'm not capable of thinking or much of anything at the moment. I am beat, and I need some rest badly. Can you stay awake long enough for me to catch a couple of hours of sleep? Once I can think straight, we can make some plans, but right now, I wouldn't want to make any kind of decisions. I'm two burritos short of a combination plate when I'm this tired."

She nodded, and to his relief, she did not seem put out by the fact that he didn't follow through on her tacit invitation. *But the Shar I know—knew—think I know would understand.* "Get some rest, then," she said with surprising gentleness. "I'll keep watch."

Could he trust her?

Did it matter?

Not really. If he couldn't trust her, he was already doomed, and he might as well get some sleep. And if he *could* trust her—

—he might as well get some sleep.

"Thanks, Shar," he said, and smiled. He reached out and squeezed her hand. "Thanks a lot. It's nice to have somebody watching at my back in this."

Her reaction—blinking as if such a thing had never occurred to her—made him wonder about her past. Living with the Unseleighe would only teach you that there could be no such thing as a partner. But someone or something had to teach her that it was possible.

Has she ever had someone she could depend on? Her mother, maybe.

"I can see that it would be," she replied wistfully. Then she shook her head and became her usual, confident self. "You get that sleep; I probably need a lot less than you do, anyway. When you wake again, we'll make some plans."

"Right." He smiled again, and closed his eyes firmly. Having her so close was such a temptation—

Go to sleep, Tannim. And—jeez, if you can help it, don't dream about Shar.

Joe padded up to the old barn a little more than two hours after he'd left it, sweating, but not even close to being winded. It had felt good to run full-out like that, with the cool night air all around him and the drone of cicadas coming from all directions. When he was doing something like running, he didn't have to think so much about things. Like how all of this was more than a little crazy.

He'd let himself into the Drake's house and had left a note propped on the kitchen table, explaining pretty much what he'd suggested to Chinthliss. Kansas City was far enough away that the Drakes would not expect to hear anything for at least a couple of days, especially since this was supposed to be an emergency. And if they weren't back with Tannim in a couple of days, then things really would have gone seriously wrong.

To lend credence to the note, Joe had rummaged through Tannim's room and his own, making it look as if some things, but not all, had been taken. Then he had gotten what he'd come for from its hiding place up inside the boxsprings of his bed. A .45 automatic, basically the same handgun as the military surplus he'd trained with. Pity that it wasn't an M-16 or some other fully automatic assault rifle, but—well, it wasn't supposed to have been a bullet-hose for all-out attacks but something to defend himself from one or more of the Chosen Ones until the real law showed up. He had to keep reminding himself that he was *supposed* to be a civilian now. Most civvies didn't even have *this* much firepower, when it came right down to it. They saw guys like Dirty Harry in the movies, and that was about the extent of their gun knowledge.

Which was why, of course, whenever one of them *did* get scared over something and get himself a weapon, the people who usually got hurt or killed by it were people in his own family. Frank had once remarked that for a bunch of paranoid nut cases, the Chosen Ones had the best gun-safety classes he'd ever heard of. Joe had not only taken those classes, he'd taught them to the Junior Guard.

He had strapped on the shoulder holster, and slung extra pouches of ammo on their web-belts around his waist. They were heavy, but you never knew. . . . Better take all he had; there probably weren't any gun shops where he was going.

He was used to running with full pack and kit; this had been nothing, really, no kind of weight at all. He had let himself out of the house, moving so quietly he didn't even make the floor creak, and took off back the way he had come.

He was halfway afraid that Chinthliss had used his acquiescence as a ruse, or had changed his mind, and that when he got back to the barn he would find the other two gone. Then what would he do?

Call Keighvin at Fairgrove, he supposed, and let him know what had happened. And hope that he didn't let anything slip to Mr. and Mrs. Drake when they asked him where their son was.

But the glow of heavy shields over the barn told him that Chinthliss and Fox were still there, and as he ran back up the track through the tall grass, intermittent flashes of bright white light beneath the golden glow indicated that they were up to something. None of this was visible if he did that little mental trick and turned what Tannim had called his "mage-sight" off. This other kind of sight—it was so strange, seeing colored glows around people, and the occasional figure that he knew wasn't "really" there for the rest of the world. It had started when he'd seen Sarah for the first time, and thanks to the training Bob and Al had given him, it was getting stronger all the time. Every time he used it, he saw more. Was this how everyone at Fairgrove saw the world, bathed in extra colors and populated by more creatures than anyone else knew existed? Or was this something only a few people could do?

Well, he'd find all that out later, if he made it through this.

If.

He had to think of it in those terms. He had no illusions that this was going to be some romp through Wonderland; Fox was terrified, and even though Chinthliss tried to seem glib about the situation, Tannim's mentor was worried. There was danger here, much more real than the "danger" his father had prophesied.

He was about to get into something he hadn't really wanted to deal with, and something he wasn't really prepared for. Magic. What the hell did he know about magic, really? Not much when push came to shove. Not enough to use it as a weapon, probably not enough to put up an adequate defense of his own.

But Tannim, in the short time that Joe had known him, had become a "big brother," just as Jamie was his "little brother." Not a blood relationship, but one that went far deeper than blood and bone and genes. Tannim was family. You stood by your family. When they were in trouble, you helped them.

Fox stood beside the gap in the wall that had once been the doorway, his tails swishing nervously. Joe trotted up. The tall grass resisted him a little and caught on his jeans. Chinthliss stood in the center of the barn, as Tannim had stood not that long ago. He didn't *seem* to be doing anything, but Joe knew better than to assume that nothing was going on.

"What's up?" he whispered to Fox, wiping the sweat off his forehead with the back of his arm.

"He's building a Gate," Fox whispered back. "The whole thing; all the Gates where we want to go are booked up and unless we build our own, we can't get there from here. I gave him all the *oomph* I had to spare, so now he's channeling in everything he can get from outside. It's not that easy, building a Gate in your world; magic runs thinner here. We're just lucky that it hasn't been tapped around here much."

Just as he finished that last sentence, Chinthliss exclaimed in satisfaction, and a tiny glowing dot appeared in the air in front of him, at just about eye-level. Chinthliss cupped his hands before him, catching the spark for a moment so that his hands glowed and the bones showed through the translucent flesh. Then Chinthliss slowly spread his hands wide; the dot became a glowing ring, which grew as he spread his hands, until it was a circle of light taller than he and broader than his outstretched arms. A dark haze filled it, a haze you couldn't see through, and which made Joe shiver for reasons he didn't quite understand.

"You've come exactly in time, Joe," Chinthliss said without turning around. "We are ready, now. You and I, that is," he amended. "Fox can journey there without the need of a Gate; one of the advantages of being a spirit-form."

"Right. See you at the bandstand?" Fox replied, and vanished without waiting for an answer.

"Will he really be there?" Joe said a bit dubiously, for all that Fox was his old "friend" from childhood. Even his memories painted Fox as something less than reliable and inclined to tricks.

"He'll be there," Chinthliss replied grimly. "If he's not, well, he knows that *I* will be looking for him when all this is over. Being called 'Stumpy' will be the least of his problems."

Joe stepped across the threshold of the barn to join Chinthliss in front of the circle of light. "So what do we do?" he asked bravely, putting the best face he could on all this. "I—I'm afraid I don't know a lot about this kind of thing."

Chinthliss looked down at him, and the dark eyes changed from hard and purposeful to warm and kindly, all in a single moment. "We simply step across," he told Joe. "There will be a moment of disorientation, then you will find yourself in the place we wish to go to. And you are doing very well, young man. You are bearing up under some very strange experiences, and doing so with more composure than many with more years than you."

Joe looked up into those odd, oriental eyes, saw or sensed *far* more years than he had dreamed, and swallowed. "I don't suppose you have any advice before we do this, do you?"

Chinthliss shook his head. "Nothing that would help. Are you ready?"

Joe took a very deep breath, allowed himself to be *conscious* for a moment of the weight in his shoulder holster, and remembered with a flush of pride how good a marksman he was. Heck, he wasn't too bad at hand-to-hand, either. Chinthliss had obviously included him in this party because of that expertise. If he simply kept his eyes, ears, and mind open, obeyed his orders, and behaved in a professional manner, everything should be all right, no matter how strange the external circumstances became.

"I'm ready, sir," he said, proud of the fact that his voice did not break or quaver, and that he stood tall, straight, and confidently. "You first, or me?"

In answer, Chinthliss gestured at the circle of light. Joe repressed a shiver when he remembered how Tannim had stepped into an identical circle and vanished. . . .

He took a convulsive grip on his belt and stepped through; his skin tingled all over, as if he'd grasped a live wire, his eyes blurred, the world swirled and spun around him, and he gasped as his stomach lurched, exactly as if he'd gone into free-fall for a moment. He flexed his knees involuntarily.

Then with a shock, he went from night into full day, and his feet landed on soft turf. Since his knees were already flexed to take the strain, he only staggered a little to catch his balance. As he straightened, he saw that he stood in the center of what looked like a city park, with a white bandstand or gazebo in the middle. By the bright light, it had to be just about noon, and where they'd come from, it was around two in the morning.

Overhead, he heard someone whistling.

He looked up in startlement to see a cartoon sun in the middle of a flat, blue sky, staring down at him jovially. You could look right *at* it without even blinking; lemon-yellow, it had round, fat cheeks, blue eyes, a wide mouth, and a fringe of pointed petal-like rays. It smiled at him as soon as it saw he was looking at it, winked broadly, and waved at him with one of the petals.

Stunned, he waved back automatically. It grinned, and went back to whistling and bobbing a little in time to the song—a *real* song—that was also being whistled by a vivid blue and red bird perched on the top of the gazebo. Puffy, flat-looking marshmallow clouds sat in the sky with the sun, a sky that was an unshaded, turquoise blue, without any variation from horizon to horizon. The emerald grass under his feet was more like carpet than grass, and did not crush down under his weight. There was no breeze, yet the air smelled fresh and clean. In fact, it smelled exactly like freshly washed sheets.

They also weren't alone. The other creatures were not very near, and they didn't seem to care that a Gate had been opened in the park, although many noticed. There were otters and foxes, though none of the foxes looked like FX. There was a massive cobalt-blue unicorn, and a centaur with a black, d'Artagnan beard. They were having a picnic with what could only be called a foxtaur, and a small golden-colored dragon, and an oddly hunched, very large bird. A white unicorn mare chased playfully after a humanoid, black-horned unicorn wearing black leather and spikes, howling taunts. And overhead, a red-and-umber gryphon with broad coppery wings glided in to join the rest.

He turned as a crackling, sizzling sound beside him startled him again. There was nothing there for a second— then a familiar arm clad in Armani-tailored silk phased into existence, as if the owner was pushing his way through an invisible barrier, exactly like an expensive special effect. The rest of Chinthliss followed shortly as Joe watched in utter fascination. He seemed to arrive suspended a few inches above the plush green lawn and dropped as soon as all of him was "there."

Chinthliss landed with flexed knees, just as Joe had. He straightened, looked around, and nodded with satisfaction.

"Good," he said. "At least we made *our* transition safely. Now, where is Fox?"

"Right here." Fox strolled up from behind them, although Joe could have sworn that there hadn't been any-one there a moment earlier. He was in the fox-footed, three-tailed James Dean form, the one with the red leather jacket. "Now where?"

"One moment." Chinthliss glanced at Joe. "Young man, would you please grasp our friend?"

Joe didn't understand what Chinthliss was trying to prove—he couldn't touch Fox, he already knew that—but he shrugged, reached out, and made a grab for Fox's arm.

And with a shock, realized that he was holding a very solid, completely real, red-leather clad arm.

"What—" he said, startled. "How—but—"

Fox looked at Chinthliss in irritation.

"So what were you trying to prove?" he growled. "You *know* I'm real here!"

"That's what I was trying to prove," Chinthliss said with ironic satisfaction. "That you were not playing any of your *kitsune* tricks with me and projecting a spirit-form here as well, rather than risking your real self. Thank you, Joe."

"You're welcome," Joe responded automatically, dropping his hold on Fox's arm and backing up a step. He hadn't expected that. If Fox was real here—was that cartoon sun up above real as well?

He didn't want to think about it.

But then he suddenly realized that he really didn't *have* to think about it. His part in this mission was very simple. He didn't have to try and figure out what was real and what wasn't; all he really had to do was keep a lookout for trouble and hit it or shoot it if it got too close. And if it turned out that all this was just one big hallucination, well, no problem. He'd wake up from this dream, or in the looney bin, and pick up his life where he'd left off. Right?

Yeah. Sure.

"I think our first logical destination would be the Drunk Tank," Chinthliss continued, unperturbed. "All news comes there, sooner or later—and if any of Tannim's friends are here, that is where they will go."

Fox sighed with resignation, but shrugged. "Suit yourself," he replied. "You know this place as well as I do, and you know Tannim's friends better than I do."

"Are you going to build a Gate again?" Joe asked nervously. He hadn't liked the sensations of crossing into this place, and he wasn't certain that he wanted a repetition of the experience quite so soon.

"Build a Gate?" Chinthliss said. "Here? Good heavens, no."

"Then how are we going to get to this place?" Joe asked, more than a little confused now, since there didn't seem to *be* anything here except lush grass, a few fairly normal-looking trees, some benches, the gazebo, and the cartoon sky. Literally; the sky appeared to intersect with the ground no more than a few hundred yards away on all sides.

"How?" Chinthliss said, and whistled loudly, waving an arm.

And a fat taxi, bright yellow with black checks, shaped rather like an overgrown VW Bug, pulled up beside them. Joe blinked; he *knew* that thing hadn't been anywhere near them a moment ago, yet there it was!

A creature like a mannish badger leaned out the window. "Hiya folks!" the thing growled. "Where to?"

"The Drunk Tank," FX told it blandly.

"This is how," Chinthliss said to Joe, opening up the door and gesturing for him and Fox to enter. "We take a taxi, of course. It's too far to walk."

"Of course," Joe echoed in a daze, climbing into the rear seat. "A taxi. Of course."

"Well what else would we use?" Chinthliss retorted, as he wedged himself inside as well, with Fox squeezed between them making Warner Brothers cartoon faces. "A dragon?"

The taxi accelerated toward the flat blue sky, which looked more and more like a wall as they drew nearer. Joe closed his eyes and gripped the seat—they were going to hit! He waited for the impact, his teeth clenched tightly.

But a second later, the taxi screeched to a halt. "Here we are, folks!" came the cheerful voice from the front. "Thanks for riding with me! See you soon!"

The door popped open on its own, and Joe stepped cautiously out onto the pavement.

Real pavement. Real, cracked cement.

The sky above them was dark here, with a haze of light-pollution above the buildings. This looked like any street in any bar-district in any big city he'd ever been in. The street was asphalt, the sidewalk and curb were chipped and eroded concrete with cracks in it, but there were no cigarette butts and other trash scattered around. Dirty brick buildings on both sides of the street stood four or five stories tall, with darkened storefronts on the ground floor, and lighted or darkened windows that might lead into offices or apartments in the stories above. The taxi had pulled up in front of another brick building with a neon sign in a small window, set into a wood panel where a much larger window had once been. The sign flashed *The Drunk Tank* twice in red, then flashed a green neon caricature of a tipsy tank with a dripping turret the third time. To the right of the building was a parking lot; to the left, a vacant lot with a fence around it. The lot was about half full of the kind of "beater" cars most people of modest means drove in a big city. They were just about in the middle of the block, which seemed to be pretty much deserted. A couple of cars and a panel-truck were parked on the other side of the street, in front of a black-and-silver sign which read *Dusty's Furley-Davidson*. Below it was what could only be an authentic Springer Softail. With a warning sticker.

The cartoonish taxi did not belong here, but the driver didn't seem to care. It waited until Chinthliss got out, then buzzed off down the street.

Fox still had his fox-feet, but he'd lost the tails somewhere. Chinthliss still looked entirely human.

"Do bullets work here?" Joe whispered to FX as Chinthliss led the way to the red-painted door.

"Oh, yeah," Fox replied, a little grimly. "Yeah, bullets work just fine. You're not in some kind of cartoon, no matter what it looks like. The last bunch of city planners were animation buffs and made the sky and all look like this, but this is real. This may look weird to you right now, but bullets work, knives work, crossbows and darts work, getting hit hurts a *lot*, and dead is very, very dead. No second chance, no resurrection, no magic spell to bring you back. Keep that in mind if trouble starts."

Joe gulped. "Right."

Fox followed on Chinthliss' heels into the bar; Joe followed on Fox's.

Inside, the bar looked a lot bigger than it had from the outside. A lot nicer, too—kind of like one of those fancy nightclubs in movies about the Roaring Twenties and the Depression. They stood in a waiting room at the top of a series of descending tiers that held two- or four-person tables. Each table was spread with a spotless white tablecloth, centered with flowers and a candle-lamp. Wall-sconces made of geometric shapes of black metal and mirrors fastened invisibly to the white walls held brilliant white lights. To Joe's left was a check-room with a hat-check girl and the hostess' stand; beyond those was a curving balcony looking out over the tables, with a few doors leading off of it. To his right was the bar, which curved along the wall behind the top tier of tables as one immaculate, unbelievably precise arc of mahogany. Everything else was done in shiny black, chrome, and glass. At the bottom of the tiers was a dance floor with a geometric pattern in black and white marble laid out on it—and somehow lit from below—and behind that a glossy black stage large enough for a complete big-band orchestra. From the stands pushed to one side and the classic grand piano, it often held such a band, but right now there was a combo composed of a keyboard-player, a drummer with a full electronic rig, a guy with an impressive synth-set, and a female vocalist. They were covering "Silk Pajamas" by Thomas Dolby, and those in the crowd who were actually listening seemed to be enjoying it. And singing along.

But Joe had to do another reality check when he looked the crowd over.

Around about half the folks here were human; plenty of them were wearing outfits that would have had them barred at the door in the real world. Said "clothing" ranged everywhere from full military kit to as close to nothing as personal modesty would allow. In the case of some people, that pretty much meant clothing-as-jewelry—or, as Frank had once put it, "gownless evening straps." Joe tried not to stare at the blonde girl in the G-string, fishnets, diamond-choker, and heels; she was centerfold-perfect—and her brawny, saturnine escort could have picked him up with one hand and broken him over his knee without breaking a sweat. *He* was done up in what looked like medieval chainmail, the real thing. The sword slung along his back was certainly real looking.

Fortunately, both of them were too busy watching the stage and the dancers on the dance floor to notice his stares or his blushes.

The rest of the patrons—including most of those on the dance floor—were definitely *not* any more human than the creatures he'd seen in the park. The couple drawing the most attention at the moment was a pair of bipedal cat-creatures, one Siamese, the other a vivid red lynx, who were showing off their dance steps. But sharing the floor with them was a female with green hair and wearing what appeared to be a dress made of leaves who was dancing alone, a couple of elves, two fox couples, a pine marten dancing with a large monitor lizard, and a pair of beautiful young sloe-eyed men, dark and graceful, with the hindquarters and horn-buds of young goats, who were dancing together in a sensuous way that made Joe blush as badly as the blonde girl had.

He averted his eyes and fixed them firmly on Chinthliss' back. The dragon was speaking to the hostess—who seemed to have a wonderful personality, if you didn't mind the fact that otherwise she was a dog. She nodded, and wagged the tail that barely showed below her Erté dress. Chinthliss made his own way towards the bar. Joe and Fox followed him.

Chinthliss ordered "yuppie water"; Fox, with a defiant glance at Chinthliss, ordered a rum-and-Coke. Joe waved the bartender away. First of all, he had no idea how he was going to pay for a drink, or in what currency—and secondly, it was a bad idea to have your hands busy with something else if a situation came up.

Chinthliss scanned the crowd, then turned back to the bartender as the man (Arabic-looking, but with pointed ears) brought him his drink and Fox's. "So, Mahmut, have you heard or seen anything of Tannim?" the dragon asked casually, as he pushed what appeared to be a coin made of gold across to the bartender. The being slid it expertly out of sight, as he pretended to polish the bar with a soft cloth. "Not recently, Chinthliss," Mahmut replied, rubbing industriously at a very shiny spot. "Why? Are you looking for him? He *never* comes here anymore; in fact, as far as I know, he never goes out of the Seleighe Elfhames these days, if he leaves America at all."

Chinthliss sighed, and sipped the bubbling water. The band finished its number to the applause of the dancers and some of the people at the tables. The lights came down, and a pair of women, one very, very pale and in a long, white, high-collared dress, and one with long blond hair right down to the floor, wearing what appeared to be a dress made of glittering green fish scales, took the stage. The one in white sat down at the piano; the blonde took the microphone. A spotlight centered on the blonde, who lowered her eyelids for a moment and smiled sweetly.

The bartender tapped Joe on the shoulder; he jumped. When he turned to see what the man wanted, the fellow was holding out a pair of earplugs.

"You single?" the man asked. Joe flushed, and nodded. "You wouldn't be a virgin, by any chance, would you?" the bartender persisted, this time in a whisper.

This time Joe flushed so badly that he felt as if he was on fire.

"Thought so." The bartender nodded. "You'd better wear these if you don't want to end up following Lorelie around like a lost puppy for the rest of your short life." He held out the earplugs. Joe looked at Fox and Chinthliss, who both nodded.

"We're protected. I wouldn't worry so much about Lorelie, but her friend has appetites you wouldn't want to satisfy," Fox said solemnly. "Lamias are like that."

"Th—them?" Joe stammered.

"Yeah, them," Fox said. "Think of them as the Cocteau Twins gone horribly wrong. The L&L Music Factory, embalming optional."

Lamias? Lorelie? Something about both those names

rang a dim and distant bell in his mind, but he couldn't put a finger on what they meant. Still, if not only this bartender but Chinthliss and Fox thought he ought to put in those earplugs—well, maybe he'd better.

He took them gingerly and inserted them. And he discovered, rather to his surprise, that even with them in his ears he could hear perfectly well, if a little distantly.

There were waitresses circulating among the tables, he saw now, and they were handing out more earplugs. But oddly enough, only to the men—or rather, male creatures. The two young men with the goats' legs laughed and waved them away, as did one or two others, including the pine marten and the lizard, but most of the men took them and fitted them into their ears.

Interesting.

The pale girl at the piano began singing as soon as the last of the earplug-girls retired; Joe recognized the song as "Stormy Weather," and after a few bars, Lorelie began to sing.

She had a low, throaty voice, rather than the bell-like and pure tones Joe had half expected; there was no doubt, though, that in *his* world she'd have a lot of people offering her record contracts. Especially with that face and figure behind the voice. But he couldn't help but wonder what all the fuss was about—and why the earplugs?

Oh, well. When in Rome . . .

He turned his attention back to Chinthliss and the bartender.

". . . and we think he might have bitten off more than he can chew," Chinthliss was saying, as Mahmut listened attentively. "Look, I know you're on the Seleighe side of the fence, so to speak, at least most of the time. You know some of the kid's friends. If any of them show up here, can you pass that information on for me?"

Mahmut nodded gravely. "For a dog of an infidel, that one is a good boy," he replied. "For me, he arranged a lager distributor from America. He has done several of my friends a service or two in the past. For a chance to even the scales, I think that they would do much."

"What kind *is* his kind?" Joe whispered to Fox. FX

shrugged and muttered something that sounded like "gin," although that couldn't possibly be right. It was probably the earplugs. Joe made a move to take them out; Fox grabbed his hand to prevent him—

Just as someone entered the bar, stared at the singer below, and stopped dead in his tracks, as if transfixed.

It was a young man; one with branching antlers rising from his head, but otherwise quite normal-looking. As Joe paused with his hand on the plug in his ear, the newcomer shook his head violently, turned a deathly white, and made a kind of odd moaning noise.

His eyes glazed over, and he stumbled down the stairs between the tiers of tables, ignoring everything and everyone in his path. He staggered across the dance floor towards Lorelie, who ignored his presence completely, and dropped down at her feet in a crouch, gazing up at her with the adoration of a saint at the feet of the Almighty.

If Joe hadn't chanced to look in her direction, he might never have seen the piano player's reaction. If Lorelie was indifferent to her worshipper, the pale girl was *not*.

She stared at the young man with such pure, naked hunger that the word "hunger" simply did not describe the expression she wore. He might have been a thick, juicy steak, and she suffering starvation. Then she licked her lips and smiled.

Her teeth were all pointed, like a shark's.

"Poor kid," the bartender said distantly. "She got another one." And somehow Joe knew what he meant. Lorelie might have snared the man, but her accompanist was going to devour him somehow. Not just figuratively, either.

Joe rounded on the bartender, suddenly suffused with anger. "So why aren't you doing anything about it?" he hissed, one hand on the Colt. "Why do you let her sing here?"

Mahmut's eyes narrowed dangerously, but his voice remained calm and even. "Look, kid, we have placards in the lobby announcing that Lorelie's singing in here. The hat-check girl would have offered him earplugs. The hostess would have offered him earplugs. How much more do you want us to do? Shove the plugs in his ears?

This is a neutral realm; Lorelie's free to sing, we're free to hire her, and he's free to ignore the warnings. Who knows? Maybe he was suicidal. You may not like it, son, but you're not in Kansas anymore, either."

This is a neutral realm. Maybe he was suicidal. They know he's going to die, and no one is going to help him.

Joe felt cold all over. He looked at Mahmut's flat black eyes; looked back down at the bandstand, at Lorelie, at her admirer, at the piano player. He shivered, and briefly considered the ramifications of running down there and trying to save that poor guy—

Then he caught Fox's eyes. The *kitsune* shook his head slowly. He remembered all of Fox's warnings, shuddered, and turned away.

Mahmut spoke to him again. "Sometimes we get people doing that because there are a lot of ways to drain a man. Those two know most of them. I have been told that many are pleasurable and leave the man more alive than before. Some think the risk is worth it for the experience. The young buck there isn't likely to die—and he might enjoy it."

He *still* might have tried to think of some way of getting Lorelie's victim free, but he never got the chance.

At that moment, one of the waitresses (a delicate creature like a winged lizard with veil-like wings sprouting from her shoulder blades) came over and tapped Chinthliss on the arm. "Sir," she said, "the lady over there would like you and your friends to join her in the Blue Room."

Chinthliss shook his head impatiently, as the young creature pointed. "I do not have time—" he began, looking in the direction she indicated.

Then he stopped speaking, frozen with shock that even Joe could read. And beside him, Fox went as white as the girl at the piano.

Joe turned to see what they were looking at.

On the other side of the room, behind the last tier of tables where the bar was on this side, there were several doors that presumably led to private dining rooms. There was someone standing in front of one of those doors.

She wore the kimono and elaborate hairstyle of a traditional Japanese woman—Joe could only think "geisha," since he had no idea who else wore the kimonos with the long, trailing sleeves, or the hair pierced through with so many jeweled pins that her head looked like a pincushion. But although the body beneath the gown was that of a human woman, the face was that of a fox.

And behind her, fanned out like the glory of the peacock, was an array of fox tails that clearly belonged to her.

"Oh, shit," FX said weakly. "It's—it's—"

Chinthliss cleared his throat with difficulty.

"Tell the Lady Ako," he managed, after several tries, "that we would be honored to join her."

CHAPTER NINE

Shar watched Tannim out of the corner of her eye, hoping it wasn't obvious that she was watching him. If he felt her gaze resting on him, he probably wouldn't be able to sleep; he'd assume she was waiting for him to fall asleep so that she could do something unpleasant to him.

Well, she wouldn't *mind* doing something to him, but it wouldn't be unpleasant. If she had gotten his hormones dancing with that kiss, she'd sent her own into orbit. There hadn't been anyone who'd had that effect on her for a long, long time.

At least she knew one thing, now. She knew he'd had the same kind of erotic dreams of her that she'd had of him. The way he'd responded to her impulsive kiss had left no doubt in her mind of that. Enthusiasm under the surprise—and a great deal of heat under the control. He would feel *so good.* . . .

But Shar knew he was also not going to presume on those dreams. He didn't trust her yet and she couldn't blame him. But there was another thing: he didn't assume that her personality was anything like the person he'd dreamed about. He didn't know anything at all about her, and he acknowledged that. *I knew he was a cautious and clever man,* she mused as his breathing deepened, and he began to relax minutely. *This is just one more example of*

498

*that. I have the advantage here; I know that the lover in
my dreams is virtually identical in personality to the real
man—or at least, as much of the real man as I have been
able to observe over the years.*

And yet, even though he didn't trust *her* yet, it seemed
to her that he was willing to give her the benefit of the
doubt; he was apparently willing to give her the time to
prove to him by her actions that she could be trusted.

She sighed quietly. If that kiss was anything to go by,
he was just as talented and considerate as the dream-lover
had been. A far cry from the Unseleighe, or the relatively
shallow and skittish *kitsune* males. Those were the only
creatures of male gender she'd spent any time with; she'd
avoided human males simply out of disinterest. And if
Charcoal and Chinthliss were examples of dragonkind—

*They're either manipulative, selfish bastards who'll run
over the top of anything and anyone to get what they want,
or they're fast-talking, charming rogues who'd rather lose
everything they have than make a commitment.*

Bitter? Oh, a tad.

Tannim sighed and nestled down a little further into
his seat. Was he truly asleep? She shifted slightly, touched
the door handle and made it rattle just a little. He didn't
stir; his eyelids didn't even flicker. There were dark shadows
under his eyes, shadows that spoke eloquently of just how
exhausted he'd been. In sleep, he looked frighteningly frail,
and now she realized just how much of his appearance of
strength depended on his personality.

Well, now what? They couldn't stay here forever; they
probably shouldn't stay here longer than it took Tannim
to catch up on some rest and recover a bit. So, how to
get out of here?

There was the Gate in the garden; that was probably
their best bet. As she had pointed out, there would be no
difficulty in simply driving the Mustang out into the hall
and out the door into the garden. The Katschei had used
that particular Gate to get into the mortal world to steal
his collection of princesses, but there were five more
settings on it. They'd have to take their chances, but at
least she *would* recognize a potentially dangerous setting

for a destination she had encountered before. That would keep them out of Unseleighe domains, even if it did dump them off into unknown territory. If they kept traversing Gates, sooner or later she'd find her way back into a place she knew.

A pity that the Katschei hadn't left at least one setting empty; she could have used that to Gate somewhere friendly. Or at least, to somewhere neutral.

I would be very happy with neutral, she decided. *Particularly neutral and familiar. Most neutrals can be bought, and usually remain bought. In neutral territory I might be able to buy some help, or a way out of Underhill.*

Tannim slept very quietly; barely breathing, it seemed, head turned slightly into the seat that cradled him, one hand curled up beside his face. She touched his hair hesitantly. *So soft,* she thought with wonder, as she pulled her hand back before it betrayed her by turning the touch into a caress.

There was nothing impulsive about the strength of her reaction to him; in a way, it was inevitable, given how long she had studied him. If he had not interested her, she would have given up on her studies a long time ago, and none of this would be happening now. If he had not attracted her as well as interested her—

I probably would have done exactly what Madoc Skean wanted me to. I'd have gotten rid of him a long time ago.

And if she had not met him in her dreams? Difficult to say. She'd enjoyed her little glimpses into his life. She found him in some ways completely alien to her. Perhaps that was part of the root of her attraction; she couldn't predict him, and her *kitsune* heritage would always be intrigued by anything she didn't understand and couldn't predict. Just as she would always be repelled by something that bored her.

Tannim was anything but boring. . . .

On the other hand, Madoc Skean was *quite* predictable, and she ought to be trying to predict what *his* next move would be, not hovering over Tannim like some lovesick nymph.

She sat back in her own seat, reclining it to match

Tannim's, but turned her gaze outward, staring at the wall. Madoc had fled the dungeon with his own guards, and probably went straight to the isolated wing of the keep that contained his own quarters. Paranoid as any Unseleighe, he would not live in a place where he could not defend against all comers.

But as his allies fought their way to his Gate and left, and nothing whatsoever happened, he would collect his courage and his few functioning brain cells. What conclusions would he come to?

The most obvious would be that Tannim—or Tannim's impersonator—was somewhere in his stronghold still. But he had means to discover if that was true, and he would put those means in motion as soon as he knew his people had cleared the entire holding of potential troublemakers.

Sooner or later, he would learn that there his fears were completely groundless. He would learn that Tannim was not in his dungeon, nor anywhere else in his own domain. Then what?

Well, his allies had all deserted him. Even if he decided to first go after them, it would take a great deal of coaxing to bring most of his allies back. It would be possible to chase after Tannim without them, but Madoc Skean was a cautious sort, and he always preferred to operate from a position of strength. He really had two options at this point: try to mend the mess that had been made of his alliances and then pursue Tannim, or go after Tannim without any help.

She could hope that he would pursue his allies; she must plan that he would pursue Tannim. She would *have* to assume that Madoc would figure out that she was with Tannim, given that she had been there when they all discovered he'd "vanished."

Madoc would waste some time trying to figure out where she had gone in order to escape his stronghold. Sooner or later, he would narrow the possibilities to the Gate in the courtyard. Then he had six possible destinations; eventually he would find the Gate that led here, but unless he had a way to trace her movements, every succeeding Gate they took would lead to no less than three and as many as six more possibilities. So it was safe to assume that they had time enough for Tannim to get some sleep.

But after that—they should assume that Madoc could be no less than a single Gate behind them. Tannim and Shar could even have the misfortune to Gate into the same place at the same time as *they* tried to find them.

So who or what is Madoc going to have with him? Probably all of the Faceless Ones; they were the most faithful of his fighters. Madoc's own ego tolerated no better mage than himself among his followers, and she was better than they were. Madoc himself would be the one to watch out for, magically. Unseleighe got to the top of the "food chain" by cutthroat competition. Literally cutthroat, sometimes. She didn't know exactly how powerful he was, and she didn't want to find out by going head-to-head with him.

The trouble was, it was going to take a lot of work to find a way out of Unseleighe domains. Gates generally connected like with like; out of every three Gates, the odds were that only one of them would have a connection to neutral lands, and then only a single connection out of the six possible. Their best hope was that the places those Gates *did* go to would be empty and unused, deserted like this one, or only a transfer point.

The best thing will be to keep moving, she decided. *The more we can muddle the trail, even by simply moving at random, the better off we will be.*

So—given that they had no choice but to use the Gate in the Katschei's garden, where was it *likely* that the settings on that one went?

No love lost between him and Baba Yaga; I doubt he had one set there. In fact, he didn't have any alliances with any of the other Russian myth-figures, not even the neutrals. He did have an arrangement with some of the Chinese demons though. . . . No, that would not be a good idea. The yush eat human souls and use the bodies. I'd be safe enough, but if they all ganged up on Tannim, they might be able to take him before we got out. He had a private hunting preserve that would probably not be a healthy place to go, either.

She rubbed one finger behind her ear as she tried to recall the rest of his historical alliances. *Something from India ... oh, no, I remember now! He had something going with the* rakshasha! *That would be a very, very bad place to end up!*

The only remotely safe places she could think of were with other national equivalents to the Unseleighe and certain minor Unseleighe folk: ogres, trolls, and the like. Most of those folk were a great deal like the major lords Madoc Skean had courted; they had shut themselves off from the human world a long time ago, and the sight of the Iron Chariot that was Tannim's Mustang, moving through their realms and causing no end of damage in the process, could be enough to frighten them into panic. Certainly they would be confused and wary enough to leave the two of them alone while they studied the situation. She and Tannim should have time to find another Gate or another setting on the one they had just used and get out before anyone mustered up enough courage to oppose them. The only awkward part was that she would have to physically get out of the vehicle in order to read the Gate and reset it; that created a time of great vulnerability. Ah well, it couldn't be helped.

Once they found such Gates, they could only hope that the creatures there did not decide to find Madoc Skean and tell him where they had gone.

Damn. We'll be moving; it won't be possible to keep those special shields on the Mustang for long. We'll show up just by the disruption we cause. The more magic there is in a domain, the more disruption will take place.

No help for it; while she could not tell from in here just how much magic Tannim had infused into this vehicle, there was no doubt that it represented a major undertaking. Protections were layered on protection; and was that an energy reserve? It could be. They would be much safer in the Mach I than without it.

So it'll be a lot like taking a cross-country trip in a tank. Maybe we'll leave a swath behind us, but most of what people shoot at us should bounce off.

She massaged the back of her neck with the ends of

her fingers. *I got myself into this,* she reminded herself. *I have to get myself out of it. There were a hundred things I could have done to prevent all this, including simply taking shelter with Mother when Madoc Skean demanded I help him. I was so sure that I could stall Madoc and have a good time doing it—and I just didn't want to hide behind my kitsune kin.*

No point in pretending that if she hadn't done what she'd done, Tannim would still be in trouble from some other ally of Madoc's. Whether or not that was true, it was irrelevant. *She* had made her decisions, *she* had put her steps on *this* path, obliterating all other possibilities. Now she was the one who must deal with it all.

And she had never felt quite so alone and uncertain before. Or quite so vulnerable.

Joe followed in Chinthliss' wake, walking just behind FX, as the dragon moved slowly toward the fox-lady on the other side of the balcony. Fox had sprouted all of his tails again, but they trailed dispiritedly on the ground behind him, telegraphing major submission. And as they neared the door which presumably led to the private room that Lady Ako had reserved, past a very attractive and very large female bat, Fox's clothing was mutating as well.

By the time they actually reached the door, the red leather jacket had become a short, wrapped red jacket along the lines of a karate *gi,* and the jeans had become some other kind of loose blue pants. Both looked like silk to Joe; both were very rich and shiny. Chinthliss' silk suit was impressive enough without turning it into anything else. Joe wished *he* had Fox's talent; he felt terribly underdressed in his fatigue pants and white t-shirt.

Well, maybe if he pretended as if he was Chinthliss' bodyguard, he wouldn't look as conspicuous as he felt. No one ever expected a bodyguard to be dressed in any kind of fancy outfits, after all. They only wore tuxes in the movies, right? The rest of the time a bodyguard surely dressed comfortably. They weren't there to provide scenery but protection, right?

Whatever.

He kept his eyes on Chinthliss' silk-clad back as they reached the doorway, resisting the urge to stare at Lady Ako. Her head wasn't precisely like a fox; the lips were more mobile, he thought; the muzzle blunter. Her eyes were lovely, large, and exactly the same color as melted chocolate. Her hands were entirely human, but like Fox, she had fox-feet. Then there were all those tails. . . .

He tried to tell himself that she wasn't any different than those cat-creatures down on the dance floor. She certainly was not at all cartoonlike. Her wide brown eyes rested briefly on him as he passed; she blinked, and he got the oddest feeling that it was with surprise at his presence.

Now why should someone like her be surprised at him?

Then again . . . he hadn't seen too many *humans* down here, only people that looked human from a distance. If he'd gotten closer, who knows what he would have seen? Scales, fangs, more tails? His kind might be pretty rare, actually. He might look just as outrageous to her as she did to him.

What an odd thought that was! It made him feel acutely uncomfortable. He'd been trying not to stare at the other creatures around him, but what if they'd been gawking at him all this time?

Lady Ako closed the door behind him. Chinthliss stood off to the far side of the room, and as he took his own place, standing in a kind of parade rest behind Chinthliss, he saw that the Blue Room contained only four flat cushions, a very low table with four brown-glazed cups and a teapot on it, plus a couple of things he didn't recognize. He wasn't sure what he should do next, but Lady Ako solved the question for him.

"Please," she said, in a gentle voice that nevertheless brooked no argument. "Sit. We will have Tea."

The way she said the last word, with a subtle emphasis on it, made him think that this was not going to be a silly affair with cookies and cream and sugar. She made it sound rather like some kind of holy ritual.

"Ako!" Chinthliss exclaimed, his voice pained. "Please, we don't have time—"

"We will have Tea," she repeated firmly. "You have accepted my invitation. You will find the time."

"Don't argue with her, lizard," Fox hissed, and then bowed deeply over his knees and took his place on one of the cushions. With a grimace, Chinthliss did the same; after a moment, Joe did likewise. Fortunately, a great deal of his martial-arts instruction had been very traditional, so he was used to sitting Oriental-style on the floor.

"What's going on here?" he whispered to Fox behind Chinthliss' back, as Lady Ako clapped her hands and another brown kimono-clad fox-woman entered, carrying a few more implements on a tray. This one didn't have the elaborate hairstyle of Lady Ako, and her kimono-sleeves were much shorter.

"The Tea Ceremony," Fox breathed back. "I'll explain it all to you later; just be quiet and don't fidget. It's very important and very meaningful, and you're supposed to be contemplating the cosmos through all of this."

Well, that confirmed his feeling that this was supposed to be some kind of ritual or other. But "contemplating the cosmos"? How did that have anything to do with drinking tea? It must be a fox thing.

The only tea he'd ever had much to do with was in the form of the gallons of iced tea he usually put away in the summer, and there wasn't much *there* to inspire a ceremony.

Oh, well. Hopefully, Lady Ako would ignore him. Hopefully, he wouldn't get involved with this at all.

"Who is this young human, Chinthliss?" she asked in a quiet voice with no discernible accent. "I do not know him."

"He is the pupil of my pupil, Ako," Chinthliss replied with a sigh of resignation, as she took up what looked like a small bowl and a shaving brush. "My pupil is missing; this young one wishes to help me find him. When last seen, Tannim was Underhill, but we do not know where. We fear that he is in some danger. He has enemies Underhill."

Is he going to say something about Shar challenging Tannim? Joe wondered. *Is he going to say anything about Shar at all?*

Chinthliss said nothing more, however, and after a glance at Joe, Lady Ako's eyes twinkled for a moment with some secret amusement. "Then, since this young man you bring is new to both Underhill and the ways of the *kitsune*, this will be a new experience for him," was all she said.

Oh, great. "A learning experience." The traditional three-word preamble to a burial. Terrific.

It was certainly that. Joe had never seen anyone make so much fuss over a cup of tea in his life. Lady Ako went through so many ritualistic passes you'd have thought she was concocting the Elixir of Life. It made as much sense as gold-plating popcorn kernels by hand. She was very graceful at it, however; she made the whole thing seem like a dance. Maybe that was the point. Who knew? He hadn't understood Fox all the time when he'd been a kid, and this Lady Ako made a fine art out of creating mystery and obscurity.

Anyway, when he finally got his cup of tea, he was rather disappointed, much as he had been the first time someone gave him a glass of what was supposed to be a fine vintage wine. The tea was odd, rather bitter, very strong. On the whole, he would have preferred a cola. He would have liked to add sugar at least to make it more palatable, but there didn't seem to be any, so he hid his grimaces and sipped at it while Chinthliss and Lady Ako discussed poetry and music. Joe tried not to fidget while they exchanged what were probably terribly Meaningful and Insightful remarks.

It all took *hours*.

Finally, *finally*, she clapped her hands and the other fox-woman came and took the tea things away. They all sat in complete silence while the other female carefully placed each object on her tray, bowed, and took it all away.

But when the serving-fox was gone, and Chinthliss started to rise, Lady Ako tilted her head to one side and gave Chinthliss a warning look that made him sit right back down again.

"You are seeking Tannim," she stated. "I suspect that you are also seeking my daughter."

Chinthliss wore no discernible expression at all. "There

was some indication that she has challenged him or intended to challenge him in the near future," Chinthliss replied levelly. "I don't see any demonstrable connection between that and his disappearance. I am not making any accusations, nor can I imagine why Shar would want to—"

"Please," Ako interrupted. "Don't take me for a fool. You know why Charcoal asserted his rights over her. You know what he intended to do with her. Must I put it in simple terms for you? *He wanted to make her the enemy of your human, this Tannim.* He sees all that you are, and ever moves to make himself the image in the darkened mirror. Charcoal would steal from you whatever he can. *I* do not know why." She glared at him, and the mighty Chinthliss, much to Joe's surprise, seemed to shrink into himself a little. "I *never* knew why. I never understood this rivalry of yours."

She drew herself up in profound dignity, and Joe suspected that she had said a great deal more with those words than he had perceived. Chinthliss closed his eyes for a moment, as if in acknowledgment of that.

"Well," Ako said after a moment. "He did not succeed in his endeavor; I had far more influence over her than he ever guessed, and she broke off all connections with him four years ago. She refuses to see him, speak with him, or communicate with him in any way whatsoever."

"She did?" Chinthliss showed his surprise, briefly. "But—in that case, why challenge Tannim? What's the point?"

Ako sighed, and carefully arranged the fold of a sleeve before continuing. "She maintained some alliances with some of Charcoal's Unseleighe connections; I do not know why. She told me that these alliances amused her. I think there was more to it than that, and I can hazard a guess or two. I believe that these alliances were too powerful to flaunt, and she was too stubborn to seek shelter with the *kitsune* from their anger. One of those connections, an Unseleighe elven lord named Madoc Skean, wanted your pupil, Tannim. I warned her that pursuing this human would have grave consequences; she disregarded that warning, and due to her meddling, this young man was trapped by Madoc."

"What?" Chinthliss roared, starting to leap up off his cushion.

"Calm yourself!" Lady Ako snapped, before he could get to his feet. "Do you think that I would have brought you here and led you through Tea if I thought he was in any danger? We of the tails have obligations to this world and the other and to the Balance between them!"

Chinthliss sat down again, slowly, but Joe sensed that he was smouldering with anger and impatience.

Ako's nose twitched with distaste. "I advised Shar that she would have to remedy the balance herself. She agreed, and took herself back to Madoc's stronghold. Madoc had Tannim but briefly, and he has the young human no longer. Further, his allies have scattered, and his own domain is in confusion. I don't know where your young human pupil is right now—and I *also* do not know where Shar is. I believe that we can assume that they are together, and that she at least took my advice and freed him from the captivity that she sent him into." Lady Ako directed a chilling look at Chinthliss; the dragon gave her back a heated one. "I told her that by leading this human into captivity, she had seriously unbalanced the scales not only between them, but between our world and his; that she and she alone would have to bring them back into balance. Her actions attracted the attention of the Elders, and she will be called to account for what she has done before a Council. I informed her of this, and that how she fares will depend entirely on what she does now to rectify the situation."

"Did she tell you what she planned to do?" Chinthliss asked, after a long moment of silence. Joe glanced at FX; the *kitsune* gazed at Lady Ako with rapt astonishment, all of his tails twitching. Evidently, all of this was news to him as well as to Joe and Chinthliss.

"No," Ako responded. "She came to me for advice and I could give her none, other than what I just told you. I assume by the confusion in Madoc Skean's holding that she rescued him successfully, but she has not attempted to contact me nor to put herself at the disposal of the Elders, as she would do if she had also returned him to his side of the Hill."

Chinthliss nodded, slowly. "So they are still Underhill,

somewhere. Where? Her own domain? I assume she has one—" He smiled, ironically. "I cannot imagine her sharing a domain with anyone."

"Oh—" Lady Ako said very casually. "*I* can. Eventually. Still, that does not matter at the moment. If she had reached her own domain, she would have been able to bring Tannim out of Underhill, for she has a direct outlet to the human side there, in America. So, she has not. I suspect that she is wandering Unseleighe Underhill, searching for a Gate that will bring her into neutral holdings, or even out of Underhill. I think that we must begin looking for her ourselves. Where she is, your pupil will most certainly be."

"We?" Chinthliss did jump to his feet this time. "*We?*"

Joe blinked. They had been looking for an ally. He hadn't expected one like this.

Wonder how good she is in a fight, he thought. Then he sized her up with a practiced eye, ignoring her sex, the fancy outfit, the hair, and the fox-face, concentrating only on the strength of the muscles, the lithe body. *Huh. Pretty good, I bet!*

"Of course, we," Ako said with complete composure. "You didn't think I would allow you to go chasing off after my daughter without my presence, did you?"

Shar had slept in less comfortable places than the front seat of a 1969 Mustang. The front seat of *her* Mustang, for instance. She had chosen her own car with the view to personifying the "modern" version of Tannim—but after seeing all the electronic gear in here, and experiencing the greater comfort-factor at first hand, she was having second and third thoughts.

Tannim woke, rested and cheerful, after a few hours of very deep sleep—so deep that he had hardly moved, and Shar had needed to check him now and again to make certain he was still breathing.

It was her turn to be yawning. She was happy enough at that point to let him stand watch while *she* caught a quick nap; by then, even she felt the strains of the past several hours and needed to recharge.

She thought, just as she finally dropped off, that he was watching her just as surreptitiously as she had studied him, but she was just too tired to be sure. . . .

She woke with a start at a noise from outside the Mustang, a shuffling sound, the scraping of a pair of feet. She sat bolt upright in alarm, but there was nothing in the amber room with them, the noise was coming from the hallway outside. Tannim wasn't alarmed, either. He just shook his head at her.

"Don't worry about that sound," he told her, watching the hall door, a shadow of melancholy in his eyes. "I know who it is; I ran into him the last time I was here. It's just a poor old man that the Unseleighe left here. He might be more than half mad by now. I think he was English, and I'm afraid he was taken more than a hundred years ago. I can understand him—barely—so he can't have come from much longer ago than that."

The cursed human. But why would he be here? Why would the Unseleighe put one of their captives here? It's horribly hard to get to this place! Unless—they got tired of him, but they wanted to keep him alive, just in case they ran out of amusements.

That would certainly be like them. And it wasn't as if they managed to get *too* many humans to play with these days. Not like in the old times, when they could kidnap people at will, practically. No, by the late 1800s, they probably *had* figured out they couldn't snatch people off the face of the earth without it being noticed, and when they got a toy, they kept it, even if they were tired of it.

She forgot all her questions, though, as the old man shuffled into the room, pushing his broom and dragging his cart. She felt an unexpected surge of pity for the old creature—and then she caught sight of his eyeless face.

She stifled a gasp with the back of her hand. Not that she hadn't seen the cruelties that the Unseleighe worked on their captives before—but there was something about this man. He struck something unexpected inside her, clothed in his rags, with his wrecked face—held captive here, in this magnificent room, a prison whose beauty he would never see—

The contrast was so great, it shocked her. Tannim watched the poor old wreck with an expression she could not read. Then, before she could say or do anything, he popped the door and was out of the car, walking quickly, heading for the old man.

She opened her own door and hurried to catch up with him, wondering what he thought he was going to do. Tannim was already talking to him, when she caught up with them.

". . . aye, sir, an' thankee," the old man was saying, with something like a smile, if such a heap of misery could produce a smile. "I hae' bread enow for many a day, thanks to ye."

Shar couldn't help but try to analyze the accent; English, obviously, and probably from the Shires. It was an accent that hadn't changed much until the advent of a radio in every home. "Would you like more than bread?" Tannim asked, leaning forward with nervous intensity. "Would you like to be free of this place forever?"

"Free? Free?" The old man shook his head, alarmed, and shuffled back a pace or two. "There's nought free for Tom Cadge!" He held up his hands before his face in abject fear. "Are ye one o' them blackhearts, that ye taunt me wi' bein' free, an—"

But Tannim seized one of Cadge's hands and put it over his ear before the old man could pull away. "Feel that, Thomas Cadge!" he ordered fiercely. "Is there a single one of the People of the Hills that has *round ears?*"

The old man stopped trying to escape and stood as still as a statue except for the hand that hovered over Tannim's ear. The trembling fingers explored the top of the ear as the face assumed an expression of confusion. "Well, sir," the old man said very slowly and in great perplexity, "I dunno. I don' think so—"

"And here, follow me!" Tannim yanked the improvised rope free, took Tom's wrist, and led him in a rapid shuffle across the floor of the amber room, to end up beside the Mustang. He put the old man's hand flat against the Mach I's hood. "Feel *that!*" he ordered. "That's steel, Thomas Cadge; Cold Iron, from nose to tail! It's a carriage, a Cold Iron carriage, and *that* is how we plan to escape from here. In it! Could *any* of the Fair Folk, kindly or unkindly, bear so much as the presence of a carriage like this? Could any of their magics ever touch someone inside it?"

Thomas Cadge began to tremble, though Shar could not tell if it was from excitement, apprehension, hope, or all three. "N-n-no, sir," he whispered. "That they could not, and there's an end to it. They could no more bear the touch of yon carriage than I can fly."

"Then come with us, Thomas Cadge," Tannim urged. "I won't pretend that there won't be danger—we're in a strange and dangerous place, and we don't know our way out of it yet. I have to admit to you that we're just a bit lost at the moment—and that the same Fair Folk that put you here are probably after us."

Thomas Cadge shook his head dumbly. "I canna think what worse they could be doin' to me, sir," he replied, in a kind of daze. "They could only kill me, eh?"

Tannim sighed. "I don't think we can get you *home*. I don't think you want to go back to your home, anyway—"

Tears dripped horribly from the dark sockets where the old man's eyes had been. "Nay, sir, 'tis one'o the things they mocked me with, that the world I knew is a hunnerd years agone an' more. An' I knew it, aye, I knew that in that they spake true enough. Ye think on all th' auld ballads, an' how a day Underhill is a year in the world above, an' I knew they spake truly. Nay, sir, I canna go back—"

"But I have friends Underhill, if we can find them," Tannim interrupted. "*Good* people—people who will help get rid of your pain and take care of you. I'd like to leave you with them. Will you come with us, Thomas Cadge?"

"Us?" The old man was quick; he swung his blind face around, as if searching for the other person. "Us?"

"He's talking about me," Shar said hastily. "Please, come with us—I don't want to leave you here. If the Unseleighe decide they want entertainment again, and come back for you—" She left the rest unsaid. "I don't want that on my conscience," she added simply.

And although she had been aghast when Tannim first urged the old man to join them, she was surprised to find that she meant the offer as the words left her mouth. Tannim cast a surprised smile at her, one with hints of approval in it, and she was even more surprised to find that the idea of rescuing the old man felt—rather good.

Ah, well, why not? Perhaps the Elders will think of this as a sign that I am striving to rebalance my earlier actions.

"I—ye hae a sweet voice, milady," old Tom quavered shyly. "If ye will ha' me, aye, I'll come wi' ye."

It took some work to wedge Thomas Cadge into the backseat of the Mustang, but once there, he exclaimed over the softness of the seat, the smoothness of the "leather" on the cushions. And when Tannim put an unwrapped sports-bar into one hand, and a bottle of spring-water into the other, the old man nearly wept with joy. It made Shar feel very uncomfortable, and very much ashamed. To this poor old wreck, the cramped back seat of the Mustang, the sweet treat, and the bottle of pure water were unbelievable luxury. And a few hours ago she had felt slightly sorry for herself for "having" to sleep in the front seat and "make do" with a sports-bar and a Gatorade.

Admittedly, it helped that although Thomas Cadge was shabby, he was clean. She had to admit to herself that she would not have felt so sorry for him, nor so willing to take him along, if he had been filthy and odorous.

Thomas Cadge devoured his meal in a few bites and gulps, and promptly curled up in the blanket Tannim got out of the trunk. Tannim came back with an armload of things besides the blanket; Shar welcomed the extra crowbar with fervent glee, and with another body in the car, the extra rations were going to come in handy.

So were the heavy flashlights, the highway flares, the first-aid kit, and the bayonet-knives he piled into the passenger's-side footwell. Other domains would not necessarily be lighted, and there were plenty of creatures who would fear the flame of a highway flare.

She swiped one of the breakfast bars and went over to the other side of the room to open up both doors into the hallway. When she returned, Tannim had strapped himself in—and Thomas Cadge was asleep in the back seat with an improvised bandage of white gauze from the first-aid kit thankfully covering the ruins of his eyes. Now the old man was truly a sight to inspire anyone's pity, rather than horror or revulsion. He looked like a wounded, weary old soldier from some time in the long past; still trying to keep up his pride, though the infirmities of his own body had betrayed him.

Taking her cue from Tannim, she strapped the seatbelt across her shoulders once she had shut the door. "Go out those doors, take a sharp right, and the door to the gardens will be at the end of the hall," she directed. "You'll have to use your lights; I'll get out and open the doors into the garden once we reach them. Then it's down a set of four very shallow stairs, and follow the garden path. The Gate will be at the end of it, and it will be night out there."

He nodded, and started the car. The sound of the engine seemed terribly loud in all the silence, but Thomas Cadge did not even seem to wake up. It occurred to her that this must be the first time he had slept with any feeling of safety or security in decades.

Poor, abused old man. No home but yourself.

"Now what?" Tannim asked from the front seat.

Artificial stars gleamed down from a flat-black sky; the Katschei's round, silver moon sailed serenely in its track above them. Although no one had tended the garden for centuries, most of the plants here were much as they had been when their creator died; that was part of their magical nature, to thrive without being tended. Flowers bloomed on all sides, all out of their proper season. Trees had flowers, green, and ripening fruit, all at the same time. Perfumes floated on the faint breeze, and bowers beckoned, promising soft places for dalliance. All a cheat, of course—there had never been any dalliance here. The Katschei's captives had been quite, quite virginal; this was merely the appropriate setting for a dozen of the most beautiful maidens in Rus. The Katschei had surrounded them with fresh beauty and all the stage-dressing of romance. The setting was still here, and it was more romantic in its overgrown state than it had been when neatly tamed and pruned.

And even if we weren't in a hurry, we have a chaper-one, damn it all.

The Gate here was a rose trellis; the rose vines had overgrown it somewhat, but it was still quite useful. Roses of three colors cascaded down over it, saturating the air with their mingled fragrances of honey, damask, and musk. Only the Katschei would have had night-blooming roses. Only the Katschei would have covered a Gate with them.

And only the Katschei would ever have placed the Gate back to their homelands in the heart of the garden his captives had been imprisoned in.

None of them could use it, of course. He would never have carried off a princess with even a touch of magical power. But he surely enjoyed the irony: his prisoners danced in and around the very means of their escape, if they could only have learned how to make it work. Doubt-less, he told them that very thing. He had been an art-ist, in his way, juxtaposing cruelty with beauty, wonder with tragedy. If *he* had been the one who had captured Tho-mas Cadge, he would not have blinded the old man. No, he would have done something artistic with him; perhaps gelded him, shaped his face and body into that of a young god, and left him to guard his flock of lovely virgins.

Shar studied the Gate with her eyes closed, testing each of the six settings. One, she already knew, came up in Tannim's world, but only a few miles from present-day Moscow. However improved current conditions were, he would have a *damned* hard time explaining his presence there—and such a destination was likely to be as hazard-ous in the end as anything Underhill.

One definitely ended in the domain of the *rakshasha;* man-eating shape-changing creatures of India, and another was set for the realm of the *yush.* Bad destinations, both of them; neither she nor Tannim could ever hold their own against a group of either monsters.

That left three other settings, none of which she rec-ognized. They all felt very old, older even than the set-ting to the other side of the Hill. They might represent alliances the Katschei made before he began his collection of human maidens.

What the heck.

She returned to the car and reported her findings. "And I can't even tell where those last three go," she warned. "The third one is the nearest, and that's all I can tell you about it."

Tannim only shrugged. "Door number three sounds all right with me," he opined, as she got into the car and strapped herself back into her seat. "If you don't recognize it, chances are whoever lives there won't recognize us, right?"

"That's the theory, anyway." She lowered the window and leaned out from inside the safety of the steel framework. Feeling very grateful that *she* knew the effect of Cold Iron on her magics, and knew it intimately, she reached out with a finger of power and invoked that setting.

The rose vines quivered for a moment, and then lit up from within with a warm, golden light. The magic ran through every vein, illuminating the flowers from within, as Shar stared, transfixed. How had the Katschei *done* that? She'd never seen anyone incorporate living things into a Gate before, at least not in a purely ornamental fashion.

Trust the Katschei to do it if anyone would.

"Now there," Tannim said with detached admiration, "was a guy who had style."

The center of the arbor filled with dark haze. Whatever lay on the other side, they were now committed to it.

"Ready?" she asked, pulling her head and arm back into the steel cocoon of the Mach I, and rolling her window back up again. Not that the glass would provide any protection at all, but at least it gave her the illusion of shelter.

Tannim managed a wan smile, and a thumb's-up. "Here we come, ready or not," he said lightly, and put the Mach I into gear, driving slowly up to and into the arbor.

Shar repressed a shudder as the dark mist seemed to swallow up the light, then the headlights, the hood, and crept toward the windshield. It was just as well that Thomas Cadge was not only asleep but blind. He'd have run screaming from the car if he'd seen this.

She closed her own eyes involuntarily. Her skin tingled as the magic field passed over her; her stomach objected to the moment of apparent weightlessness.

Then, with a jolt, it was over.

The Mach I bounced slightly as it dropped about an inch, and she opened her eyes.

And her jaw dropped as Tannim quickly hit the brakes, stopping them dead. Just in time, since they had a reception committee, and a few more feet would have put the Mach I within range of their weapons.

The weapons were the first things that *she* noticed; the headlights gleamed from the shining surfaces of huge battle-axes, smaller throwing-axes, spear points, and knives and swords.

Evidently someone here had sensed the Gate coming to life and had gathered a crowd to greet whatever came through it. From the looks of the group, they had not expected the visitors to be friendly.

"A little strong for the Welcome Wagon, don't you think?" Tannim said, as the twenty or so armed warriors stared into their headlights.

Whoever these fellows had been expecting, Tannim figured it wasn't Ford's Finest. They obviously didn't recognize him, Shar, or the vehicle; the way they glared at the headlights suggested that they didn't even notice the passengers, only the car, and they didn't know what it was.

He didn't recognize them, either. Sidhe of some kind, that was all he could tell; pointed ears thrust through wild tangles of very blond, straight hair, and the slit-pupiled green eyes were unmistakable in the bright lights from the headlights.

Elves. Why did it have to be elves?

But the clothing they sported was not anything he recognized. In fact, by elven standards, it was downright primitive. That was the amazing part.

The elves he knew, even the Unseleighe, reveled in the use of ornament and lush, flowing fabrics, of intricate goldwork and carved gems, of bizarre design and exotic cut. The elves he'd associated with wore armor so engraved

and chased, inlaid and enameled, that it ceased being
"armor" and became a work of art. They carried weapons
of terrible beauty: slim, razor-sharp swords as ornamented
as their armor, knives that matched the swords to within
a hair, bows of perfect curve and silent grace, so elegant
that their bowstrings sang, not *twanged*.

These warriors carried small, round shields of plain
wood with copper bosses in the middle; they had no
helmets at all, and only corselets, vambraces, and leg armor
of the same hammered copper. The blades of their swords
and heavy axes also appeared to be of copper or brass.
None of the metal-work was chased or engraved; there was
a tiny amount of inlay work, but not much. Under the scant
armor, they had donned short-sleeved woolen tunics of
bright colors, with bands of embroidery at all the hems.
They wore sandals and shoes, not the tooled leather boots
favored by the elves Tannim had seen. Their hair looked
as if it had never seen a pair of scissors; a few of them
had it bound up in braids, but the majority sported lengthy
manes that would have been the envy of any human
female.

They seemed frozen in place, staring at the Mach I in
horrified fascination.

"You don't recognize these jokers, do you?" he asked
Shar quietly. She shook her head. While the reception
committee stayed where it was, he took a moment to get
a look at *where* they had landed. Maybe the setting would
tell him something.

Except that the roof took him rather by surprise.

A *cave?* He blinked, very much amazed. Even when an
Underhill domain had originally looked like a cave, those
who inhabited it usually took pains to make it look like
something else—someplace outdoors, usually. This was the
very first time he had ever seen a domain that looked like
what it was.

It was an awfully big cave, though. Bigger than Mam-
moth Cave, or Meramac, or the largest room in Carlsbad
Caverns. The ceiling had to be at least a hundred feet up,
a rough dome of white, unworked, natural rock. The rest
of the place was on a scale with the ceiling; from here to

the other side of the room was probably fully half a mile.
The floor between here and there was not of stone, though,
but of wood, smoothed only by time and wear, and not
put together with any level of sophistication. In fact, it
looked something rather like a deck built by drunken
beavers or very, very bad industrial-arts students. At regular
intervals a round platform of stone rose above the level
of the wood for about a foot, and these platforms were
topped with huge bonfires. Oddly enough, though, the fires
didn't seem to be giving off any smoke. That was the first
evidence of magic he'd seen here.

Spitted over these fires were the carcasses of animals;
deer, pig, and cow. Beside the fires were barrels that he
presumed contained beer or ale—but these barrels had not
been tapped, as the kegs he knew were. Instead, the end
was open, and people came along and dipped their cups
into the liquid to fill them.

There were fur-covered benches around each fire; some
of them even held prone figures, possibly sleeping off that
beer.

Most of the people in this place, however, were staring at the Mach I with the same postures of surprise as
the warriors directly in front of it.

There were women out there—or, at least, Tannim
assumed they were women, since they wore dresses. Hard
to tell with elves, sometimes. Simple T-tunic dresses, of
the same bright colors as the tunics the men wore. Over
the dresses, most of the women wore a kind of apron.
The straps were heavily embroidered and were attached
to the embroidered panels of the front and back by large,
round brooches of copper, silver, and gold. Their blond
hair was bound around their foreheads with ribbon-
headbands and covered with small veils; some of them
wore their hair unbound except by the headbands, but
the rest wore it in two braids. Their ears were as pointed
as those of the men, and the nearest had the same
cat-slitted, elven eyes.

One of the nearest men, one who had a gold headband,
finally got over his shock. He gestured with his copper
sword and shouted something to the rest. It was a fairly

long speech and involved a lot of sword-waving and pointing at the car.

It wasn't in any language Tannim recognized. He'd heard his own elves spouting off long strings of Gaelic curses often enough when they dropped something heavy on a toe, or a wrench slipped and skinned knuckles. Whatever this was, it wasn't Gaelic, and neither were these lads. Funny, it *almost* sounded like the Swedish Chef from the old Muppet show—

Shar narrowed her eyes as the leader continued his speech to the headlights, pointing and threatening with his blade. At that point, Tannim realized something. *Huh. He's shouting at the* car! *Does he think it's alive?*

To test that theory, Tannim tapped lightly on the horn.

With a yell, *all* of the fighters leapt back a pace and stared at the front of the car as if they thought it might suddenly shoot out flames.

"Oh hell—" Shar said into the silence. "I know where we are. These Sidhe haven't seen a human for fifteen hundred years! They sealed themselves off so long ago that not even Madoc could get them to come out. They're Nordic—we're in the Hall of the Mountain King!"

Tannim bit off an exclamation as all the clues fell into place. *Right—copper and bronze weapons, copper armor— these were some of the first elves to be driven Underhill and seal themselves off from Cold Iron and the world above.* "I don't suppose you speak their lingo, do you?" he asked hopefully. Those axes might only be bronze, but they could do plenty of damage if the fighters decided to attack the Iron Dragon. They'd go through glass just fine, for instance. "It would be really nice if you could apologize for breaking up their party, tell them that we're just passing through."

"No," Shar said shortly. "Sorry. I don't think there's anyone alive who does understand them without a telepath. They not only sealed themselves off from your world, they sealed themselves off from the rest of Underhill. *Maybe* there's a scholar in your world who speaks Old Norse, or Old Swedish, or Old Finnish—but I wouldn't count on it, and I doubt he's going to suddenly teleport into the back seat."

Tom Cadge? Tannim thought—

"I can't help ye, sir," came an apologetic voice from behind them. "Whatever yon spouted, 'tis pure babble to me."

Tannim studied the situation: the leader finished his speech, and he and his followers went back to staring into the headlights, as transfixed by the light as a bunch of moths.

"Shar, can you reset the Gate behind us to somewhere friendlier?" he asked quietly, and glanced out of the corner of his eye at her. She bit her lip, then cranked the window down.

Slowly.

Just as slowly, she edged one hand and a bit of her head outside, turned to face the rear of the car, and stared back at the Gate behind them.

"There's a very shallow stone platform the Gate rests on right behind us, just past the rear wheels," she said quietly. The elves didn't seem to have noticed her head and hand sticking out; maybe the headlights were obscuring whatever he and Shar did. "That was why we bumped down when we arrived. The Gate is one of those stone arches like at Stonehenge, and it looks big enough for an elephant. I think the Mach I will fit in there with no problem."

So far, so good.

"One of the settings is the Katschei's palace, obviously," she continued. "I just don't recognize the others—but if these people have been cut off for as long as I think, I wouldn't. There are plenty of places Underhill where I've never been, and plenty more that sealed themselves off from the parts that continued to progress. I don't know a darned thing about this lot, who their allies were, or anything else."

"Okay," Tannim replied after a moment of thought. "Pick one, I don't care what. I'm going to drive slowly toward these guys, and see if I can't get them to clear off enough to give me room to turn around."

This *was* a "dragon" made of the Death Metal, something these elves had gone Underhill to avoid completely.

With luck, they were too terrified of it to touch it. With equal luck, if he was very, very careful, they would realize in a moment that he didn't want to hurt them.

Then again, maybe they were too busy thinking about hurting him to notice.

He put the car into motion, creeping forward an inch at a time.

The elven warriors backed up, an inch at a time, staring at the headlights. From the way they glared at the Mach I, they evidently read this as an aggressive move. The moment of truth was going to come when he spun the car and turned his back to them. Would they rush him?

They might. If they realized he was going to escape, they might very well.

Look, Sven, we killed the Iron Dragon and it had eaten three humans!

"Can you gear that Gate up so as soon as I get these guys cleared, I can pull a doughnut and get the heck out of here?" he asked anxiously. "I don't want to have our back to these guys for more than a minute, max."

"No argument here." Shar poked her head a little further out of the window, as he continued to creep the Mustang forward. The elves cleared back a bit more, their eyes narrowing, their knuckles going white as they clutched their weaponry tighter.

"Got it," she said, after far too long. The elves in front of him were beginning to look as if they resented being backed up, and he didn't think he'd be able to force them back much further. He took a quick glance in his rearview mirror, and another over his shoulder.

There was enough room for the maneuver he wanted to pull. Barely.

Barely is still enough!

"Hold on!" he said through gritted teeth; then he leaned on the horn.

The elves screeched and jumped back; he'd succeeded in frightening them back another precious foot or so. He floored the accelerator, smoked the wheels, and slung the steering wheel over.

The tires screamed; the rear slung sideways, then around in a complete half-circle, while the elven warriors shrieked in answer and threw themselves wildly out of the way. Tannim stabilized the spin, until the nose pointed straight at the dark haze under the trio of huge, rough-cut stones looming up in front of them. He let up on the gas for a moment, then floored it as the elves leapt at the rear of the car with hideous war cries.

The Mach I roared through the Gate as Tannim saw the blade of a throwing-axe sail past the rear end, and in the rearview mirror, the leader buried the blade of his huge battle-axe into the wooden floor, scant inches from the rear bumper.

Then there was a moment of darkness, and of dizziness, and then they were through.

He slammed on the brakes quickly, and looked up at a full moon and a sky full of stars under a snow-filled and seemingly endless plain.

"Maybe you'd better turn on the heater," Shar suggested mildly, and rolled up the window.

CHAPTER TEN

Tannim reached over and automatically turned on the
dash-heater, and a moment later was grateful that Shar had
prodded him to do so.

It must be thirty below out there!

Cold penetrated the window glass, and the side-window
on his side frosted over between one breath and the next.

"Where the heck are we?" he asked, peering up through
the windshield at the sky. Only the fact that the stars did
not twinkle proved that this was another Underhill domain
and not some place on the other side of the Hill: Sibe-
ria or Manitoba. Otherwise the sky was a much more accurate copy of the real thing than the one over the garden
they'd left.

Except that there didn't seem to be any constellations
he recognized.

"I have no clue." Shar craned her own neck around to
look up through the glass at the stars above them. "No
clue at all. I don't recognize the stars up there; for all I
know, they might not even represent the constellations,
they were just thrown up there randomly. This could be
an analog of anywhere: Alaska, the Arctic, the Gobi Desert
in winter—heck, even the Great Plains. Your guess is as
good as mine."

Maybe if he got out and took a look, he might get a

clue. "Hang on a minute. Keep the heater running." He was going to have to get into the trunk again, anyway; it was just a good thing the trunk on a Mach I was so big and he never took his survival supplies out, no matter what. They were going to need some of his winter emergency stash.

He opened the door and got out in a hurry; his nose was cold and his fingers were frozen by the time he reached the trunk and extracted two Mylar blankets and three of green wool. Army surplus, of course.

There wasn't a lot of snow; it wasn't much past calf-deep at the worst. It formed an icy crust over long grass, beaten flat, and held down by the weight of the ice. He crunched his way back to the front of the Mustang, hands and feet numbed, grateful for the warming effect of his armor. The driver's-side window was completely frosted over, and the air was so cold it hurt to breathe. Hopefully they wouldn't be here much longer; the Mustang's heater was not going to keep up with cold like this. He could make do with one of the wool blankets, but old Tom and Shar had probably better have the Mylar as well as the wool. . . .

He pulled open the door and slid in quickly, then turned to Shar and stared.

"Hi," Shar said, turning a pointed muzzle and a pair of twinkling eyes at him. "You didn't seem to have a fur coat around, so I grew my own."

He dropped his jaw and the blankets; fumbled the latter up off the floor. The warm air curled around him as he stared at the lovely fox-woman with Shar's eyes sitting on the passenger's side of the Mustang.

An arctic fox, no less, with thick, white fur, and a blunter nose and smaller ears than the red fox FX usually morphed into. He stared like a booby, and she winked at him.

I'm taking this all very well, aren't I?

"Eh, excuse me, young sir, but if ye've brought a bit more blankets—" Tom said humbly from the rear seat as Tannim sat and gawked. "—'tis gettin' a bit chill here."

He didn't move. It really was Shar. And it really was

a human-sized fox. It was one thing to know intellectually that Shar was half-*kitsune*, but to actually *see* the proof of it—

"Oh, yeah, of course." Tannim shook himself out of his daze, passed back the Mylar and one of the wool blankets, and kept one of the wool ones for himself. He turned back to Shar and offered her the remaining blankets. "Do you—"

"Just give me a wool one," Shar replied. "I may have fur, but I want to spend some time studying the Gate this time before we jump, and I'll have to do it from outside the Mach I."

Wordlessly, he handed her the scratchy old wool blanket and left the little silver packet of Mylar for later.

He couldn't keep from staring at her; *this* had never happened in any of his dreams! Jeez, if anything came of this between him and Shar, he was going to have one heck of a fascinating love life . . . or did something like this come under the category of bestiality?

Boy, I hope not. Otherwise I'm a lot kinkier than I thought.

And to think that he'd had trouble explaining some of his other girlfriends to his mother!

"Hi, Mom, this is my girl. By the way, have you got a spare flea collar around? And she's due for her shots." She gets one look at Shar like this, and she'll be praying for me to go back to Teresa and her red Mohawk!

Shar didn't seem to be in the least offended by all of his staring. "I—ah—" he began.

"You're taking this very well. Oh, I don't do this very often around humans, not nearly as often as Mother," she offered casually. "Being brought up around the Unseleighe, I tended to keep to the elven look. It was bad enough that I wasn't Sidhe; they tend to regard any of the anthropomorphic forms as very much inferior. Has Saski Berith—FX—ever gone completely fox on you?"

"Not for long," Tannim admitted. The thick, white fur looked so incredibly soft—and the eyes were still human, still Shar's. And never mind that the voice came from a muzzle full of pointed teeth, it was still Shar's voice. Shar's clothes, for that matter; she'd left them on when she changed. Fascinating.

"It has its points." She regarded her hands—very much fur-covered human hands, except for the long claws. "I can inflict a lot more damage this way if there aren't any weapons available. And raw meat and fish taste much better in this form than in the human. Still, does it disturb you?"

He shook his head. "I don't think so." Belatedly, he remembered what he'd been looking for when he'd gotten out of the car. "Oh—I think we might be in a Native American analog to the Great Plains, or to the steppes of Russia. The grasses look right, anyway. Tall grass, I think, or whatever equivalent grows on the steppes. If that's true, there's going to be a lot more Spirit Animals around here—the steppes-herdsmen have a lot of the same shamanic equivalents to the Native Americans. That's one massive generalization, of course, but what the hell."

"Really?" she said with acute interest. "I wonder why the Gate went *here*, then?"

"Eh, who knows?" Tom put in. "The Fair Folk, they ne'er did make allies an' enemies th' way us mortal folk do. It don't matter t' them whether a land were across the sea Above the Hill; 'tis all Underhill here."

"True enough," Tannim agreed. "The other possibility is that this place was abandoned a long time ago. Who wants to live in eternal winter? Even Spirit Animals prefer summer to winter, on the whole. It might be that this is only used when someone is doing a Vision Quest in winter, or needs to make part of the Quest through a winter setting."

"I don' know naught about quests, sir," Tom replied, "but there's a mort 'o places down here that go beggin'. Some 'un gets t' playin' with it, an' it goes wrong, they give it up an starts over, like. Could be some 'un was tryin' for a nice place for winter huntin', long gallops an' no places for your horse t' bust his leg, an' this is what they got."

"Well, if so, it better not be fox hunting that they were

planning," Shar replied, baring her teeth and snapping playfully. "This fox might just chase them!"

Tannim grinned. It really felt *good* to be working with Shar, even though they really knew so little about each other! He'd have to be mindful of those teeth, later, when they—

The old man had a point, though; it wouldn't do to linger here. Just because the place looked abandoned, that didn't mean it was. And if it was someone's private hunting preserve, it would be a good idea to get out of here before the hunter returned. Not that they needed any more reasons for urgency!

"Whenever you're ready, Shar," Tannim said quietly. "Take all the time you need. I've got a near-full tank, and at idle, the Mach I won't be drinking too much gas." He thought a moment. "Actually, I have an idea."

We're both in trouble together. She's made the effort to get me out. And just in case I don't make it—I can add to her chances to survive this. Even if everything goes to hell.

"Hold on a minute before you go out there." He closed his eyes, sank his own awareness into the fabric of the Mustang, and began to chant quietly.

He didn't leave his body this time, but with his magesight tapped into all the myriad possibilities Underhill, he had to blink a few times to get *here and now* clear.

Beside him, Shar was particularly disconcerting. Lovely woman, flirtatious fox, and—something else. Not *quite* like Chinthliss' draconic form; Shar was more delicate, graceful, *entirely* feminine. But the resemblance was there. The three forms washed in and out of focus, but the strongest was not the draconic but the human, followed by the fox.

Jeez, and I swore I wasn't going to date outside my own species. Even at Fairgrove. She's so sexy!

He reached out with his real hand; Shar put hers into his without any prompting on his part. Physical touch gave him physical linkage; he pitched his chanting a tad higher and plugged her into the Mach I's energy reserves.

"Oh!" she exclaimed. And then thoughtfully, "Oh . . . my."

He sealed the connections to her and dropped back into the real world. She was sitting in absolute, Zen stillness, head cocked to one side, eyes unfocused, her attention concentrated on what he had just given her.

He watched her face; interestingly, it was as easy to read the vulpine expressions as the human ones. Finally, her eyes focused again, and she came back to reality, turning a face still full of surprise to him. "Tannim—" she said very slowly, her expression full of wonder and gratitude. "You didn't need to do that."

He shrugged, covering his mingled feelings. He was filled with pleasure at her thanks, and nervousness at having given her the key to so much of himself. "Gives us both an edge," he replied. "Gives us both a source of power to draw on when we don't want to let the locals know that we're mages. Now, you go out there and study that Gate. Here, take the other Mylar blanket, too. Put it over the wool. Sit on the hood. The engine'll keep your—ah—tail warm, and you'll have a pure and reliable power source to draw on."

Tom took all this in, head tilted to the side, a slight smile on his face. "I'll be havin' another bit of a nap, if ye won't be a-needin' me, eh?" he said, when Tannim had finished.

Tannim chuckled weakly. "Sounds good to me, Tom," he said, and the old man curled up, tucking his head under an improvised blanket-hood so that his face could not be seen.

Shar laid her hand on the back of his. "Thank you," she said quietly. "Thank you very much. It is a noble gift, and a generous one. I'll never forget it."

Then, before he could reply, she popped the door open and slipped out with a crackle of plastic. She stood wrapped in Mylar in a reversal of "woman in a silver dress, wrapped in a fox-fur cape." He turned the car around carefully, so that the nose faced the Gate. Like the one in the Mountain King's Hall, this was a simple arch of three rough stones and appeared to be the only structure here for as far as the eye could see.

She slid up onto the hood of the car and sat just in

front of the air-intake, breath steaming up into the air, pointed ears perked forward. Tannim took it upon himself to sit guard for her, watching with *every* sense, in every direction except the one she faced, for any sign of living things.

He sensed her slipping into deep meditation; she must have felt him putting out warning-feelers, and trusted to him to guard her back.

It was the second such evidence of trust she'd granted him, the first being when she had slept for an hour or so, back in the amber room.

And despite their precarious situation, he felt his mouth stretching in a silly grin.

Or maybe not so silly. *Because maybe, just maybe, this is all going to work out. . . .*

"You will come with me, please." Lady Ako rose gracefully to her feet; Joe discovered that he was not as practiced at sitting on the floor as he had thought, when he tried to follow her example.

Chinthliss and FX didn't seem to have much more luck than he had, fortunately, or he'd have felt really stupid.

The *kitsune*-lady led the way not to the door into the nightclub but to the door through which their *kitsune*-server had come.

"We will use the private entrance," she said, turning her head to speak over her shoulder.

"I didn't know there was a private entrance," Chinthliss observed with mild surprise.

Lady Ako smiled slightly. On a fox-head, that translated to showing the barest tips of her teeth. Definitely an unsettling sight. "You were also not aware that the majority partners in this establishment are five-tail *kitsune*, I assume."

FX started with surprise. "I'd wondered about the Tea Ceremony," Chinthliss replied with equanimity. "There aren't too many nightclubs equipped to perform it at a moment's notice."

Lady Ako said nothing; she only opened the door for them all and bowed without a hint of servility. They all filed through, Joe taking the rearmost position.

The door led into a perfectly ordinary, utilitarian hall-way, white-painted, terrazzo-floored, with ordinary light fixtures overhead. Odd creatures squeezed by them as they passed, emerging from other doors along the hall. Some were in the uniforms of the cocktail waitresses and waiters, some in full tuxedos, a few in very little other than strategically placed spangles.

Joe blushed; he couldn't help it. Bad enough when these females were at a distance, but they brushed past him without a trace of embarrassment, full breasts practically in his face. His cheeks and neck felt as if he had the worst sunburn in his life, and he was certain he looked like a boiled lobster.

"Two sequins and a cork," Fox muttered in his ear as they threaded their way past another group of girls with butterfly-wings in matching—outfits. "Placement optional."

Joe blushed so hard he could have blacked out from the rush of blood to his skin. And elsewhere.

Finally Lady Ako brought them to a door at the end of the corridor and opened it for them. Joe had only a moment to notice that the doorframe seemed filled with a hazy darkness—

Then, before he could stop, his momentum took him through.

His stomach lurched for a moment. *A Gate?* he thought in confusion; then his leading foot came down solidly on the "other side."

His eyes cleared; he shook his head to clear it as well, taking a firm grip on his weaponry.

"No need," Lady Ako said mildly from behind him.

He blinked, finding himself in bright sunlight on an immaculately groomed gravel path. Sculptured mounds crowned with carefully placed, twisted trees, stone stat-ues, and iron lanterns rose on either side. Ahead of him was a bridge that arched over a tiny stream, with a curve as gentle as a caress. Beyond the bridge, on a perfectly shaped miniature hill, stood a pavilion with a peaked roof and white paper walls.

"You are at our embassy here; you have not left your original section of Underhill," Lady Ako stated calmly. "We

will be able to search for Shar and Tannim from here—
and we will be able to alert our allies and agents in
unfriendly domains to watch for them."

It was not until she came around in front of them that
Joe saw she had changed significantly. She was no longer
a fox-woman, but was, to all appearances, perfectly human.
She still wore her kimono, but she had discarded the elaborate black hairdo somewhere. Now she wore only what Joe
assumed was her real hair: a long, unbound fall of fox-red,
with a streak of white, ornamented by a single clasp in the
shape of a carved fox of white jade. That hair color looked
distinctly odd on someone with otherwise Oriental features.

She moved to the front of the group, but did not lead
them to the pavilion as Joe had expected. Instead, she brought
them, after a short walk, to another building altogether.

Joe got the oddest feeling that Lady Ako was giving
them the runaround. But why would she want to do that?
Wasn't it her daughter that was in trouble here?

He put his feelings aside; surely he was mistaken. It
was just because this was all so weird that the only way
his mind could cope with it was to be suspicious.

This was something like a bigger version of the pavilion; it had a wide, wooden porch around it, with more little
flat tables and cushions arranged neatly and precisely. Lady
Ako brought them up onto the porch and took her place
on one of the cushions; they did the same, arranging themselves around her.

"Now," she said, when they were all settled, "we shall
have Tea."

"We will *not* have Tea!" Chinthliss exploded, shattering the serene silence and frightening some little birds out
of a sculptured bush near the porch.

Ako fixed him with a look of stern rebuke. "We will have
Tea," she repeated stubbornly.

But Chinthliss had evidently had enough. "We will not
have any damned Tea!" he shouted, leaping to his feet.
"Tannim is missing, you don't know where Shar is, an
Unseleighe enemy of Tannim's *and* mine wants Tannim in
small pieces, and *you* want to serve us another bowl of
your damned green glop?"

"She's stalling!" Joe blurted.

All eyes turned to him—including Lady Ako's, and she was not happy with him or his observation. But Joe couldn't help it; now that his subconscious had come up with what was really going on, he had to report it to Chinthliss, his "superior officer."

"She's stalling, sir," Joe said to Chinthliss, deliberately avoiding Lady Ako's gaze. "I don't know why, but she's been taking as much time as she possibly could to do everything. It isn't just that tea-stuff, it's everything; if she really wanted to get something done, couldn't she have met us at the park? Or if she had someone watching to see if we came to the Drunk Tank, couldn't she have brought us straight here?"

The sheer numbers of people crowding that hallway, too, had been way out of line. "She even had everybody working in the club out there in the hall, just to keep us from moving through it too quickly." Now he cast a quick glance at Lady Ako; she looked distinctly chagrined. "Sir, she's been throwing every single delay at us that she could. She probably even had some kind of 'emergency' planned, so that she could shut us up someplace for a while."

Chinthliss stood, towering over her as she remained seated on her little cushion. "Well?" he asked icily.

She averted her eyes. "I haven't the least idea what the boy is talking about," she protested, though it sounded to Joe just a bit feeble. "Why would I do anything like that?"

"The reasons are as many as your tails, Ako, and only you know which of them are true." Chinthliss was clearly out of patience. "The only thing useful to have come out of this is that you have told me that Shar and Tannim are likely together, and that Tannim is pursued but no longer captured. Thanks to all this taradiddle of yours, that may no longer be the case."

He jerked his head a little, and Joe took his place behind him. FX vacillated for a moment, then joined them.

"You may do what you like, Ako," Chinthliss said, his voice coldly emotionless. "*I* am going to find a taxi. I suggest that you do nothing to stop us."

❖   ❖   ❖

Tannim's nose and feet were awfully cold, but the rest of him was warm enough, wrapped up with his armor beneath it all. Tom Cadge slept blissfully on in the backseat, and Shar contemplated the Gate from the hood of the car, a fox of white jade wrapped in shiny silver gift wrap.

She could have been an incense burner, with the fog of her breath for smoke. *Or a baked potato in a microwave? No, she's not at all potato-shaped. And potatoes explode. Hope she doesn't do that.*

Finally, though, she stirred and climbed carefully down off the hood of the Mach I. Still wrapped in her silver cloak, she padded quickly to the door of the car, opened it, and slipped inside. The Mylar crackled annoyingly as she slid into her seat.

"This was good. With leisure to study the Gate, I was able to trace all of its destinations as to *type* if not actual location. Six settings, so I can't add one of my own," she said. "One is back to the place we just came from. One goes directly to the domain belonging to the yeti. We *could* take that one—they have another Gate that goes to the other side of the Hill—but we'd wind up in the Himalayas near Everest, and the Mach I is neither a yak nor equipped with oxygen and climbing gear."

"And I'm not a mountain climber," Tannim added. "We'd have to be damned lucky to survive the Himalayas long enough for Tibetans, monks, or some expedition or other to find us and rescue us. And if we arrived in the middle of one of their killer snowstorms, we're ice cubes. Next?"

"One leads to a swamp. I don't know who owns the swamp, but I suspect something like the Will-o'-the-Wisps." She waited for his reaction, keeping quite still, so that the Mylar wouldn't crackle.

Tannim shuddered; he'd encountered one, the real thing, not swamp gas. Will-O'-the-Wisps were not little dancing fairy lights; they were horrible creatures who lived only to lure living beings into sucking morasses in the swamps they called home. Like the other Unseleighe, they thrived on fear and pain; when their victim was well and truly trapped, and sinking to his death, they would perch nearby and drink in the panic and despair as he struggled and died. The Will-o'-the-Wisp Tannim had encountered had not been content with trying to lure him away to his death; when he had not cooperated, it had tried to frighten him into a morass. Then it decided to take the matter into its own hands.

The experience had not been a pleasant one, to say the least. "I don't think that's a good idea," he said. "Next?"

"Nazis," Shar supplied succinctly.

"Pardon?" he replied, sure that he could not have heard her correctly.

"Nazis," she repeated. "And I must admit, this does solve a little puzzle for me. The Nazis had a secret program of research into magic and the occult. I always wondered where all the Nazi sorcerers went when the Third Reich collapsed; they were too powerful to have been caught, the way the Nazi leaders were, but there was no sign of them after the end of the war. Apparently, they discovered or built a Gate, found a vacant realm and took it over for their very own. They must be some of the very few mortals to succeed in living Underhill without elven aid."

"Nazis." He shook his head. "I hate those guys."

"I doubt that even the Unseleighe would care for them," Shar replied. "They were approaching magic as a science, and their attitude would have turned even Madoc Skean off. So, that's four of the six destinations. The other two end in the Unformed."

Tannim gave that some thought. The Unformed was the generic term for pockets of odd, thick mist in completely unclaimed and untouched areas. There were a few realms that were so large that they were still surrounded by a dense and impenetrable cloud of the Unformed. Elfhame Outremer had been like that—and it was out of the Unformed that their destruction had come, for the mist was psychotropic, and anyone with strong enough psychic powers could influence it, create things out of it.

In the case of Outremer, disaster had come at the hands of a seriously unbalanced child with powerful psychic and magic powers: a deadly combination, when put together with the Unformed.

Anyone who was both psychic *and* a mage could find himself facing down his worst nightmares out in the Unformed. In the old days, that had often been a test of a new mage, the test that proved how good his control was not only of his magic but of himself. There were a lot of mages who hadn't survived this particular ordeal.

There were a number of unclaimed pocket domains that were the results of these trials-by-fire, as well. The one that they were in might well be one of those, come to think of it.

"Any idea how big the pockets are?" he asked finally.

Shar shook her head. "Not even a guess. Can't help you. The only thing I can tell is that one of them might have more than one Gate in it. The other might have a physical connection to another realm. You have to remember that it is very likely that every setting on the Gates there is taken up by a destination we wouldn't like. The Unseleighe and their ilk still prove out young mages in trial-by-Unformed."

"Go for the one with the physical connection?" he hazarded. "That would be my choice. The drawback I can see to the Unformed with two Gates in it is that there's twice the probability that there's something really nasty still roaming around in the mist out there, left over from a trial—and twice the chance that some new Unseleighe mage is going to pop in on us while we're there, and maybe even break the Unformed down around us while he goes through *his* trial."

Shar nodded thoughtfully. "I hadn't thought of that, but you're right. It's going to be hard enough to keep our own thoughts pleasant; I'd hate to meet some Unseleighe nightmares. Actually, a Nightmare may be exactly one of the things we'd meet out there."

"A Nightmare?" Tannim had only heard of those, and he had no real wish to meet one in person. Sometimes a skull-headed white horse with her retinue of nine black, man-eating foals, sometimes a grim woman in a robe of storm clouds, with the head of a fanged horse in place of her own, she was, as Dottie succinctly put it, "mondo bad news." If you were lucky, she would only force you to mount and ride her through your greatest fears.

If you weren't lucky . . .

"Anytime I can avoid a Nightmare, I'd prefer to," Shar replied, echoing his own thoughts. "They're classic Unseleighe, so they wouldn't like the Mustang's Death Metal, but why take chances?"

"Heh. Mustang versus Nightmare—now that's something I'd like the video rights to!" He cracked a smile, and Shar pretended to swat him. "So, you want to aim for what, then? The destination with the possible physical outlet?"

She shrugged. "They're all bad; that seems the one with the least risk. With luck, that physical connection will be to something neutral."

"Right." He was under no illusions here; they were in enemy territory, working without a map, and their best hope was to end up *somewhere* Shar recognized. Only then would they be able to make their way to safe ground.

And home. . . .

Unexpectedly his throat closed for a moment, as longing for home hit him like a physical blow, and he bit his lip. God, he was so tired of running. . . . Home had never felt so far away, so unattainable; at least in the past, he'd known where he was, what to expect, what the limits were. Here, it was all up in the air. And he would give almost anything to see a familiar face. Would he *ever* see anyone he knew again?

"What's the matter?" Shar asked, quickly putting one soft hand over his cold one, as his face reflected some of his feelings despite his effort to hide them.

He shook his head, intending to say nothing, but it came out anyway. "I want—to go home," he whispered hoarsely. "All this—it's all so strange. I've never been this far Underhill before. I've never been anywhere but Elfhame Fairgrove, Furhold, and—I just want to go home."

He couldn't continue. *Fairgrove was a short step, and I was back on my side of the Hill. I wasn't lost. And even if someone was trying to kill me, it didn't matter, because I was standing by my friends.* He had to face the reality of the situation: he could die here, and no one would ever know what had become of him. He was pretty sure by now that Shar was on his side, but they could be separated— they would be separated if they were caught—and he would die alone here.

"I've never had a home, as such," Shar said wistfully. "I have my own domain, but it's really just a place to live. I've never felt comfortable enough with the *kitsune* to live in their realm. I certainly don't want anything to do with my father, or his allies. I have a few friends, but not many. Maybe that's why I spent as much time on your side of the Hill as I did." Her tongue flicked out thoughtfully. "Things are simpler there. At least on your side of the Hill I know the rules, and they don't change."

"Simpler—" He nodded. "That's not a bad thing." Then he shook off his mood of melancholy with a heroic effort. They didn't have time for this. Maybe Hamlet could take time in the middle of a firefight to soliloquize, but real people had to keep on running and shooting.

"I'll go set the Gate," she said, as if reading his mind. "Be back in a few seconds."

She slipped out of the blanket and the car at the same time; a rush of cold air numbed his ears as she opened and shut the door. She stood beside the Mustang for a full minute, staring at the stone arch, one paw-hand raised to it, palm outward.

The stones began to hum.

He didn't realize what it was at first; he thought that the cold might have introduced a new note into the rumbling of the Mach I's engine. But then, as the sound built, he realized that it came from the stones in front of him, a deep note just barely in the audible spectrum, that vibrated in his chest and made his hands and feet tingle.

Shar slipped back into the car, bringing with her another rush of cold air and a sparkle of frost. "Whenever you're ready."

He put the car in motion, creeping slowly forward, as the dark mist filled the space defined by the three stones. This scene was beginning to take on the uncanny feeling of familiarity; as the Gate swallowed up the lights, the hood, crept toward the windshield, he simply braced himself slightly, the same way that he braced himself against the lurch of an airplane take-off.

This time, though, the moment of disorientation was much shorter. The blackout lasted barely long enough to blink twice, then the Mach I moved smoothly into a thick, gray fog, illuminated from everywhere and nowhere.

He hit the brakes as soon as the tail cleared the Gate; red light washed up behind them as the brake-lights reflected through the mist. He killed the headlights and turned off the engine. There was no point in advertising their presence here with the glare of headlights, even though the fog swallowed up most of the light. Behind them, the Gate was a smooth arch carved of white stone, easily lost in the mist of the Unformed now that the haze of activation was gone.

That was probably the point. If a mage blundered too far away from the Gate, he'd better be able to use his powers to find it again, or he was going to be in trouble.

The Unseleighe were great believers in Darwinism, it seemed.

"Tannim—" Shar said suddenly. "Look at what the mist is doing!"

At first he wasn't sure what she meant; a moment later, though, as he followed her gaze to the hood of the Mustang, he realized what it was she saw.

The mist of the Unformed curled away from the Mach I, leaving a shell of clear space between the metal and the mist. Was the car repelling the mist? Was the mist reacting to the metal, trying to avoid it? The mist *was* charged with raw magical energy, after all. Or was the mist reacting to the spells of protection on the Mustang?

Whatever the cause, here was a visible sign that the Mach I affected the world Underhill, one that he didn't need to invoke mage-sight to read. He watched in fascination as the mist pulled back into itself, for all the world as if it reacted in pain.

Shar's features blurred briefly, and returned to the human ones he knew best. She had shifted as suddenly as a sigh, and as noiselessly as the mist. He was not entirely certain she had done so consciously.

"Probably we ought to both recon this situation," Shar said into the silence. But she made no move to leave the Mustang.

He didn't blame her; there was something about this mist, uncanny, sinister. Sad, too; his depression returned in full force, and it was all he could do to keep from giving up and curling up into a fetal ball right then and there.

Right. And if you do that, there's no way you're going to get out of here, bonehead!

Shar stared out the window, her own expression pensive, her eyes full of secrets.

"Your parents," she said out of nowhere. "I watched you with them, and I envied you for having *two* such people to care for and who cared for you. I could not understand why you left your home so eagerly."

It was not a question, but the questions were there, nonetheless. "It's hard to explain," he told her, knowing that it sounded feeble. "I think the world of my folks, and I know that they are prouder of me than they ever let on, but—" He snorted, as a little more of his depression lifted. "This is really going to sound trite, but they honestly don't understand me."

"Well, you *are* a mage, and they are—good, normal folk," Shar replied sensibly.

But Tannim shook his head. "That's only part of it. They would never understand me, even if I wasn't a mage, but that makes it astronomically worse. They don't know why I do what I do for a living, test-driving, all that. Half the time they think I'm going through some kind of a phase, and after a while I'll get tired of all this and become an accountant, or a car salesman." He ran his hands through his hair in distraction. "They worry about me, that I'll wake up some day as an old has-been driver with nothing to fall back on. And that's just the *surface* problem."

"And the deeper problem?" Shar prompted.

"There's the magic, the Sidhe—which I *can't* tell them about." He clutched his hair. "I've tried; they literally don't hear it. Won't hear it. I'm afraid to try anymore; they might think I was on drugs or something. Mom half hinted at that the last time. Usually they just act like they think I'm talking about a book I read or some movie."

"But they love you—" Shar said blankly.

"Love doesn't mean understanding," he replied, letting go of his hair and staring at his hands. "They don't share the same values I have anymore. How can I pay *any* attention to the package a person comes in, when so many people I'm proud to call my friends aren't even human? Then I get home, and Dad starts bitching about the 'foreigners taking over' and signs a petition to forbid every other language in America but English. And that's only the start of it. Dad's a great man—but he's coming down with hardening of the attitude; looking for some group to blame for problems, and not bothering to do something about the problems. Instead of trying to fix things, he's bitching about it."

Shar's mouth formed into a silent "oh." Tannim's lips twitched. "That's one reason why I try to keep my visits brief, because I know that I let things slip that they worry about. Mom isn't happy about my lifestyle; Dad isn't happy that I've turned my back on three generations of Drakes farming in Oklahoma. I'm not happy knowing that, deep down, they wish I was someone more like Joe." He rubbed the side of his head unhappily. "Sometimes I think I'm a changeling. I couldn't be more of a misfit in my family if I'd been left on the doorstep in a basket."

Shar was very quiet for a long time. "But I thought— you said—"

"I said I loved my parents. I do. And they love me. They just don't understand me." He laughed weakly. "Oh, Shar, it's awfully difficult to explain. Sometimes you can care a great deal about someone, and simply not understand him at all. Especially if you're related to him."

She blinked at him. "Forgive me for saying earlier that life in your world is simpler."

"Life is ne'er simple, lass." Tom Cadge spoke softly from the rear seat. " 'Twasn't when I was a lad, and likely has got no better. There's more grief 'twixt relations than strangers."

"Don't misunderstand me. I love my folks, Thomas," Tannim protested. "I just don't fit in their lives anymore. Their home—just isn't home for me now. I don't belong there anymore. I can't go back without feeling like an alien."

"Well, now, that's as it should be, eh?" Tom cocked his head to the side and turned his bandaged face toward Tannim. "The chick don't go back in the shell, do he? Nor the wee bird go back to his mam's nest come spring again? Ye can't *go back* to a home, lad, not once ye be a man grown. Ye have to *make* your home, your *own* home, or it ain't really *your* home, if ye take my meanin'."

"What about those who've never had a home, Thomas Cadge?" Shar asked softly, with a note of bitterness in her voice.

Tom turned his head toward her, creating the odd impression that despite his blindness, he still saw right through the layers of bandage over the grisly ruins of his eyes. "Those who've never got a home has all the more reason to make one, milady," the old man said with odd gentleness. "Even an old man, half mad an' all blind has a reason t' make a home. An' them as never got a home, well, mebbe they ought t' look to them as knows what a good home is, to show 'em how t' build one. 'Specially summat who's a friend. Bain't that what friends be for?"

Tannim stared at the swirling mist as the silence lengthened. "Well," he said, finally, "Before we get out of the Mustang, we'd better get ourselves in a better mood. That mist out there is going to react to what we're thinking, and even more to what we're feeling. The car's got shielding enough to keep us from creating any nightmares, but once we get out to study the situation—"

Shar straightened visibly, and her face took on an expression of determination. "Absolutely right. I think we're letting this miserable place get to us. And absolutely the *last* thing I want to do is conjure up my wretched father out of the Unformed." She made a grimace of distaste. "One of him is bad enough; two would be unbearable."

"Oh, I don't know," Tannim replied, managing a chuckle.

"From what you've said, if you created a second Charcoal, they'd be so in love with each other we'd never have to worry again."

Shar actually smiled. "You have a point," she agreed. "Still, let's not take any chances." She pulled her hair back from her face, and closed her eyes for a moment. "Right. I assume you don't know anything about the Gates, since you haven't volunteered to examine them with me."

Tannim spread his hands helplessly. "Not a hint. Haven't the vaguest notion how to look into the things. I make my own Gates when I need 'em, but only back in America. However, I *do* know a bit about the Unformed, since Fairgrove got involved in the cleaning up after the disaster at Outremer. If the Gate doesn't pan out, I can probably find that physical connection to the next realm."

"You can?" Shar brightened visibly. "Oh good—I can tell there's one out there, but I can't locate it."

"Then I think we have our two tasks laid out for us; nothing like a proper division of labor. And I believe I'm ready for the mist, if you are." Tannim put his hand on the door and gave Shar an inquiring glance.

"As ready as I'm likely to be." She sighed, and opened her own door with an expression of resolution on her face.

The Unformed was not precisely "mist" as any human knew it. It was neither cold nor damp. It had no odor, no taste, nothing to feel—in fact, if Tannim had closed his eyes, he would not have known it obscured everything in every direction. Anything more than three feet away might just as well be invisible. As he understood it, the theory went that the mist was a physical manifestation of the available energy in these pockets of Underhill. Raw energy at that; the theory was that once that energy was given a form, it ceased to be random and started to obey normal laws of physics. Until then—you had this mist, potential in its purest form.

It tried to trick you into giving it a form, too. There were phantom shapes out there, shapes that teased the mind and made it strive to put definition on the vague shadows. The more the unwary person peered, the more his mind tried to match the half-seen shape, the more the half-seen shape fitted itself to the image in a watcher's mind.

In the case of one particular child, in a sea of Unformed mist outside Elfhame Outremer, those images had been very terrible. . . .

Forget that. Don't look out there. Don't let it trap you. Just hunt for the pathway into the next domain. Shar might be the expert on Gates here, but that was something he *could* do, though it was a tricky bit of work, and akin to echolocation.

There was a peculiarity to the rock walls of Underhill pockets; they reflected magic. Real rock didn't do that, so Tannim could only assume that the caves of Underhill were not exactly made of rock.

I wonder if they only look like caves because that's what the creatures who first came to this place expected. The mist was psychotropic, after all. . . . If you had enough mist, could you form rock walls out of it?

But that wasn't getting anything done. The point was that the rock walls reflected magic, but a place where the rock wasn't obviously didn't. So he had to become the human equivalent of a bat.

He walked around to the front of the car, settled himself on the hood of the Mustang, absentmindedly pulled a cherry-pop out of his pocket, and unwrapped it. He tucked the cellophane neatly back in his pocket and the candy in his cheek, crossed his legs, and went to work.

Shar faced the Gate, the Mach I a solid and reassuring presence behind her, and closed her eyes, sinking her awareness into the fabric of the pale stone arch. One of the settings she already knew; the frozen plain they had left behind. Her first action would be to count the number of settings this Gate had; after that, she would worry about where they went.

She tended to think of them as directions in three dimensions; forward and back, left and right, up and down. "Filled" settings pulsed with power; the "empty" places where settings would be—when there were any such empty slots, which wasn't often in a public Gate—held power, but not as much, and always felt to her as if she touched the surface of a glass, warmed by sunlight, holding a gentle glow of magic.

"Up" is the plain that we just left. Damn, the rest are active, too. No chance to add a setting of my own. Ah well, it had been a *faint* hope, after all. In pure reflex, she checked "down" first, and got a nasty shock when she recognized it for what it was.

One of Charcoal's domains? As a destination for us? I don't think *so!* Of course, as a powerful mage as well as a dragon, her father had more than one little pocket kingdom. He might not be using this one; as she recalled, it was smallish, as small as the ersatz apartment she had built for herself. Charcoal preferred grander dwellings; he mostly used this one as a place to leave people he wasn't sure were guests or prisoners. It was one of the places he had graciously allowed her to use when she was a child.

It's tempting, though. There's at least one setting on every Gate he builds that goes someplace neutral. Charcoal might be insufferable, but he wasn't stupid, and he always kept his options open.

Long familiarity with the Unseleighe let her quickly identify the other four destinations. They all were Unseleighe Sidhe holdings, and all of them places she had visited, thanks to her father's habit of playing both ends against the middle: the Shadow Tower of Bredna, the Hall of Tulan the Black Bard, the private hunting preserve of Chulhain Lorn, and Red Magda's stud farm.

Best not ask what she raises. She might feed you to them.

All of them grim destinations, and all too small to escape from readily. Smaller, even, than Madoc Skean's holding.

The one saving grace was that none of the four were on good terms with Madoc. In fact, Red Magda and Tulan had little private feuds with him that virtually guaranteed they would turn him away with a curse if he came to them on the trail of Tannim.

Of course, this did *not* mean that they would help Tannim. Since the young human was an ally of Keighvin Silverhair, they would probably be perfectly happy to hunt him down on their own. Magda hunted any humans she could find or kidnap just on general principles; she preferred the Great Hunt over any other kind. And as for Shar—well, they'd probably treat her the same as a human.

I have no notion how I'd stack up against them. Rather not find out by meeting them head-to-head, either.

It was rather interesting, though, to discover that she recognized all the destinations of this Gate. Were they finally getting back into familiar territory? That could be good or bad news. Good, if it meant finding a neutral destination at last—bad, if all that happened was that they worked themselves deeper and deeper into the holdings of the darker creatures. Shar had heard rumors of those who'd worked themselves into places where even the Unseleighe Sidhe were afraid to go. And once, when she was a child, her father had returned silent and stiff from one of his own journeys of exploration—and he would not talk about where he had been, only sealed off the setting on the Gate that had led there. Now that was an unsettling recollection.

It almost made a foray into one of Charcoal's holdings into a tempting idea.

She disengaged her awareness from the Gate carefully, making sure to leave behind no traces that she had been there. No magical "footprints" or "fingerprints"; nothing to betray her presence.

Moving that circumspectly took time. She only hoped that Tannim had been able to find the physical opening out there in the mist, since this Gate was pretty much a washout. Of course, they could always go back to the plain and try the other pocket of the Unformed that Gate went to. They might have better luck there.

Behind her, she heard Tannim stirring, the *shh-ing* of denim on the hood of the Mustang. Good! He must have found the opening into the next domain. They could compare notes, make some further plans.

The sound of fabric sliding over the metal ended with the faint *thud* of sneakers hitting the soft, white sand of the ground of this place. She was turning to greet him when a hint of movement out of the corner of her eye caught her attention.

Is there something out there? She peered into the mist, trying not to think of anything in particular, but whatever had been there was no longer there.

She still wasn't certain if the momentary curdling of mist had been the result of the mist "wanting" her to see something, or if it had been something very real slinking through the fog, when Tannim screamed.

CHAPTER ELEVEN

Tannim slid off the hood of the Mach I feeling rather pleased at how quickly he had found the entrance he'd been searching for. He was straightening up, his defenses momentarily down, when the mist-thing streaked out of nowhere and sank its teeth into his arm.

He never got more than a glimpse of it; his brief impression was of a long, lean creature about the size of a Great Dane, as white as the mist, and impossibly fast.

It was possessed of an obscene number of sharp, white teeth, thin as razor blades, most of which seemed to be scraping his arm bones.

Maybe it was a giant white shrew, or a wild dog or an albino weasel. More likely it was someone's worst nightmare. That was certainly the way Tannim felt when the thing's teeth met in his arm as it knocked him to the ground.

He screamed, unable to stop it, no macho posturing or stoicism—he screamed.

He didn't resist the fall, he continued it, rolling over on his back and kicking at the beast as hard as he could with both legs, feet planted firmly in the creature's belly.

The thing let go of his arm as the breath was knocked out of it in a fetid puff, and the force of his kick sent it sailing over his head.

Into the side of the Mach I.

The monster screeched like a chainsaw ripping through an oil barrel. For a moment, it hung over the front fender, body convulsing as it encountered some of the protective spells. It screamed again, and a crackle of energy arced across its body, a tiny display of fireworks that obscured whatever the beast had looked like. Not that he was in any shape to notice details.

In fact, he wasn't in much shape to notice much of anything, since he was lying on his side, eyes unfocused, trying not to scream loudly enough to attract another one of the creatures.

The thing hung on the fender for a few more moments, then it slid to the ground and burst into flame.

Within seconds, as Shar ran toward him out of the mist, hands ablaze with magical energies, it was gone, leaving nothing behind to show it had ever existed. Except, of course, for the ragged remains of his shirtsleeve, which hardly amounted to more than a few ribbons of cloth over the armor.

And the bleeding puncture wounds, where the beast's teeth had gone *through* the armor.

He clamped his teeth shut on his own pain and stared at the sluggish blood dripping down his arm in shock as the pain turned to numbness, though he knew *that* state was only temporary. The shock was not only because he had been wounded, but because he had been wounded *through the armor.*

Shar dropped to her knees beside him but did not touch him. "Is that arm broken?" she asked, her voice tight.

He shook his head, unable to speak, for *now* the pain began all over again, worse than before, and his arm felt as if he had—he had—

Ah, God this hurts!

With that assurance, Shar carefully picked his arm up by the wrist, and with one crooked finger, deftly made a slit along the joining of the top row of scales. The armor peeled back from his wounded arm, revealing a half-circle of wide, oozing punctures, all of them turning an ugly shade of purple around the edges.

"Is that poison?" he asked in pain-filled and masochistic fascination.

"No," Shar replied absently, "just fast bruising. Mother taught me some Healing; I'm not in her league, but let me see what I can do."

Shar's reaction was automatic and immediate: *I've got to help him!* Without a second thought, she dashed in the direction of the scream, war-magics ready and burning to be thrown, only to see Tannim go over on his back and flip his assailant against the fender of the Mach I.

That was the end of that; Shar didn't need to watch the beast convulse and burst into flames to know that it was finished.

She dropped down beside him and went to work, ignoring the blazing mist-creature, although she thought it was a species that she recognized. The beast, before it had vanished, seemed to be one of the guard creatures Charcoal had created, or else something cooked up along the same plan. Charcoal did that sort of thing on a regular basis, rather than recruiting other creatures to his service. In fact, when she was young, he had made a habit of going to pockets of the Unformed specifically to create such monsters and chimera, bringing them back to his own domains to serve as watchdogs. Madoc Skean had gone Charcoal one better, creating the Faceless Ones the same way. Both of them preferred the expenditure of personal energy in order to obtain servants that were utterly loyal. The only trouble with these little expeditions was that it was quite difficult to keep the new creations rounded up. They always lost one or two every couple of trips, leaving the creatures roaming the mist, waiting for unwary prey.

That explains why Father had a Gate set here, she thought, as she engaged the little set-spell that parted Tannim's armored scales and slit it along the top of his wounded arm. *This pocket of the Unformed must be particularly sensitive.* The mists were not uniformly psychotropic, and those who used them to create living creatures kept the locations of the best mist pockets as a valuable resource.

She couldn't help but notice Tannim's start of surprise at her ability to open his armor. But at the moment her greatest concern was with his damaged arm; if that creature really was one of Charcoal's "shrogs" (her father's "clever" name for a thing based on shrews and dogs—what an idiot), the wounds could and would go septic in a heartbeat, and there wasn't exactly an emergency room with antibiotics handy.

She sank quickly into a Healing trance, held her hands around the wounds, and forced Healing energies into his cells. She worked from inside out; that way she wouldn't Heal the wound only to leave the infection still active inside. There was no telling if there were any more of the creatures nearby, nor when they would appear if there were more, but Tannim's injury *had* to be dealt with *now*.

As she penetrated his defenses, she realized something else.

There was something very erotic about this; it was the first time that she had Healed anyone other than herself of a serious injury. Shar had closed up other peoples' cuts and soothed abrasions, but this was deeper, much deeper. She was aware of him in a way that she had never experienced with anyone else; the touch of her hand on his arm sent pulses of sensuous electricity through *her* arms; she felt what he felt directly, from the tiny ache where he'd hit the back of his head, to the caress of the silk-smooth armor over the rest of his body, including the places where it was so closely fitted that it held swelling down.

Hmm. They didn't allow for it to expand much, did they?

She had never been so *aware* of a male in her life, or on so many different levels. Not the level of telepathy; neither of them were telepaths. No, this was on a visceral level, where the instincts lived. Was this how an empath felt? Small wonder most of them got into Healing of one sort or another and pursued all Arts of the body.

She wasn't good enough to mend the bites completely; she cleaned out the sites of possible infection, dulled down the pain, and stopped the bleeding. Then she accelerated the cell growth as much as she had the skill and the power to do. In another day, he would have a half-circle of mostly healed punctures, and in two, a half-circle of tiny scars.

She got into the car for a bottle of water and washed the blood off him with it, then got a pad of gauze from the first-aid kit. Figuring that nothing preventive was going to hurt, she dabbed each wound with a spot of antibiotic salve, then wrapped the arm in a thin layer of gauze and resealed the armor over the whole.

It was only when she looked up from the final motions of sealing up the scales that she looked up to see his expression of complete disbelief.

"How are you doing that?" he asked, voice a little harsh from the screams, but harsher still with suspicion. She would have been a little hurt by that suspicion if she hadn't been well aware that *she* would feel the same if a secret of hers had been uncovered. "How did you know how to unseal my armor?"

"Very rapid deductive reasoning," she replied as she let go of his arm, and he flexed it to test it, wincing at residual pain. "You're Chinthliss' pupil, there are only a limited number of ways you can seal armor like this, and I know all of the ones Chinthliss uses. The easiest would be the most logical, since you're obviously going to have to get in and out of it at least once a day, and you might have to get into it when you're hurt. Like now. So I tried the first spell, and it worked."

She tilted her head to the side and waited for his reply. It wasn't long in coming.

"Oh—" he said, "but—Chinthliss told me that no one had ever had armor like this."

"He was right," she told him. "No one has. Most people simply work spells into standard armor. A few more have enchanted Kevlar, or something else high-tech. No one has ever combined anachronism, high-tech, and magic to make something like this. But there are still only a limited number of ways armor like this can be opened."

Tannim sighed explosively. "Well, *damn*. And damn it again; he told me the armor wouldn't stop everything, but I'd gotten kind of used to it doing just that."

Shar nodded, with sympathy this time. She recalled the time that she had first discovered that *she* was not invulnerable in her draconic form. It had been a painful revelation. Literally.

"It's not going to stop everything—maybe in your world, but not here. Any time you have a situation where there's a seam, there's a weakness," she told him. "I still have scars on my ankle to prove the truth of that."

"I'm sorry," he said, as if he meant it. "You shouldn't have scars anywhere."

She held her breath, and looked up, to meet his intensely green gaze. "Oh," she said, unable to think of anything else.

What are you doing, Shar? You're a kitsune, *you're supposed to be unpredictable, wild, willful. What are you getting yourself into?*

Just because you've always found this man fascinating, intriguing—just because he's the only male you've ever imagined trusting at your back—and at your front—that's no reason to sit here like a love-struck ninny, gazing into his eyes.

That's no reason to want to kiss him. Or to pull him right down next to you on this relatively soft ground and finish stripping off that armor.

Like hell it isn't!

"Bloody hell!" said a voice just above her head. "What was that 'orrible screeching?"

Tom Cadge had his nose stuck out of the open window; apparently he'd managed to figure out the mechanism to lower it. Both she and Tannim jerked upright; he with a curse as it jarred his arm, and she with a curse for a different reason entirely.

"Nasty piece of Unseleighe work," Shar said, as she got up off the ground and offered Tannim her hand. He was not too macho to accept it, or to accept her help in getting to his feet. "It bit Tannim," she continued, trying to sound matter-of-fact.

"I'll be all right," Tannim added hastily. Then, in an undertone, "I will be all right, won't I?" he asked Shar. A stray lock of hair fell over his worried eyes, and his complexion was pale. "I don't feel all right."

"Don't play any tennis with that arm for a little, and go have a Gatorade. You're just in shock," she assured him. "In fact, it might not be a bad notion to move the car just to that opening you found, and then sit there for awhile. The intersections of domains tend to be rather chaotic and stressed, and I think perhaps that the Mach I won't make as much of a disturbance there." She gave him a sharp look, as she noticed that he was leaning very heavily against the side of the Mustang. "I can drive, if you can direct me."

"I think maybe you'd better," Tannim replied honestly. "I really don't feel very good at the moment."

He went around to the passenger's side and opened the door with a little difficulty. She slid into the driver's side and found the keys waiting in the ignition. As soon as she settled herself, she cast another long look at him, and did not like what she saw. Pale and sweating, he was obviously still in a lot of pain, and very shocky. "Here," she said, fishing behind the seat for another Gatorade. "Just tell me where to go, and I'll get us there. You rest—and when we get there, you should take a longer rest."

"I'm not going to argue," Tannim told her, as he leaned back in his seat and closed his eyes. "Not at all. Forward, about two o'clock."

She followed his directions, murmured between gulps of Gatorade, through the absolutely directionless white mist. Finally, the rock wall of the boundary loomed up in front of them, gray and smooth, rather than craggy as a natural rock face would be. "Right," Tannim said. "I mean, go right, along the wall. You'll find it in a moment."

She did; in fact, she spotted the place where the opening was by the turbulent swirling of the mist ahead of them. The mist itself was no longer white or drifting; stained with pale colors and random shifts of light, it eddied and flowed restlessly. It still avoided the Mustang, however, which was comforting; anything that lived in it would probably be as vulnerable to Cold Iron as the creatures spawned in the quieter areas.

She parked the car and turned off the engine. "Rest," she told him. "The problem might just be a bit of shock;

give your body and mind a chance to catch up with what I did."

He started to protest, then evidently decided better of it. "How bad are ye hurt, lad?" Tom Cadge asked with evident concern.

"Not too bad," Tannim replied, as Shar rummaged for a Gatorade of her own. "Been hurt worse."

"But we are not going any further until you are completely ready for anything," she told him in a voice that would permit no argument. "I never got a chance to tell you back there, but we've got more than one choice. We can try this unknown pocket of Unformed ahead of us, or we could try something that has—well, risk. The Gate goes to one of Charcoal's smaller domains. He might be there, he might not—but it's a place I know, and I can get to neutral territory from there."

He sipped his Gatorade, a lock of his hair falling over his eyes, as he sat in thoughtful silence. "So, the choice is the total unknown, versus a place where we know there's an enemy, one who may or may not be home right now."

She grimaced, but nodded. "If it were me—I'd go for the mist. I haven't been in that particular place for a long time, and Charcoal may have laid some nasty traps for the unwary in there. And anyway, even if he isn't there, his serving-creatures will be, and I don't think I could pass them anymore. But I thought you ought to know that the option is there; you have as much say in this as I do. If you think we should risk the known danger for the sake of a known way out—"

But Tannim shook his head decisively. "I'd rather take the unknown. You probably know Charcoal better than anyone else, and I'm strongly in favor of trusting an expert." He raised an eyebrow at her. "I take it that the rest of the destinations were equally unattractive?"

She smiled thinly and recited the other four destinations. His eyes widened for a moment at the mention of Red Magda and the Black Bard, confirming her guess that he just might know something about them.

And they just might know something about him, too.

*I rather doubt that they want to make certain he gets
invitations to all their weddings and bar mitzvahs.*

"The last possibility is to go back where we came from,"
she finished. "We could try the other settings on that Gate.
The drawback is that if someone is following us, we might
meet them."

"The other side of this rock wall sounds better all the
time," Tannim said after a significant pause.

"A little rest, first," Shar said firmly. "You need it."

*And I am not going to drive his car into another
domain. If there's any trouble—I know who the good driver
is in this car, and it isn't me or Thomas Cadge.*

Chinthliss stalked off down the garden path, with Joe
right behind him, and Fox making a reluctant third. "You
really shouldn't do this, you know," FX said plaintively.
"Lady Ako has some powerful friends. She could cause us
a lot of trouble."

Chinthliss did not reply. His stiff back said it all. As their
feet crunched along the gravel path, Joe glanced from side
to side, nervously. He could not believe that Lady Ako
would let them go so easily after detaining them for so long.

He was right. Two massive guards in fancy lacquered
armor stepped, literally out of nowhere, to bar their path.
It was really *weird*; they unfolded out of the air on either
side of the gravel walkway, then stepped onto it with curved
swords bared. Chinthliss stopped abruptly; Joe loosened
his weapon in its holster.

"I told you she could cause us trouble! We're doomed,"
Fox said from the rear of the group.

With a growl, Chinthliss turned abruptly; Joe stepped
out of the way, leaving Chinthliss face-to-face with FX. The
kitsune backed up a couple of steps after one look at
Chinthliss' expression of rage. The guards didn't move, and
Joe opted to disregard them for the moment, in favor of
keeping Chinthliss from disemboweling Fox right then and
there.

Fox held up his hands placatingly. "Hey, it was just a
comment, you know? A little information? A bit of a
reminder?"

Chinthliss took another step towards him.

Fox's hands transformed into a pair of fur-covered paws.

"Wee paws for station identification?" FX continued, with a nervous, feeble grin. "Ah—please accept my apology for the social fox-paws?"

The corner of Chinthliss' mouth twitched, although Joe could not see anything that would have been funny in that last sentence. But evidently the dragon did, and Joe breathed a little easier. Maybe Chinthliss wouldn't kill the *kitsune* quite yet.

"I did not bring you along as my court fool," Chinthliss replied coolly. "Whatever capacity Tannim has you in. I brought you because you are a *kitsune* and Shar is half *kitsune*, and I assumed your knowledge of her would be useful."

"What about the information Shar's mother could give you?" The sweetly feminine voice coming from behind Joe had a distinct edge to it. Joe turned again, and the two armor-clad bulwarks parted to let Lady Ako pass between them.

"Your information would be damned useful, my lady, if you could just bring yourself to part with it instead of offering endless Tea Ceremonies," Chinthliss replied, his own voice honed to an icy sharpness. "Failing that, we will simply seek help elsewhere."

"I have not been *your lady* for a very long time. You will not need to look elsewhere." Lady Ako made this a statement without a hint of apology to it. "There are circumstances surrounding this sad state of affairs that required you be detained." Her tone said, as clearly as words, that she did not intend to apologize for anything, nor did she intend to give any further explanation than this. She matched Chinthliss stare for stare.

Finally Chinthliss broke the silence. "Fine," he said abruptly. "I suppose I'm going to have to assume this has something to do with internal *kitsune* politics, the secrets of which mere mortals are not free to plumb. As long as your little game is over with, I'll put off looking for that cab."

He crossed his arms over his chest and waited, wrapped in dignity, for her to reply.

She bristled. "Do not presume to dictate my actions to me, Chinthliss!"

"I wouldn't dream of it," the dragon replied dryly. "Nor will I be drawn into an argument so as to permit you to delay us even further."

Fox looked from one to the other of them, and finally held up both paws. "He's called your bluff, Lady Ako," the *kitsune* said bluntly. "You might as well admit it, and give us some real help."

Lady Ako stared for a moment longer, then sighed. "He has indeed called my bluff. And the best I have is a pair of twos," she admitted. "All right; I can't seem to delay you any further, so we might as well get down to the business of actually finding them." She started back toward the building they had all stalked away from, and with a glance to the rear at the impassive guards, Chinthliss, Joe, and FX followed her.

"I've had someone watching the boy's car since it came Underhill," she said, as they mounted the steps to the graceful porch, and a few *kitsune* sitting on the flat cushions watched them with covert curiosity. "Not actually watching it, you understand, but keeping track of it by means of the disturbance it causes in the magic-fields. Shar managed to cloak it somewhat, but that much Cold Iron was bound to wreak a certain amount of disturbance no matter how skillfully she shielded it—a disturbance of a distinctive flavor, as you know."

"That makes sense." Chinthliss mounted the wooden steps of the building, keeping pace beside her. The steps creaked slightly under him, as if he weighed far more than his appearance would suggest. "But why track the vehicle instead of the people?"

"Because Shar is better than I at cloaking spells, and I do not know Tannim." Lady Ako held the scarlet-painted door open for them, and they all filed through—except for Chinthliss, who took the brass handle from her and bowed her inside. It seemed to Joe that she smiled faintly at the gallantry. "I knew that Shar would bring Tannim to his vehicle if she found a way to free him, because it represents a powerful weapon of defense," she continued. "And

I know that Madoc Skean has no allies other than Shar who could do anything with so great a concentration of Death Metal. Further, I suspected that only Tannim would have whatever other devices were needed to make it work, such as a key. So it followed that no one but Shar or Tannim would be able to move it. Not long ago, my intuition bore fruit; the car moved, and as soon as it moved, Shar's cloaking-spells destabilized, making it easier to track. Since we saw no motive-spells working, it must have moved under its own power."

Chinthliss stopped right in the middle of the white-paneled room. "It did? Where? And where is it now?"

Lady Ako beckoned them to follow, past a room full of flat cushions on the floor, through a sliding paper screen instead of a door, and into the kind of room Joe had not expected to find here.

It was a room full of computer equipment, mostly deep blue and bright red, with huge screens. There were at least a dozen SPARC stations and Silicon Graphics computers that they could see, with about half of them being used by creatures that were more or less foxlike. Some only had fox tails, some fox tails and feet, and some were humanized foxes as Lady Ako had been when they had first seen her.

They were all dressed in varying costumes, from futuristic jumpsuits to the full kimono-kit that Lady Ako wore. The lady bent over the shoulder of one of the silver foxes in a pearl-gray jumpsuit; this one had long, flowing white hair crowning her fox-mask and cascading down her back.

"It isn't that easy, Chinthliss," Ako said at last. "We know that the vehicle is moving, and we know in general where it is, but we can't tell specifically." She shrugged helplessly. "You simply cannot *map* Underhill; I have tried, with no success. You can go north, then east, then south, and find yourself facing north again. You can go up several levels only to find yourself four levels *below* the place you had started. The Gates do not connect domains in any kind of logical fashion. This room holds the closest thing anyone has to a map of Underhill."

"They're somewhere in the predominantly Unseleighe region, my lady," said the silver fox, tapping the screen with one furry forefinger. "If they can just get into one of the larger domains, one where we can pinpoint them by what Gates they are near, I can give you coordinates. But now— well, the sensors and programs we are using only show that they've used Gates to make domain-jumps, but since we don't have those specific Gates in our lists, it can't locate them precisely." The silver fox looked at everyone assembled. "We have magical sonar, and there's a lot of noise. We don't get a ping on them until they *do* something."

"You see?" Ako held up her hands helplessly. "We can track the perturbation and know that they are moving. Once they reach and use a Gate that we have in the computer, we know where they truly are. But until then, we'd be jumping blind."

Joe nudged Chinthliss. "Sir," he said hesitantly, "what about the trim-ring? Tannim used it to find the Mustang. Couldn't we do the same thing?"

"I wouldn't do that if I were you, sir," the silver fox replied respectfully, before Lady Ako could say anything. She turned around to look Chinthliss right in the eyes. "That much iron and steel is warping the magic fields down there in ways I can't predict, and neither can the computers. We just can't model chaos that well. If you tried to use that artifact to create a Gate, you might end up tearing a hole in the fabric of Underhill. Or you might just end up Gating somewhere you wouldn't like. The odds of actually going where you wanted to go are pretty low. We could run a simulation—but if we had enough data to make an accurate simulation, we'd have enough to find the vehicle, too."

"Laini is my best tech," Ako said, placing a hand on the silver fox's shoulder. "If she says it's dangerous, I'd believe her. And if she doesn't like the odds, I wouldn't take the risk."

Chinthliss eyed both of the *kitsune* dubiously. "So what *would* you do if you were in our position?" he asked.

Laini thought for a moment. "You might use the trim-ring as a magic-mirror, just to *show* you where they are. We use an optical link through a magic-mirror to connect to Internet from here. The Internet is great for hiding things and communicating with obscure locations on Earth—Underhill enclaves with outerworld fronts, allies, informants—just bounce encrypted files from one anonymous site to another. Anyway, we use a tuned laser beamed through two stationary mirrors—one here in Furhold, and one on the other side. If you use a magic-mirror, you get a super clear image most of the time. You might recognize something we could use, or get a photograph sharp enough that we could cross-reference it through our Silicon Graphics image systems here." She pointed one delicately-clawed paw—hand—at the crimson boxes whirring away. "We have thousands of subrealms identified and imaged, and some of them are mapped down to ten-meter grid squares with local magical data. We just don't know all the Gates that lead to them, because that takes a lot more than remote viewing. But we do have some."

Laini looking thoughtful again and tapped at her silvery-black snout. She flicked an ear. "If you can determine a *place*, or give us enough data that we can find it, we might be able to plot a route that could get you there, using the Gates that we know of."

Joe grinned. *Now that's a little more like it!* he thought. Evidently Chinthliss felt the same.

"I didn't realize that you had an artifact," Lady Ako said, "or I would have offered all this a little sooner."

"Is there somewhere secure that we can use to set up a scrying-spell?" Chinthliss asked. "You know what I mean by 'secure,' I trust."

"Of course." Ako smiled sweetly. "This *is* the embassy, after all. We have some very secure places. If you'll follow me?"

Once again, Lady Ako led them all down a maze of corridors, this time with walls of white paper and bamboo rather than white-painted wood. How such a place could be considered "secure" was beyond Joe, but if Lady Ako said it was, he might as well take her word for it. At least no one would be able to eavesdrop on you here—you'd see his shadow through the walls first.

Maybe that was what made it secure?

At length she pushed aside a sliding door and led them into a room containing what was either a very small building or a very large box, lacquered in black, with graceful images of cranes and carp—and, of course, foxes—on the sides, formed in strokes of gold paint. "You will be secure enough in there," she said. "It will be a little crowded, but it is very well shielded."

She opened a door into the box; it looked rather like a sauna inside, with benches against two of the walls and a low table in the middle. Somehow all four of them managed to squeeze inside; Lady Ako and Chinthliss on one bench, FX and Joe on the other.

Ako shut the door; after a moment of darkness, a gentle, sourceless light came up all around them. Chinthliss placed the chrome trim-ring down in the middle of the black-lacquered table.

Here we go again. . . .

As all three of the others bent over the shining circle of chrome, Chinthliss chanted under his breath. A drift of sparks came from his outstretched hand and settled on the ring, exactly as if he had sprinkled glitter down on it. But these sparks spread and grew, until a skin of light coated the whole trim-ring.

Mist gathered inside the ring, and all four of them leaned a little closer. "Damn," Chinthliss muttered irritably, "that tech of yours is right. The Mach I really is warping things all out of shape down there."

Ako laid one hand over the top of his, and a second shower of sparks fell on the ring. The light strengthened, and for just a moment, a picture formed in the middle.

It *was* the Mach I, all right; Tannim was in the passenger's seat, though, and in the driver's seat was the woman who'd shown up at the barn. There was someone else in the rear seat, too, and the whole car was surrounded by a white mist that eddied around the car as if it didn't quite want to touch it.

Then the picture faded, leaving only the shiny black lacquered surface of the table.

"Well, at least we *do* know that they're together," Lady Ako said into the silence.

"But who was that in the rear?" Joe asked. "And where were they?"

"The Unformed," Chinthliss growled. "There are only several hundred places they could be, with that Unformed mist around them. Damn."

But surprisingly, it was FX who shook his head. "That's the bad part; don't forget, the Unseleighe and the Seleighe both have Gates into those pockets. So do the neutrals, for that matter. It's not a big deal; we just need a little more time. We just wait for them to Gate out of there, and see if we can identify where they came out."

"Which means we sit here until the car moves again." Joe sighed.

Chinthliss nodded abruptly, scowling.

Lady Ako looked from one gloomy face to another, and finally ventured to speak. "I don't suppose," she said doubtfully, "that any of you would care for some tea?"

Shar stared at the swirling, pastel-colored mist and wondered if it was half as unsettled out there as she felt. Most disturbing was the feeling that things had gotten completely out of her control.

Her reaction to Tannim being attacked was entirely out of character. If Tannim hadn't already slain that mist-creature, she would have reverted to Huntress-mode and leapt upon it to rend it with her own, sharp teeth right then and there. She *never* leapt to anyone's defense; she always assumed that they could take care of themselves. After all, no one was going to leap to *her* defense. . . .

The strength of her own feelings had shocked her; more shocking had been the way she had automatically reacted on seeing that he had been hurt. She had *never* expended Healing on anyone else before. Not once. She was not a "natural" Healer as Lady Ako was; it cost her a great deal to invoke a Healing spell. There had never been anyone worth the effort before.

And before my mind could weigh all the consequences, I found myself Healing him without even pausing to think about what I was doing. Very strange. Very unlike her.

Tannim did not sleep this time, but he rested as Shar had ordered, slowly regaining color as he sipped at a Gatorade and nibbled at packaged crackers. After a glance at her, which she met with a smile, he fished under the seat and came up with a car magazine. His inquiring glance asked "may I?" and her answering shrug replied "be my guest." He immersed himself in its pages as she stared out at the mist, still sorting her thoughts.

It was logic, she told herself firmly. *Pure logic. This is his car, we need each other at top form to guard the other's back. I Healed him because of that. It has nothing to do with how I feel about him.*

And pigs were certainly flying in tight formation over LaGuardia at this very moment.

"Ready to switch places?" he said into the silence. When she gave him a measuring look, he grinned at her with a good measure of his old cockiness.

"I would certainly not care to take the blame for anything that happened to your beloved car if I ran it into something out there," Shar replied dryly. "Please, Captain, take the helm by all means."

But before popping any doors, they *both* checked the mist for the telltale swirls that signaled something hiding in it. And Shar noted with some amusement that both of them scooted around the car and into their new places so quickly that it would have taken a photo to tell which of them hit the seat first.

She snapped her seatbelts in place. He quirked his eyebrows at her. "Paranoid?" he asked.

"Of course," she retorted. "They *are* out to get us."

"Point taken." He started the car and drove into the mist, heading for the place where the colors and eddying were the strongest.

The gap in the rock walls must have been larger than she had thought; when the rock disappeared on the left, there was no answering darkness up ahead to show where it might resume. Tannim turned the Mach I into the gap, still keeping the wall on the left. The mist was at its most turbulent here; the predominant color was a blue-green, but there were swirls of red, yellow, even purple.

"This place makes me think of an explosion in a tie-dye plant," Tannim muttered under his breath.

Shar peered ahead into the psychedelic fog, every muscle and nerve alive with tension, and started when Tom Cadge tapped her shoulder.

"Please, lass," he said quietly, "can ye tell me where this magical chariot is goin'? All I know is we been someplace cold, an' now we're someplace else."

"Did you ever—ah—see any of the places that the Unseleighe Sidhe call 'Unformed'?" she asked. She hated to ask it that way, but Cadge didn't seem to mind.

"Before they put out me eyes, ye mean?" He shook his head. "I heard tell of 'em, but I ne'er saw one. I didna see much but Lady Magda's Hall, an' not much o' that."

"Well, that's where we are. It's a place full of mist, and not much else, and someone with a strong enough will and magic can make it into anything he wants," she told him. "Somebody left something nasty behind the last time he was here, and it attacked Tannim."

"Mist?" Tom shook his head. "What can anyone be doin' with mist?"

"It's a special kind of mist," Shar replied absently. "Think of it like clay. That's how most of the domains were made in the first place, right out of the mist. Either one incredibly powerful mage, like Lord Oberon or Lady Titania, or a group of mages with a single plan in mind, would move into one of these places and turn it into what they wanted."

"So?" Thomas replied. "Is that where we are, then? One o' them mist places?"

"Exactly. There are often Gates in there, and that's what we're looking for." Shar continued to stare ahead as she talked to Tom; was it imagination, or was the color slowly leaching out of the swirling mist? "People can make small things out of the mist, too, so they'll come here when they need something and create it."

"So—if ye can make anything ye like, why don't ye make a Gate now?" Tom asked with perfect logic.

Shar sighed. "Partly because I'm not certain either of us is up to creating a Gate at the moment. Partly because this iron carriage that protects us also warps magic around it, and I'm not certain what the effect of making a Gate around it would be. Partly because a Gate is one thing you can't make out of the mist with any certainty at all—it would be like you trying to juggle a dozen sharp knives at once. And lastly, making a Gate makes a fearful disturbance; there are people watching for us, and they'll know where we are and what we're doing."

"Ah." Tom nodded wisely. "So I see. This workin' of magic, it just purely isn't like—like magic, is it?" He grinned, amused at his own wit.

"Precisely." She forced a tired chuckle since he wouldn't be able to see her smile. "Well, we're going to see if we can't find another Gate in here to take us somewhere nearer to our friends."

By now the mist had definitely gone to pastel. In a few more moments, all the color would be gone, and it would be time to stop the Mustang and see if she couldn't locate another Gate on this side of the wall.

But as the color leeched out of the mist, the mist itself thinned. Shadow-shapes appeared, not the moving shapes the mist itself produced, but stationary shadows, with solidity to them.

The mist thinned further as the Mustang rolled forward, and the shapes took on substance, color, and texture. "Are you seeing what I'm seeing?" Tannim asked quietly.

"I think so," Shar replied, while she cobbled together the most apt comparison *she* could come up with. "This is really weird. It looks like somebody's rock collection."

If it was, the collector had to be a giant. Ahead, behind, and on either side loomed huge slabs and boulders of polished, formed or crystallized stone, each piece as big as the Mach I or bigger. These slabs balanced upright somehow, defying gravity, even though their bases might be no bigger than a foot or so across. The impression of being in the midst of a rock collection was inescapable now that Tannim had pointed it out; no two of these huge "specimens" were alike, and they all appeared—at least to Shar's uneducated eyes—to be purely of a particular "kind" of rock. Here was a cluster of quartz crystal points, the smallest of them as long as her arm and the largest taller than Tannim—

there a polished boulder of amethyst big enough to crush
the Mach I—ahead a single giant violet diamond-shaped
fluorite crystal balanced precisely on one point.

"This is bizarre," Tannim said softly, staring at the next
rock, a milky yellow multifaceted crystal which balanced
on a single point like the fluorite crystal now behind them.
The one next to it looked for all the world like an irregular
slab cut from a geode and polished on both sides. "Have
you ever heard of anything like this?"

"Never," she said firmly. "But I'm not sure I like what
it implies. *Someone* had to create all this out of the
Unformed; that's the only way you'd get things like this,
right? So that person had to not only be some kind of
rock-nut, but he had to be a complete monomaniac."

"Rock is my life, man," Tannim said automatically, but
the joke fell rather flat.

Mist writhed away from the Mach I as they passed the
balanced slab and a round boulder of pink quartz appeared
to the right. "To the exclusion of everything else?" Tannim
hazarded. "Boy, I hope we aren't disturbing his collection,
wandering around in here!" He ran a hand through his
tangled curls worriedly.

"Why don't you stop for a moment, and let me see if
I can find a Gate," Shar suggested, feeling as worried as
Tannim looked. "If someone got in here to create all this,
there has to be a way out. I think I'd like to find it before
he finds us."

Tannim nodded, and stopped the Mustang between a
colorful metallic cubic aggregate of selenium and a polished granite egg the size of a Kenworth. Shar got out,
checking all around them with such caution that it felt as
if every nerve was an antenna, tuned for danger.

Only when she was certain there was nothing within the
reach of her senses or her magics did she take a seat on
the hood of the Mustang and send her spirit out quest-
ing for the peculiar magical signature of a Gate.

"Want to try again?" Joe suggested, as the rather stilted
conversation in the crowded room died into silence again
for the fourth time.

Chinthliss looked at Lady Ako, who alone of them had not lost her outward serenity. She shrugged. "I told my underlings to come inform us if the Mustang made a sizable change of location. That would indicate a Gate-passage, of course. There's no telling, though, if they were able to locate a domain *within* the Unformed where we saw them. Elfhame Outremer is such a place; I'm certain the Unseleighe also have domains within the mist. I know that the Grand Bazaar is in the mist, and that it is not the only neutral hold to be in the center of the Unformed."

"Is that a 'yes' or a 'no'?" Chinthliss asked in open exasperation. "Oh, never mind. *I* want to see if your precious daughter is up to anything." He bent over the chrome trim-ring, and once again chanted until a shower of sparks drifted down from his hand and settled on the chrome ring. This time the lacquer tabletop enclosed by the ring fogged over with no help from Lady Ako.

The haze cleared, and Joe leaned over the table for a closer look.

Shar sat on the hood of the Mach I, her eyes closed and a frown of concentration on her face. Tannim stood beside the car in a protective stance, his bespelled red crowbar in his hands, watching warily to all sides. The Mustang itself was parked in front of a huge gray boulder, a rock as big as two cars put together and polished to a glossy sheen. The mist of the earlier vision was thinner here, but there was still nothing really identifiable about the place.

Joe looked up at Lady Ako to see her reaction. She was smiling: a satisfied little smile compounded of equal parts of approval and relief.

"It seems they truly are working together," the lady said with a faint air of satisfaction.

Chinthliss only grunted. "I should give a great deal to know how my foster-son's sleeve came to be so shredded," he replied.

Joe glanced back down at the little scene imprisoned in the chrome circle, and saw with a start that Tannim's right sleeve *was* hanging in rags. But beneath the shirt-sleeve was something altogether unexpected; armor

of some kind, he guessed. Iridescent green, of tiny hexagonal scales invisibly joined together, it covered his arm
as smoothly as Spandex from wrist to shoulder.

"Pretty," Lady Ako remarked, indicating the armor with
a fingertip that did not quite touch the image. "I assume
that this is your doing, this armor?"

"As much Tannim's as mine," the dragon admitted with
a touch of pride in his voice. "I happen to think that it
is very good work. Something must have attacked them,
though."

"If so, it learned that he bites back," Ako observed.
"Honestly, I do not recognize this place, although I will
inform my techs with a description, and we will see if the
computer has a match. What of you?"

"Not a clue," Chinthliss admitted, as Ako slipped what
looked to Joe like a palmtop computer out of her sleeve
and laid it on her lap, quickly scratching something on its
screen with a fingernail before returning it to her volu-
minous sleeve. *I always wondered what they used those
huge kimono sleeves for. Heck, you could smuggle Mexi-
cans in there!*

"You seem to be having an easier time holding the vision
this time, old lizard," Fox observed. "Got any idea why?"

Chinthliss shook his head. "Probably has something to
do with the area they're in. Less instability, maybe. There's
a lot less of the Unformed mist, anyway." He turned to
Ako. "What's *she* doing?"

"I would guess that she is searching the area for a
Gate," Ako told him. "Shar is particularly sensitive to the
energies of Gates. Even if she does not recognize a
setting, she can sometimes tell general things about the
destination."

"No—" Chinthliss took his eyes from the vision in the
chrome trim-ring for a moment to stare at Ako in astonishment. "Where did she pick up that trick? From—"

"Yes," Ako confirmed. "I myself do not know how she
does this. It is not a *kitsune* gift."

"It isn't a dragon-talent either." He shook his head. "Evidently she is not simply a meld of *kitsune* and dragon; she
is something more."

"As I have always maintained." Ako was too composed to beam with pride, but there was a great deal of pride in her voice.

Inside the chrome circle, Tannim walked a wary patrol around the car as Shar remained perched on the hood. There was nothing in Tannim's behavior that suggested to Joe that he was at all worried about Shar or what she might do. If anything, his prowling suggested that he was determined to protect her from anything that might come at her out of the mist.

That certainly suggested they had come to some sort of arrangement, an agreement of cooperation, perhaps.

The vision still wasn't clear enough to make out who was in the back seat of the Mustang. The figure was blurred, as if the focus was a bit out in that one spot, although the rest of the scene was clear enough.

"I can't see what is in the backseat," Chinthliss said with a frown, echoing Joe's own thought. "That's odd. Look, you can see the front seat itself clearly enough, so it isn't the Mach I's shields that are interfering." He glanced sharply at Ako, who only shrugged.

"I could not tell you who that might be," she replied. "Shar has no allies that she would trust in a situation like this. Perhaps it was someone they met along the way?"

"Maybe another prisoner of Madoc Skean," Chinthliss muttered. "Tannim wouldn't be able to leave someone like that behind. Especially not if it was a Seleighe Sidhe."

"Can you blame him?" Fox made a face. "I wouldn't leave a dead cat in the hands of that lunatic."

"Maybe if I—" Chinthliss held his hand over the trim-ring again, his eyes narrowing as he focused his magic. "I would feel a lot better if I could just see who or what that is—"

But his efforts were not only in vain, they undid everything else he had accomplished. As Joe watched in dismay, the vision flared, then faded, leaving only the hint of haze on the black lacquer.

Then even the haze faded, and only the shiny surface remained.

Chinthliss cursed, but Lady Ako remained philosophical.

"You can only hold such a vision for so long," she reminded him. "And what good would it do you to sit here and stare at it? You cannot help them until you know where they are."

Chinthliss growled under his breath, but had to admit that she was right. "But I don't have to like it," he added. Joe agreed silently. At least, if they could watch, they had the illusion that they could do something.

"I can—" Chinthliss began, then pulled his hand back before he even began the spell again. "No. No point in wasting magic that we might need later."

"A messenger *will* come if the Mustang makes a large enough movement for a fix," Ako promised. "I gave you my word."

At that, Chinthliss actually smiled. "I do not recall that you actually gave your word before, my lady, but now that you have—I am inclined to trust you."

Ako looked at him in some surprise, and Joe thought, she also looked a little hurt. "Have we grown so far apart, Chinthliss, that you no longer trust me without my given word?" she asked softly.

Chinthliss blinked, and turned to meet her gaze completely. The two of them stared deeply into one another's eyes, unable to look away.

Joe cleared his throat, and they both jumped and looked at him as if they had forgotten that he and FX existed.

Maybe they did forget we existed.

"Can we—ah—take a break, lady?" he asked carefully. "All that tea—"

"I don't—" Fox began, and Joe jabbed him fiercely in the side with an elbow. FX emitted a strangled grunt and fell silent.

"Certainly," Lady Ako replied, ignoring FX. "Saski can show you where everything is. Can't you, Saski?" Now she smiled at FX, to his obvious discomfort.

"Yes, Lady Ako," FX managed. Joe slid the door to the little room open, and he and Fox climbed out. The door slid shut again as soon as they were outside.

"What did you do that for?" FX hissed angrily.

"They *wanted* to be alone, dummy," Joe replied scornfully. "Jeez, man, couldn't you see that? Don't you remember what Chinthliss told us about him and the lady and all?"

"Of course I remember! That's why I wanted to stay there and watch!" Fox told him. "And—*ow*!" he exclaimed, as Joe elbowed him again. "What did you do *that* for?"

"Because you're rude, crude, and not even housebroken," Joe told him, shaking his head in dismay. "Man, I can't take you anywhere, can I? Why don't you show me what passes for a bathroom around here. I really did drink too much of that tea."

Fox sighed and cast a longing look back at the closed doors of the little room. "Oh well," he said philosophically. "We'll figure out whatever they've been up to when we get back anyway."

"You're impossible," Joe retorted.

Fox only snickered.

CHAPTER TWELVE

Tannim prowled around the car restlessly, the comforting weight of his crowbar filling both hands. He studied the mist as it eddied around the giant mineral specimens, watching it with wary suspicion. Mist alternately concealed and revealed the farthest of the rocks, moving in no pattern he could discern. Unless he was greatly mistaken, the farthest of those rocks was a slice of watermelon tourmaline, a huge irregular wedge of transparent pink and green. He wouldn't even have known that watermelon tourmaline existed, much less what it was called and what it looked like, if Dotty hadn't been so infatuated with the stuff.

She'd be going ape right now, trying to figure out how to cart a five-ton rock out of here. Boy, this place is surreal. I feel like I'm in the middle of a Lexus commercial.

He kept thinking that he saw things moving, just out of the corner of his eye. But any time he turned to see what it was, there was nothing there but a swirl of mist.

Too bad I'm not some kind of superhero. I could sure use an edge right now. Heros in books had magical senses to warn *them* of approaching danger; all he had were his eyes and ears and mage-sight. *My crowbar-sense is tingling!* The mage-sight wasn't doing him a heck of a lot of good; the mist itself was full of magical potential and obscured everything else.

574

It's doing me about the same amount of good as a guy with a heat-scope in the desert at high noon.

That left eyes and ears. Plain old human senses, backed by red-painted iron and a bit of experience. Maybe a little good sense. It would have to do.

His feet made no noise at all in the sand. None. He might just as well have been walking on a foot of packed feathers. The ground here was as strange as the rest of the place. You could dig down just as far as you wanted, and all you'd find was sparkling white, utterly dry sand. Yet neither the tires nor feet sank in more than an inch, and there was firm, excellent traction, as good as the sands of Daytona Beach. Better. As good as the Bonneville salt flats. *If I could just export this stuff, I'd make a fortune selling it to dirt-tracks.*

He glanced over at his companion every time he passed her, just to see if anything had changed. Shar's face was utterly still, without expression of any kind. Once again, she looked like a statue sitting there; if he hadn't seen her chest rising and falling in slow, even rhythm, he'd have thought she was dead, spellbound, or otherwise incapacitated.

And that chest, rising and falling, up and down, slowly—

It looked as good as the rest of her. He prowled a series of full circuits around the Mustang, still without seeing anything. This bit of magic was taking her a lot longer than the last time she'd done something. Of course, the last time, she'd had the Gate right in front of her, and this time they didn't even know if there *was* a Gate over here.

What would they do if there wasn't a Gate here? *A good question. Turn around and go back, I guess. Take our chances with one of the unfriendly settings, or with the place before that. It was cold and not very hospitable, but we wouldn't have to be there all that long. I hate to backtrack, though. We might meet something on our tail. That would be bad.*

It shouldn't take them all that long to get on our tail, either. All they have to do is figure out that Shar didn't move the Mach I like she said she did.

By now, Madoc Skean must have figured out they'd slipped through his fingers. He and his cronies were surely on their trail in some form or other. How long would it take him to sort through all of the possibilities? He wasn't stupid; he wouldn't have amassed as many allies as he'd had if he was. He had to be on his way already.

There—something flickered at the edge of his vision again. This time he patrolled a few more soundless steps, then made an abrupt about-face, hoping to catch whatever it was in the act of eluding him.

Nothing. Not even an eddy of mist.

Maybe this place is getting to me, making me see things. Haven't been this jumpy in a long time.

He decided that he might as well prowl in the opposite direction, since he was facing that way anyway.

Madoc's not stupid, and he's got a lot of ears in other domains. So, given how good a spy-network Madoc has, by now he's surely heard about our little visit to the Hall of the Mountain King. From there, there're only five destinations besides the one we came from. Given enough people to check them out . . . yeah, he could be on to us right now.

"Eh, lad?" Tom Cadge called from inside the car, sounding anxious. "How long ye reckon afore the blackguards follow us?"

Even the old man was following his thoughts.

"I don't know, Tom," he answered truthfully, leaning against the car to talk through the window. "Could be they're after us right now. The one thing we've got going for us is that they've got to tread the same maze that we do. With any luck, they'll get as lost as we are."

Tom nodded, his mouth solemn below his bandaged eyes. "Mayhap they'll blunder into a nest 'o their own foes, eh? Like knockin' over a beehive. That'd be a choice jest."

"Oh, that'd be the best thing that could happen," Tannim told him, with a mental image of the Black Bard's surprise on finding his home invaded by his old rival Madoc. That would be a lovely sight to see! If Madoc got out of there with half his followers, he'd be lucky. The

Black Bard was without mercy when it came to his few friends—and when given a chance at a foe . . .

Tom cocked his head to one side for a moment, then grimaced. "This place is mortal strange, lad. I keep thinkin' I'm hearin' summat off i' the distance, an' then when nothin' comes of it, thinkin' it's nobbut m' addled wits."

"Well you're not alone. I keep seeing things, but when I turn to look at them, there's nothing there." He pushed away from the car as Shar stirred. "Well, it looks like the lady may have found us something. Keep your ears open, all right? They're probably keener than mine."

"Aye, I will," Tom promised solemnly.

Tannim reached the front of the Mustang just as Shar opened her eyes. "There *is* a Gate here, but it's a long way off," she said, stretching her arms and blinking to clear her sight. "I wouldn't have believed this pocket was so big—that Gate must be six or eight miles from here. I can't think of too many places Underhill that are this size, and all of them have huge populations."

Tannim raised an eyebrow at that. "I wouldn't have thought it could be that big either; I would have thought that a pocket this large would have been claimed by now."

"Maybe it has," she replied ominously. "I caught distinct traces of Unseleighe magics out there. Only traces, so this isn't truly a domain of theirs, but they use this place for something."

"Grand." He sighed, and hefted the crowbar just for the reminder of its comforting weight. "Well, let's get on the road, shall we? If we're moving, we're a harder target to hit."

She slid off the hood without a comment, and landed lightly on the sand. He turned around and headed for the driver's side. He reached his seat a fraction of a second before she took hers, but this time they both fastened their safety belts.

She pointed directly ahead when he looked to her for directions. "Straight on, the way we were already going," she said.

He nodded, with a quick glance at the gas gauge. He'd

started this trek with darn near a full tank of gas, and he'd tried to be careful—

And we're still a hair above the three-quarter margin, he noted with a bit of relief. *Hard to find a gas station out here, and neither of us are Sidhe, to be able to* ken *and replicate whatever we want.*

He started the Mustang and drove on, slowly, in the direction she indicated. Visibility still wasn't good enough to warrant going faster than fifteen or twenty. Another towering rock-sample emerged out of the mist right in front of them, this one a huge nugget of pure copper, constructed like a branching coral formation.

Weird. Just too weird. He shook his head, and drove on.

A half an hour later by his watch, the mist had thinned to no more than a veil, upping visibility to about half a mile. The landscape had been changing for about the past fifteen minutes. The rock formations grew smaller, replaced by groves of dead and leafless trees, stretching blackened limbs against the white haze in the distance. Overhead was exactly the same as the nonexistent horizon: white haze. Lighting was a constant semidusk, nondirectional. All the place needed was a vulture or two for atmosphere.

The terrain itself had changed in that time; getting rougher, with increasingly steep hills and deep valleys, and nothing like a road in sight. The Mustang wasn't built for territory like this; heck, the Mustang wasn't built for anything but a real road. The only way to handle this kind of situation was to work his way up and down the hills in a zig-zag pattern, or travel along the ridge until a better crossing place showed up. The ground was still made of that strange sand; why it didn't slide and behave like dune-sand he had no idea. The top layer would slide down a little as the Mustang's wheels touched it, making the going a bit treacherous and tricky to drive, but beneath the top layer, the ground was firm.

That didn't help much, not when his jaw ached from clenching it and his knuckles were white from clutching the steering wheel.

Finally, they topped a rise only to find themselves looking down into a valley with a fifty-degree slope. Tannim stopped the car altogether.

"We can't take this in the Mach I," Shar said abruptly, before he could say a word. "Nothing short of a Land Rover could negotiate a slope like that. Tannim, I'm amazed you got this far—I'd have given up a mile ago. I almost asked you to quit when we passed that hematite boulder."

Tannim stared down the smooth slope, unbroken except for an occasional boulder of some highly polished stone or by a trio or quartet of spindly black trees, and nodded. Finally, after a long silence, he coughed.

"I'm pretty much stuck here without you," he admitted. "I don't know how to work those Gate things without already knowing the setting I want. I guess it's going to be up to you. Do we ditch the Mach I and try for this new Gate on foot?"

He was hoping she would think that was a bad idea. *I'll argue with her if I have to, but we're partners in this. I'm not going to make an arbitrary decision for both of us.*

Shar shook her head immediately. "No," she replied decisively. "Not a chance. This is one we're going to have to do without. It'd take us hours to get there on foot, Tom couldn't do it, and we'd be without our protection, our ability to move quickly, and our power source. That wouldn't be stupid, it would be suicide."

He ground his teeth to relieve his frustration, then gave voice to the only other solution, the one he'd already contemplated. "We go back. And try the other Gate."

She nodded, her own face displaying her distaste for the obvious. "And unless we're willing to take the chance on running into the people following us by going back to the frozen plain—the only other setting we stand a chance with is Charcoal's holding."

"We'll decide that when we get there," he replied. "One problem at a time."

At least he had a good idea how to *get* back. The soft sand didn't hold tracks forever, but he could still make out a clear trail behind them. While the tire-tracks in the sand were still visible, he could follow them. And after that—he'd kept track of the various rock-samples they'd passed. Unless the unknown collector (if there was one) had a habit of swapping them around on a regular basis—or they moved on their own—he'd get back to the point where the mist got so thick he could use *his* talent to find the gap in the walls again.

It didn't feel right, though, turning back like this. Besides being frustrating, it felt as if he had missed a point somewhere. Granted, this wasn't a video game, where you always got the next level if you did things in the right order, but still—turning back felt like a mistake. There *ought* to have been a way, but if there was, he hadn't seen it, and neither had Shar.

One thing was oddly comforting, though, and that was Shar's behavior. Not only had she refused to give up the Mustang—she'd refused to dump Tom Cadge.

That was automatic, too. She didn't lean over and whisper to me that we ought to abandon him with the car. She didn't suggest we leave him and come back for him with help. It wasn't, "we could leave the passenger behind, but that wouldn't be right." Instead, it was, "it would take us hours on foot, and Tom couldn't do it." As if there was no question of keeping him with us—it's a given.

He could trust her. He *could*. That single sentence had told him that much. She had nothing to gain and everything to lose by continuing to help the old man, and she hadn't even given it a second thought. It had been a completely natural response; that she accepted him as a responsibility along with her "debt" to Tannim.

His mood now much lighter, he surprised her by smiling at her once they got the Mach I turned around and headed back the way they had come. The furrows cut by the tires pointed the way, and he followed, retracing their path exactly. And hoping that he was doing the right thing.

Now as long as there isn't someone laying false tire-tracks for us to follow, we'll be all right.

"I suppose it could be worse," she said after a moment.

"There might not *be* anyone following us yet. We do have options still, and there's—"

Her head and Tom's came up at the same moment in identical startled movements, like a pair of deer alerted by a danger signal. "Oh, no—" she whispered.

"Tell me I didna hear a huntin' horn, milady," Tom begged, his wrinkled face white beneath the bandage. "Please tell me it was just th' wind, or summat like that. There's only one kind o' pack a-huntin' Underhill—"

He was interrupted by the sounding, faint but clear over the Mustang's rumble, of a hunting horn. At least, Tannim assumed it was a hunting horn, since they both shivered when they heard it.

"The Wild Hunt," Shar whispered, her eyes wide. "Oh no—we don't need that kind of trouble!"

"Whoa, whoa, what Wild Hunt?" Tannim asked, responding to the fear on both their faces by speeding up just a little. "What hunt? What's it mean to us? Who're the hunters?"

"The lost gods," Shar said fearfully, looking back over her shoulder as if she expected to see them at any moment, topping the hill behind them. "The spirits that once were gods of death and darkness in your world, who lost their worshippers and were banished Underhill. They hunt the living, led by their pack and their terrible Master. Even the Unseleighe fear them and hide when they hear that horn. It's said that there's no escape from them. Once they have the scent of you, they *never* give up!"

"Won't all this Cold Iron stop them?" he asked, as the horn sounded again, and sent a chill running up his spine. "I mean, we're talking pre-Christian, Bronze-Age guys here, aren't we? Shouldn't the rules that hold for the Sidhe hold for them?"

"The Master of the Hunt bears a spear tipped with the Death Metal from a fallen star," Shar replied, dashing his hopes. "That is why the Unseleighe fear him. They are no more bothered by iron and steel than a *kitsune*. They can cross running water with impunity, and holy things do not bar their way. Only sunlight stops them, and I doubt we're going to get any of that piped in to us on request!"

Tom Cadge had hunched down into his blankets, shivering, his head completely covered, like a child trying to hide from the monsters in the dark. It didn't look as though he had anything coherent to add.

"Great," Tannim muttered. "So what *do* we have going for us? Anything at all we can use against them?"

"We're not predictable." She stared through the back window; the horn-call sounded again, and it was definitely nearer. "They are more powerful than you, I, and all the Seleighe in Fairgrove put together—they used to be *gods*, for heaven's sake! Their horses never tire, nor do their hounds. But they will never have seen anything like this car, and they won't know what it, and we, can do. For that matter, they may not realize that the Mach I isn't alive— remember how the elves in the Mountain King's Hall reacted? If we can get out of this, it'll be by our wits."

"If I can get us into the heavy mist, can we lose them?" he asked. "Do you think that the turbulent area where the two pockets join is going to be confusing enough that they might lose the scent?"

"I don't know—but that just might work." She bit her lip and closed her eyes for a moment, thinking furiously. "Come to think of it, I know more than a few tricks along those lines. If you can get us some lead, *I* can kill the trail so cold they'll never find it, once we get into that mist!" Shar said at last, with determination replacing the fear in her eyes. "There wasn't a clever fox worthy of his tail yet that couldn't baffle any pack, on this side of the Hill or on the other, and haven't I nine tails?"

"That's the spirit, milady," Tom quavered from beneath his blankets. Tannim was surprised that he could respond at all, as obviously terrified as he was.

"All right then," Tannim said firmly. "Just let me get down where I can do some real driving, and I'll buy you that time."

In answer to that, the horn sounded a new set of notes entirely, and faintly beneath it came the deep and baleful baying of hounds.

Not the excited belling of foxhounds, however. These howls had a strange and doleful sound to them, as if the dogs themselves were in pain and wanted nothing more than to inflict that same pain on their quarry. This was a howl of bloodthirsty despair, a cry of doom approaching on four sore paws, whipped on by something even more terrible behind it. The deep cries called on the fear in the soul, the terror of the *thing behind,* the monster in the darkest shadows of childhood.

"They don't have hawks or anything, do they?" Tannim asked, suddenly struck by a horrible thought. If he had to contend with attacks from above as well as the hunters on the ground—granted, a hawk wouldn't be able to do a lot against the Mustang, but if this Master had complete control of them, there were things he could do *with* them. Having them drop rocks on the windshield—or hurl themselves against the windshield in kamikaze attacks.

"Not that I ever heard," Shar assured him. "Hawks can't be forced to course the way that hounds can. Turn a bird loose, however you have coerced it, and it can and will fly away."

One less thing to worry about. "Good."

As the ground gradually leveled, it became easier to drive. The sounds of the Hunt behind them grew ever nearer, as if the Hunters realized that *they* had the advantage here, and were determined to catch up while they still had that advantage. "What kind of rules are they limited by?" he asked, negotiating the downslope of a hill studded with gemlike boulders. "Can they go faster than a normal horse would?"

"I don't think so," Shar replied after another moment of thought. "The whole point is that the Hunt is their sport, and it wouldn't be sporting if they could just run anything down, would it? The quarry has to have some chance."

"Well, how would they react if the quarry fought back?" he asked. "If we took some of them out before they caught up with us?"

"I don't know. I'm willing to find out, though." He glanced quickly at her, to see that she looked determined and stubborn. "I'll throw everything at them I can think of."

"Take everything you can from the Mach I," he told her.

"Try not to erode the shields too much, if you can help it, but drain whatever you need."

But she shook her head. "We need the shields too much, if what I've heard is true. No, I'll be throwing everything I can back there, and most of it *won't* be offensive." Another glance at her showed she was smiling thinly. "My training is primarily from mother's side; the *kitsune* way is trickery and illusion. That's what I'll try first."

The horn-call behind them sounded as if the Hunters were close, very close; perhaps no more than three or four hills away. He made out the calls of individual dogs within the general belling of the pack.

Not good.

"I see them," Shar said, as they topped another hill. Her voice was strained and tight. He glanced into the rearview mirror and caught a glimpse of a darkness, a swiftly moving shadow in the distance, a mob of *something* that poured over the top of the hill like a dark flood. Something about that shadow sent a chill across his heart, and a touch of frost into his soul.

But beside them were the last of the dead trees, and ahead of them the first of the really large rock formations. This hill was the last bad one; after this, he could take them straight on, and since he knew what they were going into, he could accelerate down the hills to get momentum for the climb.

Shar was twisted around in her seat in a position that couldn't possibly have been comfortable, but she didn't release her safety-belts. *Probably a good idea,* he decided. *I don't know what kind of evasive driving I'm going to have to do.*

Tannim dropped the accelerator another half-inch and the Mustang's velocity increased. The white sand went up in a rooster-tail behind them as they put some serious distance between them and their pursuers. The sparkling shapes of the stones blurred past, while the speedometer needle swept toward three digits.

"Tannim, driving like crazy will buy us some time, but it won't stop them. Ten-second quarter-miles won't stop the Wild Hunt."

Tannim grinned. "Here. Hold the wheel. I'll slow 'em down." He rolled down the window on his side, and Shar leaned as far sideways as she could manage with her seat-harness still buckled to grasp the wheel. Tannim let off the throttle, and the Hunt closed on them.

The wind whipped his curly hair around his face as he hung his left arm, still somewhat tattered, out the window. He chewed on his upper lip a moment and sighted along the rearview mirror before turning his head to face the bad-dreams-on-hooves behind them. The Hounds, canine sacks of sharp bone, were solid black with glittering eyes, loping along as fast as greyhounds on a track. The Hunters were all in black—barbarian types in fur and flying capes, crude tunics, but all of it in dead black. They all wore helms that hid their faces completely, which was fine by Tannim. The horses they rode were also black, but they had fangs instead of horse's teeth. What disturbed Tannim the *most* right now was that they were close enough he could *see* such details through the white sand the Mustang was clouding up behind itself!

It was that rooster-tail of sand that had given him this idea, though, so maybe it wasn't all bad. Tannim conjured up one of his planes of force, the same kind he had been using as ramps for the Mach I. He laid it down behind the speeding Mustang, a few feet behind the rear chrome, and dragged it along. The plume of sand grew even taller while Tannim adjusted the angle of it to make it a scoop. He then called another plane into existence. This time it was vertical, and caught the majority of the sand the other one was kicking up.

Then he snapped his fingers and the vertical one dropped back behind them, braced between a monolith of beryllium and a bus-sized lump of coal. He snapped his head around to face forward, grinning like a fool. *What are you doing, you idiot? Are you actually showing off? You are! You are! You're showing off for Shar!*

"That's one!" he said as he dropped the accelerator pedal again and the engine's rumble went up in pitch. "Now for the clincher—take the wheel again—"

Tannim changed the angle of the trailing plane of force,

simultaneously making it both wider and taller. In a few moments more, they had a perfect square of white sand following them as they shot between rows of semiprecious stones the size of student apartments. Tannim laminated a second thin wall of force over the sand, let off the throttle again, and to Shar's obvious amazement, stopped the car.

"What are you *doing*?" Shar demanded.

"Hang on. You'll see," Tannim said tersely. He unbuckled and stepped out of the car. With a few hand gestures, he slid the upright square of compacted sand to one side, and then split it in half horizontally. He shuffled that half down to ground level and pushed it off to the other side, then placed one slab of white sand on either side of the tire-tracks.

"What are you doing?" Shar asked again, a note of frantic worry in her voice this time.

The sand they had left in the air behind had settled enough that he could see, with disconcerting clarity, that their pursuers had split around the wall he had put up a minute ago. Some had simply punched through it with impunity. It had, after all, just been compacted sand, held together by the vestiges of a walling spell.

The hellish horses were lathered. They had no eyes, only dark holes where the eyes should be. The Master of the Hunt was the only Hunter whose face was visible; he wore an open-faced helm crowned with stag's antlers, and his horse was practically a skeleton. The Master *looked* like the ultimate predator; there was obviously only one thing for him, and that was the hunt and the kill.

And they were all gaining.

Tannim kept his hand gestures to a minimum, so he wouldn't telegraph to the closing horde what he was up to— by now they must be thinking their prey was exhausted, stopped to make a hopeless last stand.

Well—if that's what they're thinking, I sure hope they're wrong.

Tannim called up three more planes of force, dropped them into place, and dropped back into the driver's seat as fast as he could. His foot was on the accelerator before his door was even closed, and an eyeblink later, the Mustang was moving again. The thickness of the ever-present mist was increasing. Behind them, the Hunters' horn sounded again, audible over the growling engine—

—and was abruptly cut short. Tannim looked in the rearview mirror.

Behind them, the Wild Hunt's dogs and horses were being cut down by the planes of force he had left at knee-height on either side of the upright, double layered, and very rigid walls of force. Horrors of ages past, spectres of ancient armies and spirits of death were being clotheslined at the kneecaps and vaulted, deathless faces first, into the white sand. By a kid from Oklahoma in a fast car.

And beside him, a half-dragon, half-*kitsune* lady was feverishly concentrating on—something—glowing in her hands.

"This is it!" Shar shouted over the howl of the engine. "This is my trump card! If this one doesn't work—"

She didn't finish the statement. She didn't have to. They both knew what the outcome would be if the Hunt caught up with them.

The mist was so thick now that Tannim's effectiveness as a driver was cut in half. The rocks weren't spaced apart at predictable intervals in this section, and there was always the chance he might run into one if he wasn't careful. That would bring a swift end to the Hunt, but not the one they wanted.

So now it was up to Shar to shake their followers off the trail.

There were no fireworks this time; Shar simply held something small in her hand, visibly pouring every erg of energy left to her into it. She finally tapped into the resources of the Mach I as well; Tannim sensed more power draining from it into whatever it was she held, as if she had suddenly opened a spigot at full force.

Then she dropped it—whatever it was—out the window. And collapsed into the seat, her face drained and white, her eyes closed.

A flash in his rearview mirror startled him into glancing up, taking his attention off her for a moment. To his amazement, there was another Mustang behind them, with two occupants in the front seats, speeding away at right angles from their own path!

She's built a decoy! But how—

"A hair from me, a hair from you, and a loose screw from the dashboard," she said faintly. "Wrapped up in a swatch of silk. It won't create tire-tracks, but it's made to leave a strong scent, magical and physical. I hope it'll hold them until we pass the wall into the other pocket. The decoy will incinerate in about twelve minutes . . . but by then, our trail should be cold enough that they'll give up."

However she'd done it, it had taken everything she had in her, and then some. It was obvious that she had held nothing in reserve. She lay back in the seat, pale and drained, so tired that only the seatbelt was holding her erect.

So now it was up to him again; he'd bought her the time to create the decoy, now her creation was buying them the time to escape.

Time to find the gap in the wall, and get the heck out of there.

Tannim waited until the last of the color and turbulence was gone from the mist around them before bringing the Mach I to a halt and turning the engine off. Shar had not moved in all that time; she was as spent as a channel-swimmer or a marathon-runner at the end of the race. She hadn't even noticed that they'd left the realm of the Hunters.

"Are you all right?" he asked, wanting to touch her, but not certain that he dared. As a sort of awkward compromise, he took both of her cold, limp hands in his to warm them.

"Are we there yet?" she replied, without moving or opening her eyes. "Are we on the other side?"

"Yes—and I can't hear the Hunt anymore." That had been a relief; the moment he'd crossed the barrier of turbulence, he'd lost the last sounds of horns and hounds, and they hadn't returned. It looked as if Shar was right; the Hunt couldn't track anything past all that magical confusion. They might not even be able to find their way in it.

"Nor can I, lad," Tom put in from the rear seat. "An' I think I got sharper ears nor ye."

Shar heaved an enormous sigh of relief, and finally opened eyes that mirrored her own complete exhaustion. "I think we've lost them. I didn't dare believe it, but I think we managed to lose them."

"You mean *you* managed to lose them, clever fox," he said, squeezing her hands. She smiled faintly and squeezed back. "If you hadn't created that decoy, we'd never have gotten away from them."

"There ain't many as escaped the Wild Hunt," Tom Cadge said, with awe and delight. "I didn' think e'en the two o' ye coulda done it!"

"I couldn't have done it," Tannim said flatly. "Not alone. All the fancy driving in the world wasn't going to shake that bunch." He shook his head at her shrug. "No, I know what I'm talking about and—look, Shar, I want you to know something. I know we aren't out of this yet, but—you're free of your debt to me. You've put in more than enough to get us both out of this mess."

At that, a little life and color crept back into her face. "But I haven't gotten you back yet—" she protested. "You were right. I got you into this, and the only way to balance the scales is to get you home again."

"I know," he replied, "but you've done more than you had to. It's not your fault we couldn't go back the same way I came in. So, no matter what else happens, the scales are balanced so far as I'm concerned, all right?"

"If that's the way you want it," she said slowly, "all right. But I'm still going to get you home, and I'm going to get Tom somewhere that will be safe for him."

"I know," he said, letting her hands go, with a smile. "I know. Now, help me find that Gate again, all right?"

Finding the Gate was a great deal easier than he'd thought it would be; Shar didn't even need to stir herself to help. On this side of the wall, with no wind to disturb the sand and no hills for it to slide down, the tire-tracks were still as plain and as clear as if they'd just driven by a few seconds ago. He simply followed his own trail back to where it ended at the alabaster arch in the midst of the shifting mists.

Now there was only one decision left to make.

"Back to the tundra?" he asked out loud, staring at the translucent rock of the Gate. "Or somewhere else?"

"The only 'else' we have available is that little domain of my father's," Shar replied, sitting up and running her hands through her hair in an obvious effort to revive. "It has to be the tundra. We'll just have to go there and hope that we don't meet up with Madoc."

"And if we do?" he countered. "Shar, if we have a plan in place, we'll be one up on him. If we can move while he's still staring, we have a chance to get away."

She nodded slowly. "You're right. The worst that can happen is that we don't use that plan. Do *you* have any ideas?"

"Actually, I do." He stretched and popped a couple of vertebrae in his neck. "I think we ought to keep the Gate live behind us. And if we run into Madoc on the tundra, we duck back through to here before he can react. He won't know where we went, so we'll have a little lead time. *Then,* from here—we go straight to Charcoal's pocket holding."

She stared at him, eyes wide. "You have got to be kidding. That's crazy! Why don't we just stand off in the mist and let them search around, wait until they give up on this destination and then go back to the tundra?"

But he shook his head. "Because Madoc's going to leave someone to guard that Gate on the frozen plain. If we stand off and wait, they can still follow the tire-tracks and find us. But if we go to Charcoal's domain, when they come through here, they just might see the tire-tracks on this side and follow them out across to the other side of the wall. If they do that—they'll run right into the Hunt."

He waited while she absorbed all that and gave it some

serious thought—particularly the part about leading Madoc to the Hunters.

"At the worst," he continued, "they'll figure out which setting we used and follow us there. By then, if we haven't gotten into trouble, we'll be following Gates that *you* know, and we won't be flying blind anymore."

"Those are all good points," she admitted. "And I can't think of a better plan." She ran a hand across her eyes and rubbed her temple wearily. "I hope we don't have to make too many fancy maneuvers, though. I don't have too much left in me."

He knew then exactly how much had been taken out of her by that last heroic effort. She would never have admitted her weakness if she hadn't known there was no energy, no strength in her to call on anymore.

And now he was in the uncomfortable position of trying to decide what was the most risky proposition. Should they stay where they were until Shar recovered a little, taking the chance that the Wild Hunt might find them, or some other, equally nasty inhabitant of *this* pocket jumped them—or Madoc found them?

Time is running out, either way. We're getting hemmed in.

Or should they go on, and take the chance of running into Madoc with Shar in a dangerously weakened state?

"I wish I knew where Madoc was right now," he muttered, running his finger nervously across his chin.

"If I had my old air elementals, I could tell you," she replied, her eyes growing suspiciously bright and wet. "They used to scout things for me, until Madoc murdered one of them, and the rest of them ran off in terror." She rubbed her hand across her eyes. "My favorite . . ."

He sat down beside her and offered his shoulder. He half expected her to refuse it.

But she didn't. She put her head down on his shoulder and wept silently, tears soaking into his shirt, her whole body shaking with quiet sobs. He held her, sensing that the tears were long overdue.

For the moment, decisions would have to wait.

❖   ❖   ❖

Joe tapped quietly on the door of the black-lacquered room, after intercepting FX just before he yanked the doors open with no warning to the occupants.

The door slid aside after a moment's pause. Lady Ako was the one who opened it, but Joe thought that Chinthliss looked a little less out-of-sorts. He still looked *worried,* but not as annoyed as before.

There was no change in Lady Ako's expression, at least not that Joe could read, but then she surely had a doctorate in inscrutability. He hoped that the two of them had gotten *some* of their differences ironed out while he and FX had left them alone.

He'd never have admitted it out loud, but he was kind of a romantic, and he had heard the pain in Chinthliss' voice when the dragon had told the story of how he had lost Ako. Maybe if Ako knew that, it might make some difference to her. Maybe if Chinthliss got over some of his attitude problems, she'd be willing to give him another chance.

But Lady Ako's first words had nothing to do with the relationship between herself and Chinthliss. "The computer has a tentative match with some of the things Chinthliss and I have seen while you were gone," she said. "If the match is a true one, it is most imperative that they make some move to get out of there before very long. It is a most dangerous pocket of the Unformed."

"Aren't they all?" Fox asked, as he took his place behind the table.

"Not all pockets are accessible to the Wild Hunt," Lady Ako said shortly.

"*What?*" Fox yelped, every hair standing on end. Joe blinked in surprise at Fox's reaction. He'd never actually *seen* anyone or anything but a cat bristle with fear before. It was a very interesting effect; Fox became twice his normal size for a moment, before Lady Ako's soothing hand motions calmed him.

"Tell me we *aren't* going there," FX begged. "Please, Lady, tell me we aren't going there after them! I'm only a three-tail, I can't take on the Wild Hunt!"

"Not unless we have more than just a 'tentative match'"

from a collection of silicon chips to go on," Chinthliss replied. "The lady has graciously put one of her best sorcerers at our disposal; when we *know* where they are, he will give us a Gate that will take us directly to them. But we are not going to waste that advantage until we have no doubts."

"Indeed," Ako added with a decisive nod. "I wish that we could work your Tannim's trick with the chrome circle a second time, but while we are all Underhill, the mere presence of even this much steel—" she tapped the ring with one claw "—changes the effect of our magic. We have not practiced in the presence of Cold Iron as Tannim and Shar have; we do not know how to use the effect."

Joe stared at her as something hit him. Oh, surely the lady had thought of this already! It was so *obvious*—

Oh, what the heck. "Then why not go up?" he blurted, face and ears reddening as he thought about how stupid he must look. "Why not go to our side of the Hill, where your magic won't be affected as much?"

"Oh, it will still be affected," Ako said with a sigh. "The problem is the magic itself, and not entirely the place where it is cast. Your Tannim *knows* those effects, we do not. He could compensate for them, but we have never had the need to learn to do so."

"A mistake, and one that I have pointed out to others," Chinthliss rumbled. "No point in rehashing old debates. I—" He broke off, suddenly, and his expression changed. "Ako, the boy is right! I had forgotten that Tannim used the ring to *build* his Gate! We cannot use the trim-ring to do more than scry here, for a number of reasons—but we *can* make a Gate out of it on the other side of the Hill *because we will make the Gate from it exactly as Tannim did!* You've been assuming we would create a new Gate, not that we would use the chrome circle! And it won't *matter* if the Mustang warps magics where it is, because the trim ring is *part* of the Mach I! It *would* matter if we were trying for Tannim himself, say, or Shar, but *not* if we're linking into the Mustang directly! Magical resonance should . . ."

He went on at some length about "Laws of Magic" and

spouting some kind of mathematical equations—Ako replied in the same vein, with great enthusiasm and growing excitement. Within seconds, Joe was hopelessly lost. Fox's gaze went back and forth between the two of them, like a spectator at a tennis match, but Joe couldn't tell if he was actually following the increasingly esoteric conversation or not.

Well, it hardly mattered. Chinthliss thought his idea was going to work, that was the point, and it looked as if he was convincing Lady Ako. Finally she nodded.

"I believe you are right," she said. "And what is more, I believe your logic is absolutely sound, magically and mathematically. There is no need for us to sit here in idleness any longer."

She slid the door to the tiny room open, and the three of them followed her out into the larger room. "Come," she said with an imperious gesture, showing no sign of stiffness after all that sitting in cramped quarters.

Chinthliss winked broadly at Joe and FX behind Lady Ako's back, but followed her with no other comment.

She paused only to shed her fancy outer kimono and collect a belt hung all over with a variety of implements. Beneath the elaborate robe she wore a much more utilitarian outfit, something like the jackets and loose pants that karate students wore, only in a scarlet silk as red as blazing maple leaves in autumn, bound at the waist with a scarlet scarf. She slung the belt over the jacket and pulled it snug.

"So where is this sorcerer you promised us?" Chinthliss asked mildly, as she gestured again that they should follow and headed down a corridor that ended in a door. She waited while Chinthliss got the door, nodded gracefully, and preceded Joe and FX through it. It let out onto a perfectly ordinary sidewalk bordering a paved street in the middle of a well-manicured park of the kind that would surround an English manor-house. Grass as perfect as a carpet of Astroturf undulated beneath huge oak trees and immaculately groomed bushes, and made plush paths between beds of flowers in full and riotous bloom. Behind them, the building, which Joe *knew* was huge, was nothing more than a single-storied one-room cottage surrounded by more beds of flowers, picturesque as anything in a fairy tale.

Lady Ako advanced to the street without a single backward glance. "Taxi!" she called, waving her paw-hand in the air, although Joe hadn't seen a single sign of anything like a cab. But within a few seconds, one appeared—this time it wasn't a cartoonish taxi like the last one, but a perfectly normal London cab.

"Where to, mum?" the driver asked in what was definitely an English accent.

"Grand Central Station," she replied, getting into the front, next to the driver, leaving the rest of them to pile into the rear. It was a bit of a squeeze, with Joe stuck in the middle, but they all made it. The cab smelled pleasantly of leather and metal polish; it made a U-turn and proceeded down the tree-lined avenue at a modest pace. There wasn't any other traffic, and no one on foot, either.

Fortunately, the ride wasn't long. "That's it, up there," Chinthliss said, waving at a building rising above the trees ahead of them. Joe had no clue what the real Grand Central Station looked like, but it probably wasn't anything like this. . . .

Carved of white marble, the place rose several stories tall, covered in arches and staircases—and it made Joe dizzy just to look at it, because it was all so completely *wrong*. Staircases were at right angles to one another, even running upside-down, arches gave out onto platforms that were at the tops of staircases that nevertheless went up from the platform, even though the platform was already higher than the staircase. . . .

Worse yet, there were people walking all over this thing, upside-down, sideways—though always at the correct angle to the surface they were walking on.

"Don't think about it," FX advised him in a kindly voice. "It's all right, it just isn't operating by the rules you're used to."

If that wasn't the understatement of the century! At least the *bottom* story looked normal enough as the taxi pulled up to the single entrance. Joe decided that the best thing he could do would be to fix his gaze firmly on the ground in front of him and not look anyplace else.

Lady Ako paid and tipped the driver, and they all piled out of the cab onto the white marble sidewalk. Joe refused to look any higher than the first floor, but that was impressive enough. The whole thing was white marble, and every inch of it was carved with patterns of flying birds that became fish that became birds again, or lizards, or rather bewildered-looking gryphons.

"The sorcerer?" Chinthliss prompted. Lady Ako just smiled.

"I've always said that if you want something done right, you should do it yourself," she replied. "Why should I delegate something this important to someone else?"

"Ah." Chinthliss only nodded. "Hence Grand Central Station."

She shrugged. "It will save me some effort," she replied, as if that answered everything. "The price of four tickets is far, far less than the cost of the safety of my daughter."

Chinthliss only bowed, and gestured to her to lead them on again. She did so, taking them under an archway upheld by two pillars carved with sinuous, intertwined lizards.

Once inside, Joe forgot his resolution to only look down at his feet. He stared upward, gawking. They were inside a single enormous room of white marble that reached into the misty distance. Around the edge of the room was a ramp spiraling upward until it dwindled far above them into a mere thread. Giving out onto the archway were doors with names carved over them and inlaid with black marble. Joe simply couldn't read most of those names; they weren't lettered with anything he recognized. The words were as foreign as Arabic or Chinese.

People were coming and going from those doors; not many, and not at any regular intervals, but there did appear to be a certain amount of steady traffic.

"Don't worry about those," FX told him, nudging him to get him moving again. "What we want is over there—"

The *kitsune* pointed to another arch, this one quite plain, but with a ticket booth at one side. Lady Ako was already there, buying tickets, while Chinthliss waited beside her. There was a single word carved above this archway as well: *Home*.

Home?

"Come on," Fox urged, as the lady turned away from the booth with tickets in her hand.

"What the heck does that mean, 'Home'?" Joe asked. "What's going on here?"

"All those doors you see up there are Gates," Fox explained as the two of them hurried to catch up. "You can get here from just about any domain Underhill—this is the other side of the park from the gazebo where we came in. If you don't want to use up your own magic in building a Gate to somewhere, you can always come here and use the public Gates. Underhill couldn't exist without this place, actually, it's sort of the center for everything. This is *the* most neutral spot in the universe. You could meet your deadliest blood-enemy here, and no matter how much you hated each other, you'd both better smile, nod, and ignore each other. The guardians of this place don't interfere with much, but break the peace, and they'll squash you flat."

FX giggled. "We call 'em Sysops."

"What's that got to do with 'Home'?" Joe persisted, as they came up to where Chinthliss and Lady Ako were standing just beneath the archway.

"This is a unique Gate in all of the domains," Ako supplied, handing him a ticket. "It requires an enormous amount of magic to operate—and it will take you home. Wherever your home is. It responds to *your* desire, to the place you feel is truly home to you—anywhere Underhill, or anywhere on your side of the Hill, from Warsaw, Poland, to Warsaw, Indiana; from Athens, Greece, to Athens, Georgia. For that reason, although the other public Gates here in Grand Central Station are free or of nominal cost to use, use of *this* Gate is very expensive—but I do not grudge the expense. I will need all my powers once we reach your side of the Hill to build the Gate to reach Shar and Tannim; this will help me save them for that."

"So Joe, it's up to you," Chinthliss said quietly. "We need to get back to the barn, or somewhere near it, so we can

use the trim-ring as a Gate." He handed Joe a different
ticket from the other three: metallic gold, it felt very much
like a very thin sheet of metal, embossed with odd characters. "You're the one with the Master Ticket for this trip;
the Home Gate will take its setting from you. Take us
home."

Home? For a moment, his mind was a complete blank.
He'd never *had* a home, not really, so how could he take
the others there? Not the succession of low-rent apartments
that he and his parents had lived in while his father was
working out his Grand Plan. Certainly not the old mansion outside Atlanta. *Definitely* not the bunkers of the
Chosen Ones in Oklahoma. Not even the military school,
which was the only place until now where he'd ever felt
comfortable. . . .

Until now. Suddenly his thoughts settled. What was
wrong with him? Of course he had a home now! Tannim's
parents had made that clear, that he was welcome and
wanted there. Needed, too, when it came to it; he could
pull his own weight there and know he was useful, and
be sure of getting thanks afterwards.

No, there was no question of where home was. Not
anymore.

"Ready?" Chinthliss asked, looking searchingly into his
eyes.

He nodded, confident now, and led the way under the
vast, white arch of stone, knowing what he would find at
the other end of it.

Home, he thought with a longing, and yet a deep contentment, as he felt that now-familiar disorientation take
hold of him.

CHAPTER THIRTEEN

There was the usual moment when he was blind, deaf, and directionless; this time Joe flexed his knees automatically and stepped forward confidently, walking out of blindness into—

Darkness. It took his eyes a moment to adjust to the dark after the dazzling whiteness of Grand Central Station. *Don't panic; we left at night, it should still be night, shouldn't it?* How much time *had* passed while he was Underhill? Several hours, certainly. Should it be dark, then? Shouldn't it be dawn by now? Were they even where they were supposed to be? What if they were in Atlanta, or even the military academy?

Then, to his immense satisfaction, the bulk to his right resolved itself into the Drake house at the end of the driveway, and the flat to the left became the road.

"Good job," came a whisper to his right; Chinthliss, he thought. "Right on target."

"When are we?" FX whispered urgently.

Joe swiveled and reached out involuntarily, only to find that his hand passed right through FX. So they were definitely home, the world he knew, where Fox was nothing but a spirit. *When? What does he mean by that?*

Chinthliss raised a shadowy arm and a bit of blue light flashed up from his wrist. "Good," he said with satisfaction.

"Very good! Only four in the morning, same night that we left."

Another shadow-shape touched his arm, this one slim and graceful. *Lady Ako.* "The time between Underhill and your world runs at different paces," she offered in low-voiced explanation. "Your sense of *place* is very strong, and includes a solid feeling for the exact time you came Underhill. Because Underhill has not been precisely real to you, your sense of *place* was not influenced by the apparent time you spent there."

If that's supposed to be a simple explanation, I don't want to hear a complicated one! he thought, bewildered. Nevertheless, he bowed his thanks to the Lady without revealing that her explanation left him as baffled as before.

"I'd like to get back to the barn," Chinthliss said, scanning the house and the road quickly. "The shields on it are good ones, and I don't want to leave a live Gate open behind us without shields. The only way we're going to get them out will be if we leave the Gate open at our backs."

"A good point," Ako murmured. "This is your place of expertise, Chinthliss, and I will follow your instructions. I have only visited here on this side of the Hill, and none of those visits was very recent."

"Which way is the barn from here?" Chinthliss asked Joe in an undertone. "I don't remember."

"Not a problem." Joe took the lead with confidence, even in the thick darkness of the last hour before dawn. The others followed, accepting him as the temporary leader.

The Junior Guard had followed him and his orders once—but it had been out of habit to obedience, and not because they were particularly confident in his ability.

But this was different. At this moment, despite anxiety for Tannim and worry about what lay ahead, he was as content as he had ever been. He was trusted for himself, now, and not because he was Brother Joseph's son, or the duly authorized leader of the Junior Guard, or even an officer in the ranks of the Chosen Ones.

It felt good.

He owed this, all of it, to Bob, Al, Tannim, and the other

Fairgrove people he hadn't even met yet—a family of his own choosing, if it came right down to it. They'd given him a place where he belonged, where he could find out what *he* was all about. He owed them for something beyond price, something not too many people ever got, really.

Well, he thought, lengthening his strides when he sensed that the others would be able to keep up with him, *in that case, it's time for some payback.*

"I'm sorry," Shar said, wiping her nose on the tissue Tannim offered. Her eyes were sore; her throat and lungs ached. She felt vaguely as if she should have been embarrassed; she'd never broken down like that before in front of anybody, not even her mother. Charcoal, Lady Ako, some of the Unseleighe had seen her anger, her rage, but never her tears. Grief until now had been a private thing.

But she wasn't embarrassed. It had felt so *good* to lean on someone else, even for just a little—so good to let loose all that grief, all the frustration. So good to be held by someone who wasn't going to expect the very next moment to be a passionless roll in the sack.

"Hey," Tannim said, patting her hand awkwardly, "you were just tired, that's all. You still are. Just wait until we're somewhere safer, and you get a chance to rest; you'll be all right then."

She sniffed and blew her nose, then looked up at him to meet his peculiar, weary, lopsided smile.

He handed her another tissue. "I wish all I did was cry when I get tired. When *I'm* beat, you can't trust my aim with anything. That's one reason why I don't carry a gun around."

"Really?" she said, seizing the chance to change the subject gratefully. "I can't imagine you being unskilled at *anything*."

He nodded solemnly. "Honest truth. Scorched one of my own friends with a mage-bolt once during a firefight with the Unseleighe; gave him a reverse Mohawk."

"No!" She giggled as he nodded with a touch of chagrin as well as amusement.

" 'Fraid so." He sighed and looked around at the eddying mist outside of the Mustang. "Look, I hate to try and push you, but we really need to make some decisions here. What are you going to set the Gate for? The frozen plain first? Or do we jump right into the fire and try Charcoal—"

Without warning, the Gate flared into life.

Tannim's reactions were faster than she would have believed possible for a mere human. He had the Mustang in reverse and skidding away from the Gate in a flash.

It just was not quite soon enough.

The sand came to life with a roar and rose up in a barrier behind them. It acted as if it was alive, or something was alive and burrowing beneath it, heaving upward in a towering mound with sides too steep for the Mustang to climb. He slammed on the brakes, and spun the wheel to the side, throwing the Mach I into first and accelerating into the mist at right angles away from the brand-new mound, only to find the way barred by something entirely unexpected.

A wall of shadow and dulled silver. A living wall.

A wall with ten talons, each as long as an arm.

He slammed on the brakes, just short of it. Shar stared through the windshield at the two enormous foreclaws, each half as large as the Mustang.

A dragon. . . .

There was only one dragon in all of Underhill that peculiar metallic gray, like polished ash, or matte-finished hematite.

Charcoal.

Father.

She bit back a gasp of fear, and felt a wave of chill wash over her.

Her hands were on the door handle. She tried to take them off and couldn't. They would not obey her.

She found herself opening the door of the passenger's side, *entirely* against her will; found herself getting out, standing beside the Mustang, mist eddying around her ankles. Her hands shut the passenger's door as she strove to regain control of them, to no avail. She should have been angry, but all she could feel was rising panic.

Charcoal shares my blood; he must have—the ability to control my body—

More shapes moved in on them, out of the mist: bipedal shapes in black armor, with surcoats and cloaks of midnight black, a dozen or more altogether. They paused in a group for a moment, in complete silence. One of them strode out of the midst of them with his sword drawn and his faceplate up.

Madoc Skean. He looked rather pleased with himself. *Bastard. He got Father to track us down!*

"Ah, Charcoal," Madoc said with false good humor. "I see you've found them. Now, just hand them over to me, and—"

The dragon coughed, and warm air laden with the scent of aged stone washed over her. He bent his neck down to stare at Madoc, his sulfur-colored eyes wide with amusement. "Hand them over to you? Aren't you getting above yourself, Madoc Skean? It was *you* who came to *me* for help, as I recall, and not the opposite." Charcoal's voice boomed overhead, kettledrums and distant thunder, a vibration in the breastbone. "If it had not been for me, you would never have found them, would you? If it had not been for me, you would not have known the Gate into this domain, nor would you have been able to hold it."

Shar found herself free to move again, as Charcoal's attention was momentarily on Madoc, and she backed up, one slow step at a time. *So he doesn't control me unless he's concentrating on it!* Maybe if she could get a little out of reach, where the mist was thicker, she could make a run for it. And if she broke and ran, that would give Tannim an opening to try something. Her magic was exhausted, but there was still his, and he was no amateur. Tension corded every muscle in her body as she edged past the rear of the Mustang. A little more. A little more. . . .

Madoc's expression changed from genial and self-satisfied to petulant and angry. "I thought we had a bargain, Charcoal," Madoc replied harshly. "You would find them, I would—"

"You would what?" Charcoal laughed so loudly that Shar winced involuntarily. She knew that laugh. Charcoal was sure he held the situation completely under his own control. "Dispose of the human? Punish *my* daughter? You would *presume?* I claimed this human as my prey a *long* time ago, elven fool—and such as *you* are not fit to polish the talons of one of *my* kind! However she has offended you, she has previously offended *me*, and she is *mine* to deal with, not yours!"

Charcoal's tail lashed, scattering Madoc and his followers, and the barrier of sand collapsed as Madoc took his attention from it. But the overall effect, when Madoc's Faceless Ones gathered around him again, was to put Shar and the Mustang directly between Madoc and Charcoal, with the Faceless Ones between her and freedom. This was not an improvement.

"I will challenge you for them if I must, impertinent lizard!" Madoc shouted, gesturing with his sword. "The human has slain my kin, wrought havoc among my kind! She broke faith with me! She violated the terms of our agreement! I have first claim on her and on him as well!"

"My claim takes precedence over yours, oh cream-faced loon," the dragon retorted, raising his head again. "She broke faith with me long before she broke it with you. In fact, I would say that *you* owe *me* for making a separate peace and an alliance with her when you knew that she and I were at odds."

The Faceless Ones were creeping up on Charcoal from behind, working their way across the sand silently, using the mist as cover. Shar wondered if he noticed—

Then his tail lashed again with sudden, deadly purpose. Most of them evaded it, but one did not; the creature was caught across the midsection by twenty feet of scale-covered muscle as big around as the trunk of a tree and sent hurtling, broken-bodied, out into the mist. It did not return. Not surprising; most created creatures disintegrated when damaged beyond repair.

And what will happen to me when I am damaged beyond repair?

"And as for the other, the human, my prey," Charcoal continued, as if nothing had happened, "I will deal with him as I see fit. His very existence is offensive to me, and has been since my rival chose to make a protégé of him."

Tannim opened the driver's-side door and slowly emerged from the Mustang to stand beside it. But Shar got the distinct impression that *he* had not been forced, as she had been, that he was getting out under his own control.

Tannim, no—don't do anything, don't say anything—

The young mage ran a hand through his tangled mop of hair and looked up at Charcoal with no sign of fear. "Don't you think it's a little early to start calling me 'prey'? I mean, we just met," Tannim said mildly.

Shar stiffened at his casual tone, now more afraid for him than she was for herself. *Oh no—no, Tannim, don't provoke him!*

Charcoal bent his gaze on the human below him, his eyes glowing with pent-up hatred. "Oh really? Perhaps you need to be reminded of how tiny you are."

Tannim folded his arms across his chest, and casually leaned against the car. "If you're trying to intimidate me, it's not working. I know all the tricks. And size doesn't impress me in the least."

What was he trying to do? Did *he* have some clever plan to get them both out of this? Shar clenched her fists until her nails cut into the palms of her hands, desperately trying to muster up even the tiniest amount of energy. The sparks of her magic sputtered and died as she tried to fan them into life. Surely he couldn't be counting on her to back him up—he *knew* she was exhausted!

This was a hazardous gambit Tannim was playing, if what he was doing was trying for time by bluffing—and she didn't think it had a snowball's chance of working.

Charcoal's eyes narrowed. "You are an arrogant fool," he rumbled, his talons flexing in the soft sand as if he longed to sink them into Tannim's body. "As big a fool as that Unseleighe idiot who was hunting you."

But Tannim simply shrugged and leaned a little more against the car, dropping his left hand down behind the open door, paying no attention whatsoever to Shar. "Really? You think so? Then you haven't been paying attention."

His left hand flickered once, quickly, out of Charcoal's line of sight; the keys to the Mustang fell at Shar's feet, the sound of their impact muffled in the soft sand. Charcoal was so busy concentrating on Tannim that he didn't notice.

The dragon's eyes narrowed to mere slits. "You tire me," he hissed. "I believe it is time to squash you, and—"

A whiplash of mage-energy crackled across the distance between Madoc and Charcoal. Shar ducked involuntarily as it arced over her head, and Charcoal's head snapped back from the impact on his muzzle, precisely as if Madoc had slapped him.

"First there are *my* claims, worm!" Madoc cried, his voice high and tight with anger, his hands glowing with the residual energy of the mage-bolt. "This mortal is *mine!*"

"Don't you think both your claims are a little premature?"

Shar turned, for the voice had clearly come from behind her. Another figure loomed out of the mist.

Tannim oohed. "The gang's all here."

Loomed was precisely the word; the shape moving through the mist towards them was just a little shorter than Charcoal—although in this mist it was difficult to judge. In the next moment, a blast of wind from a pair of huge, fanning wings blew all the mist away from the immediate area.

It all began to drift back immediately, of course, but not before Chinthliss made an impressive entrance in the wake of the wind.

Shar had never seen Chinthliss in his full draconic splendor before, and she felt her eyes widening with surprise. He stalked onto the sand, bronze scales shimmering subtly as the muscles beneath them moved, head held high on his long, flexible neck, wings half-spread behind him like a golden-bronze cloak. Beside him, the rest of his party looked like dolls—

Dolls? Perhaps that was not the best comparison. Perhaps they were no match for him in size, but that did not mean they were not formidable in their own right.

On Chinthliss' left, and nearest Shar, was the young blond human Tannim had been partnering before Shar kidnapped the Mustang; he had a drawn weapon in his hands, and Shar might have been the only creature present other than Tannim who knew just how deadly that tiny piece of metal really was. Beside him, in full battle arousal, was a three-tailed kitsune, his fox-mask convulsed in a snarl of rage, every hair on end, his paws crackling with mage-energy.

And on Chinthliss' right—

Mother!

Lady Ako was as serene and outwardly unmoved as a statue of a Buddhist nun; only someone who really knew her well would see the anger in her eyes and sense how close she was to the boiling point. And Shar knew that scarlet outfit she wore so regally, that belt with all of its many surprises. Lady Ako had come prepared in her own way for battle.

Tannim hadn't moved a muscle, although both Charcoal and Madoc Skean had backed up and shifted a few involuntary feet. Shar allowed herself to hope, just a little. Charcoal stared at the newcomers with the first signs of surprise Shar had ever seen him display. Shar took advantage of the distractions to bend down and snatch up the keys to the Mustang, knowing what that had cost Tannim— and what it meant to her.

He had sent her a message, as clearly as if he had spoken it to her. *If I buy it—it's yours, the car and all the power in it. Everything.*

Her heart ached. It wasn't the Mustang that she wanted. . . .

Shar, Tannim, and the Mustang were now the exact middle of a triangle, the points of which were Madoc and his Faceless Ones, Chinthliss and his allies, and Charcoal. Shar was already several feet behind the tail of the Mustang. With the change of position, Madoc was nearest Tannim, Shar nearest Chinthliss, the Mustang between Tannim and Charcoal.

"*Chinthlisssssss.*" Charcoal's hiss of recognition was so full of hatred that Shar could taste it. "I might have known *you* would show up."

The bronze dragon shrugged; an oddly human gesture.

"I am not as careless of my protégés as you, it seems. Nor am I inclined to abandon my allies as my whim suits me."

Charcoal ignored the sally and dropped his gaze to Chinthliss' feet. "Ako," he said in a tone that Shar could have *sworn* was one of reproach—if she hadn't already known that Charcoal was a master of manipulation. He assumed an expression of noble hurt. "Ako, I am surprised to find you with—this brat. I thought you had more dignity and pride than to be taken in by a manipulating charlatan."

Lady Ako looked Charcoal up and down, her face so full of open scorn that even Tom Cadge must sense it. "I do," she replied shortly. "That is why I left *you*."

Charcoal reared up as if he had been struck. The three-tailed *kitsune* openly snickered. Chinthliss' mouth widened slightly in a draconic smile.

"I believe," he said genially, "that we have a stalemate, Chinthliss."

"Foolish worms!" Madoc Skean shouted furiously, startling them all. "You are forgetting me!"

He rushed Tannim, sword held high over his head, the blue-black blade alive with crawling actinic-white tendrils of mage-power. But Tannim was not as unready as he had looked—nor as relaxed.

Tannim reached down into the Mustang's front window, and turned with one smooth motion to face Madoc's charge. As Madoc's blade slashed downward toward his head, Tannim brought up both hands with something between them. Madoc's sword met Tannim's red crowbar instead of Tannim's head.

However tempered the elven blade was, it was no match for a solid bar of Cold Iron, doubly-tempered with spells. With a scream that sounded almost human, the blade snapped in half, leaving a charred stump in the hilt in Madoc Skean's hands.

The Unseleighe lord stared at the remains of his weapon for a single stunned second. That was long enough for Tannim to make his countermove.

Showing all the expertise of any battle-honed elven warrior Shar had ever seen, Tannim swung the crowbar in a two-handed slash toward Madoc's head. The elven lord ducked aside at the last moment, and the crowbar only caught his upraised arm.

Sparks flew from Madoc's spell-strengthened armor, and Madoc staggered back a few steps.

But now the fight was no longer one-on-one. The Faceless Ones closed in to come to the aid of their master. Tannim whirled to parry their blades, but there were many of them and only one of him.

Tannim! He could never fend them all off—not without help!

Shar managed to summon up the power for a magebolt. Her hands blazed with magical energy; she screamed at the top of her lungs with the pain it cost her, but she blasted the nearest of the Faceless Ones full in the unprotected back, just as Tannim connected with a second, a raking blow straight across the chest with the pointed end of the crowbar.

Both disintegrated in a shower of sparks, empty armor dropping to the sand with a clatter.

Tannim dove through the opening presented by the loss of a faceless warrior, turning the dive into a somersault that brought him up onto his feet much nearer Shar, and outside the circle of Faceless Ones. Out of the corner of her eye, Shar saw that the young human with Chinthliss was trying desperately to find a target, but was clearly afraid of hitting Tannim. Tannim swung on another Faceless One, catching it in the back. Another shower of sparks and tumble of empty armor marked the loss of another of Madoc's creations.

Now it was Madoc's turn again; he charged Tannim with a wild war cry, his hands full of a much cruder weapon than his prized mage-sword. This was an ancient Celtic war-club, a massive piece of lead-weighted wood, previously strapped across his back. Tannim's crowbar was no match for it—and Madoc was a warrior trained since his birth hundreds of years ago in the art of wielding such weapons.

The club came down; Tannim deflected it rather than blocking it, but Madoc recovered swiftly and used the momentum of the deflected swing to come in from the side. Tannim deflected it again, but only partially; he got a glancing blow in the ribs that made him gasp and go double for a moment.

Madoc brought the club around again—

No, you bastard!

Shar's mage-bolt to the side of Madoc's head was weak, but enough to distract him for a moment. She crumpled to her knees, gasping with pain that brought tears to her eyes, but Tannim took advantage of Madoc's distraction to recover, and landed another blow against Madoc, this one a solid hit to the knee with the full weight of the crowbar behind it.

Madoc's leg crumpled and he went down on the other knee, as Tannim shuffled backward, getting out of range of the vicious club.

That gave the young human enough room to begin shooting.

Yes! Shar exulted.

Faceless ones dropped like puppets with cut strings as the human's bullets connected. Joe emptied one clip, and slapped in a second without pausing. He wasn't just a good shot; he was an expert. For every *crack* of gunfire, another Faceless One fell, until the only set of black armor still moving was the one containing the Unseleighe Lord.

Madoc was in full battle-rage, oblivious to the decimation of his followers. In this state, only his own chosen target had any place in his maddened mind. In a condition of berserker mindlessness, he felt no pain, and would not notice injuries or even broken bones. He regained his feet and charged again, limping slightly, heading straight for Tannim.

But the young human beside Chinthliss wasn't finished either.

In a flurry of rapid fire, the young man emptied three well-placed torso-shots into Madoc Skean's breastplate.

Madoc's body jerked backward with each of the three shots. Three fist-sized metallic dimples appeared in the carapace of Madoc's armor, where the spent bullets hit metal after passing through breastplate and flesh.

Silence. Shar's ears rang from the noise of the shots.

Madoc dropped down to one knee with a clatter of armor, leaning on the war-club.

Blood poured from every seam, every hole in Madoc's armor, yet the Unseleighe lord somehow remained erect.

The young human ejected the second clip and slapped in a third, leveling the sights on Madoc, although he did not resume firing.

Madoc's helm came up, the eye-slit pointing at Tannim. There was a gurgling sound as Madoc tried to speak, but nothing coherent emerged. Then, like a tree falling in slow motion, he dropped over sideways to land sprawled in an ungainly heap, blood still oozing from his armor.

The young man swiveled instantly to train his sights on Charcoal, but the dragon's attention was not on him, nor on Chinthliss, nor even on Tannim.

Shar met her father's eyes and could not look away from the burning yellow gaze. His eyes grew until they filled her entire field of vision, until she was lost in them, drowning in them, helpless to look elsewhere.

Once again, fear overwhelmed her, chilling her very soul.

She felt her body moving forward, one slow step at a time.

"This is no stalemate," Charcoal thundered, his voice vibrating her bones and shivering along the surface of her skin. "If you try to stop me, you will all suffer. Chinthliss, you are no match for me, and never were. Ako, your powers lie in cunning and in Healing; the lowly three-tail beside you cannot even muster the latter, much less courage. *No* human born could ever harm me. Even if you should conquer me against all odds, some of you *will* die, and all of you will suffer. You cannot risk that."

Shar fought Charcoal with every atom of her will, to no avail. Her feet continued to move, dragging reluctantly through the sand, taking her ever nearer to him. She sensed the Mustang within reach; it might as well have been on the other side of the Hill for all the good it did her. She could not even feel her hands clutching the keys: they were completely numb.

"Nevertheless," Charcoal continued maliciously, "I shall grant you this much. You may go; even the human called Tannim. I will permit you to escape this time. But I will have my daughter."

"No!" Ako cried, and Shar bled inside to hear the pain in her voice.

"Yes." Charcoal's icy tone sent a frost of fear down Shar's spine. "She is of *my* blood; see for yourself how I control her body. As I created her, she is mine, and I will have her."

"You couldn't hold her the last time, Charcoal," Tannim said defiantly. "She isn't *yours*, she isn't property. She'll slip your leash and run."

But Charcoal laughed, and the sound froze the blood in Shar's veins.

"Not when I am through with her, she will not." The dragon chuckled maliciously. "I shall see to it that there is nothing left in her mind that I have not placed there, no image that I have not approved. *This* time my dear Shar will be everything a doting and dutiful daughter should be—body, mind, and soul. And the body, mind, and soul will be *mine*."

She knew he could do it. He had the power to erase everything that she was, and replace it with whatever he wanted.

To unmake her.

No! she cried out in horror, but only in her mind. *No!*

And her feet stopped moving.

Fear gave her strength she didn't even know she had. Encouraged, she continued to fight: she stared into Charcoal's eyes and forced them *away* from her, fought against the control of her body until she shook as if she were fevered. Feeling came back to her hands, her arms—

Charcoal's eyes narrowed in anger; his breath escaped in a hiss, and he snapped his jaws together with impatience.

"Do not fight me, girl," he snarled. "Do not fight me, or I shall make your friends suffer."

She ignored his threats, knowing that while she fought his control, he would not be free to turn his attention elsewhere. With a snarl like cloth tearing, he changed his tactics.

She screamed as pain struck her with a thousand fire-tipped lashes, convulsed and dropped to the sand, holding her head in her fisted hands as agony lanced her in both temples.

"*Stop it!*" cried Ako, in shared agony. Shar saw through eyes blurred with tears of pain that her mother stood as rigid as a stone, her face a mask of anguish. In answer, Charcoal only sent another assault of pain through his daughter.

"I can continue this as long as her mind resists," he said with a laugh that filled her ears and mind, and echoed in her heart. "And you can do nothing to prevent it."

"I'm—not your property!" Shar managed through teeth gritted against the pain. "I—will—not—surrender!"

"Then you will suffer," Charcoal replied, and suited his actions to his words. "And when I am finished with you, if the rest of these fools have not taken advantage of the opportunity to escape, I shall turn my attention to one of them."

A different kind of pain grated on her nerves, racing up her arm from her left palm. She realized that she still held the keys to the Mustang.

And she still held the key to the power *in* the Mustang.

In the brief interval between waves of excruciating pain, she reached for that power. Held it.

Used it.

She threw up a shield between herself and her father; a crude thing, but strong, and she panted with relief as the next wave of pain broke on it and failed to reach her.

She used the moment of respite to refine it and reinforce it, before he realized what she had done, and that his punishment no longer reached her. Slowly, she got her balance back; slowly she raised her head, defiant once again. She got to her knees, then to her feet, and stood staring at him, daring him to try something new.

Charcoal was clearly taken aback by this development and stared back at her with open astonishment.

"I am not your property, Charcoal," she said in a voice hoarse from screaming. "I am not anyone's property. Anything I owed you before, you lost all right to when you tried to control me."

Charcoal's eyes widened in speculation, and she sensed that he was thinking furiously. "Shar—" he said then, his voice sweetly persuasive and hypnotic, "I don't know what this human has been telling you to turn you against me, but humans are by nature deceitful creatures. Whatever he has promised you, there is no way that he intends to make good on his promise. It is easy for humans to promise more than they can deliver—they never live long enough to be forced to account for those promises! You have not seen as much of the worlds as I have; I have only been trying to protect you from all the lies and trickery that—"

"That you are the master of," Shar snapped, holding her head high. "That always has been your way, hasn't it? When you can't force someone, you hurt them, and when you can't hurt them, you try to manipulate them. It isn't going to work with me."

Charcoal reared up to his full height, and only then was it apparent that he was *much* larger than Chinthliss. But his voice remained smooth and calm, even though malice underlay it.

"In that case, daughter," he said silkily, "I shall simply have to destroy you, as I destroy any flawed creation."

The fear returned, fourfold, holding her helplessly hostage. Shar sensed him gathering his power, and winced back behind shields she *knew* were inadequate, waiting helplessly for the blow that would be the last thing she ever felt. She closed her eyes, trying not to show that she was paralyzed with terror.

Any moment.

Her skin crawled as she threw the last of her power into her poor shields.

Now . . . now. . . .

"Stop it!"

The blow did not fall. Shar opened her eyes.

"Stop it, Charcoal," Tannim said wearily, stepping away

from the car. "That's enough. Leave them all alone. Leave *her* alone."

Charcoal turned his burning gaze on the battered young human.

"And why, pray, should I?" he asked.

What is he doing? Shar stared, trying to fathom what new trick he was going to pull. Did he have anything left?

Surely he must—

"Because you don't want her. If you want revenge on Chinthliss, you want *me*. So take me." He held his arms wide, and her breathing stopped as she realized what he was saying.

"Take me instead. I surrender."

CHAPTER FOURTEEN

"Take me. I surrender," Tannim repeated, dropping the crowbar to the sand with a dull *thud* as if to emphasize his words. A dispassionate part of his mind noted the shock in Charcoal's eyes with grim amusement. This was the last thing the old lizard had expected.

"An interesting offer," Charcoal replied slowly. "I fail to see what prompts you to assume that I will take it."

"Oh, please, I'm not that dense." He allowed a weary sarcasm to color his words. "Don't you think Shar's already told me *why* you spent all that time training her? You wanted her to be my opposite, right? The counter-weapon to Chinthliss' little 'Son of Dragons.' That's all you ever wanted her for. Well, here I am; all yours. You won't need her anymore, you make Chinthliss unhappy, you get rid of me, you've got the whole enchilada."

He had known the moment Charcoal started in on Shar that the gray dragon was right; they *couldn't* fight him. If they did, they'd all get hurt. Probably at least three of them would be killed—Shar definitely, Joe the most likely after her, Fox and himself as a tie for third victim. Joe would die because he had no idea what he was up against, and a fight with Charcoal was no time to learn. Like the new recruits in the trenches, he wouldn't have time to gain the experience he needed to survive.

They couldn't abandon Shar, leave her to be murdered or mind-wiped by her father. *He* couldn't abandon her. And even if they *did* abandon Shar to her father like a bunch of cowards, the moment Charcoal finished with her, he'd start on the rest of them anyway.

No matter what happened, *Shar* would die, physically or mentally, and she didn't deserve any kind of death, much less the kind that Charcoal would give her.

Unless *he* gave Charcoal what he really wanted.

And if I'm going to die, I'd like it to be keeping my friends safe. Keeping Shar safe.

Right, Tannim. Very brave. Very noble. Very stupid.

What the hell. When we played soldiers, I was always the one who fell on the grenade and got the terrific funeral. Too bad I won't be around to see this one. Damn. Life's been good.

He took a slow step forward, feeling every bruise, and savoring the pain as the last thing he was likely to feel. He was acutely aware of the soft, shifting sand under his shoes, the oddly clean taste to the air, the faint ache where that mist-thing had bitten him. "Here I am," he repeated. "I won't fight you. It won't cost you a thing. Take me."

Shar could not believe her eyes and ears, as her throat closed, choking back her cry of horror. What was he doing?

He was sacrificing himself, that was what he was doing.

She tried to grab him, to stop him, to counter his offer with one of her own, but she was held frozen, paralyzed. And what *could* she offer? She had just defied her father—should she make Tannim's offer worthless by surrendering herself now? Charcoal would never take her surrender and let Tannim go. Tannim was right. Charcoal didn't want *her* and never had; he wanted the human. She had never been more than the means to get Tannim.

Tannim stepped forward again, arms still wide. "Think about it, Charcoal," he said, as calmly as if he was not writing out his own death warrant with every word he spoke. "Think about how much you gain. You make Chinthliss *miserable*. Since you let Shar loose, you *don't* make Ako unhappy; in fact, you might even stand a chance of getting her back. Ako doesn't give a damn about me, she only wants her daughter safe, and she knows you won't want her once I'm gone. You get rid of *me*. As an added bonus to that, there's a bunch of Unseleighe who'll be so happy with you for getting rid of me for them, you'll be able to write your own ticket with them. Madoc Skean wasn't the only Unseleighe lord who wants me dead."

Everyone's attention was on Tannim, so only Shar saw that Thomas Cadge had crept out of the rear seat and was stealing out of the Mustang on all fours. He had taken the bandage off his head, and although she could not see his face from where she stood, he did not appear to be acting in the *least* blind.

He waited for a moment, crouched behind the shelter of the driver's-side door, then twirled his fingers in a peculiar gesture.

A thick eddy of mist twined up to the door, and he slipped off out of sight under its protective cover.

Shar nearly choked on bitterness, and fury shook her along with her grief. *He must have been Charcoal's confederate—he was the one leading Charcoal to us, and here we thought we were trying to save him! I should have thrown him to the Wild Hunt.*

If she ever saw his cowardly face again, she *would* throw him to the Wild Hunt.

"Well, Charcoal?" Tannim waited, now just within Charcoal's reach, the droop of his head and his slumping shoulders reflecting weary resignation. "How about it? Is the offer good enough?"

No— Shar wailed silently. *No, Tannim, please—*

—don't leave me alone—

Charcoal looked down with smoldering eyes for a long moment at the small human at his feet. Silent tears cut their way down Shar's cheeks, and her heart spasmed with agony.

"Yes," he said at last. "I believe that I shall take advantage of this situation."

He stared down at Tannim for a moment longer; then, before anyone could move or speak, he struck.

He lashed out at Tannim with a foreclaw, all talons extended, striking sideways, like a cat.

Shar reached out—uselessly, with agonizing slowness. Every second became an eternity, enabling her to see the tiniest of details. Charcoal's talons hit Tannim in the chest and bent against his armor, tearing at the remains of his shirt. Only one of the five three-foot-long talons caught and penetrated the armor, but it was enough. It pierced his chest completely, going through the armor, the entire torso, and emerging from the back, a needle-shaft of blood glistening in the light.

Charcoal flexed his talons open, then closed his fist around the body for a moment, as it convulsed in his foreclaw, and he screamed in triumph. Then he flung it contemptuously at Chinthliss' feet.

"Tannim!"

Shar screamed.

Her heart caught fire in mingled pain and anguish, despair and rage, and something broke within her, unleashing a fury she had never known was inside.

She reached for power, found it in her rage and hate.

Charcoal was going to pay in blood. No matter what it cost her.

Right up until the last moment, Joe was sure that Tannim was going to pull some rabbit out of the hat. Even as the gray dragon lashed out, he was positive Tannim was going to do *something* clever.

It wasn't until Tannim's broken and bleeding body flew through the air to land at Chinthliss' feet that he understood the truth of the situation.

There had been no way out. Tannim's offer had been genuine. And Charcoal had taken it.

He didn't realize that he was screaming until he ran out of breath; didn't realize he was shooting until the hammer clicked on an empty chamber. He ejected the clip and slapped in another, emptied it, and slapped in the last, tears running down his face and into his open mouth.

Then he paused for a moment, for now Fox was a streak of red lightning, launched into the air, then slashing at Charcoal's muzzle and eyes until Charcoal roared and slapped *him* down into the sand, where he lay stunned and unmoving.

Lady Ako was on her knees beside Tannim's body; Joe didn't bother to wonder why. Once Fox was out of the line of fire again, he emptied the last round into Charcoal, trying for the eyes.

Just as he dropped the last bullet into the dragon, *Shar* opened up on him.

She stood in the center of a pillar of white-hot flame, her two hands aimed for the gray dragon, and from those hands she poured the fires of the inferno itself down onto Charcoal. She looked like a living flame-thrower.

That, Charcoal felt.

He screamed and tried to fend the fire off with his fore-claws; the webs of his wings withered in the yellow-green flames and started to crisp around the edges—

Then the fires died, and Shar stood wavering for a moment, then collapsed bonelessly onto the sand.

Charcoal was still standing.

All the damage seemed to be superficial. Joe stared at him, frozen in place, unable to breathe or move, tears still scorching his face.

What does it take to kill this bastard?

Charcoal turned toward Chinthliss, and shook himself once. Flakes of ash fell away from him as he glared at the bronze dragon.

"Now," he snarled. *"You die with the human."*

Chinthliss gathered himself, preparing to spring at Charcoal's throat. Joe looked frantically for a weapon and saw nothing even remotely useful.

We're all going to die—

A huge shadow uncoiled itself out of the mist behind Charcoal. A dark bronze, fisted foreclaw lashed out of the shadow and slammed into Charcoal's head in a fearsome backhand *smack.*

The gray dragon rocked back on his heels, as a second bronze dragon, darker and larger than Chinthliss, and faintly striped with deep gold, strode past him across the sand to stand beside them all, facing Charcoal.

"I don't think so," said the newcomer.

"*Thomas?*" Chinthliss gasped, his fanged mouth gaping open in blank astonishment.

The new dragon grinned toothily. "You haven't been home in ages, Chinthliss. Just keeping up the tradition of bailing you out of trouble, little brother." Thomas turned his attention back to Charcoal. "*You,*" he said, contempt dripping from his voice. "You may take your miserable carcass out of here and slink back to whatever hole you call home. You may do so *only* because we have other concerns at the moment, more important than dealing with you."

"And if I don't?" Charcoal hissed.

Chinthliss drew himself up to his full height. "We, my brother and I, will kill you. This I pledge."

Charcoal looked from one to the other and back again, and evidently believed them, for he snarled and limped off into the mist.

Now Joe unfroze; his knees turned to jelly and he sank down on the ground, closing his eyes in despair. *Oh, Lord God, what do I tell Tannim's mom and dad? He must have had some kind of premonition this was going to happen—he asked me to take care of them if anything ever happened to him. Now he's gone—oh, God, what do I do now?* His shoulders shook with sobs, his throat was tight, and his chest ached as he hugged himself in his grief.

"Boy—" Someone was shaking his shoulder. He looked up, to find an old man—well, older than Chinthliss, anyway—shaking him. "Boy, go help your *kitsune* friend. Lady Ako needs me to aid her."

He nodded dully, responding to an authority automatically, and stumbled to his feet. He shuffled across the sand to Fox, who was stirring and moaning faintly. Just as he reached the *kitsune*, Fox opened his eyes and looked up at him, clearly still in a daze. He'd reverted to the semi-human form, the one with James Dean's face.

"Dial nine-one-one, would you?" FX asked weakly.

"Yeah, sure," Joe replied. "Is anything broken? Can you sit up?"

"No. Yes." With Joe's help, Fox managed to get into a sitting position, holding his head with one hand. "Ah, hell. Being physical is *not* all it's cracked up to be. For every kiss I get when I do this, seems like I catch ten punches."

"Right." Joe had no idea what he meant, and right now, he didn't much give a damn. He hurt too much inside to care about much of anything. All he could think of was the last time he'd seen Tannim, standing beside the Mustang, trading jokes with Chinthliss. . . .

Never again. Never again.

Chinthliss was a few feet away, back in his human form, helping Shar to her feet. The old man and the other dragon were nowhere in sight.

Or was the old man the other dragon?

The young woman leaned heavily on Chinthliss' shoulder, and Joe thought she might be crying, for she hid her face behind the curtain of her hair and her shoulders shook. He was saying something to her that Joe couldn't hear.

Chinthliss led her over to Lady Ako; lacking any other orders, Joe got Fox up and helped him stagger in that direction as well. He averted his eyes as they neared; he just couldn't bear to look at—

"I believe I have him stabilized, with Thomas' help," he heard Ako say in a voice so faint with weariness that it was hardly more than a whisper. "If we can get him to further help quickly, I believe we can pull him through, but he shouldn't be moved without more Healing than we can give him. We are at the end of our strength."

For a moment, the words made no sense to him. Stabilized? Healing? *What?*

Could she mean Tannim?

He let go of Fox's arm, and stumbled the remaining few steps to where Thomas and Lady Ako knelt on either side of Tannim's body. A body which was breathing, shallowly. There was an awful lot of blood soaking into the sand around him. Although the green, hexagonal-scale armor he must have worn under his shirt gaped open over the chest, there was no huge wound, only a raw red line, the kind you saw on a wound that had just been sutured.

"The talon missed the heart," the old man was saying. "Just. It would seem your protégé's luck is holding."

"How long can you hold him?" Chinthliss asked, as Shar picked up one of Tannim's hands and held it as if she was willing her remaining strength into his body.

"With Thomas' help, an hour, perhaps more." Ako smoothed the hair over Tannim's pale forehead. "I am not sure that anyone will ever be able to heal the damage completely. I fear he will always bear the marks of this encounter. And he may well still be lost to us."

Chinthliss looked straight at Joe. "The Gate to the barn is still open," he said. "If I send you through it with the Mustang, can you get to a phone, call Keighvin Silverhair, and get him to us within an hour?"

Joe had no hesitation. "Yes, sir!" he replied.

"I'll stand watch for trouble," Fox offered. "I've got enough left in me for that."

"I'll hold the temporary Gate for you and Keighvin. It'll be faster if he Gates to the barn, then takes my Gate here. He'll waste time trying to find us otherwise," Chinthliss said. Then he looked at Thomas. "I'm going to want to know everything later," he said firmly. "But now—let's move. Tannim is still near death, and slipping away."

Joe did not need any urging. Shar pressed the keys into his hand, though how *she* came to have them, he had no idea. He ran for the Mach I, and with Chinthliss leading through the mist, took it to the Gate they'd made of the chrome circle.

This time he drove out of the barn under a dawn sky— and headed straight for the nearest Quik Trip. There was a quarter burning a hole in his pocket.

There were some tense days ahead.

Reality seemed to float like a feather.

Even now.

Concentration returned to him easier now, despite the fact that his mother was on the phone.

"No, it's all right, Mom, really. Mr. Silver has taken care of everything. Don't worry. Really." Tannim hung up, sighing—carefully, since any movement of his lungs hurt like hell—and Shar took it from him, putting it out of the way in the headboard of The Bed. She handed him a Gatorade and made a little face of apology.

Fox—insubstantial, Tannim assumed, since he was in the real world—perched on the top of Tannim's TV set on the bureau at the foot of The Bed. He shrugged sympathetically, and twitched *four* tails.

"How are they taking it?" Shar asked. "I hated to make you talk to them, but they've been calling here three times a day, and this was the first time you've been awake enough to deal with them. I've been passing myself off as a private-duty nurse, telling them you've been taking pain-pills and you're sleeping."

He coughed, and a sharp stick stabbed him under the ribs again. "About as well as you'd expect. They hate it when I get hurt."

Shar nodded, her face full of sympathy, and sat crosslegged on the foot of his side of The Bed. He slowly tucked up his feet to make room for her.

At least his legs weren't broken this time.

"Hey," Fox said, "look at it this way. If they'd actually *seen* you, they'd have been having fits, followed by lots of really expensive therapy."

"He's right. It could be worse," Shar told him. "Joe was very quick to think of a plausible accident, to account for—" She nodded at his chest. "*I* certainly would never have thought of a runaway glass-truck."

"At least you can tell your mother the truth," he said, just a little bitterly. Then he shook his head and grimaced. "I'm sorry. It's just post-injury depression. I'm a rotten patient." He managed to drag up a little smile for her. "Usually, once Keighvin's Healers get done with me, there isn't anyone here who has to put up with me. That's why I bought this monster bed. As long as I'm not full of IVs, I can pretty much take care of myself if I have to until I'm mobile again."

"Wait. You bought a *huge* bed to be all alone?" she replied, one eyebrow arching. Fox smirked.

"Let's say it works out that way." He shrugged—carefully. "It's got room for my electronics, anyway."

"I found the fridge and the microwave in the headboard, and all the controls to everything else," she said with a fellow gadget-lover's admiration, "but I was afraid to try any of them; I didn't know what they did and I didn't want to turn you into a sandwich."

"Jeez, or worse," FX put in. "I can just see trying to explain to Lady Ako how come Tannim's laminated!"

Glad for the change of subject, Tannim demonstrated his prize for her. The Bed was the only piece of furniture he'd ever really hung onto through all of his many moves, after he found it in a Goodwill. The years of ordeal-after-injury-after-trauma had all been survived with this one item intact. Though he'd modified it for the electronics, someone somewhere had spent a lot of money designing a bed for a market that didn't exist. Or a market of one, depending upon how you looked at it.

He had awakened more than once in The Bed after one of his close encounters with severe pain—but never after quite such a close encounter with death. His last memory—looking down at his chest, his vision filled with seeing Charcoal's talon sticking into it, deep into it, as everything went red and black—played back. He wasn't certain he really wanted to think about that very hard; but he couldn't help it. If he did think about it, he was going to start shaking, and he was afraid he'd never stop, never have the courage to leave this room again. Still, the sequence of events played through his mind, and he felt his control slipping again. Then his mind cleared and the memory mercifully faded away.

His next clear moment had come a couple of hours ago: waking up in The Bed, and finding Fox on the TV and Shar sitting on the edge, pretending to read, but watching him. *That* had been enough to drive all other thoughts from his mind, at least temporarily. Then his parents had called, frantic with worry, and some story about a wreck—that he'd gotten hit by an out-of-control glass-truck and had gotten a huge shard of glass in the lung. Joe was with his folks, keeping them calm.

Just like I asked him to. Am I getting prescient?

In a few more days Joe would "fly" here, once the

Drakes were sufficiently calmed. Actually, Keighvin was going to send Alinor after him. Joe had said, with a laugh, that Al had orders from Keighvin to "outfit him."

God. Al has great taste, but he's gonna turn the kid into a bigger gadget-hog than me. At least Joe no longer had any problem with accepting Fairgrove's generosity.

He *thought* he'd come to a few times in between that moment Underhill and now; he had vague memories of Chinthliss and Keighvin hovering over him, of a woman with long red hair and oriental features, of Lidam, one of Keighvin's Healers, of Fox and Shar, and of Thomas Cadge. He did think he remembered waking up in terrible pain several times only to be soothed back into sleep by a gentle hand on his forehead, a hand he associated, for some reason, with Shar. He thought he'd dreamed of voices, of Shar and Fox talking together about him.

And he had a particularly vivid memory of awakening in the middle of the night to see Shar asleep in an exhausted tangle of hair and pillows and a blanket, on the other side of The Bed, her face tear-stained and white with weariness. He would have chalked that up to a hallucination if he hadn't come to this morning to find her here.

This was certainly a new experience; the very first time he'd ever awakened in The Bed after an injury to find that he wasn't alone.

"So, you were starting to explain just what Thomas Cadge has to do with all this when the phone rang," he prompted.

"Yeah, I wanted to hear this, too," FX said with interest.

She thought for a moment, then resumed the interrupted explanation. "Thomas is Chinthliss' older half-brother," she said. "Chinthliss says that while they have the same dragon-father, Thomas' mother was a human, one of the Sidhe fosterlings who was a very powerful Healer. Thomas used to feel very strongly against cross-species romance, partly because of all the trouble he had growing up. So when Chinthliss got involved with my mother, Thomas was against it from the very beginning, and did everything he could to break the romance up."

Tannim shook his head, puzzled. "All right, that much I've got. So why did he get involved now? And what the hell was he doing, pretending to be a crazy old blind guy?"

"That was part of his plan—you see, he got involved because he saw how unhappy Chinthliss was after Mother left him. He says he heard from some of his friends that Mother wasn't exactly full of cheer either, and he—reexamined his feelings." She fell silent for a moment. "He told me after we brought you back here that he felt at least partially responsible for their breakup, because of all the things he'd said to Chinthliss. He decided he was wrong, and he wanted to make it up to them. He loves Chinthliss; all he ever intended to do was to try to protect him from getting hurt. And whether or not he'll admit it, Chinthliss adores him, too."

Tannim nodded; he could understand that. Chinthliss had often remarked on how unfortunate it was that Tannim was an only child, how he missed out on a great deal by not having a brother. Tannim had never known, before now, that it was because Chinthliss himself had a big brother who watched out for him.

"So. Thomas decided that he was going to have to find a very subtle, clever way to get Ako and his brother back together." Shar paused. "*He* is the reason we used to dream about each other."

Tannim blinked. "W—wait. You mean, since he couldn't get the two of *them* to talk to each other, he forced the issue by getting the two of us—what would you call it? Curious about each other? Involved?"

Shar shook her head, puzzled. "I'm not quite sure. I think his original intention was just to have us get glimpses of each others' lives, so we'd be sufficiently intrigued to see if we couldn't track each other down. He *certainly* didn't intend for us to have the kind of dreams we've been having since we discovered the opposite sex!" She laughed then, the first time he'd heard her laugh with no sign of strain in her voice. She had a beautiful laugh. "He was *very* embarrassed when I came right out, described the dreams, and asked him if he was the cause!"

"I guess the only thing we can blame is our own subconsciouses for that." He chuckled—very carefully, more of a wheeze. Laughing hurt too much. "So, he figured that if *we* went looking for each other, Ako and Chinthliss would have to go along with it. And if we became friends, Ako and Chinthliss would be forced together, is that it?"

"Pretty much. Then things got out of hand." She licked her lips and stared at the wall for a moment in thought. "He wasn't prepared for Charcoal molding me into your opposite number."

Tannim sipped his Gatorade. "So what did he do?"

"He said he worked with it, keeping an eye on me through my air elementals. He figured he could get things back on track when I broke away from my father, but then I made alliances with the Unseleighe, and that was almost as bad. The *last* thing he wanted me to do was—well, what I did, kidnapping the Mustang. He knew you were going to come after it as well as I did. That was when he decided he'd better get involved directly, disguised as Thomas Cadge." She shrugged. "He freed the real Thomas Cadge, took his clothes and his cart and all, and folded so many disguise-shields on himself I didn't have a clue, and neither did you. He said he didn't know what he was going to do, he just knew that if he didn't come along, we'd probably get caught again, and Ako and Chinthliss would never reconcile and never forgive him."

"Well, that's where I came in," Fox said lightly. "Shar, since you don't need me to talk to to keep you awake, I've got a date with a pretty lady fox." He winked at Tannim. "Glad I'm seeing you on this side of the spirit-world, buddy."

With a *pop,* FX vanished, leaving his glowing "FX" hanging in the air for a moment, like the grin on the Cheshire Cat.

"Huh. That's Fox all over. Vixen chasing." He finished the Gatorade and put the empty glass down. "So that's what Thomas Cadge was all about. I wish he'd pulled his rescue a little sooner." He tried to say it lightly, to make a joke out of it, but it came out badly. The implications hung heavily in the air, and he flashed on the talon penetrating his chest again. . . .

He shivered, and caught a pain-filled breath. How long before he'd stop seeing that in instant replay?

Shar bit her lip. "I saw him sneaking out of the car. I thought he was the one who had led Charcoal to us in the first place when I saw that. Then, when I realized what he really was, I was almost as mad at him for not showing up sooner, too. For what it's worth—he demonstrated draconic shape-changing to me, and since he's half-human, it takes a *lot* longer for him to go from human to dragon than it does to do the reverse. Chinthliss told me that if the dragon is interrupted halfway through, it kills him. He feels really awful, Tannim. As badly as you'd like him to feel, I think. The only way he'd feel worse is if—if you weren't all right."

"Oh." Tannim digested this, and to buy himself a little time to think, picked up the audio controls and triggered the CD player. He didn't remember what he'd left in there, but it would probably help lighten the mood a little—

But the first selection hit him between the eyes and left him stunned. "I'll Find My Way Home," by Jon Anderson and Vangelis.

Home. He'd thought he'd lost his home forever; that he didn't fit in the old one, and hadn't found a new one. Shar had never *had* one. What was it that Thomas had said—something about not being able to go back to your childhood home because you outgrew it? And that part of being an adult was building your *own* home?

And building it meant finding someone to share it. Home wasn't really more than a place to live if it meant being alone.

So why did this room feel so much like a home?

"Ah—are Chinthliss and your mother—getting along?" he asked carefully.

She smiled, and it was clear that she approved of what was going on. "As a matter of fact, I think they're doing just fine. Mother confessed that she was stalling him to let me get you out of the mess on my own, but by then, Chinthliss was so grateful for the way she'd spent herself for you that if she'd confessed to murdering his parents and sleeping with Madoc Skean, he'd have forgiven her." Her green eyes softened, and her smile softened with them. "He really cares a great deal for you, you know," she said quietly. "He could *be* your father; he loves you that much."

Another revelation that left him a little stunned. "I think maybe you're exaggerating a little."

But she shook her head. "No. No, I don't think so. I watched him with you here; I listened to him browbeating the Healers, swearing he'd search through every domain Underhill if he had to, in order to find the best for you. He nearly did that, too—he's going to owe a lot of people a lot of favors for a long, long time."

"Oh, hell," Tannim muttered numbly. "He's never going to forgive me for that—he *hates* owing people—"

But she leaned over and placed both her hands on his. "He *doesn't care*. Didn't you hear what FX said? You nearly died, not just Underhill, but three more times after we brought you here."

"I did?" Some of those confused memories began to make appalling sense. . . .

"You have no idea how much damage Charcoal did to you," she said soberly, the color draining from her face. "Mother thought that the talon missed your heart—it didn't. Thank the Ancestors there were Healers *here* when—" She shook her head. "I can't talk about it. I thought Chinthliss was going to go mad, or I would. Fox was the only one who stayed calm. He was always here, the least powerful and the most hopeful, when we were feeling like hope was lost."

He took a slow, careful breath. "So what's the real damage?" he asked. He didn't want to know—and he did. Hell, he had to know; he was going to have to live with it for the rest of his life.

"The permanent damage is in your left lung and your heart," she said bluntly. "You've lost the bottom lobe of that lung. The rest—broken ribs, torn muscles, internal damage—is either healed or is going to heal." She blinked, and her eyes glistened suspiciously. "You're going to have to be careful. It's always going to hurt when you really exert yourself, like a stitch in the side, only worse. That's the best they could do, and Chinthliss would have sold himself into slavery to make you well."

Then she added in a very quiet voice, "So would I."

There it was, out in the open.

"You were here the whole time?" he asked softly.

She nodded. "I never left. I couldn't. When I thought you were—when Charcoal—" Her voice faltered and died. "Fox kept me company. I never saw much of the lesser *kitsune* before this. He's a lot deeper than he lets on. He couldn't do anything physical on this side of the Hill, but he watched you for me when I just couldn't keep my eyes open anymore."

So the "memories" were real. . . .

He thought very carefully about his next words, picking them with utter precision before he spoke them. "You're probably the most unique lady I've ever known, Shar. It's kind of funny—Charcoal tried to make you into my opposite, and failed. But you wound up becoming my— complement. Or else I became yours."

She licked her lips nervously and nodded, clearly listening very carefully to what he was saying.

"What I'm trying to say is that we went through a pretty wretched experience together and I *think* we make a good team." He grinned, just a little. "And, dreams aside, even though we haven't known each other very long, I *think* we know each other pretty well." His grin faded as he turned his hands over and caught both of hers. "What I'm trying to say is that I would really, really like it, Shar, if you would decide to stay here. With me. Maybe we can make this place into a home together. If you'd do that— every bit of this will have been worth it to me."

She stared at him, and her hands trembled in his. He bit his lip. "The three best words on this earth are 'I love you.' Would you believe me if I used them now?"

She blinked rapidly, and nodded.

"I love you, Shar," he said softly. "I really do. I gotta be crazy, lady, but I do."

"I—I guess we both are." She smiled tremulously. "What a pair we are! A half-*kitsune*, half-dragon, and a human racer-mage! If Thomas hadn't changed his mind, he'd be having a litter of kittens. I—" Her voice broke. "Tannim, I love you."

He looked into her eyes for a long time, then gently lifted one hand and kissed the back of it. "I'm afraid that's the best I can manage at the moment—" he said with a rueful chuckle. "You're not getting much of a lover right now."

"You'll just have to make it up to me later," she replied, regaining some of the mischievous sparkle he remembered from dreams. "And you'll have to remember, I *am* a *kitsune*—half, anyway. I won't be tied down. I won't be Suzie Homemaker."

"I never thought you would," he replied, with growing content. "There's a lot more to life than picking out drapes."

She looked at him for a long time, a penetrating stare that weighed and measured the truth of everything he had said and done. He just smiled, knowing that she would find he meant exactly what he had said.

Finally, she returned his smile and moved forward, arranging herself very carefully against—not *on*—his shoulder. He managed to get an arm around her without hurting himself.

He closed his eyes, savoring the moment, and realized that it was this that he had been looking for, without knowing what it was he had been in search of. Somehow, through pain and fear and long loneliness, they had found their way home.

Together.

Tannim held her, lovingly, as they drifted off to sleep. They had a lot of new dreams to catch up on.

EXPLORE OUR WEB SITE